BLACK DRAGON

Novels published by Midnight Fire Media

Your Own Fate
Night on Earth
Dreams Belong to the Night
ShadowWalk
Alarums of Reality
Afterglow Dust

The Janus Clan series:

The Defenseless
The Slaves
Birds Flying in the Dark
At the End of the Rainbow

Poetry:

Amos Keppler: Complete Poems 1989 – 2003
Secrets - Descriptions of what cannot be described

(A few of the) novels to be published:

Afterglow Rain
Season of the Witch
Thunder Road: Ice and Fire
Falling
Red Shadow
Lewis of Modern York
Fangs and Claws of the Earth

For a «complete» list of current and current future Amos Keppler and Midnight Fire Media projects see the Midnight Fire/Midnight Fire Media web pages.

BLACK DRAGON

BY

AMOS KEPPLER

MIDNIGHT FIRE MEDIA
2015

Midnight Fire Media

http://midnight-fire.net/mfm
For more about Black Dragon:
http://midnight-fire.net/bd

E-Mail:
Amos13@midnight-fire.net
manofhood@yahoo.com

Cover, text, design, premedia, art and photos Amos Keppler

ISBN 978-82-91693-18-7

V1
Part One:
Gimmick

Chapter 1

Lucinda woke up with a troubled look on her face, sweat pouring from her soaking wet skin. It burned like acid in her eyes.

She frowned, attempting to remember what had made her so... made her so... feel so... feel so bad.

Melinda knocked on the door. She knocked two times before opening it and rushing into the room.

– You had the dream again, the girl said, rushing to the bed, sitting down by her side.

– No, I...

She relented, sighing, brushing wet hair from her forehead.

– Yes, she admitted.

Melinda kissed her on the cheek, comforting her the best she could, and Lucinda felt comforted, felt a little better.

– I still can't remember many details, she said. – It's mostly dread and even horror, and a sense of... When I see myself in a kind of mirror I'm not really seeing me, but someone else.

– It's definitely weird, Melinda grinned, – but you're entitled, right? If there are inevitable results of living a double life identity problems certainly are one.

Lucinda looked at her sister, at the smaller, more slender and innocent version of herself and smiled. Melinda always had the ability to make her smile.

She rose, stretching her large, muscular and curvy body, noticing how the carpet hair played with her toes, widening her grin.

– Breakfast will be ready soon, I trust?

– As soon as you step out of the shower, Melinda assured her.

– Good, we don't want you to be late for school.

– «We» won't be, the girl replied lightly.

Lucinda walked into the bathroom, closing the door behind her, stopping in front of the mirror, studying herself, the sweaty face, the swollen eyes, shaking her head, shaking it off and stepping into the shower.

The water hit her face and front body. It was always a shock at first, but quite pleasant after a while, and today she felt she needed it, needed the pleasant rinsing of her body.

She stepped away from the water and soaped herself in. The soap quickly covered her entire frame. She used shampoo on her hair, her long and thick bright hair. Hands cleaned her body while allowing for the shampoo to work. Muscles were a little sore. They always were, and it wasn't strange, the way she strained them. She began rinsing her hair, cleaning it of shampoo and remaining dirt. Then she began rubbing her body again, standing too long under the pleasant waterfall as usual.

Thoroughly rinsed and refreshed she finally emerged from the bathroom, drying herself with a large towel with slow, deliberate movements. She didn't cover herself or didn't set out to cover herself, when she walked into the living room. The thought that someone, with binoculars hid in one of the apartments across the street or even further away didn't really faze her.

Let them see, she thought. Let them watch.

The admiring look in Melinda's eyes did please her, though. The girl idolized her, perhaps a bit much.

Lucinda began dressing. She did so slowly, languishingly. There were the panties with the blondes tightening around the thighs. And there was the pink dress, and that was all. Melinda joined her before the mirror, dressed exactly like her.

– IF YOU GOT IT, FLAUNT IT! They choired, grinning from ear to ear.

They sat by the kitchen table, having their breakfast, wolfing down the food, the huge heap of sandwiches and stuff, plagued by the hunger that had been a part of her life for close to ten years, and it persisted, until she had downed more than half of the meal.

Melinda also ate her share and fed with an eagerness that in polite company would have been called gorging. She noticed her older sister glancing at her and reddened.

– I'm really hugging in, am I not? She acknowledged glumly.

– You sure are, Lucinda nodded kindly.

– I'm so ashamed, Melinda cried. – I used to look at your... your gluttony and be... disgusted, but lately I've grown ravenous enough myself to rival you and I understand how you feel.

She had grown taller and had been putting on weight lately, and would certainly, in time, grow as big as her sister.

– It's all right. Lucinda took her hand.

– No, it isn't, Melinda snapped, – I have treated my own sister like a freak, and should be severely *punished*.

The intensity in the young girl alarmed Lucinda a little, also because she could see it in Melinda's mind, but she kept her mask on.

– Oh, my God, Melinda exclaimed glumly, – now there are two gluttonous amazons in the house. How are we going to *survive?* It was difficult enough to get the necessary funds before.

Lucinda began laughing, attempting to keep it inside at first, but then giving in, surrendering completely to its healing qualities, praying that the laughter's sore subtext would go unnoticed.

It was a moment of pure joy when Melinda joined her in the loud, healthy laughter, when they laughed themselves silly in each other's company.

They prepared themselves for leaving. There were the shoes with the high heels and that was all. At the exit Lucinda grabbed the other's arm.

– Perhaps you shouldn't really wear such a revealing dress at school anymore?

– What's the worry? The girl snorted. – I'm stronger than any of the boys, and getting stronger by the day. Besides, I wear one bra more than you…

There was that rebellious streak again. Lucinda sighed.

It was chilly in the hall and baking hot outside. Thankfully there was a wind, warm but pleasant, and playing with their hair and body and dress, and just about keeping them from sweating.

The school bus stopped right outside the block of flats. Several other late teenagers waited for it.

– Hello, Melinda, the forward, very forward Stu Adams greeted her.

– H'lo, Melinda mumbled.

– Hello, Lucinda, he grinned, staring at her breasts, at the very visible nipples under the pink fabric.

– Hello, Stu, she replied sweetly.

He reddened like the bumbling schoolboy he was. It was nothing to her, but she still took some satisfaction in it.

And best of all: it made Melinda feel a little better.

The other girls giggled, and the boys looked patronizingly at good ol' Stu, as well. Success on all fronts.

I told you he was nothing, she told Melinda, and Melinda cracked a big smile.

The sisters looked fondly at each other, as if sharing a secret, demonstrating to the others how close they were.

Lucinda watched the bus leave. She waved goodbye and headed in the opposite direction. It was truly a great day, one of the first warm of spring. She enjoyed the walk down the street and was glad she had decided to dress lightly and bring the office clothes in her bag. Males stared at her, but also at the other light-clad females. She didn't draw too much attention to herself, and that sort of comforted her.

Her stop was two blocks away. She reached it just as the bus was pulling in by the sidewalk. The doors opened and she and the others pushed themselves inside. It was cramped in there. She saw that and sighed, before pushing herself to a spot by the open window. The bus pulled out from the sidewalk, and doing so quite abruptly, well before most of the newly entering passengers had found their spot. Warm, sweaty bodies pushed at each other.

Taller than everybody present Lucinda stood there, bowing her head to not bump into what to her was a low ceiling, sweating and breathing hard with the others, even after the bus speeded up.

Cramped, she thought feverishly.

A hand moved towards her breasts, its intentions clear. Lucinda didn't even have to read the mind of its owner. She let him almost reach his target before grabbing the hand and squeezing, harder than she had to, and she got a perverse pleasure of hearing the howl of pain in his mind added to the loud shriek everybody heard.

Hands, even bodies stayed away after that. She got a little room, a chance to breathe, but mostly it left a sick felling in her stomach. The other passengers looked at her as if she was the rabid dog, and looked at Hands with a bit of sympathy. Her eyes started wandering, to seek outside, to the other world there.

The bus stopped for red light again, and there was a long line of cars ahead of the bus. The familiar pain started as a low pressure in her arse, spreading quickly to her entire lower parts. She had to focus all her will to not shit herself that very moment. She had had some experience in doing that, but it was still hard. The world blinked out, and the vultures closed in on her again, closing the gap, and Hands and compatriots grinned wickedly. At least that was how she perceived it (perception is reality). She muttered silently under her breath and swore she wouldn't reveal her plight, her weakness to them, to anyone in any way.

She hurried out of the bus. Flickering eyes caught the pale, cold-sweat face in the windows. She hurried on, but experience told her she couldn't move too fast, or disaster would strike. It was clear to her, more than clear that she walked in a stiff way that gave her away in the most revealing manner. She heard people's wicked laughter in her mind.

The public toilet on 6th street stank of shit and piss as usual. Fortunately, probably precisely because of that very reason there weren't that many people there. She rushed down the stairs with the coin ready, paid the fee, and to her sick relief she found several unused stalls. The closest available was number three closest to the exit. She ran inside and closed the door and locked it behind her in one single frenzied move.

She pulled down her panties, pulled up her dress and set down on the bowl, and it wasn't a second too early. The shit pushed itself out and dumped into the water with a loud splash.

Sweet, sick relief flooded her. She sat there, listening to the silence of the

10

room, while the shit fell from her arsehole and dumped into the deep sea of shit already down there. There was a frown, as unpleasant thoughts haunted her. She rose quickly, and stared down at the heap in the bowl. Determined, very determined she pushed the button on the wall, and water flooded the bowl. She cursed silently under her breath when her worst expectations were realized. The shit, all the shit had blocked the pipe. She struck the wall in frustration. Fortunately, it was a solid wall, not easily swayed by even her considerable strength, but that minor encouragement made her feel no better. She listened with her ears and her mind. As far as she could tell there was no one out there. She hurried outside and into another stall, closing and locking that door, too.

She sat down again and the shit kept coming. It was easy for her to picture Melinda doing the same, going through the same *shit* at school. She rose quickly this time, flushing the toilet before the shit had blocked the pipe. To be on the safe side she probably should have moved on to a third stall, but she found she didn't give a damn and that pleased her, pleased her a lot, for a second or two before she realized the obvious truth: that she was merely putting up a brave front in front of herself, and cared, cared a lot about all of this.

The restroom remained empty. It took less than a minute to change clothes. She exposed her body, slipped her dress off and her pants and blouse and jacket on. The added layer of clothes made her turn hot in just a few seconds and she began sweating in earnest, in spite of the extra layer of antiperspirant she put on.

The stench stuck in her nose outside. It always did, and she knew it would for hours, until the next time, until her next necessary visit to this or a similar horrible place. She walked through the streets in a daze. A loud horn made her jump. She hurried out of the way, but the car still almost ran her down, and the driver hissed at her. It didn't take a mind reader to know that, but it helped.

She thought glumly.

The office building wasn't far away, just one more block. It towered over her like a vulture. She went inside and into the elevator with her colleagues. They greeted her with a mumble, and she responded in kind. She fixed her hair and face in the elevator mirror, like the other females. The males already looked sharp and didn't need additional grooming. They would go to the restroom and fix themselves a bit later that day, though. Office work was tough on everybody's features, but not as much as the wind and the sun and city dust.

The work day passed in a daze, as it usually did. Nothing of consequence happened, really. Time stretched, as she devoured coffee nonstop and strived to stay awake.

She remembered lunch, as usual. It was impossible for her to forget that in any shape or form. They stared at her as she strived to feed in any kind of civilized way, while consuming twice the helpings of the others. She was the only one of the big people there, though they certainly were not unknown to the others. They watched her rush the meal, before hurrying off to the toilet. Lunch wasn't really relaxation to her, just more stress and anxiety.

The hours before the end of the workday slowed down to a crawl. They always did. It felt like pure torture on her already tortured soul. She fumed while noticing the others' patronizing glances. Holding herself and her temper in check became an effort, as always.

She walked through the streets again in the afternoon, forgetting work, remembering everything else.

The stench still stuck in her nostrils (she thought glumly).

Well, she was awake now, and vowed to stay awake, to not slumber again. Eyes moved, wandering from person to person, across the street and back. Head turned naturally, the girl seemingly straightening her hair in the wind. Still a little undecided she stopped on a corner, before crossing the street.

She hurried across, as if the light was about to change, but it wasn't, wasn't even blinking. People didn't blink either. They were used to people being in the hurry in the big city.

Another block passed in rushed awareness, in rapid breath. She suddenly reached a fairly less crowded part of downtown. In fact, even though she spotted some people here and there, the sidewalks were almost empty.

She noticed the nondescript building immediately. It drew her to it with a pull she couldn't explain. She shivered, bathing in the hot rays of the fiery sun without having any idea why.

Feet moved, up the marble stairs and stopped her in front of the oversized door. She hesitated, before ringing the single door bell.

– *Yes?* An electronic distorted voice queried.

– My name is Lucinda Patterson, I'm here for the...

There was a click and the door slid open. Lucinda hurried inside.

The door slammed shut behind her. She purposefully ignored that.

The hall inside was empty and silent. There was another staircase leading up to another closed door, presumably leading into what would probably be an office of sorts. She picked the pocket mirror and hairbrush from her purse and began fixing her hair, her thick and wavy hair. It was done fairly quickly this time, with confident and self-assured moves, merely a continuation of the work done earlier. She proceeded to her face, saving it from the ravages of the wind and sweat, first using a cloth to dry the skin and then smaller brushes to repaint herself. Nodding pleased to herself in the mirror she put her tools away and opened the door.

She entered a lush and large room. Nine other women, big like her, muscular like her studied her, like she studied them.

– Hi, she greeted them sweetly.

– Hi, some of the others mumbled or replied just as sweetly.

A couple of them didn't say anything.

They looked remarkably similar to her in built, even though some of them were slimmer, and some had visible excess fat around their hips. Aside from that they exhibited all the differences in a given population.

She sat down in one of the large, clearly custom-made sofas. It felt so pleasant, so different from what she was used to, so… right.

– Hi. A girl reached out a hand. – The rest of us here have all been introduced to each other. I'm Myra. This is…

Lucinda forgot the names instantly. She said her name and took the black girl's hand.

– You guys have been sitting here long? She asked lightly.

– A while, a redhead nodded. – We were told there would be one more arrival before the freak show was ready to roll.

Everybody giggled, the sore subtext being clearly noticeable. Lucinda looked at them with a bit of disdain under the mask. They sat there chatting and giggling like young, irresponsible girls, not having a care in the world. She played along, but didn't give anything away of herself.

It took about ten minutes, before another rather big woman appeared in the door.

– Hi, I'm Miriam, she greeted them. – We're ready for you now.

She was dressed in a smart suit, with a short skirt, elegantly integrating her large breasts and wide hips. It was clearly tailor-made, to her specific, unique challenges.

Her size wasn't a surprise to them, but her confident and relaxed manner was. They rose and followed her through the door.

They took it all in. Miriam let them, waiting patiently for their impressions to settle.

– It's… pleasant, Myra, noted.

They found themselves in a living room of sorts.

– Welcome to the classroom, Miriam grinned.

They looked surprised at her.

– We prefer a more informal setting, Miriam confirmed.

She was so well dressed and groomed. Her clothes, her make-up, everything matched. Some of the girls sighed in envy upon studying her.

– This is probably a question you get a lot, Jasmine grinned and blushed, – but where are the boys?

Laughter, not unkind.

– As you know we also cater to males here, Miriam replied calmly, and they envied her even more. – We prefer to split the sexes at first, to ease the transition, but will mix you later, when we feel you're ready for it.

– But some of us are adults, a woman, clearly on the wrong side of thirty pointed out.

– Yes, Miriam acknowledged, – but no matter your age you are all cast into new and difficult circumstances. Let me ask you something... Lois. You've handled your problem for close to ten years, am I right? But you still aren't in any way *comfortable* with it, are you? That's why you, all of you, have come here, in your desperation, to finally take charge of your lives.

She was so smooth, so pleasant, verging on being patronizing, but Lucinda sensed no deception in her, no reason for being cautious.

Miriam walked to the blackboard (or whiteboard).

– You will be given laptops later, and the teaching will be done more through presentations, but today, also for the reasons I mentioned earlier and also for the more personal touch we will do it the old-fashioned way.

More laughter. She was good at this, good at communication, at gaining trust.

– You should be aware that you will be guinea pigs of sorts. In the contract you will be signing that, too will be covered extensively, along with the nondisclosure agreement and the rest. I advice you to read all of it very carefully. We don't want any misunderstandings, but pleased and active participants.

She wrote GUINEA PIGS on the board.

– What happened ten years ago is, as far as we know unprecedented in history, or at least in recent history, even though experiences of unexplained phenomena may have been mentioned in historical texts and mythical fables. But during those ten years, in spite of all the amazing events we have witnessed since then, there has been conducted very little formal research, at least little leaked to the public. There's a requirement, a growing need to understand what's happening to us and what may be humanity as a whole. So far what we've heard is mostly philosophy and the meaning of comic books in today's brave new world. But comic books are mostly static environments. By necessity nothing ever truly changes there. They're useless when it comes to explain real-life events and dynamic systems. You will be asked to write a diary of sorts on your laptop from your first, official lesson here. Today I will take you through the various teaching environments, to give you an idea what to expect. There's a lot here, a lot to digest. That's why we will give you a month to consider all sides of our proposal, so when you return here you will do so willingly and dedicated to both the task of improving your own lives and participate in our essential scientific research. The one doesn't exclude the other, but is intricately linked.

She put the pen back in her chest pocket.

– Shall we?

They all glanced at each other, still a little apprehensive, before sending each other uncertain smiles, following the tall, confident woman out of the room.

Lucinda felt weird and nauseous for a moment as they passed through a dark hallway, but it passed quickly as they reached the great hall ahead. It was basically a gym, but more than just a gym, well equipped with extras.

– Who's behind this? Lucinda asked casually. – Where does the money come from?

– We're self-financed actually, Miriam replied proudly. – That's why you don't have to pay a fee or anything. It is public knowledge, but I guess we're not that well established in the public mind yet. You will hear more about that later.

– I've heard it, Myra commented rather quickly, – and seen the ads, too.

And she went into acting mode, in a parody of a sitcom black girl:

– «The new woman for the new age».

They laughed, Lucinda, too, even though she studied Myra while she did, glanced at her from the corner of her eye.

Both women and men, young and older exercised in the hall. A group of men, dressed in mostly fairly common clothes like Miriam's group studied it all from the opposite point of the hall. A tall oriental woman did a casual somersault while they were watching and eyes widened over the remarkable feat.

– That is Jordan Matthews, Miriam told them smugly. – She was overweight and generally in bad shape when she came to us a month ago…

– But won't that, won't exercise… compound the problem? Jasmine wondered incredulous.

– No, not really. Miriam took on a pedantic role. – You see, exercise will only to a minor degree further excite your metabolism. It will increase your appetite, like it does with all people, but not to an uncanny degree. It will be worth it when you see the relative control and comfort it gives you.

Lucinda looked proudly at herself in the wall-to-wall mirror, at her flat belly and well trained body.

– Those of you already exercising might think that part of our program is of less use to you, but you would be wrong. Even though you believe you know the meaning of sweating and hard exercise you will discover you're dead wrong…

If Lucinda hadn't known better she could have sworn the woman was reading her mind, talking directly to her, but she would guess that the others felt the same way. Miriam had had several classes before this one, and she knew from experience what their concerns were.

– If you take a closer look at Jordan, Miriam continued, - you will see that she's just as tall as the other women here. And she's a typical new, big phenotype. The old general differences in height and size between the Asian and Caucasian and Negroid population have been nullified by the Great Darkness.

They kept studying those exercising, those in the room excelling in physical hardship with big eyes and increased excitement.

A few of those exercising ran on a treadmill, with wires attached to the body and head. Their prowess was being monitored by women and men in white coats.

– We're taking the scientific approach here, Miriam said pleasantly, – the thorough and patient path to knowledge, understanding and wisdom. We will help and aid you all, if you let us, like we've helped so many like you. We'll help you handle both the changes within, and the often cruel perception of society.

– You can say that again, Jasmine cried.

Miriam smiled softly and professionally, clearly on top of the situation.

– It's been ten years for some of you and almost that for the rest. You've learned to deal with it, live with it, somehow, but you haven't really tapped into your potential or even gone beneath the surface much. That's what we do here: we unlock the potential within. We show each and every one passing through here what it means to be human.

She looked at them. Lucinda looked at them through her eyes, and she saw them nod, saw herself nod.

– We'll give you one «free» hour, Miriam smiled, – one without commitment, so you can deem for yourself what we can offer you, and what you will be required to offer us.

She brought them to a rather small, quiet room, with a circle couch at the center, light brown and darker brown and dark beige, so pleasant colors, such pleasant surroundings. Lucinda sat down and even though the couch had a firm surface it was like landing on soft, soft velvet.

They sat there, in the circle, talking, a little awkward at first, but then the words flowed like water.

16

The presentation started casually. Miriam spun a bottle on the table and the person it pointed at when it stopped was the first to go. And it continued from left to right.

– My name is Rhonda. A big girl with curly brown hair began. – I'm eighteen. I began… *growing* a few days before my thirteenth birthday not that long after my first period. At least that was when I first noticed. I got the cravings for food, for protein and before the month was up I had shit myself, and I had never done that before, and I cried the entire day afterwards. It got progressively worse after that, especially after my brother began exhibiting the same signs a couple of years later. We practically bankrupted our parents, before my father got lucky and landed a better, far better paid job. After that he spent a fortune on «finding out what was *wrong* with us». I guess it could have been worse. My parents didn't grow big and only had us to «worry about». Sometimes I think we would have been better off if they, too had experienced the… the transformation, so they could have understood us better.

She looked very somber, quite subdued.

– My father was, is big, Jasmine said. – He was caught stealing and ended up in prison.

As the others related their personal tale, some worse, some slightly better it became clear that their experiences were fairly similar and that they were quite similar in their approach to what had happened to them.

Lucinda opened her mouth to speak, but was cut off.

– You girls were lucky, Lois said bitterly. – You were given the chance to adapt gradually, while I had to deal with the fact that it happened over just a few weeks. I almost… lost it…

She uttered the last few words in what was hardly more than a whisper.

– I had to feed in the middle of the night, until I learned to adapt to the new demands of my body. When I woke up in the mornings I often discovered that I had grown bigger during the night. It hurt, hurt all the time, and I feared I would go… insane.

Lucinda felt a dread while looking at Lois. She couldn't explain it, but there it was. There was nothing there to justify her… her anxiety, no matter how hard she probed the older woman's mind.

– Yes. Miriam nodded. – Since you were already an adult, fully developed when the Great Darkness happened, you and others felt the full effect of it without the transitional period enjoyed by teenagers. Their Change happened sort of naturally while they grew to adulthood, even though it was no picnic to them either.

– That was what I was gonna say, Myra cried.

Brittle laughter, rough around the edges.

– Quite a few have lost it, Myra cried, – and they've received little or no aid.

The news had reported quite a few cases in that regard the last ten years. Lucinda and the others were all aware of that fact. Lucinda was very aware of it. She wanted to speak, to add more to what she had said during her presentation, but everything just turned itself to knots inside her.

– My boyfriend left me, Kelly said, speaking in a very low and subdued voice. – He even started spreading v-vicious untruths about me. I had to move to my grandparents to get away from it all.

She sent Miriam a look of absolute despair.

– I guess he couldn't handle that you were stronger than him, Miriam said lightly and shrugged, very deliberate.

They all looked at her, looked at each other, and brightened visibly.

– Come, the teacher beckoned them. – Come!

The ten prospective class participants followed her further through the large building. They passed through another dark hallway, making Lucinda feel weird again, but as before it passed quickly.

Pleasant smells assaulted their senses. They entered what basically looked like a restaurant, except that there was only one table in the room, one long table, one filled with dishes. Everybody looked astounded at Miriam.

– My guess is that you have spent most of the day walking around hungry, she said. – As stated, here you will learn that that is neither necessary nor desirable.

It was like a dream. They sat down with an incredulous expression painted on their faces. Miriam lit candles and poured wine. She began serving herself from the hot plates, and slowly, with dawning determination and grins the ten visitors began doing that, too.

– Eat as much as you can muster or desire.

And they fed, with a hunger they had never allowed themselves to feel before.

She pushed a button on a remote control and low, pleasant music filled the room. Conversation was light between the munching and crunching of great food and sipping of tasty, tasty wine.

– I and my boyfriend were making out in his car, Allison related with a huge grin. – He had attempted to wear me down and get me there, to that point in our «relationship» for weeks, and I finally conceded. We drove to Harper's Cliff, where cars are lined up every Friday night. Troy is tall and quite big for a… mundane guy, and he plays football. He was one of the few on campus that could match my size, so I guess most people, myself included

18

saw us as a natural couple.

She was good at this, at telling stories, relating her obvious glee and visible melancholy both.

– His hands were all over me. He was quite the eager kid, and I started to feel it, really feel it, turning hot and queasy, and excited, very excited. I began returning his affection, his clumsy advances, returning it tenfold… and, at some point I grabbed his arm, and broke it like a *twig*.

Her southern drawl became evident at the last word, as she dwelled on it, dwelled on the memory, taking great pleasure in reliving the moment.

– I didn't even notice or realize I was squeezing it at all, until he cried out and pulled back, and his excitement faded like dew in the morning, and he was as horny as a neutered cat, and I saw fear in his eyes. And suddenly I felt so very empowered and horny and eager, and I wanted him, wanted him more than anything else in the world right then, until the fear in his eyes changed to horror and revulsion.

– That's poetry, Jasmine sighed.

– To poetry, Lucinda cried and raised her glass.

– TO POETRY, everybody cried.

And glasses met and parted.

Lucinda served herself, at least two more plates than she usually did, and she suspected the others did the same. They weren't exactly the image of wealth any of them, and they took the opportunity to for once fill their belly.

– You will probably start feeling the urge pretty soon, Miriam said. – I know I will.

They cast her grateful glances. She was witty, informal and a friend in need.

– In case you're wondering, she added smugly, – our toilets are custom-made. They're made for big people and also adopted to our unique problem. The pipes are broader and can handle a lot more shit, so to speak.

– That's amazing. Lois frowned, not really getting it, repeating it just to be certain. – That's just amazing!

Several of the dinner guests started growing restless and began shifting on their chair not long after that. Lucinda did, too. She was the fourth rushing off to the restroom. There was no immediate need. She could have, if necessary put it off for a while longer, but she wanted to take her time, to savor the fact that she didn't need to rush it.

The restroom was large and pleasant, even though the stench ripped her nostrils, ripped them here, too. It was such a powerful smell, one no cleaner could overwhelm. She opened the door to the toilet, and found that Miriam hadn't exaggerated. The bowl was wider and further from the floor. Her butt was a perfect fit and her feet reached the floor exactly right, or at least as right as they had ever done since her early teens. She dropped the first rolls of shit and it actually felt good, for a change. Eyes closed and opened with an exalted smile, as her personal body stench rose from the bowl and surrounded her.

The ten left together, about an hour later, clearly upbeat and encouraged.

– I'm not drunk, Lois said. – It takes a lot more wine to get us drunk, right?

– Yeah, Rhonda said. – Even getting drunk is more expensive for us. It's the added, more compact body mass, I guess.

– We aren't drunk, Lois said, – but I still feel practically *euphoric*.

The bitterness was still evident in her features, but not as much as it had been when they had first met her, just a few hours ago.

Lucinda wondered what was wrong with her that gave Lucinda the willies. It wasn't there all the time, but in glimpses and when light struck the other in certain ways… something entangled itself in the younger woman's gut.

They walked down the early evening street together, laughing, enjoying each other's company. It was still hot, the dusk not quite as hot as the day, of course, but with a mellower, more pleasant heat playing their skin, both exposed and beneath the clothes. They walked together a few more blocks than what was absolutely necessary, reluctant to part, to end this beautiful day, before stopping on the corner of Wilshire and Sixth, hugging and kissing, and eventually walking their own way.

She suffered on the cramped bus again. It was always cramped. Whether it was morning, day, afternoon or evening made no difference. She bit her lower lip and endured. Strangely enough she had more trouble keeping the other passengers' thoughts out of her head, now, as if her powers had grown, as if the events during the day had made her cross a threshold of sorts. She endured and suffered in silence, determined to not make anything ruin her day.

The television was on when she returned to the apartment. Melinda sat on the couch, watching the news and consuming two large bowls of popcorn and a large bottle of soda in the bargain.

She didn't say anything, incredibly enough, but looked encouragingly at her sister, waiting for her to speak. That alone told Lucinda how anxious she was to hear the report.

– It was truly amazing, Lucinda said. – We all got the feeling that they actually cared about us and our special needs there.

– So it works? They will be able to help us?

– Yes, in more ways than one actually, at the very least alleviate our troubles greatly.

She sat down on the couch, and she began helping herself to a share of the

20

popcorn. Melinda looked astounded at her.

– AND NOW, the voice on the TV declared, – AN UPDATE OF TONIGHT'S HEADLINES!

Images flared across the screen, glimpses of reality. It wasn't really an update, Lucinda ventured, but actually a repetition. The anchorwoman faded into view, a calm and professional presence in people's living rooms.

– To those of you just joining us. Welcome to DBC Nine O'clock news. I am Sabine Finelli. The time is nine thirty, and it's time for an update of tonight's main news.

What earlier had been old footage, used for months and even years as a collage changed to recent images, to today's stories.

And Sabine was on again.

– Today, at four sixteen precisely it was ten years since our world changed forever, and on this night we examine the event itself and its aftermath, its quite conclusive results. After this broadcast there will be an hour-long program on this channel on this issue, but for now we will take you live to our reporter Willard Jenkins at the national observatory in Jaynagar, where many of our nation's best thinkers and respected citizens are gathered. Willard, are you there?

Sabine faded out and Willard faded in. He stood before a large building, one resembling a library.

– I'm here, Sabine, in front of the building where the very defining incident took place three years ago, the incident definitely changing our perception of the world and ourselves.

The image on the screen changed yet again. The viewers still heard Jenkins' voice, but his face and the building behind him were exchanged with moving images and computerized images of Earth from Space illustrating what the natural images couldn't.

The Great Darkness lasted only for a tiny moment, an inverted flash on a bright day, but its power was felt everywhere, everywhere on the globe.

There had been wise old wives, and there had been prophets speaking in tongues, in an otherwise unremarkable world, but that changed in an instant that hot afternoon.

No one knew at the time, but the world had changed in dramatic and fundamental and irreversible ways.

It was an astronomical event, or at least that was what they called it later. They showed it on the evening news, showed the Earth from various satellites, how the planet itself had seemed to blink. Everything had turned black for a moment seemingly endless, but that had actually lasted for less than a second. The darkness had surrounded the Earth, blotted out the Sun.

Jenkins' mug reappeared on the screen.

– As you know I spoke to Professor Henry Marvin earlier today about the various stunning events we have witnessed since that day.

They saw Marvin's face, and heard his nasal, childish voice. A message, TAPED EARLIER, was shown in the upper right corner of the screen.

– I have to point out… Willard, Marvin stated, very smugly, – that there is no proof that the Great Darkness is linked to the other quite remarkable events the last ten years. There's a lot of supportive evidence to suggest that it is, but we can't be certain without further research.

– They don't know anything, do they? Melinda stated rhetorically. – Not really!

– No! Lucinda replied. – No one does. At least no one we know of. They're only guessing, stumbling through the night, like small children afraid of the dark.

She spoke with both contempt and despair evident in her voice.

– Not even your bright comrade in arms, Mechanic?

– No, Lucinda replied. – If you asked him, he would be the first to admit to how little he knows, and my guess would be that he's closer to the truth than most. After he gave us his albeit stunning rundown of his conclusions two years ago he hasn't really made much progress to speak of.

They sat there watching, not really watching, listening, not really listening. The long, unusually long news report approached its end.

– The guests have started to arrive. Willard Jenkins spoke excitedly into his microphone. – And yes, I have been told that two particularly honored guests are on its way.

The camera caught what were clearly two flying people, slowly descending in front of the building. They wore what were clearly very practical costumes and hoods, masks covering their heads, and even dark glasses, making it very difficult to make out any detail of their faces.

– There they are, the two the world has learned to know as Flight Captain and Raven Bird.

He rushed forward with his cameraman in tow, one of countless reporters surrounding the two recent arrivals.

Lucinda grabbed the remote, and turned it off, turned it all off. Melinda looked at her, but didn't protest or anything.

They sat there, gobbling popcorn and drank soda for a while. The eerie silence in the apartment bothered Lucinda a bit, and she was quite relieved when her kid sister finally spoke.

– So… do you think they will accept me, too… at the Center?

– I don't see why not, Lucinda said graciously. – They seem quite flexible and even reasonable there.

Somebody turned on the TV in the neighboring apartment, or at least somewhere close, and cracked the sound up loud. They heard Willard Jenkins speak again, finally ending his report.

– Some agree with Dr. Marvin. Others disagree. Vocal groups claim there's no connection what so ever between the Great Darkness and what followed, while other equally vocal groups claim the connection has been proven beyond doubt. But one thing is certain: Events similar to what we through decades before this one only read about in comic books and watched in movies are now an undeniable reality...

Lucinda walked to the window and shut it, and it worked. The loud sound no longer reached them.

The eerie silence returned.

– Are you going out tonight? Melinda wondered, a little anxious.

– Yes, Big Sister confirmed, – I'm definitely going out tonight.

– Can I come with you? Kid Sister implored her.

– No! A decisive shaking of the head. – You're too young, far from being strong enough yet, and you lack my essential power.

– But you started out when you were at my age, and even before.

– The world was not such a dangerous place then, not even close. You stay put, and when I say put I mean it. If you disobey me I will beat you to death. *Understand?*

Melinda shivered and nodded.

– Don't be like that, the girl whimpered. – I won't go out. Honest!

Lucinda's expression softened. She patted Melinda's cheek.

– I'm sorry. I'm concerned for you, that's all.

– I know that. Melinda nodded vigorously. – Don't think I don't and that I don't appreciate it. But I will count the days until I can join you on patrol.

– One night that day will come, Lucinda stated softly.

She went to the bedroom and changed into something more practical. Light, dark fabric, pants and shirt and a jacket. Then she picked up a small bag in the closet, and that was all it took. She was ready.

– Be careful, Melinda said. – You, too may encounter something out there you can't handle, you know.

Big Sister kissed Kid Sister on the forehead, and left.

It was close to midnight. Not many people were out. It was Tuesday and people had to go to work tomorrow. The streets were quiet. Lucinda made a sweep with her telepathic powers. No suspicious thoughts revealed themselves. A man waited for the late bus. He was the only one outside that she noticed. People had mostly retreated to their bedrooms or were already fast asleep. She sensed their fleeting thoughts dance at the edge of her mind.

Lucinda Patterson walked casually to the old construction site nearby, a project that never seemed to be completed or even continued. Funding had dried up years ago, and she and her friends had used it since then. A few walls had been erected, enough to shield her or anyone else walking in here from potentially spying eyes.

She put on the mask first. It was a loose, pleasant hood to wear, really, but still with a tight fit, having openings for just eyes and mouth. She removed the jacket briefly, before putting on the Kevlar west, her utility belt, with ropes, crossbow, stun gun, and a lot of light ordinance. When she was done to her satisfaction she turned her jacket inside out, and put it back on. It still had the dark hue, but looked completely different. She now wore her uniform, her strip jacket and spotted shirt and pants, the soft leather boots with the low heels.

As a final touch she put on the ring. It wasn't an ordinary ring, but a kind of gadget. She turned it on. It glowed briefly before stopping, and looked like a ring again. There was a shimmer in the air. An indistinct doorway appeared in front of her. The costumed woman stepped casually through it, vanished, and reappeared in a dark alley in another part of town.

She listened, with her ears and her powerful, buzzing mind. People passed by, in the busier street ahead. They didn't notice her, but she noticed all of them. She jumped, a giant leap up on the wall, and grabbed the solid pipe there. Strong hands held on and equally strong arms pulled her up. She climbed the tall wall and reached the roof in a matter of seconds.

A draft hit her, pushed at her, but she resisted it easily, and turned slowly, surveying her surroundings. There was no one up here with her, at the top of the world. She tensed, just a bit, and then she charged forward, and began running across the roof, towards the edge. At the exact moment, at the last step before reaching the end… she leaped. She flew across the fairly narrow street, another dark alley, to the other side of the abyss and landed there, safely, after the jump that would have beaten all previous world records in leaping, those measured before the Great Darkness. She kept running, and jumped across the next divide, too, and the next and the next, until she reached a main street several blocks away, one way too wide to bridge.

A few of the people below spotted her and pointed at her, crying her name.

– Look, they cried. – It's Gimmick!

The name she had chosen, the powerful name of her mask, the persona that had become her life.

She looked at the many people below and felt a warm, warm tingle down her spine.

24

Chapter 2
TEN YEARS AGO TODAY

The light turned from red to white. Howard Eisenhouse limped across the street, supported by his crutches, crossing on the zebra stripes. He was breathing hard after just a few «steps», his thin arms hardly able to utilize the crutches the way he was supposed to. His even thinner and practically useless legs were just dragged along.

There was movement all around him, people rushing back and forth, from and to all sides. It was a four-way cross-section, where everything blurred and dissolved and reformed simultaneously. A tall, slender girl looked at him with contempt, or so he imagined. He was sweating, sweating hard, and his armpits itched, itched terribly, but he couldn't scratch them.

It was a typically busy afternoon in the big city. Many impressions warred with each other for people's attention. Even an outward observer would have trouble gauging what was going on… or perhaps an outward observer was the only one capable of seeing the whole picture.

– Look at that cripple, thirteen-year old Lucinda Patterson said with glee to her friend Toni Farlani. – It's a wonder that he manages to stand at all.

Toni, and Lucinda's seven-year old sister Melinda, giggled wickedly.

A pained look in Eisenhouse's eyes told them that he had heard them, and it made them feel even better and triumphant.

The traffic lights flickered. Lucinda frowned. During one, prolonged moment both the red and white man flashed at her. The white, predominating at the time faded and the red not there at all glowed brighter, until they both glowed weaker than usual. In a flash she looked at the sun, and it wasn't there. She looked, in a fraction of a second at the sky. It was still blue, light blue. She looked where the sun had been a moment ago, and it wasn't there.

And
Then
The
World
Blinked

The world turned inside out, and Lucinda could swear she saw herself from above.

People stood frozen on their spot. The full, bright light of the sun, of the star embraced them, melting their chilled flesh and bone. The traffic lights kept flickering, like everybody's fast-moving eyes.

The man on the crutches fell. It was as if every iota of the remaining strength left his limbs. The girl swayed, Lucinda swayed and fell. The two sisters fell, colliding with an older girl. Lucinda fell on her, grabbing her hips in a hopeless effort to keep herself from falling. The grown girl screamed in pain. Lucinda looked astounded at her, feeling very dizzy and very confused.

– Get away from me, you dumb bitch!

Before Lucinda could respond or even thinking about responding, the grown girl was on her feet and running off.

Lucinda threw up, all over her clean, new dress. She heard cars blow their horns from far away. The white man had turned red again, and the zebra stripes were still filled with people, with confused and bewildered people. She heard them speak, but she didn't see their lips move. They didn't speak very loud. In fact she couldn't understand what they were saying. It was all a jumble in her head.

Toni stood upright. She reached out her hands to the two sisters. They reached out with one of theirs and allowed her to grab them, and she pulled them on her feet.

People rose. Just a few had fallen in the first place, but those standing didn't move much either. Someone finally helped the man with the crutches up. The drivers in their cars had given up on their horns. The street had turned quiet, deadly quiet, like a forest in winter.

But it wasn't winter. It was hot, hot spring and early summer and people stood there sweating their cold sweat in their light clothes, not really knowing what to do with themselves. Lucinda rubbed her head, her still wobbly head. It still hurt, as if she was hung over, an unpleasant condition she had had first hand experience with for the first time just a few weeks ago. Melinda had tears in her eyes, but she didn't scream or anything, just stood there with tears flooding her cheeks.

Everything seemed to have... stopped. People were moving, but not really going anywhere. Lucinda spotted a bunch of doves by a bench where an old lady had given them bread. They didn't move either. The young girl couldn't recall she had ever seen doves that weren't moving, weren't moving with a fast, energetic pace, pushing and pulling back and forth their little heads.

– I'm a doctor, a medical doctor, a woman in a white lab coat cried. – Is anyone... is anyone hurt?

People glanced at each other. A few had cuts and bruises, had blood trickling from small wounds, but all in all everyone seemed to be okay. Sirens slowly grew in the distance. Two cops began walking among them, studying them all carefully. Melinda giggled a bit, a sound totally out of context with the surroundings. The ambulance passed the square a few blocks away, fading in the distance.

– This must be happening all over the city, a man pondered nervously. – I guess there are people worse off than us, people in need of some serious medical attention…

They all looked at the woman in the white coat.

– I should probably be heading back to the hospital, she said. – If any of you feel the need to join me… feel free.

She hesitated a bit before moving, moving away from them. No one else moved, moved at all. She was used to handle a crisis, a busload of them on a daily basis. They watched her disappear around the nearest corner.

Slowly, almost like in slow motion people began moving, began removing themselves from what seemed like their designated spot. They left the square, and met others like them, other sleepwalkers. The line of cars also began moving, began their snail-like speed through the heavy afternoon traffic. No one used the horn. Everything seemed mechanical, still frozen. The doves rose in the air, seemingly suspended in their flight, the wings flapping very, very slowly and everybody heard the sound as they did.

The three friends continued on their way, taking first one, then several more steps forward. The light was red, but no cars honked and no drivers shouted obscenities at them to make them move faster. Lucinda watched as the cripple reached the other sidewalk. He looked as out of it as ever. The three of them hurried to the mall not far away. It hadn't seemed very far away, but now, somehow it did. The world stared back at people with an eerie look, and everyone seemed to move slowly, as if walking underwater.

But the air wasn't thick like water. Everything looked normal, looked the same.

Lucinda and Melinda's parents met them at the mall's entrance, anxious beyond words. The adults embraced the girls, also Toni.

– Are you girls all right? Brenda Patterson asked breathlessly. – We were so afraid, so afraid for you, all alone out there, in the madness.

– You are all right, Gilbert Patterson whispered, touching them, even squeezing them feverously, repeating his words again and again and again. – You're all right. You're all right.

– What *happened?* Toni wondered with a shrill voice.

– The whole world turned *black*, Melinda cried excitedly.

People around them stared at her, not all of them friendly or curious. The adult couple pulled the girls away, hurried off the fastest they could.

– We don't know anything yet, honey, Brenda said quickly. – I'm sure the authorities will tell us eventually, when they are ready.

– But they never do, mother, Lucinda protested weakly.

She still felt faint, her vision blurry, not quite right.

– Nonsense! Brenda dismissed her.

She looked at her oldest daughter with disdain.

– You've made a mess out of yourself. Let's clean you up.

She took Lucinda's hand and pulled her away, like she would Melinda, like she would a child. Lucinda wanted to protest, but she had no strength to give voice to her conviction.

Mother took her to the nearest restroom. She closed the door behind them, and began wetting toilet paper and carefully rubbing the girl's dress with it, at least partly successful in removing the stain of the vomit.

– That will have to do, she nodded. – We'll have the dress completely cleaned, eventually, of course.

Lucinda, still in a daze followed her through the crowd outside, up the escalators, and to the table father had chosen for them at the mall's top floor restaurant.

Everything seemed… off. A hectic, nervous mood dominated the venue. Everybody, or at least all adults, attempted to pretend that everything was normal, but everybody failed miserably. Lucinda and Brenda joined Melinda, Toni and Gilbert at the center table.

– Let's order right away, Gilbert said hastily. – It looks like there will be a while.

Lucinda looked at her parents, as if seeing them for the very first time.

They looked sweaty and agitated without necessarily that being the case. Their eyes flickered and wavered like leaves in the wind. They looked… different. She looked puzzled at them.

Gilbert ordered for them all. He let them slip in a few comments here and there, but didn't really consider them, or the few half-hearted objections coming to light. Lucinda got a headache. One moment it wasn't there, the next it was. A weird, eerie melody flowed from speakers somewhere in the mall. The discord seemed to dig into her brain and eat away at it. She bit her lip to not let out a whimper of pain.

The food arrived at the table. It was vegetarian. Gilbert was a vegetarian buff and zealot. Lucinda liked vegetarian, but she didn't really feel hungry. She took a bite, and stopped, taken back. It was delicious.

– This is *good*. Gilbert nodded eagerly, taking a *big* bite, adding a bit pensive. – They must have hired a new chef or something.

Lucinda nodded to herself. Her parents ate here because the food was cheap, in both meanings of the word, not because it was good.

She thought perhaps everyone was just hungry. Excitement did that, she had heard.

28

Toni hardly ate anything. She merely tasted it and that was it. She looked faint, grimacing, as if she didn't like the food at all.

The excited buzz in the mall didn't dissipate, but increased with every heartbeat. It was like the fluttering of wings, flapping, flapping, not visibly moving, but still sending ripples through the air, the ether of thoughts and mind created by all the people inside the large building.

The doves flapped their wings outside, inside. A bunch of them had entered the building. They flapped their wings loud and clear, a vibration touching the very foundation of the building.

Below a sign saying

DO NOT FEED THE PIGEONS

the birds fed to their heart's content.

Lucinda looked down at her plate. There was nothing there. She looked astounded at it. And then she noticed that her father and mother stared at their plates, too, at their empty plates.

The three of them looked at Toni and Melinda, watched them eating. Melinda was half done. Toni still hadn't touched much of her food at all. The meal ended. Lucinda noticed a strange throb in her belly, something previously totally unnoticed, alien. The ripples were both inside and outside her.

Outside afterwards, she still sensed it, the waves sending the buzz at her, momentarily overwhelming her. She grabbed her mother's arm, sore afraid. Brenda was preoccupied and didn't notice.

It subsided a bit on their way home, but not completely. Lucinda kept feeling woozy, and saw some of the people around her in a strange light, and they seemed distorted in a way. She wanted to tell her parents about it, but they looked creepy, too, and she kept her mouth shut.

People rushed back and forth and to the sides around her. Most of them didn't rub her feathers, but occasionally she spotted that eerie light, the same her parents emanated, and she shrunk in her tracks. It was just a few blocks to walk, but it felt much longer, as if the world had changed imperceptibly before her eyes. They said goodbye to Toni on the corner of their street, a strangely muted scene. Toni hurried away. Lucinda stood there and stared at her back, until her mother pulled her with her.

The apartment was dark and humid, as depressing as it always was. She went to her room, and put on her headphones, and threw herself on her back on the bed and stayed there, and let the music drown any sound, any loud sound and unpleasant voices from the living room.

She turned up the music. It did her no good.

Her head hurt and she had to turn the music back down. She had to turn it off altogether. The apartment, the entire building had turned quiet, it seemed. She opened her eyes, looking at her watch, wondering if she had slept. Her watch had stopped, showing the same as it had the last time she had checked. Mother cried her name. Lucinda frowned. She stayed in bed a few seconds longer, before leaving it, throwing the gear on the wrinkled sheet.

She combed her hair, sitting in front of the large mirror, doing just a few strokes… before she stopped. In the mirror she saw the same, distorted vision of herself, as she had seen of mother and father. She put the comb down, drawing breath hard. Eyes closed tight opened slowly. The eerie, shimmering light was still there, surrounding her like mist. She looked like a shadow of herself, of sorts. It faded eventually, when she had looked for quite a while, and she sighed in relief.

It was about to turn dark when she returned to the living room. She noticed the smell of food and frowned, and went to the kitchen.

– Ah, there you are, mother said.

– Did you call for me? Lucinda wondered.

– No, I didn't, Brenda replied brightly, – but I was about to. Your father and I have grown hungry again, and decided to have an extra dinner today. I guess that restaurant doesn't serve full meals anymore, but is cutting portions in an effort to save money. Well, they won't have us as customers anymore. I'll tell them that for free if the issue should ever come up.

And as if on cue Lucinda noticed the rumble in her belly.

She noticed her father the moment she returned to the living room. He looked restless and even antsy, constantly moving in his chair, looking at his watch, staring, casting long, anxious glances towards the kitchen. Finally fed up he turned on the television.

The top news was today's uncanny incident, as one would expect. They showed images, films taken by cell phones, showing streets, bright streets invert. A news team had been covering a rock star arriving at a hotel, and here it was, in high quality detail. People closest to the camera were actually visible in the blackness covering everything.

– There was… a man cried. – There was a… a Great Darkness embracing us, taking us in its arms, pulling us into its lap.

And that was how it was baptized, was given a name.

A panel of experts (or the usual pretence of such) sat around a table in a bright lit studio, having a typical flimsy discussion.

– There were warnings, I tell you, a man insisted, – minor things happening before and after, clearly a direct or indirect result of the Blink.

– God Blinked, a hysterical participant declared and looked up at the

30

ceiling, at the heavens.

The man that had spoken first looked at her and frowned, clearly…
bothered, not certain what to believe.

Lucinda heard Melinda complain, as was her want.

– But I'm not hungry, mommy.

– Sure you are, Brenda brushed her off. – C'mon, don't make a fuzz. We
will have a nice, pleasant family dinner and enjoy ourselves.

– Allow me to call your attention to these facts, the bothered man told his
fellow debaters.

The image on the screen zoomed in on the nearest traffic light, and they all
saw it, saw the flickering in the moments before the Blink, before the Great
Darkness.

Another stub showed people halt in their tracks and… frown right before
everything turned dark.

And there were other signs, and it was so amazing to see them all put
together like this. Lucinda felt the tiny, tiny trickle hammer her spine.

Brenda and Melinda had set the table and the four of them sat down
around it. The smell of the food played with Lucinda's vibrating nostrils.
Brenda had made lots of food, quite a lot. In the steaming kettle there was
far more than she usually put there. Lucinda looked amazed at it, not quite
able to wrap her mind around the fact her eyes told her, not able to make
sense of the constant buzz in her mind, of the dizzying pain in her frontal
lobe. She touched her head. It was as if she felt it move in there, felt it grow
and expand, as if she could actually see it expand.

They began eating. Lucinda ate. Melinda didn't really. The adults *fed,*
putting as much food in their mouth as humanly possible, and had
difficulties chewing and swallowing, and were forced to take it easier. The
two girls stared at them with distinct worry in their huge eyes.

Lucinda ate. She finished her first helping and started on another. By then
her parents had already started on their fourth. Melinda had stopped eating.
She just stared at her plate and just rearranged the food on her plate with
the fork. Lucinda saw that she had eaten over half of the heap, but she had
forced herself to most of it. She hadn't really been hungry.

It was some time later. Lucinda heard her sister in the bathroom, throwing
up. The sound seemed to shake the air in the apartment, somehow, making
Lucinda shiver slightly in the warm living room. The wind had picked up
outside, but none of it seemed to find its way into the building, in spite of
the open terrace door. Her father paced back and forth on the floor. The
moment Melinda returned from the bathroom he rushed out there. After
that it was her mother's turn. Lucinda sat there, waiting. She sensed the

beginning of a pressure in her arse. It felt unpleasant, even more so than usual. There was a sense of great relief when Brenda flushed the toilet and opened the door.

Lucinda rushed inside, into the room filled with the powerful stench of her parents' shit. It was gone from the bowl, but its stench lingered. She opened the window, opened it wide, before pulling down her panties and sitting down on the warm seat. The shit came fast, creating a strange relief in her. There was a bit of it. Two dinners in a day would do that to you, she surmised. In spite of the open window the stench seemed just as strong. She felt like puking, pushing as hard as she was able below. It took a while. Time seemed to stretch on forever in there. The strong draft from the open window, created by the powerful summer winds outside, made her cold and weary. Finally she was confident that she had let go of all the shit.

She dried her arse, flushed the toilet, pulled up her panties and pants and hurried out of there. Melinda sat in her room, pale and down. Lucinda glimpsed her face through the narrow opening of the door as she passed by. Brenda did the dishes. Gilbert watched television. He kept changing channels in the hope of avoiding the startling news from earlier today, in vain. It was everywhere, if not on an actual broadcast, there was footage on the advertising, amazing as that was. Father didn't look pleased. He had never had a temper, but now he looked like a storm cloud invading the living room with its lightning and thunder.

And he seemed confused as well, as if he couldn't really get a grip. The frown on his face kept deepening, and he shook his head ever so often, perhaps even without being aware of that fact. Lucinda returned to her room and stayed there for the rest of the evening, convinced, with her full stomach that there wouldn't be any more meals that day. Her stomach still felt full, felt content hours later, even though it often released rumbling sounds that made her embarrassed and ashamed.

She got tired fairly early. It wasn't even completely dark before she realized that she had actually closed her eyes and almost dozed off. She undressed and went to bed, and before long she was fast asleep and dreamed disturbing, vivid dreams.

The traffic-light flickered. She stood there, on the zebra stripes, staring at it, shaking her head, wanting to cry out, but no sound came from her shivering lips. Slowly the gray man flickered. Lucinda looked at the people, all the people, their faces and details. In the dream she had the time to turn and focus on everybody present. But something was not right. Her parents were there, too, looking very concerned, their frowns deep furrows in their skin.

It turned dark, a brief moment in time stretching on forever, and she could see, see in the dark. She would swear she could actually see better than before. When she looked at Melinda she saw that strange light or mist dance on her skin, and she saw her features twisting into something frightening and hardly familiar. Her parents looked like that, too, and several other people in the street, both in front of and behind her and on both sides. Those not changed didn't really look like people at all, but more like mannequins, unreal and dull.

And then she saw herself, a creature virtually bathing in the misty glow, changed by it, transformed by it, into something new and alien and terrifying.

The teacher spoke to her, sharply, a second attempt. She replied to the woman with the usual dull and fake eagerness, not sure whether or not the adult was fooled or if she just didn't care.

She grew aware of the first pangs of pain in her belly. Minutes passed while she made every effort to fight it off and hide the obvious signs of discomfort she imagined on her face. She reached up her hand and caught the teacher's attention.

– May I be excused? She whimpered and hated herself.

She was up and heading for the door without actually having seen or heard the teacher give her approval. The hall's quiet darkness comforted her a bit, while she hurried down the stairs to the restroom two floors below.

It was such a relief to get it all out and into the bowl that she almost broke into tears. She knew it had been close, closer than it had been since she had been a little girl. Everything practically forced itself out in one, powerful burst. There was a loud splash down there and her thighs got soaking wet. She got up, dried herself, dried herself thoroughly and flushed the toilet. There was a loud, deafening sound when everything was sucked down the pipes.

She returned to the classroom. The teacher looked at her with dismay.

– That was quite the trip, Miss Patterson…

– There was quite a lot of it to go around, Miss Johnson, she replied innocently.

The adult woman grew tomato red. She had trouble breathing and just stood there, frozen, paralyzed, without being able to act at all. The other pupils snickered and hummed, and that made Lucinda feel a little better, made the cold sweat pouring from her skin a little less cold.

Toni and a score of other girls approached her during the break.

– That was so *cool*, Toni giggled, and the rest of the chicks giggled with her.

– Yeah, Trish Markham chuckled wickedly. – You turned the tables on the ugly witch *magnificently*, making her look like a *lunatic*.

– I felt… inspired. Lucinda nodded graciously to her subjects, swelling in pride behind her stoic mask.

She noticed it easily back in the classroom, the admiration from everybody present, the wary look from the other teacher, and she enjoyed it.

The school day passed in a daze, even more so than it usually did. Lucinda's sense of triumph, of empowerment passed quickly, as it always did.

But Trish, Toni and the gang joined her after school, and the good feeling persisted. They went to an ice cream bar down the street. It was crowded there, but Lucinda didn't care. They bought their ice cream after standing in line for quite a while and sat down around a table outside.

Lucinda wolfed down the ice cream. The others looked stunned at her. She had finished devouring it before they were half done with theirs.

Toni glanced worriedly at her, one more worried glance added to those since yesterday's afternoon.

She knows, Lucinda thought startled.

Knows what?

Lucinda wanted another ice cream, but held back. The curious looks of her peers already made her cringe.

They prattled on as they made their way back. She didn't really listen, but walked in silence. The others didn't notice. She felt like everybody's eyes were on her the moment they entered their street. All of them lived here, or close by. Everybody knew everybody or knew of everybody. She did her best to ignore the unwanted attention.

– See you guys later, she said upon leaving them when reaching her place.

The replies from the others were far more heartily than it had been only yesterday, the admiration in their eyes obvious.

It made her feel good, really good as she ran up the stairs to the apartment. She found the key in her pocket and locked herself in. The apartment was empty. She was the first to arrive. Melinda stayed longer at school today, taking part in a new tryout program called «children's safety first», until either mom or dad picked her up after work.

Lucinda went straight to the fridge, for the ice cream there. She began feeding, in a more or less controlled frenzy, not even taking the time to savor the flavor. After less than ten minutes she had to sit down, looking stunned at the large, empty box.

She ran to her room, and stayed there, sat on the bed and didn't leave the room or even move when she heard the familiar sound of people in the hall.

Everything turned dark around her, and she didn't understand it, and began shaking, shaking hard.

When mother stood above her and spoke to her some time later she didn't

34

see or hear her at first.

– … I even shouted, mother said, her voice and shape fading into Lucinda's consciousness, – and you still didn't reply, and I got concerned.

– I ate all the ice cream, mom, Lucinda said sullenly.

– You what? A sense of relief mixed with the sudden smile in Brenda's face.

– I ate all the fucking ice cream. I couldn't stop. It was like a… craving, an itch I couldn't scratch. Am I pregnant, mom?

– WHAT? Both incredulity and concern returned to Brenda's face.

– I've read about it, the girl sniffed. – You get cravings, insane cravings for sweets. You even have to get up in the middle of the night to eat.

Weak-kneed Brenda felt an almost overpowering urge to sit down, right there, on the floor. Instead she pulled herself together and sat down by her daughter's side.

– Lucinda, she began, striving to keep her voice even, – I want you to be honest with me, and this is very important… you haven't… been with a boy, have you?

The girl looked stunned and incredulous at her.

– No, mom, *of course* not.

Realization and relief lit up her face, for a moment, before the anxiety returned.

– Perhaps I have a worm or something… perhaps that's it… a big, fat worm stealing all the food I eat, and perhaps she had a lot of b-babies filling up my belly, all of them growing hungry and g-greedy?

– It's time for dinner, Brenda said sternly. – Don't be such a baby.

Lucinda shrunk under mother's stare and let herself be taken out of the room and to the kitchen.

It was raining, raining hard. The Patterson-family sat around the dinner table. They didn't talk much. Lucinda didn't feel much like eating, but she did anyway. It was amazing how that rather large heap on the plate faded before her eyes. She noticed Brenda's worried glance, no matter how hard her mother attempted to hide it.

– So, how was school today? Brenda asked lightly.

– T'was okay, Lucinda shrugged.

– T'was okay, Melinda shrugged solemnly, looking at her older sister for appreciation, for acknowledgement of her undying loyalty.

– It seems like it will rain tomorrow, Gilbert said to no one in particular.

– It's raining every day these days, Brenda conceded.

And that was pretty much it, really. After that they fell silent in fact, not only in spirit.

Brenda took her to a physical checkup the next morning. As if by an unspoken agreement they didn't discuss it or anything, but quite simply went ahead with it. It wasn't far to go. This particular family doctor actually had an office in the neighborhood. The waiting room was cramped and probably had been long before they arrived. Half an hour after they had secured the two last seats it was filled up to such a degree that the nurses had to deny people access and ask them to return the next day.

Lucinda got a headache almost instantly in the crowded space. Every time she attempted to focus on a person's face it seemed to dissolve into an indistinct, misty glob, and the voices in the room rose to a noisy roar, a choir threatening to split her head. She kept rubbing her temples, to no avail.

A strange feeling came over her, as she looked at the others gathered in the room. Quite a few of them didn't look good either, and some of them stared at her with burning eyes.

She and mother had their lunch, the dry sandwiches and lemonade. Others had not been bright enough to bring food and they looked envious at those who had.

People were called into the private office of one of the three doctors and returned after a while, and the process repeated itself, time and time again, seemingly without helping much on the queue. Two extra doctors had been called in today. It didn't seem to be helping much either, even though it most certainly did. Lucinda knew that, intellectually, mathematically. It didn't make her feel any better.

She had no idea how long they had been sitting there, when her name was finally called. Looking at her watch didn't help. She saw nothing but a glob of incomprehensible dots. The world had been blurry for a while, now, but now it just faded away on her.

Doctor Hughes was indeed local, a mainstay in this part of the city. He serviced the upper middle class or those in the middle class with health insurance. Lucinda's father had a package that came with his job as a salesman. Times were fairly good. The package included random visits like these.

Lucinda wondered, once again, with her keen intellect about the numbers of people still queuing up in the waiting room. Hughes had a fairly good reputation, but he wouldn't help people unable to pay for his services, and there was quite a few in the neighborhood that couldn't do that, but still the place was crowded, practically overcrowded, and she wondered where everybody else went for their checkup.

It was obvious to her that a lot of people went for checkups today.

The doctor did her blood work, took her pulse, and did the most thorough check she could ever recall going through. He wasn't exactly the most considerate person she had encountered, and acted mostly as if she wasn't there at all, but right now she didn't mind that much. She felt detached, not really there, so his treatment of her felt strangely fitting.

He hummed while working, and she found it damn irritating, or she would have, if she had cared. The nurse did most of the work, of course, but she didn't seem to be present either. Lucinda attempted to catch mother's eyes, but she stood by the window and seemed to look at nothing. The girl began shaking, to the point of the nurse having trouble setting the needle for the blood work in her vein. They had to wait until the girl had calmed down somewhat.

Not that long afterwards it was she who stood by the dirty window, looking out at the yard, while mother and the good medical doctor walked into another room. They didn't think she could hear them, but she could.

The endless prattle hurt her ears, and she wondered if they had thought about that, if they considered her feelings at all.

– I think you can take it easy, Mrs. Patterson, he insisted. – We have to wait for the results of the tests, of course, but in my professional opinion there's nothing wrong with your daughter. In fact she's one of the healthiest people I've ever seen.

He hesitated. Lucinda saw it. The door was slightly ajar. That was sufficient, or at least she imagined that it was.

– Yes, doctor? Brenda urged him.

– It's quite remarkable, really, he finally added. – It's quite the change from last time I examined her. Oh, she was quite okay then, too, but not this very image of health she is today.

– So, why does she have the dizzy spells and… everything?

– It could be a number of… explanations, he replied. – Everything from nerves, to… euphoria.

– *Euphoria?* Mother cried nonplussed.

– Precisely. Everybody I've spoken to has been a little on edge since the… incident. It's well within the parameters of possibility that people's defense mechanism has kicked in, and thereby triggering a surged mood of some kind. It's not unheard of and in this case mass hysteria is far more likely than in most other cases I have on file.

That was the last Lucinda heard. The buzz in her ears or in her mind rose to a crescendo, and when she came to a little later she feared she might have blacked out.

Brenda stood behind her, ready to leave. She knew that, before she turned around, and before Brenda had spoken.

They left, both feeling an enormous sense of relief. The noise in the streets hammered them. She heard people speak on the walk back to the apartment.

– This was no eclipse, a man cried. – At least there wasn't the usual case of the moon covering the sun, and certainly not its shadow engulfing the entire Earth. For that to be happening, the moon would have to have momentarily jumped from its orbit, and grown to an enormous size from one moment to the next and shrunk back to normal size again just as fast.

It made no sense to Lucinda.

She followed mother home, like a dog following her master, except there was nothing of the eager servitude usually displayed by any given dog. It was just a dark cloud of despair.

They passed a friend of her on the opposite street corner. Lucinda didn't wave, but kept walking blindly. The other girl hesitated a bit, before shrugging and continuing down the street, away from Lucinda and mother, on their way home.

She stayed home from school the next eleven days. A shrink, after another long day in a queue, diagnosed her with «acute depression» and prescribed anti-depressive drugs, a «treatment» making her feel even worse, until mother finally wised up and stopped administering the shit.

The results of the tests came through. They were totally conclusive and confirmed Doctor Hughes' conclusions. In a way it just made Lucinda even more depressed. She did eat, breakfast, dinner and at least two more meals a day. It made her feel sick, but she couldn't keep herself from eating. The hunger was like a howling wolf inside.

Being cooped up in the apartment finally got to her, and overwhelmed her dislike of leaving it. She returned to school. Everything had changed. It didn't exactly look different, but the feel was so vastly dissimilar that she felt the distortion like a big, bad lump in her throat.

She sat in the back of the class, shrinking in her seat, attempting to look as inconspicuous as possible. Miss Johnson needled her, but she didn't really deal with her or it at all. She did sort of return to her circle of friends, and they took her in, not giving her too much grief, but it didn't feel right, didn't feel wrong.

It didn't *feel!*

The gang went dancing at the local disco. It was an afternoon gig for young teenagers with a *strong* parents' presence, and none of the teenagers really enjoyed being there, but it was the only show in town or in their part of town, so they went there by default.

– What are we gonna *do* with all those guards ogling us, anyway? Trish exclaimed exasperatedly. – They're even in the restrooms, for god's sake.

The others unanimously agreed, their prattle hurting in Lucinda's ears.

She shrugged. Right now she didn't care. The blinking lights, the moving shadows took her mind off things outside.

Lights flickered on the dance floor. She threw herself into the moving and shaking with the rest of them. It felt strangely liberating, quite different from her previous visits to this dismal place. She danced, light on her feet, suddenly feeling good, feeling great over the surprising strength in her limbs. They weren't really allowed to dance *with* anyone, but she danced with a boy, feeling strangely liberated. He moved across the floor from her, but each time their eyes met there was... a connection. It hurt. It hurt every time, and she felt like crying.

She sat on the toilet bowl, pushing out her shit. It hit the water surface below with a loud, plump sound. She dried tears all she was good for, and couldn't believe all there was of the aching water, wondering where it was coming from.

When she excited the stall, the chaperone was there, ogling her. She knew her eyes were dry, but could do nothing with the swollen tissue surrounding them.

She basically ignored the grown woman, pretending she wasn't there, and it worked, and as she left the restroom, she felt a kind of empowerment rise within.

The dance clearly empowered her, with each new step. Elation grabbed her, and she rode with it, deliberately taking it a step further, making others glare at her, without caring.

The gang studied her afterwards, as they sat in the «bar» with each their milkshake, with both admiration and unease in both their posturing and their eyes. She read them like open books, and it felt so good, good, good.

– That was some *moves*, girl, Toni said, with both envy and relief evident in her voice. – You haven't been taking secret lessons or anything, have you?

– Nope, I guess I'm just a natural, a late bloomer finding my calling.

They laughed with her, not of her, and it created a well of good vibrations inside.

Everything had worked so well. The dance stayed with her, long after it had ended. She recalled the strength in her muscles, the sensation her easy use of them created in her mind.

The first signs of dusk had begun to show when they made their way home. Lucinda sensed it as well as she saw it. The others prattled on. She heard whispers in the shadows, and couldn't help but listening to them, even though she didn't understand what they were saying. The others spoke about boys, about fashion, clothes, purses and shoes and fancy watches. Lucinda studied Trish, her pink dress, her lipstick and make up, and wondered about how it would feel to be in her stead, to be the most popular girl at school.

She imagined how it would be, and just for a moment there, she imagined she could actually see through Trish's eyes.

It freaked her out, and she almost cried out in surprise, and the illusion faded.

They reached what was familiar home turf to most of them, but it no longer looked familiar to Lucinda, but alien and threatening. She wanted to speak to the others about it, but she didn't dare.

People stared at her, as if they could look straight through her, and see her for what she was. She knew most of them, but they looked at her with menace in their dark eyes.

– What was that, honey? Toni wondered.

– They have dark eyes, she repeated.

Toni considered it, but finally shaking her head.

– Nah, I don't think so. It might look that way, on a day with a lot of dark clouds in the sky, but it's just a trick of the light, you know.

They reached her street and bid her farewell. She walked the last, short stretch to her entrance alone. A man stood close to it. He just stood there, hardly even moving. A man dressed in light, non-descriptive clothes and white shoes stood on the lawn right by her entrance and she had to pass him, and butterflies flapped their wings in her belly, and a pang of pain gripped her.

He stared at her, and at this time she could no longer pretend he wasn't focused on her.

– You are pregnant, you know, the old man told her, leered at her. – But not with a child. You have a demon inside of you, and it will grow and grow. It will wax and you will wane until it is everything and you are nothing.

She hurried inside. On the next floor she glanced back out, through the large window to see if he was still there, and he was. A convulsion rattled her, and she whimpered in terror.

The silence loomed in the apartment, even more than it usually did. She made herself some sandwiches and finished them all in what seemed like one bite. Mother and father sat in their designated chairs, not saying much of anything. Silence loomed.

She stayed in her room all night.

Chapter 3

Tobruk had been called the rain city for centuries, but that designation no longer applied. During the last five to ten years it had turned into a dustbin of sweltering heat. There had been several instances when there had been a severe drought and use of water had been restricted. Night or day, it didn't really matter. Now, just after sunset was still boiling hot, and would remain so, until next morning, when the sun once again would begin boiling the streets of Tobruk.

Gimmick moved through back alleys and dark streets in her stealth mode, alert and ready for anything. She was sweating, inadvertently in the heat. This, her «summer costume» had exposed thighs and no sleeves, but it hardly mattered. She heard and also listened to the whispers of the night, still after all the years after her powers had manifested not being able to tell if there were real whispers or in her head. A man, a homeless, with a sweaty and dirty face stood by a burning oil barrel, cooking some suspiciously looking meat. He stared at her with insane eyes, and she felt the familiar shiver slide down her spine.

A colleague of hers, Jolene Masters, codename Oracle had used her power to create a maze of portals throughout the city and the world at large a while after she had been accepted into their organization, their club, The Maverick Crew. No one knew exactly how Oracle's powers worked, but she was also psychic, a Seer, able to glimpse and sometimes know the future. Jolene was missing. She had been for some time, for two years, and that created no small amount of concern in Gimmick and her colleagues.

Jolene was the only one of them with a known civilian identity, and that clearly made her vulnerable.

The portal was in an alley around the corner at the end of the street. Gimmick could almost sense it, or imagined she did. Oracle had made sure it didn't work for anyone but the Maverick Crew, or anyone accepted by them, another aspect of her power. The rings made them see the portal, by slightly extending their eyes' way of perceiving light, making them see more of the so called electromagnetic spectrum. Mechanic, their resident Whiz kid had whipped up the rings for them. Other people might still glimpse a shimmer in the air when they approached, but it wouldn't work for them.

This was the second portal Gimmick had to go through. They had deemed it unsafe to have one directly to their homes or close to them, and they didn't know each other secret identities anyway. Another safety measure Lady Grace had insisted on.

Of course, she, like Gimmick, being telepathic knew everyone intimately.

There were other people along her chosen route, but she masked herself to them. She couldn't make herself totally unseen, but she was able to keep their attention off her, when there weren't too many of them, when she wanted it. Gimmick was a shadow stalking the city. She smiled, an expression only marginally visible through the mask.

The mask… she watched herself through the glimpse of a dark window. It didn't seem like a face at all, but like a body and no head. She shuddered and hurried on.

The hard muscles on her thighs tightened further when she turned the corner. She spotted the gate ahead, in all its glory. There were just a few more steps. She reached it, and with a slight hesitation she stepped through.

She appeared at the other side, feeling nauseous and disoriented. It always felt this way, as if she had been shaken apart and put together again. She appeared in a pleasant-looking entrance hall. It felt like the very building itself was greeting her, welcoming her.

There was a door on the wall behind her, an ordinary door, but it hadn't been used for years. This was why no one could see any of them come and go. It was a genius setup.

She walked the short distance from the gate to the assembly hall. Most of the others had already arrived. The Bowman arrived as she was sitting down in her chair, the chair with her name on it.

– Sorry I'm late, he grinned. – I had to stop a hold up in progress at Chester Avenue. It could have turned ugly.

He looked completely unfazed. It couldn't have been much of a struggle.

He was dressed in a black and dark gray uniform pretty much like hers, without the spots, his jacket a little tighter, showing off his muscles. His grin warmed her.

She deliberately ignored him and focused on each and every one gathered around the table.

The table was a kind of soft, stretched triangle, pointed at one end and rounded at the others. At its head sat Flight Captain and Lady Grace, at each side of the point. They were the co-leaders of The Maverick Crew. The others present were Gimmick, The Bowman, Raven Bird, Mechanic, Martial Athlete and Energetic.

Gimmick was the tallest of them all, and also the biggest of the females. The Bowman was the tallest male, and clearly both strong and agile. Most of them had the growth gene, as it had been named. Only Energetic was totally without visible signs of it. The others had it, to some degree or the other.

– I call this meeting to order. Flight Captain rose and everybody straightened in their chair.

His uniform was basically shades of deep blue, creating a match to Lady Grace's light blue and light gray. They clearly fit together, in more ways than one. Everyone could easily see that when they saw them standing there.

The Bowman had his eyes on Gimmick, as had been the case from the moment he had entered the room. She felt his attention and had difficulty focusing on what went down. His mind was extremely well focused… on her, and she couldn't help responding to it. She had to change her position on the chair every tenth second or so. His grin widened.

A young, innocent face revealed itself on the wall, one they all knew well, and they all, even The Bowman felt the familiar sense of loss and despair.

– Oracle, Jolene Masters remains missing, in spite of our prolonged, strenuous effort at locating her. During the two years that have passed since she vanished, no significant clues have turned up concerning her whereabouts. We have all gone that extra mile in order to find out what *happened* to her, but all we have to show for ourselves is half baked rumors and hearsay. No body has been found, but aside from that there is no way to tell if she is alive or dead or captured or injured or something else.

– She vanished just after Cougar went underground, Raven Bird cried. – Surely that's no coincidence?

– But no one has heard from Cougar either, Gimmick said. – Shouldn't she, if she's truly behind this surface at one point or another.

– She's biding her time. Lady Grace struck the table with her fist. – Waiting for her spot, her chance to fulfill Oracle's prophecy. There are many people out there that have never put on a costume she could recruit and train for whatever her plans are.

– It doesn't make sense. The Bowman shook his head. – Even if there is another, yet unknown major player out there he or she or It isn't any less of a ghost than Oracle and Cougar.

They talked about this for a while, like they always did, venting their frustration, before finally having worked up the nerve to move on. This was a sore spot, and had been since that fateful day two years earlier. They avoided each other's eyes.

– One thing is certain. Flight Captain stated ominously. – It's growing increasingly dangerous out there, with ever more empowered groups and individuals popping up everywhere.

– We need to re-establish control. Lady Grace nodded, giving Flight Captain an affirmative smile. – We have allowed it to deteriorate for way too long.

– We were the first, Energetic said. – That should count for something in terms of clout… right?

He was in fairly good shape. In fact it could be said he was in extremely good shape. Everybody would have said that about him ten years ago. Now, he hardly looked average.

The others nodded and voiced their agreement.

Gimmick jumped to her feet and began pacing back and forth in front of her side of the table.

– Oracle was… afraid, she stated, frowning. – She knew what was coming, or at least enough about it to give us her warnings. Perhaps if we hadn't let Cougar go or let Oracle go alone that day…

Calm yourself, little one. Lady Grace spoke in her mind. Nothing is gained by such theatrics.

Lucinda wanted to give her an angry reply, but relented, and sagged and stopped, feeling like a little girl again.

Everybody looked down. The big woman's sentiment was shared by all.

They had been shocked, practically paralyzed because of the events that day. Cougar had just left, and no one had lifted a finger to stop her. Everything had started to go sour from that moment on.

– I have to pee, Gimmick said weakly.

The Bowman looked like he wanted to throw her a funny remark, but even his mood wasn't up for it.

Gimmick rushed to the toilet, suddenly feeling very full. Being upset always made her bladder act up.

The restroom was bigger than most public toilets, with room for everybody and then some, if they should all need to use it simultaneously.

She closed and locked the door to the stall closest to the door, pulled down her short pants and sat down on the bigger, specially designed bowl. The heavily scented water flooded like a waterfall less than a second after her thighs had touched the seat. The stench burned like acid in her nostrils.

Her eyes stung when she closed them. She struck the marble wall with her right fist and the entire room shook. The piss kept on coming, as if there was no end to it. It was merely yet another result of her heightened metabolism, and hadn't given her as much grief over the years as the shit, but still more than enough.

She heard them out there, could easily follow the conversation and moods through others' eyes and ears.

And as a constant she sensed, no felt Lady Grace's probing of her own mind. No deep probe, but still there, an ongoing presence in Lucinda's consciousness, at least on occasions when they were in fairly close proximity, like now.

She saw her own sweaty face as a reflection in the marble, and also the gathering, as she made the mistake of watching it all through the Bowman's eyes, and picked up on his lewd thoughts. He watched Lady Grace openly. Lucinda knew that irritated her to no end. Lady Grace wouldn't be caught dead with a man she considered to be an inferior among inferiors, and he knew that, and it made him even more eager and bold.

The flow of retching piss finally ceased. Lucinda sighed once again in sick relief. Sometimes, at her worst she feared it would never stop.

She dried herself. The piss seemed more like soup. She hadn't been drinking enough water, and paid the price for that now.

Everybody deliberately didn't look at her when she returned. She saw through their pretense easily, but didn't say anything.

— Martial Athlete was telling us about his last encounter with the Brewery Boys, Flight Captain said, clearly to lift her spirits.

That made her smile, inevitably. The Brewery Gang was a standing in-joke in the superhuman community.

— Those geezers never get it right, Martial Athlete grinned. — They are as inept today as when we first encountered them.

He was thinner than most with the growth gene. Even though his genetic potential leaned more towards a more powerful build, he had gained a mean, lean body through rigorous exercise and the knowledge of ancient techniques.

Flight Captain studied her, to gauge her reactions, to see if she needed further encouragement, like an officer with his troops before a battle.

He was a great fighter, very good in a combat situation, but quite a softie otherwise. She suspected that was why Lady Grace stayed with him; because he was so easy to handle.

— Ulysses and Trevor came at me with their fists, showing themselves as incapable and inefficient fighters as always. I took them out in a few seconds and threw them back at their gang, before any of the henchmen could fire a shot at me.

Ulysses and Trevor Rogan, the Brewery Brothers had the growth gene and were quite strong, but without the training necessary to utilize it properly.

— They have a nice sister, Mechanic whistled.

He glanced around at the females present, as if to apologize for his sexist whistle. They ignored him.

— She's the white sheep of the family, Lady Grace commented curtly, making Mechanic shrink like a slug before Her Majesty. — Generations of Rogans have a rap sheet, but she works as a teacher in the Pit in Jaynagar, working to improve people's lives.

The Pit was the pit to end all pits, the worst of the worst of downtrodden areas in any modern city. Jaynagar was the largest city in the southern part of the West Coast, one of the largest in the world, and hot as hell.

– I wonder what happened to them, the Bowman wondered. – They disappeared along with the other convicts, didn't they?

– Disappeared like dew in the morning sun, Martial Athlete confirmed.

There had been a mass escape from the Folson Penitentiary recently, a prison with an entire wing dedicated to those that could break out of an ordinary prison without breaking a sweat. Every single inmate, both enhanced and not had escaped… and vanished without a trace, as if they had all been dropped into a black hole or something. Even all the guards and security personnel had disappeared. Not one had resurfaced in the close to two months since it had happened. It was a source of great mystery and great concern.

Silence fell among those gathered around the twisted triangle, their good mood gone they refused to look at each other.

There was a draft, in a room with even ventilation and regulated temperatures. They couldn't tell where it originated from, only that it was there.

– We have to step up our efforts, Flight Captain insisted (and Lady Grace approved), – do it all full time for a while. I imagine most of you need a few days to make arrangements. We'll meet back here when everybody is ready.

Lucinda felt a thrill inside. It was happening, finally happening.

Lady Grace turned to Mechanic.

– What about your search efforts? Any improvements?

– Not so far, he replied, clearly nervous under her pointed stare. – As you know I calibrated the machine to locate Oracle based on her recorded brainwaves, but either they've changed or she's in a place where she can't be found, a place with powerful magnetic currents or similar, or…

– Or she's dead, Lucinda cried.

There, it was said, a festering wound had been opened wide. She felt the others' despair and anger.

– I'm not ruling out any possibilities, Mechanic insisted. – I'm also working on ways to boost the machine's capacity. We have a lot of the disappeared on file, anybody we've ever captured actually, and most of those we've cooperated with. I can usually track the latter quite well, and have learned a lot doing so, but there is much to work out before I can actually making it work on a bigger scale.

He had been bright also before the Great Darkness, and it had only enhanced his natural abilities.

46

Name anything mechanical and he could do it, and he wasn't bad with electronic gadgets either. The man had an uncanny ability to know how things *worked*.

Gimmick often got the creeps because of the way he looked at her. He wasn't sexually interested in her. She knew how that felt.

He looked at her, studied her, like he would one of his gadgets.

– Well, then, Flight Captain stated, – if no one has more to add, I declare this meeting for adjourned.

– We'll rendezvous back here at the regular time, Lady Grace said before anyone had a chance to say anything, – but be prepared to stay for quite some time.

– To kick some serious butt, the Bowman cried. – Finally.

– A-men, Martial Athlete said pleased.

The two of them did a high-five. Lady Grace looked displeased at them. They ignored her.

Then she grabbed Flight Captain's hand and kissed him on the lips in a very possessive move, very deliberately, smiling sweetly to the two other men.

Gimmick and the Bowman remained, as the others left. Raven Bird waved cheerfully goodbye to her. Lucinda returned the wave meekly and red-faced.

There was a swooping sound as the others stepped through the portal in the hall, then silence. Gimmick and The Bowman were alone.

He stepped close to her and grabbed her, kissing her possessively without delay. She stiffened and attempted to hold back, before relenting and eagerly returning his affection.

– I should go back, she mumbled. – My sister…

– … is more than capable, from what you have told me of taking care of herself, he grinned.

Lucinda sighed. It was true. In her zeal to join her sister on patrols and eventually join the Maverick Crew Melinda exercised and trained Martial Arts fanatically, even though she had quite some ground to cover before reaching the necessary level where she could take care of most mundane threats.

He began undressing her with great skill, as he pulled her with him into his private quarters. She began tearing at his clothes, too, though not with the same efficiency. He managed, somehow to remove his own clothes while he kept undressing her. She tore off her vest with growing impatience, several of the weapons concealed on its inside loosened from their straps and hit the floor. He began fingering with the straps to her mask.

– No, she mumbled, then repeating it firmly. – No!

– But I want to see your face, he protested.

– I'm scarred and ugly as sin, she grinned wickedly, twisting her lips into a snarl.

– You know who I am, but you won't let me know who you are.

– I do, she spat. – I know all your dirty secrets, peeled away like the skin of a fruit…

– It isn't *fair*.

– Everything is fair in love and war…

He grabbed her top, and she stretched her arms above her head. She stood nude before him. He grabbed her, and began fondling her, kissing her wildly. They tumbled down on the bed (the large bed). He began caressing her from top to toes, making her skin beyond sensitive, making it burn with a low flame. She felt her nipples grow hard and large, felt her pubic hairs turn wet as sin, and she gasped, and then a loud moan rose from her throat. He grunted in anticipation. She kissed him and grabbed his cock, and began rubbing it, rough, very rough, without any sophistication, only with an impatience born of an insane desire. He grabbed her. In one single, effective move he had placed her on all fours.

– NO! She gasped in protest.

– Yes, he chuckled.

He touched her between her thighs, in her moist weakness. She moaned long and deep.

– Yes, she mumbled. – Yes! YES! YES!

He grabbed her hair and pulled, pulled her head hard back. She hardly noticed. In a brief, but indefinitely long loop she glimpsed his erect cock, saw him, felt him push it teasingly between her thighs, push it at her hole without penetrating her aching large lips.

– Please, she mumbled. – *Please!*

There was a slight delay, almost making her insane with need, before he pushed himself deep within her. She shouted in wild joy. They began moving, back and forth, back and forth, back and forth. He was big. He filled her up, or so it felt.

– Yes, baby, she cried. – Do it, *fuck me,* fuck me *hard.*

She was in his mind, sensing his passion, but everything was jumbled, incoherent, and even if it hadn't been she would have been way too far gone to perceive it. What had begun as an itch spread through her body like wildfire. Both bodies were soaked in sweat. The moves turned even wilder, more uncontrollable, totally dominated by instinct and devoid of reason. Then… then it finally exploded into a beyond savage pleasure. They fell on the bed, gasping and kissing each other in wild abandon.

They lay still in each other's arms afterwards. She held around him and granted him wet, sultry kisses, a beyond pleased look painted clearly on the visible part of her sweaty face.

– My lovely, lovely Bowman, she whispered sweetly.

Again her lips twisted in the mask's opening.

She rubbed her breasts at his chest. He buried his face in them, and she cried out and laughed in surprised delight.

– You're such a crook, Richard Pearce, she chided.

He bit her nipple, a bit too hard. She bit her lip, but had to release a slight moan.

– You *enjoy* this, don't you?

– Do you enjoy doing it? She countered.

She scratched his skin, leaving a long and bloody mark. She licked her fingers, challenging him to do something about it.

They wrestled a bit, fighting for control. He was stronger, but she was craftier, and they both lost, as mindless passion struck them yet again, as they rocked back and forth on the bed. She couldn't recall him entering her this time. It seemed like he had always been there. He squeezed her thighs. She cried his name again, but heard no sound. She heard only him repeating Gimmick, Gimmick, lovely, lovely Gimmick, and then the hot water rolled in from the sea, and all rational thought faded into darkness.

The smile showed afterwards, not only on her face, but also on her body. She knew it did, saw it in his eyes as they showered, as they fucked yet again, and again, and she lost count over how many times it happened. He made sure her mask got wet, that shithead. She struck him, struck him in ever weaker strikes, as her fist crumbled to an open hand, and they both fell on the floor and the water kept falling on their steaming, steaming bodies.

She dried herself with a large towel, feeling wanted, desired, and making sure he got a good look at her, at her luscious body, knowing that he, in his mind wanted her again and again and again. He dressed. She dressed. They exchanged kisses and parted, there in the hall, before the shimmering portal.

The smile stayed in place, as she walked through the portal, through the shimmering city heat, on her way home. Her mask was still wet, but it was no big deal. She had made it to take a little rain. If her mind had been sharp and open before, it was even more so now. She reached out with ease to the city surrounding her, to its crowds of people, touching them, and even allowing them to touch her a bit, just a bit. But she could do so much more, she knew she could. She wanted to.

A lingering flash stayed with her for a while after she appeared at the abandoned construction site. Changing clothes was done in a whiff. She removed the mask and frowned. It was full of stain, his stain. She would have to clean it.

There was no one close when she left the half-erected walls. She reached out far to make sure, and could only sense active minds far away, at the edge of her consciousness. There was no immediate danger. She walked in a languished, relaxed pace towards the block of flats she called home. There was a street of stores, not far off her route. She chose the detour without really considering it much. A few of the places had late night opening hours. She could easily make out Melinda's tall frame behind the desk of one of the grocery stores.

Still in Gimmick-mode she remained in the shadows for a while, like the shadow she was, carefully studying the scene before her, before crossing the street.

The place resounded with loud music. This was a modern store, not exactly a quiet place to fill the fridge, but one with a lot of stuff beside stuff on their plate. Melinda and the other girls' scarce fashion clothing, among the other «hip» stuff designed to draw costumers illustrated that in excellent ways.

Melinda waved. Lucinda returned the wave.

There were just a few late customers. The store was about to close.

– Goddess, what happened to you, Melinda asked.

– Nothing much, Lucinda shrugged.

Kid Sister touched Big Sister's sore jaw. Lucinda cringed.

– What about this?

– I hardly noticed. Don't worry, he got as much as he gave.

Melinda wanted to say more, but the manager came within hearing distance and she pretended to be busy with counting the money in the cashier. It had to be exactly the right amount. If there was too little she would have to front the rest. If there was too much she would still be given grief from the manager. There was hardly ever the correct amount.

The girls and boys (the sweet boys) gave today's sale to the manager and in return he gave them a receipt. Lucinda and Melinda and the others left the store. The manager was closing shop. Lucinda saw no signs of trouble, no one moving in on the man as he took the cash to the (very solid) night safe, and she relaxed some more.

– Hey, Melinda, a boy cried, – we're going to Henrec. Are you coming?

– No thanks, she replied, – I'm beat. Perhaps another time.

They looked at her with pity. Lucinda knew that look, knew it very well.

The sisters walked home. Melinda had bags under her eyes. Lucinda spotted them easily, even in the bad light.

– Are you okay? She asked carefully.

– It *is* a strain, Melinda conceded willingly, – to go to school all day and then work at night, but I'm good. I have to be, right?

That was true, especially now, when Melinda, too, had begun devouring food like a beast. They needed the money, needed them badly.

– The Center's model agency may have some work for us, Lucinda said, cautiously optimistic. – If everything goes well the money will be quite good.

– Oh, Melinda frowned, then grinned happily, – but that's wonderful. Isn't that *wonderful?*

– It might be, Lucinda acknowledged, – but remember what I said: It's a possibility, not a certainty.

– Don't worry, mom, Kid Sister said insulted, – I'm a big girl and can take a little disappointment. But I've checked out these guys on the Grid, and they seem to be on the level. Very few have anything profoundly bad to say about them.

The Grid was the world-encompassing communication and information network that had arisen the last twenty years, a mix of a library, a market and a place where everybody could post their thoughts, and discuss any topic they wanted. It was, essentially the greatest library in history.

Lucinda had also made a thorough check, both on the Grid and elsewhere.

They strolled the few blocks back to the apartment. The night hummed quietly around them.

You're scanning, aren't you? Melinda thought. If you want to conceal that you should learn to avoid that wary look. It shines through your cheerful mask anytime.

I do, Lucinda admitted willingly. There is something…

… something *out there*. At that very moment she felt it more than sensed it, a chill, a dark laughter, something or someone… studying her.

There had been nothing, nothing substantial, until this second, one stretching into an eternity, as if whoever or whatever was out there allowed her to notice, or deliberately let itself be noticed. It was an instant of profound fear that Lucinda had never quite before experienced.

She speeded up, inevitably and didn't care if Melinda or anyone else noticed.

Melinda noticed her fear and therefore, by default she got scared, too.

– What is it? She asked anxiously. – Tell me!

– I don't *know,* Lucinda replied, striving to keep her voice even. – I've never felt anything like it. It's hard to tell whether or not it's directed at me, at us or not. It could be that someone wants to send me a message. That he or she knows my secret, but it could just as well just be a general sweep or something, by someone, something looking for enhanced people.

– But it freaked you out, right?

– Yes, Lucinda admitted, unable to keep her voice even. – It was a vicious, menacing presence which equal I've never before sensed, far less encountered.

She speeded up further. Melinda sought closer to her, shivering, not even attempting to put up a brave front. They turned the corner to their street, and saw the entrance to their block. It was silly, even stupid, really, since whatever enemies there might be might just as well be waiting to ambush them in their apartment, but Lucinda felt an overpowering sense of relief.

The neighbors' familiar faces gave her a kind of comfort, provoking a cautious smile on her face. The two sisters headed up the stairs to the loft they cohabited. Lucinda walked with closed fists, her nails digging into the skin of the palms. She was scanning, probing the upper floors as hard as she possibly could, so much harder than she had ever done before.

The apartment waited for them, dark and ominous. Lucinda pushed the button by the door, fully aware that she was giving any would-be attackers an easy target as a silhouette against the hall light.

There was nothing there, only their worn-down and somewhat cozy loft apartment.

They slipped inside and locked the door behind them, doing a quick search through their home, but found nothing, nothing unfamiliar or threatening.

– I don't understand, Melinda wondered. – Why are you physically searching everywhere? Shouldn't your mind power...

She stopped, getting it.

– The presence I felt was powerful, Lucinda whispered or thought she did. – I can't be certain it can't... mask itself from my probes.

– Your bad dreams, Melinda cried. – Is that it? You've dreamed about this... threat?

– Yes, Lucinda acknowledged. – Perhaps. I don't know!

She put down her bag and turned towards her smaller, weaker sister.

– Attack me, she said curtly.

Melinda understood and didn't object in any way. She crouched, balancing on her toe balls and rolled her hands into fists. She threw herself at the giant before her. Lucinda struck her with her flat hand and sent her sprawling across the floor.

– No, Lucinda spat. – Attack me, with everything you've got. You fear and hate me. I'm your enemy, and you'll do anything to defeat, to vanquish me.

Melinda dried her lips and was astounded to see the blood on her hand, to taste the warm blood in her mouth. She snarled and attacked, kicked out at her opponent.

Lucinda grabbed her foot, twisted it, making Kid Sister scream, and struck her, struck her hard in the belly.

The girl lay there, on the floor, gasping, defeated, humiliated, looking at her enemy with fear and hatred in her swollen eyes.

– Now, you know, know how helpless you would be against virtually any well-trained assailant.

Melinda nodded, tears of frustration and pain filling her eyes.

– Strike at me with your mind then.

– But I can't, I haven't... I can only see and hear and smell and taste well, Melinda said incredulous and bitterly. – My power is as dangerous as a kitten without claws.

– In my experience all powers have an active, aggressive component, Big Sister said. – Find it! Strike at me with all the hate and fear and passion you can muster.

She virtually saw it, saw and even sensed how Melinda focused, how she attempted to strike out with whatever rested there, inside her skull.

Nothing happened.

Lucinda relaxed, her tense pose slackened, and Melinda seeing it, relaxed, too.

– We can't train properly here, Lucinda shrugged. – We would be evicted in an hour. You will accompany me to the next meeting of the Maverick Crew. We need to make you a costume.

It took a few seconds before the relevance of her words dawned on Melinda. The girl's expression changed between shock, elation and fear.

– You're spooked. She spoke softly, her voice a hoarse whimper. – You're seriously spooked.

Lucinda walked to the window, but not quite. She half hid behind the wall, glancing outside, as if being fearful of something invisible hiding in plain sight, right in front of her.

– She's out there, she mumbled. – I know she is.

She turned back to her wide-eyed Kid Sister.

– I'll talk to the principal at your school. We'll be having an extended vacation. Flight Captain and Lady Grace felt we had to remain together full time for a while to search for Oracle, and there are other reasons, other increasingly pressing matters. This will be just one more on an extended list. Your organic tracking abilities will actually be quite useful, complementing Mechanic's technology.

Melinda looked hurt at her. Big Sister could be so cruel, such a manipulative bitch sometimes. Lucinda ignored her.

– I'm thinking dark green. What do you say, little snowflake?

– I like g-green, Melinda said, with tears in her eyes.

The pressure in her ass, the pain in her stomach came sudden, like it usually did. Lucinda sensed it in her, almost before she noticed it herself. The girl rushed to the toilet. Not long after that the powerful stench filled the apartment. Lucinda nodded to herself, strangely pleased.

She stood there, by the window, reaching out with her mind power, reaching further out than ever before. It was growing, like a living thing, feeding on itself, hardly needing any necessary sustenance to sustain itself.

But there was nothing, nothing beyond the mundane thoughts of ordinary life, of ugliness, longing and despair. She felt Melinda shiver there, in the darkness of the bathroom, in the pale light of the bulb far above, sensed every person in this building, and many buildings in the surrounding blocks, sometimes as individuals, but mostly like a homogenous mass not standing out in any way, nothing like the menacing presence that had practically invaded her earlier.

Perfidious thoughts coursed through her, and she couldn't keep it from happening, keep them from overwhelming her, and she believed she heard the vicious laughter again.

Melinda returned from the bathroom, weak and pale from the ordeal of having emptied herself.

– It burns, she said. – Does it burn all the time?

– It does, Lucinda nodded, striving to keep her voice even.

They made their meal together, like they always did, when at home. It was a ritual, a renewed bonding. They made large sandwiches. It was a guilty pleasure, but they didn't care.

As always the food was consumed in a feeding frenzy, no matter how much they attempted to slow down.

– It's like watching wild beasts feed, isn't it? Melinda asked Big Sister. – Like gorging?

Big Sister didn't voice any reply, but her expression told the girl everything she needed to know.

– T-that was what I thought when watching y-you, Melinda spat. – I was ashamed, ashamed of having you as a s-sister. F-fuck m-me!

Her last words were virtually unintelligible. She finished her meal, and pushed her plate away... and then she broke down in her sister's arms.

Lucinda sat there, staring straight ahead, patting Melinda on the head, not speaking, and not breaking the silence brought on by heart-wrecking sobs and self-recriminations.

They slept together that night, like they sometimes did. The bed was large, more than able to take two large females. Melinda fell asleep quickly, like Lucinda had suspected she would, fell into a stupor of restless sleep. But Lucinda couldn't sleep. She stayed awake for quite a while, keeping her eyes

54

on the girl sleeping in fetal position and sucking on her thumb. Lucinda pushed back the sudden and powerful feeling of contempt with an effort.

The silence, the night was filled with sounds. She listened behind the sounds, for the dark, contemptuous laughter, but didn't hear it.

But in her dreams she did. She saw the dark shape by her bed. Melinda was nowhere to be seen. Lucinda was alone and shrunk in the presence of the horrible dark shape.

Lucinda took the morning after pill at dawn, took two of them, recalling once again how her mother had gobbled them like candy, and been sick for most of the day. Big people needed more of everything.

They began working on Melinda's costume. Lucinda took a sick leave from work, and called the principal at Melinda's school. She considered going to the school for a personal meeting and smothering his resistance with her mind power, but she managed to charm him without it, using old-fashioned feminine wiles.

The two sisters worked with a frenzy that scared them both, and they exercised, hard enough to make sweat pour from their sore skin, and they were rewarded with hard knocking on the floor from their neighbor below. Lucinda smothered his anger without thinking twice about it. She redacted, calmed every single neighbor, making them shrug indifferently no matter how loud the noise turned out to be.

Melinda noticed, of course. She always noticed when Big Sister used her power. Lucinda couldn't calm her or herself, no matter how hard she tried. And it was good, good when Melinda was so worked up that she reached new levels in her fighting, good when she, against all odds hit Lucinda hard on the jaw, making blood flow, great when she continued fighting in her fervor, even when she was hit and was down.

They treated each other afterwards, treated sore skin, with band aids and herbs.

– You have made quantum leaps both in terms of skill and execution today, Lucinda said softly. – Perhaps fear truly is the key.

An icy wind trickled down Kid Sister's spine.

They fed again, gorged on the food again, and it felt so good, with just a little of the usual shame asserting itself. They slept, too tired to dream. Lucinda woke up with a frown on her brow, but less fear.

Lucinda washed and cleaned her mask, scowling at Melinda for her knowing smile.

– The Bowman again, I gather, she grinned, rubbing it in. – You *like* him.

– He's ignorant and a thug, Lucinda shrugged, – but he's not without his uses. And, as stated you can be confident that I give as well as I get.

– That brute, Melinda gasped in mocking shock. – That *fiend!*

They went to their regular shooting practice again. In spite of the protection covering their ears, their hearing started suffering as they fired rounds and more rounds at an imaginary enemy, one without face, blood and soul, an invisible creature without form and tangible existence.

Melinda suffered more, of course, with her far superior hearing, in spite of her even better protection.

The instructor studied them carefully afterwards. Lucinda considered alleviating his worries, but decided not to bother.

It was early evening a few nights later. They packed their bags with their costumes. Melinda felt inevitable pride and excitement when her fingers traced the lines of her uniform. She sent Big Sister an uncertain smile. Lucinda smiled confidently back.

The night was the same dry and hot, as it had been for so long now. They headed towards the abandoned construction site using the city's shadows and blind spots. Most people wouldn't notice anything special about their movement. Others with skill and cunning and intent, however would. That worried Lucinda, but it couldn't be helped.

Melinda walked, practically in her footsteps, clumsily and nervously. She moved her head constantly, as her various enhanced senses were kicking in. Usually she managed to control it, but not now, when she was beside herself with anxiety.

– Do I need to put you on a leash? Lucinda prompted.

That did it. The frantic movement stopped, even though she occasionally tilted her head and sniffed in the air, like a dog on the trail. She hung her head in shame.

They reached the half-ruins, half constructed building. Melinda walked behind with a very stubborn look on her face.

– You know, nobody can sneak up on me, she stated, deliberately lacing her voice with pride. – They might be able to block your scans, but I can always tell if someone is sneaking up on me. People can't keep themselves from smelling, or making sounds or triggering waves in the air while moving, or at the very least not everything simultaneously. They will always give something away.

She saw the portal, too, sensed it, or a combination. It shimmered in the air like moonlight.

They changed clothes. It felt strangely easy to Melinda, the transformation. The world itself seemed to change, but she was the one who was changing. She became something different, different from what she had been before.

– Take my hand, Lucinda bid her.

– But I can…

– It doesn't matter that you can see it. You still need to touch one favored by Oracle to walk through it.

They held hands and walked through. The passing was virtually instantaneous.

– That was amazing, Melinda cried. – We're in a completely different part of town, aren't we? I…

She swayed, crouched and vomited. When she looked up again her eyes were filled with tears.

– You'll get used to it, Lucinda shrugged. – At least better used to it. C'mon.

Melinda followed Lucinda down the badly lit street.

The sensations she picked up with her five senses were so much stronger here, at the center of town, where there were so many more people. Normally she handled the increased pressure easily, but now she was woozy and generally out of it, and she felt it like she was assaulted from all sides.

They reached the second portal. Lucinda grabbed her hand and pulled her through. At the other side the girl doubled over once again and threw up on the shiny floor.

She straightened while drying her lips, staring defiantly at her older sister.

– I've waited so long for this, she stated. – I'm here. I'm finally here.

Wonder took over for the nausea, as she finished speaking, and she took pride in the pleased look she spotted in Lucinda's eyes.

They walked into the main chamber, the meeting hall. Everybody was there, absolutely everybody.

The conversation faded and the room turned silent, as they spotted and studied carefully the newest arrival.

– Guys, Gimmick grinned, – I want you to meet Sensor, our newest bloodhound. She's inexperienced and a little overwhelmed by this, but she can be of immense use to us.

– She looks quite capable to me already, the Bowman remarked.

Sensor turned red as a tomato, and forgot everything she was about to say.

– You threw up, huh? Energetic remarked.

– Yes, she admitted glumly.

– I did, too, he said, – the first fifteen times I walked through the portals.

The laughter was not unkind. Sensor (she was Sensor, now, from now on) laughed, too, a high pitched squeal resembling a whine.

The two sisters took their place around the table, Sensor on an extra chair by her sister's seat.

– You have more to share with us, little one, Lady Grace said to Gimmick.

Little one… Sensor couldn't help herself and glanced at the regal woman. Gimmick was the tallest here. Sensor knew Grace could read her mind, but right now she didn't care.

– Yes, I have, Gimmick acknowledged. – That's the reason I feel that my plans and all our plans have to be completely redrawn and rethought.

She drew breath, several times before continuing.

– I've felt a… growing presence lately, mostly in my dreams, more like nightmares than any solid, substantiated event. But a few days ago, on the evening of our previous meeting I felt the presence as a tangible and undeniable force, a threat unlike anyone or anything we have ever faced.

– What was the nature of the presence? Lady Grace prompted her.

– It was a *sweep*, Gimmick cried out. – It was as if it was searching for something, seeking something… or someone, or perhaps seeking anyone with Power. I… recognized it.

Sensor put a hand on the shoulder of the shaking form. Flight Captain leaned forward, as if he wanted to ask a question, but changed his mind.

They knew what she was going to say, somehow. She knew their reaction to her words in advance… somehow, saw, and more than sensed their shock, incredulity and bleeding wounds.

– It was… it was Cougar, or rather a horrible, improved version of her. I dreamt, more than dreamt about her… about a giant shape looming above the city… about the Black Dragon…

Chapter 4
EIGHT YEARS AGO TODAY

Lucinda returned from the restroom, weak and pale from the ordeal of emptying herself. Everything seemed to be burning in her, burning on a low flame.

The world seemed to shiver and shake around her, as if the ground was shaking, but it wasn't. She sensed no or little shaking in her feet, but noticed it mostly through her hands and lips.

On the wall in the hallway was written in blood and large, erratic letters:
FEED AND YOU SHALL NO LONGER BE HUNGRY

The words echoed within her, ever pleasantly and disturbing.

She returned to the classroom. They didn't look at her and she didn't look at them. She sat down in absolute silence.

The clouds in the sky moved above her head, as she walked down the street. People stared at her, especially those in her home street. They knew how much taller and bigger she had grown the last two years. Strangers might mistake her for an adult, but these strangers wouldn't.

Lucinda didn't recognize them at all. They looked ugly in her eyes, with their stares and scorn.

As unpleasant as that was she didn't want to go home, and walked around for hours after school. She wandered aimlessly at the harbor, looking at the boats, distracting herself with their shape and size, removing herself from her thoughts, until the hunger grew too adverse, and she practically ran home, and all her thoughts centered on food.

She ran up the stairs, instead of hitching with the elevator. Doing so felt easy. It didn't make her breathless much. When she reached the eight floor, her floor, it didn't feel like she had exerted herself at all. It lifted her spirits. She walked inside and her spirits fell again.

Her father sat by the table in the living room, consuming a large steak. He seemed to be eating, feeding all the time. Lucinda didn't see her there, but for some reason she still knew Melinda stayed in her room, overwhelmed by gloomy thoughts. Lucinda walked to the kitchen, and there, as expected sat her mother, eating with her hands, feeding like an animal.

– Mother has made a snack for you, mother said hoarsely. – Dinner will be done soon.

The day had passed in a haze and the large piece of meat first on the pan and seconds later on the plate occupied her attention. She poured on vegetables and salad, filled a large glass with lemonade and rushed to the table, where she began feeding, not bothering more with knife and fork than her parents had done.

Brenda finished making the dinner not long afterwards. The entire family sat down around the table, very relaxed and civilized. They used knife and fork, and were very careful to display any single table manner they had ever learned. Outsiders looking in would easily mistake this for a very harmonic group.

– So, how was school? Gilbert asked casually, merrily.

– T'was okay, Lucinda shrugged.

– T'was okay, Melinda shrugged solemnly, looking at her older sister for appreciation, for acknowledgement of her undying loyalty.

Lucinda was still hungry, like her parents, but it was muted, not such a desperate gnawing in her belly. She could enjoy the dinner, somewhat.

Both Brenda and Gilbert had also turned visibly bigger. Grownups had stopped growing, Lucinda had learned. But that was evidently not true anymore. Gilbert had become very strong physically. She had seen him lift insanely heavy weights at the gym two blocks away, and he had acquired a body both a professional weight-lifter and fighter would envy. Nobody fucked with Gilbert Patterson anymore.

Everybody knew what would follow soon, the queue outside the bathroom, the stinking toilet and all. Melinda looked at all of them with a deep furrow on her forehead and her still childish face twisted with anxiety.

They had worked out a system, each day changing who would be first on the toilet. Today Lucinda was last. The pains erupted like clockwork, long before it was her time.

She and Melinda sat on the couch in the living room, in uncomfortable silence.

– Does it hurt? Melinda asked with a whimper, clearly sympathetic to her big sister's plight.

Lucinda ignored her sister's niceties, solely focused on keeping herself from shitting herself. At first there was only the wrecking pain, but soon she had to squeeze tight the hole in her ass to keep it from leaking, and eventually from not releasing most of its considerable content. It was harder to walk with this kind of problem, and she had managed that, but this was still hard, so very hard. A tear formed in her left eye, and that made everything even worse. The pity in Melinda's eyes made her squirm.

Brenda finally pulled the handle behind the door for the second time. The relief created by the sound of the suction almost made Lucinda release her precious load prematurely. She rushed past her mother when Brenda opened the door. Shaking fingers pulled down her pants, just as her butt hit the bowl. The wet and hot shit jumped from her ass and hit the water, and she almost cried in relief.

She made sure to flush the toilet before continuing to empty herself. They had needed a plumber to clean up their mess before they had learned that the pipes couldn't handle all their shit at one go.

Sweaty and weak she retreated to her room afterwards. She heard her parents argue, surely about money again. Their financial security had slowly drained away the last two years, as their grocery expenses had skyrocket. She heard them extraordinary well, no matter how hard she attempted to close her ears and mind. It was as if she could hear them without hearing them, so to speak, and it only served to add to her confusion and sense of alienation. Finally she had had enough, and headed out.

It had just turned dark. She preferred that. It made it harder for people to see her and for her to see their accusing stares and hateful snarls. Without really thinking about it she headed for the harbor, where it was quite and pleasant. She saw no people there and met no one. There were only lots of boats, very expensive boats.

They looked like giants in her eyes, and cast their shadow over her, and she shuddered without really knowing why.

She walked to the edge of the pier and sat down there, staring at the dark waters. They were mostly still, but tiny waves still struck the shore around her, licked the wood under her feet. She sensed their movement, their latent power.

It resonated within her, in ways she didn't comprehend.

The young girl enjoyed the peace and quiet, sitting there without a single discernible thought in her head. The thoughts returned, though, unbidden, and she began to glance around her, and her eyes started flickering. She saw Gilbert with his steak, saw him devouring it, saw the children at school, and their parents, with their scowl and scorn and heartless laughter.

She rose abruptly, stood still at bit, staring, glaring at the lit city above, before leaving the pier with slow, reluctant steps.

The draft in the air caught her momentarily, before letting her go. She glanced around her, but there was no one there.

She walked up the dark road to the city. Something made her hesitate, and she stopped several times before continuing.

The three boys met her halfway up. They approached her with lewd grins painted on their faces, not really hiding their intentions at all.

– Hello, Lucinda, the biggest of them greeted her.

– H-hello, she replied, cursing her stuttering.

She knew of the three of them, even though she didn't know them. They were two classes above her, and attended another school.

– You go down here often, don't you?

– Yes, she replied hoarsely.

– So, we've heard, he nodded. – You go down here by yourself, without telling your parents where you're going.

They were pretty much fully grown, fairly tall and with well-developed muscles. She tried not looking at them, but still saw them with uncanny clarity, both their features and intentions. They stepped forward. She stepped backwards, looking warily at them.

– Ah, don't be like that, Lucinda, one of the other boys chuckled.

Don't call me Lucinda, she thought. Don't say my name like *that*.

– Look at her, such a peach.

The leader stepped close to her. The other two circled her, surrounded her.

Their close proximity made her dizzy. When she looked at the leader's flushed face it was like he touched her, and he clearly didn't. She didn't know what was happening, and they scared her.

– You're such a big, beautiful piece of flesh, he told her, – and we just want you to be nice to us.

She knew those looks, those desires, knew what they wanted from her, and it made her squirm uncomfortably.

– Give us a kiss, the commanded her.

– I want to go home, she whimpered.

– And you shall, he assured her, – but not quite yet.

He grabbed her arms and pulled her close, and held her, and then he kissed her on the lips, first once, then twice. The second time was much more potent, far more demanding. She returned the kiss, and sensed their triumph and cruelty that much stronger.

It made her blush and gave further fuel to their patronizing grins. One of the other boys grabbed her and turned her towards him. That angered her further. She tore herself loose and pushed him away.

– Ah, don't be like that, girl, he grumbled.

The big one, the leader attempted to grab her again, but she grabbed him instead, as he reached for her. She pulled hard, and he yelped in pain. Another pull, and his arm was almost yanked from the shoulder. She felt his pain and would have done so even without it being visible in his face. When she lifted him up and threw him over her shoulder, at the others, it happened so easily, effortlessly.

He hit the ground hard, and yelped aloud, unable to help himself. She stood there, looking at them. Then, as he strived to get back on his feet she suddenly realized they were afraid of her.

62

– Go away, she told them curtly.

They hesitated. She took one single step forward, and they pulled back. When she took another step they ran, ran until they turned and saw that she didn't pursue them. They faded away in the darkness.

She stood there for a long time, filled with conflicting emotions.

Her attention was drawn to a tree nearby. It was old, with many thick branches. She approached it with a frown on her brow. The lowest branch was high above her head and well outside her reach. She crouched slightly, preparing for the jump, and then she did it, reaching the branch easily, miscalculating and reaching too high, grabbing the branch on her way down, hanging there, for a moment before pulling herself up, reaching up to the next branch, pulling herself up into the tree.

And then she stood on the thick branch, breathing a little harder, but that was mostly in excitement. Thoughts raced through her head. Except for the compulsory classes in school she hadn't really exercised much, but she still had developed quite a nice muscle tone. The gym teacher had given her compliments for that, with the usual frown in place. She remembered standing in front of a mirror, remembered her embarrassment. Every time she even passed one she had felt shame, because of her tall and curvy frame. She imagined she was standing before one, now, and for the very first time she felt something akin to pride.

After a while she looked up, and then she climbed higher up, all the way to the top of the tree. It didn't feel hard at all. She had never been very athletic, not before… not like she was *now*. Breath wheezed in and out of her lungs, but not because she was really breathless, but because of the excitement riding her. She climbed back down, jumped off a branch fairly high up, and landed on the ground without noticing much. The sudden need to use her muscles and her body did feel invigorating in itself. In a moment's arrogance she started on a wheel across the lawn, doing gymnastics she had never been close to achieving before, and even though the execution clearly left something, no, a lot to be desired she did it, actually did it.

A large grin appeared on her face as she set off, as she started running back towards the city. Its bright lights embraced her. She ran flat out for a while, and then stopped, astounded over the fact that she didn't feel tired.

It was in this excited state of being she entered Almond Street, a part of Tobruk's famous shopping area. This was after closing time for most stores, but lights were still on in the closed places, like it was all over this part of town. She looked around her with wonder in her eyes.

A few late stragglers were leaving the closing shops. It was noisy there, even with just the few people and no cars nearby. Lucinda frowned. Something felt… off. She imagined she heard someone speak close to her, or behind her, but when she turned there was no one there, no one even approaching close. A shiver passed through her. Every single shadow in the street seemed to pull closer to her.

She hurried on, suddenly afraid, not knowing why. Running from the bright lights she sought the quiet shadows. She stood on a corner, breathing, breathing far harder then after her recent run. This was also a shopping street, but a few blocks away from Almond, enough for it to be a different world. Tourists and the filthy rich usually stayed away from this place.

A deep, hard sound rocked the ground. She almost lost her footing, because it happened so quickly and unexpectedly. An explosion. After regaining her bearing she realized it came from the nearest building, the store selling used jewelry. She rushed, without thinking to the door. It was locked. She stared into the smoky room. A man wearing a mask was well under way with the task of putting money and jewelry into his large bag. Two people, the elderly couple running the store lay on the floor. They were tied up and gagged. Lucinda shook the door, shook it hard, making the entire wall shake, but the door didn't budge.

– Help, she cried. – HELP!

She screamed her lungs out. It came off as hopelessly ineffective, even in the quiet street. The man, the masked man spotted her and waved, waved to her. She watched him smile, a wide smile highlighting his pearly-white teeth. Before she knew it she had kicked the door, kicked it hard. It was reinforced metal and didn't budge. The glass was smashed into thousand small pieces, but it was special glass, designed to splinter and not break, to keep people out. She stepped to the side, to the big window and kicked at it. It splintered. She kept kicking at it. It didn't break, but she kicked it off the frame, and worked herself a hole in which she could enter the building. She felt good, kicking loose like this, experiencing the strength in her legs as such a pleasant feeling.

The burglar didn't seem overly worried when she climbed inside. She walked towards him with a cautious look in her eyes.

– Ah, he said, putting down his bag, – so why are you here, girl? Have you also come to loot? Seeing you are also special, like me, I'll be willing to share.

Special? She frowned, giving him an even closer scrutiny.

He was young, but still tall, and big… like her.

– Have you had a lot of unpleasant and unexpected trips to the toilet lately, sweetie?

She stopped, thunderstruck.

– I have, he nodded, smiling when he saw the truth dawning on her. – I thought I should use the better aspects of the changes in me to something positive.

The money would be good. Her parents were struggling, and she supposed this was only the beginning of their plight to feed themselves and their daughters.

Then it was as if she could look straight into him, see him undress her in his mind.

– Surrender, she heard herself say, – and I may go easy on you.

He produced a rope from his bag, and it looked almost alive in his hands. She jumped at him in a fit of rage and fear, striking him down.

– Wow, he said, drying his bloody jaw, – that's impressive, so inexperienced, but still so strong and brave and fast.

She just stood there, letting him get back on his feet. He attacked her, struck her. She staggered back, the salty taste in her mouth making her dizzy. Before she managed to recover he was all over her. He grabbed her and pushed her upper body over the desk. Then he struck her in the ribs, making her loose her breath, paralyzing her. He grabbed her waving arms and pulled them back on her back. She felt the rope around her wrists. It seemed to move by itself and gave her the creeps. He tied her up, tied her up hard. She gasped in pain.

– Sorry about this, love, he said with regret in his voice, – but I just don't have time to play any longer. The nasty men in uniform may show up any time, even as slow as they are.

He tied her ankles together, too, and gagged her, and she was totally helpless, at his mercy.

– But don't worry, you're a spunky kid, and I feel confident that we will meet under far more pleasant circumstances.

His strong hands grabbed her again and carried her to the back of the store, where the owners lay tied and gagged. He dumped her there. It hurt as she hit the floor. She choked, and tears began wetting her face. He patted her cheek in what was probably or possibly meant to be comforting, and then he left her, then he was gone.

She lay there, sobbing, making half-hearted attempts at getting loose. The ropes didn't budge. The owners lay a bit away from her. They stared accusingly at her. She sobbed harder.

He had handled her, taken care of her easily, swatted her like he would a fly, and stamped on her pride like it was nothing. The shame and humiliation burned within her.

She just went away then, really. When the sirens sounded in her ears and the red and blue lights blinked outside she didn't really notice.

The big, black boots trampled on the floor of the store, approaching her, but she didn't acknowledge their presence. She remembered sitting in a van with her hands cuffed behind her back, remembered more pain, as the metal squeezed her wrists.

Then it was the morning after, in a square gray room. She recalled faintly spending the night in the arrest with a lot of hookers and drunks.

The room had one table and two chairs. It was the interrogation room. She had seen similar places often enough in the movies.

A man, a detective stared at her from the other side of the table.

– He let you down, huh?

– Who? Lucinda asked incredulous.

– Your boyfriend.

– I tried to stop him, she whispered. – I couldn't.

– I understand, he said sympathetically. – You robbed the jewelry together, and things went awry. It happens, right.

She frowned, not quite getting his meaning.

– Your boyfriend is a greedy asshole and didn't want to share.

Her jaw hurt even more than it had last night. It had swollen to twice its size, or so it felt.

– He isn't my boyfriend.

She shook her head vehemently.

– Of course not, the detective acknowledged willingly. – An asshole like that...

– No, you don't understand, she protested. – He *isn't* my boyfriend.

– Of course not, the detective repeated.

There was this buzz in her head. It rose and faded in waves, but it never quite went away. She kept frowning and slowly her head cleared somewhat.

– You think I participated in the robbery, she stated, straightening in her chair.

He looked at her across the table, his fingertips placed against one-another, and his eyes very, very serious.

– I didn't, she cried, – I tried to stop him, and have never even met him before tonight, before I entered the store to stop him.

– That seems a little hard to believe, the detective said, shaking his head in a very patronizing manner.

And this time she didn't misunderstand him.

– I'm strong, she protested, – stronger than all the boys at my school. And I chased away three guys attempting to rape me tonight.

Sure you did, his eyes mocked her.

She heard his laughter, and the laughter of those behind the large mirror,

66

and then she realized that he, at least wasn't openly laughing, and she didn't understand how she could hear him.

– Look, she said, feeling the first signs of desperation. – The couple owning the store can vouch for me…

– Nope, the detective grinned, – they were drugged, and can't remember shit.

It was at that point Lucinda felt a headache coming on. The unpleasant sensation settled between her eyes and wouldn't let go.

She's such a peach.

The voice came to her from a strange place. She watched his lips at that very moment. They didn't move, didn't move at all.

– I was drugged, too, she said, begging him with her eyes. – The asshole did it to me, too. The drug was in the gag.

– Who was he? The leering detective asked sharply.

– How the fuck should I know? She cried. – It's your job to find out such things.

– Don't be a smartass, young lady. The big man's fist struck the table.

The girl jumped in her seat.

That's right, now we're getting somewhere.

That «voice» was coming from behind the one way mirror. She was certain of it.

Go for the kill.

The last word echoed in her mind, as if several people spoke it simultaneously and repeatedly. She saw herself in the store, being captured and tied up by the burglar, and felt the excitement of those who were watching, watching the curvy young female lying there, tied up, watching the…

– You better start cooperating, now, young lady, or there will be hell to pay, the interrogator said curtly.

She began smiling, smiling ever so sweetly to him. At first he smiled, too, but then he frowned, as he began to get the feeling that something wasn't quite right.

– The surveillance cameras, she stated slowly.

– What about them?

He blurted it out, before he could catch himself.

– They recorded everything happening in the store. You watched them.

I see you!

He stared at her with an open mouth.

A lot of what had happened to her recently suddenly made sense, very much sense. Excitement and apprehension rode her like a mare.

– You never believed I was guilty, she said, grinning a little, suddenly very calm, relaxed, triumphant. – You just wanted a bit of sport with the defenseless little girl. She, in her predicament would have done anything to accommodate, *please* you.

Contempt entered her voice during the last, few words.

You little bitch, the tiny voice in his mind whimpered. *How did you know?*

– You were really quite transparent, she said sarcastically. – It didn't take much intelligence to see through your ploy, and I'm far smarter than most.

And she had an advantage he wouldn't dream of. Joy made two jumps in her excited mind.

– My parents are here…

– Uh…

– My parents are here, waiting for me, and before you release me, you will tell them that I tried to stop the burglar, that I'm a hero, or I'll fucking press charges.

He practically jumped to his feet, sweating like a pig, fighting to somewhat stay in control of himself. She watched as he hurried out of the room.

As if on cue her stomach began acting up. She almost started crying in relief and couldn't understand how it had left her in peace for so long. The toilet was right outside the interrogation room.

Figures, she thought.

And when she consciously formed thoughts in her head it was as if her ability to read other people's thoughts grew in strength. She heard the leering men behind the one-way mirror. No one spoke, and they wouldn't look at each other in their anxiety and shame, but she heard them still.

The headache subsided fairly quickly and what remained actually felt kind of good, reminding her of her empowerment. She hummed an unknown melody when she went and relieved herself. The tiny space seemed to be filled with voices. It took some effort, but she learned to control it eventually, to shut them out, at least to mute them. They became part of the background noise of the city, except when she focused on them. When she directed her attention on one person she could listen to that person's thoughts almost without distortion. It kept spooking her, but less so, as time passed. She knew what this was, had certainly read more than enough about it. The smile widened when she stopped momentarily outside the restroom, before joining her parents outside.

The Great Darkness had done this to her, had empowered her, enhanced both her body and mind.

Thus she realized the connection well before most people on the planet.

She walked to her parents, outside, in the blinding light. They rushed to her and embraced her and coddled her, as if they were being paid to do so. She studied them, both outside and inside. They showed no sign of exhibiting any ability of the mind as far as she could sense.

– They told us you were being held at the hospital for observation, mother said, clearly distraught, – and wouldn't allow us to see you.

– It was just a precaution, mom, Lucinda comforted her.

– How could you do something that stupid? Father chastised her.

– It felt like the right thing to do at the time, dad, she shrugged, focusing on sending them relaxing vibrations.

It seemed to be working, even though she couldn't be certain. The cop had been pretty slick and had probably done a great job convincing them of the fact that there was nothing to be worried about, and she, in turn, with her relaxed behavior had probably done the rest.

Possibly.

They took her home, like good parents, and she followed them home, like a good daughter.

People stared at her, at them, at the people physically changed. They spoke to her, but didn't move their lips. The hostility was palpable, even more, now, when she could better perceive it. She began shaking.

– You poor girl, Brenda said in a comforting tone. – You may be a tough cookie, but I'm afraid there's a limit even for tough cookies.

You don't know the half of it, mom. You don't know what's lurking beneath people's pleasant surface and fake smiles.

Mouthful, she caught from Brenda's unfocused thoughts.

She can be a mouthful.

It was just a stray thought, but it made Lucinda fall deeper into anguish.

– You will of course stay home from school today.

Gilbert rubbed her head (and messed up her hair).

That didn't stir any emotion, high or low in Lucinda. She accepted it with a shrug.

They followed her to the apartment, but she sensed their restlessness, their eagerness to leave her.

– We must return to work, Brenda said quickly. – Will you be all right, dear?

– Yes, mom, Lucinda replied quietly.

She sensed the lethargy in them both. It had been quite evident for some time, but not like this, like an open wound. She kept a brave face until they had gone. Then she threw herself on the couch, and lay there despairing.

Not many people were home this time of day, but she knew whom. They were an evident presence in her mind, no matter how much she attempted to lock them out. She was tired, and the tears flooded her cheeks. Awareness and sleep warred within her briefly, and awareness won easily because of the sudden pangs pf hunger in her stomach.

She stumbled to the kitchen and made a heap of large sandwiches, and began devouring the first before she had completed making the second, in an orgy of feeding. It felt so good to feed, so uncannily well. She swallowed it all with a large glass of lemonade. The pangs of pain began before she finished the meal and she ate the last slices of bread and drank the last drops of lemonade in the glass while sitting on the bowl and shitting. It hurt and the putrid stench made her want to puke.

The very first thing she did afterwards was to wash the entire bathroom, the bowl, the floor, the walls, using a lot of perfumed water, and then she took a shower. It didn't help much. The stench stuck in her nose, in her very mind.

She walked nude through the apartment, while drying herself. The curtains covered all the windows. No one could look inside and see her. She stopped before the large hall mirror, and looked at her changed and more or less adult body. At least it looked that way, and had become so during the rapid change the last few months. She suspected she would grow even bigger, even though she was already as big as her mother.

The three boys appeared in her mind. They had wanted her. Their palpable desire had worked on her, too, especially because she was able to read, sense their thoughts and emotions. A part of her had wanted to give in to them, but her anger had been more powerful and won out, and she had vanquished them, easily, and pride had surged through her, like it did right now. She had handled the detective, the adult male with contempt and class, showed her superiority down his throat, treated him like dirt under her feet, and it had worked.

Her nipples hardened and grew. When she dried herself she began to itch, also below. She bit her lip. The young girl knew what this was. She was well read and listened in on the older chicks when they whispered among themselves, when they with anxiety and awe described forbidden acts of liberation and pleasure.

The building remained quiet and empty. She «listened» for several seconds more, before she rushed to her room and slammed the door shut behind her. Her eyes caught the key in the lock. She grabbed it and turned it in a feverish movement.

The towel began moving on her body practically by itself, bolder closer to the growing pain below. She stumbled towards the bed, her feet almost failing to support her several times. Her hands, also moving of their own volition rubbed her breasts, cautiously at first, then harder, fondling,

70

squeezing them. Then they moved down the belly, to the moist place between her thighs. This was what the boys wanted, the prize they sought. She visualized the burglar, the big boy with the hard muscles in her mind. A low moan escaped between her lips. She pushed a hand at the hot and wet place, and cried out, almost shouted. The hand began moving uncontrollable up and down, and now she knew she had no control of it. She writhed on the bed, tossing and turning, unable to stop herself. Her breathing turned labored and sweat covered her recently cleaned body. Her body turned rigid, and then the release erupted from her loins, and she cried out in rapture, in an exalted expression beyond joy.

She lay there without moving for a while. The smile lingered. Her breathing returned to normal. She enjoyed the heat in the room and there was no need for her to cover herself. Sounds and voices from the street once more seemed close. She studied the flustered faces of those she watched through others' eyes and chuckled raucously. They *had* noticed, ever so little. She *had* been projecting subconsciously in her fervor, through her empowerment. When she tried doing it, tried influencing people deliberately she couldn't do it, no matter how hard she tried, but she suspected she would be able to, as she and her power matured.

Hunger ravaged her. What she had experienced hadn't been enough for her, and she began again. This time she controlled it more, consciously guiding her hands as they moved across her body. The sensation felt so pleasant, such a delight, and she knew she would keep doing it, doing it often, also when her parents were home. She didn't scream this time, even though she couldn't keep the low moans and noises from rising from her sore throat, and didn't really attempt to.

When Lucinda Patterson stretched her body, when her hand once more turned soaking wet a huge smile blossomed slowly on her face.

She fell asleep fairly quickly after that, and her mind was filled with confusing and pleasant and terrifying dreams.

Her eyes instantly sought her watch. Fortunately she hadn't slept more than a few hours. She jumped out of bed and pulled the sheets and down off it, and rushed all of it to the washing machine, and poured soap into the dispenser, the mechanism that would distribute the soap to the centrifuge, and turned the machine on. Then she showered yet again, rubbing herself hard, deliberately, in an attempt to keep the hunger from awakening again. It worked, sort of. There was a faint itch, but not more than that, and she felt kind of relieved.

Back in the kitchen she wolfed down yet another tall heap of large sandwiches. The meal didn't sate her completely, but it didn't need to.

Dinner was only a couple of hours off, and she would be able to savor the wait.

She studied herself in the mirror, her still glowing face. If Brenda had walked through the door right now she would know what had happened in an instant, no matter how little she would like it. Lucinda was grateful for the extra time.

Melinda returned home from school an hour or so later. Lucinda pretty much ignored her, like she always did, like big sisters did, but studied her, hid her curiosity behind random glances. Her kid sister still retained her slender body. There was no sign of her growing as big as her sister and parents. She didn't eat more than normal kids and didn't really divert from them in any way.

It wasn't hard for Lucinda to know why. She was pretty much convinced it had to do with puberty. From the day hormones began ravaging Melinda's body she, too would grow tall and big, and change far more than the average teenager.

Lucinda started on the dinner. It took all four plates, one large pan, two giant kettles, and then some just to get it all going. Steam rose and filled the kitchen. She felt the first pangs of the hunger (Hunger).

Melinda stared at her. She could tell. The child's curiosity was a hunger, too. Mel had always been a precocious child. Lucinda turned and looked at her, nodding her approval, momentarily overcoming the kid sister's caution towards the older, wiser and ominous sister.

– Was the boy *mean* to you?

– Not really, honey, he was just being an asshole. Boys are like that. You'll discover that eventually.

And with that casual remark, that shrug, she returned to her pan and kettles, dismissing the irritating fly buzzing her space.

Their parents returned, fairly synchronized. The four of them sat down and had dinner. The three oldest *fed*. It was quite different from the family dinners two years ago. To call it gluttony (she chuckled quietly) was an understatement. Lucinda was grateful for her own Hunger, distracting her from that of her parents.

The growth had done one thing for them, though. It had reignited their stale, passionless marriage. Lucinda knew they would rush to their room shortly after dinner and start fucking their brains out. In the years after Melinda's birth they had hardly done it more than twice a week, if at all, but now they did it twice a day, at least that. Brenda gobbled prevention pills and took pregnancy tests regularly.

The girls couldn't avoid hearing them when they went at it. Lucinda found out that her newfound awareness made her notice in an even more pronounced way. She had half expected that it would make her horny again, but it didn't.

The two sisters did the dishes. They stood there by the kitchen sink and listened to the grunts and moans from the large bedroom. They giggled and sent each other cheerful glances.

The evening dragged on, though, as it always did. Gilbert sat in his favorite chair, watching football reruns. A little later all four watched the newest reality show.

Lucinda rose abruptly.

– I'm going out for a while, she declared.

– Is that wise? Brenda frowned. – This isn't a night where you should walk alone in the streets, you know.

– I thought about joining the new self defense club at Feron and Shutter, Lucinda argued, without arguing. – It's just a few blocks away and the streets are well lit and filled with people until midnight. I'll be okay, mom.

– I guess that will be okay, Brenda frowned.

– It's free, Lucinda added.

She didn't receive or was denied permission. Brenda and Gilbert exchanged glances. Gilbert shrugged. Lucinda was out of the door faster than fast. The moment she left she heard Gilbert speak and imagined him shrugging again.

– Kids should learn to defend themselves today.

The well-lit streets filled with people hardly made Lucinda feel safe. She didn't know what the burglar looked like. The few tall, bulky men she met were older, not young like him. But he had been sort of nice in his meanness. Others wouldn't necessarily be.

Feron & Shutter was a community house. It had been a mall in the nineties, but had seen better days, and was now used to all kinds of varied activities by people that wouldn't pay rent. They were called squatters and worse by the city's elite and people supporting them. The elite wanted them gone, but the people that wouldn't pay rent weren't so easy vanquished. There was talk, and had been for years in the city council of selling the building off to real estate developers, but every time the question came up passionate protests ran rampant, and any possible development project was once again shelved.

She kind of enjoyed the sight of the forlorn, old building. It looked far nicer than any result of an «urban renewal project» she had ever seen.

The people currently running the place had an open door policy, everybody was welcome, and it was indeed what met Lucinda when she approached the entrance. She hesitated momentarily, before stepping inside. No one looked at her when she entered the entrance hall. She had half expected that they would and relaxed a bit.

Then it hit her, the clear and present sense of hostility. She stopped, gasping, attempting to get her bearings, to focus on wherever the powerful emotions came from, but it seemed non-localized, unfocused. A hard ball of frustration and disappointment formed in her throat. She hurried through the room to the next, and the pressure let up a little. It was all so new to her, and so difficult to define, to differentiate between the new sensations coursing through her.

She was relieved to find herself where just a few ventured. In one room people were singing, or attempting to. It faded both in her ears and her mind, as she made her way to the back of the building.

Five teenagers and one grownup man sat on their ass in a circle in the dirty hall. She stopped at the threshold. He waved to her. She stepped inside. They made room for her in the circle and she joined the others on the floor. She was the only big one present. The others glanced stealthily at her, from the corners of their eyes. She ignored them, happily aware of the astonishing fact that she didn't have to look at people to focus on them anymore.

Her telepathy was a little hard to control, but not excessively so. The initial confusion had already been supplanted by a growing confidence. Pondering the subject she realized that her gift, her power had been there almost since the Great Darkness, and perhaps even before, in a limited capacity. It had just taken its time asserting itself. She had always been intuitive, good at reading people, and surmised that this was simply an extension of that.

– Thank you for coming, the man said, greeting them. – You should see this as an introductory meeting only, where we all get to know each other, and see if we want to be better acquainted.

She noticed how he was studying them all, and her, especially her.

– Training Martial Arts is a sacred trust. So is teaching it. You don't teach it to unworthy students, and sully the art.

He was boasting, being a pompous ass. She realized that slowly, and after she had realized it, she realized that it wasn't hard, wasn't hard at all to identify specific emotions and similar. The others spent most of the «interview» focusing on the potential teacher. She spent the time slowly learning her new ability, her gift, her power, taking her first, difficult steps on her new path.

– Martial Arts aren't truly violent or about violence at all. It is self defense, and a way of life you will certainly appreciate. As long you don't abuse what I teach you, our relationship, the one between the teacher and the student will be long and fertile.

74

They were teaching opera on an upper floor. The students' cracked voices made people cringe all over the building. Lucinda experienced it in more potent ways, because she also experienced it through others. She giggled in initial euphoria. The teacher liked her laughter, and she overdid it a bit, but not too much. Her upcoming classmates laughed, too.

They were all accepted, in a move that had been evident to Lucinda from the start.

– I look forward to teaching you.

– The honor is ours, sir, one of the boys said, very polite. – And we certainly need it, need it in a hostile world.

The teacher frowned, but eventually nodded and agreed.

I need it, Lucinda thought.

The six stayed together for a while, in the building's cafeteria. They exchanged pleasantries and looked like a group. Lucinda sensed insecurity in them all, one slowly dissipating as their reason to come here was validated in the company of common purpose and desires. She didn't really recall afterwards what the conversation had been about, but knew it had circled around their need for improved physical prowess. They had all been victims of assault, or feared being one.

The six parted company with their new friends outside, feeling a little better, now, when they had taken one of several steps in order to be better at defending themselves. They were still jittery because they had to walk home through darkened city streets, but she wasn't. A strange ambiguity she couldn't quite identify coursed through her.

She ran to the harbor, to the darkness and silence there, and there, at the pier, as she stared at the distant lights the voices in her head faded to insignificance.

Chapter 5

The headquarters had a state of the art training hall, with equipment. The sisters went at each other there first, far beyond breaking a sweat, under the watchful eyes of Lady Grace and Mechanic. Sensor was also run through a trial of hard exercise, to test her limits. Gimmick let herself be a part of that to support the newcomer. She noticed Lady Grace probing her, even more invasive than she usually did.

The intrusion was there, like a buzz, virtually permanent when the two was in close proximity. Lady Grace had done that since they had first met. It felt almost like second nature by now.

Gimmick focused on her fight with Sensor, on tutoring the young girl. They didn't need to hold back here, and there was also equipment allowing them to cut loose without the risk of harming themselves. Everything was padded. If they fell from the climbing ropes they would be caught by a safety net spanning almost half the floor. They climbed the ropes, changed from one rope to another, striking out at each other. She struck the novice to the ground yet one more time, having forgotten how many times she had done so. Sensor hit the net and was rocking up and down a few times before lying still. She shook her head and rubbed her jaw, the pain visible in her face. Gimmick let go of her rope and made a controlled fall, like a gymnast. She reached out a hand and grabbed the younger girl's hand when she reached out hers, and then Gimmick pulled her on her feet. They stood there, facing each other. Both were sweating profusely.

– That was *amazing*, Sensor cried out. – I'll become so good at this.

Her hands were clearly sore. She had hammered on sandbags, both with and without boxing gloves. She had made enormous progress during the two days they had spent here. Gimmicks eyes turned a little softer, a little less condemning.

They hit the big shower in Gimmick's room, removing their costumes and masks and turned on the water. Melinda whimpered, inevitably, as she had to touch herself.

– I will be yellow, blue and black all over tomorrow, she said ambiguously. – Even my bruises have bruises.

– Your natural strength makes it much easier for you, compared to most others, Lucinda noted. – Just like it did with me. Soon you will be so tough that this initial unpleasantness will be a distant memory.

They dried themselves, yet another trial for Melinda, but her overwhelming excitement proved victorious over the pain.

– Who is *paying* for all this? The teenager wondered. – I can't remember reading anything about a secret benefactor or something.

– Alan is an inventor, Lucinda shrugged. – He has made a fortune on his inventions and patents.

– Alan?

– Mechanic. He was bright before the Great Darkness and his intelligence took completely off afterwards.

– Alan Prescott, the *inventor?*

– The same, Lucinda nodded.

– He has more money than *Bill Gates…*

– Not even close, I'm afraid, but what he has, he shares generously with us. Melinda frowned.

– Correct me if I'm wrong… You know who he is, but you don't share your secret with him, with anybody here, am I right?

Lucinda wanted to say something, anything, but found that she couldn't.

– That's right, Kid Sister teased Big Sister, – you, you and Lady Grace read the others' mind. There is no way of keeping secrets from the two of you, is there?

She was part kidding, part not. There was an aggressive, underlying subtext to her good mood that worried Lucinda a bit.

– As you well know Raven Bird, Lisa knows, Big Sister said defensively.

Kid Sister practically ignored that statement in total contempt.

They dressed in their spare underwear and refitted their costumes, once more becoming Gimmick and Sensor.

Next stop was Mechanic's laboratory. They were both placed on tables, and fitted with electrodes, like lab rats. All kinds of machinery surrounded them.

Lady Grace was here, too, probing them just as much as the machines.

You told her his name, Grace sent sternly to Gimmick. That can be a problem if she forgets herself.

I… slipped up. I'm sorry. It won't happen again.

Mechanic focused on Sensor, checking the electrodes attached to her head.

– We will now try to determine the limits to your enhanced senses, he told her dryly. – And also see if there is more to it.

– More…?

– There usually is, he noted distracted.

He was always distracted, she suspected.

She smiled sweetly to him, but realized that he probably didn't notice because of the mask. Or perhaps the little opening for the mouth was sufficient for him. Perhaps he was the kind of guy that noticed everything. She cringed and covered her mouth with a hand.

He pushed a button and the sound of a voice flooded her auditory canals.

– Can you hear this? He asked.

– Yes, she frowned. – Can't you hear it?

It sounded like perfectly normal and casual conversation in her ears.

– Most people would have to strain to understand the words, he said. – Would you please repeat what you hear word by word?

She did, without straining herself at all.

– Morrison Quackbacker walked down the road.

A giggle threatened to push itself from her mouth, but she kept it contained.

He punched a bit on the keyboard, before pushing the button again. This time she heard low conversation, but had no trouble when she was asked to repeat it.

– The rest of us hardly heard anything, he enlightened her, – anything at all.

She looked astonished at him, and turned towards her sister on the other table.

– I heard it through your mind, Gimmick said, – but no audio.

– What did I have for breakfast today? He asked, when he turned back towards her.

– Bacon and eggs, she said automatically. – Toast, burned…

She shook her head in amazement.

– And? He prodded her.

– Tomato, she continued. – Sausage… mushroom… apple…

She stopped.

– The apple was a little later, she added.

Gimmick sensed her sister's anxiety, her elation and fear, clear as glass.

Black lines appeared on a white screen on the opposite wall.

– Can you read it?

– «Apples are orange», she read, read what for Gimmick and the others was nothing more than blurred black lines. – «Oranges are green».

And thus it continued for a while, until Mechanic's curiosity was somewhat sated.

– I would like to do more tests on you, he told Sensor, – if that's all right? It would require more time and a more thorough examination.

– Sure, she replied, drowning in his penetrating blue/green eyes. – I would love that.

Gimmick frowned, fully aware of what «a more thorough examination» meant.

– This preliminary excursion is sufficient, though, to conclude that your five ordinary senses are far above that of an average human being or big human being, are far from ordinary.

The attention shifted to Gimmick, and she returned to her own head. Mechanic and Lady Grace gathered around the table. She rested there on her back and felt inevitably vulnerable.

– Yours is also a curious case, he said. – to this point you and Lady Grace's powers have worked in remarkably similar ways, but now you are displaying a kind of telepathy clearly varying from hers, either different or more advanced or both.

– What I felt…

– Yes? He said quickly.

– What I felt, the sweep didn't seem to be related to telepathy at all. It was a probe, but not really searching for minds at all, but… but power.

– I will make you relive the memory, Lady Grace said, – take you back, and thus we may be able to recreate the conditions when you experienced it, at least from your point of view.

Lucinda wanted to object, but that wasn't really an option, so she nodded glumly.

– Another curious thing about it is that Cougar never displayed any kind of mental powers before she… before she disappeared. How do you know it was her?

His voice was clearly strained. They had all been affected by Cougar leaving and its cause, but perhaps he had been affected the hardest.

– I recognized her… mental signature. It was distorted, but still easily matched by how it was just before…

– She never revealed any kind of mental powers, Lady Grace, said decisively, dismissing his objections. – But she may have deceived us, or it is her blooming, second power.

Many had indeed displayed a second power years after the first had emerged.

She began her examination. Gimmick sensed the buzz, the intrusion in her mind. It was deeper, more thorough compared to the fairly light contact they usually benefited from, more one-sided. Lady Grace probed her mind, penetrated deep within and not being very considerate about it. Grace, or Claudia Malone was the oldest, and had always been the dominant of the two since they had first met, had always taken advantage of that fact. Gimmick bit her lip. It didn't really hurt, at least not in a traditional sense, but it was… unpleasant.

Relax, the voice said. Let go. Let me in. Show me, show me everything.

Lucinda felt like she was floating. The cold fingers at her temple burned her skin. She got a sense of those around her and the room, all the equipment, machinery in a way she never had before. It displayed itself to her, humming and buzzing, and she couldn't tell whether or not it was the technology, herself or Claudia.

Then there was a pull, and suddenly she was back on the streets, and she relived the moment she had sensed the overwhelming presence, and this time the desire to scream was actually stronger than the first time, because Claudia prolonged the moment in order to study it better. It was only one fraction of a moment, but so powerful.

Lady Grace pulled out and pulled back, literally, clearly shaken, and Gimmick couldn't deny she felt slightly pleased by that.

– Such a malevolent spirit. Grace shook her head, clearly distraught. – I wouldn't believe it possible.

Mechanic, Alan Prescott didn't ask, not aloud, but his expression said it all. One didn't need to be a mind reader to know the question burning on his lips.

– Gimmick is correct, she acknowledged. – It is Cougar, incredibly more powerful and dangerous, compared to when we knew her, unlike any enemy we have ever faced. Oracle was right, about everything.

Relative impasse was substituted for hectic, even frantic activity. The quiet place… woke up. The final preparations began and concluded in less than an hour. Everybody gathered in the entrance hall. Sensor studied the commotion with huge eyes.

– This is unprecedented… isn't it? How many of them are there?

– This is indeed a record-high number of costumed crime fighters gathered in one place, Lady Grace granted her, – including two affiliate groups. And we will be meeting up with others as we go. There is a growing need for cooperation between the various factions, and we need to bring in the solitary figures at the fringe of society.

Sensor frowned a bit, pondering the subtext of Lady Grace's words, before her excitement once more proved ascendant.

Presentations and introductions were made between «faces» new to each other. Most wore masks, though not everybody bothered with that. Some had either chosen to reveal their «civil» identity to the world or had been exposed.

Members of the affiliate groups aren't given any rings of course, Lady Grace told the recruit in her head. They need to travel here, and through the portals with one of us. When you gain the honor of wearing a ring you will also have the privilege to travel alone through the portals, and bring whoever you wish, within limits, of course.

80

Gimmick followed the «conversation» through her sister. Sensor had long experience in mind speak with her, and that aided her in the talk she had with Claudia, making it a little less awkward.

Everybody directed their attention at Lady Grace and Flight Captain, at their potent authority, as they walked to the center of the hall.

— We have all struggled through rough times lately, Flight Captain cried. — It's getting dangerous out there. All three teams, the Maverick Crew, Asphalt Cowboys and Junior Mavericks have noticed that. It's time we take control of an increasingly dangerous world, taming the chaos threatening to overtake our society.

The members of the Junior Mavericks and Asphalt Cowboys looked at him with misty eyes. Both teams had indeed suffered through rough times the last few months and sought closer ties to the mother organization.

— We will sweep all probable and improbable places, looking for information, for villains. Lady Grace spoke aloud, with a fist raised to her face. — We will shake all trees in our path, make all possible rotten fruits fall. We will move with military precision through all places available to us, looking for those empowered convicts on the run and the forces behind them, and doing that I'm convinced we will eventually also find our lost friends. You have been briefed. You know that unpleasant surprises await us out there, that some of our friends may have deserted us and switched sides. Yes, there are indications, strong ones even that Eleanor Sharpe, Cougar has joined the enemy. Don't let that distress you, but rather let it inspire you to do better, better than the *mockery* she has made of our fellowship. When and if we find her, and if our intel is confirmed to be correct, we will show her no more mercy than we do our other foes. We've been lax lately, let things slide, and it's time we reestablish ourselves as a force to be reckoned with in our country and the world at large. Our society needs us. The world needs to be put back on track.

Everybody stood straight, like soldiers. Lady Grace had that effect on people, on them, on everyone she met.

— I will take command of one group. Flight Captain, Gimmick and The Bowman will lead the others. One group will at any time remain here, at our command center, so it may quickly assist or come to the rescue of one in dire need of aid. We will visit all the places the portals can take us, and then we will use our choppers to cover other hotspots.

— All places? Cracker wondered. — Jagadir, too?

— Especially Jagadir, Lady Grace snapped. — We're through pussyfooting.

There were gasps of anxiety and excitement both among the youths. Every single individual present was fully aware of what her words signified or might signify.

Are you ready? Lady Grace sent to Gimmick.

I am, Gimmick replied, finding herself straighten a little more.

You know what is required of you, what you may need to do?

I know! Gimmick assured her leader, very consciously projecting calm surface thoughts.

Lady Grace and Flight Captain picked the teams. The entire process was surprisingly smooth. This was, after all the first time the three teams had cooperated in an organized manner.

Gimmick projected calm to her team, at Sensor, Oil, Raven Bird, Brick, Lavender and Stalco. It was like the other teams, well balanced and put together, even though Raven Bird was the only other member of the core team. It was sufficient. Gimmick kept herself from shrugging with an effort.

Everybody fed well before they left, and drank a lot to go along with it, and then they went to the toilet. There was no queue. Even for this increased number of residents the number of toilet bowls was sufficient. The stench filled what Lucinda always thought of as an overgrown public restroom, even though the fans worked overtime.

We prepare ourselves, she sent to the team. It's good.

Everybody appeared from the restroom, weary as always, spent, empty, only Energetic being spared the unpleasantness.

The other teams passed through the portal. Lady Grace and her team stayed behind. They pulled back to the control room, to act as command central and backup.

Gimmick studied her selected six. They waited eagerly for her word with trust in their hazy eyes. She found a small box in her jacket and handed it to Sensor. The girl looked curious at her, at it.

– What is it?

– Open it! Gimmick bid her, a bit sharper than she had intended.

Sensor obeyed, and pulled out a blue, silk scarf with engravings, golden letters.

– It is beautiful.

– Smell it, *hound*, Gimmick prompted her.

Melinda understood. She shook imperceptibly and pushed the soft fabric at her lower face.

– There are several scents here, she reported, – but only one fairly recent, overpowering all the others.

– It belongs to Oracle, Gimmick informed them. – For some reason she left it behind before she disappeared. It used to be her mother's, a keepsake, a family heirloom passed down through the generations. Will you be able to hold on to its scent?

– Yes, Sensor confirmed proudly. – I've done similar things before and...

– Will you be able to recognize the smell among thousands of others in busy streets?

– I believe so. My power has grown so much stronger lately.

She lit up.

– We'll see if you can prove yourself, Gimmick remarked.

The smile turned itself off like a light.

Lucinda steeled herself.

They walked to the portal. Gimmick noticed again how it began shimmering upon her approach.

– Focus on the scent, she told her sister. – Focus hard. Think of nothing else. Slip into the world of your senses, relaxed and alert. Stay there.

She felt how the girl made use of the meditation techniques she had taught her, how she created a realm within her mind, like Gimmick did herself, like Lady Grace had taught her. It created a kind of detachment to the outer world, like floating in a bubble of quiet air. She put one hand on Sensor's shoulder and another on Oil. Raven Bird did the same with Lavender and Stalco, and Brick sort of embraced them all with long and strong arms. Then, they stepped through the portal. The journey was practically instantaneous. It wasn't like they could stick their head in, and see the other side, but close.

The relative silence was exchanged with noisy and smelly streets. They found themselves in the Pit, Jaynagar's seedy and forlorn downtown, also called the Valley of Lost Hope by popular vote. Despair besieged Gimmick the moment she began catching the mood and thoughts from the pedestrians. The Pit had started out as a fairly small area, but had grown to cover a vast expanse of the vast city of Jaynagar.

Jaynagar was one of the world's largest cities and covered most of the south-western part of the country. Lucinda felt it as they began moving within the derelict, abandoned building, imagining she felt the entire city stretch on, stretch on forever...

Melinda knowing her well, knowing that she had one of her «episodes» discreetly put a hand on her shoulder, rousing her from her trance.

Gimmick shook her head, doing her best to mask her confusion, found the communicator in her uniform and signaled the headquarters.

– Yes. Lady Grace said.

– This is Gimmick, reporting in, signal 3973. We have arrived.

– Good, Claudia said. – Everything is good here, signal 4822.

Lady Grace had given each squad leader the numbers telepathically in advance.

– We begin our mission. Gimmick out.

The communicator turned silent, and Gimmick returned it to its place in the uniform.

Sensor began her task, began sniffing out various places in the room, the ground in front of the gate, and a trail leading away from it, crouching, going down on all fours, before getting back on her feet.

– Oracle was here, she reported. – Her scent is faint, but tangible. She came here several times, both alone and with others, both with and without you.

She looked at Gimmick and Raven Bird.

There was no glass in the windows here, in the glaring openings. The traffic and noise from the outside reached them practically undiluted. When they left the building and appeared into the busy street they hardly noticed the difference.

– The trail is gone, Sensor reported. – It disappeared the moment we stepped outside. The sidewalk has been scrubbed countless times, I guess.

The loud sounds and confusing sensory input hurt her, now, when she strained her abilities.

Gimmick caught her attention with a slight nudge in her mind. Sensor looked at her in pain, understanding before Big Sister spoke.

– You once told me that your sense of smell was sharper than that of a dog…

Sensor had already resumed her effort. She began sniffing on lampposts and the wall, up and down the street. People stared at her, at them, but they were a fairly familiar sight in the city, and no one interfered.

– Perhaps we should put her on a leash? A man across the street cried and laughed himself silly.

They ignored him. Lucinda pretended to ignore him. She gave no outward sign that she was studying him, but she was, probing his weak, easily influenced mind.

He kept laughing, a very enjoyable state of affairs at first. The puzzled frown appeared on his face when he discovered that he couldn't stop.

Choke on it!

He heard the voice out of nowhere, and looked confused around him.

Choke on it, like the *dog* you are.

He laughed, and couldn't stop laughing. Others, even those that had shared in his joke initially began glaring at him with condemning eyes. He let out a howl of laughter reminiscent of a horse's neigh. Sweat burned in his eyes (she knew it did). He began coughing, but he was never able to do it properly. The laughter just kept going by its own accord. The first hints of fear showed in his eyes. He hurried down the street, occasionally crouching, sometimes running, or attempting to.

Lucinda forgot about him, closed him off in her mind, even though the horrible, pained laughter kept echoing through her thoughts. The others looked at her with respect and fear. Their reaction pleased her.

– I found her, Sensor cried out in excitement.

She stood by a pole at the end of the street.

– She bumped into this one, and it's the last time she passed by here.

Before Gimmick or any of the others managed to comment on her find she had rushed on to the next pole, and the next, and the next. She stopped by one across the street, waving for them to follow her, excited like a child. Lucinda choked on a hard, hard ball in her throat.

They passed a playground. Kids in worn clothes were playing with balls and balloons. The engine of a car driving by coughed hard. Sensor almost jumped out of her skin, but kept going. Gimmick began feeling the beginning of a headache.

– My mouth is parched like paper, Lavender said. – We should have brought bottles of water.

The seething hot air quickly made it worse. Gimmick cursed herself for not thinking about it, for not taking such a basic precaution or at least taking care of it the moment they arrived in Jaynagar. This city had been built on what was basically a desert. The extensive irrigation system bringing water from faraway mountains didn't change that. It was failing. Drought threatened to make large parts of the city and surrounding area a wasteland and forcing countless people to flee.

Then she shrugged.

– Endure! She told Lavender, told them all, sending them all silent, unnoticeable reinforcing thoughts.

One of the children cracked a balloon. Sensor gasped, the loud and abrupt sound wrecking havoc with her enhanced senses.

Another balloon burst, louder than the first. Gimmick looked instantly at the kids, but she couldn't identify the culprit. She stared long and hard, and scanned them with her mind, but still couldn't do it. Her headache grew worse. Sensor looked distressed at her.

A series of balloons burst, like a machinegun or a battery of cannons. Sensor screamed short and sharp. This time Gimmick didn't look at her, but directly at the children.

– It isn't them doing it, is it? Oil shouted. – It...

– Ready yourselves, Gimmick admonished them.

She studied them, taking a certain pleasure in the way they prepared themselves for battle, how their rigorous physical and mental training kicked in. Forcing herself through the red haze of a headache she scanned their surroundings in all directions.

Nothing, nothing she could identify or perceive.

– Anything? She first turned to Sensor, then to Raven Bird, then to Oil and Lavender.

They all shook their head.

All of them were sensitive in one way or another, but they sensed nothing moving in their immediate vicinity. Nothing caught their attention, no danger or anything out of the ordinary.

There was nothing there, no one to point at, no one to fight.

Slowly, only slowly they emerged from the extreme battle readiness they had descended into.

– Move on! Gimmick said. – Someone is working very hard to distract us. They won't succeed.

They heard her, looked at her in confusion at first, and then increasingly attentive. Evidently she had a good hand with them. Sensor began sniffing again. The others were able to move, beyond frozen muscles and fixed attention, to once again study the scene unfolding before them. It seemed unreal, though, as if they were dreaming or were drunk or high. A cluster of balloons slipped from the children's grasp and rose along the wall, until it reached above the roofs. A driver pushed his horn in order to make another bunch of children in school uniform hurry across the zebra stripes. Brick moved ahead of Sensor in her obvious direction. Gimmick sensed how Raven Bird used her power over magnetism to create protective fields around her, making them lesser targets. Lavender used her power of hard shadow to do the same.

Her power wasn't really visible either, except like transparent implications in the air, but it was still there. Lucinda sensed it, felt the pressure points it created around her.

Lavender and Raven Bird didn't use their powers all the time, or they would have been exhausted and useless very soon, but they used it every time something happened, a sound, a man in training gear running towards them, seemingly charging them, passing them on the sidewalk, or other initially perceived suspicious activities. Gimmick used her power on the running man, but sensed no threat there. He was just exercising, that's all, actually exercising in this hot, hostile environment.

It took quite a bit of time, several blocks or restless rushing back and forth before their tracker stopped, before she shook her head in frustration and despair and dawning realization. Then she had searched several blocks in a wide square around her last point of contact.

By that time they were thirsty, hungry and weary. They realized hours had passed. Nothing had happened. There had been no overt attack, and everybody, especially Lavender and Raven Bird, the squad's foremost defensive capability were exhausted.

They sat in a cafeteria, wolfing down food and fluids.

— Too much happened, didn't it, Stalco began, his practically hairless jaw shaking, — for it to be coincidences? Someone prepared a welcome for us.

He was worried, frustrated and angry, like all of them.

I think that is a safe assumption, Gimmick thought, not sharing with them, giving them an imperceptible nod. They all nodded.

— But to plan and execute all that? Lavender said incredulous. — That takes a lot of organizing… and power, and just to… to *ire* us?

— Our enemies are sending us a message, Gimmick said. — They want us to know that they could have attacked us, but chose not to.

The heat no longer felt pervasive, the pearls of sweat on their skin cold.

— They know us, Sensor cried distressed. — They knew about… me.

— That's by no means a certainty, but certainly a possibility we must consider, Gimmick acknowledged.

The guests at the cafeteria stared at them, like people always did, but aside from that they left them alone. Gimmick couldn't sense any major ill intent in any of them, but she had begun to seriously distrust the effectiveness of her mind power lately and felt some of the same ambiguity of relief and anxiety her charges did when they looked to her for guidance.

— Cassandra Rogan teaches just a few blocks from here, Gimmick said. — That includes afternoon classes, as I recall.

— Perhaps we should pay her a visit! Raven Bird more than suggested, on an unusually aggressive note.

— I was thinking the same thing, Gimmick nodded, pleased with her friend's ability to cue in. — It's been a while since we checked her out. It's growing increasingly unlikely that she hasn't heard from her brothers. The Rogans may be small fish, but if they have joined a bigger organization we could collect information about it through them, and find information about them through her.

They kept eating. Even in their accelerated feeding mode they used a long time to devour everything on the exaggerated plate.

Brick, the biggest of them all took a break from eating. The others looked astounded at him.

— It didn't sound like a balloon bursting at all, but as if one of the kids stomped on it… all of it very deliberate, as if they weren't into hiding themselves at all.

Silence greeted his words. They all threw themselves into the feeding, as if by a quiet agreement.

Gimmick paid for the meal with her Crew golden card. It was a considerable amount, one she could never cover in her civilian identity.

The school was just up the street. Gimmick kept an eye on it through people passing by and those inside, well before they reached it. Still no immediate danger.

She frowned.

If you keep doing that with the current frequency you'll grow old before your time, Melinda teased her.

– Cassandra isn't here, Gimmick said. – At least I can't sense her.

The building was in old, gothic style. The late afternoon sun split in red, but Gimmick saw the stairs and entrance in blue silver, as if walking in moonlight.

And then it was as if the late day sky started bleeding, and it was no longer moonlight, but a red, thick and dry air stealing the breath from her lungs, a pervasive reality filled with fighting people and the cruelest, most brutal violence.

– What is it? Sensor asked, noticing her distress.

– Nothing, big sister replied. – Nothing important.

The vision, or whatever it was, faded.

And then they were inside, in a no less sinister moonlight.

She and Raven Bird led the way through the building, to the principal's office, one they had walked quite a few times. Raven Bird opened the door. They walked past the secretary and approached the woman behind the big desk.

– We're looking for Cassandra, Raven Bird said sharply.

– Haven't you bothered that poor girl enough? The aggravated woman cried.

She was big as well, middle-aged, tired.

– We just want to talk to her, Gimmick said. – Ask her about her brothers.

– Her brothers, the principal chuckled darkly, – as if she would have anything to do with them.

Gimmick probed the woman's mind.

– Anyway, she isn't here, and hasn't been for weeks. I reported her missing weeks ago after checking her apartment. It was practically abandoned. Don't you guys check with the legal law enforcement? I have heard you've got an *excellent* working relationship with them.

She didn't have any idea where Cassandra was, and was concerned for her.

– Her brothers would have contacted her sooner or later, Gimmick said curtly to the woman behind the desk, – and apparently they have. Thanks for your cooperation.

They retreated to the hallway.

– We should have checked up on her far more often, Raven Bird swore. – This is clearly not a coincidence.

– No, Gimmick agreed, – it fits well with everything else that doesn't fit.

She turned towards Lavender, noticing her distress, both her mental state and her restlessness, how her eyes never stopped moving around.

– What is it?

– It is this place, the girl said. – It... it gives me the creeps. I don't know if you have noticed, but it has grown darker in here.

As incredible and unlikely that was... she sounded afraid of the dark. Her thoughts had suddenly become a murky rubble Lucinda could only glimpse.

– It is the shadows. They move of their own accord and... *whisper* to me.

A chilly draft surged through the narrow passage.

– But the shadows are your friends, Oil said. – It's what you've always said.

– I know, but something has changed, or something is different *here*.

– What is here? Gimmick asked patiently. – Where is it?

– Not anything I can p-pinpoint. There is no fixed direction, nothing to grab h-hold of.

Gimmick kept projecting her calm, until the girl finally calmed down from her anxious state. It turned visibly brighter around them.

– Can you pinpoint it, now?

– No. Lavender shook her head. – It, whatever it was seems to be gone.

She still shivered a bit, but that, too faded away with each passing second.

They walked through the entire school, all its levels and rooms, even the basement, but found nothing suspicious or notable anywhere. Wherever they went they saw misery. They walked through classrooms filled with adults dressed in rags, chairs and people missing a leg, dirty floors and broken windows. This was where Cassandra Rogan had worked.

– Anything? Gimmick asked her squad.

Everybody shook their head, confirming Lucinda's conclusions. There was nothing here, nothing suggesting that this was anything but a desert walk, a useless venture retracing its own tracks.

– Let's leave, Gimmick said.

The sun had vanished when they stepped outside. This far south the dark came abruptly, with a very brief transitional twilight. They didn't waste time, and took the shortest route possible back to the portal, but it still felt like a stretch, like they walked twice as far as they were supposed to. Suspecting foul play they began checking and rechecking street-signs and markings, without discovering anything amiss. They looked bewildered at each other, and fear yet again entered their thoughts.

Gimmick pulled the communicator from its hiding place in her uniform and sent the signal. Almost instantly they heard Mechanic's voice through the speaker.

– Yes?

– This is Gimmick, reporting in, signal 3416, Lucinda said, very focused. – Is everything all right at your end?

– Everything is calm, Alan replied. – Signal 5784. What about you?

– We are not in any immediate danger, as far as we know. The frustration bubbled in Gimmick's voice. – Aside from that it's difficult to tell.

There was a brief moment of hesitation before they heard Lady Grace:

– Return to base.

– Very well. Gimmick out!

They hurried on, as astute as they possibly could be after hours of exhausting focus and alertness.

– Lady Grace is clearly military, Stalco giggled, – and high ranking to boot.

– At least she sounds like she is, Sensor agreed.

She was a colonel, but the others would never be told that. Gimmick laughed with her squad, masking her sense of inadequacy and shame.

The mood lightened a bit, even though Gimmick didn't need to prepare them when they entered the derelict building where the portal was hidden. They approached the invisible hole in the air cautiously, pushing beyond the fatigue the best they could.

– Everything seems to be okay, Gimmick said, noticing nothing different with the shimmer exposed to her eyes.

They repeated the procedure from earlier that day, and stepped through.

The familiar surroundings of the headquarters surrounded them, and the very familiar masks of Mechanic and Lady Grace and the rest met them, and they felt an enormous sense of relief.

The other teams had returned long ago from their mission.

Gimmick opened her mind to Lady Grace and allowed her to see everything that had transpired. It didn't take more than a few seconds, and a few seconds more with repetitions and questions and answers.

– Debriefing will commence immediately, Lady Grace declared.

They walked with their peers to the meeting room, and began relating their experience, relating it through speech, to everybody present, not leaving out anything, from the initial tiny events, to the gathering sense of unease and of being watched.

– It was like we were being led by the nose, Lavender cried distressed. –

They knew we were coming or at least were prepared for it.

Then, catching Sensor's glum look, she reddened.

– No offense, she said hastily.

– None taken, Sensor shrugged.

Lady Grace turned to Gimmick. She didn't have to say anything or even sending her a message with her mind.

– I agree, Gimmick said. – We were caught up in a web from the moment we stepped through the portal. I noticed nothing casual about it at all. The entire setup was very deliberate. They told us, in no uncertain terms that they could have attacked us at any time, but chose not to do so.

– I've never experienced anything like what I experienced at the school, Lavender whimpered. – It's difficult to explain, but it was like something or someone moved under my skin. I've always been more than my body. The shadows extend my reach, and I've always been comfortable with that... until today. If that someone also exerts control over shadows her or his control is far more precise than mine.

– It seems like our unknown foes, at the very least knew the place, the people and the powers, Mechanic mused. – If that is indeed the case that makes them very, very powerful.

– C'mon, people, the Bowman cried, – it's a con, a magic trick. They knew we would come looking for either Oracle or Cougar or revisit Cassandra Rogan sooner or later, and set the stage well in advance, with several parameters, in order to rattle us, an impressive feat, for sure, but nothing approaching what they want us to believe. Why didn't they attack? They didn't *dare!*

People looked astonished at each other and then they nodded, and laughed a little, nodding some more to themselves. Even Lady Grace sent the Bowman a grateful look.

– The Bowman's point is well made, Flight Captain stated. – The fact that none of the other groups experienced anything similar more than suggests it. We rustled some feathers, knocked a few skulls, in short doing very much like we usually do, without tangible results. Jaynagar could be a false lead, a deliberate attempt at diversion, but right now it's all we've got, and we should certainly keep that in mind as we widen our search. We have made significant progress today, people, for the first time in years. We should be *pleased.*

Everybody smiled at each other. As usual, even more than the Bowman he had put everything in perspective, restored the balance of the gathering.

He rose and raised a fist in front of his chest.

– We are the most powerful group of people ever assembled on Earth. Of course our enemies fear us. We stand in the way of every possible dastardly scheme they may entertain.

The applause began, and it made no sign of ending for what seemed like minutes. Lucinda felt like she stood at the center of an orchestral drum roll striking her deaf.

Most of the gathering stayed on the premises during the night. It had turned quiet when Gimmick stood by a window in the simmering twilight in the bathroom on the upper floor and looked down at the Tobruk warehouse district, unpleasant memories haunting her. Even her colleagues' minds had fallen quiet, even though she could perceive their fevered and chaotic dreams.

Lady Grace stopped in the hallway outside. Lucinda had sensed her aware thoughts all the time. She sensed her approach.

– Is everything okay, little one?

– Of course, Gimmick replied without turning.

– You did good today. You have no reason to be ashamed.

Which were exactly the right words to make the younger woman feel ashamed.

She turned, bowing her head in the other's powerful presence.

– I failed, she said. – We didn't achieve *anything* of significance.

– Your first command, Claudia Malone said, – and you handled your troops like a seasoned veteran. You have reason to be proud, little one. We had our first encounter with what well may be our ultimate enemy, and it didn't dare attack because of your battle readiness, your ability to strike fear in their hearts.

Lucinda soaked up the praise like a sponge would moisture.

– You think so? She sniffed.

– I know so, Lady Grace stated with utmost confidence, one stunning Gimmick. – They waited for you, were ready for you, and still didn't attack.

– But I couldn't sense them, couldn't sense any hostile thoughts, and that has happened a lot lately.

– You need to work on that, of course, need to work on improving yourself, to be prepared for the confrontation that will come, but I know you will do it. I have faith in you.

She sounds like an army recruitment drive.

Lucinda thought, and was scared shitless that Claudia would notice.

– What about your sweet sister? How would you rate her?

What a strange wording, Lucinda thought.

– She handled herself well. She's tough.

– Good, good. I agree. It was the right call when you decided to bring her into the fold. She has prepared herself for years, and is finally ready for bigger things.

– Thank you, Gimmick said with pride in her voice.

Lady Grace nodded, as if to herself, as if she had made a decision.

– Well, we should get some sleep. There will be a hard day tomorrow. Good night.

– Good night.

Lady Grace didn't salute, but Gimmick felt an almost irresistible need to do so. She stood straight long after the commanding presence had vanished through the door.

And don't worry. The Bowman will sleep soundly tonight. You won't be bothered.

Bothered? Lucinda thought.

And this time she didn't care if Claudia heard her.

There was no further communication. Gimmick returned to her bedroom. Every senior member had their own room, where they could have all the privacy they wanted. She locked the door, didn't leave it open like she usually did. Removing the uniform was no problem. She managed, no matter how distracted she was. The mask, usually staying on was also removed. It felt good to move without constraints again, to move her eyes without encountering the boundaries at the edges. The distant lights from the city below cast the room in yet another kind of twilight. This place reminded her more of a hotel room than of a home, but it sufficed. She crawled onto the large bed, and pulled the blanket over her body. Scenes and sounds began replying themselves in her head. In the silence and emptiness of the night there was no way to hide from what was lurking in her mind. She wished Richard was here, holding her, fucking her brains out. The large body writhed on the bed, making the furniture shake beneath her, creating more disturbing sounds. Gimmick crouched restless on the unfamiliar bed, waiting for sleep, wide awake, her mind working overtime, and only slowly, slowly was she falling into a kind of pitiful dormancy and dreaming disturbing dreams about yesterday and tomorrow.

Chapter 6
SIX YEARS AGO TODAY

Everything faded when she fed. Every detail surrounding her vanished into mist and shadow, bringing brief respite from the everlasting Hunger.

She probed the trashcans in a fever pitch only increasing when she found something to fill her belly. The surrounding streets turned indistinct while she re-experienced yesterday and tomorrow.

Mother was clearly distraught. Lucinda didn't need her increasingly enhanced senses to tell her that. The older woman did the dishes, her skin whitening where she clutched the plate.

Lucinda danced on the living room floor, the music reaching her through the ear plugs. It was peaceful, but the world, represented by what the girl heard through Mother's ears kept distracting her. She tried to close it off, but she was drawn to the glum thoughts and unable to stop them from manifesting in her mind.

The plate broke in Brenda's hand and practically turned to dust in her powerful grip. Lucinda rushed to her. It practically took her forever to reach the kitchen, or so it felt. Mother stood there, totally beside herself.

– It's okay, mother, Lucinda soothed her, held her in her soft grip. – It's okay. Don't bother with it. It's just a plate. Why don't you go and sit down. I'll clean up here, take care of everything.

– Thank you, Brenda said weakly. – I think I'll… do that.

She walked into the living room. Lucinda heard the soft sigh when she dropped into the big, soft chair, daddy's chair.

There were quite a few broken pieces, both in the sink and on the floor. Lucinda looked at it with dismay. Her mother's depression kept distracting her, as she let out the water, and started cleaning each and every item in the sink, both for food remains and powder. Mother had become so strong that she had made mincemeat of the plate. Lucinda concentrated on not breaking anything. It was a slow, methodical and tiring process.

She was sweating in the hot kitchen, already wet after the meal, and the mandatory visit to the toilet. Melinda was there, now. She was always the last after the meals, since she could afford to be patient. There was no rush in her. Except for feeling bad because she didn't suffer the others' affliction she was basically okay. Lucinda sensed her in there, or remembered sensing her in there long ago.

Someone had left a large piece of meat in the trashcan at the corner. She grabbed it quick as lightning and put it in her bag before any of the others had the change to even come close. They scowled at her, but didn't try anything. The rusty knife in her hands spoke volumes of both her ability and willingness to defend herself.

There were sixteen trashcans lined up from the corner and to the first entrance of the block of flats. There were four «Trashers», including herself tonight, an average number. That meant there was usually enough for everybody, but not always. And Hunger ruled them all and made reason fly away.

One of the other girls found a loaf. The man grabbed the food right out of her hands.

– It's mine! He glared at them, clearly gloating. – Mine!

He was tall and big and strong, an adult male. The girls shrunk in his presence.

Lucinda looked quickly at her catch. It was less than she had hoped for, more than she strictly needed tonight. She pulled away, never taking her eyes off the other three, still using her eyes and expanded awareness to be on the lookout for other potential threats.

It was late night, silent, of sorts, even to her, the constant buzz in her mind less than when people were awake. She left the immediate block with fast, decisive steps, like a thief in the night. No one was following her, no one waited for her in the shadows ahead. If there was it would have to be one without feet, mind and breath.

The very thought made her shudder in belligerent fright.

The building ahead lacked most of its windows. The entrance door was long gone. She walked through it, into the deeper shadows, where the only light was from distant streets and buildings. Thoughts from a tearful, frightened girl grew to the forefront of Lucinda's consciousness.

– It's me, she said in front of a battered, but still somewhat solid door.

She heard the small yelps from both Melinda's mouth and mind, and the sound of running feet crossing the floor, the turning of the the key in the lock. The small, scrawny body embraced her, the tiny hole of a mouth choking against her chest.

They pulled inside. Melinda slammed the door shut. She panted excitedly in the bad light, but Lucinda didn't need to see her face. Big Sister showed her tonight's catch before she could ask. They walked to the next room, through something resembling an office landscape, the nightmarish kind. There was furniture there, a mothballed couch and a few chairs and a table, a dusty carpet, and their bed, as it was.

– You feed first, Melinda insisted.

– No, Lucinda said, – if I start I may not stop until I've devoured everything, and you need to eat, too. Your bones are sticking out everywhere.

The child hesitated only briefly before she grabbed some half-digested fruit and began feeding. The meat was cooked, but cold. She didn't care, but munched it as if it should be the most delicious course. Lucinda began feeding when Kid Sister slowed down. Reason left her almost immediately, and Melinda pulled back, clearly cautious, even scared. Lucinda sensed that, in her feverish mind.

There were only a few pieces left when she was done, some smoked meat, of all kinds, but nothing even resembling a full meal.

Lucinda sat down, with her back to the wall, waving the child to her, prodding her mind slightly, and calming her.

– Come here.

Melinda crawled close to her large and warm body, snuggling there, needy, as starved for attention as she was for food. Lucinda put an arm around her, careful not to use too much force.

– I'm sorry I struck you…

– I know, the child said, in a very adult way. – I told you not to worry about it. You can't help yourself when the Hunger grabs you.

Lucinda relived the moment days ago, when she had struck the child. She had been like a wild beast, hardly able to reason at all.

They wanted to speak more, making the attempt several times, failing to bring sound to moving lips.

Lucinda listened to the outside. She always did. There was nothing, no humans in the vicinity of the building. She sensed life, animals, mostly what was probably…

– I can sense the rats in the sewers, she said, she finally managed, – always hungry, always feeding, never sated.

The child rubbed a hand back and forth over her head, doing her best to comfort her.

– It is late night, Big Sister continued, – silent to others, but not to me. Even if there were no cars or machines I would hear the noise of life everywhere, the sound of loud dreaming wherever I walk.

She rose, making sure to touch Kid Sister's cheek before leaving, before walking to a hole in the floor on the opposite side of the building. She removed her pants, spread her legs over the hole and began the easy process of pushing the shit out of her arse. It fell, the long way down, until it hit the floor on the ground floor. There were rolls of toilet paper below the dirty window. She walked there and tore off a considerable piece. As always she had to use a lot of it. She returned to the room where Melinda sat still on the same spot and rejoined her there, where they both embraced again.

96

They sat there, unable to note the passage of time. It just slipped away. Lucinda looked at her watch, but it didn't really tell her anything.

– If only we could get the fridge to work, Melinda said, after a while. – Then we could at least store food, and you wouldn't have to go out every night.

Words slipped away like thoughts. They looked at the bed, the big mattress, longing to move, to undress, to unwind and go to bed, to enjoy sleep, but sleep came, like it often did, quickly, unbidden, lovingly, and they never knew where they would wake up the next morning.

Gilbert Patterson walked the city streets with a large bag in his left hand. He had a determined expression inscribed in his feature, his attention directed forward to the point of hardly looking to the sides at all. It was a typical busy afternoon in the financial district. Most people had just quit their job for the day and were on their way to the bank and subsequently to the stores to buy groceries. They rushed back and forth without direction, without a plan. It was all random. They might have a destination in mind, but then again, they might not.

He stared at them from above, like at mice running through a mace. There was no need to focus his concentration or anything. He only needed to squint his eyes a bit, in order to see it all cast in shadow.

Gilbert Patterson stopped briefly, across the street from the bank. He waited, patiently for the traffic light to change from red. One man crossed on red, maneuvering between the even flow of cars and loud horns. An old man stopped, frozen in time. The light changed. The old man remained on his spot, unable to move. Gilbert crossed the street on the zebra stripes. He pulled the mask from his jacket and pulled it over his head. People looked at him cautiously, but kept their distance and avoided his empty stare.

The automatic doors to the bank slid open and closed, swallowing him whole. He pulled his twelve-round shotgun from the bag, firing once into the ceiling. A part was blown off and fell to the floor, hitting it with a crack almost louder than the firing of the shotgun. People screamed. No one moved.

– On the floor, he said calmly, keeping his attention on the people in the cashier.

Everybody threw themselves down.

He walked to the cashier.

– If anyone touches any button I will know, he said, – and the button pusher will pay.

He placed the open bag on the desk, signing for the people behind it to rise. They did and began filling the bag with bills. All of them made it their task in life to not even glance at the alarm button under the desk. He turned once, surveying the room. No one had moved.

The personnel hurried up, on the verge of hysteria. A few bills happened to drop outside the bag.

– Forget about it, he shrugged.

The bag filled up and did so surprisingly fast. This was one of the biggest branches in the city, and even though most of the money was either in the vault and locked in a time code there was still quite a bit of «change» left.

The bag was over half full, and began to turn heavy. He looked at his watch, hesitated a few seconds before he closed the bag, grabbed the handle, turned and headed for the exit.

One eager employee pushed the alarm button. It was a silent alarm, but Patterson heard it. He turned abruptly and fired. The man behind the desk was dissolved in blood and guts. Patterson turned back towards the exit, continuing his escape.

He put the shotgun back in the bag, left the bag open and walked more or less calmly through the door sliding open for him. The street looked calm and peaceful. The light was red, but changed before he reached the zebra stripes. He began the crossing. The whining of tires disturbed his sense of peace. Police patrol cars arrived from both sides, at least four of them. He stopped counting by then. With an abrupt turn he walked to the closest car. He fired at the two officers before they managed to even open their doors. They remained in their seats, penetrated by hails and glass.

– FREEZE! Another pointed his gun at him.

Patterson shot him with a slight shift of his aim. The man vanished from his sight.

The man's partner fired his gun. Patterson shook a bit, staggered a couple of steps back before killing his fourth cop. He rushed the fifth and sixth. They fired, mostly missing, but hitting, too. He shot them, kept shooting them, but they charged him in droves. He reloaded the shotgun, firing while he pulled one of the bodies from the driver's seat of the closest car. The engine was still running. He fell down in the seat, and in just a moment or two the car jumped forward with a mighty roar. The street was practically closed, in both ends. He crashed into two cars like a rocket, pushing them backwards, leaving several officers with broken bones and skulls in the bargain.

He backed off the car and repeated the procedure. Yet more of a possible opening revealed itself. He fired through both windows at the moving targets. A rain of bullets hammered him. Slowly both he and the borrowed patrol car were shot to shreds. The explosion rocked the street and the buildings. The car was done for, but these cars were well protected from explosions and the blast hadn't really hit him. He left the car and continued to fire, even as bullets kept hitting him. A few of the officers fled. Others were too afraid or stunned to move. Others kept firing at the demon in their midst. It was like on a firing range. He had some experience with moving targets, and these fleas ran pretty much like rabbits. The giant smoking figure went down on its knees, swaying a bit in that position, before falling on its side. Hands kept holding and firing the shotgun. All the officers hid, now, waiting like vultures for the prey, the predator to fall. He still managed to hit a few, easily spotting the legs and bodies displayed under the cars. The creature fought to get back on its feet. For a moment or two it seemed like it would be successful, pushing against the pavement with its huge paws, but then it fell back, breathing one more time, two, before lying still.

The officers stayed in relative safety for quite a while, before emerging, before cautiously approaching the cooling, torn asunder body of Gilbert Patterson.

They stood there for a long time, their guns cocked, before finally lowering them, staring stunned at the disaster area the usually so busy city center had become.

Lucinda woke up, choking a bit, drying a tear or two from her eyes.

Melinda woke up, too, looking at her sister with a sad face, pulling close to the big body.

– You dreamed about father again, didn't you? You're projecting your dreams, somehow.

Lucinda caressed the girl's cheek.

– You're a wise and spunky little girl, she joked.

The child pulled back a little, staring sullenly at the older sister.

– Yes, I dreamed about him, Lucinda admitted. – It is as if I'm actually there, when it happened. Sometimes I think he was in contact with me the moment he died, and that he downloaded everything into my cerebral cortex. I can smell the blood, the stench of the guns, hear the sounds, the screams, the firing of the guns… see every detail of the street surrounding him. I can't feel the pain as the bullets hit him, though. Perhaps he wanted to spare me that.

Melinda looked at her with wisdom beyond her years. She had always been a wise kid, and lately been forced to grow up fast.

Lucinda turned fully to her, grabbing her hands, making contact with the wet eyes.

– Listen to me, Kid Sister, and listen *good*.

Melinda nodded serious minded.

– No one will help us. No one helped mommy and daddy, even though they went everywhere in their desperation and growing despair. We are on our own, in survival, in *vengeance* and everything on the long list on our path. *Swear* to me that you will never let go of those things, no matter what happens.

She clutched the child's hands in hers, drawing blood as her nails burrowed through skin, and then Melinda did the same with her, the sweet face transformed by fury.

– I *swear!*

They sat that way for seconds , minutes, before letting go of each other, slowly smiling.

– C'mon, Lucinda said, kissing her sweet Kid Sister on the brow, – let's get you to school.

They devoured the rest of the food. Lucinda went and did her shitting for the morning. They washed themselves in cold water, in a sink with a cracked mirror and dressed. They still had a few clothes from their old life to choose from, somewhat clean, stored in suitcases, but their number dwindled week by week.

The two of them placed themselves in front of the mirror for a final check, the drawn faces, the low pole child and the tall pole, a young, practically grown woman.

– If you got it, flaunt it, Lucinda cried.

Melinda giggled, spontaneously embracing the other at the hip, tiny tears in her eyes.

– Hey, little one, Big Sister said softly, – that's no attitude. Remember «attitude»?

– Attitude! Melinda emphasized.

The child stubbornly dried her tears. Lucinda touched her jaw, checking her face for stains. There was none, the days old bruise not too visible. They left the apartment, left the building, suddenly finding themselves walking down busy streets.

With people surrounding her on all sides it happened again to Lucinda. She caught snippets of thoughts, words and emotions unintentionally and had to focus to keep it to a minimum. The world seemed to, in a strange way to stand still around her. She kept walking, fighting the sensation's mesmerizing effect.

They passed an ice-cream parlor. She couldn't help lingering there.

– The cravings again? Melinda said sympathetically.

– It's just like I am pregnant, the way I've heard it, Lucinda said glumly, – but I am not. I don't get a big belly or anything.

Suddenly, her thoughts were pulled to her memory of the old man. She had never seen him again, but remembered him and his words so well.

– You are pregnant, you know, the old man told her, leered at her. – But not with a child. You have a demon inside of you, and it will grow and grow. It will wax and you will wane until it is everything and you are nothing.

It wasn't too far to walk to the school. They still kept themselves within their old haunts, no matter how agonizing it was. A group of kids recognized them and pointed, and giggled wickedly.

They stopped briefly by the gate.

– Will you be all right? Lucinda asked.

– I will be. Melinda nodded. – Since I made that bitch Clara a bloody nose, the kids don't really bother me anymore. They fear I am strong like you, and that I will grow up to be big and strong, like you.

– Good, Lucinda whispered. – Very good!

They parted.

– You will, you know, Lucinda pointed out. – You just have to be patient.

– I can hardly wait, the child cried, and waved, as she was walking through the gate.

Lucinda left. The school was just a detail in the streets, the jigsaw puzzle her mind made of everything.

She headed for the nearest shopping mall. It would have been easy to find, even if she had never visited it before. Coincidentally it was the same she had visited with her sister and parents and friend Toni the day of the Great Darkness.

It seemed altered, so different from how she remembered it. All possible shadows everywhere seemed to reach for her. She caught a glimpse of the wide-eyed, needy young girl in windows and mirrors wherever she went and hurried on with fast, short steps and frantic breath.

She sat on a bench outside and gasped for air, shaking hard.

Slowly, only painfully slowly she was able to calm down.

Everything passed by her, on her spot.

A couple had a nasty quarrel. She didn't want to listen to it, to give it any of her time, but she was drawn to it, not just to their loud voices, but to their loud minds as well.

Asshole, the girl thought.

Cunt, the boy snarled.

And so it went, went on for minutes. Lucinda curled up on her spot, rocking back and forth, her eyes glazing over.

The couple had left. She didn't notice the moment it happened. When she looked up after a while, they were gone and there were no more nasty sounds in her head.

A man, a boy not that much older than her sat down by her side.

– Hi, he greeted her.

She frowned, pretty confident he was talking to her. There was no one else around.

– Hi, she replied.

He wasn't very tall, but had fairly well developed muscles, and a nice smile. She couldn't help but return the smile.

– I noticed you, he said, very straightforward. – My name is Leon. I think we can help each other out.

– Oh? She said, rather naughty. – How so?

– You're one of them, aren't you? You have the Growth Gene…

– What if I do? She said sullenly.

– You have the Growth Gene, and you need insane amounts of food in order to not starve.

She wanted to say something, anything, but nothing came to mind.

– I am a photographer and a movie producer, he said.

You don't look like a movie producer, she wanted to say.

– I'm not the kind of movie producer that get much time in mainstream entertainment, he grinned, – but I can tell you right away that my films are *very* popular.

It dawned on her exactly what kind of movie producer he was. She waited for the blush to erupt all over her body, but strangely it didn't.

– The pay isn't bad, he said, – and I believe that you and others like you can be quite popular, the new, exciting thing, if you like, one even transcending the… limitation of the genre.

– You're not shitting me, are ya? She said, filled with resentment. – It isn't something you're just saying to get in my pants, or for some other shitty reason?

– No, no. He shook his head hard. – I'm telling you the god honest truth, girl.

– I believe you, she said. – I believe that if you are lying, you're so good at it that you believe your own lies…

She rose, and instantly dwarfed him, in both height and size. He was taken a little aback, but not that much, as if he was familiar with the little intimidation she attempted to create.

– My name is Lucinda, she said brightly, – I think I will come with you and see what you've got to offer…

At one, brief moment she changed from young, innocent girl, to a dark, sinister creature. Her intimidation gained a sudden different and poignant reality.

And somewhere inside he was visibly shaking.

They shook hands. She squeezed a little, and he, obligatory rubbed his hand afterwards.

– You know, perhaps you should consider a career as a debt collector, he joked. – And not only because of your physical strength either. That intimidation tactic of yours is very effective…

She looked at him, with her large eyes, and she knew it unnerved him.

He grabbed her hand and pulled her away. She followed him. Glimpses of what was on his mind revealed themselves to her, and she reddened, and was glad he didn't turn and look at her. She saw him with his camera, and herself and other girls, all big together on a large bed. It was painfully obvious to her what dominated his thoughts right now.

They left the mall and its general, surrounding area, the more modern parts of the city and entered into the older parts, in the same, general direction where Lucinda and her kid sister had taken up residence.

– You know, Leon said cheerfully, – there are rumors that some of you guys are actually flying.

– There are?

Suddenly out of breath in anticipation she squeezed his hand a little too hard. He yelped and pulled it free, and glared at her, clearly not pleased, before regaining his jovial self.

– Honest to God. He nodded vigorously. – I haven't seen it myself or don't know anyone that has, but a friend of a friend works in a newspaper, and they have interviewed several witnesses, not quacks either that claim to have seen flying people lately, after the Great Darkness. They're sitting on it, though, until they gain irreversible proof.

Suddenly Lucinda's mind was in utter turmoil, the implications slowly dawning on her.

– That's… that's amazing, she said weakly.

– Yeah, wouldn't that be cool beyond anything?

He took her hand again, both her hands, his eyes sparkling. His intentions would have been plain even without the added tool of her enhanced mind. She reddened, and this time she didn't care if he noticed. His smile lit her up, and she closed her eyes, waiting for his kiss.

She opened her eyes again and blinked. He looked at her, or seemed to be looking at her, but his eyes stared at nothing, empty and unmoving.

Hello, little one.

She heard, and looked frantically around her, unable to tell where the voice was coming from. He kept staring straight ahead with empty eyes. She waved a hand in front of his face, but he didn't move. He stood there, frozen, like a statue.

I'm here.

The voice echoed in her head. This time there was a prodding of some kind, and she knew where to look. She noticed a big, muscular woman across the street. The woman wore a military cap on her head and a top, one with bare arms that displayed her upper body quite prominently.

– W-what?

Do not speak, little one. Speech is a barrier. Come to me, and we'll talk.

Lucinda realized, beyond certainty that the woman was speaking to her in her mind. The girl glanced briefly at Leon.

Forget him, he isn't your destiny. He would have used you, and discarded you, left you to rot. That isn't what awaits you, dear one. Your future is glorious, enviable.

Who are you?

Lucinda managed, somehow, to form a thought she knew the other would pick up. She crossed the street. There weren't any cars, not anywhere close to her, left or right, but there was still a buzz roaring in her head.

– My name is Claudia Malone, she said softly, as Lucinda stopped in front of her. – The world will know me as Lady Grace.

And she looked very much like grace to Lucinda. Grace was bigger than her, adult, fully grown, with hard, visible muscles.

The boy will hardly remember your meeting, remember you, except as a forgotten dream, haunting him in lonely moments.

– You can do that, alter his thoughts and memory, cloud his perception?

– Can't you? Claudia smiled to her. – Have you never tried, never even projected your thoughts?

– No. the girl shyly shook her head. – I wanted to…

But I didn't dare.

Claudia chuckled softly in her mind, applauding silently.

– See how easy it is, what greatness awaits you on your new path?

Lucinda looked wide eyed at the woman. She wasn't that old, that much older, but clearly so much more experienced and mature, oozing of the confidence Lucinda lacked.

– C'mon.

The girl followed the woman down the street, unable to take her eyes off her.

Where are we goinggoing? Lucinda wondered, unable to stay completely coherent, in her eagerness and excitement.

– I'm going to introduce you to some people, colleagues of mine. They, like us have been enhanced in various ways, and together we will create the future.

She waited a bit, pausing deliberately for effect.

– They are similar to us, but not like us. They won't know our civilian names, but we will know theirs. We will be privy to all their secrets and will have a special standing, even among our peers.

But…

Claudia pulled two similar masks from her purse.

Everyone is masked during the meetings, and during our nocturnal activities. What did you think, little one…

Flustered and embarrassed and increasingly excited and grateful Lucinda accepted the gift.

– We will put them on just before the surveillance cameras catch us, not before, not after. I know this isn't much, is a bit poor taste and inadequate, but know that this is just the beginning. We will make better costumes for ourselves eventually, with proper protection and equipment.

Lucinda opened her mouth to speak.

– And don't give your current rather poor financial standing much thought either, Lady Grace replied in advance. – Alan Prescott, codename Mechanic is loaded. He's basically a genius, and has made a fortune on his inventions in just a few years. He probably won't be able to support all of us indefinitely, but will set up those of us in need of money with enough of it to establish ourselves and live comfortably, to catch our fall, so to speak.

– You know everything there is to know about me, don't you? Lucinda wondered, whimpering a little.

– I know everything I need to know about you and the others, Claudia replied softly, – and soon, you will, too. I will be your mentor, your teacher in all things, including matters of right and wrong.

They walked fast, and crossed a vast area in a surprisingly short time, the entire downtrodden part of the city, to its other side, bordering on the suburbs. Lucinda got a little winded, in spite of her being in great shape, but she grew increasingly excited as well.

It is *fun*, isn't it, to use your strength, to do something that would make virtually anybody else dog tired?

Fun, Lucinda agreed. Fun fun fun

Almost boiling over with enthusiasm and eagerness to use her newfound ability, so much in awe of her companion.

Having grown more astute she was able to catch more of the thoughts and moods in the apartments they passed. A couple was quarreling about expenses. A mother gave her daughter a hard time. Two children fought over a ruined doll, ruining it even more.

– People live in such squalor, Lucinda said in despair. – Many are poor, not only those enhanced, but many more than that, and it's nothing *new*.

– That isn't our problem, Claudia said. – At least not for a while. We'll fix that, too, of course, fix everything, but not until we've dealt with crime and the criminals, not until we've gotten society back on track.

The image of her father during his last seconds revisited Lucinda. She saw her mother again.

Lady Grace, big and strong comforted her with a rub on the cheek, stopped a tear from breaking from the girl's eye.

They reached the most desolate area of the city, a wasteland of unfinished projects and condemned buildings. Lucinda noticed a subtle change in Claudia, a sign that they were about to reach their destination, noticed a few seconds before she held up a hand.

Can you sense anyone, anyone close?

No, Lucinda replied, reaching out really hard with her power, not certain it did any good. No!

Except for her companion's focused, structured mind she sensed not a soul, only what she surmised was the faint background buzz of the city's entire population.

She put on her mask. It covered the entire head, except the eyes and the mouth. Claudia put hers on, too, after ditching, putting away the military cap. Lucinda giggled darkly.

We look like criminals.

Thus is the old, ongoing dichotomy with vigilantes.

Claudia shrugged.

They turned a corner and entered a street with somewhat intact buildings. Lucinda knew their destination. She saw, sensed which direction Claudia looked, where her attention was focused, and exhilaration touched her once again.

Yes, sister, you're learning. We will be like one, you and I.

Claudia sent a message when they were halfway across the street.

I'm here.

And the large door ahead began opening before they reached it, and it began closing before they had walked inside.

They entered a dusty, clearly incomplete foyer.

It takes its time, Claudia remarked. We have to hire sets of workers independently of each other, and I have had to mind-wipe them, as we go. Now, I will thankfully have help. Trust me, it will be great exercise for you in developing your power.

The words made Lucinda shudder so pleasantly.

106

They walked further in, into what was clearly the main hall, also in an incomplete state. Five people waited for them in there. They stopped. Lady Grace put her hands on Lucinda's shoulders.

– Ladies and gentlemen, allow me to present to you the newest branch of our tree...

Gimmick, Lucinda told her.

– Gimmick, Lady Grace continued, eloquently, virtually without a break. – Gimmick, this is Flight Captain, The Bowman, Cougar, Mechanic and Raven Bird.

– Welcome, Gimmick, Flight Captain greeted her and reached out a hand.

– Thank you, Flight Captain, she said, striving to sound casual, giving him the sweetest of smiles, sensing Claudia's approval.

Reading him was easy, wasn't hard at all. She did it without him being any wiser. An image of him without the mask and in ordinary garb appeared to her. He looked almost common then, not being that big compared to many men with the growth gene.

– You can fly, she cried excitedly. – You can actually fly!

Everybody looked at her, and at Lady Grace. The big woman put her hands back on her shoulder.

– Gimmick is like me, a rare jewel in the jungle the world has become.

They looked at Gimmick with... It dawned on Lucinda that they looked at her with respect. A thrill shot through her.

– Welcome, the Bowman grinned.

His thoughts were painfully apparent. She blushed hard, and was very grateful for the mask. His lewd, beyond lewd thoughts blocked out everything else. When she tried reading him she saw only herself in a slightly... *distorted* version. It turned hot, so hot under the mask.

Cougar only nodded to her, didn't speak or reach out her hand.

– Don't mind her, the Bowman said. – She isn't exactly the most civil person you'll meet.

The fragmented impressions Gimmick received from Cougar was of an animal running through the forest, the strongest scents and sensations.

Raven Bird was open, greeting the new kid with a genuine smile.

– You can fly, too.

The black woman grinned.

– I can ride the magnetic airwaves of the world, she cried dramatically. – Everything magnetic is mine to command.

Mechanic was like a clock, logic, reason, an even keel, at least on the surface.

They were all young, in their late teens or early twenties.

She looked amazed at them, at herself in the mirror of their eyes and mind.

– So, what do you think? The Bowman asked her. – About our humble abode and all this?

– I am… speechless, she stated slowly. – It's really happening, isn't it, just like in the comics? How many… how many of us are there in the world?

They all looked at Mechanic.

– It's impossible to tell without more specific data, he said. – Even if we knew how many with the Growth Gene that have also developed or will develop powers there is no way to ascertain the number.

– But if you're asked to speculate? Raven Bird said sweetly.

– Based on available, woefully incomplete data? Everything from several hundred thousand… to millions.

That stunned them. Gimmick saw that, sensed that.

– You haven't considered this before? She asked incredulous.

– I guess it didn't cross our mind.

Gimmick heard Cougar's raspy voice for the first time.

– Our new member has an imaginative mind, Lady Grace emphasized pleased. – She dreams big dreams.

And Gimmick felt warm and fuzzy, bathing in the pretty glow of their acknowledgment.

– It's time to give her the welcome she deserves, the Bowman kept grinning. And he had the widest grin she had ever seen.

– Come with us, fair maiden.

He bowed and reached out a hand. So did she, and allowed him to take hers. He led her into the next room, into the dining hall, to a room with a table covered with dishes, with food, and wine, the loveliest cuisine. The stench of spices overwhelmed all her senses.

– You're among your own kind, now, Claudia said, a strange dichotomy in her voice. – We know your desires, because they are our own.

They sat down. Flight Captain pulled out the chair for her (of course he did).

– Who said gluttony was a sin? Cougar joked, agitation tangible in her mind, but perhaps not in her constantly strained voice.

– We have a lot of toilet bowls, too, Mechanic said. – There will be no queue, here, in the maverick crew's shiny manor.

– That's your… that's our name? Lucinda asked in a girlish voice.

They glanced astonished at each other.

– I was thinking something more forceful…

Lady Grace hesitated, before relenting, undoubtedly sensing the acceptance and almost childish excitement in the others' minds.

– The Maverick Crew it is, she acknowledged.

The Bowman raised his glass. One second later they all did.

– To the Maverick Crew, he cried. – May they long live!

– THE MAVERICK CREW, everybody choired.

Glasses met and parted. The wine, and later the hot curry burned in Lucinda's stomach.

Gimmick, I am Gimmick.

As Gimmick I have named you, as I have defined you.

It was just thoughts, not something they could pick up. She studied Lady Grace, both her thoughts and features, but found no sign of her picking it up either.

A loosely knit group had their very first bonding, their first celebration together.

– This is the first step to something great, Lady Grace (not Claudia Malone) stated solemnly. – A modest beginning of what will grow and multiply in stature, to become what will one day carry great weight in the world at large.

– Hear, hear, Flight Captain tuned in.

– The lady has a way with words, Raven Bird snorted, taking a huge sip of the wine.

Seven sweaty people sat there, having a party with uncomfortable masks covering their head, dreaming huge thoughts about tomorrow. The mood made Gimmick giddy, or giddier. Even Lady Grace went a little over the top. The others' good mood supported and reinforced their own.

Lucinda couldn't tell afterwards how long the party had lasted. She could only note that it was still daylight, that the sun hadn't really moved that much on the sky and that Melinda was still at school.

– You did good! Claudia praised her. – You didn't actually slip a single time, didn't make one remark revealing anything about yourself. I wasn't wrong about you.

– Thank you, Claudia.

The girl blushed. They were both drunk and their mind fuzzy.

– Mechanic sat you up adequately, I presume?

– He gave me more than enough money, enough cash for the down payment on a new apartment, and for months ahead.

Thankyouclaudiaohthankyouthankyou

Fuzzy, very fuzzy.

You're welcome, littleone. Pleasure is minemine

Not that fuzzy, but noticeable, which was, Lucinda suspected a sensation in itself when Lady Grace was concerned.

They parted, there, in the middle of the street, where they had met such a short time ago. Claudia kissed her on the cheek, and Lucinda responded by kissing the other on the lips.

Lucinda was alone again. It seemed strange and lonely. She didn't see Leon anywhere. At least he was no longer standing frozen like a statue where they had left him.

It dawned on her after a while that she had chosen a detour on her way to the school. She faltered briefly. Then she shrugged and with an excited smile she went with the flow.

She spotted the ice cream parlor. Thought and action were one, and she approached the booth, focused her attention on the fat man in the apron behind the counter.

– One hell of an ice cream, please, she told him. – Three flavors, vanilla, chocolate and strawberry.

– I hear ya, the man said. – You enjoy your ice cream, I take it?

– I absolutely love it, she stated calmly, brimming with triumph and a sense of accomplishment.

He handed her the giant tasty thing, and she handed him her empty hand. *This is a hundred dollar bill.*

– You don't have anything smaller? He frowned.

– I'm sorry, sir, she wheedled. – I'm afraid not.

– That's quite okay, young lady, he said unconcerned, – I always make sure I have a lot of small change at the start of the day.

– That's wise, she told him and gave him her best smile. – Well prepared is halfway there, right?

– As I live and breathe, the man nodded.

He gave her a lot of bills and change. She put it all in her pocket and began devouring the ice cream.

A girl stared at her, at both her and the man behind the counter, probably not sure what she had seen, if she had seen anything.

Lucinda just shrugged it off and walked away, so pleased with herself. It had been so easy, done with no effort at all.

Melinda waited outside the gate for her. It had been just a few minutes. She lit up when she spotted Big Sister.

Everything is okay, now, Kid Sister. Our trouble is no more.

The girl frowned in incredulity, realizing after a few seconds of contemplation what had happened.

Yes, my sweet one, it is I, your mighty Big Sister that is communicating with you without spoken words.

In a moment or two of frantic, condensed communication she told Melinda everything that had happened. Melinda strived to make sense of it at first, but quickly got the hang of it.

That's wonderful, she thought, so wonderful.

Just you wait, wait until you see the apartment. Lady Grace showed it to me mind to mind, but I'm certain that didn't do it proper justice.

– You're going to be a fucking *super hero*. The child practically jumped up and down in excitement. – That's so cool, so fucking cool!

The kids around them stared, but right now the two sisters couldn't care less. They walked away arm in arm.

Lucinda finished the dishes, throwing away the remains of the one that Mother had broken. She dried sweat with her sleeve, staring at the not very appealing red face in the kitchen mirror, feeling very, very down and miserable.

Brenda was talking in the phone when she entered the living room.

– I'm calling again to inquire about the insurance policy my husband left us…

The laughter at the other end of the line was so loud that it made the very walls in the apartment shake.

Brenda put the phone quietly down, choking with eyes brimming with tears.

– It will be all right, mom, Lucinda assured her. – Something will come up. You'll see.

She helped mother back to the chair, helped her sit down.

Then she walked to her room and threw herself on the bed. She wanted to cry, but no tears came.

The noises from the outside sounded more distant than ever in her mind. They slowly faded away to nothing. The world didn't reach her, there on the bed.

Later she would always wonder why she didn't notice anything, why there had been no warning and no alarm what so ever when it happened.

It was Melinda's high-pitched scream that shook her, that made her jump out of bed and rush back to the living room.

Melinda stood there, in mute horror, looking out of the window, down at the pavement below. Lucinda forced herself to walk forward, to go to the window and out on the balcony, and look down at the pavement, at Brenda Patterson's broken body, at her bloody and twisted remains.

The two sisters stood there, frozen like death, until medics entered the apartment and took them away.

Lucinda kept searching trashcans for scraps of food. In her mind she never stopped, not in all the yesterdays and tomorrows that would ever be.

Chapter 7

Lucinda awoke as she had done a lot lately, soaked in sweat and dread.

Lady Grace woke her up with a light nudge. Her eyes opened wide, hurting, the pain fading quickly, but lingering, a constant backdrop in her consciousness.

Are you all right, little one?

I'm peachy, Lucinda replied sourly. Why do you ask?

There was no response, no words, not thoughts.

She crouched briefly in fetal position, before throwing off the down and rising, crawling off the large bed. The building was still fairly quiet. She had no trouble hearing the distinct sound of her feet as she stumbled across the floor to the mirror. Fear touched her, just before she looked, but when she stopped in front of the mirror she saw only her own drawn face and puffy eyes reflected back at her.

A light concentration, and she began the process of waking up those yet not awake. It was easy. They would have woken up on their own in an hour or so anyway. Access was instantaneous, unresisting, using the pathways to their mind she and Claudia had long since established. She saw them, experienced them, and got a sense of their mood and surroundings.

Her stomach rumbled already, making its demands known. There was a fairly big slice of a pie in the fridge, the remains from a hasty nightly meal. She devoured it in less than a minute. It only served to stoke her appetite. She went through the hasty motions, pulling the mask over her head and slipping the shirt over her head, only covering herself in a miniscule part of her costume, of yesterday's smelly clothes.

She made sure to scan the hallway before unlocking and opening the door. There was no one there. She sensed that some members of the gang were already gathering in the kitchen down below, Melinda among them. The Bowman had started singing, something he often did in the morning. She hurried on her bare feet down the stairs.

Raven Bird worked in the kitchen, a work in which she was uniquely suited, juggling pans and kettles with her power in ways that an outsider surely would have called amazing. It made Gimmick smile.

– Morning, she mumbled.

– That good, huh? Lisa Carlton said.

Lucinda stopped. Lisa put down the pans and kettles.

– I think I had the dream again, Gimmick whispered, feeling very haunted
– but I can't remember any of it, at least not in anything resembling a

distinct manner. I think she's doing it to me, on purpose, taunting me with meaningless clues, bragging about her might, telling me she can come and f-fetch me anytime.

– C'mon.

Raven Bird pulled out two chairs, using her hands. Gimmick sat down on one of them, Raven Bird on the other. Lisa grabbed her friend's hands.

– I think my… Hunger is growing.

– Uh, huh. Lisa nodded.

– It's hard to tell, of course, since it has never been a walk in the park, but I fed well last night, during the night and swallowed the big remains of the pie this morning, and it feels like a black hole in there. It was in Jaynagar as well.

– Uh, huh. Lisa repeated patiently.

And then the outburst finally came, like a deluge, the expression of deepest despair and anger exploding.

– Why only me? Why not one of the younger and inexperienced? Am I weak? Is that it? Am I only a toy, a puppet on her stage?

She sagged on the spot, crumbling before the other.

– My guess is that she needs a sensitive, Lisa said, comforting her friend with a light touch on her cheek, – an able receiver for her spite, and she has only two to choose from. Perhaps your power is sufficiently different from Grace's in some way we have yet to determine.

And then the big black girl shrugged deliberately.

– Or perhaps there is no sane explanation. Perhaps, for some obscure reason she just doesn't like you.

– He he.

It wasn't exactly a hearty laughter, but it made Lucinda feel better, a little better. She rose, grabbed Lisa's head and kissed her on the brow.

Thank you.

Gimmick continued into the dining area, still feeling sort of distant, disconnected, not really present. Melinda laughed at something Oil said. They were clearly flirting. Several of the others were also included in the girl's happy sphere. It looked like Sensor fit in well with her new peers.

– The Hunger is like a beast, Lavender told the other kids, – residing inside us, feeding on us with its fangs and claws, drawing blood and pain.

They nodded in solemn agreement.

Everybody looked attentive at Gimmick when she entered the room. That… pleased her. Sensor kept her added excitement contained, fairly hidden, but she lit up when she spotted Gimmick, to Gimmick she did.

Thanks for taking me here. Thank you, thank you, thank you

The others also looked at the member of the original team with admiration in eyes and mind. She sat down and became the center of their attention. They were not surrounding her physically, but in thoughts and words.

Notice, Lady Grace sent. They adore you, see you as one of them. You have always had it easy with them, gained their companionship without trying.

Gimmick wanted to protest, at least a bit, but found no voice.

It's a good thing, Lady Grace told her graciously. Use it. Add to it. Open them further to our teaching.

Gimmick hesitated a bit before turning to Lavender.

– You've had bad dreams lately, haven't you?

She took the startled girl's hand.

– So, as you know have I, she added. – What is yours about?

Star Bartlett's conflicted mind was unusually open to her. Gimmick calmed her down, soothing her fears and the anger and betrayal she felt because her teammate had read her mind.

– It's the shadows, she whispered. – They've always been my friends, but now they are laughing at me, *spiting* me, similar to what they did in Jaynagar.

Her mind was more difficult to read than most others. Whatever the source of her power, it made her thoughts more fleeting, harder to grasp... like shadows.

– Is there any... intelligence behind it, you think?

Star looked stunned at her.

– I don't know... I have never really considered that before. They are separate from me in a way, I know that, not something I create, but forces I control, like loyal dogs or something. But now I felt something, something truly... malevolent.

She shed a few tears. Gimmick comforted her, while searching for proof of manipulation in the other's mind, but found nothing.

– The fight is intensifying, she stated, including everybody present, – turning more into the war we feared would always come. We must be prepared.

They nodded solemnly, silently supporting her words, lining up behind her. She knew them so well, recalling every shred of info she had ever learned about them, not even needing her power to remind her.

Her attention turned to Oil. She studied him without studying him for a while. He stank of oil, as he always did. It was visible. He always appeared unwashed, unclean, like a car mechanic after a particularly messy job. She didn't grab his hands, even though he was wearing gloves, and fought against the sense of revulsion.

– What about you? She asked gently.

– Me? He asked incredulous.

114

– Yes, are you okay?

He tried to meet her eyes, but it was no contest. It pleased her when he looked down, submitting to her stronger willpower.

– The stench is getting worse, he blurted out. – It doesn't matter what I do, what kind of good smell I put on, how many times I shower. I'm a walking freak show, even more than...

– ... the rest of us? Gimmick completed the sentence.

He stared at her. His eyes, too, were filled with tears. She patted his knee. The others, too, comforted him, as much as they were able. Jenna Morgan, Dancer did so demonstratively, kissing him on the cheek, rubbing herself at him.

Jenna was tall and big, too, but clearly leaner than most of the others, reminding them a little bit of a cat, and of Cougar.

Gimmick felt both relieved and irritated when the others started to arrive, the strange dichotomy that had plagued her lately. The Bowman bent down and kissed her, and she allowed it. The laughter around the table made her even queasier.

Lady Grace and Flight Captain joined them, holding hands, their flushed faces leaving no doubt about their recent activities. In spite of the cheerful snicker that created in youthful minds, the fairly light mood and exuberance still settled somewhat.

... theQueen andcrony arrives, Gimmick caught a stray thought around the table, unable to discern its source.

– Good morning, Lady Grace greeted them all brightly.

– ... morning, everybody replied.

As if on cue the bell rang, and Raven Bird called from the kitchen:

– BREAKFAST IS READY!

People rushed there to fetch their food, almost colliding with Brick, as he carried big kettles to the table. Their meals were usually both cold and hot, to cater their hunger properly.

The meal, the consummation began. Conversation faded, even though there were a few words exchanged here and there, now and then. Everybody was caught up in it, inevitably. Even If Lady Grace and some of the others attempted to stay dignified somewhat, they didn't quite succeed.

They had learned to keep themselves at bay in public, but here nothing held them back. There was no need. They were among friends, among likeminded people.

Lady Grace waited until the feeding frenzy had calmed a bit in them both before using the usual nudge to catch Gimmick's attention.

I noticed that you probed Dancer...

Both kept feeding, having practiced a long time to hide their non-vocal conversations.

Yes, I used the opportunity to deep-read her mind.

And did you… find anything?

There was very little there, very little cause for worry. The girl is angry, sure, but no more than the rest of us.

Lady Grace waited a bit, before nodding.

You did good, little one, a great initiative on your part. I am proud of you.

Lucinda couldn't keep herself from reddening, the involuntary happiness she conveyed to the older woman a waterfall of emotion.

She fed and forgot everything else, all other concerns.

The pain began, as it always did well before the meal was done. She sensed it rise in everybody present, even in Energetic, as a kind of sympathetic event, returning in full to her. Experience kept her from panicking, from letting go, but some of the younger, like Sensor and Oil fled towards the toilets like migrating birds.

Gimmick finished everything on her plate, like Lady Grace and a few others, before giving in to the pressure, before rushing off, flying south.

The stench struck her like a hammer. She felt everybody's smell, through their nostrils, like a blow. Weak legs almost gave up under her, and she managed to remain standing only with an effort of will. The need to turn around was almost overpowering, but the pain in her gut and ass quickly regained priority. She stumbled towards the nearest stall, and pulled down her pants and panties as she did, her butt hitting the bowl the second before her ass spat the first roll of shit.

Lucinda Patterson sat there, cursing silently under her breath, half sick, half delirious, everything fading away, until she became the pain, transformed into the shit pouring from her lower hole.

It rose from her, and she rose with it, filling the restroom, experiencing it all from countless different viewpoints simultaneously, choking in misery and degradation.

The pain and discomfort subsided fairly quickly afterwards, as it usually did. She, Sensor and Raven Bird returned to her apartment on the upper floor. They undressed quickly, tearing off clothes stinking of shit. Lucinda threw hers into the washing machine, like the others would do, upon returning to their own room.

– That feels *so* good every time, Lisa said.

– Goddess, Melinda said, – wearing the mask is a bother. I feel like I couldn't breathe properly, even though it isn't really that tight, even during the brief use today.

116

– You'll get used to it, Lucinda said. – It isn't the worst thing facing you out there.

– How do we keep the place clean? Melinda wondered. – My guess is that we don't have servants on hand?

She was just as astute as she always was. Big Sister nodded pleased to herself.

– Mechanic has created the perfect automated robots for the task, Lucinda enlightened her. – His personal inventions are, as you know far more advanced than any other technology out there.

– We just worry what he may make next, Lisa said lightly.

The three of them went into the shower together, completely nude, feeling light on their feet.

– I can't believe I'm finally here, Melinda cried excited.

– You've waited long enough, girlie, Lisa said cheerfully, – at least from your point of view.

Melinda scowled happily at her. Laughter stuck in Lucinda's throat.

They soaped each other in, as the water wet their sore skin, soaped in their hair and skin and ass and cunt, rinsed and soaped in and rinsed again. The stench finally gave way to a somewhat more neutral scent. They dried each other with large towels, slowly, languishingly, or at least the appearance of it.

After a while, having taken their time, they started dressing in new clothes, a perfect match of their old and temporarily unavailable. Sensor didn't have her own, personal wardrobe yet, a copy of her newly made suit on hand, but easily found what she needed by picking and choosing from the others' stockpile.

– I don't mind, she assured the other two when they sent her compassionate looks. – I'm new and I'm here, and can wait for the extra luxury you old gals enjoy…

They returned to the ground floor and headed for the conference room. It was the same there. Only the established members had their own chairs. The others took place behind them. It was happening, what they had expected and dreaded for months. A nervous excitement dominated the assembly.

Flight Captain and Lady Grace entered the room. Lady Grace walked right to the computer and the monitor, and turned it on. They studied her, knowing fully well what was on the disk she held in her hand, but still curious, inevitably.

When the system was up and running she inserted it. Images and sound filled the room. Cold sweat broke on their skin and terror erupted in their mind.

Pay attention! She emphasized to them all.

It was an unnecessary admonishment. Their eyes were glued to the screen.

They recognized the woman the moment she showed herself on the screen, the landscape and architecture as well. It was all very distinctive, very chilling, and very visible on the youngsters' faces.

– Greetings, the woman on the screen said. – My name is Alysse Montgomery. I am the Governor's First Secretary in our proud state, and I will guide you through this Ultra HD presentation.

She was tall and big, but not tall-tall or big-big. Her dark red jacket and skirt forming a suit stuck to her, framed it, her female form. Her brown hair was set up in a top. She wore a dark brown tie, non-descriptive, relating well to the red suit, her entire appearance clearly designed to convey authority.

– Look at her, Martial Athlete mused. – How measured and deadly she moves. That's one bad mother.

– In more ways than one, Lisa choked.

– We are the associate self-governed free state of Jagadir, Alysse Montgomery said, in the voice-over. – Associated with the United States of America, enjoying all its privileges and duties.

More pictures from clean city streets and waterfalls and wilderness filled the screen.

– Jagadir City, the woman said, unable to contain her pride, – surely one of the modern seventh wonders of the world?

She stood on a hill with the city behind her. The city faded out and other places faded in, the natural beauty of the land, the mountains, the forests and the shore, the coastland, with the beaches and the casinos, the tourist destinations.

– We are a compassionate society based on the rule of law, Alysse continued. – Our citizens take their duties seriously. The crime-rate is among the lowest in the entire world. This long-time experience has aided us, also recently, upon dealing with a more recent threat to both our great society and the world at large...

Those watching froze, very aware of what was coming.

Four tall and big people, two males and two females worked in a field. They fell on their knees and bowed their heads, as Alysse approached them.

– Good morning, Lester, she greeted the closest male.

– Good morning, My Lady, he replied humbly and devoted, smiling brightly.

– How are you today, Lester?

– I feel great today, My Lady, Lester replied.

– Do you like it here; Lester? She asked him lightly.

– I love it here, My Lady.

– Tell us about yourself, Lester, the Lady bid him.

– I was a *bad* man before coming here, My Lady, but you straightened me out. Thank you, thank you.

She turned towards the camera.

– All the people carrying the «Growth Gene» are prone to rages and criminal behavior, according to our esteemed scientists, but here they get the proper treatment, here they can live full, productive lives.

The field and the kneeling big people faded out, and a laboratory and a man in white coat faded in.

Down to the left in the picture a text said: **Robert Milner Dr. Med.**

– They are little more than children, really, the man in the white coat said, shaking his head. – They are not very bright, very much like children in an adult's body, and need a firm hand in order to behave properly, to learn the difference between right and wrong. We teach them that, taking them under our wings, so to speak.

– And you're quite convinced this method is the best for them, Doctor?

– Our results speak for themselves, Milner bristled. – Both in the United States and the world at large these... people figure prominently on all crime statistics, but here, in our benevolent system they're not.

Nausea grabbed all those watching, as the final image and patriotic music faded away.

– They wear the collars. Raven Bird turned enraged towards Mechanic. – The rumors are true, *true*.

A lot of those present directed their anger at him, one way or another, also those not looking directly at him.

He didn't look good, flustered and embarrassed and angry and everything between.

– How do you figure they got their hands on them? Lady Grace asked him unusually softly.

– I don't know, he said exasperated, – not more than any of you, okay? If I should guess they would only need to get their hands on one, and reverse-engineer it. I don't know if any of you noticed, but the collars we saw looked smaller than... ours, a bit more developed, possibly more effective.

Everybody exchanged glances. They hadn't noticed. He was as astute as ever.

– No matter, Flight Captain said, curling his right hand into a fist, – even though this is just yet another disturbing detail in the overall and growing threat we face, from a number of sources, it shows it's finally time to make Jagadir a priority. We need to be proactive, to grab the bull by the balls, so to speak.

– But we were also warned, by our own government that there would be consequences if we took on Jagadir's government directly and breached its sovereign borders, the Bowman said. – What about that?

– I have been… assured by my sources in our government that those restrictions no longer apply, Lady Grace said curtly. – Make no mistake, we are on our own and they will disown us if we should… fail, but we have their blessing if we choose to deal decisively with the Jagadir problem.

She nodded to Mechanic. He nodded, too, as he put a box on the table. Everybody looked curious at it. When he opened it and displayed its content everyone's eyes grew big and they looked startled at each other.

The box contained rings, a lot of new, shiny rings.

– From this moment on, Lady Grace declared, – everyone present is granted full membership in the Maverick Crew, with its privileges and duties. From this moment on we'll start fighting back in earnest, against all the forces threatening us. Whatever happened to Oracle and Cougar must never be allowed to happen again. We'll make sure that it won't.

Lavender and Sensor and the others stared in awe at the rings before quickly grabbing them, as if they feared they would go away, would dissolve before their eyes.

Sensor put it on her finger. It glowed and buzzed momentarily, before settling down.

– You have now full access to the portals, Gimmick told them. – Visualize where you want to go and the portals will take you there, anywhere there is any. It may feel a little awkward at first, but will get easier every time you do it. Lady Grace and I will aid you with our minds until you get a handle on it.

This is suchathrill

Sensor's thoughts bubbled over with excitement. All the youths looked beyond grateful at the senior Maverick Crew members.

– It's time, for us all, Lady Grace stated, very deliberate, – to put childish things behind us. We have, in the past, for lack of a better wording… held back, held back in fear of harming our opponents, and paid the price for our caution. From now on we will use our gifts to their fullest. We have trained on letting go of everything holding us back. Now, the time has come to put it to good use. We're soldiers in a vast war, and it's about time we start acting the part.

Everyone understood. They would have, also without the accompanying images and sensations. A series of chills passed through them.

Lavender bowed her head.

– I don't know if I can kill…

Lady Grace stepped close to her and slapped her on the cheek, hard enough for it to be felt through the mask.

Lavender stared at her, startled at first, touching her burning skin. Then Gimmick sensed how a dark, smoldering anger began asserting itself in her.

Lady Grace chuckled.

– Behold the warrior awakening…

She turned towards them all, or so they imagined.

– I won't tolerate any of you being a slacker. Don't expect the rest of us to come to your rescue if you fall behind. We will try, of course, but we may not be able. Not all of you have active, aggressive powers, but you still have your hands and feet and cunning and are proficient in handling various weapons. I expect you to be at your *best!*

If anyone had been in doubt about her military background, that faded now, completely.

They rose and stood straight before her, Flight Captain as well. Her eyes softened when she glanced at him, but only briefly.

– Flight Captain will act as my second in command, she declared, – Gimmick, The Bowman and… Lavender will be my lieutenants.

Lavender looked startled at first, but then as Lady Grace soothed her fears and grew her confidence with her mind, the young woman looked at the older with dedication and devotion.

They moved out, towards the portal.

Are you okay? Gimmick asked Sensor.

Yes, Sensor brightened. Yes, I am. Don't worry about me. I can take it and I can dish it out. You'll see. You'll be *proud* of me.

Everybody checked their equipment and weapons. Gimmick checked her gear, the small and bigger items, the climbing hook with the rope attached to a crossbow, her other crossbow shooting arrows… and her gun.

– Everything smells oiled and smooth and ready, Oil told her.

– The metals slip well between each other… lieutenant, Raven Bird reported. – I can sense no faults in them.

There was only a slight acrimony in her voice and her thoughts. Gimmick corrected that automatically, without thinking twice about it, just like Lady Grace would have done, and Raven Bird's hardened facial expression visibly softened.

Still prepared, all her anger directed towards what was ahead, towards present and future enemies.

– We're ready for this, Lady Grace stated proudly. – We're finally ready!

Mechanic appeared from his lab, carrying his miniaturized electronic gadgets.

– I have been tinkering a lot lately, he stated, clearly proud, too, no matter how muted his pride revealed itself. – The portable satellite feed, the remote chopper control and stuff, all of it vastly improved and more user friendly. Any of you, even the Bowman could master it in a pinch. The backup plans are in motion. We're set to go.

The Bowman scowled at him. The others nodded in acknowledgement, silently saluting his skill.

They gathered in front of the portal. All of them were able to see it, now. The awe in their mind was very noticeable to Gimmick.

– We'll do a little combined reconnaissance and recruiting on our way, Flight Captain said. – You'll be able to prepare further, fight several battles in our unending war.

Lady Grace gave him a smile of approval under the mask.

They stepped through the portal, focusing on the image Lady Grace and Gimmick sent to their mind. There was a tiny, prolonged moment until they appeared on the other side, surrounded by the noise of Mastich Harbor in the north-western part of Tobruk.

Sunset Alley was bathed in even brighter than usual sunlight today, or so it seemed. Some of them had to blink a few times in order to adapt.

No one saw us arrive, Gimmick reported to Lady Grace.

Very good, little one, Lady Grace acknowledged.

She sent a note to Flight Captain. Gimmick sensed that, even though she couldn't «hear» the exact words.

– Ok, people, Flight Captain cried, – move on, like we practiced.

They spread out in a pre-arranged pattern, as they entered the large Coleman Square. It took one second, three, until people began noticing them, began staring, curious and apprehensive.

– Behold, my soldiers, Lady Grace noted pleased. – Bear witness to how our arrangement with the authorities benefits us. Without it we couldn't have moved around in bright daylight without the risk of being bothered by either civilians or the local law enforcement.

They all noticed how she spoke the word «bothered», as if it was a nuisance in itself.

There were quite a few police officers present, like it always was in this troubled spot of town, but except for the occasional burst of resentment Gimmick didn't sense any threat from any of them.

The sound of gunshots echoed between the brick walls. There was no open fighting, but people were withdrawing from the building right ahead, and the officers were surrounding it.

– She's here, Lady Grace said, and the others were astonished to discover a grin on her lips. – We don't have to draw her out.

They crossed the street. Lavender and Raven Bird surrounded them in a protective bubble. They walked straight through the door, broke it open like they would paper. Two men inside fired at them, just before they saw what they were up against and threw away the guns and dropped to their knees. There were several more shots fired elsewhere in the building, several cries of pain and loud sounds of bones breaking.

An enhanced woman appeared in the doorway, firing airwaves from her hands. It pushed half of the Crew back towards the door. Raven Bird pushed a number of metal chairs at her and she vanished back into the room. Brick pushed through the door, taking a lot of the surrounding wall with him. An enhanced man struck him in the head, struck him hard with an iron bar. The iron bar broke in two pieces, but Brick went down. Gimmick jumped the man and struck him with her right hand. He shook his head, a little dizzy, but still standing. She struck him again. He fell, but still reached for the gun on the floor. She stamped on his arm. There was a loud crack when something broke there. He screamed short and sharp.

The others entered the room, a large storage hall. There were other unconscious people, but no more enhanced. A tall and big woman rose cautiously from behind her cover. They recognized Crimson Mask. She looked weary at the approaching group, also after she had made them.

– I could have taken them without help, she said.

– Of course you could, Dancer said caustically.

– You broke my arm, the man on the floor cried at Gimmick.

Sensor looked at him with wicked eyes and he fell apart instantly.

– You broke my arm, he whimpered, not really speaking to anybody but himself.

Mechanic put a collar around his neck, and his eyes turned hazy and distant, as if his brain activity was just switched off. He stopped moving and just lay there, totally helpless. Mechanic pulled his arms behind his back, ignoring the muddled cry of pain and slapped chains on him.

– I'll be on my way, Crimson Mask shrugged. – You take the credit, if you like. I don't care.

She rose into the air, her powerful telekinetic powers easily carrying her.

Lady Grace stopped her with a slight suggestion, making her land again, easily disrupting the concentration she needed to stay afloat.

The redhead stared sullenly and stunned at the taller and bigger woman.

– The time you could remain independent is long gone, Lady Grace said. – There is no middle ground anymore, Adeline. You shouldn't further try my patience.

Adeline Goddard shuddered and glanced at the chained, inarticulate man on the floor.

— That was uncalled for, she said, not hiding her anger.

— No, it was me, telling you in no uncertain terms that I have no patience left, Lady Grace snarled. — You will come with us. You won't slip away in an unguarded moment, because if you do, we will come for you. Do you understand, soldier?

— I do, Crimson Mask replied, clearing her throat, straightening before the regal woman. — I understand.

Gimmick knelt down by the other enhanced woman.

— You are new, she said, — calling yourself Wind, right, Ashley?

— You're a mind witch, right? Wind grinned, wincing when Gimmick grabbed her sore jaw, looking at the other with spite in her eyes. — There aren't too many of you guys in real life, is there?

What do you know about Black Dragon? *Tell me!*

Ashley Hastings shook under the onslaught. Gimmick knew she wasn't hiding anything when denial echoed through her mind.

Nothingnothingnothing… neverheardofher SCARE you, does she?

Gimmick found a collar and chains from her bag. Wind's cocky demeanor vanished like smoke.

— No, please, she begged, — not the collar, please, no. I visited a friend in prison and she was totally gone, as if she had become feebleminded or something. And everybody knows abuse is rampant there. She attempted to tell me something, I could practically see it in her eyes, but she couldn't articulate herself, no matter how much she tried. It was *horrible!* Please don't send me there. *Please!*

— But you've got nothing to offer us, Ashley, the Bowman said.

— I can join you, can't I? The girl implored them. — Pay my debts to society that way? That isn't unprecedented… right? As you said, I'm new at this. I'm certain that I can… develop my powers further under your guidance, making it one to be feared. I'll be a good soldier, *honest!*

Her mind confirmed her words, confirmed everything she was desperately conveying.

Gimmick hesitated a bit, looking without looking at Lady Grace.

It's your call, little one.

Gimmick put the collar away.

She sensed no triumph or cunning in Ashley's mind, only sick relief and gratitude, one easy to play on and reinforce, as she took Wind's hand and pulled her on her feet.

Very clever, little one, Lady Grace granted her. She will be loyal and devoted to you, until death.

124

Gimmick gave Wind her spare mask. She put it on with a beyond grateful smile on her face, her relief a sickening presence in Lucinda's mind.

Crimson Mask stepped forward, very attentive, standing straight before Lady Grace, because that was what Lady Grace desired.

– So, where are your associates, the Lustful Carnage Gang this morning?

There was a bit of snickering following that one.

– I guess they're nursing a hangover or ten, Crimson Mask shrugged. – It's a slow morning.

– Lead on, then, to their lair.

– Are you serious? Crimson Mask cried incredulous, then catching herself nodding. – I guess you are. You're always serious…

The extended group left the building. The police officers entered it to do the mop up. Wind glanced nervously at them. Gimmick calmed her down, soothed her, and reconfigured her.

– We don't really need directions, Sensor said brightly, squeezing shut her nostrils, – I can already smell the stench of days-old alcohol and vomit…

And sweat and body juices and tobacco and illegal substances and and and…

The rest turned into a jumble in her thoughts.

– They started almost two full days ago, Wind giggled. – We heard them from blocks away, and figured they would keep it going at least over the weekend, leaving more than enough time for us to…

She glanced anxiously at her new teammates.

– … do our thing.

The Lustful Carnage Gang had more or less laid claim to an old factory at the edge of the Old Brewery district. They had never really set out to clean the district up, only to fight against the many low-lives there.

– After you guys put everyone behind bars and in collars we figured all the competition was gone, and we could move in… Who do you think freed them all?

– We don't know, Lady Grace shrugged, deliberately.

– Was it… Black Dragon?

– We don't know.

Ice burned through them all.

– There have been rumors and stuff lately. We didn't have any name to connect to the horrors we heard about, but judging by the reaction from you guys every time her name comes up, I'd say it's connected, all right.

– Who's she? Crimson Mask asked. – Do you know that much?

– She's Cougar, Flight Captain revealed, – real name Eleanor Sharpe, Cougar changed, altered, transformed beyond recognition.

His voice was unusually and uncharacteristically laced with bitterness.

Dancer, Cougar's sister, cringed in shame and resentment somewhere to Gimmick's left.

– They call themselves the Cadre, Wind said quietly. – They were recruiting, I heard, through others not directly connected to them, recruiting «the new masters of the world». I made it fairly clear that my ambitions were slightly more modest, and it was evidently sufficient for them to leave me alone, at least for the time being.

– The Cadre… Mechanic said slowly.

Finally there was a name, something somewhat tangible to connect their woes to.

The rusty gate squeaked when Raven Bird pushed it open with her power. They listened as they spread out, but there was nothing, no suspicious sounds.

– Secure the perimeter, Lady Grace commanded. – No one gets in or out.

They did, acting on the experience gained during combat and countless training sessions. She gave some instructions with her telepathic power, whispers in the ether that Gimmick had no trouble listening in to, but all in all they weren't necessary.

– Perhaps I should go first? Crimson Mask wondered. – If they aren't half dead from binge drinking there might be trouble.

– No! Lady Grace shook her head. – You come with us. You do as I say, when I say it, understand!

– Yes, ma'am, the redhead replied.

Lady Grace, Crimson Mask, Wind, Gimmick and Flight Captain made their way into the derelict building. Birds rose towards the hole in the ceiling. The sound of flapping wings echoed between the worn brick walls, cutting into Gimmick like shards.

They walked up the stairs to the upper floor. Crimson Mask could have lifted them all through the air, but she didn't offer, not even in her mind, following Lady Grace's orders to the latter.

The Bowman, Raven Bird, Lavender, Brick and their support group took up position on all four sides of the building. If they had been headed into combat Gimmick and Flight Captain would have joined in and led instead of Brick and Raven Bird.

This is a matter of diplomacy, Lady Grace sent.

Crimson Mask almost let out a giggle.

Wind didn't. It was like Lady Grace had noted. The girl would be loyal and devoted until death. It was evident in her eyes, her mind and in her body language, in every move she made.

126

The door topside had been left wide open. Vomit covered half of the doorstep and a lot of the floor on both sides of it. Lady Grace stepped over it without a second glance. The others had to focus in order to successfully repeat the feat.

The stench hit them like a sledgehammer. One toilet, clearly out of order had been cleaved in two. The other, of the special-sized type was in working order, but quite a bit of shit was still left in the bowl. Bottles, broken and not, covered substantial parts of the floor.

After a long trail of garbage, vomit, the occasional heap of shit and broken glass they finally arrived in the large bedroom with the giant bed, where eight nude big people of both sexes were lying around, stretched out in every possible position.

One man had his ass and legs on the bed and much of his upper body outside it. Several of the others were also caught in similar positions.

– Amazing, isn't it? Crimson Mask said to a grinning Gimmick.

Lady Grace walked to the man «hanging» outside the bed and kicked him in the chest. He tumbled from the bed and hit the floor like a rag.

– W-what?

– You are dead, she told him.

He rose to his feet. He attempted to jump, but couldn't quite do it.

– What's it to you? He blinked at her. – You want to join the party?

She woke up all of them with a mental command. They blinked sleepily at the light. Gimmick looked at the half erect cocks of the men, attempting in vain to focus on Lady Grace.

The females rose, too, with a lazy expression in their eyes and body language. Two of them were visibly pregnant. A third had recently given birth. All of them were covered in semen. Gimmick felt the beginning of an itch below, a heaviness in the breasts.

– No, I want you to join our party, Lady Grace said firmly.

He looked stunned at her, until cracking up with laughter.

– You ARE kidding… right?

– We are going to invade Jagadir, she stated calmly, detached. – It will happen a few hours from now, whether you join in or not, but since you guys for a long time, now have impatiently stated your desire to do just that, we thought we should give you a change to join in on the action. Are you *ready*, soldier?

– Now? He said dumbfounded. – Today?

– We will set out as soon as human possible, she confirmed. – We have to. They may know we are coming. At least they may suspect if they hear that we are recruiting, and our arrival here was very public.

He winced, inadvertently straightening before her, before realizing the utter silliness of that position, and letting out another loud burst of laughter.

– I'll be damned, he said, shaking his head, – are you serious?

Then shaking his head again.

– Of course you are...

Gimmick almost giggled again.

Attend me, little one.

Gimmick did, rushing to Lady Grace's side.

Look at this one, more beast than man. His kind may be useful, but need to be held in tight reins, and look how easy it is.

– Look at you, Ashton Kramer said to her with an appreciative glance, – you're a cutie.

Gimmick blushed.

– You guys should get going, Lady Grace said icily. – You clearly have a job to do to get sober, in order to not get us all killed or captured.

It was just the right amount of contempt in her voice to take all play out of him. He stumbled towards the shower with bowed head. Gimmick and Wind and Crimson Mask looked at their leader, their commanding officer with admiration and respect in their eyes.

The other seven also made their way to the showers.

– We will be ready, one of the women, one of those pregnant said. – It's just those of us that can take a lot of drinking without being affected by it much that have been drinking bottoms up, anyway. I can't because of the baby.

Gimmick felt guilty in a very irrational way.

They heard the sound of the water flowing, of more laughter. Lady Grace walked into the «living room» and Gimmick and the others followed her there. The couch and chairs were covered with dust. No one sat down. Flight Captain walked to the window, looking down on the street. Gimmick saw through his eyes. There was nothing overly suspicious down there, or anywhere else he cast his eyes, no sinister movement in any of the windows across the street. Gimmick checked with the others as well, sensing Lady Grace's approval. There was nothing.

A female laughed in the showers, drawing Gimmick's attention there, and Gimmick instantly regretted that it had. Ashton showed interest, strong interest in Lauren Harris. Gimmick broke contact, but it was too late. She suddenly had trouble breathing.

Wind approached her, a welcomed distraction.

– Thank you, the girl said.

Thank you, thank you, thank you, echoed endlessly in her undisciplined mind.

128

– I will always be grateful, she stated firmly, solemnly. – You didn't have to be kind to me, but you were, anyway.

Gimmick wanted to explain it to her, to crush her naive schoolgirl view of the world, but held back.

Wind took her silence for modesty, and was even more grateful and beholden because of that.

– You will earn your keep, Gimmick told the girl.

– Yes, I will, Wind said. – I will prove to you that you did the right thing, that you made the right choice.

– Ashton, you ASSHOLE! Lauren cried. – You… AH!

Scones were thrown in a circle on the floor.

A scone of scones, Wind thought, suddenly very clear and distinct in Gimmick's mind.

Lauren's increasingly horny moans echoed through the factory. They heard them all the way out. The Bowman touched his cock. Gimmick blinked. He began rubbing it as if she was there, with him. She bit her lip. Lauren began banging on the wall, in a steady, ongoing rhythm following her moans on her path to fulfillment.

The other six left the showers and began drying themselves. It was easy to get sweaty again on this hot day.

– Who wants pizza? The other pregnant woman cried. – We all need a lot of proteins to burn off the next day or so.

Flight Captain had a hard-on. He glanced at the women's swaying breasts and inviting smiles. He was soaked in sweat from one moment to the next.

– Pizza sounds good, Gimmick heard herself say, as if from far away.

They needed to forage extra food anyway. Their generous rations, rich on energy and stuff wouldn't be even close to sufficient to cover their appetites.

– I need even more than you lot, the woman said. – If you gals thought that the growth gene plays havoc on your system, just you wait until you get pregnant.

Lauren shouted in pleasure the moment it exploded in her, the moment Ashton grunted loud enough to make the walls shake.

Gimmick sensed, beyond sensing how Lady Grace also reacted, how she mentally bit her lip, how the pace of her breathing speeded up, and how she pictured Flight Captain in her mind, how she exposed herself, and revealed she was human after all.

The echoes of Lauren Harris' moans were still roaming the building as the initial stink of hot pizza hit vibrating nostrils, as the Bowman's eyes burned Gimmick's already sweaty skin, and the first stirrings of the approaching sunset began manifesting themselves in increasingly restless souls.

129

Chapter 8
FOUR YEARS AGO TODAY

Lucinda noticed it long before she arrived at Coleman Square, the unrest, the hushed whispers and quick glances people sent each other. It quickly grew more agitated from there.

There were clearly more people on the Square than what was normal on a given midweek afternoon, especially those of the big and tall variant, participating in a public meeting of some kind.

A protest.

Perhaps it hadn't started out as one, since nothing had been announced in advance, but as Lucinda approached the car-free area at the center, she sensed emotions running high, some of the most powerful she had encountered since her telepathic powers had manifested.

Her attention was drawn to the young woman on the low stage.

She had dark hair and a dark complexion, clearly of mixed Mexican origin. Her raised fist flared in shadow. She wasn't very tall or very big. Compared to most of those present she almost looked skinny. She could be confused with one of the mundane people glaring at her, almost.

– We haven't done anything wrong. She spoke quietly in a way, but was still easily heard. – But we're still treated like pariahs, like lepers and criminals. Some claim we are sick. Others say that we have «a criminal predisposition». Very few will publicly acknowledge the obvious fact: that we quite simply are human beings longing to be treated as such. Since the Great Darkness we have been ignored, condemned and brushed off. If some of us break the law to survive one more day, I'd say they are entitled. We aren't the criminals here. The decision-makers sitting on their fat asses are.

Thunderous applause and feet thundering against the pavement followed.

– There isn't one among us that haven't been touched by tragedy caused by criminal neglect after the Great Darkness. We have all seen a relative or close friend turn to desperate measures in their despair. In their darkest hour they have fallen either for their own hand or for police bullets, or they are unjustly incarcerated under inhuman conditions. We're all, one way or another treated worse than *animals*. They make us feel ashamed of ourselves, but can't stifle the justified pride we feel…

Lucinda felt like the girl was speaking directly to her, and she surmised that she shared that with everybody present.

– Fucking overgrown gypsy, a man mumbled.

Almost everybody.

There was a bunch of average-looking people standing a bit to the side, scowling at the girl and those cheering her on. They didn't speak up or anything, but aside from that made no secret of their views.

Lucinda felt a catching in her throat, of anger, resentment and the stirrings of unpleasant memories.

She looked at her watch and hesitated, before pulling backwards, making her way further down the harbor, casting longing glances back at the assembly.

There was a tavern by the sea called The Tavern by the Sea. Loud music already flowed from speakers in there and through open windows. The dark girl's words drowned in it. A burst of irritation rose within Lucinda, as she opened the door and walked inside.

The man behind the desk would have been seen as tall and big more than five years ago, but had fallen quite a bit on the rank, now.

Lucinda went straight for the kitchen to change.

– I won't need you today, anyway, Chuck Storm said.

– You said you did. She blinked. – I have planned for it and said no to another job.

– Things have changed, he shrugged. – The offer to perform at my other establishment in Old Brewery still stands, though.

«His other establishment» in the Old Brewery District was a notorious lap-dance bar with a high percentage of tall and big females among the performers.

– No thanks, she said.

– Suit yourself. He shrugged. – I'll have to offer the spot to someone else then.

She struggled against saying anything more, even though she wanted to. He had made her come here, to frustrate her. She saw it in his mind, saw his lust, how much he desired her, wanted to possess her, to make her join his... stable of girls.

– Perhaps if you had paid anything approaching decent wages, she said calmly.

That would do it, she thought glumly. He wouldn't call on her again.

– They are whores, he said. – They don't deserve it. No whore does.

She saw an image of herself, stretched out on a bench and tied up in his mind. He towered above her there with only an apron covering his cock. She giggled a bit. He stared hard at her. One brief moment she hoped he would actually try something, but he didn't. She turned and left the place without a word, with his stare burning her back.

It felt good to breathe outside, to be able to, to not be choked in the presence of someone like him.

She walked back, towards the Square and the bus station, catching herself in making haste.

The protest had ended and the Square was mostly quiet and abandoned. She spotted a few of those that had participated. They had gathered in groups and engaged in loud and intense discussions.

The girl was nowhere to be found. She saw her in people's thoughts, but none of those present had any close relationship with her or had any idea of where she could be found.

Lucinda hurried on. The cruel voice and image of the pub-owner and pimp echoed in her head.

– They are whores, he said. – They don't deserve it. No whore does.

The contempt in his voice rattled her, made her shiver in the warm summer afternoon, and confusing and conflicting emotions ravaged her.

There was a lot of recently started construction work around the bus terminal. Many of the old houses had been demolished and new constructs of steel and concrete and glass and plastic rose towards the heavens. Lucinda glanced at her watch. She was early, also for the first, upcoming bus.

The place was cramped inside, as usual, making it hard for her to breathe, in both meanings of the word. She hurried back outside. The heavily polluted city air suddenly felt very good.

She sat down on the long bench reaching the entire length of the building. There were only three others on it and they were far away and left her in relative peace, even though their incessant obsessive troubled thoughts continued to trouble her.

The city, represented by Hammond & Shuster Construction was constructing the tallest building a little to the right, across the street. It was hardly more than the construction skeleton yet, but the mere sight of it still made her dizzy. When she looked up it was as if there was no end in sight to it at all, and that it split the sky. It wasn't a skyscraper, but still gave her that almost overwhelming feeling.

A girl crossed the street, seemingly appearing from nowhere behind a bus. She sat down further down the bench, right across the emerging giant structure. Lucinda recognized her as the angry speaker. She was still angry. It seethed within her and made Lucinda's headache take a turn for the worse.

She lit a cigarette. Lucinda felt the smoke being pulled down her throat and into her lungs. The girl didn't cough. Lucinda did and her eyes were flooded with tears.

Damn you, she thought. Damn…

It was as if she was sucked through a giant hole in the air, in reality itself.

She didn't move, not a finger, but suddenly, from one moment to the next everything had changed.

The sun shone from a different position in the sky, casting different shadows. There were more people in the street. The building... had been completed. The entire block had been transformed. It was... was clearly the same place, but still totally different. There was only one constant: the girl. She sat on the same spot. There was a loud breaking sound. Suddenly Lucinda was inside the girl, was the girl, was Jolene Masters. Jolene was strangely calm. In fact she displayed no form of distress or strong emotion at all.

One of the supporting columns for the completed building broke, broke like a dry twig. The sound was even pretty much the same, slightly off, more in the line of metal. The others broke, too, one by one, until nothing on that side supported the structure anymore. The building toppled over. It happened so fast, so incessantly slow. The building fell, right at where Jolene sat. It fell on her and countless others, crushing them and the parking house attached to the bus station, creating havoc of seemingly infinite magnitude, like an earthquake or similar. Smoke rose and filled the street, the entire block, as a thousand windows broke and rained death on the people below, shards cutting flesh and bone and veins and skulls wide open.

Lucinda blinked. Everything had returned to the fairly peaceful afternoon scene she faintly remembered from long ago. Breathing was more difficult than ever. It felt like an eternity before she felt like she could breathe again.

Jolene rose from her position further down the street. Lucinda watched as she approached and felt a tinge of fear, of overwhelming apprehension.

– Hi, Lucinda, she greeted the other, as if they were old friends.

Lucinda stared hard at her, or tried to, through a web of confusion.

– We are old friends, aren't we? You were filled with the totality of my experience and I with yours. We experienced a sympathetic event, not so strange that, you being a telepath and all, and well versed in your power, isn't that right, Gimmick?

– Why here, why, now? Lucinda wondered and worried, not finding it worth it even attempting a denial.

The totality of the girl's being and even to a degree her memories swirling within her mind.

Jolene Masters grinned.

– Because this is the moment I always seem to choose to approach you. It seems appropriate. I could have approached you sooner, of course, right after my speech today, or long before that, months ago, not long after my powers first manifested. I, being a precognitive, among other things knew our paths would cross, like rain will hit the ground.

Lucinda looked up, at the still standing building, at the Tower that it would be known as in colloquial speech.

– Neat, isn't it? Jolene said in a deliberately upbeat manner. – We know where we won't be at a certain date four years into the future.

– They won't listen, Lucinda nodded. – They never listen.

– No, they won't, not even after my precognition has proven itself in the public eye. That building is just as much destined to fall as we were fated to meet.

Lucinda frowned a bit, considering the other's wording. She waited for the other to elaborate, but she didn't.

An oracle never did.

Icy bursts trickled down the big girl's spine.

– You'll remember it, too. The power of memory you enjoy will keep the experience, if not your sense of my being in your consciousness. The overload will take care of most of that, but not all.

– My power of memory?

– Sure, don't tell me you haven't noticed, how everything, even homework goes that much smoother for you since the Great Darkness. You're among the lucky few that can take one look at a written page and recall it word by word.

– But I already have two powers: strength and mind witch. Do you know anything about that?

– Sorry. Jolene shrugged and shook her head. – Can't help you there. Perhaps it is a function of your telepathy not shared by Claudia. I'm confident the answer will reveal itself, in time.

– In time, Lucinda echoed.

She smiled.

– It's so cool to hear you talk about people you've never met, as if you've always known them.

Jolene looked somberly at her.

– In a way I have.

– In a way, Lucinda echoed.

She rose to her full height, looking down at the slimmer dark girl. They both giggled.

– Boy, girl, you're tall…

– I'm a giant in a world of dwarfs, Lucinda joked proudly.

She crossed the street. Jolene followed her, walking with light steps and with her hands behind her back.

– So, where are we going? She asked innocently.

– Nice try that one, Lucinda praised her.

– I work out and I have nothing against a stroll through the city. Jolene sniffed the air. – But I find us a bit pressed for time. You should find a place to dress up.

Lucinda wanted to protest, to resist, but then she shrugged and relented.

They needed to walk a while before they found a secluded spot. Lucinda sought the less traveled areas with her power, and Jolene did the same. They stopped in a narrow alley where no sunlight reached and no camera recorded your every move. Lucinda pulled her gear from the bag and changed clothes within a couple of minutes. She was used to do it quickly in a pinch.

– This was the very first image I saw of you, Jolene said, – of you changing, transforming yourself. It isn't a mere change of clothes, but also in attitude, in total appearance. It's truly amazing, sister.

The warm, warm trickle within added a little more to itself.

– Aren't you gonna change? Gimmick heard herself say, cursing the catching in her throat.

– No. Oracle shook her head. – I have no need to hide my identity. I want the world to know who I am and where I come from.

Her accent wasn't pronounced, but noticeable.

She turned and put her hands on Gimmick's shoulder. Gimmick suspected what would happen, even though she wasn't certain. Oracle's mind was hardly readable under ideal circumstances, and was often, like now a jumble of conflicting images and impressions and thoughts.

– Visualize where you want to go. You need to be very precise. Your mind is always very focused and disciplined, so that won't be a problem, but you need to project it into mine, which may pose a challenge.

Gimmick pictured Mechanic's lab behind closed eyes. Then she focused on Oracle, focused harder then she had ever done to penetrate the seething whirling mist in there.

– Yes, Oracle mumbled. – YES!

Once again, but not in exactly the same way as before the world turned itself inside out. The two appeared in Mechanic's lab exactly at the spot where Gimmick had wanted.

Nausea overwhelmed her. Before she knew it she had puked on the floor.

– Sorry, Oracle said lightly, very lightly, – the transfer takes some time getting used to...

It had been like being twisted inside out.

Anger warred with wonder within Lucinda and wonder won with a mile.

– A teleporter, she cried amazed, – you're actually a teleporter, too.

– It's probably connected to my other power, is my other power, somehow.

I can Travel both physically and in my mind's eye.

It didn't feel real to Gimmick. Nothing did, except the man on the floor.

Mechanic - Alan Prescott lay unmoving on the floor close to his board, his laboratory control section. Apprehension coursed through Gimmick, as she shifted to full combat mode.

Be ready for anything, she sent to her companion.

She reached out with her mind power, making a swipe as wide and far as she was able. There was no one, no one in the entire compound, except the three of them present in this room.

– There is no one here, she frowned. – I can sense no hostile thoughts, no thoughts at all.

– That fits pretty well with my impression, Oracle said. – I can sense no immediate threat. My impressions aren't always reliable, but I usually get something when danger is present. Now, I'm not.

Gimmick studied the laboratory, looking for clues about what was wrong, but she was no scientist, and didn't understand shit about what she saw.

– Something is wrong with him, she said. – His mind is a jumble. It's almost like he's drugged or something, but not quite. He's conscious, but… absent. It's horrible! I've never sensed anything like it.

A button was flashing in red on the main control board. She realized it had been doing that since they had arrived.

His hand moved. It startled her. She kept her eyes on it, on him, but there was no more movement. Her attention returned to the flashing button. His hand moved again, not much, almost unnoticeable, but sufficient.

– Do you want me to push the red button? She asked him. – If you want me to push the button, move your hand.

His hand moved. She pushed the button.

Two or three seconds passed, while she wondered if she had misunderstood him somehow, before he sat up.

– Thank you, he said, filled with relief, a little aghast, not directed at her, – that wasn't exactly one of the most pleasant experiences in my life.

He moved on all fours under the desk, picking up a piece of paper, showing it to them:

PUSH ME

There was also a drawing of the red button with an arrow pointing to it.

– I thought I had prepared for any eventuality, he said and shook his head, – but I missed the random gust of wind surging through here, as the two of you arrived.

He looked at the unknown woman.

– Hello, there, he said.

136

– Mechanic, Gimmick presented, – this is Jolene Masters, Oracle. You'll have a field day studying her.

– Hello, Oracle replied, blushing under his direct stare.

– What were you doing to yourself, Alan? Gimmick wondered.

Now, he did look aghast at her.

– Don't worry. Gimmick grinned. – My guess is that she already knows far more about you than I do.

He grabbed the collar around his neck, what she hadn't noticed before, what had been partly concealed under the collar of his uniform. There was a click and he removed it.

– Remember how we and our esteemed authorities have despaired over the fact that the villains break out of jail almost as soon as we arrest them? He asked rhetorically, and before she managed to do more than nod, he continued proudly. – This will take care of that. It will probably need a bit of fine-tuning and possibly be accompanied by a mild drug

The authorities had certainly despaired, and been very vexed, and threatened very decisive action if not a solution was found.

– The collar renders people helpless, right? Oracle said.

– Yes, Mechanic replied. – It interferes with people's brainwaves, making it very difficult for a given person to think coherently, far less act.

– And you consider handing this invention of yours over to the authorities, with the possibility of misuse that will represent?

Gimmick looked at her, sensing how upset she was,

– I can't say I'm thrilled about it myself, he drawled, – but I can't see we have much choice. The government has threatened to add extensive emergency powers to the police, granting them the permission to kill enhanced lawbreakers on sight. There is even talk about incarcerating *everybody* with the growth gene as a «preventive» measure.

– I don't think that's the way to go, Jolene said, visibly upset. – I don't think giving in to an oppressive government is the way to go at all. I'm sorry, I just don't.

Mechanic didn't respond verbally, quite upset himself.

Gimmick watched Jolene, watched her pull herself together, forcing a smile on her lips.

She turned towards Gimmick.

– There is somewhere we need to be quite soon, now.

– There is? Gimmick said startled. – How so?

– You'll see. Come!

Gimmick hesitated a bit, before stepping close to Oracle.

Jolene turned briefly towards Mechanic, delivering a final poised outburst.

– Do you know what the most probable outcome I saw coming out of today's event was? I saw you being loaded into an ambulance, lying comatose in the hospital with lots of needles sticking out of you, and that it would take days before we finally found the note.

He paled, knowing very well what she was speaking of, easily grasping the concept of her powers.

The two women vanished in the shadows emanating from the dark girl, faded from the room and reappeared in a public restroom.

– This was the closest I could come where we wouldn't be seen, Jolene said.

– Closest to what? Gimmick wondered.

– Come! Oracle said excitedly. – You'll *love* this…

She was like a child almost, in her eagerness.

The restroom was below street level. They rushed up the stairs to the busy early evening streets.

There were just a few blocks to the back alleys and less traveled paths. People glared at them. She heard someone mumble «Gimmick». They turned a corner, and the crowds virtually disappeared, reduced to just a few other people that also had business in the gray zone between the area where the successful people lived and the Brewery District.

Lucinda recognized the downtrodden jewelry store instantly. Four years vanished like smoke, even more so, as more steps brought her forward, and she stared through the dirty window. She spotted the masked man in there.

The door wasn't locked. She almost lost her footing when she attempted to tear it open. She walked into the store. He turned towards her, taking a break from the task of lifting the jewelry.

– I guess you haven't come here to aid me in the chore of reliving this place of pretty baubles, love?

He grinned.

It was him. She recognized him in a thousand ways, even though he was dressed differently. He put down his bag. She attacked him, striving to stay calm and centered, using what she had gained through teaching and experience since she had last fought him.

Her hand connected with his jaw. The pain, both hers and his felt good. He struck at her, but missed. It was so easy to anticipate his moves. She saw them before he did them, and she didn't even have to use her active mind power. Trashing him felt so good, so thoroughly satisfying.

She hit him in the abdomen with her left. Air wheezed from his lungs. He crouched and she struck him, brutally hard on the head with her right. He just stood there, bent over, dizzy and weak. She grabbed his hair and held on, hard, and then smeared his face on her knee.

He fell and lay still. She looked down on him a bit, savoring the sensation, the triumph.

– You weren't much help, she said to Oracle.

– As if you needed any, the dark girl said unconcerned. – Besides, I enjoyed seeing you in action.

– And, she added, – without me, you wouldn't have been given the change, and you and the Catcher would never be the hot item you'll become.

Gimmick shuddered in disbelief and knelt down by the practically unconscious man. He wasn't completely submerged. His eyes moved a bit, the eyeballs swam in his sockets.

She put him on his belly and pulled his arms, hard, behind his back. He cried out in pain.

– So, what do you call yourself? She asked him. – The Blunder?

– The Catcher, he groaned. – Damn you, bitch!

She struck him again, not hard, just enough to make it hurt. He yelped.

– No, you are meat, she told him softly. – We're going for a walk, now, to the nearest police station, and you'll be a nice little boy, or I'll beat the crap out of you.

He didn't recognize her, and she wanted to keep it that way, and was cautious about what she said. She removed his mask, pulled it off in a brutal pull. He shook as his bloody face was displayed to the two women.

– Troy Franklin, alias the Catcher it is, she nodded, easily picking his birth name from his mind.

– How did you know that? He cried. – Do I know you? Who are you?

– I am Gimmick, she replied, – and we will be seeing a lot of each other, I guess.

She found the reinforced chains in her bag, and slapped the bracelets on his wrists. Then she removed his boots, and slapped another set of chains on his ankles. The ankles chain was also short, but long enough for him to walk, or stumble. She pulled him on his feet and pushed him forward, into Oracle's arms.

The old couple, the owners was tied up behind the desk, just like the last time. She freed them. They bubbled over in gratitude. She hardly heard the words they spoke over the noise in their mind.

The Catcher attempted to move, to free himself from Oracle's grip, but then Gimmick noticed something. A shadow grew from Jolene's hand and The Catcher cried out in pain.

– This is a neglected area, in so many ways, Jolene snarled at him. – The police wouldn't ordinarily care about what they consider a petty crime here, wouldn't care about anyone preying on the poor, but they don't like us growing girls and boys much and that means they'll take good care of you.

There was a meanness to her just then, something beyond the anger of the moment, making Gimmick frown.

They walked Franklin to the nearest police station. He shook the chains a few times. Gimmick allowed it, to show him the futility of his actions. People observed them while they approached the station. Some people cheered, others stared in silent condemnation. They walked inside, straight to the arrest desk. Oracle smiled sweetly to the sergeant.

– Hi, there, we have a package for you, she said lightly. – Included in it there is even a video recording where this handsome man is the star.

The two girls laughed a lot about that later, when they walked through town, towards the Old Brewery district, to its slightly less derelict entertainment area.

– Thank you, Gimmick said. – That did make me feel better.

– Think nothing of it. I figured you needed a little closure. I also have the pleasure of informing you that you'll be arresting the Catcher quite a few times in the years to come…

– Thank the Goddess! You implied earlier that we would become an item.

– In a way you will be…

– And I'll have just as much fun every time we meet, and he won't?

– Precisely. He won't exactly be the Threat of the Year or anything.

– It *was* fun, Gimmick admitted, – like receiving a prize or something.

She began noticing the sound of glasses meeting and parting, and music and the buzz of people's conversation. More neon lights began brightening the streets.

– What did you do to him, anyway? She asked cautiously. – It sounded pretty heavy.

Franklin's scream hadn't been pleasant.

Jolene wasn't put off or insulted or anything.

– There is an active, physical component to my powers fairly useful in combat, and to punish scum like Franklin, people stealing from the poor. What I use to open portals I can also use to hurt people, if I choose to.

Gimmick felt the other's rage like lye in acid. It flared, before quickly subsiding.

– I'm a little more opinionated compared to other people you know, am I not? The dark girl said.

– I don't mind, Gimmick heard herself say.

– I know you don't. You've got just as much reason to be angry as I do, if not more.

It hurt somewhere inside Lucinda. She shrugged it off.

140

Oracle's expression softened.

– What do you say? Wanna go celebrating our eternal friendship?

Jolene nodded towards the noisy establishment across the street.

– I don't know, Gimmick said. – I usually don't drink in these clothes.

– Well, you can't go out with me in your civilian identity, since you will expose yourself then, since I'll quickly be known as a member of the Maverick Crew and all.

– I can't, can I? Gimmick grinned, glancing across the street with longing in her eyes.

Grinning wider they rushed towards Holland Tavern, light on their feet, dancing to the beat already reaching them from inside.

They walked through the door, and Gimmick felt the pressure wave of all the excited thoughts in full. It was still early and not that many guests present, but everybody present turned and stared at her, or so it felt, a feeling that didn't exactly dwindle as they made their way to the bar.

– Two pints of Guiness, please, Jolene told an absolutely astonished bartender.

He took her bill and made his way to the cashier, and returned with change. Tapping of Guiness took time and patience, and they made their way to a table in a corner.

They sat down. Oracle removed her jacket. Gimmick kept hers on.

– I guess you don't want to display that arsenal of equipment you carry on you, Jolene grinned.

– You got that right…

Lucinda caught herself smiling fondly to her companion.

The bartender brought them their glasses. He lingered a bit by the table, as if he wanted to say something, but he didn't.

– Cheers, Oracle cried out. – To the true Dynamic Duo.

– Cheers.

Gimmick cried out, too. Glasses met and parted, a little too hard, almost too hard, but they didn't break.

They drank. The tasty cold fluid flowed into Lucinda's mouth and down her throat.

– No foul taste, Oracle said. – He didn't pee in the glasses. He considered it, you know.

– I didn't read anything specific like that, Gimmick said, – only a general dislike. Your power is amazing.

– It has its moments.

– How is it like? Lucinda wondered wide eyed, leaning forward, closer to the other girl.

– It can be wonderful, Jolene replied with wonder in her eyes. – Sometimes I can see so clearly, trace the threads and pick those most likely to happen with unequivocal accuracy.

She hesitated a bit, before adding glumly.

– And sometimes it's nothing but mud.

– Cheers to clarity, Gimmick said sympathetically.

Glasses met and parted again. They drank.

A new song began. They sat and rocked in their chairs for a while, enjoying the relative silence between them.

– You were amazing at the Square, Lucinda said, filled with visible admiration, – so brave and articulate.

– Thank you, my dear, Jolene bowed from sitting position, mischief in her eyes, – it's so great to meet the fans.

– I mean it, Lucinda insisted, – I don't think I could have done anything like that, ever.

– That is *so* sweet of you, and you even missed the final part, about president Burton.

– I take it you don't care for him much?

– You've got that right. I loathe him, and with good reason. I knew he would get elected, knew he would eventually reveal himself as yet another liar and charlatan, but still I felt my heart beat faster every time he made his pitch about Change, and he's even slightly better than Oboto was.

She shrugged, not really shrugging at all, but looking at Gimmick with clear eyes, eyes not dimmed by alcohol fog at all.

– It's all a deception anyway. Presidents and prime ministers and such are nothing more than janitors, figureheads for the power behind the scenes. It's all about smoke and mirrors. Poverty, inequality and injustice have existed for a long time. The vast problems facing this world began long before the Great Darkness. We're merely one more convenient target in a long row, someone to blame for the people at the top, so people won't blame the people at the top. Fear is the key. They rule by it, and are ruled by it. They put names on the unknown, in an effort to make it known, to make the fear go away.

Gimmick shivered inadvertently, both in dread and excitement. She couldn't stop herself.

– To the absence of fear, she said.

– The absence of fear, Oracle whispered.

They drank a lot, almost emptied their glasses.

– We should buy another round before this one is gone, right? Jolene giggled.

142

– It's important to keep the flow going, Lucinda agreed.

– I'll be back.

Jolene jumped up and rushed towards the bar.

Gimmick looked at her glass. There was still a little left. She resisted the urge to drink it in solidarity with her new friend.

Oracle returned, light on her feet.

– The... gentleman at the bar will be here soon with our further refreshment, she giggled.

She was clearly in a good mood. Gimmick sensed that without even trying. They emptied their glasses, at the exact moment when the scowling bartender brought their refills. Lucinda dipped her upper lip in the beige foam at the top of the glass, and Jolene did, too, tipping the glass, digging their way to the holy water beneath.

Skin began to lose its sensitivity, and their thoughts turned hazy, as the initial stages of alcohol poisoning took its toll on them.

– It's interesting, isn't it, how humans use various poisons to further their celebrations?

– Some parts of the brain are dulled, others aren't, Lucinda said, – opening up for new and startling thoughts. Any artist worth anything has used one thing or another to do just that.

– To new and startling thoughts, Jolene said.

Lucinda repeated it. Glasses met and parted and they drank.

– And it works just as much on us as on everybody else, Lucinda pondered, stated.

– Sure does. Our body mass is greater, of course, but not that much greater. We can take more than the average human, but not that much more.

As Lucinda noticed how Jolene's mind opened more up to her, as her powers waned, she felt how her own power of the mind weakened, how the buzz in her consciousness turned less obtrusive.

The haze grew, until it became a pleasant, ongoing hum.

– Time for tonight's first pee, she declared, the pressure in her bladder suddenly increasing by the second.

– I'll hold the fort, her friend said generously.

Gimmick rose, clearly unsteady on her feet, with a huge grin on her face, stumbling towards the restroom. She noticed the eyes on her, the lewd thoughts and she couldn't keep her muted giggle contained.

The ladies' room was fairly filled up. All eyes turned in her directions. She ignored them. There was a queue, as she had feared. Another big girl stamped her feet in impatience. There were lots of stalls, though, and everything proceeded smoothly. Holland Tavern had become fairly popular with the big people, precisely for that reason and Lucinda had also sought out the restroom fifteen minutes before she strictly had to, wise by experience. For once there was little rush when she pulled down her pants and panties and sat down on the bowl.

It still felt like sweet release when the fairly free-flowing piss flushed the water below.

She dried herself. The alcohol muted her senses and made it less of an unpleasant experience compared to how it usually felt like. She opened the door to the stall and walked to the mirror, one of several night birds displaying her mirror image. Seeing her face only as eyes and lips still felt new to her. Every display of teeth looked like a grin and not a smile, no matter how hard she tried.

A big man had joined Jolene at the table. They both looked up when Gimmick returned.

– This is Marcus, Jolene said. – He asked *humbly* if he could be allowed to join us...

– Hi, Marcus, Gimmick said brightly (a little too brightly).

– Hi, the big man said. – I just told Jolene here that the two of you are a sight for sore eyes.

Lucinda blushed hard. It spread to absolutely every piece of her skin.

– Marcus was kind enough to buy us more beer, Oracle grinned widely.

– That's so kind of him, Gimmick cried. – Isn't that kind?

Both looked hotly at him.

She noticed with some satisfaction that he turned red under the collar.

– To kindness, he coughed and raised his glass.

– TO KINDNESS! They choired.

Three glasses met and parted. They drank deep.

– So, what do I call you, my beauty?

– You, kind sir, may call me Gimmick...

– I liked that name from the moment I first heard it, he said. – It opens for so many... possibilities.

She didn't really have any problems reading his mind, no matter how fuzzy everything was. He was completely open about his intentions.

– My turn, Oracle said and rushed towards the restroom.

Gimmick silently cursed her, as she remained there, left alone with the charming man.

He grabbed her jaw lightly.

– I like your mask, too, he said, laying it on way too thick. – You look so sweet in it, except from the viewpoint of the bad people you catch so effectively, of course.

144

She pulled back a little, pulling free of his light grip, but she couldn't help but smile to him.

— To masks, she cheered, feeling bold and free.

They drank, keeping their eyes on each other.

Oracle returned, grabbing her glass and sitting down on Marcus' other side.

— So, what have the two of you conspired about while I was gone?

— We have only breathtakingly awaited your return, my dear, he said.

She was blushing. Both girls felt a pleasant heat rise within.

Gimmick didn't feel jealous, not the slightest. She enjoyed herself in both people's company.

A new melody flowed through the speakers. She once again met Marcus' eyes and she began breathing faster. Oracle smiled in anticipation, and if Gimmick needed more encouragement that was it. All three of them emptied their glasses in one turn.

She rose, slowly and began swaying, as she walked out on the floor, where there weren't any tables, a shadowy part of it that was used as a dance floor occasionally. Feet moved. She reached her hands above her head. The dance began. Oracle rose and reached out a hand to Marcus. He grabbed it and she pulled him with her out there, on the dance floor, to the siren calling to him.

Gimmick did call out to him. That was obvious in her hazy eyes and fevered thoughts. Oracle began kissing him before they reached the floor. Soon, as they danced the slow dance the girls surrounded him, yelping happily as he squeezed them in his strong arms, returning their fever in equal measure.

Lucinda caught people's stares, their increased desire, dynamics that in turn increased her own further. She gasped, and others did, too. It was almost audible in her mind.

— You had... sex before your transformation, didn't you? It's... more *potent*, now, isn't it?

He was in his middle to late twenties. She saw the images of him, a different him and girls making out and fuck.

— Yes, he gasped, so much stronger.

The strong, experienced man stood there and panted like a bungling boy between the two needy females.

— It's like the Hunger, Lucinda whispered, — impossible to resist, and I don't want to.

Jolene nodded and nodded and nodded.

Others joined them on the floor, both those attempting to join their party and others forming their own groups. The smaller boys didn't really make any attempt to endear themselves to Gimmick, but they took a few shots at

Oracle. She smiled wickedly, as she touched them with her pain, and they pulled back, suddenly not very endeared at all.

The party took off, almost from one moment to the next. It quickly turned wild out there on the floor. Beer flowed and people began fumbling at each other's clothes. A button was loosened here, a shoulder bared there. The bartender and the staff took swift action and acted decisively, and pushed all of them towards the exit and out on the street with a whiff of panic in their eyes and mind. Gimmick chuckled darkly.

She remembered walking through lit and dark streets and alleys, fighting now and then to stay somewhat lucid, before giving up, giving in to the storm raging through her, raging through them all.

There were about a dozen people around her at some point, everyone buzzing excitedly in her immediate surroundings and her mind. A few left, but a few males and females remained in addition to Jolene and Marcus, big people all. They stopped frequently to fondle and caress each other. A guy fumbled with the straps of her uniform. She slapped him on the hand.

Bad boy!

She giggled and pulled him to her. He looked at her with a puzzled expression in his face, a large bit of lust and a little fear. She kissed him on the lips and all the remaining fear melted away.

– You're so beautiful, he gasped.

– Why, thank you, my boy, she said sweetly, – what a nice thing to say…

– I love your eyes, and your… lips, another man chuckled.

Marcus grabbed her, very possessive. She let him, melted back into his embrace. Jolene and another female writhed against the brick wall, besieged by horny males.

What a love doll, a man thought, very distinct, even through his and her own fervor haze.

She grabbed his cock and squeezed, a little too hard. He yelped, but then it hardened, and rose and pushed hard against his pants, and he groaned in his sudden, increased need.

There were only flashes of reality from than on, the brief fear of throwing caution to the wind, the glimpse of dark shadows in the passing alleys, the dissolved features in the faces surrounding her, Marcus fumbling with the keys to a door.

They walked, no, flowed up the stairs to a rather large apartment, to one big room, with one big bed. Gasps echoed in the largely empty room. They began undressing, unceremoniously, unashamed. Lucinda felt good, so very good, as she loosened the straps of her uniform.

– That's some arsenal, girlie, Marcus said and shook his head, – especially

146

that ugly-looking thing on your hips.

She drew the crossbow and pointed at him. He paled.

– I'll use this ugly-looking thing at anybody attempting to remove my mask, she grinned.

Everybody laughed, a little spooked.

– Please, be careful with your finger on the trigger, another male said nervously. – It may slip, you know, especially when you….

– Nonsense! Gimmick snorted. – I can control it in my sleep, if I have to.

Giggling hysterically.

The others had a little head start on her because of all the straps and equipment, but they took it slow, like her, enjoying the process like her. She enjoyed their stares, like pleasant shower pinpricks of warm water against her skin.

All the weapons and gadgets thrown on the floor, she could finally pull her shirt over her head and join the others in nudity.

It felt so good, standing there, having the hot summer wind from the open windows caress her sweaty skin, the wet wide spot between her thighs.

Everybody was, through the seemingly endless groping on the walk here long since more than ready, eager and willing for what was coming. There was no more hesitation, only anticipation and excitement.

She used the arrow tip to caress her right nipple, and then, not believing how bold she was she moved it down, to Marcus' cock and played with it, the cold metal not swaying his lust at all, but building it further.

– Goddess, one of the females said. – I'm so wet. I can't believe how wet I am.

They sought close, all of them, first on the floor, and then on the bed. There was no noticeable gap between them on the floor and them on the bed.

Gimmick and Oracle kissed, entertaining the others. Lucinda touched Jolene's mind again, beneath the joy of the moment.

– I have bad dreams, Jolene whispered, as Lucinda looked startled at her.

– Don't worry, honey, a girl said, caressing her from behind, – we'll make them go away.

Oracle closed her eyes and relented and smiled in anticipation, in beyond anticipation.

Gimmick pushed Marcus down on his back, sat on him, with her knees on each side of his body, and pointed the crossbow at his head.

– Serve me, sir Knight, she declared. – Serve your Queen.

Everybody laughed themselves silly, Marcus with a little worried frown. He pushed himself at her, his cock going the final distance to full growth. She moved a bit forward and impaled herself on him. Both gasped, as they instantly began moving against each other, more and more fiercely. Everybody gasped, as they watched, as they sought closer, as they began fucking, too, as the night walked that extra mile towards the total and enduring haze.

The sounds of the other couples' gasps and moans surrounded Gimmick, as she moved up and down on the big male. It felt like she was immersed in it, like the flesh rubbing her skin, just like the whirling hot wind. Marcus fondled her breasts, playing with the large and hard nipples. Both hips moved faster.

Her finger twitched around the trigger. At the last possible moment she managed to turn the crossbow, and she fired the arrow away from him, from everybody. It hit the wall with a loud TWANG.

They looked incredulous at it through their hazy vision. A wild and crazy laughter echoed in their ears.

Then it happened. She gasped, and the others' gasps echoed hers. Suddenly, it was as if she couldn't get air, any air at all. The sweet pain increased to an unimaginable degree. The choir of moans filled the room, filled her consciousness, her total perception. He emptied himself in her in hard, beyond potent pushes. She flooded his groin with hot water and everybody's mind with her explosive joy.

Her heavy body fell on him, and she covered him in wet, grateful kisses. She began moving from person to person and everybody else was, too, swimming in a sea of bodies, so much enjoying the close proximity of another human being.

– What was that? One of the other males, Roy wondered, his eyes shining.
– What the fuck happened?
– That was my telepathy, Gimmick grinned widely, – totally out of control.
– Not like in the comics, he nodded exalted.
– Not like in the comics at all, Oracle nodded vigorously. – They keep that part out.

She kissed him, kissed him again and again. His cock began rising again. All the cocks did. Everybody present felt the need, the beyond powerful lust return.

A fuck doll indeed, Gimmick caught from Bart, the fourth male.

She ignored it, as she pushed herself at him, hard and demanding.
– Fuck me! She challenged him. – Fuck me hard!

Everybody changed partners, and the fucking just continued, without any break to speak of. Bart grabbed her arms. They wrestled a bit, before his greater strength overpowered hers

He put her down on her back and pushed himself into her without delay.

148

Everything turned a pleasant haze of black and shadow after that.

– Harder! She shouted. – *Harder!*

A timeless time afterwards everything exploded for a second time, and not so long beyond that a third time. It just went on and on. She couldn't tell the males apart anymore, only acknowledge the fact that they were there. Brief moments of clarity were exchanged with prevalent, unending and undulated pleasure.

And when the eternal moment ended, and she died slowly there on the bed, bathing in the sea of flesh she touched Oracle's mind again, and she glimpsed a dark, imposing figure standing in the shadows, one making everybody moan fear-struck in their sleep and suffer disturbing dreams about yesterday and tomorrow.

Chapter 9

It was such a pleasure waking up. Nude skin pushed at her at all sides. She lay still for a while, enjoying the others' warm bodies and joy-filled minds. They were all spent, like her, all content beyond measure, like her. She wanted to rise, feeling the first stirrings of a full bladder, but it was so pleasant here, and she quickly fell asleep again.

Next time she woke up she did so with his arms around her. It felt so good.

– Good morning, precious, he greeted her, mumbling in her ear.

– Good morning, lovetoy, she grinned and kissed him on the lips. Letsdoitagainrightnow.

His eager thoughts impressed themselves on her mind.

He began kissing her, roaming her.

She felt it instantly, how he raised her need, how she had to struggle in order to resist his advances.

Sorry, my boy, a girl has to pee and she has to feed.

He didn't really lose his good mood when she writhed out of his grip and fought herself free, but just gave her a smack on the butt. It burned so pleasantly and she couldn't help but smile as she made her way to the bathroom.

She drank a huge glass of water. There were several of them in the bathroom cabinet. She refilled and drank it empty again. Her eyes and lips looked different in the mirror. Her smile widened as she sat down on the bowl. The pee burned as it always did, but it didn't diminish the smile dancing on her lips.

The sounds and stench and sensations from outside her tiny cubicle imposed themselves on her. They changed, as she changed. It was as if her clothes, her uniform grew back on her skin, as if four years passed, slowly, in just a few seconds.

They had been forced to briefly return to the headquarters for everybody to empty themselves of shit and piss.

– Nice digs! Ashton Kramer whistled.

It wasn't really that much of a detour, anyway. With the access to the portals they enjoyed, they weren't really that much further from Jagadir than they had been. Distance had become truly relative.

– I knew you had some kind of advantage, Kramer said. – I just knew it!

Gimmick dried herself quickly. Everybody speeded up their actions. They hurried out into the entrance hall, gathering there in greater number and force than ever before, gathered before Lady Grace.

– We're still pretty much on schedule, the imposing woman said. – Luckily I prepared for the extra time.

No one cracked a joke or a smile at her expense. The seriousness of the situation, of what was immediately ahead filled their mind, made them focus on the last few preparations in their head.

– We're *ready!* Lady Grace continued. – We will never be more ready.

– Like we practiced, Flight Captain said. – We strike hard and relentless, and never let up the pressure. We go to *war* this day, one long coming, one that has become inevitable.

They rushed to the gate, threw themselves through the shimmering air with apprehension in their gut, and appeared at the other side on a mountaintop overseeing a vast landscape. Brick took point. Everybody followed him as he descended a slight slope. Those not able to fly ran through tight vegetation, striving to move through the thick heather. Their feet sank into it for every step they took, but they didn't slow down.

Another shimmering hole in the air appeared around a sharp turn, beyond a cliff. The sun's rays shifted and burned at its edge. At some point far closer to the Jagadir border five remote-controlled choppers took off from a secret base in the ground. Doors slid open, and they rose into the twilight air.

Oracle knew this day would come, Gimmick sent to those unapprised. She made a portal to what was then open landscape inside Jagadir.

– But Oracle has disappeared, Lavender said. – She might have been captured and forced to reveal everything she knows.

Yes! Gimmick acknowledged.

But we're prepared, prepared for anything that might meet us the other side.

And she instantly sensed Lady Grace's approval.

And then there were no more distracting thoughts, no more distractions, except what was ahead.

They appeared inside a warehouse, Lavender and Raven Bird first, both using their powers to surround themselves and those arriving right after them in a protective bubble. Lady Grace and Gimmick linked everybody together by thought, something that was straining them, but they did it, they really did it, and felt really, really good about it.

They had done it before, but only under what had been far more ideal conditions.

Everybody stood there, alert and posed for trouble, taking their positions, but nothing happened.

– People are far away, Gimmick reported.

– Confirmed, Oil stated.

He could sense organic life forms and also distinguish between humans and others.

They relaxed just a little, and looked around at their surroundings.

– It's like Oracle described it, Mechanic marveled, – like she said it would be. If there are a few details wrong...

– There are, Lady Grace remarked.

– There aren't many, Mechanic completed his reasoning.

Those that had known her heard her voice, both the actual and the recordings they had played over and over again, also in their head.

«On the left you will see a large crate, with a blue mark on top».

Energetic ran to it and touched it, as if to stress the point.

There were other markers that they identified one by one.

– Her precognitive power was truly blazing that day, he said. – Strange to ponder the fact that she didn't know what was coming, whatever happened to her.

– Her power was unreliable, at least in part, Gimmick pointed out. – It was one of the first things she told me. «Sometimes it's nothing but mud».

– She didn't say anything about her own appearance here? Crimson Mask wondered.

They stared at her in wonder, as they pondered the new angle she had presented to them. Lady Grace looked at her in appreciation.

– No, she didn't say she would be here, or that she wouldn't be. I guess that's just one more fact we must write off to the quirkiness of her power.

– She told us that we would arrive here safely, Flight Captain said. – And that the changes were high that we would leave and leave with mission accomplished. I guess the rest is up to us...

– It is. Lady Grace nodded. – And I know you will all make me very proud this day and all days to follow.

They straightened, inevitably, prompted by their commander's words and presence.

It... began. They felt it, as they once more moved, as they obeyed the tactical map Lady Grace imposed on them. The layout of the area was revealed in their mind, as they spread out through what was basically one giant combined prison and military camp, surrounded by several layers of fences and barbwire.

The security was so tight and so far-reaching that any mundane escape attempt would be considered ridiculous.

– I can see us come here as prisoners, Lavender mumbled with a noticeable chill in her voice, - us be prisoners here. We wouldn't stand a change of escaping. No one would.

Fences upon fences upon fences reached far into the terrain. There seemed to be no end to them.

Gimmick moved, her body as well as her mind, venturing into enemy territory. Sensor was right behind her. So were Oil, Brick, Raven Bird, Stalco and Wind. They moved through and between what were first empty buildings, but then one building drew attention to itself in the map in Gimmick's mind.

She was there, right between the closing-in walls before she could consider her options, the muscles of her thighs burning with the effort.

A familiar mind appeared to her, and she strived to keep herself on a somewhat even keel, and she realized that was what had drawn her to this particular spot.

Ten. Gimmick easily caught Oil's thoughts. Ten... adults inside.

She had trouble confirming that. To her mind it seemed like there was no one there. Even the one she had sensed seemed elusive, slippery. Added fear and repulsion warred within her, as she suspected the truth. The others glanced curious at her, unable, as she was at hiding her suddenly raw emotions.

The closest door wasn't locked. They rushed into the building prepared for anything. Brick, with his heavy frame was first, as he often was. Gimmick pushed him at his back, to make his forward momentum even more powerful.

Their battle-readiness was, at this instance a wasted effort. They met with no resistance. Everyone had a frown on their face when they moved through what resembled ordinary living quarters. They passed what was clearly a nursery, filled with cribs. The soft noise of a dozen tiny minds filled Gimmick's consciousness. She closed them off without making a conscious decision about it.

They reached a bigger room, one filled with nude adults, people in deep sleep after extensive sexual activity just a few hours earlier. It still filled their dreams.

– What IS this? Wind said incredulous and aloud.

Gimmick knew what this was. Nightmarish sensations filled her waken dreams.

It dawned slowly on Wind and the others, too.

– It's a production facility for mindless soldiers, Gimmick said flatly. – This is merely one of many in this camp alone. There are many more camps.

She lost control of her powers momentarily, rocking one of the nude men. He opened his eyes and looked directly at her.

– Hi, Gimmick, he greeted her happily, dull, like a child or a retard.

She recognized Marcus somewhat, even though there was only an outward resemblance, and hardly even that, to the man she had briefly known.

He and everyone here had been broken, brainwashed and «reeducated» into eager servants of the people ruling Jagadir. Gimmick quelled the vomit rising in her throat, doing so just as easily as she returned the ten nude people to their pleasant sleep. No more effort than fine-tuning of their already practically dormant state was needed.

– We're going to burn Jagadir to the ground, she said, she swore, as she turned towards her companions, as her thoughts went out to everybody in the attack force, – burn everything in it until there is nothing but ruins left.

Her companions looked briefly at her, and then nodded.

They don't know, she thought, don't know what I know. They see and have seen, but don't truly realize what has happened here.

That's hard, without our vaunted ability to see beneath masks, little one.

Perhaps we should *show* them? Lucinda responded angrily.

Perhaps, but not now. For now it's sufficient to share our rage, our determination with them.

Share! Gimmick nodded, without nodding.

She turned towards the others. They faced her rage head on.

Everybody rushed back outside, moving their legs, their bodies, pushing their paranormal abilities to the max well before they met with resistance, readying themselves.

Their incursion had happened at a very opportune moment. The soldiers supposed to be guarding the camp at the second night shift had gone to bed, had just fallen asleep, leaving only one set of sentries. Gimmick and Lady Grace could easily make those close to them stay asleep, and also make quite a few of those awake fall into dormancy. They moved from barrack to barrack granting them deep dreams. The others knocked out the rest, knocked those not handled by the telepaths into oblivion.

It went well for quite some time. Then, as was bound to eventually happen, a soldier managed to cry out, waking up those not handled or knocked out.

Loud shouts filled ears and minds. It took only seconds after that before the general alarm sounded.

The first shots were fired. The first few skirmishes began.

The remote controlled choppers began firing at the other soldiers' barracks and at the fortified fences surrounding the camp. Explosions rocked the ground for miles. Soldiers, part of the black-clad elite force flowed from one of the barracks. Raven Bird pulled their weapons from their hands with a gesture. She wasn't quite able to move their bodies, but her effort clearly hurt them. Oil did affect several of them severely, made them gasp and scream

154

and fall to the ground in pain. Wind pushed them through the air and stole air from their lungs. Then Gimmick and her group were in the midst of whirling, uniformed bodies. Brick struck each of them down with one single hit. Gimmick began attacking them, too, using both her mind and body, with a ferocity she welcomed. Her blazing thoughts burned their mind. Feet and hands made contact with jaws and soft bodies. She didn't hold back, none of them did.

Gimmick kept an eye on Sensor at first, in glimpses and flashes of blood and rage, but Kid Sister did good, kicking ass like she was born to it. The girl felt fear, but she, too, was caught up in the heat of battle.

Hands and feet turned sore. Faces twisted themselves in intense concentration. They fought on, beyond pain, beyond the passion ruling them.

– Major troop movement, Mechanic informed them. – Two hours, perhaps three away.

Gimmick glanced at the flashing images on her wrist monitor, showing a map of Jagadir. A soldier in front of her picked up a gun. She struck him. The pain shot through her entire arm. She kept fighting in a haze, and even the haze was blurring around the edges.

Oil used his full power on the advancing soldiers, twisting the flesh of their bodies, killing many of them instantly, making most of those remaining fall and shake and howl on the ground

Only a few soldiers occasionally managed to fire their weapons. Most were struck down well before they got the chance. Wind was hit in the arm. Gimmick kicked the female soldier in the head, breaking her skull and killing her. Wind swayed.

Keep fighting, Gimmick told her. *Don't stop, not as long as you breathe.*

Wind bit her lip, bit it so hard that blood flowed.

Dusk set and faded into night as they kept charging forward, kept rolling over any resistance they encountered. Pain itself turned numb as the members of the extended Maverick Crew abused their flesh and minds moving through the brutal, insane reality of the enemy camp.

Stalco took a bullet in the chest and went down. That woke them up, somehow, from their relative trance, made them focus even harder on the task at hand, and they briefly wondered what their limit was, how long they could keep up this constant, prolonged battle engraving itself so deeply into their body and thoughts.

Those with active, flesh and mind-rendering powers kept wrecking havoc among the soldiers, showing little or no signs of tiring. Rage and fear and desperation and the determination burning deep within them all kept fueling the invaders.

It was first when soldiers started fleeing that Gimmick and most of those others carrying arms drew them and started firing at their backs, as if being on a firing range.

They closed in on the camp's command center from all sides, a sight glimpsed through the red mist that had become their lives.

Crimson Mask waved her hand and a large truck flew through the air and hit the fortified steel door. The explosion made a giant hole in the wall. The red mist grew thick and heavy. Body parts decorated floors and ground everywhere.

They rushed inside. Parts of the floor were gone. Gimmick jumped easily across the divide. The others followed her in a frenzy feeding itself as they penetrated further into the building.

Gimmick cut into the people they encountered with her mind power in a manner she had never before mastered. The rage gave her the added edge. People fell and writhed on the floor, crying out in distress. Those following her took care of them with brutal kicks and attacks, using their powers and fists and feet to the very best of their ability. Sensor killed one of them with a brutal kick to the head, breaking the soldier's neck, moving on to the next in an even flow.

A briefly concerned Gimmick probed Kid Sister, but there was no regret in the heat of battle, only stronger fueled rage.

Dust and fumes hovered in the air, didn't fall the slightest according to her perception. A guard pointed her gun at her. Gimmick made her shake her hand and the bullet went awry. Martial Athlete jumped ahead and kicked the armed woman in the face.

SURRENDER, Gimmick shouted in their mind, OR WE WILL SLAUGHTER YOU ALL. ONE MORE ATTEMPT AT RESISTANCE AND YOU'RE DEAD

They experienced it as an extremely loud voice. Many of them were downright stricken and rushed to surrender. Others took their time, but made no attempt at resisting.

– ON YOUR KNEES! Sensor shouted at them, striking those dawdling. – HANDS BEHIND YOUR BACK!

They obeyed and were handcuffed, or rather striped or sedated quickly and effectively. Darts were fired into their thighs, and they fell unconscious to the floor. The invaders reached the inner sanctum, the control room, where monitors showed almost every single spot of the top-security prison. Gimmick noted that the warehouse they had arrived at was one of the exceptions, and that the nursery, all the nurseries, the extended breeding facility consisting of many buildings wasn't.

We were lucky, Gimmick told Sensor. The guard on monitor duty granted himself a prolonged absence.

He was back now, from his extensive visit to one of the pens, way too late. Gimmick easily glimpsed in his surface memory how he had abused and brutalized two female slaves and thoroughly enjoyed the act.

She grabbed the man with her mind, instantly realizing that he had training in resisting telepathic intrusion.

STOP RESISTING ME OR IT WILL HURT!

He moaned, as pain seemed to fire up every nerve-ending in his body and relented immediately. She found everything he attempted to hide. Then, with a snarl she let go of him. He fell to the floor.

Resistance faded away in the mist and the smoke. All enemy combatants surrendered.

Premises secure! She reported to Lady Grace.

PREMISES SECURE, Lady Grace confirmed to everybody from her command position not long afterwards.

We must hurry, Gimmick admonished. There are plans for gassing the entire area if an infiltration is successful.

She had seen it in the guard's mind. The man was practically glowing in sick anticipation.

The signal has been sent. It will take some time to implement the procedure. The facilities aren't ready for use. No one among the decision-makers reckoned there would ever be a need for it.

Gimmick made sure it hurt when she gauged the final pieces of information from the man's mind.

– Elite forces are leaving the capitol, Mechanic reported. – Their planes are in the air and heading for us.

The elite forces were the only units with access to jeg fighter planes.

Triumph rose in the Crew members, hard and fast, to the point of hurting. Gimmick armed the self-destruct mechanisms with a few simple pushes of buttons, setting explosives all over the camp to go off in half an hour. Only the facilities inhabited by brainwashed slaves were spared.

– We're turning their perceived power against them, Sensor cried excited. – It's so cool, so fucking cool.

She was covered in blood. The blood wasn't hers.

They made their way back the same as they had come, carrying Stalco and others with serious wounds. Wind had a white, turned red bandage tied around her arm, looking tough and mean. They were numb, most of them, but with blood boiling in their veins.

The one nursery they had previously visited looked strangely unaffected by all the carnage. It was, of course, since there had been no fighting there, but it still seemed strange to them. They picked up the adults and the babies, and rushed back towards the warehouse.

– We will return for the rest, all the rest of them later, Lady Grace told them, – if there is a later.

Everybody easily understood the further implications of her words. The cold and hot chill, always present beneath the cold and hot triumph moved and thrived.

The nude adults were like children and easy to lead. There was a frantic, but controlled run into what had been their point of origin in a place that kept making them shake in fear, disgust and rage.

They ran through the portal, bile rising in their throat. At the other side, at the mountainside it still did that. They couldn't shake it off.

Lady Grace placed herself in front of them all, somehow.

– You did good, she said. – I'm proud of you.

Her approval washed over them all like a warm, warm wind.

– We kicked ass! Ashton Kramer bristled.

Gimmick noticed he looked at Lady Grace with devotion in his eyes.

– The plan proceeds apace, without delay, Lady Grace said. – I know you're sick and weary, but I also know that you will rise above it, and continue doing what we must.

She… filled them with purpose and dedication. They ignored the remaining sickness in their gut and allowed the rage to flow freely, let it grow even stronger, more powerful. Those with wounds too grave to fight, but still standing took the badly wounded, the babies and the adult children back to the headquarters. Those left, the majority of the original force returned to Jagadir, but chose a different route through the portal, to Jagadir City. They emerged inside the government building, the Whitehall, in an empty, silent room. The sounds and sensations from the streets outside and the rest of the building rose in Gimmick's consciousness.

Spread out, she sent.

They did, on this floor and to the rooftop.

And then her attention focused on the adjacent room.

They're all there, she sent, all the important people, everybody pulling the strings in Jagadir.

There were two guards, too, two lower ranking officers serving the elite, but they were not important, in any way, more for show than anything else. The people around the long table felt safe and confident in their power.

The attack was coordinated to the second. They charged the main conference room the moment the first cries of distress and struggle sounded from elsewhere.

The two guards screamed and fell the very moment Brick broke down the door to the «War Room» inside. The main attack squad rushed forward, quickly covering the parameter. The entire upper part of the building was quickly covered and neutralized, the squad facing no major resistance.

– Nobody move! Flight Captain shouted. – Or it will *hurt*.

Everybody in the room froze. Nobody made more than one or two steps before they stopped and looked angry and stunned at the invading forces.

They were all here, «Governor» Fredrik Stanton, Jason Carnegie, the industry captain, Alysse Montgomery, the pretty face they showed the world and all the rest that had brought Lucinda close to nausea for years. Hatred and fear and self-loathing coursed through her.

– What's the *meaning* of this? Stanton cried out, and succeeded somehow to put all his vaunted authority into his voice.

– You're our prisoners, Lady Grace declared with exactly the right amount of chill in her voice.

– What gives you the right...

– You're prisoners of war, Flight Captain snarled, unusually excited.

– War? Montgomery gasped. – What war?

She shifted uneasily, her muscles tensing. Gimmick stepped forward and struck her down before she could act.

– The undeclared war you and your like have waged on our kind since the very first day our presence became known to the world. Fortunately for us you've also broken quite a few federal and international laws while doing so...

Montgomery dried blood from her lips and jaw. Gimmick felt the full power of her hatred behind the doll-like, serene paste-up face. She burrowed deep within the woman's mind, paralyzing her, making sure it hurt. Montgomery whimpered under the onslaught.

Consider this the modest, initial payback for all the suffering you've inflicted on random and innocent people.

She saw what Alysse had done, how she had been at the forefront of things, not only in public relations, but at the laboratories and in the dungeons, the torture chambers and brainwashing facilities.

Lucinda fought to stifle the gasp and bile rising in her throat, the horror burrowing itself deep in her mind. She heard Alysse Montgomery's cruel, cruel laughter.

All stations are covered, Lady Grace told her troops. All is well.

Gimmick knew that Kramer had roughed up a few people more than strictly necessary. She shrugged.

We've talked about this, little one, Lady Grace sent exclusively to her. We need to instill respect, even fear in our enemies and in people in general, show them we can take it as well as dish it out.

I know. Gimmick shrugged again, more deliberate this time. I'm good.

He was entitled. They all were.

Consciousness fueled by rage and determination kept spreading from those central points. The two women were in constant light rapport with those they couldn't see with their eyes.

Mechanic began setting up his equipment on the table. The council members were pushed, not exactly polite or kind into the deep corner of the room. Gimmick sensed shock, indignation, fear and smoldering, rising righteous anger. A light prompting and it exploded into the open.

– You dare? Carnegie cried nonplussed. – You actually *dare?*

– Of course we do, Gimmick nodded, very patronizing, her grin containing all the contempt in the world. – Why shouldn't we?

He stared at her with his tiny eyes, practically frothing around the mouth, only keeping his self control due to years of practice.

– I don't know how you managed to penetrate our defenses, he frowned, – but I can guarantee one thing: you'll never leave here, except as the chained and collared *beasts* you are.

Gimmick giggled darkly, further encouraged by the approval she sensed in her comrades.

– You have no idea, have you, no fucking idea of what we're capable of? I guess you're judging us all by all those poor wretches you've captured and broken and trained and become so jaded because of that, because of the easy lane you've enjoyed.

Mechanic's setup began buzzing, began glowing, almost at the point of being a presence in the room.

– Jamming device activated, he reported.

The lights blinked a few times. Stanton stared in horror at the infernal machine.

Mechanic pushed the second button.

– First chopper swipe plotting completed.

Stanton turned to Lady Grace.

– Tell us what you want, he said exasperated. – Just tell us, goddamn it!

He was sweating and breathing hard, like after a long and strenuous run.

You can stop dehydrating him, now, Gimmick sent to Oil. He manages that quite well on his own.

– You will tell your forces to stand down.

160

Lady Grace calmly told the gasping man.

– Stand down…

The frown on his forehead turned deeper and bigger.

– You will tell them to surrender. You, they and the entire state will submit to our authority.

Several of the council members broke in laughter. Stanton didn't.

– Your… authority? By now he was gasping like a whale on land. – What gives you…

She struck him, hard. He fell. Blood filled his open mouth.

– Our power gives us the right, a power also backed by the US government and everyone else of the world leaders you've pissed off by your many intrusions into their sovereign soil the last few years. You didn't think we would have come here if we didn't have permission from the very top, do you?

He faltered. Everybody saw it.

– Everything you have done returns in your face with interest, Gimmick informed him.

– They're bluffing! Montgomery snarled. – Don't fall for it. Our rescue is being prepared this very moment.

Like the experienced politician and power player he was Stanton watched his fellow council members, easily seeing where the chips were about to fall.

– Go to hell! He said.

– I was so hoping you would say that.

Lady Grace's laughter sounded unusually harsh, in a manner they had never seen her display herself during her photo opportunities and public appearances.

She didn't sign to Mechanic or give him any signal, covert or otherwise. He just stood there, taking no action.

– We anticipated your reluctance, she shrugged.

Nothing was happening at first. Gimmick listened in on the minds of those using the glowing communication lines in and around the building. Plans were being made. Actions were being prepared.

The loud sound of approaching engines was clearly audible, and increasingly so, as the choppers closed in on the city.

– We have choppers with the latest stealth technology, Mechanic stated proudly. – One slightly improved by yours truly the last year or so.

– Fire! Lady Grace shouted.

The entire board on the box began blinking. The choppers fired the first array of rockets. Everybody heard the distinct whining, as the deadly metal charged through the air. The building right across the street was hit and blew up in an inferno of smoke and fire. People and assembled soldiers died and continued dying. Gimmick felt them, a wave of death and pain. All the four buildings surrounding this one were hit. Soldiers on the street were hit by falling debris. The next wave of explosions began taking out buildings further away.

– Attack! A general shouted from the first floor with bulging eyes. – ATTACK!

A few of the soldiers had reached the first steps on their way up when they howled in pain and collapsed on the spot. Something seemed to come out of the very air. Whatever it was, it decapitated the general instantly.

No soldiers attempted to move after that. They dropped their guns right there and didn't move, did hardly breathe.

Flight Captain directed his gun at Secretary Bailey and shot him in the head. He collapsed like an empty sack on the floor.

– Who will be next? He asked the remaining council members.

They looked in horror and shock at him and their dead colleague on the floor.

– In what way did you think we were bluffing? Lady Grace wondered.

She turned her attention back to the box.

– NO! Stanton held up a hand. – No, please! We surrender… unconditionally.

She granted him the sweetest of smiles, the kind she reserved for journalists and photo ops.

– You will give very strict and explicit instructions. Be aware that we will be able to listen in, on all communication, at all times. You will tell your elite guard to report here, unarmed and to submit to our authority. You will prepare the dungeons for them.

She kept giving him instructions, hammering them into him. He looked like he was sleepwalking, and he sounded like that, as well.

The first wave of the attack force began drifting towards the restroom. The stench began filling the building, the street, drifting in the wind.

Filth. Vile filth.

Gimmick shuddered by the words and venom she picked up from Montgomery's mind.

She ignored it with an effort as she walked to the Bowman, as they both appeared from the restrooms with a smile on their lips.

– Notice the smell of victory in the air.

And she pushed herself at him, giving him a lingering kiss on his lips for all to see.

They felt it all, and it was further noticed and amplified by Gimmick and

Lady Grace, of course, the triumphant cry rising from within. An unarmed aide passed by. She could smell his fear, even without reading his mind.

– How do you feel, now, she spat, – when you know the truth about us, know that we aren't unthinking beasts?

His hatred boiled over, just like it had done with Montgomery.

– But you always knew that, and you still did what you did. You're just another stinking racist.

Your dreams will be *nightmares,* she told him, her silent laughter rocking his core.

He wanted to run off, wanted to charge her, but she didn't allow it. She froze him in place, and her rage made her power flow like never before.

– Yessss, you know about the dungeons. You have visited them, and also the internment and training camps, and been quite active there. I'm happy to tell you that you will soon see it at a completely different angle. All those nice and pleasant places are your fate…

She showed him, made him feel everything waiting for him.

He shouted in horror.

– No, please, he whimpered. – NOOO!

It was so imaginative, all of it. She marveled at it all. His stark fear was music in her ears.

The shout became a scream, joining many other screams of previous Jagadir public servants.

Lady Grace appeared on state television, very strict and very foreboding.

– Jagadir's very *existence* is an affront to human dignity, she told everybody watching.

Everyone not watching was told the same thing, in national papers, on the Grid and the radio and any possible media outlet, forced to look at themselves in the mirror.

– Your penance, as a people and as individuals for accepting, aiding and abetting the vilest criminals such as your leaders will be long and hard. This place will be put under administration, and every citizen required to take lessons aimed at preventing bias and racism and the atrocities we've unearthed today. You're all guilty and you will all suffer the consequences of your inhuman deeds. Your children will be raised in orphanages and told repeatedly what cowards and assholes their parents are…

And so it went on and on, for hours and hours, with repetitions running constantly, day and night.

The elite soldiers, the long arm of the previous government were called in for screening and subsequently thrown into the deepest dungeons the Maverick Crew could find. Those residing there were freed. They had been among the few protesting or who had done anything to fight the previous regime, and now became an integrated part of the new, provisionary government.

– People fall in line so easily, don't they?

Sensor kept shaking her head in horror.

– Yes, little one, Lady Grace confirmed. – Most people will do anything, no matter how horrible, to obey the orders from above, eagerly succumbing to their unpalatable instincts. They need stern guidance to see the light.

Sensor frowned, looking at her leader, wanting to say something more, not able to put further words to her thoughts. She walked to her sister.

– Did you... did you hear?

– You're... worried, aren't you? Gimmick said, touching the girl's jaw. – Don't be. There's nothing to be worried about.

– Nothing, Sensor whispered.

– This will be the end of it, Gimmick said. – No more people kidnapped by this oppressive state and brought here from all over the world, no more big children being terrorized by state-sponsored bigots. This might even turn out to be a free haven for us, if we should ever need one.

– All those people persecuted, now free, and in charge, the Bowman grinned. – That is as close to poetic justice I've ever seen.

– Tainted, Crimson Mask said, – ruined by their prolonged ordeal, eager for vengeance on their torturers, their eyes open, easily seeing the leaders and so called freedom-loving people in the rest of the world as the hypocrites they are.

Gimmick shivered by the sound of her voice alone, and her words... they penetrated deep within her.

Don't listen to her, Kid Sister, she sent. Her hard life has marked her, made her bitter.

– Oracle gave us this victory, Lisa said with a noticeable chill in her voice. – Without her...

– Without her we would have needed to be far more cautious and planned it quite differently, Lady Grace acknowledged. – Everything would have been harder and far more dangerous, inevitably so. We owe her even more after this.

Big people were liberated from breeding facilities, servitude and medical experiments all over the country. They counted in the thousands. The sight meeting some of the liberators made them sick to their stomachs.

Some soldiers, particularly those black clad, the elite of the elite soldiers didn't surrender, at least not immediately, but they were losing ground fast to those fighting for the new regime, aided by the Maverick Crew utilizing

164

the brutal and tactical advantage of Lady Grace, Gimmick, Lavender, Raven Bird, Oil, Mechanic and the others in full. The uniformed men and women stubborn in their loyalty to the old government were slaughtered in the thousands, and the survivors ended up in the deepest, deepest dungeons.

The wrapping up took more than a few days. There was a time when the Maverick Crew feared they would never escape the graveyard of the human spirit called Jagadir. They became the enforcers of the new regime, brutally and enraged striking down the riots in the streets, those shouting for the big people to burn. The former leaders and many of the elite soldiers were shipped off to international courts to face persecution for crimes against humanity, for genocide and torture.

– They will face a long list of charges, Flight Captain swore. – It's over for them.

– It's quite funny, isn't? Wind giggled darkly. – Many of those charges would fit the leaders of the United States and most others as well.

She shrunk under the stare of Lady Grace and Gimmick and the rest.

– I meant no disrespect, she said low and subdued. – But it's true… right?

– It *is* true! Lady Grace acknowledged.

The others looked stunned at her.

She shrugged.

– The sad truth is that our leaders aren't up to the standards we aspire for them. That means our job becomes that much harder, that much more a steep and greasy slope. As I've told you time and time again: we need to be at our very best to prevail.

Everybody straightened, yet again inspired by their leader's words and uncompromising stance. Wind, too. She looked at Lady Grace and also Gimmick with more boundless gratitude in her wet eyes.

Gimmick's platoon received another bout of elite soldiers later, received them with full honors of fear and triumph, beating up on the slackers.

– You're a SORRY bunch, aren't you, Wind cried, – when you're not holding all the cards.

The nude men and women were pushed down the stairs, into the dungeons that had previously been their domain, joining the many already there. Most of them would never see anything like daylight again, and they would be the lucky ones.

How are the troops holding up? Lady Grace queried.

She was always doing that, asking questions where she knew the answers, and Gimmick always replied, obediently and eagerly giving her report.

They are fine, ma'am. A little weary, but still keeping the glow of victory burning inside.

And soon rewards will be theirs, Lady Grace granted her. We will take our leave tomorrow, and only need to return here for the occasional checkups of the new republic we've helped create. We have every reason to be proud.

– Proud, Gimmick breathed and thought simultaneously.

The new army, loyal to the new government had now gained close to total control over the state. The few remaining skirmishes were just that, minor pockets of fighting quickly subsiding.

Control was handed over in a pompous ceremony the next day. Lady Grace held her obligatory speech, surrendering her iron fist to the newly appointed general.

– Jagadir was a rogue state, she cried. – Today, it has once more joined the free world as an equal member of its fellowship of nations, and we are all better off for it…

– She's good at this, Mechanic said ironically, – the punctuation, the exactly right tone of voice. It's quite remarkable.

– Shh, Wind said, punishing him with a cold gust of wind.

Lady Grace ended her speech. She saluted the general and he returned the salute.

The marching band marked the Crew's departure. They left, entering the government building, rushing up the stairs, to the shimmering point in the air, the music cut off the moment they entered the portal.

A beyond pleasant surprise awaited them, when a jubilant crowd cheered the moment they left the empty street of the portal and stepped out on the large square. Lady Grace had made them all focus on this particular exit. Gimmick had thought nothing of it, until now. She and the rest of the returning heroes felt a warm glow inside as they let themselves be praised by the population of Tobruk. It was so unexpected and unusual that it overwhelmed them completely.

They waved and the crowd filling the plaza outside the City Hall cheered some more.

– It's almost… eerie, Raven Bird whispered in Gimmick's ear.

– It feels so great to finally be accepted, Oil sniffed, close to tears.

They all waved frantically, re-experiencing the triumphant victory far away.

– We're soldiers, Claudia Malone said, – defending our country from foreign and domestic threats. Of course they love us and cherish us.

After years of distrust and revulsion the city of Tobruk and its people embraced its heroes, the weary but increasingly happy men and women returning home from the war.

Chapter 10
TWO YEARS AGO TODAY

The guys were relaxing (or trying to) at the headquarters after a workout, watching television, a program about the Growth Gene and those carrying it.

– We don't know exactly how many with the «growth gene» that has committed suicide during these eight years, a guest lectured his audience in the studio and those watching it at home, – but we know that those carrying it make out about one in a thousand of the population, give or take and allowing for local variations, and that they consist of about ten percent of the crime statistics figures, a fact more than suggesting their trouble at adapting.

– And that's a *fair* and balanced program? Jolene cried out in frustration.

– We also have to take into consideration that people have developed powers without the Growth Gene being apparent. They can more easily hide among the ordinary population, of course.

– Certainly an important fact to be aware of, the hostess noted with a sweet smile.

– Precisely, her guest nodded solemnly.

– A fair and balanced program indeed, Martial Athlete sighed.

Oracle changed channel, changed it again and again. It was no use. Virtually every single one covered the issue, in one way or another, and not very favorably.

– I feel like an alien… or something, Raven Bird said.

She had been pacing the floor in front of the television for minutes. She kept pacing.

A news anchor appeared. He was doing his daily routine, ending the program by commenting on «current issues».

– Tomorrow's date has been chosen by its participants as «big people rights day». Since its inception on Coleman Square two years' ago it has been marred by controversy and unrest. During last year's protest major riots were avoided only by the resolute encroachment of the riot police.

– Where does he get off? Oracle cried. – «The resolute encroachment of the riot police». Is he thinking through his statements at *all*?

– People are asking themselves if any member of the costumed crime fighter community will join the protest this year, after being strongly advised to stay away by representatives of the police and local and national government. Oracle, Jolene Masters of the Maverick Crew has been one of the movement's staunchest supporters for years. Will she stay away this time, in order to ease tensions?

– Don't bet on it, she mumbled.

– Government sources have talked about «decisive action to deal with the problem if it persists», especially in our bigger cities and in «hotbeds» like Jaynagar and Tobruk, and in the old confederate states, where the conflict between the Big People and society has been… *strained* from the start.

Jolene finally turned off the television, and no one present voiced any protest.

– I wanted to see it, she mumbled, – wanted to see how bad it has become.

Gimmick soothed her the best she was able, both with the touch on the shoulder and in her attempt to access the seething cauldron that was her mind.

It was twice difficult, since Lucinda had to fight the surge of her own anger and that of almost everybody present.

– We should feel angry, Cougar cried. – My God, we have every right to be.

Gimmick couldn't really access her thoughts either, not when her anger crossed over to rage like this.

The anger shimmered in the very air like something physical, tangible. She gasped and crouched as the pain coursing through her rose in ever stronger waves from her belly. Everybody turned bewildered towards her.

– We're hurting her, Raven Bird said softly. – Our anger is hurting her.

The powerful emotions eased somewhat, and Lucinda could once more breathe.

They all found it… odd that Mechanic should choose that particular moment to appear. He stepped into the opening in the wall at the other side of the large room and addressed them.

– I'm ready to begin.

He stepped back and vanished into the hallway and returned to his laboratory. They followed him there, glancing at each other.

– I've always found him strange, Energetic said.

– I have, too, the Bowman grinned.

It felt good to laugh a little.

– Haven't we all felt strange both to ourselves and to others?

Oracle didn't laugh.

They imagined they saw him in there, in his lab coat, before they actually entered the room filled with the buzzing machines.

Lady Grace joined them. Lucinda realized stunned that she had kept away during the worst of the emotional storm Gimmick had suffered.

He stood in front of the large monitor screen, facing them with a keyboard in his hand. They found their spots in his space. Gimmick could see fairly easily how his mind worked, the whirling mass of thoughts in there. She could also see what was on his mind, even though she couldn't quite grasp its meaning.

– Thank you for coming, he said. – I'm recording this, both for posterity and hopefully to help shed some light on the subject for everybody interested.

Some of them mumbled something unintelligible. Most stayed quiet. There was a sense of anticipation and apprehension present, also dancing in the air around Gimmick, as something she could almost reach out and grab.

– Many have speculated about the Great Darkness, Alan Prescott began, – speculated on its origin, on why and how and what. Many theories have been put forward… none of them very helpful or complete.

He pushed a key and the familiar images began playing out on the big screen behind him.

First there was the actual satellite footage and then the computer images, and then the actual footage again, slowed down, slowed down a lot. They could actually see how the darkness flowed across the Earth, embraced it like a living thing.

– It isn't instantaneous, Raven Bird cried, – but flows from one part of space to another.

– It does. Mechanic nodded. – It's also spreading. Computer models where all data is plotted in are more than suggesting that it originated from one single point in Space, one fairly close to Earth.

– A… hole or tear in Space somewhere, Flight Captain suggested.

– My, oh my, my Captain, Cougar flirted, – you are a nerd at heart, aren't you?

She looked very feral then, very sensual and even gorgeous. Most of her was covered in clothes, but it didn't matter. Gimmick knew the present males were more or less turned on, some in very fast and powerful ways.

There were giggles and chuckles.

They knew the good captain read a lot and he had also admitted to «quite a fondness for reading» before his powers had developed. Some laughed even harder in an effort to distract themselves from Cougar's advances.

Mechanic waited until the ruckus had faded and the room once more had turned quiet.

– That might be it, he agreed, – but will, until we find out more be only more conjecture. We might speculate that its point of origin was somewhere between Earth and the Sun, but we can't be certain. For all we know «It», whatever it is or was traveled a long way through space like a thin beam or something else entirely, before it suddenly «decided» to do whatever… it did.

He was patient, and they, his audience were, too. They knew he usually got to the point eventually.

– Persistent theories link the appearance, the actualization, the «switching on» of the Growth Gene to the Great Darkness… and I agree with that assumption. Even though there's no definite proof, and probably never will be, I find it unlikely that two such major paradigm shifts happen independently of each other. I see it as a boost, really, a supercharging of pre-existing conditions. There have been people with modest paranormal abilities on Earth for a long time, but the brief Blink that some people have described as «the longest second in their life», whatever it was or is made everyone with that potential far more powerful, increased it hundreds of times. Its dramatic social impact is obvious. What we have seen so far is nothing compared to what is ahead. One in a thousand seems like such a modest number, but that means there are one thousand enhanced individuals for every million, five thousand in Tobruk alone, seven million on Earth altogether. It matters little if only a few of us have powers or obvious, active powers, or if none of us had had any. Our visibility and added circumstances are sufficient. Every single individual with the Growth Gene has big children. It has become a dominant hereditary trait. We are a new order, a threat to *what was* by our very existence or nature. It doesn't matter that we aren't all of one mind or political inclination. We are here, and we need to address the arising problems in a sane and scientific manner no matter how bad the government's… grasp of the situation is or will be.

– You touched upon a very important point there, Lady Grace noted solemnly.

– You must be kidding me! Jolene cried and turned towards her.

– It is an explosive situation, Flight Captain countered her, – and we must contain it, both among ourselves and in society as a whole. We must be a standard to uphold, like the legendary Round Table of old.

– Oh, *please!* Oracle snarled.

Tempers flared again. Lady Grace and Gimmick both crouched. Gimmick bit her lip so hard that it started bleeding. That calmed them down again, but only to a point.

Lady Grace wiped sweat from her brow.

– Please continue, Mechanic, she stated softly, but with the foundation of authority present.

– Knowledge is power, Mechanic said. – By finding and/or understanding the origin of the situation we may be able to device a better strategy of dealing with its more… lasting effects.

He's so *slick*. He should be a damn politician.

Gimmick caught easily the stray thought from Oracle's usually so difficult to read mind.

– I still don't know the why and how and what. It has frustrated me beyond belief, but that is how things stand right now. Sometimes I fear we must invent an entire new science to even start on anything resembling an approximate of a satisfying explanation.

His words, his carefully worded speech showed how far his frustration went.

– I believe however that I've managed to find a new angle that may be helpful. Watch carefully, please.

There were more footage of people and streets, of traffic lights and people's eyes. The focus switched back and forth, back and forth. He showed them the flickering lights and frowns they hadn't seen before.

– I don't get it, the Bowman said. – We know both electronics and living beings showed unmistakable signs of reacting to it both before and after, but...

– This footage was recorded an entire month from the date in question, Mechanic told him, told them.

Gimmick realized that this was recorded on a cloudy day. There hadn't been a cloud in the sky on the day of the blink. They looked stunned at him, and each other, as more close-ups were added.

– I've found documentation in samples five months before and after. That was just a test, and I called you in immediately upon my discovery. So this is it, people, I'm confident if we seek further we will see ripples years both before and after the event itself, perhaps decades in advance and beyond. The Great Darkness clearly transcends time and space.

Silence claimed them all, before Martial Athlete finally spoke up.

– So, what is it doing right now?

– I can't tell. I can't even measure the damn thing directly. This is no known form of energy. It isn't dark energy or at least not «typical» dark energy, which we could have measured indirectly through gravity. There is no machine or method we know of that can even register it properly. It can clearly affect both organic life and electrical systems, so I made an extensive study in that direction first, but I found nothing substantial. My mind and its grasp have grown beyond any known previous existing parameters, but this one keeps eluding me in all important matters.

They had to smile a bit, by the ruthless exposure of both his prevalent arrogance and frustration.

– The «why» seems obvious, in light of... of us, of the result, doesn't it? Since it created paranormals it stands to reason that was the intention.

– Only if there is an intelligence behind it, Mechanic shrugged, – and it could still be an unintended and even undesired effect, a byproduct of something else. Perhaps something far more pronounced we haven't so far been able to observe has happened.

– An... intelligence, Flight Captain said stunned. – I hadn't even *considered* that.

The room seemed to turn colder, as most of those present seemed to shrink and fade and their surroundings changed into something completely unrecognizable.

– It has turned dark outside, Raven Bird said, rubbing her arms. – For a moment there I thought, I believed...

Everybody stayed put that night. There were no immediate pressing concerns to take care of, and that usually made most of them head back to their private homes, but they stayed and had low-keyed discussions among themselves, the unrest visible in wavering eyes.

– Either the culprit is a beyond mighty being we might not be able to comprehend or a seemingly new and totally unknown natural cosmic phenomenon, Jolene chuckled. – I must admit I find that thought amusing...

Most of the others didn't appreciate her wit.

People gathered around the table for the evening meal. It was more like another dinner, really, both in quantity and content. They started wolfing down the food in the usual unceremonious way, but there was more talk than during an ordinary dinner. No matter how much they had to chew they still managed to speak.

– It is a paradigm shift to end all paradigm shifts, Mechanic said admittedly. – Ten years ago it was hearsay and myth. Those propagating such things as facts were ridiculed and even harassed. Now, it's full-blown reality.

– And our lives have changed dramatically because of it, Lady Grace said, – for the better.

– My point is that we couldn't possibly dream that this would happen, Mechanic said, – and yet it did. It was like lightning from a blue sky, something far beyond statistic probability.

Everybody, as if on cue looked at Oracle.

– I've always had bad dreams, she shrugged, – just like Gimmick was empathic and intuitive, and Mechanic was smart.

– Honey, Raven Bird said, – that isn't exactly «just like», isn't exactly the same.

– Isn't it? Even though they've become more intense they are as confusing as ever, their... truth eluding me.

She frowned and didn't shrug this time. A haze seemed to cover her almond eyes.

172

– They've intensified further lately. There have been nights when I've been unable to fall asleep, as if there is a cloud of impending doom hanging over me. It has always been unpleasant, but now… It seems clear that someone will attack us, but I can't say whom. It's just a shadow standing there, by my bed. I can sleep with many people on the bed, but in my dream I'm always alone, and the shadow stare at me with cruel eyes and a vicious, triumphant smile on its lips.

She and Gimmick did the dishes that night. The others had completed their final visit to the toilet and retreated to their rooms. Gimmick could sense their uncertainty, the shiver occasionally passing through them. Everybody was, in one way or another marked by today's revelations, as if they somehow shared Oracle's night terrors.

– You will come with me tomorrow, won't you? She besieged Gimmick, as they prepared to go to bed.

– I'm still thinking about it, Lucinda replied, attempting levity.

– Please, the dark girl said, – I need you to come.

Her mind was as chaotic as ever, but there was an open anxiety at the base of that that hadn't really been noticeable before, at least not as anything but an unease in dreams and below the surface of the mind.

– I will! The big girl said.

Jolene embraced her, choked and kissed her on the lips, before pulling away with a relieved smile filled with gratitude. She walked to her room, visibly happier.

The door closed behind her, but her presence remained. Lucinda froze in the warm, twilight hallway.

We need to talk, little one.

Claudia's voice filled her head.

We do?

We need to dissuade our friend from moving forward with her plans. It's the wrong call and she will put us all in jeopardy. We must soften her ridiculous disrespect for authority, making her more susceptible to our arguments and aid her in the process of becoming a more harmonic and useful human being. It's about time.

NO! We can't do that.

We must. You know we must.

Lucinda bowed her head.

But why must I be a p-part of it? You could easily…

Her mind is an inaccessible quagmire. We need to work together on this one, little one. You are her friend. She trusts you. You, with my backing will be able to guide us into her innermost being.

Lucinda bowed her head more.

Of course.

Very good, little one...

Claudia appeared at the end of the hallway and walked silently towards her. They waited patiently until everything had become silent inside, and Lucinda sensed that the girl inside had fallen asleep.

They joined minds, preparing themselves, breathing even, before pushing gently into Jolene Masters' stormy mind. It was turbulent in there, more so than they had ever experienced in any person, even in schizophrenic minds. The surroundings battered them, but by supporting each other they managed to keep the worst at bay.

Will you look at that...

They saw themselves, saw the others and probabilities shift and change, as her psychic ability revealed itself to the... the intruders. Lucinda swallowed hard, instantly sensing Claudia's calming influence and instructions.

It's amazing, isn't it, how her power dominates her perception, her entire consciousness. It's almost as if that is all she is.

They saw her speak at the gathering, saw her raise her fist in anger, all of it very lifelike, almost as if they were there. Lucinda saw herself there, an active, dedicated supporter, standing behind the agitator, the powerful political radical shouting into the microphone.

Join with your image, your avatar, Claudia bid her.

Lucinda did as she was told. The scents, the sounds and sensations became even more pronounced and real.

You know what to do. Do so!

Jolene had hardly started speaking when Lucinda stopped her.

«This isn't right» she told her. «We need to think this through and come back with a better plan. I'm leaving».

«Don't leave», the dark girl begged her.

«I must».

The crowd had turned silent and looked stunned at them. The tall and big blonde stepped down from the platform. The last she saw before leaving Coleman Square was the doe-eyed vulnerable girl staring at her back.

Gimmick, Raven Bird and Oracle were on their way to Coleman Square to participate in the protests. At some point Lucinda and Lisa glanced at each other and stopped in their tracks. Jolene stopped and looked at them in despair.

«This isn't right» Lucinda told her. «We need to think this through and come back with a better plan. There will be other protests».

«I agree», Lisa said. «Lady Grace has the right idea. We need to hold back

174

and not push so hard».

«Don't do this. Please»!

«Come with us», Lisa said. «Give me your hand».

And Lisa changed to Claudia.

«No», Jolene's avatar choked.

– No, Jolene mumbled on the bed.

«Come on», Gimmick said, «don't be such a girl. There is work to be done for the strong and powerful in this world».

Jolene choked, hesitated for a few more moments before reaching out her hand, before letting both Lady Grace and Gimmick grab her and whisk her away.

«No more bullshit», Lady Grace told her. «From now on we will tell you what to do and you will do it. Do you understand, little one»?

«Yes, Claudia», Jolene whispered.

– Yes, Claudia, Jolene whispered.

«You will be a dedicated soldier in our war, eager to perform to my expectations and design».

Statement and response repeated itself several times. More scenarios played themselves out, all with the same decisive result, removing Jolene ever more from her point of origin, tying her stronger to Claudia and especially Lucinda, with a stronger affinity, a bond long since established.

Gimmick and Lady Grace pulled out. The girl on the bed fell into a deep sleep. Claudia looked pleased at Lucinda, petting her cheek.

I think that was a qualified success. It's hard to tell, of course, before the result reveals itself, but we rocked her world in excellent ways, played on her insecurities and showed her the better path. She won't remember more than the usual confusing sensations, but the instructions and education will hopefully stick and stick deep. Well done, little one.

A final pat on the cheek and Claudia left her alone, there, in the dark.

They had breakfast the next morning.

– Today is the big day, Raven Bird grinned at Oracle.

– Yeah, I guess, Jolene said a little defensive, strangely reluctant.

Raven Bird looked a little closer at her.

– I can understand if you're a little tense. Things might turn ugly out there.

– It might, Jolene agreed.

She frowned, before continuing her ravenous feeding.

– You've started feeding harder lately, Raven Bird said, – putting on weight.

Jolene looked confused at her.

– I have?

– Yes, most definitely, Lisa grinned. – I can see such things, honey.

– I guess you've finally decided to catch up with the rest of us, the Bowman joked.

– She isn't taller, is she? Lady Grace inquired and studied the girl carefully.

– Not yet, no, Raven Bird mused, – but I would guess it's only a matter of time. I've seen it happen with others. Because she's a late bloomer, it will probably happen very fast, an explosive growth, instead of the after all fairly slow transformation most big people went through.

– Mechanic will do a check up on you, pronto, Lady Grace told Oracle. – If your Change can happen anytime we must be reasonably sure it doesn't happen today.

– Okay, Jolene shrugged, and added: – I agree, actually.

The others exhaled in relief. They had feared it would turn ugly between the two women.

But both seemed very reasonable today.

Jolene, usually the last to the toilets rushed there as one of the first.

– I can see it happen, you know, the Bowman grinned lewd to Gimmick. – She starts growing right there in the crowd and bursts out of her clothes.

Lucinda gave him an elbow in the ribs, straining to hold back. She wanted to strike him, wanted to strike him hard, and the catching in her throat threatened to strangle her.

Don't worry, little one, Lady Grace assured her. We didn't do this to her. She has moved towards her destiny for quite some time, now, you know that. Soon, she will be far more useful to us.

Jolene stepped back into the room. Lucinda felt her eyes on her, but when she turned and briefly glanced at the dark girl Oracle stood with her back to her.

– I would like to join you in the lab, Raven Bird told Mechanic when Jolene approached him. – There should be a medical doctor there, too.

– I thought you would never ask. He shrugged. – Would you both come with me, please?

I didn't ask, Gimmick heard in Lisa's mind, but the brown-skinned woman didn't voice her venom.

Gimmick wanted to follow them, too, but she remained, and tailed them on the crippled wings of her mind.

It was easy latching on to Lisa. She had done so before.

Mechanic worked quickly with Oracle. He strapped her to one of his tables and put virtually every single piece of equipment to work. Gimmick knew he had been waiting for this moment, this opportunity for a long time.

The machinery hummed and buzzed. Oracle writhed on the slab, clearly more than a bit uncomfortable. Mechanic ignored her. She gritted her teeth

176

when one of the needles penetrated too deep.

– You're hurting her, Raven Bird cried.

– We're measuring her reaction to adversity, Mechanic replied calmly. – The transformation has been known to occur frequently in prolonged moments of stress.

She strained in the harness. It was a kind of fabric, but evidently incredibly durable. She was able to stretch her bonds to a certain point, but not break them.

– Don't move, he instructed her.

She stopped moving. He nodded pleased and set a needle in her arm. Her arm began twitching almost immediately. She cried out in pain.

– It… hurts, she gasped.

– It's supposed to, he admonished. – Lie still!

She tried, but her body started moving of its own volition. It writhed there on the slab, and she was merely a victim of its whims.

Look at her, Claudia spat, how compliant and eager to serve she has become, and only one day after the first treatment. Mechanic is the authority in the lab and she knows that, knows he is to be obeyed. Her nasty streak is gone and her silly bouts of rebellion are brought under control. You did good, little one.

Jolene screamed. Everybody shook in discomfort. Gimmick shuddered.

Everybody sagged in relief when the loud wailing finally stopped, when Mechanic let her loose. It dawned on Gimmick that she had shared her experience with everybody and not even realized it. She looked at Claudia. The woman didn't look angry at all, but rather pleased. She wanted everyone to know, to learn discipline, regimentation.

Go to her, little one.

Jolene rose from the table on shaky legs. She sought Raven Bird's embrace, her comforting proximity. They both looked at Mechanic through a film of tears.

– There's a curious physiology involved, Mechanic said. – You're storing energy and mass for the transformation to make the transition easier. I suspect there is an evolutionary adaptation of some kind at work. I don't believe it's possible to induce the chance by stimuli, though. I'm afraid it's bound to happen during a dangerous, real life situation.

Gimmick entered the room and walked to her. She sought her friend's close comfort. Lucinda held around her and patted her head.

– You're an amazing case, you know, Mechanic said in wonder. – Amazing! I look forward to study you further as your physiological and cerebral changes progress.

Lisa, Lucinda and Jolene stumbled out, side by side, supporting each other. Lucinda instinctively entered her mind in order to calm her, to soothe her fears, but the very act of touching her mind hurt. There was pure chaos in there.

– I just waited for him to put the c-collar around my n-neck, she whispered in Lucinda's ear. – He wants to do it, wants it so bad. I see him, see him put it around many a slender neck.

Lucinda wanted to say something, anything, but her effort was interrupted. Lady Grace stopped in front of them.

– How do you feel? She asked curtly.

– I'm okay. Jolene straightened before the imposing figure, pulling free from the two supporting her. – I feel fine!

– Very good, the big woman smiled. – There might be tougher material somewhere in there, after all.

– Yes, the dark girl echoed.

– Go and clean yourself up.

– Yes, ma'am.

There was laughter. The others believed she was being ironic, being her usual caustic and funny self, but Lucinda wasn't so sure.

Jolene stumbled towards the bathroom. Lady Grace called the attention of everybody else present.

– We're heading for harsh times. We all need to be at our best. There is no room for slackers anymore.

Everybody nodded with wide eyes and serious expressions painted on their rigid faces.

Jolene didn't spend that much time in the bathroom. When she returned from there she had fixed herself up, and looked more like her old self.

– Come, she said to Gimmick and Raven Bird, – let's go.

She turned her back on them and they followed her with a concerned look in wavering eyes.

The portal buzzed far stronger than usual when its creator approached it. The pale shadow spread and seemed to fill the hall.

The three of them stepped through, and one moment later they found themselves in the city centre. Hundreds of minds touched Gimmick the first second, thousands more the next.

– I'm okay. Oracle spoke up before her two friends did. – I'm also okay with what Lady Asshole made Mechanic do to me. Her reasoning is sound and there was a change the treatment could have enhanced my powers, and we need that, need more power badly.

Raven Bird giggled. Gimmick didn't.

– Torture, you mean torture right? The black woman snarled.

– Yes, Jolene Masters said curtly.

– Are you sure everything is okay, honey? Lisa wondered. – And I don't mean only Lady Asshole and Mechanic's new low today, but the fact that you haven't been quite yourself lately.

They all stopped, as if on cue.

– It's the bad dreams, Oracle said, frowning. – They've taken a turn for the worse. I see a creature. Gimmick has seen it, seen *her*, too, occasionally, through my mind...

– I have, Lucinda said, – since the day I met you.

The dark girl turned to her and held her in her gaze, as she sometimes did. Gimmick couldn't move.

– And how did the sight of her make you feel?

– Bad, Lucinda said. – I've felt a growing sense of terror and menace beyond belief.

– And you can multiply that with what I feel during the worst visions, Jolene cried. – She's tall and big and beyond cruel and powerful, unlike anything we've faced before. Sometimes it feels like she's... showing off for me, that she *knows* I'm watching her. I get the impression that she allows me to see her, as if she can keep me from doing it if she so desires.

– But how is that possible? Lisa wondered. – Does she have the same powers you have?

– Whatever powers she possesses are far greater than mine, virtually... godlike. Sometimes I'm not even hundred percent certain It is a woman, but more like an... an entity, a disembodied, formless spirit of some kind.

She searched for words in an attempt to describe the indescribable.

Saying there was a chill in the hot sunshine wasn't in any way sufficient. The chill grabbed them and pierced every slice of their being.

Jolene touched her temple and crouched a bit.

– Oh, no!

She sighed, alleviating the others' dread a bit. They looked stunned at her when she chuckled.

– Amazing...

She shook her head. Gimmick grinned, too, as she easily enough read Oracle's mind. She couldn't help herself.

– What *is* it? Raven Bird said. – Spill!

– It's our old friend, the Catcher. He has escaped, or is about to escape from prison...

– But how?

Gimmick smiled, suddenly very amused, the catching in her throat lessening a little.

– His collar will malfunction… has malfunctioned, and off he goes.

– That *is* amazing, Raven Bird acknowledged. – But is this guy really our problem? And how come you see him all the time and not many of the other, far more dangerous… villains?

– You know, that is a good question, Gimmick said, allowing the warm feeling inside to wash off the sense of dread and worthlessness dominating her since last night. – I guess he is a danger, for ordinary policemen, is disgusting for the victims he picks, his preferences for robbing poor people, but we have far greater concerns to deal with.

Oracle gasped and crouched, turning pale as they watched.

– I see him.

They looked good humored at her, used to as they were with her more or less cryptic statements and slow explanations.

They stood there, seemingly at the center of the hot sunlight, and then the shadow grew and embraced them.

– I see him with her, with the Black Dragon. He kneels before her, as her devoted servant.

– The Black *Dragon?* Raven Bird said stunned.

– That's her name… I think. I see a drawing of one, on paper, on skin, on many arms. That's why I see him. He is important to her, or connected to her, somehow, or he will be. I don't know, okay, I just know that we *need* to keep him behind bars.

Lucinda looked at her on the verge of tears, on the verge of confessing everything.

– Are you sure?

Speaking those three words felt like a monumental effort.

– What do you mean I am sure? Jolene said incredulous. – You usually take my word for it, and this time I'm far more certain than I usually am. The specific reason eludes me, but the importance of acting on the vision doesn't. It's the first time I see her while being fully awake, and in such detail. It *must* mean something.

– I'm sorry, Lucinda whispered, – but it hasn't exactly been the best of mornings.

The three of them shared a soft, sore smile.

They looked towards Coleman Square. Gimmick heard the commotion and passion there in her mind.

– You should be there. She turned towards her friend. – You should *be* there!

– There will be other meetings. Jolene shrugged. – We have a more

180

important task today. Come!

She rushed off in the opposite direction. Raven Bird followed her. Gimmick choked inside and lingered a moment, before she did as well.

They rushed back to the portal and jumped through it. Now, when the decision had been made Oracle was clearly anxious to get on with the chosen task. When they appeared on the other side, close to Folson penitentiary she kept rushing forward, towards the prison gate.

There was only one visible guard in a booth at the one and only entrance. Gimmick sensed many more minds and eyes directed at them from the many watchtowers further inside.

– Hi, Oracle smiled sweetly to the sentry, a smile hiding the anxiety boiling within, – we don't have an appointment, but we have important and urgent business in your pleasant abode.

He looked like one giant question mark, but he grabbed the phone and called the warden.

The warden spoke to him, told him the guests would be granted access «after sweating in the sun for a while». Gimmick heard him through the guard's mind and she knew that Oracle had her ways of hearing that, too.

It was hot out here. Gimmick couldn't help but succumbing a bit to the heat's ravages. The mask felt like a pressure cooker and she wanted to dry her brow, what was covered in fabric. She found herself regretting that she hadn't cut off the mask's top. At the very least that.

– We don't have time for this bullshit, Oracle cried, suddenly uncharacteristically impatient and anxious. – We believe the Catcher has escaped or is in the process of escaping.

The sarcastic, angry voice on the phone fell silent.

Less than a minute later they were taken on a guided tour. The outside path of barbed wire gave way to gloomy prison hallways. The walls seemed to bulge and lean on them. As they approached the cell blocks Gimmick and Oracle felt ever stronger the dulled minds of the prisoners. It was like a presence surrounding them, and they couldn't keep themselves from revealing their discomfort and apprehension and the three-man honor guard didn't even try hiding their glee.

– All of you freaks belong here, the way I see it, one of them hissed.

And the hissing in Gimmick's mind was far more unpleasant.

He feels like a wet cloth, doesn't he?

Jolene's growing anger also hurt Lucinda's mind.

What do you think creeps like him do to our kind in this place?

The warden met them at the main gate leading to the particular cell block.

– So, where does your information come from? He asked, very smug, without introduction.

– He's still here? Gimmick asked, cutting off Oracle before she could respond.

– The prisoner is under video surveillance 24/7, he confirmed, – and I checked on him before I left my office.

– May we see him? Oracle asked, her voice noticeably rising.

– Sure, why not, it isn't as if I can't waste even more time today.

Lucinda felt his mind like a slug touching hers. Bile rose in her throat.

He was the lord of the castle, the master of all he surveyed and he enjoyed it immensely. She felt very vulnerable, as they, escorted by an even heavier honor guard moved ever deeper into his domain.

– This one is indeed a troublemaker, he grunted, – but easily handled thanks to the invention of that genius of yours. Those handy collars should be mandatory for all of you lot…

He emphasized the word «troublemaker» and stared pointedly at Oracle.

Gimmick didn't exactly feel better because she, for the time being avoided the brunt of his venom.

Oracle didn't seem too concerned and brushed him off, deliberately ignoring him, but Gimmick, upon casually probing her found that she remained shaken, murky bundles of anxiety and confusion.

Raven Bird was also testy, anxious in their hostile surroundings.

Lucinda shook when another door slammed shut behind them.

All the dulled consciousnesses surrounded her sensitive mind. She imagined they were ganging up on her, fearing that their accusing stares would cut her open and expose her shivering insides.

Jolene grabbed her hand and squeezed it gently, telling her that everything would be all right, making her feel even worse.

Troy Franklin - the Catcher sat incarcerated in solitary confinement. That made Gimmick frown.

– He merits… special treatment?

The prison had so many inmates that most of them, by necessity were kept in groups in big rooms. Only a few could be kept in solitary containment simultaneously.

– Not really. He's scum, like the rest of them, but not particularly so. We have them on a rotating system and give them closer attention when their number is pulled out of the hat.

She knew what that special attention meant, what it signified. She shrugged it off, like she shrugged off Jolene's soft touch.

The cell door was massive. It was held in place and opened by enormous bolts and electronic locks.

He sat in there, his eyes staring at nothing. The door swung open and she saw with her eyes what her mind had seen seconds earlier.

– Reduce the output of the collar, Oracle snapped.

The warden did as she told him to do. Gimmick sensed how Franklin's mind practically woke up from its slumber. Franklin was able to reason again, even though his power was still inaccessible.

– My three pretty birds, he said hoarsely.

In that brief sentence she sensed all his hatred and rage and passion.

She frowned and then looked startled at him, and Jolene noticed easily what she hid behind an indifferent mask.

What is it, honey?

I just realized that I've never seen his face before, not even on mug shots, except as swollen collections of meatballs and that I still know how he looks like.

Images assaulted her, of him, during their previous encounters, of his mask.

It's just your memory working in conjunction with your telepathy, interpreting patterns of complexity. You're getting better at it, both consciously and subconsciously. We're all growing.

And by that thought she became aware of the process, practically saw how the patterns of complexity weaved themselves in her mind. The bloody face she had seen and the features behind the mask moved and reset, until his present face presented itself to her.

– Hola, Troy, Oracle greeted him casually, slipping into her Jaynagar Mexican-English accent, – how are you? Any plans for an extended vacation lately?

– Sure, he shrugged, – this is no place for a human being, right?

She was on him in a rush, grabbing his throat, lifting him up like he was a feather.

– I asked you a *question,* asshole!

He stared right into what appeared like a creature from a nightmare. Lucinda knew that and got the shakes. He attempted desperately to reply, but the squeeze around his throat prevented that.

– One change, chico, Jolene said softly, – before we start on you.

He shook and looked very human to Lucinda just then. Everybody present knew the inmates had no rights and that the warden would just enjoy it if they started going tough on the prisoner, that it couldn't really compete with the ongoing abuse the prisoners suffered.

– No plans! He cried. – There is no way out of this hellhole, with this cursed collar dragging you down like a stone in water. You know that, right, right, *bitch?*

Oracle didn't have to look at Gimmick to see her shake her head.

He's telling the truth, Lucinda confirmed.

Jolene showed no outward emotion, but in her mind she shook her head in bewilderment.

I was so sure.

– Looks like we were wasting your time today. Gimmick turned towards the warden, giving him her sweetest smile behind the mask. – We're very sorry.

– Don't feel too bad about it on my account, the warden grinned. – I enjoy seeing the shitheads getting roughed up, no matter how little. Looks like some of you people might be good Americans, after all.

He wasn't being ironic, right? Raven Bird wondered, as the three of them were escorted back to the outside, to the real world.

Not in any way I could detect, Gimmick replied, deliberately shrugging in a useless attempt to prevent her friends from noticing the shiver passing through her body and mind.

They removed themselves from the prison. The vast collection of buildings kept towering above them, no matter how far away they walked.

– I was so *sure!* Jolene cried. – What's *wrong* with me?

And then Lucinda imagined that her friend might be way too distraught to sense the emotion of others, after all.

– Today was a mud day, she shrugged. – It happens, right?

– It happens, Jolene agreed. – Tomorrow will bring nothing but clarity.

– Clarity, Lucinda echoed, the catching in her throat not giving her any rest.

The world faded away, as they stepped into the ebony portal, and they were all ripped further apart by the ongoing tidal forces striking them.

Chapter 11

On the press conference on the day they returned from Jagadir:

They gathered on the stage behind the classic stable of microphones usually reserved for heads of state and successful athletes.

– Good afternoon, Lady Grace greeted the journalists. – I will read a brief statement and then we will all be available for your questions.

She dominated the hall. They awaited her word, her sacrament.

– After prolonged frustration with the way the United States and the world's governments handled or didn't handle the ongoing and worsening Jagadir atrocity we decided to act decisively in the matter. After careful planning we acted alone and without any other sanction than our conscience to terminate the horror we've seen unfold the last ten years in a tyranny perceived as «one of our friends and staunchest allies» to quote our Commander in Chief. Our operation was an unqualified success. The Jagadir government and the entire hierarchy supporting it has been removed and supplanted by a democratic and benevolent system.

She kept it going quite a bit, working them all and not holding back anything. Gimmick sensed and picked up how she modified their perception and mood and even thoughts to accommodate her purpose and desires.

They would be useful tools to further her agenda.

– You have, technically speaking broken the law, a hardnosed journalist commented. – Do you expect any reaction from US law-enforcement or authorities?

– Not really, Lady Grace shrugged. – So far we have only heard good things, unofficially, of course…

– We are, as always at the disposal of the authorities at all times, Flight Captain interjected. – We will aid them, whatever they would want to ask us or want from us.

A warm, warm glow burned within Gimmick and the others when they saw how their leaders handled the hungry mob, how they made them eat from their hands.

The questions turned less aggressive, more non-threatening, to mundane matters fairly quickly.

– Why do you call yourself Gimmick?

– Well, she grinned, pondering the question a little. – I do use gimmicks, and it sounded right at the time.

Laughter, pleasant and favorable.

And so on.

It ended in laughter and on pleasant notes, and that stayed with the Maverick Crew as they pulled back, temporarily leaving the limelight they would never more leave.

Lucinda and Melinda returned to the apartment. They chose the route Lucinda usually used, both using their enhanced senses to scan for people, but sensing no one. Prolonged scanning revealed no threat or anything even reminding of one. They changed into civilian clothes and walked home.

Big Sister scanned Kid Sister, as they walked, as she stopped before the mirror in the hallway and looked at herself.

– We really showed them, didn't we?

The laughter, harder, accentuated was that of an adult, not a child or an adolescent.

– I feel like we have been away for ages.

The apartment looked eerie to Lucinda as well. It hadn't changed any more than Melinda's physical appearance, but still seemed different.

– We showed the world, Lucinda finally said.

The office at work the next morning seemed changed, too. She sort of recognized her coworkers, but at whatever angle she studied them they didn't look the same.

– Great holiday, Patterson? Tracy Longhorn cried.

– One for the record books, Lucinda replied, deliberately shaking her hips for the staring males admiring her new, fashionable killer suit and skirt.

She had to walk the entire gauntlet to her stall at the end of the office. Anonymity had never been an option for her here.

Never been desired, she thought.

She lingered by the water cooler, swallowing huge amounts of water, kind of surprised when the need to pee didn't assault her instantly.

The males' interest turned her on, but not excessively so. Her need burned on a pleasantly low flame she could easily manage.

Their thoughts weren't exactly transparent to her, only their desires, but all it took was a little focus on one of them, and she was there, cruising the thoughts of another person.

She noticed the need in her bladder the moment she was about to sit down and rushed off to the toilet, noting, glancing at her watch that she still had a few minutes to spare. The hall and the restroom were empty, which was a relief. Something was distracting her. She practically moved on autopilot when she walked into the stall, when she pulled up her skirt and pulled down her panties and sat down on the bowl. It hurt, like it always did when the piss resembling soup flowed from her hole. She hadn't drunk enough water.

186

Carter Morricombe waited for her in the hall with what she perceived as a sleazy grin.

– Great holiday, Lucinda? He smirked.

– An excellent holiday, Carter, she replied.

She realized they were alone, well outside normal hearing range and that he had even closed the door. A quick probe confirmed that no one listened in. She straightened, both subconsciously and deliberately posing for him. It wasn't hard seeing herself through his eyes, wasn't hard at all.

He didn't exactly stare, but still had his entire attention fixed on her. She sensed desire, of course, but most of all possessiveness and several other undefined emotions.

– You've just returned from Jagadir, I take it? He smirked.

She just looked patronizing at him, not giving away anything.

– It took me a while to figure out which one of them you are. There are, after all dozens of potential candidates and you could have worn a wig in your other identity.

– You're not seriously «accusing» me of being a costumed vigilante, are you, Carter?

He reddened, but didn't give.

– I still wasn't sure when I saw Gimmick in Jagadir, he breathed, – but when I checked with your sister's school and was informed that she was gone, too, everything fell into place. I saw the both of you side by side, and there wasn't any doubt left in my mind.

Desire had always been easy to read and now, more than ever. Roaming his mind hardly represented a challenge and neither did the little pulling and pushing she performed.

– So, Carter, what were you going to tell me?

His expression had changed completely from only seconds ago. He frowned and frowned harder.

– Tell you? He gawked.

– I had the impression you were awfully eager about something, she said softly.

She challenged him deliberately, feeling so good about it, about it all.

– What should that be? He blinked confused.

– There is nothing then?

– Nothing, he nodded.

– You didn't follow me here, then, did you?

– No, he shook his head, – certainly not!

– Good, she smirked, – then I guess I'll see you later. Work waits for no man or woman, you know.

– Right, he nodded, clearly shamed, but unable to tell why.

– Good boy.

She passed him on her way back, not close, not avoiding him in any way. He made no attempt at grabbing her or taking advantage of anything. She kept roaming his mind to see if he had shared his suspicion and venture with anyone, but he hadn't. He had wanted her all to himself.

When the work began she probed everybody, but no one harbored thoughts similar to cute, slimy Carter.

Work was easy that day, no matter how boring it had become. She was laughing a lot. The others glanced at her with envy, but couldn't truly fathom her good mood. How could they?

She was still chuckling when she met Melinda in the afternoon, when eyes met eyes and sisters nodded in mutual understanding.

– Look at you, Big Sister whistled, – you're beautiful.

They both wore their pink dresses. Kid Sister blushed.

She had worn the dress before, they both had, but there was a new kind of confidence in the two pairs of eyes.

– You look like you're in a good mood, Melinda said sheepishly.

– I thought I knew the people at work… my «co-workers», and I did. I just didn't know how well I truly knew them. They're exactly as small-minded and ignorant as I envisioned.

– They don't know, Melinda said softly, – cannot know the world as we do.

They headed into the fairly less crowded parts of Downtown. Lucinda kept shaking her head in wonder.

– Casual mind reading has become a simple task. It's easy, now, what was so hard before. By focusing on a single person I can read that person's thoughts, really do it. Is this it? Was all it took a little intense fighting and bloodshed? Is this what Jolene never had the pleasure of experiencing?

Somber thoughts visited them again by the touch of sadness they shared.

They headed over the street, towards the inconspicuous building ahead. Lucinda noticed the changes, subtle and major instantly. The sign above the door proudly proclaimed:

THE GREAT DARKNESS CENTER
FOR BIG PEOPLE

– Now, that's subtlety, Melinda giggled.

Several people arrived at the same time as the two sisters. Lucinda recognized Lois and a few others. Melinda rushed forward and rang the bell.

The door opened before she had spoken a single syllable. Everybody went inside. The door closed silently behind them. For some reason that gave Lucinda the willies.

Greetings and new names were exchanged. The nervous energy from the last visit had diminished, even though it wasn't gone.

– I knew instantly that this was your sister, of course, Lois grinned.

She looked much calmer, also to Lucinda's enhanced and extrasensory perception. Lucinda noted a harmony, or at least something passing like one that hadn't been there the last time they met.

All of them walked up the staircase to the next floor. That door was open this time.

– I can't believe it's only a month since the last time I was here, Lucinda said to Melinda, slipping a bit, forgetting herself. – So much has happened.

– It feels like forever, Lois declared.

And didn't really understand what the other was talking about.

What Lucinda saw in the older woman's thoughts was very ordinary, prosaic.

When they walked into the waiting room she noticed that a mechanism kept the door from closing.

The waiting room was practically full. Lucinda counted twenty women, including the recent arrivals.

The mechanism stopped working. The door closed. A chill passed through Lucinda. Striving hard to hide her bewilderment she wondered what could possibly be threatening about this place, and what had changed to make it more threatening compared to the occasional low-level sense of menace she had sensed the last time.

Melinda noticed, through their light rapport. Lucinda scolded herself.

Miriam appeared in the other, open door, the one leading to the inner workings of the building. There had been no waiting to speak of since the last few had arrived.

Lucinda scanned her, made a deep scan and Miriam was exactly as before. There was nothing there, nothing suspicious or even approaching suspicious.

– Good evening, good people, Miriam greeted them. – Welcome.

An excited buzz of both minds and voices rose to return her happy greeting.

– Follow me, please.

Lucinda scanned everybody on the premises, «patients» and employees alike. There was nothing or nothing she could pick up. Her thoughts drifted back, to the image she had seen in Jolene's mind and the invasive, beyond powerful mind that had assaulted her not that long ago. The shiver almost turned into a shake.

She relented and shared it with Melinda before Kid Sister grew too inquisitive. And then both sisters sensed the elephant feet walk down their spine.

I've been thinking...

Melinda formed cohesive thoughts for the telepath to pick up. Lucinda looked at her, resisting the urge to turn nasty.

Your unrest might not have anything to do with this place at all. Perhaps you still retain your rapport with Jolene, no matter how well hidden she might be, no matter what deplorable hellhole she is held captive. The two of you... were close. Perhaps she is still alive in a place no ordinary sensors can reach her.

Lucinda didn't trust any of her «voices» and didn't voice a reply. She nodded and fortunately Melinda seemed content with that.

The twenty big females followed Miriam into the pleasant living room, the informal classroom. They sat down in the nice, big chairs and directed their attention at the only woman standing.

– Once again, let me wish you the warmest possible welcome to your first official day here at The Great Darkness Center for Big People.

– Hear, hear, Lois cried, and several others joined her, while Lucinda studied it all.

– The classes won't be settled for a few days yet, until a few necessary procedures have been completed. Miriam gave them a professional smile. – But I can say one thing to you: Our situation has changed dramatically for the better since we last met and we all know why.

– The Maverick Crew's incursion into Jagadir, Myra stated.

– Precisely. Miriam acknowledged her with something resembling an excited snap of the fingers. – One can say much about the moral and legal validity of it, but it has led to an improved status for big people everywhere. We, here at the center noticed immediately how the commercial possibilities picked up, how several potential investors became more inclined to contribute and for advertisers to buy our products. With increased revenues in the works, we will be even better equipped to help all Big People.

– There are noticeably fewer assholes throwing insults at us on the streets these days, Jasmine nodded.

Lucinda began to feel... excited. Words and more began churning within her, rising from some primordial sea. She felt it, and the catching in her throat became noticeable, pronounced. Melinda looked at her again, but now she was smiling, and Lucinda shook her head in bewilderment.

– We will begin with testing you, Miriam said, – testing you extensively, physically, psychologically. I must warn you: there will be needles...

The laughter followed easily. Melinda's were loud and strong, and Lucinda's rose a few notches.

– And lots of paperwork, Myra groaned a while later.

And more laughter commenced.

They sat in enclosed stalls and crossed off choices on various questionnaires. Lucinda attempted to concentrate on the questions, but it was all a blur to her. There was a loud crack. She realized stunned that she had struck the table in front of her and split it in two.

Everybody stared at her. Miriam approached from a distant point at the opposite side of the room.

– S-sorry, Lucinda gasped, turning a deep red, feeling the immense, dark dread coming on.

– Don't worry. Miriam grinned with a comforting touch on the other woman's cheek. – Let's say such… material disasters aren't exactly unexpected.

And Lucinda felt comforted. The warm laughter, the touch and the kind words all did that.

And she woke up, as if from a dream, and was happy she did.

What happened? Melinda asked, a little anxious behind the bubble of laughter.

I… don't know, Lucinda replied. I guess I am more than a bit emotional these days.

The anniversary of Jolene's… disappearance is coming up, Kid Sister noted.

The second anniversary and even Melinda's inner voice had that sore catching in her throat. It had affected them all.

It is, Big Sister noted.

The final questionnaire she read, after she had sat down by an undamaged desk concerned liability, employment benefits and duties and was basically a contract.

It wasn't anything that Miriam hadn't covered in her review, though. Lucinda was just glad she would sign it with a clear head.

Even as the unrest persisted.

She signed the contract in a quick, decisive movement.

Melinda did so right afterwards. Lucinda cosigned Kid Sister's papers as her guardian. Everybody signed and left the papers at Miriam's desk.

– Very good, Miriam said to them. – I hope you're all pleased with your decision. We want you to be. As explained, enthusiasm is a major part of what we do here.

– I think I speak for us all when I say that your terms are more than generous, Lois said, – and that that comes on top of the kindness and understanding you've met us with.

Everybody echoed her sentiment. Lucinda found herself doing so as well.

They were brought to the combined gym and laboratory. They would discover that almost everything was a part of the laboratory here, again, just like Miriam had told them in the briefing.

The words GUINEA PIGS flashed before Lucinda's inner eye.

They changed to training gear in a dressing room. Some of those present looked down in shame.

– In less than a month you will all look like goddesses in those tight clothes, Miriam swore. – Don't you dare feel ashamed of yourself.

They ran on the treadmill with all kinds of wires attached to their bodies. Those wires stayed attached no matter where in the room they moved. When Lucinda lifted weights she saw how colored lights flashed on the board not far away.

– More, Miriam urged her when she started tiring. – Much more.

Lucinda wasn't exactly used to being pushed, not even from Claudia. She had usually exercised at her own pace and desired level. Now, she was being pushed beyond her comfort zone, at least as much as the others. There were other female trainers around, but Miriam walked around the room, visiting all the new recruits with her insistent demands. Lucinda began feeling the strain. Her muscles hurt. Stars began decorating her vision. She noticed that Miriam glanced at the nearest control board and monitors now and then, how her eyes lit up in interest. Then Lucinda hardly saw anything, anymore, except the cacophony of colored stars and mist. The weights fell down and would most certainly have harmed her, if not for the safety measures put in place in order to keep accidents from happening.

– Again, Miriam said, way too soon, and everybody groaned.

The weights had, after a few initial rounds been adapted to each person's strength. Lucinda lifted far more than the rest, except for Lois. Lois was clearly the physically strongest of them all.

They had trouble finding weights heavy enough for her and had to bring some from the male gym.

Lucinda noticed how she reveled in it all, how she thrived.

Melinda did, too. She could finally play and have fun with her peers without a mask and be very close to throw caution to the wind. It was evident just by looking at her.

Miriam sent them all through a hard, beyond hard series of hurdles.

– C'mon, girls, she shouted, – this isn't like the military. You don't need to suffer through mud and moors. Let's make en *effort,* now. Show me what you're made of.

She joined them and overtook them easily, led them to strain themselves even further. Lucinda made a real effort to keep up with her, but couldn't do it.

They stood before the coach afterwards with their palms on their knees, gasping for breath, all muscles in their body screaming. Miriam looked just as fresh.

– Again, she snapped. – Give me everything you've got.

They groaned, but there was laughter beneath, and that, in turn encouraged Lucinda. She led on, through the maze, in a haze of exhaustion and bright and dark colors.

Time stretched out into forever. She reached the end of the maze, again, again and again, until Miriam, taking pity on her poor charges finally signed for them to stop.

Lucinda stood there, slowly recuperating, watching as the others reached the end of the trail (and their ropes).

Melinda stumbled, straightened and stumbled again, until she cried out and fell just before completing her run. Lucinda felt a little woozy herself, but rushed to her sister.

It was like she was blacking out for a moment and Lucinda felt like she was blacking out, too, but then they both stared at each other with something akin to calm in their eyes.

– What happened? Melinda wondered weakly.

– You fell, Lucinda enlightened her, fighting to keep a casual tone in her voice.

– I know that, Melinda reproached Big Sister.

Lucinda helped her on her feet. Melinda kindly but decisively freed herself from Big Sister's grip.

– You're not used to exerting yourselves, pushing yourselves beyond endurance, Miriam said softly. – Not so strange then that there will be side effects. We are on uncharted territory here, after all…

She paused a bit, before completing her line of reasoning:

– Isn't it *exciting?*

More chuckles rose from sore throats, making sore limbs even sorer.

– And now, my fair-looking students the rewards are here. Follow me, please.

They did. There was merely a short walk into the dresser room.

– Most people would now take a shower and than have the feast, but since we are not like other people we won't do that. If we did we would have to shower twice, so we will feed first, then empty ourselves of shit before cleaning ourselves and dress properly.

– A wise turn of events, Jasmine grinned. – The stench after shitting makes a proper cleansing downright mandatory. I can't recall all the times my working buddies have chastised me for stinking after a visit or three to the restroom.

– I have been fired more than once because of that, Myra said sourly.

But amazingly, there was a grin lurking in the corner of her mouth as well.

They removed the clothes stinking of sweat, dried themselves a bit and dressed themselves in casual clothing provided by the center.

Everybody glanced at each other with a lingering smile on their lips, as they approached the long table burgeoning with culinary delights. They sat down and began feeding without further ado. Miriam joined them, just as filled with visible, ravenous Hunger.

Lucinda heard, or imagined she heard a piano somewhere. It made her pause in her gorging, made her listen for what might not be there. When she continued her munching it was still there.

They were shitting, dumping huge loads of shit into the overgrown toilet bowls. The stench kept bothering her, no matter how distracted she became.

Steam filled the shower room, one with a size equaling that of the toilets. Her arse was sore, it always was, but it felt so good to clean it up immediately after pushing all that acid shit through it.

And no matter how distracted she was, she kept her attention on all the big bodies around her.

When they were drying themselves, almost without the previously so present shame, she walked to Miriam, deliberating touching the skin on her meaty shoulder.

– That's a nice tattoo, she said casually. – Where did you get it?

It was a representation of a dragon, a black dragon. Lucinda and Melinda could hardly contain themselves, almost overwhelmed with excitement and the growing catching in the throat.

– Oh, it's just a fraternity thing, Miriam replied calmly, unworried. – We called ourselves the Black Dragons among ourselves, instead of using the generic name of our sorority.

– You did a good job of keeping your secret then, Lucinda shrugged. – I've never heard the name before.

– It's beautiful, Melinda beamed, very clever. – So well made. Where did you have it done?

– We were drunk, Miriam grinned. – Somewhere on the wharf... I think, even though I won't swear on it.

Lucinda probed her again, probed a lot, but there was nothing significant there, at least not anything significantly suspicious, no crack in any would be armor.

They dried themselves, taking their time, enjoying each other's company. Lucinda opened her mouth to speak, but no words came out. They dressed.

194

This wasn't like most dressing rooms attached to a gym or a swimming pool, wasn't steamy and hot, but one that had quite a pleasant temperature and there was little or no sweating. They could relax and use whatever time they needed.

Everybody joined in on the brushing and polishing in front of the mirror, too, feeling very little awkwardness doing so. There was a great mood between them. No one tried to score pointers or in any way harass the others.

– We should attend the protests tomorrow, Lucinda said, finally giving voice to the catching in her throat. – We should all go.

The others stared astonished at her, until they nodded one by one.

– It's long overdue… isn't it? Lois mused.

There were lots of hugging and kissing, as they parted in the hall. Both sisters walked on light feet outside, as they continued on their own.

– That was *so* cool, Melinda cried with youthful exuberance.

Lucinda looked bemused at her, the laughter loose in her throat.

– I mean, I'm sore all over my body, but…

– And then there was your dizzy spell…

– And there was my…

Kid Sister looked incredulous at Big Sister.

– How did you…

– Please, Lucinda said, – don't play dumb with me. You know that will never work.

– So, I had a dizzy spell, Melinda sighed subdued. – So what?

– You gorged in there like you had never seen food before, far more than me, than anyone present.

The laughter in her throat didn't go away, but was muted and Melinda noticed.

– You have fed like a ravenous beast for days, now, in fact since before we left Jagadir.

She put on her shades, pulled them from her purse with shaking hands.

– You're putting on weight fast. There have been several cases like yours. You are, in Mechanic's words «storing energy and mass for the transformation to make the transition easier». He said that to Jolene the day before… she disappeared.

– B-but you didn't. Your growth was even, without major leaps and bounds.

– It was, Lucinda confirmed. – But something in our physiology, in spite of us being sisters is clearly different. We have seen other signs of that, too, haven't we?

Melinda nodded.

– I let Jolene out of my sight. I won't do that with you, no matter what. I hope you see the inevitable wisdom in this…

– I do, Melinda nodded subdued, – don't worry, I do.

Lucinda faltered. She saw herself, through Melinda's eyes.

– I don't know what to do. I would have taken you to Mechanic, but aside from the fact that he would have tortured you, I don't trust him. I don't trust him and don't trust Lady Grace, and I don't give a fuck if she knows it.

There, it was said. She glanced around her, in trepidation, but Lady Grace wasn't there, wasn't in the vicinity or in her thoughts. It dawned on her that she thought of her as Lady Grace and not Claudia. The comforting touch of her sister's hand on the shoulder helped slow down the shaking, but didn't stop it.

– No matter, our plate is full tomorrow.

– Our hat is filled to the brim, Melinda echoed happily.

It came with the wind, echoing the contraction in Lucinda's gut. She glanced around her with insane eyes.

– What is it? Melinda cried. – What?

– Can't you *hear* it?

Lucinda grabbed her shoulders, grabbed them hard. Melinda moaned in pain.

– The laughter, the cruel laughter. It's coming from everywhere, no matter where I turn.

– I don't hear anything, Melinda whimpered.

(And I can hear anything).

It was another hot and sunny afternoon turning dark and moody, and Lucinda Patterson froze to ice in her tracks.

She stared hard at the open, innocent face of her sister, deep into her mind. There was nothing there, nothing to warrant suspicion and distrust and fear.

– I'm so sick and tired of being afraid, so sick and tired of it.

– I know. Melinda grabbed her hands. – I am, too.

– So we act on it, like we should have done long ago.

She made a fist, imagining she did so in all directions, at every angle and Melinda did, too, and Big and Kid sisters smiled grimly to each other.

– Black Dragon, whoever or whatever she or *It* is, is so clever, so skilled at playing on our fears and insecurities…

The sisters' eyes met.

– That would more than suggest she is human… right? Melinda said. – Any alien, anything strange and beyond human would have trouble doing that.

Lucinda shook her head in amazement, making sure Melinda understood that.

196

– Thus, the value of a fresh perspective is demonstrated once again.

Melinda was blushing. The catching in Lucinda's throat grew, grew with her resolve. The malignant laughter turned louder and filled to the brim with the wickedest spite, only slowly, slowly fading in the wind.

– We, the two of us and whoever we put our trust in will expose Black Dragon, force the coward she is out of hiding and into the open.

– Word, Melinda agreed with numb lips.

Hands clasped, eyes met. The determination didn't leave them. Not during their journey back to the apartment, not in their sleep, alone together in the large bed, where both imagined the other faded away and left them alone, clinging to each other like they had done when they were children in the old, abandoned building.

It remained while they, in broad daylight, with a lot on their plate, on their to-do list dressed up in their costumes, and Sensor and Gimmick walked openly through Tobruk's busy streets.

The two of them felt the wind around them, both hot and cold. They crossed Coleman Square, setting the course for the Wharf. Preparations had started for the afternoon protest. Holly, one of the organizers waved to them. They returned the wave. Her eyes widened.

To their right, as they walked along the shore they passed a tavern by the sea that was no longer called The Tavern by the Sea, but had changed name to Distant Harbor.

– Chuck Todd's heirs have evidently sold the establishment, Lucinda remarked. – Very good. I know for a fact that the new owners have better taste in both decorations and taverns in general.

Once again, the ambiguous sense of both triumph and sadness visited them.

The people at the first tattoo studio they visited assured them they didn't recognize the drawing of the black dragon when Lucinda showed them the photo she had taken of Miriam's arm. Lucinda easily noticed how one of them turned anxious, though. She didn't read any important specifics in his mind and decided to confront him on the spot.

– You know something, she told them. – What is it?

– I... heard something, he said, his voice clearly fluttering.

– What did you hear? She asked him patiently.

– Someone wanted someone to make... make custom needles to put that drawing on people's skin. I heard two guys talk about it at the table next to ours in a bar. I can't even remember what bar it was. We crossed town from one corner to the opposite one evening and that's when I heard it. And those guys talking about it, they were scared, man, they were really scared. You could practically hear the fear in their voices. I was pissed drunk, but it made an impression on me, made one hell of an impression on me...

He didn't know anything more. She saw the scene replayed and replayed in his mind, and no new details revealed themselves.

At the third studio they struck gold and found the guy who had actually done the work on Miriam and her friends.

– Yes, he said, – I remember this, remember her. It was the most curious thing. I had done the work for another client the day before they visited me, and I...

Gimmick and Sensor held their tongue, waiting for him to continue.

– The fact that you come here and ask about this put it all in... *perspective.* I don't know why and don't know how, and don't want to know, but I know enough, enough to leave it alone. Please do not contact me again.

Gimmick and Sensor walked in silence, once again crossing Coleman Square on their way to their next assignment that day.

He didn't know much either, Lucinda noted, but he knew...

Enough, Melinda agreed. He knew enough.

These guys had no reason to be scared, but they were still scared shitless.

The warm, warm day suddenly didn't feel so warm anymore.

– It was like she was there, Gimmick said with frost in her voice, – like she was present in the hearts of people that have never met her or even heard of her. What kind of creature can generate such fear?

She turned and grabbed her sister, burrowing her nails into her skin.

– Jolene was scared, too, practically desperate, enough to submitting to torture, enough to go to extremes in order to protect herself and the rest of us.

– Was that a mistake? Melinda whimpered.

– No! Lucinda shook her head decisively. – It was the right call. The mistake we've been making since then is to not be sufficiently radical in our approach. We followed loyally Lady Grace's cautious mainstream approach, but no longer.

– But she led us into Jagadir and has also embraced a proactive agenda... hasn't she?

– No! Lucinda said again. – What she did and does fit her political agenda, but it isn't truly a departure from her earlier actions. She has merely expanded a bit on it, that's all.

Sensor nodded slowly, as if something dawned on her.

– She's so slick, isn't she? The girl raged. – She talks a good game, but it's just posturing, a pretense, a diversion from what she's really doing.

– That's my girl, Gimmick said.

They grabbed each other's hands and held on, nodding in acknowledgment and mutual appreciation.

– We follow the plan, Lucinda said, – and we throw caution to the wind.

They approached their destination. Their determination grew. The knot in their gut did not stop them.

– Remember, Gimmick cautioned her younger partner. – We don't try to warn them on behalf of a precognition, but phrase it as a terrorist threat. They have to listen to that.

– Trust me, Sensor assured her. – I will be great.

The previous night and day, with both its terrors and pleasures had faded a bit, but the rock-hard determination remained.

The bigger crowd venturing the area in and around the bus station looked at them with big eyes, both admiring and wary, but left them more or less in peace. Sensor looked very striking in her new, greenish costume and she, being new in the public eye caught most of the stares. She waved a bit, before Gimmick stopped her with a stern glance.

They reached the Tower and the newly completed blocks of buildings surrounding it, a futuristic setting making Gimmick dizzy and queasy.

There was something deeply unsettling about it all.

The headquarters of the Tobruk Great Metropolitan Police Department was situated not more than two blocks away, yet another giant, imposing structure. There were visible guards and snipers posted everywhere in its vicinity. Gimmick and Sensor walked slowly up the stairs to the entrance, while being photographed and identified. Visible characteristics were compared with computer analysis and they were granted access to the entrance hall.

Gimmick approached the desk first, Sensor a few steps behind. The desk Sergeant looked sourly at them, giving them an even worse treatment than he would ordinary people seeking help.

– We need to speak with the Commissioner, Gimmick stated, without introduction. – We have urgent business to discuss with her.

Roscoe Lefere, the desk sergeant wanted to play the rejection game with them, but he didn't dare. He grabbed the phone in front of him and pushed a button.

– Gimmick and…

– Sensor, the costumed girl said, very helpful and amiable.

– Gimmick and Sensor are here, he informed the person at the other end. – They have… *urgent* business to discuss with the Commissioner.

It didn't take more than ten minutes, and they had probably added a few minutes just for spite. The two sisters stepped into the elevator and were brought to the top. Commissioner Burton, niece of the president and mentioned as a future president herself waited for them. Her very body language told them that they weren't welcome.

– We picked up a terrorist threat, this morning, Gimmick informed her with just the right trace of panic in her voice. – The Human Defense League has finally decided to step up from bluster to action. According to our intel they have placed or will place explosives all over the Tower and might blow it up at any time. We must act swiftly and decisively.

Burton was a member of one of many cells of HDL. So far, there was no central leadership and lots of infighting. She gave the two an ugly stare.

– And I'm supposed to take your word for it? Are you aware of the time and manpower it will take to evacuate the Tower and all surrounding premises, including ours?

Sensor stepped in front of her computer screen and showed her a few pages, a few threads on discussion boards clearly making threats. The logo of the HDL was very distinct.

– This is what is public. We have far more.

She looked pointedly at the much inconvenienced Commissioner.

– It is either a little inconvenience or heaps of bodies all over town, she shouted angrily at her. – What will it be?

The contest of wills ended before it began.

– And have you any idea of when this is supposed to go down? The fairly big ordinary woman said ironically, fighting for her last pieces of dignity.

– I'm sorry to say that our sources weren't specific, Gimmick said with distinct regret in her voice. – It might be today or next week. As you know many of your own men are members, so they can plant the explosives at any time. You need to root out all your bad seeds, I'm afraid.

– It isn't anything you and your… trusted people couldn't have found on your own, by making an effort, Sensor shrugged. – Be happy that we were around to correct your sloppiness.

It was over, and so fast. Gimmick had long since found it amazing that she often didn't need to use her telepathy to read people. The Commissioner looked like a whipped dog.

– You won't go to the media with this, will you?

The words just slipped out of her, almost involuntary.

– Of course we will, Gimmick grinned. – We will most certainly use this for all it is worth, to put you racist assholes in the worst possible position. We will spread it across the planet, in the vain hope that most people will actually see the truth, for once.

The evacuation had already started by the time they had reached the street.

First part of our two birds with one stone scheme complete, Gimmick sent to a silently cheering Sensor.

People flowed from all the buildings, from the bus terminal and everywhere nearby, creating a ruckus of another world. The two big people in costumes were pointed at and stared at more than ever.

… take charge… you're suchatakecharge woman, sister.

There was a bow of almost infinite admiration. It made Lucinda feel so good, so great.

The first shots were fired. The first screams heard.

Let's get away from here.

They ran. Gimmick tried scanning high points for active snipers, but it was impossible to read anyone's mind in this melting pot of excited thoughts.

She glanced at Sensor, but the other just shook her head. She was just as blind. Sweat poured from exposed and covered skin, reaching the eyes. Damn!

After a run that seemed to last forever they finally reached a narrow alley close to salvation, to one of the gates, the one near Coleman Square. They dived into it.

And erupted onto the abandoned construction site, stumbling a bit before recovering their balance, gasping for an eternity before catching their breath.

They listened extra hard in the sudden silence with their blazing senses. Nothing.

– No close thoughts, Gimmick said. – No spies, no laughter…

– No close smells or moves, Sensor said.

It comforted them, somewhat to speak aloud. They removed their costumes. Gimmick removed all the various weapons and put them in the bag. What remained on them both was light, practical clothing.

– We are alone, aren't we? Melinda asked, not really asking.

– We are. Lucinda confirmed. – Like we have always been. I'm afraid Sensor's membership in the Maverick Crew was brief.

– I don't care, Kid Sister declared passionately.

– We are alone, Big Sister stated, – but we won't stay that way, not for long…

Hands clasped again. Melinda's grip had become that much stronger.

Lucinda felt it and more. There was something…

It slipped away. Lucinda shook her head.

They made the necessary detour to the apartment and left their gear, taking their time, gorging on food, making trips to the toilet. They took two turns of each and looked amazed and more than a little anxious at each other.

– My Goddess, Melinda gasped, – we have…

– … cleaned the fridge, Lucinda nodded, acknowledged, confirmed.

Lucinda opened her mouth to speak, hesitated and held back.

– What is it? Melinda wondered. – Spill!

Lucinda fought a moment of despair. Damn that perceptive…

– I felt something when we clasped hands, almost a… jolt. The Hunger… increased… in a striking way. Whatever was happening I stopped it, before it was… actualized. I can't remember feeling this way before, ever.

She felt it once again, re-experienced it.

– I feel the Hunger, too. Melinda took her hand. – I thought I had felt it before, but that was just a child's pretense of adulthood in comparison. What is *happening* to us?

– I can spot… potential big people again, Lucinda said. – I haven't been able to do that since I was a child and didn't know what I saw.

Saw the children, the pre-teens, seemingly normal but destined to become Big.

– It's a dark flare, turning itself on and off, very distinct and impossible to misunderstand.

– I think you've held yourself back all these years, Melinda said, suddenly very deliberate. – You do so no longer and everything kept inside comes to the fore. Very good!

Lucinda closed and opened her eyes once, and then they stayed open.

– I think you are right, Sensor, she nodded. – I have held back, in so many ways, but *no longer*.

Two pair of eyes twinkled and twinkled and twinkled, as they sat there by the table, as they walked outside in the hot and arid air, as they took the bus back to town, to the city center, to Coleman Square.

It was packed already, and more people, both big and others made their way there all the time, filling the entire square. Lucinda felt the hot wind, felt it stronger than ever.

– Claudia would try to stop me, even unmasked from doing this, like she stopped Jolene, she told her sister, – but even if she knows what I am about to do, there is no way she can stop me in this cauldron of human emotion.

– She has held you back all this time, hasn't she?

– She has, Lucinda acknowledged startled. – She has led us all around like dogs in a kennel.

Anxiety grabbed her again, and held on, but she rolled her hands into fists and determination won without contest and it felt so good.

– You stay close to me all the time, you understand? We do this together, now, and for all time.

– I… understand, Melinda replied with shining eyes.

The speeches, the testimonies began, the official, pre-announced, the impulsive and the rest, filled with passion and rage.

Lucinda Patterson signed the long list. She was fairly high up on it.

Lois joined the two sisters. Jasmine, Miriam and all the others in their group at the center joined them. The passion and light in everybody's eyes overwhelmed their qualms and the catching grew in Lucinda's throat.

Determination burned in her, when she raised her fist in anger, when she cried her support for the other speakers, when she two hours later stepped behind the microphone.

– They've got no valid reason what so ever to treat us the way they do, she cried.

The boiling cauldron at Coleman Square replied to her.

– We are one more group in a long line of convenient scapegoats. In a society filled with inequality and injustice and destruction of life itself they point at us, making us responsible for horrors that were present long before we appeared. It's just yet another pretext they use to stay in power. Those in charge are the true maniacs and criminals and it is they who must be confronted, not minority groups and fringe groups easy to blame. Racism is practically enshrined in our constitution. We, all of us have had the power to put a stop to that, to everything unjust and oppressive for a long time. It's about time we start.

The police was there, as they always were. They did nothing.

It would have been pure suicide if they had tried anything. The mood was explosive and stayed that way during the day and night and the days and nights that followed.

– We can be arrested by the police officers at any time, in connection with any crime, even if we happen to be the victims of that particular crime. The law gives them the right to incarcerate us on a *whim*. Yes, good people, that is exactly how the establishment and their eager henchmen sees us. We are a threat to them by our very existence.

A rise of anger swept through the attendance.

Are you there, Jolene? Are you watching from somewhere, somewhere you can't escape?

– They finally did something with the hate groups today, did so because they had to. So far the hate groups have been given free reign, and we see the result.

There was still shooting around the police headquarters. More blood was spilled, joining the waterfall already becoming a pond, becoming a lake, becoming a sea.

– The hate groups were given free reign because it fits the plans of those in charge. Hate groups have always been their instruments, their true power base. That, too, ends today, when I and all the rest of you gathered here step forward and say NO MORE!

– NO MORE! The cauldron responded.

The sound, distant, close was very distinct. Lucinda realized, startled, beyond startled that it was the sound of metal breaking. Everybody turned as one towards The Tower. It and the other tall buildings were easily visible from the Square.

One of the support columns for the tall building broke and the rest followed in seconds. One snap imitating a dry metal twig turned into what sounded like a million others. The building toppled over. It happened so fast, so incessantly slow. The building fell, right at where Jolene didn't sit. It fell on her and countless others, crushing them and the parking house attached to the bus station, bombarding all the surrounding buildings, creating havoc of seemingly infinite magnitude, like an earthquake or similar. Smoke rose and filled the street, the entire block, as a thousand windows broke and rained death on the people below, shards cutting flesh and bone and veins and skulls of the people still there wide open.

Everything was captured at a thousand angles by various cameras, filmed by both pros and amateurs, with surveillance cameras and cell phones and professional recording devices from choppers and high and low points across town. The cacophonic caricature of noise seemed to blanket all other sounds for hours.

It would echo in people's consciousness for days and nights without number, never truly letting go.

Chapter 12
TWO YEARS AGO TODAY

– I see her, see the Black Dragon surrounded by flames and dancing, ephemeral skulls submerged in the dark fire. The flames don't burn her, but *feed* her. It's like she's playing with souls like trinkets, twisting them in suffering and horror. She sits on a throne. Behind her, in a hellish glow of dark red the tattoo is painted on the wall. I can see the red glow of her eyes, but not her face.

A beyond distraught Oracle was surrounded by her teammates. She had woken up screaming, so hysterical that they had felt compelled to actually break open the door, not even waiting for someone to show up with the master key.

She looked absolutely stricken, terror painted on her face, terrified beyond wits. They tried to comfort her, but had to withdraw to not be hurt by her power. She seemed to have lost completely control of it. It flared off and on. Once they even feared she would disappear on them, but she remained, a leaf blowing in the storm.

She was nude, in body and mind. The men wanted to protect her, to cuddle and comfort her. One look from Gimmick's blazing eyes and they pulled back and moved out.

– I will take care of her, she declared. – We will be ready when we're ready.

All the others left.

– What's the big deal? Cougar shrugged and turned briefly in the door, changing her face and body into a patronizing smile. – It's only nightmares.

– You try it, honey, Gimmick retorted angrily, – night after night after night and days of distress.

The door closed. The two of them had been left alone. Jolene crumbled even further on the bed, practically dissolving in shakes and sobs.

Gimmick tried very hard to calm her, to comfort her, but it was no use.

– She's here, the pale dark girl choked. – She's with me all the time.

Gimmick turned to follow her friend's blind stare and shook abruptly in repeated chills. There she was, the Black Dragon, the creature in the shadow, at the edge of human dreams manifested. It was an image of sorts, but not exactly that. To Lucinda it felt like substance, like she was real. Suddenly overwhelmed with terror she imagined that the creature grinned at her.

Before it faded, like a nightmare in daylight.

Jolene Masters crumbled on the bed, in stark relief. Lucinda shook harder for a moment, fighting to pull herself together. The two kissed and rubbed shaking bodies, comforting each other.

– She... It looks human, doesn't it? Lucinda spoke in a voice that sounded like it was created from a rusty saw.

– She does, but only in appearance, Jolene whimpered. – What's inside the... the terrifying shell is far worse t-than it s-s-s-seems.

The last word was hardly spoken at all, but mumbled, garbled like a child before it learned to talk properly.

– She is coming, Jolene stated, suddenly very collected and calm. – We need to prepare, to gather intel. Information is power. We need Power, more of it, much more.

– But what do you...

– What do I have in mind? Huge, deep eyes drowned the other girl. – There is something... old legends only fools will attempt to pull forth from antiquity. But first we need to strengthen ourselves, to gain the necessary... momentum to pull it off.

She rose from the bed, a shivering bundle of flesh and bone rolling hands into fists. When she dressed her hands were steady. Lucinda didn't spot a single move that wasn't deliberate, a part of the body's path as it moved forward.

They walked to the meeting room, where the others were waiting for them.

– I need to be stronger, far more powerful, Oracle said. – We all do. Or we will be pushovers when the Black Dragon c-comes for us.

They all looked with haunted eyes at the woman they had learned to know as confident and strong, and seeing her like this... did something to them, to them all. Even Cougar's spiteful smile grew pale and ragged.

– I want you to t-torture m-me, she said subdued and tiny. – I want you to do *whatever it takes* to make me manifest my full power.

They stared at her, beyond startled or stunned.

– Are you sure? Lady Grace asked.

– I've never been more certain of anything my entire life.

They walked towards the laboratory.

– I want you to design exercise programs for each and every one of us, Oracle told Mechanic, – programs where we're straining far beyond our perceived top level.

He stared at her as if she wasn't quite right in the head. She certainly had grown a notch or ten in intensity. They could practically observe how her manifested «dark field» sparked and danced around her body.

Gimmick and Lady Grace couldn't help but rebroadcast her fear, her anxiety and desperate determination.

She placed herself on her back on the bench. Nobody moved. Gimmick abruptly stepped forward and closed the harness around the lab rat's wrists and ankles and neck.

– You are helpless now, aren't you? She asked softly. – You need to be free to walk through your portals.

Jolene nodded with big eyes, very aware of her vulnerability.

Mechanic put a hood on her head, one covered by electronic devices. He tightened it, making it stick to her skull. It didn't cover her face, but everything else.

– The devices, what are they? She asked.

– They send out a kind of vibration similar to the collars, but not equal to them. They won't block your power, but disrupt it, disorient you, making it harder for you to concentrate, and you will need to go that much deeper into yourself, and we can measure your progress, see what works and what doesn't.

He turned a switch and a hum surrounded the girl's head. She shook it, or tried to, but it didn't look right. No matter how much she strained she couldn't fight off the dull expression in her eyes. She whimpered in her distress. Even the sound didn't come out right. It sounded like a little girl, the squeal of an animal.

He began working with the needle. Her scream rose to the ceiling, cut instantly into everybody's ears. She jumped up and down in her restraints. They held. As far as those watching in horror could see, she wasn't even close to breaking them. He pushed the needle at her calf. The loud whining rose to another level. He stopped, after something that seemed like forever. Everybody could hear the sound of their own breath.

– I'm going to feed you, now, Jolene, he told her, – feed you continuously while putting untold strain on your system, fattening it further for its transformation.

She didn't seem to hear him. There was no visible reaction from her when he pushed the tube into her mouth and down her throat.

– Don't worry, he admonished them. – She's breathing well. There is no need for concern.

He started the feeding machine. It sent a colorless porridge down her throat.

– This is a protein-rich mixture, easily digestible, practically feeding energy directly into her system.

He put giant clamps on her feet and arms, and sent repeated shocks of electricity through her body. Some of them pushed their palms at their ears in a vain effort to keep out her banshee wails. He stopped momentarily.

– I can keep her from articulate her pain if you desire, he told them. – I can keep her from screaming. It's easy.

– Can you keep her from feeling pain without stopping your «treatment»? Raven Bird snarled.

– I take that as a no, he shrugged.

Oracle started gagging, clearly attempting to throw up. He pulled out the tube quickly, turned her head to the side and made sure her acid stomach content ended up in the bucket he provided, all of it so very efficient.

She sat on the table a timeless time later, sick and pale.

– I feel weak as a kitten, she choked. – This is useless.

– Not so, Mechanic corrected her eagerly. – Look here. There is a spike the moment you were about to throw up. I missed it when it happened because I was distracted.

Distracted with helping her, with being human, Gimmick sent to Raven Bird.

He eagerly showed the nauseous girl and everybody the printout.

– Your energy level went way up, briefly but distinctly. You even caused parts of the equipment to fail. It didn't register anything, anything at all for several seconds. We're learning so much here, even though understanding remains elusive.

He looked at her with both love and frustration in his eyes.

– No matter, she's done, now. Martial Athlete stepped forward. – It's my turn.

– My gallant knight, Oracle said, as she walked past him and softly kissed his cheek.

He will make him pay for that, Gimmick picked up from Jolene's chaotic thoughts.

The screams began again and continued unabated. They seemed to go on forever.

Martial Athlete almost broke the bonds. They had never seen him like this before. He always used to be so together, with such control over himself.

Mechanic, or what Mechanic did to him (Gimmick couldn't decide which it was) made him choke and gasp, made tears flow from his eyes, and rage fill his scream.

Energetic was next. His form began shaking almost the moment the torture began.

It was torture. It had quickly stopped being anything else. They stood there indecisive. Even Mechanic showed a flicker of doubt, as his game progressed.

Energetic couldn't sit or stay still when he was done. His feet and arms shook violently, to the point where he could hardly stand, and he was leaking energy, his power completely out of control.

– Lady Grace is next, Raven Bird stated calmly, but very determined.
Suddenly silence reigned.
– Sure, Lady Grace shrugged, very deliberate, – but...
– You *started* this, Raven Bird snarled. – And you have complained over your «insufficient power levels», haven't you, wailing endlessly over your «inadequacies»?
– Stop! Oracle spoke up quietly. – Just *stop*.
She shook her head, finally having had enough.
Gimmick looked at Lady Grace then, saw the smile on her lips, and wished that Jolene had kept her mouth shut a little longer, wished she had encouraged her to do so.
– This was a bad idea, Jolene stated empathically.
– Do you have one better? Lady Grace asked her, in what seemed very much like a practical, neutral approach, on top of things again, in control again.
– As a matter of fact, I have.
She hesitated, but determination pushed her further.
– It's one that I should have suggested a long time ago, but I was afraid. I still am, but time and what we are facing have long since made such concerns insignificant.
Gimmick sensed her anxiety, her determination. Both burned inside her with equal power.
She glanced around her with wavering eyes, looking for the shadow that often was there, but there was nothing.
– Follow me, she told them, and they all did.
She led them into the gym. Everybody froze and stared the moment they stepped inside. A cold and hot wind hammered them.
Gimmick looked for the shadow, for the Dragon as well, but there was nothing.
On the floor was drawn a pentacle, a pentagram inside a circle. Torches burned on poles and on the walls. The entire room had been transformed into something new and alien.
– W-what *is* this? Lady Grace gasped.
– What does it *look* like? Jolene reproached her.
She had suddenly and undeniably taken command of the situation and them all.
Lady Grace was clearly out of it, and Flight Captain as well. They weren't used to, or even capable of handling unexpected and shocking developments.
– It's remarkable, Mechanic mused. – I'm willing to wager that the pentacle is hundred percent mathematically correct.

Gimmick saw her make it, saw her design the room for the upcoming task, saw her rise in the night and perform the task in swift and sure moves.

– It better be, or we will be in serious trouble, Oracle said. – This is a different part of the family heritage. I've only dabbled in it before and rarely done anything to develop my skills, but I realized recently that that was a mistake and have made every effort to catch up, to remember what mother taught me. It is as I said: we need all possible skills, all the power we can gain to prevail.

You did this, Gimmick sent, and still you submitted willingly to Lady Grace's machinations.

I did. Who would you say gained by it?

Gimmick shook by the sight of the burning shadows in her friend's eyes, the almost inhuman determination she spotted there.

I had to, sister. We both have to step up our game, against both external and internal enemies.

Gimmick wanted to say something, to communicate anything, to the other, to everybody, but couldn't do it.

Are you with me, sister?

I am, Lucinda replied instantly.

A dark laughter echoed through the room.

Did you hear that?

Lucinda almost panicked.

I did. She is here, or rather watching from somewhere else, hiding, biding her time.

None of the others had heard or noticed anything. That was clear just by a casual glance. The light telepathic probe was unnecessary.

But we can't… we can't do anything while she's here… can we?

Yes, we can. She isn't that strong, obviously, or she wouldn't have needed to move in stealth or attempted to soften us up before moving in for the kill or whatever her damn motivation is. We need information to expose her, before she is ready, before she does come for us.

– Form a circle around the circle, the new, assertive Jolene commanded.

They did, placing themselves at various points while glancing uncertain at each other.

Oracle stepped into the circle, walking in circles, facing each and every one of her teammates on the outside.

– I'll need one of you with me, one that will join me in my quest and see my path.

A telepath.

– I'll do it, Lady Grace stated slowly.

– No. Oracle shook her head. – Gimmick will do it. We are sisters in spirit. We will look beyond the veil together for the crucial answers we seek.

Gimmick rushed into the pentacle, casting a brief, triumphant, spiteful glance at Lady Grace.

Backfire much? She wanted to shout in glee.

– But you will all be with us, Oracle said softly, – in spirit and blood. We will all be a part of this endeavor to defend ourselves against the forces gathering against us.

She drew a knife and walked to Flight Captain.

– Give me your hand.

He did, with a slight, confident patronizing smile.

She grabbed his hand and cut the meaty part of it, right through his hard, difficult to breach skin. Howard Eisenhouse gasped in surprise and pain. She squeezed and blood flowed down on the part of the circle right in front of him.

– I take your blood, she cried. – I take your strength, in this world and the next.

Her voice changed, turning deeper, more like a chant than speech.

She repeated the procedure with all of them, everybody outside the pentacle.

Cougar hesitated a bit, even taking a step back, before stepping forward again, giving Oracle her clawed hand.

– This is quite an amazing thing you've kept hidden from us, Jolene, Lady Grace said, her sweet voice accompanied by a sinister smile behind the mask.

Gimmick saw it in her mind.

– Not hidden exactly, Oracle said, briefly casting her eyes down. – I guess I was ashamed and hesitated to reveal to you that particular part of… of my heritage.

She straightened once more.

– But as stated: all such considerations have become moot, and even though mother told me there would be risks with breaching time's curtain, she didn't have my power, my natural ability to breach it.

She had placed two things at the center of the pentacle: a drum and a small sack.

– My sorceress' paraphernalia, she said and reddened.

And that was how Lucinda Patterson would always remember her, a child getting wet on her feet, while taking her first, few steps into the vast water.

She pulled another, smaller pouch from the bigger. Her left hand dug into it and returned with a beige powder-like substance.

– Bones and blood mix, she chanted. – Bones and blood and sweat and mind and Shadow stirring the pot of the Hollow, stirring the air of the Other World. Allow us to see beyond the Veil.

– Christ! Energetic cried out.

There were hisses when the powder and the blood met. Vapors rose in the air. She breathed them, seemingly swallowing them. Gimmick joined her, a little shaky but determined.

– Power, she mumbled, – I want power. We need power.

The dark laughter shook them.

Do you know what you're doing?

There was no response, either vocal or thought.

Jolene grabbed her hand and led her to the center of the pentacle, its base and point.

– We are sisters, she told the skeptical girl, – balance of power. This is our destiny in this world and beyond.

– How long have you known that? Gimmick asked curtly.

– Since before we met…

There was her grin, with her touch of anxiety.

She sat down on her ass with her legs crossed in front and Gimmick did the same. They sat there, facing each other.

Gimmick began feeling faint, her own hazy vision echoing that in Oracle's eyes.

The big girl felt how panic swelled within and threatened to erupt into the open. The dark girl grabbed her hand.

– Do you trust me?

– With my life, Gimmick mumbled.

Oracle sent her a look of boundless gratitude.

– Good, good…

She let go of Gimmick's hand and began hitting the drum. It was a sound both hypnotic and stirring.

– Heed the sound of the drum, the sorceress mumbled, – let it stir you and bind you, wake you up, send your thoughts and self in new and startling new directions. Heed the stirred fire, smell the ashes…

Ghostlike hands put the drum away. The drum, in an unfathomable way… kept beating, its sound resonating like thick waves between the walls, beyond the walls in the city streets outside and even beyond them, into mist and Shadow. She moved her head, turned it in an everlasting circle, staring at the others, those making the circle with her huge, penetrating eyes.

– LILLITH - Mother of Demons, she cried. – We seek illumination, seek the future, the past and everything in-between.

The torches suddenly burned that much stronger, their fire reaching towards the ceiling. Everybody shook. Oracle grabbed Gimmick's hands. Both shook visibly in what felt like an electric charge.

– Grant your humble servants this boon, Lillith. We want to know the world beyond the illusion, know the secrets spoken in your kingdom. Grant us insight to do your will on Earth.

– FUCK THIS, the Bowman shouted in disgust.

He attempted to leave, to move, but was unable to do so. And then, after one look from those huge, opaque eyes cat got his tongue and his lips felt like wood. He could no longer speak.

Oracle began speaking in a foreign tongue, clearly an archaic language no one on Earth spoke anymore. Gimmick moved her lips as well, moved them in sync with her mirror image across the vast gulf that had grown between them. There was no ground, no walls or ceiling anymore, only an indistinct shadowy and misty landscape.

They were all there, sitting, standing like statues in those alien surroundings.

– The deed already done keeps happening, Jolene said with a ghostly voice.

She turned her head relentlessly, looking at them all in her elevated distress.

– The moment is born in violence and hatred.

Gimmick frowned. She blinked and in each blink was a flash. They both blinked. In less than a second they glimpsed the woman on a throne. They saw her twisted, demonic face, one they didn't recognize. A beyond powerful chill passed through them. Gimmick felt so tired, so sleepy, fatigue chasing the chills.

The woman sat on the throne. Those kneeling before her had all a tattoo of a dragon on their left shoulder. The Black Dragon looked directly at them, as if she knew they were there. The two of them moaned in distress.

– I welcome you to my court, she said.

Her voice, her voice like a rusty saw on metal.

Sleep, or something very much resembling sleep claimed them, claimed them both. They might not be sleeping, but they were dreaming still.

The dark tunnel sucked them in, like it had done the first day they met. Lucinda found herself in a room filled with sizzling, torturous heat, one of many prisoners placed in cages in a room so big that she could hardly even glimpse the walls. Jolene was there, too, a couple of cages away. Big men and women stood outside the bars, slamming big whips at the floor.

One of the men shouted something, shouted in what seemed like minutes, but Lucinda couldn't understand him, didn't understand a single word. She frowned in distress. No matter how much she strived, she heard nothing but gibberish.

– You are not prisoners, the woman said, as if she spat something vile, – you do not have that honor. You're lower than worms on the ground, but if you endure and do well for yourself, you will earn your place in our army. You may become a soldier, dying for the glory of the Ebony Goddess.

Gimmick realized startled that she, the future Lucinda recognized the woman, the woman so tall and big and strong, so dramatically changed and such an awesome and fearsome sight and felt sick to the bone. The mere sight of the powerful creature made her gasp in terror and awe.

There was more, much more downloaded directly into her cerebral cortex, fading in a flash of darkness and sickness, as if memory itself was sucked out of her.

Gimmick and Oracle awoke at the center of the pentacle, as if from a deep, deep dream, letting go of each other's hands, moaning in pain and misery.

Lethargy pulled Gimmick down, pulled them both down. The shock and horror seemed muted at first, taking what seemed like forever to surface.

The second heartbeat followed the first, followed by a third and Oracle's eyes cleared.

The room slowly returned to normal, or what went for normal. What had felt like wood became flesh again. Everybody emerged from their stupor. The circle broke.

Disorientation riddled Gimmick. She had problems with coordination and focus. Oracle helped her on her feet, helped her stand.

Oracle let her go and addressed the gathering:

– It's her, she cried, pointing an accusing finger at Cougar. – She will change and become Black Dragon, the terror from my nightmare.

Everybody looked beyond shocked at the stricken Cougar.

– Behold, the sorcerer, the familiar, unfamiliar woman told them. – Pay attention!

She showed them, with images growing from her left hand, forming in the very air, how Cougar changed, how she grew taller and grew true claws and a demonic visage, and how she used her greater power to destroy and ruin lives. They watched her beat up men and women on the floor, snarling at them and shouting brutal commands. Everyone witnessed sights beyond bad, beyond terrifying.

They all felt strangely detached from themselves as they watched the story unfold. Several of them attempted to speak several times during the very illustrative and deeply disturbing three-dimensional true-to-life movie, but no one managed to do it.

It was done. The silence kept screaming at them.

– That can't be! Cougar gasped. – I would never do anything like that, become something like that. You can't possibly believe I will?

– But they do, Oracle said softly. – They know my power, know how it works. You do, too.

It was evident by a casual glance at them all, including Cougar, how everybody almost subconsciously pulled away from her, by the sick revulsion and shame evident in their features when they looked at her.

– Fine! Cougar snarled. I wouldn't want to be one of you assholes, anyway.

She rushed out, her entire body tense like a metal spring, leaving a hole in her former teammates' gut.

– We should stop her, the Bowman said meekly.

But no one moved. They were frozen on their spot, in their stricken thoughts. The last vestiges of their innocent childhood dream ended right there and then, never to be regained.

Gimmick put a comforting hand on Jolene's shoulder, calming her shaking form.

– I'm all right, Jolene assured everyone with a pale smile.

Everything was a jumble in her head. Gimmick wanted to cry in her lethargy when all the images and sensations threatened to overwhelmed her.

– I feel like I've been sleeping, she choked, – and no matter what I do, how hard I fight I can't wake up.

– We all do, Lady Grace sniffed.

Seeing her down like that was perhaps the most shocking of all.

– We all must, she straightened, visibly pulling herself together.

The silence felt eternal.

The beeping tone reached them from far away.

Raven Bird found her cell phone and clicked on her message.

– Your snitch again? The Bowman wondered.

– My very reliable informant, Raven Bird corrected him. – Yes, it is she. I must go.

– Seems like too much of a coincidence, doesn't it? Mechanic more stated than said.

– I agree, Lady Grace said. – Martial Athlete and Energetic, you go…

– I can handle it, Raven Bird interrupted her.

Lady Grace shrugged.

Raven Bird left. Martial Athlete and Energetic remained.

– Trace Cougar, Flight Captain told Mechanic. – Never let her leave your screen. And keep an eye on Raven Bird, too. Sound the alert if anyone even breathes on her.

Mechanic rushed towards his lab, unusually agile and agitated.

– Contact our allies, Lady Grace commanded. – Tell them what happened.

Leave out nothing. Ask them to be on their guard.

Martial Athlete and Energetic headed for the communication room, eager to obey the voice of authority and to have something, anything to occupy their mind.

Everybody busied themselves with something, with the smallest of tasks.

Eventually only Gimmick and Oracle remained in the room of mist and Shadow, of torches and smoke.

– I must go, Oracle said. – I have to check on something.

– I'll go with you, Gimmick stated.

– No. Oracle grinned her sore smile. – You are needed elsewhere tonight.

It was yet another of her beyond cryptic statements, and Gimmick didn't object. It didn't even occur to her to ask what it was about.

Jolene embraced her and kissed her on the cheek. Then she left. Lucinda followed her with her mind to the gate, but after the dark girl had stepped through it, Lucinda lost contact.

Silence descended on what had once been a gym. Gimmick stood there unmoving for a while, until she, too left.

Claws of cold squeezed her neck. She rubbed her skin, until she realized that it wasn't imaginary, but a true memory. Her eyes stayed open. She kept them open and they turned dry and opaque. Then there was the inevitable blink and the snarling face of the Black Dragon revealing itself in her frozen vision.

She gasped, almost falling on her knees in terror and awe. Flashes of her recent experience kept assaulting her, never solidifying, never turning tangible, until eventually fading, at least a bit. She made her way to the communication room, joining Lady Grace, Flight Captain, Martial Athlete and Energetic there.

Lady Grace had already noticed her distress and what was ailing her. She frowned, reaching out to touch her, hesitating, letting her arm fall back down.

Endure, little one. Be strong.

How, when you can't even touch me, can't stand what's on my mind?

Gimmick glared at her mentor and perhaps it was the rage that finally made the numbing chill retire to the backdrop of her consciousness.

Something amazing happened. Lady Grace faltered and crumbled.

I'm sorry, I couldn't touch you. YourThoughtsHurtHurtMe.

The armor cracked, briefly and Gimmick gained a glimpse behind it and caught the vulnerability there.

Gimmick caught anger then, and they both tensed.

Mechanic interrupted the awkward moment. He walked fast, with an

216

expanded worried frown.

– I can't track Cougar, he said. – Her signal is gone. It disappeared in the wharf area. For that to have happened her ring must have either been destroyed or she has discarded it, removed it from her finger and thrown it away.

There was more silence.

– No one else has seen her either, Flight Captain said.

– They weren't lying, Lady Grace interjected. – They share our concerns and basically believe our version of events.

Gimmick touched her head and couldn't stifle a gasp of pain.

– She's experiencing rather bad after effects of whatever she and Oracle went through, Lady Grace said softly.

And now she did touch the younger woman.

And again Lucinda straightened herself and pulled herself together.

Her cell phone beeped. She pulled it from its pocket inside the costume. There was a message. She pushed the button. The message said.

Broken Alley, asap!

– I must go, she said.

She generously shared the message with the others.

– You alone? Flight Captain wondered. – Isn't it for all of us?

– It's only for me, she grinned. – It would have been quite a different message and probably broadcasted through the rings if she was sounding a general alert, you know that.

She left them and the awful awkward mood of shame and regret.

For once she welcomed the nausea through the gate. She had her hands curled into fists when she appeared in Broken Alley.

There was no one there. She searched her surroundings, but sensed no danger, near or remote. People tended to avoid this place even in daylight and the day was fading. Gimmick realized startled how little was left of the day. Oracle's ceremony had lasted many hours. Time had slipped away like grains of sand between fingers.

Raven Bird flew in from the south. Lisa smiled as she landed, as she and Lucinda greeted each other. They were friends these two, and had a connection beyond the camaraderie of the others.

– You got my message, I see, Lisa grinned relieved. – I wasn't certain you would.

– I heard its beep, Gimmick said distracted. – I followed its call.

– Are you okay? Raven Bird asked her softly, as they embraced. – I would imagine that today's events were almost as hard on you as they were on Jolene… and Cougar, at least harder than on the rest of us.

– I am, or at least I will be, Gimmick assured her with a choking voice. – Life must go on.

Lisa nodded solemnly.

– Good, she chuckled. – Because the way I've heard it your old friend The Catcher will be on the prowl tonight, and you will get the chance to beat the living crap out of him. He has escaped from prison again, just like our dear Oracle predicted. She was a little off with her timing this time, but not wrong.

Lucinda nodded, feeling little or no surprise.

– You're awfully chummy with that songbird of yours? She said lightly.

– She has never let me down so far, Raven Bird replied fairly unconcerned. She looked away for a while, listening in her way, like Gimmick did in hers.

– You seem… different.

– I guess I am, Lucinda acknowledged.

– You're certainly entitled, Raven Bird said softly, in a comforting gesture. – Perhaps we should let others take care of the Catcher tonight?

– No. Gimmick shook her head. – I need action, need to feel my fists *pummel* the Catcher's face.

– You feel… betrayed, Raven Bird said. – I guess we all do, but as I said, your experience of it was clearly more powerful and shocking.

– I… saw the future, Lisa. Even though it was only in bits and pieces it was impossible to misunderstand. We had been captured by Black Dragon and her minions. They held us prisoner and tortured us, brainwashed us, made us part of her army, and we had nothing to say in the m-matter.

Raven Bird once more embraced her, comforted her friend Gimmick.

And then Gimmick heard the sound of steps, caught the whiff of the Catcher's thoughts.

She stiffened and raised her head.

Action time, she told Raven Bird and grinned her sore smile.

She started running in stealth mode and Raven Bird followed her, levitating just above the ground, not making any sound except for her elevated breathing. They entered the old warehouse district, yet another disheveled area of town, the one Lucinda knew well. The derelict building where she and Kid Sister had spent months of their childhood wasn't far from here. Gimmick shook her head, focusing on what was ahead.

They rushed through a building missing a lot of its walls. There, Gimmick made contact with the Catcher without a discernible effort. Pride coursed through her, in the midst of despair.

He's right around the corner, she sent to Raven Bird, on his way to one of his old hiding places. What a tool.

Any connection to… to Black Dragon you can discern?

Even Raven Bird's thoughts reeked of sorrow and anxiety.

None! It must be something Oracle glimpsed in his future, an omen that they will connect, somehow.

We must find Cougar, Raven Bird stressed, make things right. All of this is insane. She isn't Black Dragon, isn't Black Dragon *yet*. Oracle's skills are far from perfect. I am well aware of how she has proven herself and her insane powers to us, but we know so very little about the mechanics behind them. For all we know today's events are exactly what pushed… what will push Cougar over the edge, make her the creature from the nightmares you and Jolene share.

Gimmick wanted to say something, anything, but they were out of time. It charged them like a device keeping air from their lungs.

They turned the corner and their prey appeared in the direct line of their vision. The Catcher noticed them and turned towards them with a puzzled frown.

– Hola, Troy, Gimmick greeted him, subconsciously mimicking Oracle's inflection, – any chance you will be a good boy and just give yourself up?

She actually felt his disbelief over their appearance and his anger and panic like a physical blow and nearly staggered.

– I'm not going back, he shouted, suddenly totally out of it. – No way I'm going back!

– Good, she hissed, – I feel a need to pummel something, anyway, and you certainly fit the bill.

His confusion and shock and rising anger and panic echoed within her, like hers echoed within him. The ropes seemed to come alive in his hands, writhing like snakes in the air surrounding him. She jumped at him, feeling the rising aggression like a pleasant river inside. He hit her with a rope. It was heavy and the stroke packed some serious punch. It rammed her in the chest and threw her big and fairly heavy body off course, making it hit the wall, hard enough for her to release a modest gasp.

– The boy has grown some teeth, Raven Bird cried pleased.

Lisa was also on edge, thrown off her center. Lucinda didn't have to do any deliberate probing to sense that. The air was practically filled with emotion, with passion and contempt and revulsion.

The three made a perfect triangle, fitting each other like a glove.

– I've been preparing for this, he breathed, – for everything every second I was able to think beyond the fog of that damn collar.

Raven Bird gestured and he was pushed at the wall where Gimmick was waiting for him. She struck his jaw with a hard and fast fist. He stumbled back.

– I'm so grateful, she grinned at him.

Striking him again.

She delved into his mind in the hope of finding anything, any information about Black Dragon, but there was nothing. Frustration gripped her, as she moved in on him to strike again.

Then she faltered, briefly. It was sufficient for him to avoid her and strike back. He hit her on the jaw, an ill-conceived, weak blow, but enough to make the blood flow. It flooded her mouth. Its taste spread to her body and mind.

Raven Bird looked curiously and a little startled at her.

– Oracle, Gimmick said, shaking her head in amazement. – I... can feel her.

An enhanced, powerful sensation followed realization. Suddenly a part of her consciousness shifted to Jolene's mind and she saw the world through her friend's eyes, something that had previously only happened when Oracle had seen the future.

But this was the present. Gimmick knew that, somehow, as she saw Jolene Masters approach the well known, dubious establishment at the Wharf, in the Old Brewery District. She didn't actually see Jolene, but the street, the area ahead of her. It was as if she actually rode the dark girl's mind and experienced the world through her senses.

The Catcher attacked her with one of his ropes, attempting to hit her with it. She grabbed it, still distracted and pulled him forward, right into her right fist.

This... contact actually felt more... intimate than earlier contacts with Oracle, more potent in a way, though not quite that intense.

But there was something...

Something right under the surface, where she couldn't access it.

She struck the Catcher, struck him time and time again, pushed him at the wall and held him there, until she knew he could no longer stand on his feet and she let go of him, and he slipped down the wall and sat there without moving, more unconscious than not.

– You're pathetic, aren't you? She snarled. – I could handle you half asleep.

She gasped, as Jolene gasped, as terror rode them both and the intensity grew.

Oracle was sweating, sweating hard, before slowly calming down and the heart no longer hammered in her chest. Gimmick found the collar from her purse and put it around the Catcher's neck. The final resistance left him.

She pulled him back on his feet and pushed him effortlessly down the street. Raven Bird landed by their side and walked with them.

– This was fun! Gimmick spat her contempt at Troy Franklin. – We must do it again sometime. Hopefully, there will be more *spunk* in you then…

Her voice turned deeper, more like Jolene's.

She knew Lisa looked at her with anxious eyes.

The Catcher stumbled forward, virtually unaware of his surroundings. She couldn't help but pick up his dull thoughts as well and being reminded of the horrors of the collar, and what he lived through in prison. He walked straight into the street on a red light, and she had to grab him and pull him back in order to keep him from getting run down by an angry car passing by.

The car looked very angry to her. She had no sense of the driver, didn't even see him through the clear windows. But she imagined that the car snarled at her.

She rubbed her forehead.

– Is she still there? Lisa wondered incredulous.

Raven Bird's voice sounded distant and weak, hardly audible above the buzz.

– Yes. I try keeping her out, but I can't. It… hurts.

And then it happened, the more powerful shift in consciousness, from one moment to another.

Jolene walked inside the Old Brewery dump, the smoke-filled main room where big females danced nude on the stage, where males marked her with cruel, possessive stares.

It was as if Lucinda's entire consciousness had been taken over by what she experienced as beyond powerful impressions and sensations. She gasped and kept gasping without a sound finding its way from her throat and her mouth and through her parted lips.

Jolene walked straight to the dressing room. The stench from the brewery in the basement and «homemade» liquor ripped into her nostrils. The steam of sweat and alcohol followed her into the room with the many mirrors and big girls.

She stopped before a big redhead resting in an armchair. A red half-mask, the same color as her sparse clothing covered the girl's eyes.

– C'mon, Adeline, time to go home, to leave this place.

Adeline Goddard looked at her with hazy eyes filled with dull pain. She was shivering, being in the first stage of drug-withdrawal.

– I can't d-do t-that, the girl stuttered. – Chuck will soon come with my n-needle and then I will d-dance the night away.

Chuck was the owner of this establishment, the kind man employing big girls.

– Where is the payment Raven Bird gave you? Jolene asked softly.

– I owned Chuck m-money, but now everything will be f-fine s-soon. H will take care of everything.

H was heroin.

– That won't happen. Jolene shook her head. – I'll take you out of here.

She grabbed the thin arm and pulled the girl on her feet. Adeline was skinny. The misuse and subsequent malnutrition had kept her from developing properly compared to other big girls.

A guard stood in the door, glaring menacingly at Jolene.

– Just you try it, she hissed at him.

He stepped aside faster than a shadow.

Jolene turned to the other girls in the room.

– I know several of you have been forced into this as well, she said softly. – Endure. I will return for you all.

Some of them spat curses at her. Others busied themselves in front of one of the many mirrors. The rest hardly reacted at all. They stared at the world with dull eyes.

Gimmick and Raven Bird walked the Catcher into the nearest police station, leaving him with the desk sergeant there.

– I hope you will manage to hold onto him this time, Gimmick said, shaking her head in more than one patronizing way.

She stumbled outside and would have fallen if Lisa hadn't caught her. They sat down on the nearest bench, clearly out of breath.

Raven Bird looked worried at her behind the mask.

– I don't know. Gimmick sniffed. – I don't know what is wrong. I keep attempting to reach Oracle's conscious mind, in vain.

Fear, even a growing terror rode them both.

Oracle half carried, half dragged Adeline through the dark hallways, going straight for the backdoor. The girl began sweating, sweating hard. Jolene dried her brow with her sleeve.

– I know it's hard. She spoke softly into the other's ear. – But I will stay with you this time, stay with you every inch of the way.

– It hurts, Adeline whimpered. – It hurts BAD.

They reached the alley. The door slammed close behind them. The loud music from inside turned distant and muted. The sound of the loud traffic thundered in their ears. The streetlights illuminated Adeline's exposed pale skin.

– No, she whimpered, resisting the dark girl's efforts, – they'll come for me and p-punish m-me.

– They will if we don't get away from here, Oracle said firmly. – In your condition I can't teleport you without hurting you. We need to run.

And kept pulling. The redhead was much too weak to resist.

– But, no, they won't. I will smash them if they ever come for you, and you will, too, once you're free of the chains they've put on you. We will gather evidence against them all, putting them behind bars forever.

Adeline chuckled darkly.

– That's such a *ridiculous* statement, she cackled. – You don't *know* them, like I do.

She tore herself free and faced the other with a snarl.

– Then tell me, Jolene insisted. – Tell me everything you know about them.

She reached out a hand again.

– NO!

Adeline gestured and it was like Jolene was hit and pushed backwards by a giant invisible hand. Her head and upper body met the wall with a loud crack and she fell to the ground. She didn't move. A trail of blood flowed from her temple. Adeline looked at her with terror in her eyes, her pale and sweaty face taking a turn for the worse.

– You silly cow, she mumbled. – You *silly* cow!

She stumbled away. After a few steps she managed a kind of run. She kept running, not looking back once. The loud, whining scream drowned in the loud traffic as she reached the main street at the end of the alley.

Gimmick screamed. It happened so sudden, so unexpected.

Lisa held her, doing her best to comfort her shaking form.

– She's in trouble, real trouble. We must go there. At once!

Lucinda rose on unsteady legs, and fell right back on her ass.

The Old Brewery District was on the other side of town and not in any way quickly accessible.

– You go, Gimmick cried. – Hurry!

Raven Bird nodded with a parched throat and took to the air. She couldn't fly fast, but she could fly straight. Gimmick pushed the alarm on the ring, just about managed to do it, before the dizziness overwhelmed her and she collapsed on the bench.

Oracle lifted her head, shaking it in an attempt at clearing it. Heavy steps closed in on her. She glimpsed feet through her hazy vision.

– One bird has flown, Chuck Storm said pleased. – But it will be no difficult feat to recapture her. She has left us a far more valuable gift.

They grabbed the semiconscious Oracle. Storm struck her jaw. Another buried his fist in her abdomen. She yelped in pain.

– We have to be a little rough, honey. Too bad we don't have one of those nice collars. But you will regain your beauty soon enough, in time to shine in our stable.

They were hardly more than thugs, totally lacking in sophistication, but their unmistakable skills kept her in that horrible state of semi-consciousness, in a permanent state of red and gray. She fought to activate her power, but her head cried THUD THUD THUD. Nothing worked.

He lifted her up after the collar. She hung in his grip like wet clothes.

– We can't display you at any public stage, of course. You're way too *hot* for that, but rest assured that our rich guests will pay handsomely to see you perform at private, exclusive parties. Once you're properly trained you'll become extremely popular.

They carried her back inside, into a bedroom with a giant bed. She glimpsed it through that horrible haze of red and gray. One of the men produced a needle. She writhed weakly in their grip. Yet more brutal strikes made her crumble in their grip once again.

– This isn't the really good stuff that your friend Adeline has been given, just a bit of juice making you pliable for a while, making you a good girl throughout your first *lesson*.

He set the needle in her arm and emptied the content in her veins. The red and gray turned dark gray. They started ripping off her clothes. A dull, somewhat aware part of her registered that they were filming it all. They were fondling her with crude, invasive hands. The sick cackle and expectant laughter echoed in her mind like wool. They began undressing with leering grins. Hardening cocks rose and pointed at her.

Storm kissed her lips.

– You will do us many services, he cackled. – In fact, once you're tamed there will be no *end* to your usefulness.

She attempted to scream, wanted it desperately, but she couldn't even do that, couldn't do more than a weak choke.

– You're gonna get it, now, cunt!

A deep sound shook her, as if she was being torn apart inside.

And then she found herself in the hallway, or in one hallway, she couldn't tell.

– WHAT THE FUCK, she heard.

– WHERE DID THE BITCH GO?

– SHE CAN'T HAVE GONE FAR. FIND HER!

She faced a wall, leaning against it in a shadowy hallway with pale colors.

– Lucinda? She frowned.

And then the contact was broken, cut off like a string. Gimmick crumbled on the bench outside the police station, pale and sweaty beyond words. She attempted to reestablish contact, but there was nothing, nothing there.

224

People approached her cautiously, and fear grew further.

– Stay away, she told the cops and the curious bystanders. – I'm perfectly okay. There is no need to fuss over me.

And then, suddenly her view shifted to Raven Bird, to Lisa as she flew across town.

Gimmick's eyes were open, but she didn't see those around her, those grabbing her, only the aerial view of the Old Brewery building. She hardly even felt their hands. Raven Bird and her rapid breathing seemed to fill all her senses. It was clear to her that the two of them were reinforcing each other's emotions and reactions.

There was a loud crack. The entire image that was Raven Bird's vision seemed to shake. It resembled a painting being pulled back and forth in a tug of war. The first explosion didn't seem to actually do anything.

Then the building exploded in an inferno of sound and fury and fire. It practically *dissolved* from one moment to the next. The shockwave pushed Raven Bird backwards. She floated on her back on a wave of heated air, falling down on a roof nearby, somewhat safe and sound, as the flames of the inferno that showed no signs of pulling back caressed her and blistered her unprotected skin.

Chapter 13

Coleman Square and most of the city center was at a fairly safe distance from the impact, even as a large part of the city was flattened and ravaged by the fall and its aftermath.

It was a kind of domino-effect, one toppled building toppling the next and so on. People watched the repetitions with a stunned and dull expression and kept blinking, as if they couldn't quite believe their eyes.

Lucinda saw the exhilaration in some minds, though, including that of her sister. They didn't just feel shock, but also other, more complex emotions.

The collapse and disaster mixed with the explosion two years ago in her mind, mingling, becoming one.

Her confusion lasted for long, long seconds before sorting itself out in her head. The flames filling her vision faded and only the massive dust clouds remained.

The brewery in the basement had exploded, taking with it the entire building and the surrounding blocks. Pieces of flesh and bone and blood had spread across a vast area.

They had made sure to DNA-test every single piece they could find, and they had combed everywhere where there was a reasonable change of fallout.

They had found absolutely no trace of Jolene Masters.

She had become something of a hero, even a martyr to the movement since her shocking and mysterious disappearance. Her reputation had grown to almost mythic proportions.

Other big people, a considerable number of strangers flocked around Lucinda, ignoring the ruckus and panic, joining those she already knew in congratulating her. It warmed her, even though she frowned a little.

– You made such a great speech, Melinda marveled.

– I wanted to honor her, do her justice. Lucinda bowed her head. – I'm not so sure I did.

– Trust me, Melinda said, with cheeks glowing in excitement. – Jolene would have been proud of you. In fact, the way I see it your performance and rhetoric was far more radical, went further by far than anything she ever said or did. Hell, she would have been *ecstatic*.

– I'd say, Miriam said empathically.

The others joined in, voicing their support.

Lucinda felt it flow at her, adding to the touching of hands and supporting kisses. Her reserved smile blossomed and her heart beat harder in joy.

Determination grew further in her mind and at her core. She began studying in earnest the people gathered around her, scanning their minds without them being any wiser, assessing and analyzing them, constantly picking and choosing, disregarding and accepting.

It wasn't easy in this gathering in the midst of panic and confusion, but she managed, fueled by what waxed and glowed within.

They left Coleman Square in the same great mood shared by almost everybody. The shock caused by the growing disaster unfolding in the city couldn't stifle that completely.

The dust settled only slowly behind them and in their stirred insides. The excitement and glowing hot determination persisted.

Two dozen big women entered the cafeteria on a far pier of the Wharf. They smiled and laughed a lot, causing a stir of another world.

A reporter shouted into his mike on the giant screen, the image of his red face juxtaposed with those of the ruins of the giant buildings, the smoke spreading across the city.

The other guests scowled at the big people, glancing with hazy eyes at the screen, mumbling among themselves.

The twenty-four gathered large heaps of food on their plates and began devouring it all with a more than healthy appetite and excited chatter.

They occupied two long tables, but most of the attention was directed at Lucinda. The girls looked at her with admiration and the beginning of devotion in shiny eyes. She felt a warm flow inside.

– Cops have never been my friends, Myra declared, speaking quite loud. – They have, on the contrary done the utmost to hassle me and mine from the start. Why should I care about them?

– I must admit I find it funny that most of the victims clearly shared the views of their executioners, Miriam said, shaking her head hard. – If that isn't poetic justice nothing is.

She giggled, glancing nervously around her, but with a determined look carved on the pretty face.

Lucinda leaned forward and everyone else did, too.

– Look at them. She indicated the other guests with a wave of the hand. – People recoil in horror at old pictures of blacks draped in shackles & chains, yet choose to live their lives as shackled slaves. We have been granted, through coincidence and fate the awareness to be different. I would bet all of us have suffered because of it, but without the Great Darkness we would probably have been exactly like the rest of the sheep, not ever realizing how special we truly are.

They looked exalted at her and nodded in solemn agreement.

Melinda did, too, even though Big Sister sensed her reluctance.

What… are we doing?

Lucinda smiled, pleased by the nuances in Melinda's wording.

There was no terrorist attack, Kid Sister pointed out, quite unnecessary. The building construction was faulty and the fucker of an entrepreneur is getting off easy.

We're grabbing a lucky opportunity, Lucinda shrugged in her mind. Miriam is correct. Those assholes deserved what they got and we will use the momentum of today's events for all it's worth, both publicly and with the girls.

She indicated those around the tables without moving.

The racists, through today's random events have been exposed and are finally vulnerable and we will move in for the kill.

They hurried to the Center afterwards, racing to release their heavy load in time. The walk through the ruins and dusty streets took longer than they liked, but as they had realized before they visited the place: the few toilets available at the cafeteria and at the Wharf as a whole were no alternative. Wise by experience they left the place long before the need to shit and pee revealed itself.

The cold sweat began showing on their brow before they got halfway.

– Damn! Lois muttered. – Felt overconfident, didn't we? Brazen?

No one commented on her words, both because they knew perfectly well what she meant and because they focused all their willpower on keeping the shit inside.

Melinda stared ahead as she walked with a pained expression in her pale face. What her «inner face» looked like to Lucinda was far worse.

They reached Coleman Square, with its dust and open landscape.

– We must find a spot, Lois mumbled, – an alley or somewhere.

The portal, Melinda «gasped».

No. Lucinda shook her head. Not the portal. It is too far away, anyway.

The two blocks seemed like an infinite stretch.

– We go back, she said, – into the Brewery. We should have gone there right away.

Melinda gasped, aloud, and crouched, pressing a palm at the wall, pulling her panties and pants down her thighs in one, desperate move. The others were able to cast one bewildered look at her before the wet shit started flowing between her thighs and they turned brown and ugly. She screamed in anguish. There was a dark flash of sorts, emanating from Melinda, making Lucinda blink, before full-fledged reality rushed back in, and they were right there, stuck in the busy Coleman Square, as Myra, too, let go of her load, and she started sobbing in a quiet despair.

228

The mumbling around them turned pointed, vicious. The others formed a protective circle around the two girls, in vain.

– What the fuck are they doing?

People began glaring, really glaring at them. Cruel laughter rose from sore throats.

– What's the matter with you, people? Lois cried. – Do you think they do this on purpose?

People practically ignored her. If anything, it made them worse.

– Yeah, we forgot that you guys are like small children, a man chuckled wickedly. – You can't keep your shit.

Mumbles filled the air. The voices rose and didn't settle.

– Let's go, Lucinda said, – *walk* slowly all the way to the center. We've got nothing to be ashamed of.

She pulled Melinda on her feet. Kid Sister stood on her own. With a determined look on her face she pulled her panties and pants back up. Myra did, too.

They walked the gauntlet through streets filled with contempt and loathing.

– Look at those freaks…

Lucinda wanted to do something, do something bad, but there was no way she could handle them all and she pulled back into herself, like the rest of her sisters, doing her best to endure the gauntlet and not making any attempt at beating it.

– What if… they charge us? Myra whispered, filled with shame and naked fear.

Lucinda had no answer for her or herself, terrified for what would happen if they were attacked.

– It's a mob, she shrugged, with a certainty she didn't feel. – They are capable of doing bad things to us, but right now I think they're content with enjoying their perceived superiority, their beyond ugly snarls.

And then she added, as an afterthought:

- And they know we're capable of hurting them, hurting them bad, no matter their superior number.

Her companions once more looked to her for leadership and she obliged. She led them through these loud, dusty streets, to the fortress, the shelter at the city's center.

Miriam fumbled with her keys, her hands shaking. The door finally opened, a black hole sucking them inside, welcoming them with a sick swoop hurting their ears just as much as the shouts from the people closing in on them.

The door closed by itself. Miriam crouched and threw up on the floor. Several of the others looked like they wanted to join her, but they kept it inside, kept it bottled up inside. They hurried upstairs, to the toilets, the big and comfortable toilets.

The stench once again filled Lucinda nostrils and mind, making her sicker than ever.

The two sisters sat in the lounge with the others afterwards, holding around each other, unable to speak or even move much. They held hands. Everybody touched and comforted each other.

Lucinda felt everybody's despair. She was used to it, but it still hit her harder than the rest, inevitably. The feedback made it worse for everybody. Melinda clutched her discreetly and by an act of will she managed to break the loop.

Tears of despair and rage kept flowing from sore eyes.

– What was that? Lois cringed. – For one moment it was if my... my emotions were returned to me tenfold, as if someone was *doing* it.

They looked bewildered at each other. The sisters made an effort to mask their emotions, their knowledge of what had happened and it made them feel even worse, made them feel like the worst kind of shit.

Miriam rose, visibly pulling herself together.

– It is as I have told you. She spoke up. – It's more than likely that several of you have hidden gifts we haven't discovered yet...

She straightened, swallowing hard.

– I know we haven't scheduled any exercise today, but I think, I feel strongly that we should use any opportunity to do so, to find our hidden depths and bring them forth.

There was a time of silence, unknown and awkward, before the two sisters rose and joined her there, on the floor.

Lois was next, then Myra. They all moved like a flow and coddled and caressed each other there on the floor.

– We need our hidden depths, Lucinda stated with a very visible right hand rolled into a fist, – need Power.

And emotion once again surged between them, but now it was heat. Now, it was fire.

– The assholes have been exposed, Melinda stated calmly, intensively. – And they're coming out of the woodwork, like the worms they are.

The young girl stood there, in front of them all, shaking in anger and passion. Lucinda swallowed hard and had to go deep within herself to not be overwhelmed by emotion.

They ran and lifted weights and fought themselves through the gauntlet, until stars flooded their closed eyelids.

– I can hear myself screaming, Myra gasped, – which is funny since I haven't.

There was a mix of incredulity and humor and wonder and anxiety in her voice.

– Today we start on the sandbags, Lucinda declared later, much later, when they were all pretty much exhausted beyond recovery.

Miriam glanced at her, but voiced no protest. It had been subtle at first, but Lucinda had more or less taken over everything.

– Hit it! Lucinda shouted. – Harder. HARDER

She was on the girls like a hawk, constantly prodding and even chastising them. Everybody jumped when she slammed the belt she held in her hand at the floor like a whip. The sisters gave them an initial crash course in self defense, the first of many in the weeks to come. Melinda slammed Lois to the ground. The big and much stronger woman couldn't catch the dancing dove driving her to frustration and beyond.

They fed again, safe in their surroundings, wolfing down the food without restraint or second thoughts. The smiles and laughter rose to dominance once again, even though uncertain smiles lingered. They sent Lucinda curious and uneasy glances.

One more visit to the restroom and the big toilet bowls, more stench and revulsion.

They showered and instead of dressing in their used clothes they were given new by the Center. Miriam offered and Lucinda didn't have to ask or force the issue. There were more hugs and bonding. They eventually drifted towards the exit, with more uncertain smiles and glances, at each other and Lucinda.

– We should stay a few more hours, if you don't mind, Lucinda suggested.

Some of them hesitated, but everybody returned with her to the plush room and sat down in the pleasant chairs.

Melinda pulled the curtains tight. All the windows stopped brightening the room. Several of the young girls shuddered in the suddenly dank place.

Lucinda put a stool in front of one of them. She put an envelope there and pulled back.

– Lift it, she said casually.

A hand reached out.

– Without physically touching it.

The hand pulled back.

– Lift it, push it, do anything with it, Lucinda told Ashanti. – Focus on its structure, tear everything apart.

Ashanti tried. They saw how she focused, focused hard on the envelope.

She leaned back in her chair not that long afterwards, spent like after a run, with nothing to show for herself.

Myra made the attempt as well. They observed how her brow turned furrowed with concentration.

— Don't try too hard, Lucinda said. — Breathe evenly and act casually, like when you are moving an arm and or a leg.

Long seconds passed. Nothing happened. Close to a minute passed. Nothing happened. The girl shook her head.

Lucinda turned to Miriam.

— Do you have a portable measuring device?

Miriam's face lit up in renewed respect for the other woman.

— Yes, why haven't we thought about that? She said, eagerly rushing off.

— We have just done this in a laboratory, Lucinda told the others. — Not in pleasant surrounding like these. We were told we were lab rats, but we aren't.

Miriam returned quickly, out of breath. She began attaching electrodes to Ashanti's temples and fingers, and then she switched on the machine.

— It's cold, Ashanti said, shivering a little.

— It's supposed to be, honey, Miriam smoothened her.

Lucinda looked at the screen. It was a pretty forward display. There was one needle jumping up and down, reaching for a green area.

Positive feedback, Melinda thought brightly. Green is a good color.

— It measures... Miriam began.

— Alpha waves, Lucinda said.

She turned the machine around, letting Ashanti see the display.

— Look at it, she said. — Study it. When you see the needle at a high point, do your best to note your mood and thoughts. It's known as biofeedback. Try to stay there, to find a rhythm. You will enter what is called an Altered State of Consciousness. There might be some unpleasantness, but if you feel it, don't sssshy away from it, but ssssavor it.

As Lucinda began to lisp, the others began glancing at her, staring at her. She felt her own ASC coming on. It came strangely easy to her these days, even though she hadn't really done it that much. She knew her face changed and her eyes turned deep and big and vivid and strange. Everybody's thoughts came to her without her straining herself and she wondered why she hadn't really done this before.

She gasped soundlessly, knowing beyond knowing that the others hadn't heard her. They all began glowing in a weird, eerie light. Her hands began itching. She had reached out almost all the way to Ashanti when she realized what she was doing and let her hands fall casually back to their usual position by her hips.

Melinda glowed, too, stronger than ever.

232

One of the lights in the ceiling began failing. Lucinda looked at the needle. It didn't jump.

She watched the others. Several of them clearly had emulated Ashanti and joined her in her efforts.

The needle jumped. The air surrounding the black girl started shimmering, started…

Ashanti cried out, startling everybody in the room.

– Sorry, she bellowed weakly. – Sorry. I couldn't hold on to it anymore. I couldn't!

– Don't sweat it, Lucinda said kindly and comforted her with a light touch on her shoulder. – You did it, you know.

She looked in triumph at everybody.

– And you weren't the only one.

– But nothing happened, Ashanti protested.

– That isn't so, Melinda pointed out. – Something did happen, several things actually.

And everybody's eyes seemingly brightened.

– My turn, Lucinda said.

Melinda meticulously attached the sensors to her sister's temples, both of them making a production of it. Lucinda deliberately held herself back, waited one moment, two moments, five… before she let herself go… and the needle jumped into the green area and stayed there.

– It feelsss sssstrange, she reported, – assss if I'm not really here.

She saw herself through their eyes, saw the dark aura surrounding her, visibly bigger than in every other person she had looked at, even Jolene. It was a stunning, awe-inspiring sight.

– I think I can… think I can see… more, she stated, as she kept up the pretense. – It is as if I am in several places simultaneously.

Thoughts, ideas, inspirations raced through her head, helping her implementing what she had already planned and started. She set her eyes on Tabitha, a tall, somewhat incomplete girl.

– I can see you from behind, she said, with a stunned expression in her face.

– You can? The girl gasped excited.

– Yes, it is as if I am standing right behind you, breathing down your neck. I think I am able to be several places simultaneously, or at least see from several angles without moving.

– That's so *cool!*

The others echoed the sentiment.

– What am I doing now? Miriam asked and held her hands behind her back.

Lucinda looked at her without looking at her, wondering if there was a mocking expression hidden behind the other woman's smile.

– You're making a circle with your right thumb and index finger, she grinned, portraying excitement, just like a young woman that had just discovered something amazing about herself would do.

Those able to observe Miriam's back froze and happy, excited smiles lit their face.

Miriam nodded in acknowledgment.

– You were always one of the most promising candidates, she said. – I've waited for you to express it. Congratulations, you've just taken another step on your path.

She walked forward and embraced Lucinda. The others did as well, some of them hesitant, but increasingly less so. Lucinda practically heard their young hearts beat.

The needle fell. Lucinda's triumphant euphoria and sense of power faded, but lingered.

– Your turn, she told Miriam.

She personally attached the sensors to the teacher's temples. Miriam sat there. The needle jumped almost immediately and stayed there.

– It does that every time, she said frustrated, – but nothing happens.

– Something happens, Lucinda insisted. – We just don't notice what, that's all.

The strange, eerie mood persisted, in the room and among those present.

– I hear a sound, Miriam stated.

The others didn't.

– What kind of sound? Melinda asked.

– I don't... know...

– You can't be more specific?

Miriam shook her head.

– Are you noticing any other sensations?

Miriam kept shaking her head.

Lucinda heard it through her mind. It made her shake. She seemed surrounded by a sudden and brief chill.

The needle fell. Miriam disengaged the sensors herself.

Lois took her place. Lucinda sensed her... her anxiety. Lois scratched her hands and arms, as if... the skin was itching.

Aside from that the telepath found nothing in particular in her mind, no matter how deep she scanned. The older woman's image of herself had been scarred long ago, by what followed the Great Darkness, but she had spoken about that in length in the group talk and bonding sessions.

234

She isn't hiding anything, Big Sister told Melinda.

Miriam bent down to pick up the sensors from the floor where she had thrown them, slowly halting, stopping in her tracks. They all heard it, a crackle in the air, all saw it, the shimmer around Lois' hands. She looked astonished at it. It faded a bit, while her focus inevitably broke, but then, shortly afterwards appeared again.

The shimmer turned to a glow, to a sizzling fire-like energy. It grew from her hands like wires, dancing and twisting in the air in front of her.

One wire reached out for Miriam and sliced the skin of her right hand. Her shout of pain mixed with the shocked gasps from everybody else.

The energy faded and everything looked normal again. Only in the eyes of those gathered around the big woman one could glimpse the recent past and the shadows of the future.

You can sense it, can you?

Lucinda frowned, fighting even harder to keep her composure. The voice in her head she was unable to identify made the familiar chills surge through her body.

You can sense the *dread,* the *horror* and the dark portents.

She recognized the snarl, the boundless wrath and loathing, the beyond sinister laughter of the force she had learned to know as Black Dragon.

A hand touched her shoulder. She almost jumped in her tracks.

– Are you okay? Miriam asked softly.

– I am, thank you, she assured the other.

She turned toward the others, as they left, reluctant to do so, feeling even stronger the bond between them all.

Is Lois okay? Melinda wondered.

She is, Lucinda replied confident to Kid Sister.

Melinda had sat down in the chair, too. She hadn't revealed anything or faked it, but there had been something about her trial, something Lucinda has been unable to grasp.

She relived it, replayed it in her mind.

Worry grabbed her again, but illumination eluded her.

No one had managed to move the envelope, though. It still rested on the table where Lucinda had left it, like a portent.

The women left, but a part of them stayed in the room.

– The fallout from last week's dramatic public events is doomed to be substantial, Miriam said in speech at a meeting with the Center's board of directors not many days later. – We already see further evidence more than suggesting that the Great Darkness wasn't merely a single, isolated incident, but the first in a long row that will inevitably change our world forever. One thing is the purely physical manifestations, another is, as I've stated before: the powerful social ramifications.

– So, where are we… heading? A cigar-smoking woman at the head of the table asked.

– It's impossible to tell at this point, Miriam willingly conceded. – And logic suggests that the situation will grow more obtrusive, not less. We will continue monitoring and analyzing the puzzle, the tapestry as it unfolds, of course.

The *Tapestry*.

Lucinda monitored the meeting from the outside, for the first time taking a good look at the board of perceived powerful people.

She shook her head to Melinda.

– They're mostly greedy bastards masking that behind a shell of benevolence, of «social responsibility», she said, – but aside from that there is little or nothing suspicious.

The meeting ended. Those present filed away, until that left nothing but an empty room. Lucinda heard the sound again, not through another's mind this time and she recognized it. It reminded her of an alarum, a distress call in the night.

– I felt something, Melinda said slowly.

Lucinda turned to her, working even harder in the effort of masking her emotions, her thoughts.

– What did you feel?

Melinda pondered the question, pondered her own impressions.

– I don't know. It is right there, you know, at the tip of my fingers, my eyebrows, whatever, but I'm unable to reach it.

She turned moody, withdrawn.

– I felt it just before I *shit* myself, too.

Self-recriminations and contempt dominated her features and her mind.

Lucinda touched her cheek in a comforting gesture.

Melinda dried her tears with a defiant stare.

They walked down the street, heading home, holding each other tight.

Several days passed with relative tranquility. They walked down the same street, returning to the center. They entered what seemed like a different place, the photo atelier in the attic, a bright place filled with even light and white umbrellas and cameras and tripods.

– Will there be rain? Ashanti wondered.

Nervous giggles from the others accompanied her words.

– The umbrellas are used to reflect light, Miriam explained with a smile. – They will be a very familiar sight to you the coming weeks.

Miriam had returned to her more confident and aloof administrator self. She led the twenty big females further into the room, to another big, well dressed woman waiting in front of one of the white screens.

– This is Desmonia, she presented. – She will oversee your transformation from timid hopefuls to full-fledged models making both the Center and yourselves some hard-needed cash.

More insecure laughter ensued.

– Hello everybody, Desmonia greeted them frivolously.

– H'lo, her new charges mumbled or replied in a pretty unimpressive response.

– Come with me, please.

And they were led into yet another room with plush sofas and furniture. They sat down and Desmonia... called attention to herself, and they all focused on her.

She wore a black dress, revealing her muscled arms and thighs. Her black hair was done in a fairly plain, but clearly deliberate style, highlighting her forehead and eyes, her big and deep eyes.

– I greet you, proud women, she began. – This is what you have been yearning and preparing for during all your time here: a chance to shine and excel using your talents for all they are worth.

– You're so beautiful, Melinda said promptly. – Will we be like you?

– You will! The confident woman nodded. – You will all be worshipped by male and females alike. *Big* will be the new standard, leaving small sized and size zero models behind like the yesterday they are.

Wicked chuckles and enthusiastic applause followed.

Desmonia took a bow.

– Men will desire you and women will envy you. You will be their idols, the next big thing until you are firmly established in people's consciousness and then it will no longer matter. Your birthright will already be yours.

A flicker of a frown touched Lucinda's mind and brow. She knew what the other woman was truly saying, hinting at beneath the bluster and boasting.

But the warm glow persisted and expanded within.

– I'll teach you how to stand, to smile, to be, the teacher said. – When I'm done with you, you will be outstanding representatives of our kind.

A couple of hours later they had already been given the first, precious lesson.

– Stand! Desmonia snapped.

Lucinda did, straightening, striving to find mercy for the critical eyes burning her.

– Relax! Desmonia said casually.

Which had the complete opposite effect, of course.

– That won't do. The other woman shook her head in dismay. – That won't do at all. If you do that during the photo-sessions or when walking down the catwalk, you will look completely ridiculous. There is vast room for improvement here, ladies.

Lucinda bit her lip, bowing her ahead in disgrace.

Ruby stepped forward. Ruby was used by Desmonia every time she needed to demonstrate «how it is done». The signal was given and the redhead moved like greased lightning across the floor, a smooth but powerful animal on the prowl. The girls kept gasping impressed.

– See how her big body doesn't keep her from showing grace and mobility? Look at her expression, how her face is a mirror and not a window.

They did and when the teacher sent them across the floor doing their best to copy Cool Ruby, failing miserably, of course…

Desmonia smiled, a very kind smile. Melinda shrunk to nothing in her shame.

– We have a lot to of ground to cover here, girls. Take comfort in the fact that when your lessons are done you will be confident and suave young women that no longer have to take shit from anybody.

Melinda walked down the floor. Lucinda followed her, and all the others, and when everybody had done it once, they began again. They walked down a catwalk simulating applause and an audience, all of it blurring in their mind, until the outside world hardly existed anymore.

– That's it for tonight, girl. You won't be allowed to leave and will stay the night here, of course.

– But it is Friday night, Maya groaned.

– Precisely, Desmonia nodded. – That is a good thing, since you don't have to report for work and won't be fired when you don't show up, and that will give those of you I give up as useless something to fall back on when I fire you. We are the new great wonders of the world and I will accept nothing less of you.

They were given a healthy evening meal and sent to bed. The teacher followed them there, to mattresses on the floor in one single hall.

– Good night, girls, she said from the door. – Enjoy pleasant dreams.

– GOOD NIGHT, DESMONIA, ENJOY PLEASANT DREAMS

They choired, like good girls.

– Christ! Lois snarled with savvy.

Everybody giggled in stark relief, but looked at the half-open door with anxiety in their eyes.

Desmonia is so… imposing, Melinda thought. I feel like I'm right back at the fucking dormitory.

Yes, she is, Lucinda agreed. I do, too.

Like she can see straight through you. Do you think she... can?

No, but she does have a kind of charisma-power making it easy for her to get her point through. We just have to be on guard in case she tries to do more.

It was hard to fall asleep, hard to even become sleepy, but eventually they did.

They slept on the mattresses, until they were roused early next morning. And everything started again.

They stood there, posing for the photographer.

– Lucinda, I want you to raise your jaw a bit.

A hand touched her jaw and Lucinda felt strangely detached, as if she couldn't say no to her.

– That's a good girl...

Desmonia walked in front of the line, seemingly keeping her eyes on everybody simultaneously. It was disconcerting in major ways.

– You will look into the camera often, with your pretty smile and steady look. You will remember that this is the point of contact between you and those out there we seek to sway, to bend to our will.

– Advertising 101? Ashanti wondered.

– Precisely! It is the alpha and omega of it actually, even though very few in the business dare admitting it. Advertising is plain old brainwashing in its cute, but no less sinister form, my children.

Nervous laughter. She was cute where she stood herself, giving off the innocence and benevolence Lucinda sensed in her, by probing deep.

– I want this, Lucinda stated calmly. – I want money and independence and power.

– I know you do, honey, the charming woman said, slowly, deliberately making a fist of her right hand. – I know you do. I know you want to commit to this, because a girl has to look out for herself in this world.

Nods and smiles spread through the gathering.

They had breakfast, spent some time shitting on the comfortable toilet bowl, trained some more, had dinner and shit some more, and trained and fed and shit. And days and nights passed in a blur.

Lucinda heard the music before it thundered in her ears. She saw the room change before it happened. The photo shoot was in full session. Lightly clad men and women moved accompanied by flashes and heavy beat. She hardly recalled herself as the awkward and shy amateur any longer. Desmonia's many strict lessons had faded in her consciousness and become part of her instincts and impulses.

Men and women had finally mingled, on the final days of the training and teaching. It ignited yet another level of stress and unfulfilled desire, palpable and powerful. It showed on the photographs and films, on all interaction between the newly educated models.

Lucinda watched Melinda, how the young girl stared at a particular young man with doe eyes and practically followed him around with her tongue hanging out, her still fairly innocent smile gaining another layer of sensuality as well.

Kid Sister wore a pale green flight uniform or something resembling it and moved in a manner making the males present wanting to devour her on the spot.

Lots of photographs and films were taken. They frowned at the early results, from their training, at how wooden and insecure they looked, and nodded eagerly when Desmonia used them as training videos and photos. But then, slowly a smile began playing on their lips, spreading to their entire face.

Lucinda watched herself stretched out on a couch, scantly clad, smiling enticingly to the photographer, and felt pride swell within.

The text was simple, but effective:

BIG CLOTHES FOR BIG PEOPLE

And then Melinda joined her, and a new text was added:

SISTERS OF STRENGTH

Then there was a group image with some of them standing, others sitting on the floor.

THE WAVE OF THE FUTURE

Later various other brands were added to the franchise. It remained weird, even eerie weeks after that again, when they looked at themselves, or at what looked like themselves, the strangers caught on camera.

When the sisters received their first inflated salary Lucinda and others called their old employers to terminate their old job, those moments were duly recorded and celebrated with champagne.

– I let him go, Lucinda giggled. – Cheers!

The loud choir of a response felt good beyond belief. She took a huge sip of the bubbly water.

When they went out dancing that night, they had consumed quite a lot of the bubbly water in advance. There was a lot of giggling and loud cries.

The first successful ads had been placed on posters, on the Grid and in other venues two weeks ago and they were recognized on the street. Anxiety and joy coursed through them. Lucinda, as always sensed her emotions enhanced in others twice over.

When she saw the image of herself cover an entire wall, that powerful sensation increased further. The thrill within and without made her skin tingle.

The laser lights and smoke surrounded them as they danced in the disco basement at the old tavern. They shook loose at the packed place, drawing many a stare from what was an amazingly mixed crowd.

Lucinda shook pleasantly, bathing in the sea of excited thoughts and emotions. She danced with Ronald, a guy from the Center. Most of the twenty women and twenty men in the program were present. They let loose in something resembling wild abandon and dominated the floor and stayed at the center of attention from their arrival and until they left.

She glimpsed Melinda in her green flight uniform, noted how she filled it, even though it was new only two weeks ago, how men's eyes were drawn to her long, shapely legs.

Then final worry left Big Sister, as she threw herself even harder into the dance and the abandon.

The light in the room turned red. She looked at it through the eyes of others and saw that it wasn't her imagination. She shivered. Ronald stepped close and grabbed her. His hands on her nude arms made her shiver in anticipation. It was as if his hands electrified the skin they touched. He kissed her on the lips and they were electrified, too. She responded instantly, without thought, pushing herself at him.

The dance ended, but it continued in her mind, as she stayed on the floor as the next song began, stayed with him, clung to him.

He pulled her with him, pulled her away. She panted, attempting to breathe properly, to draw air into her lungs. Everything felt hot and clammy and she couldn't get close enough to the big male roaming her body at will. She jumped into his arms, embracing him with arms and feet. Her nipples itched, her breasts were sore. She rubbed them hard against his face in an attempt to quench the pain and ascending need ravaging her. He chuckled pleased.

– Goddess, she mumbled with her lips smashed into his, – I feel so unbelievably horny.

Her voice echoed in a large room, a vast cave.

She writhed in his grip. He put her back down on the floor and pushed her at the wall. She hardly noticed the crash, the moment even more air was pushed from her already straining lungs. He had a hand on a breast, fondling it, squeezing it.

– Harder, she cried. – *Harder!*

Pain finally overpowered the need and she shouted short and sharp.

He pulled up her dress for all to see. She didn't care.

– I knew you were a firecracker, he hissed in her ears, – knew it the first time I saw you.

She frowned, reaching for his pants. He touched her all over, or so it felt. The moan rising from her sore throat was so loud that it overwhelmed the loud music in her ears.

But she heard his growls, his breath. The frown faded and she surrendered completely to his advances. She looked down. His pants no longer covered his hips, or anything. Her vision turned hazy by the sight of the big, hard cock. He held her easily. She rubbed and scratched the skin on his strong arms.

He lifted her up and pushed into her.

– Yes, she shouted. – YES!

Her feet embraced him once again, pushing his sweaty body tighter to hers. He began moving harder back and forth in her wet hole. Thought left her, cognition left her. Everything just faded away, except the burning pain rising and flaring all over her body.

– You're such a peach, he growled with triumphant scorn in his voice, – such a beyond tasty peach. This is grand. This is beyond grand.

People around them were getting affected as well, as usual, when Lucinda felt the rising pleasure ravage her flesh and mind. Not everybody acted on it, but quite a few did. She felt it, more than saw it.

The explosion, when it came blanketed everything else, took her over completely and utterly. Moans and growls escalated all around her. Her very essence seemed to fill the room, the entire building and everyone in it. Shouts of pleasure repeated themselves indefinitely. Somewhere, among all the noise she felt and heard Kid Sister cry out in vast joy, saw her ride a boy with features almost dissolved by the ecstasy brutally riding her.

Confusing and indistinct surroundings only slowly turned sharp through her eyes. She realized she sat on the floor, and that he, her fuck partner was nowhere to be seen. The big smile stayed on her lips and face, no matter how much her eyes moved and searched. Two males stared at her. They stood over two spent females across the hall. Juice dripped from half erected cocks. She sent a big grin in their direction, calling them to her, pulling them into her mind without thoughts and thoughts of consequences.

– It was so good, she mumbled with a look of profound joy on her face, – so good, so good and I want more, more, more…

Only the need mattered, the beyond powerful passion only marginally sated. The frown was back in place, but didn't move her, didn't make her reconsider anything.

The men rushed forward. One of them swept her up like a swab and carried her off. The other followed eagerly, like a panting dog. He stuck a hand between her thighs and began roaming her insides, and she mewed in pleasure and expectation.

They did her, she did them on a wide couch, on a soft carpet in a quiet office somewhere. She stretched out, performing for them between fucks, slipping down on the floor, the soft floor.

Shit poured from their holes and all three laughed themselves silly, kissing and comforting each other.

They pumped into her many times. She kept coming back for more, rubbing and caressing them and their cocks, petting and cajoling them with a frightening passion. Their eyes turned glassy and vacant, but she and her powerful mind kept their bodies going.

It just went on and on, until passing into darkness, into oblivion.

She rested on her back, holding the two men in her arms like she would babies, the two of them sleeping like the dead, empty, dried up, totally devoid of juice and with nothing left to give. Thought slowly returned to her fevered mind. The smile didn't leave her face. She, too, was spent, but feeling content, strong, powerful, bathing in the stench of her own body juices, semen and shit flowing down her thighs and hardening on her skin.

It wasn't until later that she realized that she hadn't been able to read his mind, read «Ronald's» mind and a deep chill passed through her and rocked her deepest self.

Chapter 14

I feel so cold, she thought. What is *happening* to me?

It was late at night, at the institute. She had gathered the women and men of her choice to further exercise and training, beyond what the institute would demand of them, far beyond. They looked attentive at her.

She glanced at Melinda from the edge of her vision. Kid Sister looked happy, unconcerned. Big Sister moved on.

Miriam and Desmonia were both present, looking even more eager and excited than the rest at her. Now, they had become the students and she the teacher. The warm and cold flow persisted within Big Sister.

– Kick the sandbag, she told them.

Miriam was first. She kicked it.

Melinda didn't need the sign from her sister. She walked forward and kicked it, kicked it so hard that it broke in several places and sand would have trickled out, if there had been sand in it.

The others gasped impressed. They had watched the two sisters exercise their more vicious abilities earlier, but had never watched them kick loose.

Desmonia stepped forward and kicked it.

Lucinda stepped close to her. She spoke in a low and vicious voice.

– That sandbag is your mortal enemy and you just killed it, not because you did a good job, but because it laughed itself silly before it croaked, before it killed you with a swat of its hand. NOW, GIVE ME SOME PUNCH AND SHOW ME SOME FIRE

Desmonia looked wide-eyed at her. A look of determination and anger lit her beautiful orbs.

She kicked and kicked again and again, and the bag dissolved under her onslaught.

– Bring in the next bag, Lucinda commanded. – It will hold longer, I presume.

– It is made of sturdier material, Miriam replied, pale and sweaty. – I ordered them last week, based on your... recommendation.

Desmonia looked at the ruined bag with a pleased expression spread all over her serene, sweaty face.

– A fist is a great statement, Lucinda told them. – So is a foot, a knife or a sword. It breaks and cut skin. Whatever power we may have doesn't change that. It aides us in our action, our resolve...

They trained with wands and then swords, alone and against each other, careful and cautious at first, but then with increasing confidence.

She brought in a trainer, right from the start obscuring them to him, making them ghosts he would eventually forget. After she discarded him, his memory of them would fade away into virtually nothing. She marveled at his disciplined mind, but faced no major trouble mastering it, mastering him.

I feel it, Melinda cried, feel the sword extending my reach, making me more of a… a weapon.

It was as if the katana, the light Japanese sword moved by itself in Lucinda's hands, as it increasingly extended her reach.

There were breaks now and then, even though they seemed brief to both Lucinda and the others. She studied Melinda, like she had done for a while, now, she studied herself, but saw no conclusive signs of a major physical change. There were no signs of the two of them exhibiting different powers either, even though the peculiarities persisted.

Melinda turned. She had noticed, noticed the eyes burning her back and walked to Big Sister.

– What is it? What is wrong?

– Nothing, Lucinda shrugged. – Nothing significant, at least nothing new.

Kid Sister hesitated. Lucinda waited patiently.

– What happened? The child asked softly, concerned. – What happened between you and Ronald?

– Nothing, really. Lucinda shrugged, but then she couldn't hold back a frown. – We fucked and after that I haven't seen him, and no one else I know of has either. He left or vanished into thin air. I don't think his name is Ronald, actually.

Melinda touched her in comforting ways and sent her comforting thoughts.

– Something happened that night. I think he… made me, made me fuck him, raised me to a heightened state of desire I couldn't resist. And it persisted afterwards. I forced two guys. It was me, but I still got the sense that I was outside myself, in a way. He did that, he made me do it, that asshole, and I couldn't read his mind, couldn't receive any clear thoughts from him… except a sense of elated triumph. Thinking about it, it was as if he knew me, but even though there was a certain familiarity I've never seen him before.

The monologue ended. She discovered that her hands were shaking and that her throat hurt.

– Well, everything that happened felt awesome… whatever it was, Melinda grinned, both subdued and excited beyond words. – If I can experience only pale shadows of it several times during my life, I will be content. I would certainly not call it a bad thing, you know.

Lucinda felt the afterglow of Kid Sister's beyond pleasant experience in the teenager's memory. She still practically brimmed with pleasure.

They both returned to the others with renewed vigor and purpose.

It was many days later, after the sword master's final day with them.

Desmonia followed her with her huge, expressive eyes.

– You handled him so well, she marveled, – like he was a kitten eating from your hand.

Lucinda was a little put off by the admiration in the other woman's eyes, but didn't reveal it, any of it. It made her feel good, and that, in turn made her feel even better.

Everyone stood on an improvised shooting range, holding a gun in both hands.

– Aim and fire, she told the group.

They did, badly at first, except Lois and Jordan. The two of them clearly knew what they were doing, treating the weapon in their hands like pros.

– I was in the army, Lois admitted. – My former husband, too. We competed a lot, or so I believed, until I started winning and it wasn't fun for him anymore.

Jordan wasn't in the current class, but like several other previous participants, she had stayed on at the center as part of the staff.

The line between «students» and staff had become increasingly blurry, anyway.

Lucinda made Miriam bring in another instructor. They kept struggling even after he arrived, and didn't do so well, but eventually, beyond a certain point, it was actually possible to see how their performance improved.

– We may not need guns most of the time, but sometimes, when push comes to shove we may need them desperately.

She drilled them through the same meticulous and insane regime like she had done with everything else. The results quickly showed themselves to be self-evident. They learned and they felt increased pride in their prowess and in themselves.

– You are so good at this, Melinda marveled, – giving us far more than Miriam and the center have done.

Claudia would have been proud of you.

Lucinda caught the last strain of mind speech as a stray thought, a touch of venom in her sister's flow, one the girl might not be consciously aware of.

But it didn't really lessen the pleased expression on Lucinda's face when she beheld them all on the evening of their «graduation».

The uniforms she chose for them, she helped them chose for themselves were yet another distinct statement. The Maverick Crew preferred strictly practical clothing. These were a deliberate departure from that. The minds of the assembly whispered to her when they saw her stand before them in her full new costume.

She looked at herself through the eyes of others, at the red, blood red mask covering her face, at the eyes just about visible in the twin openings. They admired the dark violet velvet covering the Kevlar vest, the tight, flexible coat and the boots without high heels, her prominently displayed muscular thighs.

– I am Tattletale Fury, she declared, – and we are The Furies.

The whisper turned to a hum. Melinda and Desmonia grinned at her behind their masks and everybody else showed similar signs of prominent affection. The males desired her with hot, potent passion. Their cocks practically pushed at the fabric of their pants.

– We need a base of operations, Miriam said, prompted or seemingly prompted by Lucinda. – I have just the place, one easily accessible and not affiliated with or easily traceable to the Center.

– Very good, Lucinda nodded in acknowledgement. – I'm confident that it will be exactly what we are looking for.

Miriam glowed in gratitude and gratification.

Tattletale Fury stood before her charges with a fist raised.

– This, all this is just the modest beginning. One day, one wretched night we will change the world.

They were with her. She knew that, saw it in every little movement and flickering of eyes. There was hardly any need what so ever to look into their minds.

– You are Radiant Fury, she baptized Melinda.

She walked to all of them and baptized them, animating them, giving them life, all of them accepting her and her gift with passionate anticipation.

– You are Piecemeal Fury, she told Miriam.

– I can feel it, Miriam mumbled, – the charge in the air, the burning within.

The others voiced their eager agreement. Tattletale Fury grinned pleased.

They left the gym, taking their first steps into the world at large. There were voices somewhere. Lucinda knew there was no one nearby, no one in the entire building. They walked into the living room. The TV was on.

– That's strange, Miriam frowned. – The janitor usually turns it off. Come to think of it, he always turns off everything.

She walked to the television set, clearly set on turning it off.

– No, leave it on, Lucinda said casually.

It was the Nine O'clock news. They all recognized President Burton, but the big woman he faced was unknown to most of them.

The news anchor's voiceover accompanied the broadcast.

– Colonel Claudia Malone, the new government advisor on parahuman affairs was presented at a special ceremony at the White House tonight.

Lucinda felt how her brows wrinkled and contracted.

– Has the President now made a decisive move to control this new wave sweeping our society? The voice asked. – Or has he instead grabbed a tiger by its tail?

A studio debate ensued. Lucinda didn't really listen to it. The noise in her ears and mind pretty much blocked any reception.

She waited, waited until it was all over and then she walked to the television set and turned it off.

– Let's go, she told her charges.

– So, what will we do on our first night out? Lois asked excitedly. – Aren't we too many to do the usual vigilante thing?

The others breathlessly awaited their leader's answer.

– We will draw on our numbers, Tattletale Fury declared. – And establish our presence in the streets, in the life of all people in this city and beyond. We will not be threatened or hassled or in any way allow ourselves to be intimidated by anyone.

Determination and excitement lit up their faces further.

– But we can't just walk out the door, can we? Jordan wondered, not really that worried, her striking Asian features not really hidden behind the mask, not to those present at least.

– It would mean taking an unnecessary risk, Miriam nodded pleased. – Fortunately we don't need to.

She looked smug, very smug at them. Lucinda saw more in her mind of what she was about.

What is it? Melinda asked, sensing her sister's more intense thoughts.

It hasn't always been apparent, Lucinda replied, but Miriam and the forces behind her sort of planned for this, or at least hoped for it to happen. They wanted their own private army of big people and feel confident in their ability to control us. Miriam doesn't mind me taking the lead, quite content to remain on the backstage and as a... guide. She and her bosses have been waiting patiently for the right mix of people and one with... the drive to lead.

– If you would follow me, Piecemeal Fury said, deferring to Tattletale Fury with a slight glance.

Lucinda granted her permission with a hardly noticeable nod.

The nuances of power can be almost indistinct, she thought.

Knowing, not caring that Melinda caught that.

Miriam grabbed a nondescript remote from the table. She held it up for all to see.

– This has rather special features. Pay attention. I will show you how it works.

She led on down the hall, and then down one of the dark halls where Lucinda got that weird and nauseous feeling, to a distant part of the building the students had never seen.

– Today I push 648988, she said. – We will work out a system where we change the codes and procedures at uneven intervals.

She pushed the numbers. A nondescript part of the wall slid aside, revealing a tailspin staircase.

– This is one of several secret pathways, she told them. – It is a feature that also has the advantage of becoming impossible to use if it should be… compromised.

– Wow, we've become secret agents, Myra exclaimed.

The anger, if there was any was easily submerged beneath the surging, ongoing excitement.

They descended the stairs, emerging into another hallway with sparse lighting, one with far less ornaments and class, one clearly part of a basement of some kind. Piecemeal Fury walked on and the Furies followed her. They reached another even wall. Miriam held up the remote again, slowly pushing a different set of numbers… 6… 7… 3… 3… 2… 8.

A part of the wall slid open, revealing a long, dark corridor. They rushed through it, with an eagerness they were unable to hide. Several high-speed walkways brought them even faster forward. The walk to their immediate destination still lasted what had to be many minutes, even though none of them consulted their watches, until they stopped at a third smooth wall. Miriam punched yet another set of numbers.

– That had to be at least one block, right? Jasmine said.

– Several blocks actually, Ramon said. – So far from the Center that it won't even occur to people that there is a connection, if they don't get a reason to think so. It is part of an old bomb shelter from the Cold War that very few people alive have any knowledge of.

A great hall appeared before them, as automatic lights turned the place from shadow to bright light, one with a supply of cars and choppers and other useful stuff to last a lifetime. They stared in awe at it all.

I knew the terms were too generous, Lucinda told Melinda.

– That is some arsenal, if I've ever seen one, Myra remarked. – The world will tremble if we ever need it.

– Way too much to carry through the streets, Radiant Fury whistled brightly.

– Can I cook or what, Miriam said in a dreamy voice.

– You're the Goddess of chefs, Leonard praised her. – We are not worthy.

She brought them to what was clearly a control room, where they could survey the entire complex, including the Center. Everyone stared at the screens with great interest.

– There are three other hidden access points, Miriam related, – gates where we can enter or leave without easily being spotted.

– There is enough stuff here to start a small war, Lois said.

They walked around a bit and admired it all, taking a closer look. Jordan checked out the bigger guns, handling them as easy as she had the smaller.

– I let myself grow fat and idle. She shook her head. – Never again!

– This stuff must have cost a fortune, Ashanti marveled, letting her fingertips rub the metal on the table.

– We got it all from a military surplus storage, I'm afraid, Miriam said. – It's all fully operational, but old and quirky and needs lots of oil.

– We'll make it work, Jordan stated darkly, with a confidence they had hardly heard from her before.

They left it behind, for the night, without regrets, eager and excited about what was ahead. Miriam pushed another set of numbers and opened another door in the wall. They followed her through it, slipped into a subway of sorts. Sounds of movement reached them, but it was clearly muted, far away.

Tattletale Fury took the lead and the group moved as one. They appeared in a derelict abandoned backyard, with another passage leading to a street.

The street was empty of people. Only a few newspapers blew in the wind. Of five streetlights only two were working. They moved like the wind through the streets, now, with slow and measured steps, with people casting long and fearful and angry and admiring glances at them.

Tattletale Fury bathed in the accolades and passion and downright hatred their presence stirred in the streets, feeling how she was drowning in it, how it weakened and strengthened her.

There was a strange mood in the city tonight. Whether or not it was caused by their presence or something else was hard to say.

– This is so great, Lois breathed, – so fucking great.

Her voice had a quality of triumph and even conquest, as if every step forward brought a seething sense of accomplishment and victory.

Tattletale Fury reached out with her power, her fervor, attempting to stretch it beyond their immediate surroundings, as if her gift was truly to see the unseen and not mere telepathy.

A haze covered the higher part of the air between the buildings, a mix of the poisonous exhaust from the cars crawling through the early evening traffic and not so easily identifiable sources.

My nose suffers, Melinda complained.

But her «voice», too had that happy touch of excitement Lucinda sensed in all the furies.

– This is better, Lois said brightly. – This is much better.

They looked at her, at least some of them did, sensing there was more to her words, more to come.

– Remember that day after the disaster and the protests? We allowed the small people to… to bother us then, but not now.

– We wear masks, now, Miriam said. – That may seem like a fairly new custom, but it isn't, really. It is, on the contrary one very old, even ancient. The mask, according to legend brings forth another persona, another part of you, one you may have hidden both to yourself and others.

– I get pleasant goose bumps, Myra shuddered.

They all did. Everybody smiled more than a little as they moved through the streets between the few admirers and many fearful detractors.

– It's quiet, Tattletale Fury said.

She heard her voice as if from far away, as if she was displaced, as if she wasn't really there. Her forward movement stopped. Her feet stopped moving without her making any conscious decision to make them stop.

– I think I know what you mean, Piecemeal Fury breathed. – The heavy traffic should be imposing, but isn't. The crowds are close, but they don't feel like they are.

And as she nodded to herself clarity imposed itself in even stronger waves on Tattletale Fury's growing awareness.

Lucinda frowned again. There had been a frown earlier, one she hardly recalled. She raised a hand. Everybody stopped right after she did.

Sounds and images imposed themselves on her reaching mind, distant flashes at first turning into nightmarish and disturbing impressions.

– Screams, she said aloud, in an eerie voice – loud and horrible screams.

– What do you see? Piecemeal Fury asked her gently.

– Faces, frightened, terrified faces, two women and one man.

The impressions faded with the distraction, but the sensations persisted. She saw through the eyes of the three present, through a fog of exhaustion and stark fear.

– They are held captive, nude and strung up like meat. The smell, oh, Goddess, the stench is horrible.

The stench of blood, piss and shit, and all possible body juices days old.

I can smell them, smell it, Radiant Fury told her in her mind.

Melinda could hardly keep it inside, keep her disgust and horror contained, and she wouldn't have been able to, if she hadn't already been hardened by war.

Lead on, Lucinda commanded, but...

Yeah, pretend that you do, I know.

There was a touch of resentment in the teenager's voice worrying the older sister.

Tattletale Fury walked first in the group suddenly crowded with anxious and frightened individuals. The two sisters timed it fairly easy, like they had learned early, learned deception.

The Furies walked through what felt like enemy territory with flickering eyes and sweaty palms and brows, no longer feeling superior or confident. The stench of oil and gas and exhaust mixed with that of the body juices in the dreamscape of their increasingly improved senses.

They trust me, Tattletale Fury thought. They look at me for guidance and direction.

She saw her back and figure through their eyes, a sight enhanced by increased respect and something resembling awe. Lips smiling mixed with the apprehension in Lucinda Patterson's eyes.

– I feel... malice, she mumbled, – pervasive and present, here.

She and Kid Sister almost fell out of the playacting. They both stopped before a door ajar, in front of an old warehouse. Lucinda realized startled that they were no more than a few blocks away from the Maverick Crew's headquarters.

Her mind, strained beyond endurance could detect no dangers, but she kept up the battle-readiness, kept her people on their toes. That particular scary something, what she for so long had felt outside her range, grew yet another notch in her troubled mindscape.

She started running, slightly breathless, not because of the running, but because of the growing chill in her belly.

They emerged into a place of mist and cold, clearly a former storage facility of some kind. Lucinda saw how they moved, determined but uncertain and she signaled them to do better, spurring them on, and they did, moving in accordance with each other and the terrain, scouting for enemies, preparing to meet them head on.

It hit her harder, the sensation emanating from the spot ahead. She bit her lips as she began to feel the pain and she saw the surroundings of the three big people in there through that haze of red and horror.

They entered the room of steam and shadows. A couple of bright lights shone straight at the faces of those hanging in chains from hooks in the ceiling. Tattletale Fury's teammates gasped soundlessly as they spotted the two women and one man, their battered and bloody faces. Three pair of eyes looked dully at the newcomers.

– There is no one else here, Tattletale Fury stated, somewhat calmly. – Whoever did this has left temporarily or permanently.

Radiant Fury walked to the three. The nearest women squirmed.

– We are the rescue team, Melinda said softly.

The words, or their truth, didn't seem to register at first.

– You are? The other woman spoke up. – You are not shitting us?

– Please, the man blurted out. – Don't hurt me anymore. I'll do *anything*.

He broke down in tears and helpless sobbing.

Tattletale Fury stood there frozen while her teammates as fast and tenderly as possible freed the prisoners.

What is it? Melinda asked, catching on almost immediately.

Ronald was here.

Ronald was... here? Melinda looked incredulous at her. What the fuck?

He was one of the attackers.

– Who did this to you? Piecemeal Fury asked the woman who had more control of herself.

– T-they told us they were the Brewery Gang.

– They... told you? Lucinda said with a hollow voice. – But you... shouldn't you have...

The others didn't really notice.

– Shouldn't I have recognized them, you mean? The woman nodded. – We didn't, but they told us. They even bragged about it, how they had changed in both appearance and otherwise, both within and without, how they had become powerful, powerful enough to not have to take shit from *anyone* anymore.

– Their sister was with them, the man choked, – and she was the worst, a sadistic bitch enjoying every little wound and pain she inflicted on us.

Ronald is Trevor, Trevor Rogan, Lucinda told her sister.

That asshole! Melinda promptly replied, not able to hide her shiver.

– Changed you say? Jordan asked, fairly levelheaded. – You mean they had had plastic surgery?

– No, the somewhat calm woman said. – At least I don't think so. When they told us I could sort of recognize them, even though I couldn't quite believe it. They have been the laughing stock of the town, the country and even the fucking world for so long. I must have seen their faces dozens of times, both live and not.

– They served a woman, the still almost hysterical and timid second woman whimpered. – They spoke about her in whispers. It was she who had changed them, transformed them from pathetic worms to truly fearsome and mighty creatures. They spoke her name in reverence, practically struck with terror by the very thought of her.

– Black Dragon, Lucinda said with a dull voice, unable to keep up the pretence anymore.

– That was it, the woman cried. – That was it exactly!

– I've heard that name, Lois said, – heard it mentioned in the community, like a demon, something unmentionable and vile.

– We leave, now, Tattletale Fury said, with a fluttering quality in her voice her kid sister had never heard before.

The tortured trio could hardly stand and their rescuers had to support them as the evacuation began.

– Everything will be alright, Lois told the scared to death woman softly. – We'll take you to the police...

– NO! Not the police! You know they will collar us and throw us in jail just for the heck of it. The law gives them the rights to do it, too.

The outburst shook them, shook them all violently.

– She's right, Miriam acknowledged. – The additions to the police «regulations» clearly states that «any enhanced human involved in a crime can be arrested and contained indefinitely», and they use that, use it for all it is worth. It doesn't necessarily matter whether or not those involved are victims or perpetrators. Only somewhat officially sanctioned teams like the Maverick Crew are exempt from that.

Lucinda and Melinda, with their enhanced senses easily noticed how the three turned calmer.

– We can't take them to hospitals either, Leonard mused. – That may bring about exactly the same result.

– It is fortunate then, that we are able to offer them alternative healthcare venues, Miriam said. – There will be no registration, no record of anything.

The former captives visibly relaxed and Lucinda recognized the typical doglike expression of gratitude in their eyes.

– Put on these masks, she told them. – It will hurt, but you won't be recognized.

She attempted to keep the chill and hard edge of her voice from expressing itself, in vain.

The three did as they were told.

The Furies moved through the streets with the people they had rescued. They kept to narrow streets and alleys as much as possible, nervous twitches very much visible in their eyes and movements, uttering low sighs of relief when they after what felt like an eternity returned to their headquarters.

Reality shifted, both in truth and in Lucinda's mind. The war-torn streets of Tobruk gave way to moist and hot tropical forest. The models and crew of the Center took a working trip to the jungle of Asbasos.

It didn't feel like much of a shift, more like someone had turned a switch instead of the prolonged, strenuous flight.

The chill from that night or horror stayed with them, even though it felt like a distant memory, down here, in the tropical heat.

They ran on the beach, in the warm, pleasant afternoon sunshine. The photographers stayed close, doing their utmost to catch every valuable moment, even during what clearly wasn't scheduled sessions.

– Believe me, Quentin Martins, the man in charge of the sessions said, – the best moments come when you're not prepared, when you don't stand there posing like a pole.

Melinda walked around with a DSLR camera mounted on a Glidecam, a pod, a technological wonder allowing the photographer to move without any shaking showing on the film.

– Hey, this used to be heavy, but it isn't anymore.

There was much play and joy, as they let go and caught every scrap of enjoyment coming their way.

They ran through the jungle, on a path of sand along a small river.

The smile brightened Lucinda's face. Melinda had caught her just as she turned, with an expression filled with radiant life.

Males and females stood in two half moon circles, half eye-flirting each other, half with the camera. They were paired off, or photographed alone or in groups. Sometimes the model was surrounded by jungle, by green and sometimes the beige sand and blue ocean of the beach or the old colonial buildings. Everything blurred in Lucinda's eyes and senses eventually.

They sat around a long table during sunset, having dinner and sipping sweet wine. Desmonia raised her glass.

– To us, she cried. – To big and curvy models.

– TO BIG AND CURVY MODELS, the rest choired.

The level of the laughter kept increasing as everybody's intoxication increased, as the evening arrived and the party truly took off...

The two Patterson sisters shared a brief, quiet moment at some point, Melinda still holding the camera on the Glidecam.

– So, how does high and mighty Patterson the older feel right now, Kid Sister giggled, very tipsy.

– Happy, Lucinda replied with a dreamy expression on her face, – happy as a kite.

They walked through the nearest town later. It was hardly more than a village, really, a community for those servicing those coming to enjoy Asbasos' exotic beauty. They walked through the few streets with glasses and bottles in their hands, shouting and screaming, and doing their utmost, in their giddiness to disturb and destroy whatever peace the small town enjoyed.

There were a few natives there as well, wearing only loincloths and carrying spears, bows and arrows on their backs.

– Don't worry, Peter, the guide comforted the slightly concerned visitors. – They just come here to trade and are basically harmless.

– Look at them, Myra, slurring a little marveled. – They're all big. How come?

– In tribal communities all are fairly close related and it is a genetic trait, Miriam mused. – There were some initial doubt about that, but by now the various sciences and scientists have reached what is practically a consensus on the subject.

– The creationists deny that and claim that we are the creatures of Satan, of course, Jordan grinned wide. – According to them we are directly descended from demons.

Grinned wiiide.

They danced on the «main street», what was hardly more than a soil-covered road with large holes. Someone beat what resembled a jungle drum somewhere, and the rhythm and the heat made the dance go even wilder and more uncontrollable.

Melinda drank a lot, emptied glass after glass and proceeded to drink from yet another bottle, and Lucinda ended up babysitting her.

– Sorry, the girl mumbled. – I'm ruining the evening for you.

Lucinda nodded empathically, but stopped herself from voicing her agreement.

– Don't worry about it, she snorted. – I'm too drunk to do much anyway.

She let out a loud, distorted laughter. One second, two seconds passed and then they both did.

A timeless time of infinite haziness later, she put Kid Sister to bed.

– They looked at me, she mumbled. – The natives fucking stared at me.

She saw it, re-experienced it, in dull flashes. Their mouths spat a word of fear, disgust and boundless respect. She was unable to hear it, then as now.

Her head hit the pillow in the twilight darkness and that was all she wrote, until next morning, when she still writhed on the bed, squirming under the ruthless onslaught of vicious nightmares she couldn't recall.

– JESUS CHRIST, she heard Myra whine all the way from the restroom down the hall. – This shit needs makeup that isn't invented yet.

Melinda was puking her guts out into a toilet bowl somewhat closer.

Most looked like pale ghosts at the breakfast table and even though their appetite re-manifested itself in inevitable ways, it was merely a pale reflection of what it usually was.

– Looks like you all have gained yet another day of relaxation today, Miriam said ironically.

Lucinda's head kept speaking to her and it said THUD THUD THUD THUD in that dull and horrible repetitive voice.

Everybody grinned or attempted to do so, failing miserably.

They went exploring and the photographers kept them company, and they ended up working, sort of, anyway, and smiling to poor Melinda, as she recorded everything.

More days and nights passed. Lucinda wanted to catch it, grab it and hold on, but she couldn't. Everything ended up as tiny, almost impossible to spot pieces in her visual memory, sensations fading the instance they appeared.

– A week is a day, Desmonia hummed, – and days are just grains of sand on the beach of life.

And Lucinda looked at her with new eyes.

There were more walks on the beach, more swimming in the pleasant ocean, photographs in bikinis, swimsuits, *wet* swimsuits, and a variety of clothes for Big People. It wasn't exactly relaxation, but in spite of the tiring hours it hardly felt like work at all.

Lucinda, wearing a wet and transparent low-necked dress emerged from the frothing waves. Her large breasts, very distinct and firm pushed at the fabric. She walked around between some cliffs with Jake, one of the photographers. Posing no longer felt awkward to her, and she did so with the casual moves of a pro. She followed his instructions like a true mannequin.

– Raise your arms above your head, he instructed.

She did, well aware that her nipples were pulled up and would show even better on the picture.

– Higher, he teased her.

She shrugged and did as she was told with a cold stare, totally exposing the nipples.

– That is a wrap, he said. – Those latest shot will probably not be useful for publishing unless you want to pursue a more… daring career, but rest assured that they are hot beyond belief.

She drank soda, feeling more than hot and queasy, avoiding his stare, almost emptying the bottle in an attempt to wet her dry throat. It didn't work.

– How come you don't join the rest of us dolls? She inquired coyly, deliberating returning his stare with the cold eyes. – You have the body and looks for it.

The last sentence came off very patronizing.

– I prefer being behind the camera, he shrugged.

He had big, hard muscles, the body of a god, but there was something there, a roughness in his features that might disqualify him as a model.

She nodded to herself. He caught that and she saw and sensed a flare of irritation in him. Her smile widened.

He stepped closer and she was suddenly very aware of the fact that she stood just a step away from him, practically nude. The prevalent heat had already dried most of the moisture on her body, but not where her swelling breasts pushed at the fabric. She knew he noticed the bigger pearls of sweat on her forehead. Her nipples rose and hardened, sore and long. He had to notice that, too, just had to. She noticed his confidence when he put the camera on the flat rock and stepped close to her. He grabbed her and pushed her at the nearest cliff-wall.

She scanned him, the deepest she was able. He didn't notice a thing. There was nothing there, nothing except his powerful desire to possess her.

– And you get full access to the cookie jar, anyway, she remarked, deliberately caustic.

– I can zoom in on any of you bitches in a relaxed and pleasant manner, he concurred.

He squeezed one of her nipples between his fingers, easily eliciting a moan from her. She didn't care, but chuckled in growing excitement and pushed herself even harder at the big and hard body.

Excitement grew to a hard, pulsing need when he held her with one hand and used the other to caress her in ever more invasive ways. He removed what little she had of clothes on her body and put her on her back on the flat rock. She noticed, through the haze her vision had become that he had pulled down his own pants, that his hard and throbbing cock pointed right at her, and she wanted it, wanted him inside, deep inside.

She knew she pushed him, spurred him on like she did all men the moment she passed beyond a certain point of need. It was involuntary, a reflex that was a part of her, but now she deliberately added to it, making him think of nothing more than the upcoming mating.

He grabbed her hips and raised them up, pulled her close and pushed himself deep into her, his upper body falling forward until it joined hers on the rock. The sight and sound of the camera falling off the edge of the rock and hitting the pond of seawater with a splash didn't really register in her

258

consciousness at all. She screamed and the fingers on her hands squeezing his shoulders formed like claws and the nails scratched his skin. All conscious thought and motivation slipped and faded.

They were in some bed somewhere, moving and breathing according to each other. Loud groans and moans kept flowing from open mouths. They shook in yet another powerful orgasm.

It felt like they fell towards the bed, like the collapse of tense limbs went on forever. He was all over her afterwards, like an eager kid after his first time.

– That was fucking fantastic, he marveled. – Unbelievable!

She wanted to give him an angry retort, a patronizing snarl, but was too spent and content, and she managed no more than the sweet, sweet smile he expected and craved.

– You have some sort of power, right, something you can't quite control during great sex?

She wanted to wipe the smirk off his face, but found herself responding like the young, innocent girl of his expectations.

– I guess I have some kind of empathy, but I have never noticed it much, except during… sex.

– I can't fathom how the guys you have been with before could ever let you go, he bristled. – Rest assured that I never will.

She reddened and lowered her gaze. He chuckled pleased.

– Hold that pose, he ordered and she did.

He returned with another camera and began snapping pictures of her from all angles.

– Wow, he whistled, – you cost me one camera, but I think, no, I feel confident that that loss will be compensated a thousand times. You're quite the irresistible cunt and that will also show on the photos.

– That is high praise for sure, she mocked him, – and very considerate wording. I knew there was a reason I got the hots for you…

The deep frown pleased her.

– Turn around, he snapped, – show off that fat butt of yours.

She gave him a defiant grin and did as she was told.

– It's your best feature, he said casually. – One look at that and every hot-blooded male turns wild. Any product you advertise for will fly off the shelves.

She wriggled it, for him, for the camera and for anyone that might be watching.

– The most enticing butt in the business and it's all mine, he boasted.

His tough macho talk made her hot again, no matter how much she chastised herself. She swayed and wriggled with an even greater effort.

– Touch yourself. Turn towards me.

She did, all over her increasingly sensitive skin. The camera filmed and photographed her simultaneously. The clicks thundered in her ears. She saw his cock begin twitching, and then growing, until it pointed at her.

He put the camera down on the floor, never taking his eyes off her.

– You're just one big tease, aren't you? He said hoarse as dry sand. – A whore showing off for anyone.

– And you're just the typical misogynist without much more than hard cock to offer, she said enraged.

He wanted to slap her. She saw it clearly in his mind, saw him raise his hand in fury, and even imagined that it was real.

But something happened, something she felt like an invasive force, a fist in the face. Suddenly something stuck out of his chest and blood was sprayed all over her.

Jake fell, dying with each breath. A male savage stood in front of her with a bloody spear in his hand. He hissed at her the word she didn't understand.

One swift continuous move and he struck her on the head with the butt end of the spear. She fell, even more stunned than the killing of her lover had made her, fell in the pool of blood on the bed. He grabbed her hair. She attempted to kick him, but he avoided her foot easily and struck her in the ribs, releasing a triumphant roar. He struck her in the face, hard. She blacked out for a moment. He kept striking her. A few more strikes and she was half unconscious. She tried to defend herself, but was more or less unable to do so. He had beaten her. It had happened so fast. She had hardly managed to react, to fight him at all.

He struck her on the side of the jaw again. Blood flowed from her mouth. Her ribs hurt. She could hardly breathe. He kept beating her up. Her scalp hurt, a dull pain overwhelmed by all the other sources in her world of hurt. Fear touched her briefly, before that, too, fell into that vast black hole somewhere below.

Thought faded, consciousness faded. She noticed when he let go of her and she fell on the bed, but it was like it happened to someone else, as if it didn't concern her at all.

Chapter 15

She woke home in her bed, her world of hurt still fresh in her nightmares.

Her eyes opened. The bright light bothered her. The painkillers still working made her nauseas, close to delirious.

Kid Sister appeared in her crooked line of vision. The Melinda now and Melinda a week ago blurred in her sight.

Melinda shot the native, shot him straight through the heart. He collapsed and died instantly.

She leaned over Big Sister, touching her cautiously, as Lucinda fought her way up from the world of hurt that had become her reality.

– You screamed for me, the girl whispered in the holiday resort in Asbasos, – You screamed in my head and it was as if a thousand needles penetrated my body. The Center's private doctors are on its way. They will fix you, you'll see. Everything will be alright.

PoorLucindaohimsosorrysosorrysorrysorry

The concern and shock were still there. Lucinda heard it, even through the haze her mind had become.

They will fix you.

– I feel awful, she mumbled.

She couldn't help herself. Everything just… leaked, like an open wound.

Melinda stood there, with her hands on her hips, attempting to sound and look cheerful.

– Well, you haven't exactly had the best week of your life.

No, she hadn't and merely the added reminder made her cringe and her body ache. Pain racked her. She rose and felt like she had pulled her shoulder off the hinges, and in her thoughts she inevitably returned to the… unpleasantness, the horror of her ordeal. It flashed through her mind as she stumbled on to the shower, as sweet water hit her body and head.

She felt, practically re-experienced the beating and heard the indecipherable word the native spat at her, felt his groping hands while she lay there beaten and helpless. Her fist hammered the wall, making the entire room and building shake. The arm fell, weak as the kitten she felt like. The water flooded her face, masking any tears that might fall.

The living room felt gloomy. The soft towel hurt her sore hide no matter how careful Melinda used it.

The food stayed on her plate, not going anywhere. She pushed the plate away.

– You need to eat, Melinda said, – need to feed to heal.

– The mere thought of food makes me want to puke.

– Oh, don't be such a *baby!*

Kid Sister's sarcastic, spiteful tone worked.

When Melinda grabbed the plate and the spoon and began feeding her, she willingly opened her mouth, and the hunger, the beast reawakened, and she fed like a predator on the prowl.

She fought herself to the toilet to relieve herself.

The stench filled the apartment and she wanted to puke.

She returned to the bed and crouched there, in fetal position. Melinda sat down and gave her a careful neck rub, comforting her somewhat. Lucinda began crying again. She had lost count of how many times that had happened the last week.

– Why did he do it? Melinda mused. – What on Earth went through his mind?

– I don't know, Lucinda replied, – I never managed to read his mind beyond the rudimentary surface thoughts.

– I killed him, Melinda said, her voice thick with emotion, – and it pleases me, pleases me greatly.

It pleased Lucinda as well, even though she wasn't able to muster much in the sense of triumph.

– Perhaps we shouldn't bother to ask why, Melinda shrugged, a dark glow burning in her eyes. – At least not making a production out of it. It's sufficient that he did what he did to you and that he suffered for it. You're the victim, he's the perpetrator, end of story. I've never felt more right than when I pulled that trigger.

Lucinda wondered if she should be worried about her sister, but she didn't have the energy to do anything anymore, it seemed.

She imagined she fell asleep again, imagined that she didn't and lived the nightmare.

It was a gray autumn day when she finally left the apartment and a private chauffeur from the Center drove her to the private hospital. They removed the final stitches.

– You will be good as new, the surgeon told her, sounding like he played in a hospital sitcom or something. – There will be only a tiny scar. We big people have *excellent* healing tissue.

She pulled away from him, from his winning smile and confident demeanor.

– Drive, she told the chauffeur. – Just drive.

He did, evidently used to get strange requests and taking the scenic tour. The existence outside the limousine she spotted through the dark windows flickered before her eyes.

The imagery of a still ravaged city passed by. The clean up was far from complete and the rebuilding hadn't even started yet, and wouldn't for some time. A local radio station played some music. She couldn't tell what melody it was or what kind. It just... eluded her, all of it.

Flashes of memory kept haunting her, the pain and humiliation returned to her defenseless mind.

She saw him, heard him, his face twisted and coarse, not real at all.

– Drive me to the hospital, she said to the driver, doing so with a hollow voice she attempted to make sound forceful. – The public central hospital.

He hardly changed direction. If he did she was unable to tell that he did.

Tobruk Central Hospital had been spared the worst of the fallout from the collapse of the tall buildings a considerable distance away. The few broken windows had been replaced, the debris outside removed or at least moved to places where it wasn't instantly visible. She chuckled darkly, unable to decide if it sounded more like choking.

She entered the reception area, not able to recall the moment when she had left the car, unable to shake off the prevailing daze filling her mind.

Then she stopped and turned around well before she reached the reception desk, shaking her head in distress, suddenly covered in sweat.

– Drive me home, she told the driver.

He did, and she dismissed him.

Melinda was there, making dinner, rushing to meet and embrace poor Big Sister when she entered the apartment.

– I went to the hospital to visit Lester and Marcus, she whimpered, actually *whimpered,* – and I almost forgot that I was Lucinda and not Gimmick.

– Poor girl, Melinda said.

She sat down by the dinner table and started feeding, feeding a lot.

– At least your appetite is returning, Melinda said lightly.

She almost shit herself before she had to rush to the bathroom. She returned pale and queasy, deliberately looking away from the pair of concerned eyes.

– You do look much better, Melinda insisted later. – Please believe me when I say you will bounce back from this.

Kid Sister didn't look so good herself, very distressed and bewildered. Lucinda choked and straightened, and reached out to touch the girl's cheek.

– You're absolutely right, she stated firmly. – I will!

And the cautious hope she spotted in the other's eyes made it all worth it.

Melinda grew even more assertive as the day progressed. She brightened, as if suddenly recalling something.

– Hey, the others didn't know I had killed anyone before. They were cautious, of course and wanted to comfort me, assure me I had done the right thing and all that, but they also looked at me with newfound *respect*, no longer seeing me as a mere attachment to you.

She nodded to herself.

– I like that.

Lucinda carefully masked her expression and kept her thoughts to herself, in that moment and during the rest of the day and evening.

Until at night, during sleep, when all her defenses broke down and she was glad that Melinda was sound asleep.

Pretty Lucinda, a voice spat at her. Give the world the cute, pretty girl.

The dark, expectant chuckle rattled her, rattled her hard. She couldn't help projecting her fears and shame, and notice that Melinda began writhing and moaning in her sleep, clearly suffering a whopper of a nightmare.

Lucinda pounded her fist silently on the softness of the bed, sleeping, dreaming, not sure if she was in truth doing either.

Pretty girl, the voice mocked her, showing her when smiling during a photo session and later, when she was beaten up and bloody and bruised, with a breathing tube up her nose.

Stop it, stop it, stop it, she cried in protest, she begged with no voice.

The pale light of dawn brought no relief, just more disturbing thoughts.

She guarded those thoughts like a jealous lover, while she kept peeking into Melinda's mind. There was pride there, and the expected concern, but nothing else, nothing... suspicious.

Melinda had left for school. The apartment felt incredibly empty and hollow.

The Black Dragon stood there and grinned at her, even if she couldn't actually see her.

There was a knock on the door. Lucinda froze.

Even if a quick, random scan revealed the visitor's identity Lucinda couldn't quite bring herself to move.

She walked to the door and opened it. Desmonia greeted her with her usual smile and model beauty.

– Hi, she said, – I thought I should come over and cheer you up a bit, keep you company in your moment of despair.

– I do not despair, Lucinda countered quickly, fighting to convey confidence and indifference, – but I appreciate your concern none the less.

She stepped aside, deliberately, allowing the woman to enter the apartment.

– You look great, Desmonia said brightly.

She looks awful, Desmonia thought glumly, her thoughts echoing in the other's mind.

— Thank you, Lucinda responded, — that's so nice of you to say.

— I mean it, the suave woman insisted. — Not everybody can take what you went through, not without going through some serious blues.

Poor broken thing, Lucinda easily picked up.

The words rose from Desmonia's storm of thoughts. Lucinda heard them clearer than she had in anyone's mind before. Lucinda smiled in triumph.

— Thank you, but I guess my model career was quite short-lived, huh?

— No, no, not at all. Don't worry, honey, hiding the scar with makeup and retouching won't be any trouble at all.

It will be a drag, but entirely doable.

— And your misfortune won't be revealed, you know. The public won't be any wiser, ever. Only unsubstantiated rumors have so far reached the public and trust me, we are very good at keeping it that way.

Lucinda sat down on the couch, feeling a relief she couldn't hide.

— Thank you, that *is* good to hear.

Desmonia sat down by her side, rubbing her cheek, the scar side in a comforting gesture.

— You're strong. You will bounce back from this.

I hope.

— We need you, she whispered. — We all need you so very much and we will all give as much support as you could possibly need. You're not the first model with a rather unfortunate start of your career, you know.

And now she was sincere, sort of.

— You know… this is a rather nice apartment, but it's time you, the both of you move on to something better, isn't it, something more deserving of your elevated stature?

There was something there, one more chill touching Lucinda's heart.

— We will seriously consider it, she replied, nodding earnestly.

We kinda like this place, she thought.

— Good, Desmonia said, — very good.

There was a feather-light kiss on the lips before Desmonia faded away. Lucinda hardly heard the sound as the entrance door opened and closed. When she walked to the bathroom and the toilet bowl and the subsequent shower she imagined both the path and the rooms she passed through had turned black, or at least dark. The sunshine world outside resembled a lifeless painting in her mind.

She found her bag with her Gimmick gear, making sure to pick clothes covering her upper body completely and left the apartment, still unable to hear the sound when the door opened before her and slammed shut behind her.

The strap of the bag felt heavy on her shoulder. She put on shades before stepping outside. The heat struck her immediately. She felt like a pressure cooker in her warm and tight clothing.

– Hi, big girl, the brother of Melinda's pushy classmate greeted her with his lewd expression and thoughts. – Trying out the winter collection?

The chuckle echoed in her ears. She ignored him, like she knew he expected her to do, feeling stark relief when he didn't contradict her expectations.

It wasn't that long to the construction site, but every step felt like a mile. She was soaked in sweat and breathing hard before she had covered half the distance.

Fits of alternately rage and despair helped her cast her thoughts far and wide around the place. She was hardly able to control it or herself, the mastering of her ability almost as bad as when it had first manifested. People within her range noticed. They shivered and glanced around, convinced there was someone or something there, but they didn't see anyone.

She changed clothes. Her moves stayed awkward, a far cry from the fast and effective way she remembered. Finally Gimmick, or someone resembling her, stood there. She put the Maverick Crew ring on her finger, unable to recall how long time had passed since the last time she had done that. It buzzed at her skin, before settling there.

The portal, a glowing shadow in the bright light appeared in her vision. She stepped through and appeared in the familiar alley. Nausea assaulted her instantly and she threw up all over the place. She fought to stay on her feet, looking around with bewildered and wary eyes, not so unlike what those normals touched by her emotional mind had just done.

She walked the fairly short stretch to her destination. Males ogled her legs and she regretted not wearing pants, knowing in her simmering rage and despair that it shouldn't matter to her, one way or another.

Soul Bellows, «the crying musician»… bellowed his soul from a car stereo in the endless queue outside the hospital. She shuddered some more, a pale smile touching her lips.

The reception area, in comparison to the outside appeared temperate and filled with shade. The ring on her finger started buzzing in a very insistent manner.

She stopped and put her hand to the ear.

– Yes, she sighed.

– Where have you been? She heard Lady Grace's very imposing voice. – We need you.

Need you need you need you, echoed on the edge of her expanded

266

thoughts, impotent and unable to impress her.

– I can't right now, Gimmick shrugged.

She pulled the ring off her finger, breaking the connection, a very deliberate act making her feel so very good.

Everybody stared at her, as she walked the short stretch to the desk. The big woman in a nurse uniform behind it smiled to her, both somber and with hero worship in her eyes.

– It's sooo good to see you, Gimmick, Claire gawked. – Lester and Marcus are still in the same room. Your visits always cheer them up.

When Lucinda looked into Claire's mind she truly felt like the idol of millions.

She walked down the dank, dirty hallway. Claire led on, eager to perform her duty for her hero. She smoothed the guards at the checkpoints, making them see Gimmick in a kinder and more favorable light.

The two of them sat together by the window, like they always did. They turned as one to face the visitor. The others present, as ever turning ephemeral in her vision.

– Hi, Gimmick, Marcus greeted her as he usually did, happily, dull, like a child or a retard.

Seeing him, experiencing his state of mind always brought the strange, sickening chill to her core.

She steeled herself, deliberately grabbing his hands, penetrating his jumbled, addled mind in a way she had always hesitated to do before.

There was only a slight transition and then she was back in his arms, in the bed with Jolene and the others, like she and he, in his dim mind remembered it. She persisted, no matter how much the catching in her throat grew.

– Good morning, precious, he greeted her, mumbling in her ear.

– Good morning, lovetoy, she grinned and kissed him on the lips.

Letsdoitagainrightnow.

His eager thoughts impressed themselves on her mind.

He began kissing her, roaming her.

Sorry, my boy, a girl has to pee and she has to feed.

He didn't really lose his good mood when she writhed out of his grip and fought herself free, but just gave her a smack on the butt. It burned so pleasantly and she couldn't help but smiling as she made her way to the bathroom.

She picked a huge glass. There were several of them in the bathroom cabinet. She filled it with water. Emptying it and having the cold water flow down her throat felt good. She refilled and drank it empty again. Her eyes and lips looked different in the mirror. Her smile widened as she sat down on the bowl. The pee burned as it always did, but it didn't diminish the smile dancing on her lips.

He was there when she emerged from the bathroom, catching her in his arms.

– Let's surprise the others with breakfast, she grinned.

– Uh, about that…

She saw the glaring empty fridge in his mind and sighed.

– There is a market not far from here, isn't it? She brightened.

And he did, too.

They dressed. She put on the uniform, but didn't bother with the jacket or the armory. He put on his shorts and a t-shirt. His large cock was very visible under the fabric, and she knew he looked at her large unbound breasts and the large, hard nipples pushing at her shirt. She reddened.

– The villains, at least the males have it easy with you, haven't they? They just charm you to death.

She gave him an elbow in the ribs. He gasped, overdoing it a bit, just a bit. They left the room. One of the girls waved to them before she fell asleep again. They walked down the stairs, and then they were outside, in the noisy street.

He put his arm around her and she let him.

– … feels so good, she mumbled.

– It does?

– The very thought of that magic in your pants makes me feel good…

It twitched down there. She felt it as much as she saw it. He put a hand between her thighs and she turned limp in his arms. His pleased and expectant chuckle echoed in her thoughts.

She frowned and froze in his grip, putting a finger in the air.

– What is it? He asked, impatiently burying his lips in the soft tissue of her neck.

– There is something… I caught hostile thoughts.

– Think nothing of it, he brushed her off, – they are as common as grass when it comes to our kind. Surely there's nothing here that you haven't sensed a thousand times before?

– No! She shook her head, clearly anxious, suddenly feeling naked, as it dawned on her that she had left her weapons behind. – This is different, a stronger, dangerous focus, a trained mind…

He stopped fondling her and pulled back a little, not letting go of her arms or his smile.

– You're really into protecting your poor, defenseless lovers, aren't you?

She giggled, unable to help herself.

268

– I'm not saying you shouldn't be paranoid. With the life you live, that is certainly a prudent course of action. Stay alert, but let's focus on enjoying this fine morning. I'm confident you can make mincemeat of any miscreant out to ruin it. Okay?

– Okay!

She nodded serious-minded, almost breaking out in laughter on the spot.

Then a sudden, horrible pain shot through her, even as her scream mixed with his. She found herself crouching on the sidewalk, glimpsing Marcus there as well, his handsome face twisted in shock.

The two bodies writhing on the ground had been pretty much paralyzed. It was impossible to make anything work, anything beyond rudimentary, involuntary actions. Lucinda glimpsed military boots, heard the hard sound as they stamped on the sidewalk. She recognized the insignia of the Jagadir elite army and coiled in fear.

– What are these «people» made of? A deep voice spat its words. – They should be out after one charge.

– Tranquilize and bag them, a voice of authority barked, – we're on a schedule here, people.

Lucinda felt a sting in the thigh, and felt how she was slipping almost immediately, how everything just went away.

She felt it when they grabbed her, though, grabbed her in feet and arms and carried her off.

Consciousness rose and fell. She knew she was out for a while.

– Look at them, still moving. We quite simply have to adjust the dosages.

– This is what makes them such excellent breeding material, another sinister voice added to Lucinda's woes.

She felt another sting and went away again.

The next time she came to she was loaded into a chopper with other prisoners. The wooziness, the proof that she was still drugged persisted, but she could move. They had cuffed her hands behind her back. She tested the cuffs, but they were the new, solid version meant for big people. They didn't budge, not the slightest.

A brutal kick in the ribs made her gasp.

– Oh, no, beastie, struggle all you want, but you're caught now, are a prisoner now, and you will remain at the mercy of your betters for the rest of your life.

She knew they saw all big people as little more than animals and she couldn't keep a violent shiver from expressing itself.

– Look at it. The poor beast is scared.

– It isn't completely mindless. It knows the fate awaiting it.

Another soldier rushed forward with a tranquilizer gun. Alysse Montgomery waved him off.

– Don't bother, let it stay awake. Let all of them be allowed to ponder their lot. It will be an excellent introductory step of their training.

Gimmick counted ten captives. They had all been thrown into the back of the big chopper like cargo, like slabs of meat.

– Look at you, the great Gimmick, Montgomery chuckled. – You weren't really that hard to catch, not hard at all. Word got out that you were having fun for the night, and once we knew where to find you, capturing you was child's play. You're all just silly beasts and easy to train, easy to mold into whatever we desire you to be.

Lucinda glared at her with hatred in her eyes.

The prod in Montgomery's hand, with its electrical charge hit her calf. Lucinda screamed like a wounded animal and felt twice bad as she crumbled under the brutal attention of the officer.

– You don't look at me, Montgomery hissed. – You don't do anything without explicit permission.

She smiled in wicked triumph.

– I know you will learn this, that you will in fact be quite eager to gain that sacred knowledge. Once you learn the difference between punishment and reward, teaching you other essentials won't be hard at all.

Lucinda tried to make her telepathy work, but it didn't, not beyond a rudimentary level. They had drugged her and knew what they were doing. She descended into the same senseless despair as the others.

The door slammed shut. The chopper took off and the destination made the cargo despair that much more. They knew, beyond suspicion and apprehension what awaited them. Jagadir and the stories it generated, had long since become many a cautionary tale among their kind.

One of the men started sobbing. Large, wet tears flooded his cheeks and the floor below.

The sound penetrated deep within them all, stuck there like the most horrible nightmare imaginable.

And then the man's sobbing descended into uncontrollable wailing. The sound and the sight sank its hooks into Lucinda Patterson forever.

The sickness brought on by the poison kept ravaging her, kept her from focusing properly. It felt like just after she had shit herself, worse. The ball of nausea stuck in her throat no matter how much she attempted to get it out, to puke her guts out on the cold chopper floor.

– Look at you, the commander boasted. – What a triumphant day. One of our most outspoken critics has been reduced to a squealing child begging our favors. It will be such a pleasure displaying you for the world, once you've learned your lesson.

He bent down and began rubbing a breast. She bit her lip.

Something hardened within her then, turning shiny and sharp. She kicked him, hit him straight in the balls. The drugged but startled part of her mind realized that they hadn't constrained her feet. Her mind worked on what could be described as autopilot. She didn't think, only did. His feet gave in and his body turned completely slack. He would fall on her in a moment. She twisted and pushed, using both the foot and an arm on him. His big body struck a soldier on his way forward. He tumbled backwards and hit the lock on the sliding door. It opened, it actually opened. Gimmick blinked, but she didn't allow herself to be distracted by her remarkably good fortune.

– MOVE! She shouted to the other prisoners.

She already did, having started two seconds ago, on what felt so long ago in her head. The wind blew all around her. Her left foot hit a head in front of her. There was movement everywhere, a whirling far more pronounced than what the mere blowing of the wind could create. Fierce fighting surrounded her on all sides. She could hear Alysse Montgomery's scream of rage somewhere.

– STOP HER!

Gimmick saw the sky ahead, the blue sky, the water below. Wild hope filled her, filled her to the brim.

The taser hit her again, hit her at close range. Everything except despair was turned off within.

She felt another body hit hers, even as she was on her way down, down, spiraling towards the floor. Marcus' face was just a blur in her vision. His heavy body pushed hers towards the opening, towards freedom. Her eyes stayed open, wide open as she practically flew out of the chopper. She stared horrorstruck at him, as they knocked him down and he fell to the floor.

Despair and horror lingered, as her survival mechanism took over and she twisted her body in the air, preparing for the landing. No more than a few seconds passed and hardly even that, before she hit the surface, before the water submerged her.

Before she fell down, down, down…

And stood by the hospital bed and stared at Marcus with eyes filled with tears.

– You saved me, she blurted. – Please help me save you.

There was nothing there, not even a glimpse of the man he had been.

She backed off, backed off and left him again. Her feet wanted to run, but she kept her steely resolve of perceived calm all the way to the entrance and even far beyond that. She wanted to pay attention to where she walked, wanted to be alert and dangerous, but everything just dissolved within, turning into mush and clay.

People looked at her with unfriendly eyes, but she didn't look at them, didn't pay attention to her surroundings. She managed to return to the alley, somehow, refitting the ring. The portal was kind to her this time, didn't ravage or shake her that much. She shook in relief when she appeared at the abandoned construction site.

The shaky legs just stopped supporting her and she collapsed there, on the spot. She removed the ring again. Seconds, months, years later she found herself stumbling forward, her surroundings a constant, horrible blur. She slammed the door behind her and rushed to the bed, and stayed there, not remembering much more than brief flashes from the walk home.

Melinda shook her once, twice, thrice before she reacted.

– You were visiting your two damaged birds again, weren't you?

Lucinda nodded.

– Why do you keep torturing yourself like this?

– He s-saved me. Lucinda's voice cracked. – Saved me from what is truly a fate worse than death, and I couldn't save him in return.

– Well, at least you're thanking him properly, Melinda remarked, sarcasm dripping from her voice, – being cooped up and brooding in your bed, doing your best to mimic his condition.

Lucinda struck her, her fist hitting her straight on the jaw. It happened so fast that none of them could react. Melinda fell backwards and hit the floor hard. Lucinda stared at her in horror.

– Wow, sis, the girl mumbled through the blood filling her mouth, – I didn't think you still had it in you.

There was no humor in her eyes or voice. She spat the words like venom.

Lucinda broke into tears and a moment later Melinda did as well. They crumbled in their respective positions. Lucinda crawled out of bed and joined the other on the floor. They embraced and cried themselves dry in each other's arms.

They moved three days later. Almost all the guys from the Center, both those already living there and the others helped out. Lucinda fought to hold herself steady each and every second in their crowded company.

The discoloration on Melinda's jaw was slight but distinct, but nobody commented on it. Instead they focused on keeping a light banter in the group. In her rather dismal mood Lucinda wasn't sure she approved. She just went along with it, like she did with everything else.

Melinda danced around in their new, impressive apartments with bright

272

eyes.

– This is... she mused. – This is...

She gave up and just kept shaking her head in wonder.

They were big as football pitches and luxurious and equipped with everything one could possibly desire.

– It's a trap, Lucinda mumbled, – yet another trap.

– This is SOMETHING, she heard Kid Sister shout from the other apartment across the hallway.

– Private tutoring is available, of course, Desmonia explained to Big Sister, appearing before her without announcing herself, melting into her vision like flowing water. – If you feel Melinda needs it, skilled tutors will be on hand at any given time. As her guardian you're calling the shots.

Lucinda signed some papers without looking at them. It wasn't important anyway.

Desmonia glanced around her a bit before pulling closer and giving her a conspiratorial look.

– I have something for you, she whispered. – Try it and see what you think.

Lucinda looked at her open palm. There was a pill there.

She looked startled at the other woman.

– Open your mouth.

She did and Desmonia put the pill on her tongue. Lucinda closed her mouth and swallowed. It was easy and there was no need for water.

– Have a happy afternoon, Desmonia chuckled and kissed her on the cheek.

Desmonia left with a «chao» and a wave. Lucinda closed the door. She stood there for a while and waited for Melinda to come, but she didn't.

Lucinda walked to the window, looking at the city below and its darkening twilight, giving way to the neon lights.

A dark chuckle rose from her throat. She staggered a bit. The sofa, the very nice sofa rose up and met her on her way down.

She writhed there on the soft ground, bathing in the scent of grass and green. A smile broke on her face. It burned so pleasantly in her veins. She felt like she was immersed in water, but remained dry. There were no sounds. Everything stayed soft and pleasant.

Suddenly her eyes opened wide. She gasped. No sound escaped her open mouth.

Suddenly everything had turned extremely pleasant. No matter how many times she tried she couldn't draw breath, but it was still as if oxygen-saturated air flooded her blood. She felt it. Every time she touched herself pleasure filled her being.

Moans sighed in the infinite space she had become. Each exhale felt like heaven. Her smile spread to her entire body, to every piece of skin she possessed.

She spiraled down into a beyond pleasant darkness without end, dreaming endless tales of yesterday and tomorrow, and not even the scarecrow resembling a dragon at the end of the fall frightened her that much.

Lucinda awoke with a smile on her lips. Pain threatened to split her head. The smile remained in place.

She stood before the mirror, staring blindly at that sick smile. It was as if she disappeared in that much bigger room in there, as if she dissolved, faded away in the vast landscape of that other world.

Weak legs carried her back to the living room. She sat there, waiting for Melinda to come.

But she didn't.

It was as if a giant hole opened up inside her, as the low point of the drug ride hit her. Giant tears slipped from her eyes. She hardly moved aside from that.

The watch on her wrist stared at her with its numbers. They didn't move, but were frozen and still. She slipped into sleep and dormancy. Her sense of reality just slipped away.

The door opened. The chilly draft made her open her eyes. She expected Melinda, but it wasn't her, but Miriam. The elegant woman took one look at Lucinda and saw straight through her.

– Desmonia gave you one of her specials, huh?

It wasn't a question. Lucinda nodded meekly.

– She did that to me, too. She's a cruel, uncaring and manipulative bitch. If you ask her for more or even accept her kindness one more time you will be hers forever.

She walked to the downtrodden woman on the plush sofa, tenderly touching her cheek.

– You need to get your act together, she said softly. – We need you, need you badly.

– So do you, Lucinda said with swollen eyes and stare fixated on her. – There will be a time, soon, when you must choose between us and your mundane masters and whether or not you are your own woman or their corporate whore.

Miriam shook. Lucinda felt power again, felt it rise within. The triumphant smile lit her face.

– I don't know if Desmonia did what she did out of kindness, if she intended to help me. Lucinda sniffed and dried her muzzle, rubbed it harder

274

in another pass in order to feel it beyond the numbness. – But it sort of worked, sort of cleared my head. I know what I'm not, now.

Miriam nodded serious-minded, like a little girl expecting a scolding from a strict mother.

– I tried, she whispered, – tried from the start to handle them, instead of them handling me, but I felt it slip away. They were just so much better at the game than I was.

Lucinda saw it easily in her mind, now, when the shame was laid bare.

– I know, but you're not alone anymore. I'm here with you.

Miriam easily recognized the iron hard conviction in the other's eyes. She fell on her knees with a happy whimper. A moment later she had grabbed Lucinda's hand and kissed it.

– Thank you, oh, thank you.

Lucinda smiled down on the girlish woman, easily comforting her, calming her fears.

– Don't you worry, we'll fix everything. It will all be alright.

It was so easy. It would be so easy… to take full control.

– It will be alright.

She repeated her words to the kneeling woman, and Miriam's face turned relaxed and serene. Lucinda saw it, how the little girl in a woman's body dreamed happy waken dreams.

– Come, she bid Miriam and Miriam followed her, followed in her tracks.

Lucinda didn't knock on Melinda's door, but walked right inside. Kid Sister stood at the center of the floor, swaying to the music in her head speakers.

Come with me, Lucinda bid her.

Melinda removed the head speakers and followed Big Sister and the other woman.

They walked to Desmonia's office at the end of the hall. The headmistress sat behind her desk.

– Stand up! Lucinda snapped.

– What… Desmonia blinked confused.

She rose hesitatingly.

– On the floor, stand straight! Look straight forward.

Desmonia obeyed, a distant stare appearing in her eyes.

Lucinda circled her, studying her with a cruel, appreciative look.

– Excellent, most excellent…

Desmonia reddened. She began breathing faster, lowering her eyes, baring her neck for the stronger.

– We will have an exercise session in the gym in ten minutes. Give the word.

– Yes, Lucinda. At once, Lucinda.

Lucinda saw how her nipples hardened and smiled in cruel triumph.

– Everybody will be there. No excuses will be tolerated. You report to me when everything is ready. Is that clear?

– Yes, Lucinda.

The three left, leaving Desmonia to her task.

Aren't you taking your emulation of Claudia a bit too far this time? Melinda giggled.

No, I am not! Lucinda snapped, chastising Kid Sister.

Melinda crumbled a bit, but kept giggling in her mind.

Sorry…

– Young and bashful, Melinda, Lucinda said softly. – I don't mind that, I really don't.

A light touch on the jaw made Melinda squirm in discomfort, but she didn't pull away, or attempted to do so.

They walked on.

Ten minutes and thirty seconds later every member of the Furies currently in the building was present in the gym. Lucinda was pleased.

– The first phase of our training ended when we took to the streets some time ago, she declared. – Tonight, and in the weeks to come, we will take it to yet another level of skill and strength.

They listened, she knew they did, and she was pleased.

She pushed them hard, harder than she had ever pushed them.

And when they felt absolutely certain they could take no more, she pushed them beyond yet another level of mental and physical exhaustion.

She stood in her bedroom later, looking out of her window, her special window. There was no more sweat, no more stench. A thorough shower had taken care of that. She felt tired, tired in a good way, as in total exhaustion, her muscles sore, her mind too worn-out to think.

She walked to the bed, the beyond comfortable bed, falling on it with a soft, hard noticeable thud. Hands moving of their own accord pulled the blanket over her big, strong and lethal body.

Her eyes closed, she spiraled down into that beyond pleasant darkness without end, where hardly more than a faint itch of worry remained.

Chapter 16

The harbor stank of chemicals and poisons. Thick fog and exhaust and the hot, arid weather made it worse.

They were just ordinary containers, in an ordinary part of the harbor, not drawing attention to themselves at all, except through enhanced and aware minds.

– Hurry, Lucinda hissed. – Straight perimeter. Be ready for anything.

She conveyed urgency and danger beyond her words without actually revealing her true powers to them. They were in full alert-mode.

There is no enemy in the vicinity right now, she told Melinda, but there might be soon.

Confirmed, Melinda nodded distressed.

She knew what the stakes were, what the others didn't, couldn't fully comprehend yet.

The two bloodhound sisters found the container they had been looking for easy enough. They were drawn to its horror and submerged in its poisonous flame. Lucinda heard the breathing inside, even as she was almost overwhelmed by the dull fear and lack of coherent thought she sensed from the bundles of flesh in there.

She nodded. Lois grabbed the lock. Energy flowed from her hand and the lock practically broke in her grip, by the onslaught of her rage.

The door slid open and the stale breath of body juices and trapped air assaulted them. The chained, nude women inside hardly reacted to their emergence. They just kept staring straight ahead with empty eyes. The Furies froze in indecision and stark fear.

– Stay alert and in formation, Lucinda hissed at them.

– What *is* this? Desmonia practically whined.

– It is like we told you, Melinda said. – Male supremacist groups have been doing this for years. The group we're dealing with here is just slightly more advanced in their plans and better organized.

– On your feet! Lucinda commanded the poor wretches on the floor. – We don't have much time.

They obeyed, like they would obey any authoritative voice. Moving like sleepwalkers they managed to stand up and stumble out of their cage.

– They told us, one of them spoke up weakly. – They told us that we were their slaves and that we would wear chains for the rest of our lives.

She had welts after the lashes several places on her body and so had most of the others. Lucinda's vision almost turned black as the pure, crystalline rage rose from her depths. She pushed them with their mind, made them move faster, while she kept scouting for the slavers, catching herself hoping they would show up.

Desmonia puked her guts out somewhere. Everybody heard it and pictured it before their eyes even if they didn't actually see her do it.

– There were only two of them, Lucinda said slowly. – Two left to affect the… transport. They ran away when they saw us.

She saw them in a speedboat leaving the harbor, quickly gaining too much of a head-start for any pursuers to catch up.

– They… ran way? Lois choked.

– They did, Lucinda confirmed.

– Those yellow assholes, Lois swore. – So they didn't have the guts to stand up to real resistance, huh?

She chuckled darkly and triumphant and the others, including some of the former captives joined her. The mood lightened up considerably. Whatever fear there had been faded to virtually nothing and rage welcome as rain supplanted it.

– Come, Melinda told the wretches just risen from the floor kindly. – Come with us!

At first it seemed like they wouldn't come, wouldn't move, but then they did, remaining impassive, as if they weren't aware that they were being rescued.

The Furies grabbed them somewhat gently and moved them and themselves away from there, from the place where horror lived.

– They took us against our will, one of the girls said, speaking in a hollow voice. – Then they told us it was their right.

– They aren't the first saying something like that, honey, Lucinda said, – but they will be one of the last.

The vans waited for them not far away. They rushed inside, anxiously glancing in every direction. The vehicles drove off. The darkness at the back smothered them all.

– We will train you, Lucinda told the freed girls. – We will make you into lethal creatures that will never need to take such crap again.

As if confirming that to herself, she made an effort at memorizing every single naked face before her.

– They ran away, Miriam stated triumphant, turning around, sharing it with everyone. – They feared facing those able and willing to defend themselves.

Everybody nodded and voiced their agreement, laughing in relief and euphoria.

The nausea didn't leave them, but scratched their insides like claws, leaving open, festering wounds.

The nightmare the girls had lived through lingered in Lucinda's - and thereby everybody's mind. A lash hit the back of the redhead, and the others felt it. Lucinda made her right hand into a fist, making her nails dig deep into the skin of her palm, making it stop.

But at night, in her troubled sleep it returned, like everything did.

A wicked grin taunted her. She writhed on the bed, moving constantly back and forth, almost like she was awake. The grin belonged to a female, but Lucinda didn't recognize her face, hardly saw any features except the grin.

Melinda stood before her with a pained expression in her face.

It hurts, Big Sister, she wailed. Why must it hurt?

Lucinda watched as Kid Sister began filling out her clothes, began growing bigger and taller. The clothes cracked at the seams. The face changed into something demonic and vile.

The creature towered above her, a wicked grin snarling at her.

It does not hurt anymore, Tiny Sister.

Lucinda woke up, soaked in sweat. It was bright morning, bright day. Melinda, still innocent and good-humored Melinda pushed aside the curtains, revealing the blue sky outside.

– Rise and shine, sunshine.

– W-what? Lucinda said dazed, still not quite awake.

Melinda turned on the television. She was clearly excited, even beyond her usual youthful exuberance.

The image showed the hospital, the reporters standing outside, a crowd of them holding microphones and/or recording equipment.

– Behind me, the woman spoke excitedly, – in the psychiatric ward of the hospital what is described as a medical miracle has occurred. Marcus Lerner, one of those freed from enslavement in Jagadir by the Maverick Crew has, according to his therapist made something approaching a full recovery from the thorough brainwashing he suffered in the hands of Jagadir officials.

She didn't hear anything anymore. All sound just faded in her ears. Melinda spoke right in front of her and she didn't pick up a single word.

Lucinda rose, practically jumped from the bed. She slowed down deliberately, picking up her Gimmick bag from the closet, outwardly calming down, but inwardly seething with anxiety, expectation, fear and hope.

A tear fell from Melinda's left eye.

– Do you want me to come with you or do you prefer privacy when you meet up with your old bed partner?

– I would love for you to come with me, Lucinda said softly. – I can always discard you later.

– Of course, Melinda grinned, and Lucinda imagined that the grin filled the room.

She took the time to shower, shower a lot, making Melinda's grin widen further. The rub of the towel hardly touched her skin.

– It's so chilled in here, she mused. – We can't feel the heat outside.

– To me that's a good thing, Melinda stated solemnly.

Kid Sister had found her own gear. Lucinda realized she had actually brought it with her when she did her rise and shine routine.

Kid Sister grinned at her some more, just as infuriating as always. Lucinda sighed.

They locked their doors and had breakfast. Many of the others had also woken early, and Lucinda's shared her good mood with them and it returned to her in an ongoing, pleasant loop.

– Today is a good day, isn't it? Lois said, clearly in high spirits.

– It is, Lucinda agreed, nodding with the rest of those sitting around the table.

She imagined his face in its radiant version, the face she had only briefly experienced close up during a few hours four years ago. The memory made her heart beat faster and she chastised herself.

The breakfast and the people around it slipped away, and she and Kid Sister walked through busy streets as Gimmick and Sensor.

Busy journalists and television crews surrounded the hospital. Guards blocked the front and probably all sides of the building, keeping the newshounds from gaining entrance. Gimmick knew the two of them had been spotted when the buzz in her head picked up. Microphones and cameras were practically pushed at their lips. The crowd, all the buzzing minds affected Gimmick, making her dizzy and disoriented.

They kept walking, pushing the people ahead of them aside with what were visibly gentle but decisive moves.

– ... and Gimmick is clearly deeply affected by the latest event, she heard a woman tell her viewers in front of a camera. – The reason Sensor is here isn't that obvious, but I would guess emotional support.

The guards stepped aside for the two costumed women and the sisters finally reached the inside of the hospital, its quiet halls. Lucinda realized that she was breathing hard, that she was actually gasping for breath, and that Melinda held around her, whispering calming words in her ear.

It helped, at least to a point. She managed to focus again, to breathe again.

Claire the nurse waited for them behind the reception desk, bursting with excitement, close to tears in her sentimental happiness, living gloriously through her heroine.

– He hasn't left yet, she sighed in joy, – even though he could have. He has truly recovered. Don't be afraid that he hasn't. The doctors say it is a *miracle*.

– That is good to hear, Gimmick heard herself say.

– I'll *bet* he is waiting for you, Claire winked. – Room 217. It's a guestroom, where the two of you can be together without any… interruption.

Lucinda choked. She wanted to thank the woman from the bottom of her heart, but could not voice her gratitude. She grasped the other's hand.

– You go, Sensor said. – I'll wait here, read some magazines, waste some time, scream if I get bored or attacked.

Gimmick rushed through the hallways, knowing the way, easily zoning in on suddenly familiar brain patterns.

She knocked on the door. His voice called out, called out her name. She pushed the door open and rushed inside. Numb hands closed the door, locked the door, and turned to face him.

He sat in a chair, still in his hospital gown, staring at her with the alert, appreciative eyes she recalled so well.

– Hi, she said shyly.

– Hello, he said, choke full of emotion as well, – aren't you a sight for sore eyes.

– I came here as soon as I heard, she said, unable to move, cursing her hoarse voice. – My sister woke me up today to the great, to the unbelievably good news.

She saw, sensed how her wording made him wonder, made his eyes widen and she wasted no more time as she started unlocking the straps around her neck.

– You're sure about this?

– You saved me and suffered horribly for it, she said softly. – I would do anything for you.

And then she pulled her mask off. She stood before him as herself and felt incredibly good about it.

– Wow, he whistled, with something very close to his old charm and wit intact. – That is certainly a well known face and indeed a sight for sore eyes.

She rushed into his arms and onto his lap. They kissed, and it felt like heaven.

He was still strong in body and as she probed him, as she sat in his lap and caressed his face, she convinced herself that he had indeed regained his faculties as well.

– You saved me, she choked, – and I couldn't return the favor, your sacrifice, couldn't do anything to help you, any of you.

– But you did, he insisted, – when you and your comrades felt it was right, when you were confident you had a high probability of success, and you were correct. You went to war for us. Who can demand more?

He caressed her cheek, drying a tear.

– And you woke me up. Even though nothing you did seemed to help, it eventually did. You never relinquished hope.

– I did, she whispered.

– You, the idol of millions, in both your incarnations came to me, cared for me, infused me with your will to live, to prevail.

– The idol thing is pretty overrated, she joked.

He touched her scar.

– Who did this to you?

– A crazy Asbasos native, she replied casually. – Melinda, my sister shot him, so you can't be my knight in shining armor here.

– But I will be your knight, he stated.

A pleasant hum filled her. Joy filled her. She closed and opened her eyes.

He began fumbling with the straps of her jacket, and then she felt it, felt him hardening against her thigh. She drew her breath abrupt and fast. He kissed her, demanding and potent. She responded without thought and resistance. He removed her jacket and all the gear.

– I've waited so long for this, he growled. – I can't even tell exactly how long.

– So have I, she gasped, rocking a little in his lap already, in anticipation for what was coming.

She helped him remove all the hurdles, doing so in fast, feverish motion. When she leaned backwards she was able to show him everything. She was suddenly sweating profusely, covered from head to toe. He was still wearing the hospital gown. She tried to pull it off him, but that was impossible, since he was still sitting. They tumbled down on the bed, chuckling and grinning. She grabbed the edge of the gown and in one, single pull she tore the piece of cloth apart.

– You're not wearing any underwear, she said triumphantly, laughing herself silly.

He grabbed her and held her. She let him. And he was still strong. His body had been rigidly exercised and hadn't lost its agility. He held her and started touching her. She gasped, loud.

– You're such a great love toy, he told her.

He bit an already hard nipple. She noticed in her fever how his big hands grabbed her breasts, how he squeezed them. He put her on her back. She was breathing hard. They both were. There was not enough air in the room. There couldn't be.

– Yes, your toy, she breathed, her face a study in ascending ecstasy. – To do with as you please. Put it to good use. Put your tool into it, please.

He waited, rocking a bit on top of her.

– One of the most famous faces and bodies in the world, and it's all mine.

– Yours, she agreed.

He pushed himself into her, deep into her. She screamed, loud enough for most of the hospital and the journalists posted outside to easily hear it. First there was incredulity. Then hungry shark smiles transformed their faces.

– You're such a wildcat, he mumbled with his mouth close to her neck. – You should change your name.

– WILD WILD WILD, she shouted.

She reached for his lips with hers. He held her jaw and kept her away. She panted and moved beneath him. He moved and she moved, their bodies pushing against each other. His big eyes expanded in her vision. She felt like she was drowning in them.

Then he kissed her on the lips. Everything, already so sweet exploded below and above. Bodies stiffened. He emptied himself in her and his heat spread all over her body, even as her water drowned him.

They moved on the bed, in hard pushes and pulls. She had imagined they floated above it and now they fell down, down, down, drowning in its deep, deep, deep waters.

She giggled, crouching in his strong arms, playing with the hair on his chest, giving him wet kisses on the cheek.

– It feels so good to be near you, to lie close to you, she said softly, – to feel your skin against mine.

His kiss felt good, too, better than better, better than best.

You're just a fly I swat.

She froze, her sweat suddenly cold and acid.

– What is it? He wondered. – What is wrong?

She left the bed and walked back and forth on the floor.

– It isn't your fault, she said. – She spoke to me again. She does that.

– Who?

– The Black Dragon.

Lucinda shook her head, clearly distressed.

– The black…? He said astonished, grinning a bit, but also anxious.

He was so easy to read, his thoughts so clear in her head. The warm feeling inside of her persisted.

– She's a… a super villain. I have never actually met her, at least not like she is now, but she has pestered me, all of us, really for years. She's... lurking, waiting out there for something, for a moment only she knows, waiting to strike.

– Sounds more like she's afraid of facing Gimmick and her gallant warriors, he said lightly.

– Yeah. Lucinda chuckled. – That thought struck us, too, at first, but it has become clear to us that she leads a... sinister network of individuals bent on expansion and domination. And the sense of menace and power she projects... if that's fake she's a damn good fucking actress.

He rose from the bed, too, and walked to her, grabbing her gently.

– You're shaking, he said astounded. – She really has you spooked, huh?

She looked up at him with haunted eyes.

– Sometimes I feel like she's a spider weaving her web around me and doing it in such a clever, sinister way that I don't notice that it's happening, and when I least expect it she will seal my one chance of escaping and trap me f-forever.

They stood there for what felt like a very long time. He held her and slowly the warm feeling once more dominated her perception.

– Sorry, she whispered.

– You've got nothing to be sorry about, he said firmly. – Of course you haven't.

Her eyes cleared.

– I know, thank you.

He kissed her again, started fondling her again, cautiously, with increasing confidence and determination.

– Listen, I must go, he said. – My father died yesterday and I have things to settle.

– Now, I am sorry, she gasped. – My problems suddenly seem very trivial compared to yours.

– It isn't really that much of a deal, he insisted. – We didn't get along at all. He was a mundane, and he practically rejected me, threatened to disown me, but he never did.

– I did have a notion that the shack didn't quite suit you, she mused. – I didn't pry, but you projected... class. I guess you're loaded, now?

– I am, but I could use your help with lawyers and such, if they prove troublesome.

She knew what he implied. It couldn't really be misunderstood. The low-keyed, warm feeling rose in her again. He *knew* her.

– You've got it.

He kissed her and she sensed the swell of gratitude in his mind.

– We are a little bit in a hurry, he said casually, – but we still have time for a much needed shower.

– We are, huh? She grinned. – We do?

– You bet!

He grabbed her and carried her into the bathroom.

– I feel so free, she mumbled, – so unrestrained with you. It is as if I am a completely different person.

The caresses turned intense fast, like an explosion. Bored journalists started paying attention again. Some of them directed their microphones at an open window.

Water flooded her open mouth. He pushed her at the wall and fucked her from behind. Each move sent shivers of pleasure through her. She was drowning in it and couldn't get enough. It was so pleasant, pleasant, pleasant. Steam rose. She felt like the steam, dissolved, like hot water, like the hot water flooding, flooding, flooding... They both shouted. Rigid bodies turned soft and malleable again. They groaned and sighed in happiness. She slipped down the wall and from his grip as her feet once again touched the floor. Her lips moved by themselves, as she turned around and smothered him in affection.

They stood there forever and enjoyed each other in the hot rain.

Later, when they dried each other, it felt like no time had passed at all. She enjoyed immensely his strong hands on her body. They eventually dressed, but did not take their eyes off each other.

– It's too bad I have to wear the mask when we're together in public, she said. – I'm thinking of giving up that secret identity shit.

– Don't do it for my sake, he grinned. – I kind of like the fact that I'm one of the few knowing what a pretty face it's hiding.

– You're really the silver tongued devil, aren't you? She purred.

She put on the mask, tightening the straps around the neck. It felt like she had trouble breathing again and this time it didn't feel like a good thing.

Gimmick stood there again, in front of him. She could see it through his eyes, sense how it changed his view on her and she fought the sense of dread it brought her.

They walked to the reception area. Sensor stood up.

– Hi, handsome, the girl greeted him coyly.

She's my sister. Play nice.

– Hi, cute girl, he returned the greeting.

She blushed instantly.

Not that nice, she admonished him.

You enjoyed yourself, did you? Melinda thought sourly.

I did, Lucinda admitted, the warm feeling instantly swelling within her yet again, enjoyed myself beyond words.

Sensor led on outside. The other two followed her arm in arm.

The flood of questions and attention hammered them immediately.

– He saved me, Gimmick said. – I could not save him in return.

– But she did save me, he countered, – First she freed me from the shackles of flesh and then from the shackles of the mind. I felt it like I awoke from a dream, a horrible nightmare I had been unable to wake up from for so long. This is such a happy day.

She looked affectionately at him with the eyes dominating the mask, making no secret of how she felt about him. The photographers had a field day.

They stood there, posing for a while, before leaving, Lucinda and Melinda, trained models as they were, instinctively finding a pose for each new step, before shaking it off and moving through the crowd.

Gimmick waved to people, clearly euphoric.

A car, a limousine picked them up at the edge of the hospital plaza.

– This is James, my father's driver and sort of mentor to me when my father couldn't be bothered to entertain his son.

– Hi, James, the girls choired cheerfully.

The man ignored them with a practiced disdain.

They drove off, leaving the area with a load of paparazzis on their tail.

The two sisters had grown used to be brought from place to place by personal chauffeurs lately, but this was different, more personal, somehow.

It was the same black windows, though. Those inside could look outside, but those outside couldn't look inside. A chill passed through Lucinda as flashes of thought from those staring at the car with their fish eyes reached her mind.

She and Marcus coddled in the wide, wide backseat. Sensor sat opposite them and tried to pretend she was passing time. She shifted uneasily in her seat. Gimmick realized stunned that she was... was aroused.

He paused a bit with Lucinda and looked across the divide to the lonely girl there.

– Why don't you come over here?

She looked stunned at him, and then at Gimmick, but the smile didn't waver on Big Sister's flushing face.

Melinda rushed over to them, clearly excited. She sat down on his opposite side. He grabbed her and fondled and kissed her. She moaned impatiently.

– Why don't the two of you give me a floorshow? He practically bid them.

They looked shyly at him and each other. After a brief hesitation and prompting from him they went down on their knees on the floor and clinched and began making out there.

Are you okay with this? Melinda wondered in her fever.

I don't mind sharing you with him, Lucinda replied, and this is... pleasant as well.

They had never done this before, never done girl play, and the instant, surprising pleasure spurred them on further. The fondling and kisses hands to body, lips to lips quickly turned more intense.

– That's my girls, the man said pleased.

Two more cunts that will soon kneel at my feet.

The girls turned towards him with huge smiles painted on their faces under the masks, smiles easily visible in spite of the small part of the skin shown.

Gimmick frowned, fighting not to reveal it, any of it.

– Come here, he bid them.

They did, beyond eager and willing in their zeal to obey his commands.

Sensor overwhelmed him with kisses, pushing herself at him.

Eager cunts, easily submitting to my superior will.

Lucinda felt chilled to the bone, even as she fought to keep up the pretense. Nausea struck her hard. She kept her hands hidden from him and pushed the hidden button on her ring. Its alarm started ringing and woke her from her trance-like condition.

– Oops, she said sheepishly. – I'm afraid that's our cue. Gotta go, lover boy.

She embraced him and kissed him hard on the lips.

– We'll make it up to you, I *promise!*

– You better! He said, slapping her on the butt.

She yelped in joy.

– This stinks, Sensor said sourly. – This really stinks.

– Duty calls, Sensor, Gimmick said, giving Kid Sister a stern look. – Play later.

– You better stop, James, Marcus said lightly, – or there will really be an emergency here...

James obliged. The two sisters gave Marcus one last, stunning smile before jumping out of the car and starting on their instant run through the street, towards the nearest gate. Gimmick turned off the alarm as she moved.

– What is *with* you? Sensor practically slurred, clearly agitated, her eyes big and unfocused. – I thought we didn't take calls from the Maverick Crew anymore.

Shut up! Gimmick sent. Shut the fuck up!

And then, stunned, as she spotted the tears in Lucinda's eyes, Melinda realized that Big Sister was agitated as well. She almost stopped in her tracks, slowly waking up from what had obviously been a trance-like state.

Keep running, the shaking voice told her, and she did.

And the frown turned bigger on her brow as well.

The paparazzis attempted to follow them, but the two quickly ditched them by choosing a few backstreets and alleys, and there it was, the portal. Lucinda practically dragged Kid Sister with her through it, both mentally and physically.

They appeared on the abandoned construction site, cast in shadow.

The ring started ringing again. Gimmick took «the call» while desperately attempting to dry the tears flooding her eyes.

It was Mechanic, understandably concerned, checking up on them.

– Everything is okay, she told him with her sweetest voice. – It was a mishap. I touched the button by accident. We are in a kind of bind here, though, so I'll talk to you later, okay?

She «hung up».

She stood there shaking, striving to pull to undo the straps and pull off the mask. Finally she succeeded.

Melinda stood there, shaking her head. It felt very much like she was waking up from a dream.

– What was that? She cried, choked. – What *happened?* He did something to us, didn't he?

Lucinda nodded.

– He did. Earlier today I got one of those nasty messages, one I thought was also from Black Dragon, but it was from him, just like the last one in the car, clearly unintended.

She slid down the wall, practically collapsing, crumbling before her sister's eyes.

– He has a specific telepathic talent: working on perception, making himself attractive in people's mind. He can impose his will on others, especially females, sort of making them see him in a much more favorable light, even making them… I-love him.

– Oh, Lucy, Melinda choked.

– It was much stronger now compared to the first time I met him. I guess his masters in Jagadir deliberately developed his gift, in order for him to aid them in their brainwashing of others. And another part of his talent is that he can hide from other telepaths, hide a part of himself, presenting the Boy Scout image, easily preying on my guilt. But I have grown, too. When he was focusing on you or was otherwise distracted, somewhat his true self… leaked, and I got flashes, flashes of his deeper thoughts. I was afraid, fearful that I wouldn't be able to fool him, but I did, using his own tactics against him, displaying to him the surface persona of the silly goose he so easily seduced.

– But he…

– … saved me? Lucinda glared at her. – He did, but my guess is that it wasn't intentional. What I saw in his mind more than suggests that it wasn't. He was probably attempting to save himself and he quite simply collided with me on his way out. And there's more…

She stopped. Melinda wanted to kneel by her sister's side, but she was also experiencing the same horrible feeling of being used and discarded, and was unable to both move and speak.

– He's a slaver, Lucinda spat. – I glimpsed in his mind the scenario of what would have happened if we hadn't been kidnapped by Jagadir forces. His fellow male supremacists waited for his word, closing the trap around both me and Jolene and the others. The irony is almost too much, isn't it?

– And now? Melinda finally managed to speak through her own snot.

– And now? Now, he would have played with us both for a while, until he grew tired of the game and then we would have been on our way to one of their «training camps».

– I felt it, Melinda whimpered, – feel the irresistible infatuation fading. I couldn't say no to him. The thought didn't even cross my mind.

Then she fell to the ground as well, hurting herself, not caring. They crawled to each other, embracing, sobbing endlessly there on the dusty ground, until it, in what felt like hours later finally subsided, and they could somewhat breathe and think rationally again.

– But why didn't you…

– … take him there and then? I wasn't certain that I could, the shaking bundles of emotion that I was. I feared that all his buddies waited in the wings, that he had stacked the cards in his favor and I didn't want him to know that I know, in the hopes that we can outmaneuver him later, use him to expose his organization and free his captives. And I want him to pay, want to make him pay hard. The seething hatred inside is still so powerful that I can hardly *breathe*.

Melinda caressed her exposed cheek. She nodded.

– He's a fucking rapist, worse.

They rose, on shivering legs. Lucinda put the mask back on, and it felt good.

– And I, in my storybook naiveté exposed myself to him, gave him a weapon he can use against us. I don't think he will reveal our identities to the public, but he knows and he will never forget. He and his misogynist pals will be able to track us wherever we go and the media will inadvertently help them.

And Kid Sister's attempt at comforting her only made it all worse.

Melinda suddenly crouched violently and vomit flowed from her mouth. She stood there with watery eyes and stared blind at the world.

And that made Lucinda feel strangely calm, collected and in control. The emotional rollercoaster stopped in its tracks.

– Look at you, she spat, very patronizing and cruel. – Look at little girl lost. Melinda blinked.

– I reach out to you, she whispered, – and you treat me like shit? Fuck you! Lucinda turned her back to her, ignored her and walked away.

– Perhaps I should have let that nice savage keep doing what he was doing? Perhaps you don't deserve my pity or my support?

Gimmick stopped in front of the portal, waiting. Sensor shook and hurried to her side.

– Follow me, little lost girl and be found.

Melinda, filled with shame and recrimination and unsteady on her legs, did.

They stepped through the portal.

And returned to the central parts of the city, not that far from their new home. Lucinda removed the ring and Melinda did as well. She sensed no people even near the quiet back alley. There was something resembling a garbage can there. Lucinda found the tiny keyhole under it and pushed a key into it. The nearest side opened. They found their bags with their civilian clothes there and changed with the efficiency that experience had taught them. Then they put the costumes in the bags and put them back into the elaborate hiding place, something they had rarely bothered doing before, but now caution dodged their every step. It took a few minutes with deliberate detours around the old, abandoned warehouse district before they encountered people at all, but not long after that Lucinda and Melinda Patterson walked through streets among many others. They were recognized and ogled and scrutinized and admired and despised, and it was worse than before. They were on constant high alert. The Center wasn't that far away, but it felt like miles and they imagined that the march lasted days. Lucinda scanned the area that much harder when they reached the block near their new home. Any small and big person was perceived as a potential threat. With bodies tense like a steel wire and their minds like hot air in constant uproar they crossed the street. Only a resolve they hardly recognized kept them from running the final stretch.

Sick relief flooded them when they stepped through the main entrance and the heavy door closed behind them.

Both walked right to the restrooms, to the special made toilet bowls. The stench quickly filled the perfumed room. Lucinda heard Melinda vomit again. She felt it, a kick in the gut.

There was a choke she could not stop. She half waited for the nausea to come to her as well and the vomit to flow from her mouth and desecrate the antiseptic toilet.

But it didn't. She pushed her hand against her mouth and bit into the fleshy part of its skin, and kept doing so until she tasted blood.

A long time passed or seemed to pass, until she studied the hand and found that the damage wasn't that bad. She rose and started drying her ass with loads of paper she didn't bother to format. Her hand hurt. She rolled some paper around the hand, flushed the toilet bowl and left.

There was no one outside. Melinda was somewhere close, but was attempting to close her out and her exact whereabouts thereby became harder to pinpoint. Lucinda walked to a living room empty and desolate. She walked to the bar. It wasn't locked or anything. She grabbed a bottle of scotch and a glass and sat down on the couch. Her strong hands opened the bottle by themselves, easily managing without a screwdriver. She poured the small glass, grabbed it and drank its content in one, uninterrupted flow. The heat burned her throat and spread from her stomach and to the rest of the body. She poured another glass.

Melinda grabbed her own bottle and glass and joined her by the table. She poured the glass full and drank and coughed, clearly straining to keep the strong liquor from affecting her too much.

She filled the glass again. Lucinda waited patiently.

– Cheers! Kid Sister said and lifted her glass.

They had a toast, and drank.

It didn't take many minutes before they had become piss drunk. They saw the world through a pleasant haze.

Melinda put on some music and began dancing with wild, unsteady moves, sipping from her tiny glass.

The singer belched his song with a loud, dreamy voice:

I once met a lost girl
And squeezed her dry
I taught her about life
And made her feel joy

The little girl lost came to me
On a bright, sunny day without clouds

I spotted her as she turned a corner
She smiled to me with the darkest gleam
Of her deep-saturated eyes

I once found a lost girl
And drenched her cold
I taught her freedom
And bliss beyond words

Melinda returned to the couch and dumped herself by her sister's side.
They had another toast, drank and choired the verses.

Glasses met and parted again. Lucinda couldn't tell how many times that
had happened. The content of the bottles had shrunk almost to half.

– Why do you hate me? Kid Sister sniffed, her eyes an open wound.

– I don't hate you, Lucinda muttered with alcohol-numbed lips.

– Why do you detest me then? Kid Sister's voice rose in anger. – You must
detest me the way you treat me.

– You misunderstand, Lucinda protested. – I'm just toughening you up,
that's all.

I'm afraid of you, she thought.

It was when Melinda's eyes widened that Big Sister realized that she had
spoken aloud in her mind.

– I dreamt about you growing, Lucinda almost stuttered, – saw you grow
into…

– … Black Dragon, Melinda completed the sentence astonished.

And just like that, it was as if the creature was present, was right there,
hovering between them, hardly a mirage at all, but something, potent,
tangible.

Lucinda broke into tears.

– I'm so fucked up, she sniveled.

Melinda studied her dark and cruel. It was as if her entire form and
surroundings shifted and burned in dark, invisible fire. Melinda moved
closer to her. Her feature softened and she reached out a hand, touching Big
Sister's cheek.

– Yes, you are, she mused. – Perhaps it isn't I that am the little girl lost?

Lucinda glanced at her through her tear-wet eyes, attempting to dry it all
off with her sleeve, with both her sleeves. Melinda tried aiding her in her
struggle. Both efforts were in vain.

A hand reached for the glass. It missed and pushed the glass off the table
and it fell to the floor and broke in a thousand pieces. Lucinda stared at

the fluid and pieces of glass. She giggled and rose, taking the strenuous trip to the bar to find another, to find several other glasses, some of them also ending up as pieces on the floor. She put all those still intact on the table and filled them up, and she drank, and Melinda drank, and they stabled the glasses as they emptied them.

They danced, giggling, laughing, cackling, their voices and sobs drowning in the thunder of music and distortion hammering them. Hands and arms around each other's shoulders they supported the other sister through minutes and hours of unsteady moves and binge drinking. Lips synced and choired to the same melody, the same discord. They danced and kept dancing, but finally felt unable to resist gravity any longer.

Lucinda opened her eyes. She awoke on the floor, convinced hours had passed, even though she wasn't sure. Her watch was…

– My watch is smashed, she giggled darkly. – I'm broken.

She discovered she was alone. The room had fallen silent. A door slammed somewhere in the building. She fought herself on her feet. The swaying continued. She detected no desire to puke. Brief relief passed through her.

– No, that isn't right, she reconsidered her previous statement. – I… I…

Whatever she intended to say dissolved in her alcohol-induced daze.

– Mel, she cried. – Sweetie?

There was no reply.

She left the living room, stumbling through dark hallways and turning abrupt corners, colliding with every wall she encountered.

Thoughts flooded her mind, but unable to decipher them as she was, they just kept drifting on the edge of her consciousness. Fleeting images and sensations filled the ether around her. She had reached the door to her apartment and fumbled with the key when unmistakable sounds reached her ears. The blushing was instant and deep. It came from the opposite apartment. She shook her head in amusement and kept fumbling with the keys.

The moaning was loud, as if it were close by, without any walls between it and her. She turned half around and spotted the door ajar.

Her feet guided her through it. She closed and locked the door behind her, half aware, half not of what awaited her in the bedroom.

Melinda knelt on the bed there. She was alone, rubbing her cunt with a steady, rough movement.

– There you are, she said hoarsely. – So nice of you to drop by.

Lucinda hesitated, before stepping forward, before joining the other on the bed.

She hesitated even more as she reached out with a hand. Melinda grabbed it and kissed it.

– Did that feel good? I know it does.

Kid Sister leaned forward and kissed her on the lips. Lucinda froze. Melinda kissed her again, softly at first, the first, few times and then more insistent.

And then Lucinda returned the affection.

Melinda grabbed her arm, looking incredulous at it.

– Your watch is broken, she said.

– That's it, Lucinda said startled. – That's what I tried to…

Another kiss shut her up.

What are you doing, sweetie?

Doing, doing, doing, the sweet voice droned on in her mind.

Lucinda grabbed Melinda's hair and kissed her hard on the lips. Two twin gasps rose from wide open mouths. They undressed each other, not too clumsy, moving against each other, caressing inflamed skin. Melinda put a hand between Lucinda's already sticky thighs, and if there had been any reluctance left in Big Sister that ended it.

– I want to suck your big tits…

They hit the soft bed. A smile broke on Lucinda's face, as she sensed the hungry mouth close around her nipple, as a content sigh escaped her open mouth, as Melinda let go of the nipple and moved further down on the body.

Someone had put on the music again, and broadcast it through the intercom, the very advanced intercom. The two of them seemed to sway to the rhythm, there on the bed. Lucinda moaned long and deep when Melinda buried her head between her thighs.

You've never had anyone eating your pussy before? Melinda's giggle and muddled speech echoed in her mind. Kid Sister will teach you, teach you *everything*.

And she did, like a responsible older sister. Lucinda shook her head. She couldn't stop doing it. Thought faded. Tasting Melinda a while later drove her totally wild.

– Wild, wild, wild, she mumbled.

And somewhere sounded the dark laughter from yesterday, tonight and tomorrow.

Darkness embraced them, like heat and release and sleep did, and they dreamed with a smile on their lips.

Chapter 17

The hard knocking on the door and panicked screams woke them up and made the smile die on their lips.

– MIRIAM HAS BEEN MURDERED, Lois shouted. – AND THE P-POLICE ARE HERE, INSIDE.

Ice cold spikes penetrated Lucinda. She watched how Melinda literally paled, how everybody gathered outside had already done so.

Images of Miriam slain on the living room floor assaulted her. Grief slammed her, hammered her relentlessly.

– We're coming, she shouted. – Stay calm.

She turned to Melinda and touched her cheek.

– Please, stay calm, she said. – Will you do that, for me?

Melinda nodded empathically, with a lower lip that wouldn't stop shivering. They dressed, without taking a shower or washing themselves in any way. Melinda rushed to the door and opened it. Anxious, terrified boys and girls rushed inside. They knew what was happening.

– Who let them in? Melinda asked beyond distressed.

– Nobody knows, Lois said enraged, frustrated. – At least I don't know who does.

Lucinda held up a finger, and the chatter faded, the room turned quiet, deadly quiet.

– Hard times are ahead of us, she admonished them. – We have only two options and both are equally bad. If we run, sneak out of here through the tunnels we will be branded as the murderers. If we stay they will take us in and keep us indefinitely. There's no middle ground here. There's nothing we can do about that, now. Even if we knew who the killer is, it wouldn't help us.

She could say with reasonable certainty that he or she wasn't present or close right now.

Everybody practically crumbled before her eyes.

We're fucked, she thought, another one she didn't share with Melinda. We're fucked good!

She couldn't get rid of the catching in her throat, the cold, cold terror clutching her heart.

The policemen were everywhere, vicious and cruel, with trouble in mind. She saw them wherever she sent her thoughts, saw them blocking all access routes and her anxiety and the sneaking suspicion that something was horribly wrong... grew.

– Desmonia said she would call our lawyers, Lois said, – but something might have happened to her, too. When I in my frenzy called them ten minutes later she hadn't done so.

– Good, good, Lucinda praised her. – Good thinking on your part. We must draw on all the advantages we possibly can.

She led her charges down the hallway, down the stairs, filled with grim emotions and forebodings that wouldn't go away.

A group of ten grim policemen of both sexes appeared around the corner.

– You will all come with us, their leader said brusquely.

– We were on our way down, officer, Lucinda said, adding a smile to her humble voice and features.

The only response was a silent snarl. They were pushed and hounded downstairs. Melinda stayed close to her, clearly anxious. Lucinda attempted to comfort her the best she could, masking her own shaky emotions.

Miriam was splashed across the table, an unspeakably bad sight. Blood decorated the floor in a wide circle around her. Steam, looking like shrapnel seemed to rise from her and rotate in the air.

It's her power, Melinda thought glumly, finally revealing itself.

A man waited for them by the body. His direct stare didn't in any way look encouraging.

– Good evening, he told them. – My name is Lestrade. I'm a detective at the city's homicide division.

– Good evening, Lucinda said.

– You're Lucinda Patterson. You're in charge here?

– No, I'm not. She shook her head. – No one is in charge, really, but you should talk to Desmonia, Desmonia Monahan, now, when you can't talk to… talk to…

He nodded curtly, and she stopped trying.

She wiped a tear from her eye, wiping hard twice.

– Everybody is here, now? He asked, he snapped.

She looked around. Her friends nodded to her.

– Everybody living here and a few more, but not everybody, she replied.

– Well, that will have to do, he nodded. – You will come to the headquarters with us. Up against the wall, all of you.

– What do you mean? She asked startled.

– You know perfectly well what I mean, he grinned.

She saw it in his mind, the pleasure he derived from this. The other cops pretty much shared his sentiment.

– Are you serious? She made an effort, useless as she more than suspected it would be to appeal to him. – Our dear friend has just been murdered, butchered in a most horrible way and you will add to our burden like this?

He looked at her with his pig's eyes.

– You won't make any trouble, will you, monkey?

All of them looked around them in desperation. There was no choice, really, and no way out.

There was hesitation, rage, before her shoulders sagged, and everybody followed her cue.

The man's expression of expectation changed to one of triumph.

– No, she choked, – we won't make any trouble.

They're just waiting for us to make a move, she told Melinda.

Melinda looked at the small big bruisers standing there with their tasers and guns and swallowed hard.

– Face the wall, he shouted, – and be quick about it.

They did, sniffing and fearful, seeing the collar in his and others' hands.

– Excellent, he boasted. – And you better not move from that position, or you will pay for it.

They obeyed him. The cops stepped behind them. Their arms were forced behind their back. Bracelets with chains were put around their wrists and upper arms. The collar was slapped around their neck. It emanated the signals interfering with the brainwaves. They all felt instantly how it was dulling their mind, their very reason.

– You've seen this being done with other criminals, I gather, their captor spat in triumph. – I'll bet you never imagined it would be used on you.

Lucinda felt how it negated her powers, how other's thoughts faded from her mind. She wanted to say something, anything, but speech failed her. She recalled how it had looked when people she had captured had attempted to express themselves, how retarded they had all looked, and she choked in misery, knowing fully well that their captors had more in store for them.

Syringes with the characteristic yellow fluid were being prepared, and the content injected into their thighs. It burned as it moved through their veins, and an even duller shade appeared in their eyes.

– According to local law 1415 you are arrested, he declared. – According to federal law 16013 concerning enhanced humans, you are drugged and whatever powers you possess are being negated. You will be incarcerated thus, until further action has been determined.

Lucinda choked. The dark laughter shook the walls. Her eyes widened and she moaned in distress, in what would have been full-blown panic if the collar hadn't dulled and wrecked her mind. She glanced bewildered around her, gasping in fright. No one else seemed to hear the laughter.

They had to, just had to. It was so loud, so triumphant, shaking her to pieces.

– Move, monkey!

Low-level charges of the tasers made them scream and jump in their tracks. It hurt, hurt bad.

The laughter turned loud as they entered the hallway, the one where she had always felt discomfort and fear.

This is it, the voice taunted her. This is your life from now on, your destiny fulfilled.

– Look at the monkey, an officer of the law chuckled in contempt. – The monkey is afraid.

They were being dragged away, stumbling along their captors, until being placed in the back of police transportation vehicles and taken away.

It had happened so fast. Everything had changed so abruptly that they hardly had been able to draw breath.

They sat there, unable to move a muscle. Lucinda imagined she felt twitches in her fingers or saw other fingers twitch, but everything had become a hazy blur of feverish dreams.

– Look at that famous body, an officer grinned cruelly. – It is all ours, now.

He began fondling her breasts with impunity. She attempted to move, to scream in protest, but nothing but mumbling and a few, ineffective moves came out of it. Others grabbed the other prisoners, and began playing with them.

– You're nothing, now, he hissed, – nothing but common crooks, and we have a certain way of dealing with your kind in our fair city.

– Oh, let them be, a woman said casually. – We will have lots of time with them, to teach them manners and proper conduct.

She scared the prisoners more than any of the others.

Lucinda frowned. The very voice scared her. It sounded so familiar. She knew it did, but couldn't place it. Her brain didn't work right anymore.

– Look at her, another man spat, touching her scar. – She is ruined.

That brought another choke out of her. She couldn't help herself. The smallest emotion strangled her.

One of the female officers sitting close, playing with the exposed cock of a male prisoner listened to music through headphones. It sounded just as garbled as all other sensations reaching Lucinda Patterson's consciousness. She wanted to scream, but nothing came out, except what sounded awfully similar to baby sounds. The cruel laughter never stopped hammering in her ears.

Hours, time itself just went away, disappeared for her, no more real than the flashes of coherent thought making everything worse.

298

Hungry, I'm hungry, hungry, hungry, hungry, hungry

They weren't in the vehicles anymore, somehow, but sat on benches in a white, white hall. Only glimpses of a gate and a dark, foreboding building ricocheted in her memory. A woman, or what felt like a woman petted her on the cheek and put a teat attached to a bottle into her mouth. A light prompt, a word, a command or some other action she couldn't identify made her suck and a fluid filled her mouth and flooded her throat.

– That's a good girl. Tastes great, doesn't it?

She felt herself nodding and smiling like a child given sweets.

Sometime later she had shit herself. The stench added to the vast unpleasantness already torturing her. She feared the pitiful moans and whimpers rising from a thousand sore throats could all originate with her.

Her wet pants turned wetter and wetter and wetter. She screamed some more in her head. More tears flooded her cheeks.

Then, suddenly, slowly there were thoughts once more, gathering themselves like dust scattered in the storm. Their arms had been freed. Blink by blink the world looked clear again.

– You will not speak, a man cautioned them.

– You will not do anything, a woman spat, – without explicit orders.

They didn't, just sat there mute and dull.

– You will now rise, the commanded them.

They obeyed.

– You will now undress, the woman ordered them.

They did, without any conscious objection, pulling off clothes drenched with shit and piss.

– You will now walk into the next room and wash yourself.

They couldn't tell which one of the two that had given the order. They obeyed. There was movement. Feet moved and weak hands struggled with turning the water on. Steam and heat filled their world.

Males and females stood there, washing themselves. Lucinda was kind of aware of what was happening, but not consciously so. She was just as gone as the rest. Everywhere her hands touched felt like steam, like mist. Eyes heard nothing. Ears saw nothing. Everything crossed itself in her brain. Commands registered sufficiently for her to obey them, but she didn't understand a word. She strived to grasp anything in her close proximity, in vain.

It was later. They dressed in new clothes, in uniforms.

– You will now stay at attention, they were told.

Frowns only briefly crossed the bland features. An image came to them. There had been demonstration and there had been training, both cerebral and physical. Helmets had been put on their head and given them both audio and visual input, repeated instructions, the beginning of... of brainwashing.

They stood at attention in a large white hall. Lucinda now easily recognized the woman approaching them and stopping in front of them.

– Good afternoon, she said, – My name Alysse Montgomery. I would bet most of you have heard about me. The United States have had the foresight to employ me, to make use of my skills and services, and that, in turn will benefit you tremendously. You will learn to serve your country with a smile on your face. The collar you wear will never more be removed, even if, like now its charge may be reduced, enabling you to reason and act without your masters' prompting. It has, like you also know several other advantages. It can dish out punishment and even at this low level it will keep you from activating whatever powers you may have. It is an excellent tool for teaching you your place in life. You will never return to the life you lived. Forget about due process and such shit. Lawyers won't be able to help you. Neither will anyone else. You will never see a courtroom from the inside. Get used to it. From now on your sole goal is to serve your country and humanity in whatever capacity we, the better humanity decide for you, the better humanity you left behind when you became the monstrosity you see in the mirror every day.

A man, Lucinda didn't know him broke ranks and bolted, or attempted to. Alysse pushed a button on a devise she held and he fell screaming to the floor. He writhed there, in horrible cramps. She pushed a button again and he slumped and laid still.

– A volunteer, she shrugged wickedly, – how satisfying.

She walked among them, appraising them like she would horses. Lucinda remembered those eyes of hatred on her and she imagined they had always been there. The shakes never stopped.

When she sat alone in a smaller white room later it was still there. She was strapped to a chair, her head, hands and feet chained so hard that she couldn't move.

– Good morning, Lucinda, Alysse greeted her.

Lucinda frowned. Was it morning?

– You may reply, Lucinda.

– Good morning, ma'am, she replied timid and fearful.

– You fear me, don't you, Lucinda? You may reply.

– Yes, ma'am, Lucinda whimpered.

– That's a good girl. Fear is the first stage in the process of making wicked girls good.

She studied the charts on the computer screen, nodding pleased to herself.

– Do you have powers, Lucinda? You may reply.

– Yes, ma'am.

– What are they? You may reply.

– Enhanced perception, ma'am, making me able to see through the eyes of other people and experience the world through their senses.

– Good girl, you didn't lie or attempted to be smart, now, but you are a smart girl, aren't you, Lucinda?

Lucinda hadn't been told to speak and held her tongue.

– And your sister's powers, what are they? You may reply.

– They are similar, ma'am, but slightly different, not so… active, at least not yet.

– Yes, yes, Kid Sister isn't quite mature yet, is she? But rest assured I have great hopes for both of you. And now, sweet girl, you have earned yourself a reward.

When she put the teat into her mouth this time, Lucinda started sucking unprompted, and kept sucking until she had devoured every drop in the bottle. The protein-rich content filled her stomach. The sick smile of child-like gratitude filled her face.

She was falling, she knew she was, even though she couldn't convince herself she was falling physically, but she descended, she knew that, into ever more utter hopelessness and despair.

Alysse removed the teat and bottle. Saliva and remains flowed from Lucinda's mouth. Alysse dried her jaw and lips. She walked behind her and whispered tenderly into her ear.

– So, which of the vigilantes are you? Big Sister may reply.

Lucinda shrank in the chair, biting her lip.

Alysse turned on the charge. Lucinda screamed, screamed herself hoarse, until Alysse made the pain stop.

– I will not ask you again, sweet girl. Reply!

Lucinda made several attempts through the haze of pain until she managed to obey.

– We're the Furies, she whimpered. – I'm…

– Their leader, yes, as I was convinced you were. Very good, beautiful girl.

There were both spite and praise in her voice. Lucinda blinked.

– Isn't confession great for your soul, Lucinda? You may reply.

– Yes, ma'am, Lucinda replied, deeply ashamed and with fear stuck in her throat.

– Call me, Alysse, beautiful girl. We will become very good friends you and I. You may respond.

– Yes, Alysse, Lucinda sniffed.

– You will tell me everything you still haven't told me, of course.

Lucinda held her breath, fighting to keep breathing evenly.

Alysse frowned, but then she shrugged and smiled in anticipation.

– You'll be such a great lab rat, in addition to your other qualities. I can hardly wait to begin phase two of the testing on you, to start your lessons in earnest.

The condescending voice kept doing something to Lucinda, kept digging into her like dull hooks.

The knocking on the door came as if from far away. Someone opened the door, but Lucinda couldn't see who it was, since she obeyed the programming and didn't turn her head, desperately betting that her gamble would work, filled with insecurities and uncertainty.

She recognized the voice, but didn't turn her head in her shock and disbelief, waiting for Claudia Malone in her full military uniform to reach her view.

Claudia was accompanied by two aides.

– Good evening, Director Montgomery, she greeted the woman in the white lab coat.

– Good evening, colonel, Alysse responded measured, with evident fake amiability, – what can I do for you?

– I have, based on the testing selected the candidates for my part of the program.

Alysse accepted the sheet of paper. She frowned.

– Are you sure? I'm not so sure if these are the best suited for what you have in mind. You could do better, in my opinion.

– I am sure, Claudia stated firmly. – I expect them all to be ready for transfer in ten minutes.

– Of course, Alysse said, very amiably. – And please let me congratulate you on your zeal. Not many top brasses would have come here to personally oversee the transfer. But I guess you are eager to have more big people join you in the army.

Claudia didn't say anything. She turned and left, not bothering with words of goodbye.

Lucinda was alone with Alysse again.

– It looks like you and I won't be better acquainted after all. Too bad!

Lucinda was almost overwhelmed by the sick relief she didn't allow herself to feel and the added worry threatening to break into full-blown hysteria.

Alysse pushed a button and set Lucinda free of her physical chains.

– Stand up!

Lucinda obeyed instantly, like always, doing her best to not show any added

302

eagerness.

– Follow me.

She followed her out in the hallway, falling unresisting in line. There was a short walk to the reception area, the place where everybody came to be processed on their arrival here. Claudia and aides waited for them there.

– This is Colonel Malone, Alysse presented, as if she hadn't just visited the lab. – You will be hers from now on. You may speak, beautiful girl.

– I understand, Alysse, Lucinda said evenly.

She placed herself at attention before Claudia, not revealing in any way that they knew each other and neither did Claudia.

Alysse delivered the list to the «receptionist».

– Prep these five specimens and be quick about it, she commanded.

Biting her lip in fear and respect the receptionist started on the paperwork.

Lucinda glanced at Claudia, waiting for a silent communication, but there was none. Claudia ignored her or seemed to ignore her. The catching in Lucinda's throat didn't go away.

Melinda appeared with four others, accompanied by guards. Lucinda knew the others, but couldn't recall their names.

– Hello, beautiful boys and girls, Alysse greeted them. – You may respond.

– HELLO, ALYSSE, they responded automatically.

– This is Colonel Malone. You belong to her, now.

The five placed themselves by Lucinda's side, facing Claudia with empty stares.

Alysse pushed a button on her tablet. It buzzed and the tablet in Claudia's hands and the collars buzzed.

– That's it, Colonel. They are yours. Will you sign here, please?

She handed a sheet and a pen to Claudia. The uniformed woman scribbled her signature at the low end of the sheet.

– Thank you, Alysse said pleasantly. – You have a good day and journey, now.

Claudia didn't say anything. Alysse grinned wickedly and left, withdrew to the inner sanctum of the premises.

– Follow me, Claudia commanded.

She walked first. They followed her. The two mundane soldiers made up the rear.

Lucinda caught a glimpse of Melinda's fraught expression, how she fought with herself to not scream at Claudia. The transport, a van waited for them right outside. They were put in the back with the two soldiers. Claudia sat in front with the driver.

There was a short distance to the gates. The screech hurt their ears. The car drove through it and soon reached the highway.

They could have detected it, if I had used my powers in there, Claudia told the sisters. I couldn't risk that.

She had gathered them in her mind. The subtext of her voice came through to Lucinda even without her powers being on.

They took us so fast, Lucinda choked, caught us so easily.

Yes, hopefully this will be a powerful lesson for the both of you. By the way, your four friends were quite lucky picks in a lottery, a smokescreen to hide the truth. I couldn't and can't just free you and certainly not only you, you see. That would have raised and will raise way too much suspicion. Lucinda and Melinda Patterson are and will forever be a part of a clandestine military program I'm sponsoring. Gimmick and Sensor, however will be free to be Gimmick and Sensor. From now on you will embrace your costumed identities. Be grateful and jubilant that I was able to save you from Alysse's clutches before she truly started working her magic on you. She is one sick puppy that one. Unfortunately my superiors find her useful.

The strict, cruel way she was «leveling with them» silenced both sisters effectively, stopped all their questions at inception.

Good, she nodded. You realize the bind you're in. You're my wards and you better wise up. I will no longer put up with any insubordination from you. You will be better off because of it.

The sisters sagged against the wall, not distinguishing themselves from the other four with collars, not speaking out, striving not to express themselves. They sat there during the entire long drive, finally slumping in their seat with the rest.

The car drove through a gate at a remote military installation. They followed Claudia and her two aides inside, where dozens of more big people and military personnel waited for them. She stood there, imposing her will on them all.

Soldiers began removing the collars. It was surprisingly easy. Lucinda gasped as her powers began functioning again. It wasn't instantaneous, but happened in leaps and bounds. It seemed like she had been head blind forever, and then after less than a minute it felt like she never had been.

– You do have a choice, Claudia told them all. – You can flee at the first opportunity, and that opportunity will eventually present itself, and thereby become fugitives and criminals and be treated thus for the rest of your life, or you can stay with this program, this service and enjoy a modicum of freedom between missions. Your old lives are over, no matter what. If you fail me or others of your commanding officers you will pay for it. You may end up in jail or be sent back to an orientation center or similar.

Everybody knew what an «orientation center» was. It was the place they had recently been saved from.

– You've been picked for two main reasons: because you have powers and because of your psychological profile. We don't want mindless soldiers here, but fairly independent and creative people. Thus your gift would be wasted most other places. As long as you remain useful tools, we will be pleased with you, and won't return you to sender.

Sender was Alysse Montgomery and her like.

When a young man spoke, he spoke for them all.

– I will do anything to not be returned to that horrible place.

Claudia's smile broadened, his words confirming what she already knew.

They had all got more than a taste of that place and had witnessed what happened to people not being fortunate enough to be chosen by alternative agencies. Images and sensations almost overwhelmed Lucinda again.

Claudia and her aides led everybody into a hall where more big people waited. The six and the other newly arrived joined the line.

– You will be processed and groomed, Claudia told them, – and then your service will begin in earnest.

She left them there. Lucinda would have missed her, if she hadn't sensed the constant, pervasive presence in her mind.

Melinda looked calm on the outside, but inside she still struggled with a sense of unrest that threatened to unravel her. Lucinda soothed her, comforted her from the distance of her mind, and it proved effective. She nodded pleased when Kid Sister rolled both her hands into fists.

They filed through the gauntlet of military life. Heads were shaved. Uniforms and other utilities were being issued.

I want to go home, Melinda whimpered, unable to hold back within anymore.

This is your home from now on, little one, Claudia corrected her. No matter where you go, you will always return to this place.

Melinda shrunk under her cruel attention. Lucinda wanted to go to her, but she received a distinct warning from Claudia and stood still.

They were brought to the barracks with both male and female recruits. Claudia rejoined them and walked in there with them.

– In case you're wondering: it has been determined that the difference in physical strength between the sexes among big people is far less compared with the dwarfs they call ordinary, she told them. – There's just no excuse to keep you apart, except for long since outdated rules of conduct.

The recruits looked at her with ambiguity in their eyes, with both the very evident hurt look and a kind of indistinct, but still apparent gratitude and pride.

– Make me proud!

Claudia left. Several of the recruits stared blindly at the point she had occupied ten, fifteen, twenty seconds ago.

A girl, Gretchen stared at Lucinda and Melinda.

– I know the two of you, she said with venom in her voice and eyes. – You were caught in your honey trap, huh?

They wanted to reply to her, to give her an equally poisonous response, but cat got their tongue and they ended up bowing their heads and staring at the floor. The vicious laughter rocked them.

A towering sinister-looking woman in a sergeant uniform entered the hall.

– AT-TENTION!

Everybody straightened. They didn't look at her, but straight ahead.

– Good morning. As you've probably already surmised I am Sergeant Tanya Hall, your Senior Drill Instructor, and let me make one thing clear: No matter how hard you believe other senior drill instructors in that other army is, they got nothing on me. I'm a mean and sadistic daughter of a bitch. There are no rules or regulations here. I can kill any of you, and no one will even bother me because of it. There are a lot more of you out there, to replace you, if need be. You better believe it, or you will be in a world of hurt you can hardly imagine.

They noticed the whip, the actual big, bad bullwhip in her hand, very visible at the edge of their vision and they swallowed hard.

– You will become killers, she stated. – You will give all your vaunted strength and dedication to what will always be your masters. They will command and you will obey. That's all there is to it.

She slammed the tip of the whip at the floor. Everybody shook. They had known for a while that they were in deep shit, but their situation grew increasingly hopeless. The sergeant drove that point home with hammer and nails.

– You will become intimately familiar with this baby, she spat and held up the whip. – You will be willful and disobedient, and you won't give your all to the army. Not at first.

She walked among them. A man winced as she lashed him a single time on the back of his thighs.

– You didn't cry out. Well done, soldier.

She stopped before Lucinda.

– You already have a scar. Did you earn it, Private Patterson?

– Ma'am, yes, ma'am, this recruit did, ma'am, Lucinda cried out.

The pervasive sickness of mind didn't go away, but lingered, festered in her consciousness.

Hall walked on to Melinda.

– I will call you Private Patterson Junior, she snorted, – just to distinguish you from your big bad sister.

Lucinda easily felt how the sergeant scared them, scared them all by her mere presence and how pleased Hall was by that.

– You will all come with me, Hall told them.

They followed her like the whipped dogs they were, out through the door and further through the camp. She brought them with her through the hurdle and running trail at a murderous speed. They were exhausted early on. She ran back and forth, encouraging them with her brutal lashes the instant they slowed down or every time she felt like it.

It was raining, raining hard. The ground had turned into mud many places and the ropes of the various hurdles quickly became slimy and slippery. Hands striving to sustain the grip hurt. They almost drowned in shallow ponds. The run continued. They shit themselves halfway. It flowed down their pants like hot soup and hurt even more than it used to. The commands turned their ears into cotton. It was as if it had stopped raining, as if they no longer had air to breathe.

Eventually there was no voice but the sergeant's, no sound except her whip, no sense except the lash hitting their body.

When they stood shivering in the shower late in the evening that was still true. Cascades of warm water hit them, and no matter how hard they rubbed themselves they still felt dirty.

The reveille woke them up abruptly next morning. Dead tired, with eyes hardly able to open or stay open, they moved to Tanya Hall's voice, to her snarling whip.

There was more cruel exercise, more imposing commands and in their befuddled minds it never stopped, but became an ongoing horror blanketing their thoughts.

They stood there, feeling like drowned rats.

– You pathetic cunts and pricks, she swore. – You think your lives have worth, that you are anything but worms crawling in the mud.

She stopped before a tall and big man.

– MA'AM, NO, MA'AM, he belched.

She struck him in the abdomen. He went down like a felled tree.

His response, somewhat modified echoed down the line.

Lucinda stood with trembling lips before her, hesitated for one moment, two, before bowing her head and shouting her declaration of servitude.

And then she found herself on the floor, gasping for air, burning with shame like the others.

And she couldn't fathom how she could stand this, how she could accept being treated like something lower than the worm on the ground. Understanding kept eluding her and her confusion and despair grew until nothing else seemed to visit her mind and self.

She was tossing and turning in her sleep, and tears were wetting her cheeks and she could never understand why.

There was fighting, one on one and then the rage had purpose, then she was able to focus and channel it. During the pugil bouts she overcame her opponents easily, struck them down and kept striking them until they lay still on the ground. She felt something akin to sexual pleasure.

They stood in the shower again, the water pouring down on and around their steaming bodies and gasping mouths, their heart still beating hard in their chest. Lucinda rubbed the shit from her sore ass and between her thighs. Others did as well. She felt it all, from everybody, as she always did. The numbness of mind and body didn't stop that, but on the contrary exaggerated it.

She bit her lip, fighting off the first stings of arousal, giving up after just a few moments. The water turned off they left the shower room. She dried herself in the dressing room, surrounded by rapid breathing. The door to the dark hallway stood ajar. She looked distraught for her uniform and underwear. It wasn't there, of course. She was so stupid. It had gone straight into the giant washing machine at the other end of the shower room. Their dry and clean clothes waited for them down the dark corridor. She rushed into the hallway, striving to appear unaffected.

He caught up with her in the darkest part of the hall and grabbed her arm. She tried to pull free. He held on.

– I know what you are, he said. – What your problem is.

She didn't need to hear his hoarse whisper and see his erected cock to know what state he was in. And he easily saw through her weak efforts to hide hers.

– They are quite correct about us, he grinned. – Males and females of our kind are better matched physically.

He pushed her front against the wall.

– I like that…

He held her, and then he pushed himself into her. She writhed in his grip, resisting less for each passing breath. The breathing, the horny shouts, the loud moans and groans were all around her.

– Your bald head is kind of annoying, he panted. – Nothing to *grab*.

He squeezed her shoulders hard enough, though.

– Why don't you stop yapping, she snarled, – and get *on* with it?

Her snarl, her challenge excited him. She sensed that, too, easily enough. He doubled and redoubled his efforts. She released a pleased moan. He was big and filled her up well enough. Then he began roaming her hole with a hand and fingers as well. Her mind, the entire her began humming and rocking. They fell to the floor, but kept going. She glimpsed the bloated face of Tracy, a very tall and big girl not far from her own head.

– You're such a peach, Ron grunted in her ears. – Such a tasty peach.

– Peach, she echoed.

Peach peach peach.

He pumped into her. They both screamed, joining the multitude around them.

Slowly, only slowly consciousness returned, the explosive pleasure fading to a pleasant hum. Ron turned her around and put her on her back and quickly was at it again. She fought herself to a moment of reason and caressed his cheek, touching his mind.

– You're sssuch a ssstud, she slurred. – Sssuch a lovely ssstud.

And grinned in triumph when his cheeks turned wet with tears.

She sensed Melinda not far away, glimpsed her face dissolved in joy. There were others after Ron. One male, she couldn't tell who grabbed her and carried her on his shoulder to the nearest living room where most of them gathered on couches and carpets, and they just kept going.

Ron was spent. He pulled out from someone and just couldn't get it up anymore.

– Tracy, attend me, Lucinda said casually.

Eyes slowly closing opened and focused attentive on the other woman.

– Blow him, Lucinda told her. – Make him work again, so we can enjoy more of his gifts.

Tracy reddened all over her body. She glanced at Ron's still big but useless cock.

– I have never done it before…

– Do it, Lucinda bid her.

It was easy making her do it, making her want it.

– He's so big, she mumbled.

She leaned forward, reaching out with her right hand, carefully grabbing the soft limb. Her tongue licked suddenly dry lips. She started rubbing the soft flesh in her hand. Ron looked at her and down at himself alternately. His cock twitched. He moaned aloud. His cock grew.

– It wasn't so spent after all, Melinda said incredulous and suddenly very, very horny again.

The words echoed in Lucinda's still feverish mind. Tracy began licking Ron's growing thing, visibly wetter between her thighs again. Melinda caressed herself.

– You want him, don't you, Kid Sister? Lucinda asked gently.

– Yes, Big Sister, the teenager gasped. – *Please!*

– He's yours, Lucinda said indulgent. – Enjoy his bounty.

– Thank you, Melinda practically shouted. – THANK YOU!

She jumped him and pushed him down on his back, cruelly discarding Tracy. It didn't take long before she was riding him, riding him hard.

Someone grabbed Lucinda from behind. It startled her. Someone put an already wet hand between her long since soaked thighs. Her mind let go of Tracy and the other woman yawned. Another male grabbed her. Her eyes reopened yet again. She leaned backwards. Lucinda managed just about to see a hazy figure climb her before she was pushed forward. She stood on all fours while the unseen male buttfucked her.

Her eyes opened and closed constantly, the image of him indistinct in her mind.

– YES! She cried out.

I want more, she thought in the upper haze of her consciousness.

More more more.

There were more after this one, too. At least she thought so. There seemed to be no end to them and she yelped happily. They returned to the showers and there were more of them. Everybody was asleep around her. She imagined that just before her eyes closed and her head rested on hard muscles. There were dreams, happy continuation of the reality surrounding her, before deep, deep sleep.

They were roused, more or less roughly an unknown time span later. There was more cleaning, but this time under the watchful eyes of superiors. Lucinda didn't mind. She glowed in her happy mind.

Later that day the females were brought to the doctor's office, admitted one by one. There was a new doctor again. Lucinda smiled to him. He kept his smug smile.

– You big bitches need a far more powerful contraceptive than most cows, he said patronizingly. – Ordinary dosages and methods just don't cut it, you know. And if this doesn't work on you either, it will be straight to the breeding farms with you. There are those that, once pregnant just can't get rid of their spawn. Believe me, we have tried…

She saw it all in her mind and vomit rose in her throat.

The breeding farms… the mere thought of it brought a sick dread, a prevailing image refusing to let go.

She opened her eyes completely and looked at him as if he was shit under her nails.

– You're obviously operating under the completely erroneous assumption that we've never heard of the flowers and the bees, she said, matching his patronizing and doubling it. – What do you think we have been doing the last few years?

He turned pale. She made him, reinforcing the sudden, unexplainable feeling of inferiority striking him, preparing to walk to him, deigning him to actually touch her person.

There was a cold draft. A door opened and closed. Lucinda faced Sergeant Hall again.

– You had forgotten, hadn't you? You had actually forgotten.

Lucinda shrunk under the cruel attention.

– You better not try any tricks on me, or there will be hell to pay.

She hadn't really attempted to read or control the Sergeant earlier and now it finally dawned on her why she hadn't. There was a black, festering hole there she didn't even dare approach.

Lucinda Patterson walked shaken and cowed to the doctor's side. She didn't need to read his mind to know how his smug sense of superiority had grown to virtual arrogance.

– Give her a double dosage, Hall spat. – We shouldn't leave anything to change in her case. I actually lost count of how many times she was pumped up. The film will be very popular and increase our funding significantly.

The sting on her thigh felt like the worst kind of torture, but nothing compared to the nausea striking her in the hours and days to come. She vomited her own stomach repeatedly, long after it was empty.

Days, nights, years later, she stood at attention before the Sergeant.

– Are you loyal to the army, Private Patterson Big Bitch?

– MA'AM, YES, MA'AM

– Are you loyal to the United States, Private Patterson Big Bitch?

– MA'AM, YES, MA'AM, THIS RECRUIT IS WILLING AND EAGER TO BECOME A SOLDIER AND TO DO WHATEVER UNCLE SAM WISHES OF HER, MA'AM. THE ARMY IS HER HOME, HER FAMILY AND SHE WILL SERVE HER COUNTRY WITH DISTINCTION

She felt pumped, drained. When she returned to the barracks with her fellow soldiers she no longer even entertained the thought of controlling them to do her bidding anymore. It was as if…

She frowned, unable to follow the trail of thought further.

With one female soldier in their platoon the treatment didn't take and she was shipped off to the breeding farm. She looked utterly lost when she was loaded onto the truck with the others that had in some way failed the unfathomable criteria of success in the camp. The others watched it happen with dull eyes.

The training continued unabated. It was always on their mind. There was more fucking and more needles, but now Lucinda was merely one of the girls, one of the happy females and males giving in to their urges.

She didn't throw up anymore. When the doctor touched her she didn't object or even cringe from his touch. She noticed how the others looked at her with pity. They fell more easily in line because she fell in line.

They were showering again. Steam rose further from already steaming bodies. Lucinda watched when a male's cock began stiffening between his legs. Her juices began flowing immediately. He took a stroll across the floor. She felt a stark disappointment when he approached Melinda. All of the others stood still, only Steven and Melinda moved.

– I don't feel like it, she mumbled and pulled away from him.

– Aw, don't be that way, girl, he said and grabbed her.

She turned fast and grabbed him, pulled him to her, striking him in the abdomen, striking him in the head. He fell and hit the floor hard. She struck him and struck him again.

Everybody stood at attention later, including Melinda and Steven. He could hardly stand, but he was standing.

– Recruits Patterson Junior and Larson, step forward, Hall commanded.

They obeyed promptly.

– What happened? The Sergeant asked. – Any volunteers?

Melinda straightened. Hall nodded in acknowledgment.

– Ma'am, Private Larson offended me, so I punished him, ma'am.

Steven kept resembling a wet dog.

– You both seem to have lots of extra energy, for some reason. That's good. That's a very good thing. We can do a lot with that.

They stood nude in the barrack's cold storage room, their bound hands stretched above their heads. Hall began whipping them with fast, brutal moves. The lashes hit their backs and fronts until they began screaming, until they had no more voice left.

Everyone was in attendance and everyone shook, made to watch, unable to look away. They even imagined that the very walls shook around them. There was no relief from the horrifying spectacle. Lucinda wanted to stop her projection, wanted at least to spare the others that, but as always she couldn't stop herself.

Lucinda felt every strike as if it hit her and turned increasingly pale as the incessant torture continued, as ruby fluid flowed down inflamed backs and it felt like it would never stop.

Chapter 18

They hung in the ropes, hung in the ropes for what felt like days, until they were untied and carried off.

Melinda crouched in bed. Lucinda rubbed ointment on her inflamed and cracked skin, avoiding her accusing look.

– It hurts, Kid Sister moaned and spat. – It hurts bad!

Her mind was just a black hole of hurt and rage. Lucinda couldn't deal with it and turned off her power, turned it off as much as she was able.

It leaked through, like the open wound it was.

There was the insane final run, the impossible struggle through mud and cruel traps. To call it The Crucible didn't in any way do it justice. There was no cooperation, no kindness, only survival. Lucinda saw Ron succumb to a horrible maw of destruction, practically being consumed alive by an artificial machine of knives and hunger. From that moment on she would recall the sight every time she blinked.

The mud turned to quicksand between them. The swamp sucked them down. They fought on.

The pain and horror remained when they stood blinking in the bright sun many days and dark nights later.

Senior Drill Instructor Tanya Hall stood there in front of them big and bad. They shrunk in her mighty presence.

– Congratulations recruits, she greeted them. – You've made it!

Relief flooded them, numb, stark relief. Strength flooded their being. They fed, devoured their food and could shit in peace afterwards for the first time in forever.

They sat in comfortable chairs while listening to Tanya Hall, a lovely, beautiful woman wearing a dress. It made them stare, stare as much as they were able.

– We will now proceed to the final phase of your recruit training, she said.

The itch in Lucinda's gut was proven correct. It wasn't over.

She squeezed Melinda's hand, squeezed a little too hard. Melinda bit her lip, but didn't cry out. Lucinda nodded pleased to her.

– You will learn to be pleasing, to be deadly in the game between the sexes, or your life will be forfeit. The very illusion of freedom will be taken away from you.

The sergeant's words... they sounded so ominous, so beyond ominous. Everybody swallowed hard.

– Come with me, recruits, she bid them.

They obeyed without thinking twice about it, without thinking at all. They had become so attentive to her commands that obeying them felt like second nature.

There was another dressing room somewhere at the other side of the main building, one where they had never been before, where they found civilian clothes. They removed their uniforms and put on their non-descriptive outfit. The brief nudity didn't bother them anymore, but the new clothes felt weird and disorientating.

They had all become good at handling weapons, all kinds of weapons. Lucinda could hardly believe how much she had improved with the crossbow. They could hit moving targets with sniper rifles from far away in virtual darkness. The repetition only confirmed that and their sense of pride grew. The two sisters excelled in physical combat, superior to most of their platoon. One of Melinda's opponents had to be carried off the fighting area. Lucinda hardly felt anything but red in her mind anymore.

The course in deadly social etiquette was in session. It was in many ways a repetition of their teaching at the model agency at the Center. They learned how to look pretty, to move and smile, not to a camera, but to a real and imagined human being, learned poisoning an enemy or target, learned how to incapacitate and execute him or her.

Hall was not present all the time, but she was always there, in their thoughts, in the expressions and faces to their various teachers.

– How do you approach an enemy in a civilian setting... Melinda? Kenneth Marshall asked casually.

– I do as I always do, she replied instantly. – I prey upon his or her weaknesses, exploiting anything that might aid me in reaching my objective.

– Very good.

The girl didn't blush, but the chilly smile lit up her doll-like face. Lucinda wanted to shake her head, but found herself listening to Kid Sister, emulating her conduct and words. Melinda had practically embraced the teaching lately and she did so even more as more weeks passed, as time turned indistinct and blurry reality clear as sky. She was clearly one of the very best students. The nausea in Big Sister's throat lessened as fuzzy time passed.

This particular batch of recruits, no longer recruits moved into nicer accommodations at the other side of the camp. Each was given their own apartment, a somewhat private space.

– This is more like it, Gretchen said.

– It is nice, Tracy said. – A nice cage.

Gretchen's smile was put out like a candle in the wind.

314

The two sisters stood on the balcony connecting their apartments, looking at the desert beneath and beyond.

– Are you okay, honey?

Big Sister rubbed the other's cheek lightly, not that different from how she had done long ago.

– Of course. Melinda looked surprised. – I'm ready and primed.

Lucinda tilted her head and looked closer at her.

– I've taken well to the lessons, don't you think?

Lucinda didn't reply, but kept her face impassive.

– I've caught up with you, now, the teenager said with luring eyes. – You're not ahead of me anymore. We're a nice pair. I think they will make us stay together, two deadly vipers prowling the night.

Lucinda didn't share her thoughts or much of her thoughts with her anymore. She had learned to keep them more private.

They walked down the hall to the living room where all the new recruits gathered.

– Remember, Lucinda said patronizingly, – we have to remain on our guard, or we will be lost.

Melinda nodded both empathically and equally patronizingly, conveying what she felt about being cautioned, but still shivering below the surface.

They wore revealing dresses, swinging their hips in challenging moves, as did all the females. The males wore suits, filling them out like heavyweight fighters. The scene brought revulsion and excitement, a sinking feeling in the sisters' stomach. The sensations from the last weeks haunted them. They fought to keep the fluttering in the belly under control and the rock-hard focus at the forefront of consciousness.

Lucinda walked to Steven, to the hard, cruel man he had become. She kissed him on the cheek. He grabbed her.

– Your touch hurts, she said.

Her arm, where he squeezed seemed to be inflamed with pain.

– It's my power, he grinned pleased.

She made him feel it, twice over, in his mind. He gasped and released her, and held his head in what seemed like a vice. It was as if he was clawing at his skull, attempting to dig himself in.

– It's my power, too, she said calmly, – and your touch is nothing compared to mine.

His was merely physical. Hers was mental, of the mind and so much more, on so many levels.

Her spoken words echoed with her telepathic speech thundering in his mind. He backed off. From then on she would always see fear in his eyes and the very memory of that would strengthen her.

Encouraged by their superior officers everybody interacted throughout the night, probing and stabbing each other. Lucinda knew of and took pride in her obvious advantage, but she never allowed herself to forget anything that had happened to her lately, how limited and vulnerable she truly was. She studied her comrades in arms with the ever-present low-burning rage serving her so well.

The night surrounded her and her male companion. She looked at the nameless one in front of her, feeling nothing but contempt. He was strong. Like with Stephen there was no evident crack in his armor she could easily exploit. His power was illusion, disorientation of some sort. She had watched him, observed him while he used it, both consciously and subconsciously lately.

The bartender served them strong liquor. The two of them sat by the bar, with a few others. Other couples had spread to tables around the room. Melinda and a male engaged in what seemed like an intimate conversation. Stephen touched Gretchen's arm and she pulled back with a whimper.

Mist drifted in from the entrance. Lucinda saw it, experienced it as if it was real. She shook in the cold.

– The heating in this room doesn't seem to be up to par, her opponent said kindly. – Are you sure you don't want to borrow my jacket?

– I'm fine, thank you, she replied sweetly.

There was mist, was shadow in the room beyond the illusion and disorientation he made her experience, she was certain of it. The Black Dragon looked contemptuously at her and Lucinda both feared that the man, the enemy was exploiting her fears and not.

– Cheers! He raised his glass.

– Cheers! She raised her glass.

They drank. The strong liquor burned in their throat and stomach.

Melinda played with her partner's senses, finally able to invert her powers, using them to influence others, not merely passively using them to record her surroundings. Lucinda had suspected that she was able to do so for quite a while, but hadn't been able to confirm it until this moment.

– What's happening? The man keeping Kid Sister company blurted out.

– Nothing is happening, Melinda said sweetly, – nothing at all.

The man sitting opposite Lucinda blinked, his eyelids suddenly heavy, very heavy. A loud yawn rose from his open mouth.

– I thought I was ready to party tonight, he chuckled embarrassed, – but I was evidently mistaken.

And then he got it. His eyes widened.

316

– You thought you put the poison in my glass, she shrugged, – and you did, but I switched them.

– I can't see, the man opposite Melinda shouted. – I'm blind, *blind*.

He rose.

– Everything is so loud, he whined, – so LOUD

The man opposite Lucinda sagged and fell off the barstool, the shock and horror only faintly visible in his dazed eyes.

Stephen was fucking Gretchen, Her shouts turned to screams, to loud whines of horror.

– It hurts! IT HURTS

Her whining turned to helpless sobs.

Lucinda sat there sweating, imaging that Black Dragon smiled to her, fearing that it wasn't real, that the seemingly unconscious man on the floor had gained the upper hand on her, and only made her see what he wanted her to see.

Gretchen's childish displays faded in everybody's ears, as the room slowly fell silent, and only faint traces of the mist and shadow remained, and the two sisters smiled to each other in wicked triumph.

They were all present at the airstrip the next morning when the losers were shipped off.

– I made it, he shrieked as they led him away, the man without a name. – I fucking MADE IT!

He collapsed in tears and helpless sobbing.

Gretchen didn't say anything. She seemed totally subdued, not really there at all. They were skipped into the truck with the rest, fading from the life of those that remained.

– Congratulations, Tanya hailed them. – I'm so very proud of you, all of you.

The fear that she was still in that cold, damp room didn't leave Lucinda.

The two sisters spent the next few weeks doing advertising and recruitment for the military. There were other suitable males and females, but it was clear who the stars were. They hid Lucinda's scar, too, either by not photographing that side of her face or covering it with makeup or by retouching the images.

She looked at the retouched version of herself in the mirror or through other's eyes and imagined she saw only her eyes and mouth and nose, as if she was wearing a mask.

– Why have you chosen this over your prosperous career? A journalist, sounding truly puzzled asked her during a press conference.

– I wanted to serve my country, she replied solemnly. – There is a need for us big people to step up our game and truly embrace our destiny as leaders of mankind.

The sweet smile made the front page and magazine covers and trended on Grid main features across the world. Recruitment of both big and small people to the military tripled.

Gimmick and Sensor returned to Tobruk and the Maverick Crew headquarters in what was supposed to be early fall. The first thing they noticed was that the heat hadn't really diminished at all. It still felt like breathing, gasping for air inside an oven, perhaps even more so than before. Putting on the masks felt bad, making them gasp even harder for air.

Welcome back, little ones, Lady Grace greeted them with her mind as they stepped through the portal and arrived in the entrance hall.

In deliberate, visible distress they walked into the meeting room while everybody was present, creating a commotion of another world.

The others, shocked and relieved embraced them and gave them a hearty welcome.

– We searched for you, Lavender choked, – but we never found you. What *happened?*

– It was the C-cadre, Melinda stuttered. – We were captured and brought to one of its «recruitment camps». It was the worst fucking experience of my life.

The abridged version clearly worked. Gimmick sensed that and relaxed, and fell into an even deeper hole.

– But we turned it around, Gimmick said. – We managed to escape and now we have so much more information about our foes.

Well done, little ones, Lady Grace praised the two again.

Lucinda and Claudia didn't really have to smother much suspicion and skepticism. Relief and happiness dominated the gathering.

The walls of her old room, her only home from now on bulged and imposed themselves on Gimmick. She was unable to stand and dumped down on the bed. She sat there, unable to stop the shaking.

There was a click, one she knew signified that her door had been unlocked and opened and by whom. When she looked up Raven Bird stood there. The door was closed again.

– I'm sorry, but I had to see you.

– You don't know sorry, Gimmick said sullenly, – don't know it at all.

Lisa Carlton crumbled even more then.

– I wanted to tell the others, she wailed, – but Claudia kept me from doing it, telling me she would «fix it», and she did, didn't she?

I don't care if she hears me, don't fucking care. Let her hear my contempt, my spite, my…

It was Gimmick that walked to Raven Bird and comforted her and dried her tears and felt very strong in the process.

There was kissing and comforting, a lot of kissing and comforting.

– Are you alright? Gimmick asked.

Raven Bird looked astounded at her.

– You're asking *me* if *I* am...

She nodded subdued.

– I am, she sniffed.

– Good girl, Gimmick acknowledged, giving her one last kiss on the exposed skin close to the left eye.

Lisa was open like a barn door and through her Gimmick could easily discern what had happened here during her absence: Lady Grace had strengthened her power base further.

The Maverick Crew gathered around the bigger, considerably bigger table, all of the old faces and several new. The mood was happy, excited, aggressive.

– This is a happy day, Lady Grace stated, the catch of emotion just about noticeable in her voice and stance. – Dear friends and fellow soldiers we thought were lost to us have returned to us. The servants of our enemy couldn't hold on to them. We've finally found a chink in her armor.

Everybody lapped up her words, bought her pitch, even Raven Bird, who knew the truth. Gimmick easily saw how excited she was, leaning forward in her chair with a blushing face.

– We have new information, Flight Captain said, – and we will act on it immediately. We're moving out in twenty minutes. Lavender and the Bowman will lead the two attack teams, while Raven Bird will stand ready with her team if... necessity arises. Gimmick and Sensor will stay with us.

He and Lady Grace stood side by side, presenting a powerful, confident united front. The others looked at them with admiration and trust in their eyes.

Everybody rushed to the toilets, the nervous flutter in their stomach making the need worse. Gimmick sat down and let it flow. It burned, as it always did.

– After everything that has happened, it still burns, Sensor told her outside.

– I figured it would stop at some point, but it never will.

Gimmick wanted to say something, but before she had opened her mouth to speak Sensor had left.

Everything proceeded smoothly and efficiently, far more so than Gimmick and Sensor recalled. It was all set in motion on several different fronts. Mechanic activated his automatic machinery and autopilot. The Maverick Crew had become a well-relating unit, had become soldiers. Gimmick and

Sensor easily recognized that and felt kind of relieved. They didn't stand out... too much.

The guys still don't know, Melinda thought. They still don't know what the world is like.

The away teams stepped through the portal. The others returned to the surveillance room. The helicopters waited for the teams at a secure location Gimmick had never seen before, only glimpsed in other's mind.

– As you can see, Lady Grace said smug and pleased, – we keep expanding in both scope and manpower. Soon we will be able to do much more, reach our objectives that much faster, and face our enemies head on.

– It's a thing of beauty, Sensor said.

Gimmick didn't glare at her, but she knew she let her displeasure be known to Kid Sister.

– Look at it, Melinda said, – how smooth the operation is. It's proceeding without a glitch.

And Gimmick knew that her sincere words, her honest expression made Claudia Malone pleased beyond words.

Cameras levitating in the air and on headbands showed the two teams as they progressed, as they entered the building, as they brought down most of the front wall and rushed inside.

They found nothing, of course, nothing of consequences, except the carefully crafted stage Lady Grace, Gimmick and Sensor had prepared for them.

– The cowards have fled the nest.

Lavender kicked a piece of wood on the floor, kicked it so hard that it hit the wall with a loud THUD.

And Lady Grace smiled.

– Search again! She ordered.

They searched the place once more, knocking on walls, looking for secret trapdoors and everything under the sun, but of course found nothing.

Everybody gathered on a previous agreed spot by the exit.

– Return to base, Flight Captain told them in his always encouraging voice, resignation only noticeable at its subtext.

He had always been sort of high strung, hiding his basic, deep-rooted insecurity behind a mask of confidence. Gimmick had seen that demonstrated fairly often in the years she had known him.

– It was a sort of long shot, anyway, Lady Grace told him kindly. – We'll get another chance at them eventually.

Claudia put her hand on top of Flight Captain's head, sort of comforting him, or at least calming him down, easing his distress.

Lucinda realized startled that a kind touch didn't have to be benevolent, that it actually was one very effective act of control.

Everybody returned. The home team met them in the hall, greeting them with an optimistic and encouraging stance.

– Our opponents aren't stupid. They may make mistakes, but they're not likely to repeat them. Gimmick and Sensor were lucky and brave and skilled to escape their clutches.

– A celebration is in order, Lavender cried with bright eyes.

Her words were met with a loud choir of agreement.

– A celebration it is, Lady Grace agreed.

They gathered around the long table in the dining room. Ashton Kramer had a drink before he sat down, and another not long after that. He scratched his chest. Lucinda felt him do it. He was horny again. His cock pushed against the insides of his pants. He was always horny. She shifted uneasily on her chair, and she knew several of the other females, including Claudia did the same.

Lady Grace, the very image of calm and authority waited until all the others had sat down. Then she stood back up and raised her glass.

– Our group has grown lately, she said, – and it is all good. Two of our missing members have returned from hellish capture. We have lots to be grateful about. Cheers!

– Cheers! Everybody choired.

Everybody drank. Gimmick felt the wine slide down her parched throat, and it felt even better when it reached her stomach and flowed into her bloodstream.

A memory caught her unaware. Ron's scream and the sight of the rotating and bloody maw filled with flesh and bones overwhelmed her attention. She had more wine. It helped to relieve the waking nightmares somewhat.

Raven Bird served dinner, put all the plates, kettles, knives, forks and spoons on the table with practiced ease. Only Lucinda saw how uncomfortable and downright apprehensive and resentful she was. Everybody cheered. Gimmick clutched the knife and fork in her hands so hard that she feared she had cut herself. She imagined she pushed both the knife and the fork deep into Lady Grace's abdomen, that Claudia fell to the floor in a pool of blood and guts.

Lady Grace sat there relaxed and confident, master of everything she surveyed. Gimmick had some food, and then had more and more. Wine and food flowed down her stuffed throat.

She danced with the Bowman, danced tight and hot.

– I feared what had happened to you, he said hoarsely. – It nearly drove me mad.

– You're sweet, she told him.

He reddened.

There was concern for her, there in his mind, but must of all he just wanted to possess her, like everyone else.

They kissed lips to lips. He pushed it, as he always did, aggressively fondling her. She snarled more than smiled to him. He yelped at the mind nudge and looked hurt at her when she gave him her cold smile. She kissed him on the cheek, liberated herself from his weak grip and walked away.

Lavender, Sensor, Wind and the other girls sat on the couch and had a moment of bonding. Gimmick observed how Kid Sister was loosing up a little, just a little.

– They… whipped you? Cracker gasped, running a hand at the still partly uneven skin on Sensor's shoulder and upper back.

– They did, Sensor said, sounding almost proud. – I had been disobedient and they punished me.

– I would have crumbled after a treatment like that, Dancer said horrified, – the thought of escaping being very far from my mind.

Dancer, Cougar's younger sister, or half sister was stricken, still fairly innocent and even childish. Gimmick studied the girl, like she had for years, for signs of her taking after the older sibling, but there was nothing. She was angry and resentful each time Cougar's name came up, but mostly at her sister, not at her teammates.

Both she and the others looked at Sensor with admiring eyes. Melinda's status had with a stroke been increased among the younger Crew members, and she soaked it up like a parched throat would water.

– Crimson Mask isn't here? Gimmick asked lightly.

– She still keeps to herself, often working in the field alone, still communicating basically through Raven Bird, Lavender replied. – She is at Lady Grace's beck and call, though, and comes whenever her presence is desired.

The veiled antagonism towards Lady Grace was casual, very matter of fact. The very thought made Gimmick smile.

The music played up again. Dancer walked to the fairly spacey floor and began moving. It was clear that she had Cougar's grace, but not her ferocity. More sick relief flooded Lucinda.

Gimmick and the Bowman danced together again. She easily sensed his growing impatience, his fervent desire. He had always kept himself in check during similar social gatherings before, but Lucinda saw that things had changed in this matter as well. The presence of Ashton Kramer and Lauren

Harris and the other former members of the Lustful Carnage Gang, all of them acting out, clearly influenced the rest of those present. Lucinda knew it swayed her, made her bold in the Bowman's arms, and she, in turn heightened the desire of everybody else present.

The Bowman pushed her at the wall. She hardly saw his face through her alcohol induced haze. He touched her, but her skin had become so numb that she didn't really feel his hands on her. She was so dizzy that she was unable to stand on her own.

And then sudden nausea struck her. She crouched abruptly and she threw up all over him.

The laughter rose from her sore throat and then, in relief from everybody present. The Bowman didn't laugh, but she didn't truly care about that… or him.

She realized that a little startled and pleased. Her laughter turned louder. It didn't fade for a long time in her head.

It was later. She kneeled before the big toilet bowl, throwing up again. It was neither the second, nor the third time this evening. She cleaned herself in the generous water-flow in the sink. Her skin stopped stinking of vomit. Her costume didn't. Her skin looked so pale that it appeared practically transparent in the mirror, the steamy mirror.

It was even later when she stumbled towards her room. She had trouble with the key, fumbling it in her hands, striving to put it into the hole. It wouldn't fit, no matter what she did. It dropped from her weak hands. She swore loud enough to make her ears hurt. It took some effort, several attempts until she managed to bend down and pick it up. The haze in her eyes doubled and redoubled. She kept swaying, her sense of balance completely ruined.

Ashton Kramer approached her with his usual lustful grin in place.

– Dream on, she snarled at him.

And felt no small sense of satisfaction when she saw that she actually got to him and deterred him from his usually so undeterred path.

She put the key in the hole without too much trouble and pushed the door open. Her drugged body and befouled mind practically fell inside. She made sure the door was closed and locked.

Later, she didn't know how much later, she found her head stuck in the toilet bowl, found herself breathing in the stinking vapors of the vomit. She imagined that there had been sleep, but couldn't verify that to herself. There was no more solid content left in her stomach and only slime flowed from her slack mouth.

She crawled back into bed. Dormancy claimed her, but not sleep, never sleep, and with her suffered also others in the building and nearby, as the poison roaming her blood and mind turned her power off and on. She found a certain perverse pleasure in that.

Nausea stuck in her throat and mind and body well into the next day. She sat by the breakfast table pale and sick, forcing herself to eat what tasted like sand, like paper and unappetizing organic mass.

It filled her belly, slowly restarting her system.

There were more trips to the toilet. Eventually the waste started coming out the right hole. She sat on her bed, her head bent forward, practically hanging from her shoulders. Slime flowed from her slack mouth and made a pond on the carpet.

– On your *feet,* soldier!

The powerful voice came from far away, but then it exploded in her drugged mind.

She obeyed Claudia promptly.

A strong hand squeezed her jaw.

– It isn't necessarily a bad thing to go overboard like this once in a while, Claudia said. – One might need to do so, in order to function better, but now it's time for you to step up your game, in order to properly make our dream of a powerful team come true.

– Yes, Claudia. Lucinda nodded eagerly. – Our dream, our glorious dream.

She repeated it a thousand times in her mind.

– You are our second in command, Lady Grace said. – Our most valued soldier.

Gimmick wanted to speak, but her voice failed her.

The voice and the words stayed with her, though, in the field, when she was leading her squad. Lucinda and Melinda were back at the containment area where Claudia had «liberated» them, where Alysse Montgomery ruled or had ruled. Alysse was gone and so was everybody else.

– This place is fucking deserted, Wind said incredulous. – And it looks like it didn't happen peacefully either.

They had been called here by Claudia's masters, to assist in the investigation of an attack, of the disappearance. There was no one here, except them and the investigation team. The entire place was cleaned out… empty.

Crimson Mask led on into the pens, where everything returned in a flash to Gimmick, everything they had done to her to prepare her and Kid Sister and the rest for Alysse's even crueler machinations. Adeline Goddard bent down and picked up a set of chains and bracelets. There was blood on it, both fresh and old.

– Our kind suffered here, she said. – All of them suffered greatly. I would say whoever freed them did them a great favor.

Gimmick related everything to Lady Grace. She sensed her displeasure and boundless frustration.

They reached the laboratory part of the pens, the tubes. The past became alive to Gimmick and she had to focus, focus real hard to not display her memories.

– Prepare the subjects, Alysse Montgomery commanded with an expectant grin on her face. – The second stage of the indoctrination will now commence.

Lucinda, Melinda and the rest of the newly arrived lab rats knelt on the floor, looking stricken at the big people with dull expressions being chained inside the big, transparent tubes, how breathing masks covered their faces, how the doors were closed and water filled the entire tube and those inside floated in the fluid and shook their shackles in vain.

– They've been carefully prepared, Alysse said pleased, – opened up so to speak. Their minds will be washed clean and then be filled with our purpose. This is you in a few weeks.

Their eyes, kept open were filled with images. Small speakers stuck in their ears spoke incessantly to them. They writhed in their bonds, pulled them, but could not break free. After a few hours they stopped struggling and received the burst of data without resisting in any visible way.

Lucinda recalled how they had stepped out days later, their eyes even emptier, conditioned further for a life in Alysse's service. Lucinda, like all the rest shook hard as they knelt before the commanding woman, begging her with lowered eyes to not make them her slaves, making it so much easier for her to do so.

The nightmare scenario faded. Gimmick struck a hand so hard at the wall that she almost broke it, and the pain briefly lessened the stark fear.

– You doubt me, don't you? Crimson Mask said abruptly. – Doubt what they do to us?

– No, I… Gimmick replied faint.

– Allow me to show you then, Adeline said. – Let me take you on a tour outside your ivory tower.

Gimmick stared enraged at her, unable to keep herself reined in.

– That got to you, didn't it? You think what happened to you was bad? I will show you that it is nothing compared to what we live through every single day.

The others looked embarrassed at the two of them, diverting their eyes. Lucinda ignored them.

They returned to the headquarters, from another milk run, yet another failed mission. Morale stayed low. Lucinda sensed it and couldn't help echoing it.

– Let's go then, Sensor cried. – Let's break some eggs.

Crimson Mask looked at her, clearly not very comfortable with her angle, the suggestion implied in her words.

They walked back through the portal. Gimmick felt it again, how it seemed to be tugging at them, an icy catching in their bones. They appeared in the alley by the Square. Gimmick, Sensor, Crimson Mask, Wind and Dancer, an all-female squad joining the mundane afternoon crowd rushing back and forth by the misty harbor.

Gimmick noticed it immediately, confirming to herself what she had sensed since her return.

– They look at us differently, now? Sensor wondered.

– They do, Dancer chuckled darkly. – They always feared us, but now, even though we don't assault them we have become a force to be feared.

– They see what we do to our own, Crimson Mask said with a shaky and angry voice. – And while that comforts certain segments of the mundane population quite a few of them don't like it and grow worried that the tame dog shall turn on them.

Sunset Alley, in Mastich Harbor, in the north-western part of Tobruk shook in the shadows of the fast-moving dark clouds. They walked through the Brewery District in full view of the locals. The squalor, always evident had clearly taken a turn for the worse lately. They spotted scrawny big people everywhere. Gimmick sensed more of them in cramped apartments. She couldn't keep herself from noticing them.

– They hardly seem... big at all, do they? Wind shook her head in distress and disgust.

– Being hooked on the worst kind of addictive drugs will do that to you, Crimson Mask growled, her voice a study in anger and despair. – Many of these suffer under the influence of a new kind of heroin developed especially for our kind. The rest is starving and have been doing so for so long that they no longer have strength to empower themselves. Quite a few of them «voluntarily» start using H+ in order to better hold out their sorry existence.

They knew she spoke from experience.

– Oracle saved me, she choked. – Then she vanished, probably because of the predicament she suffered while aiding me. I have tried all the time since to be worthy of her precious gift. And here I am, just another good dog doing more harm than good, just like the rest of you.

– That isn't true, Lucinda protested.

She heard the doubt in her voice and choked on it.

326

She sensed the hostility and despair like a blanket strangling her and those same emotions warred within her, and it made the trouble she had with breathing even more pronounced.

– These wrecks are responsible for their own plight, Sensor snarled in contempt.

The others looked startled at her, but no one voiced any protest.

They heard music, played by an old, broken player. It gave off more noise than music. They followed the sound cautiously to its origin, a large, derelict building on the deep right side of the District. Gimmick signed for the four following her to spread out, take up positions in the terrain and they did. Crimson Mask rose into the air and levitated close to the wall, more concealed than the others from potential onlookers and attackers. The other four started walking faster, approaching running.

The turning of the corner brought no danger, neither did the next. There were just more worn down people with empty stares. They entered the building. The entrance room was big as a hall, with more skeletons coated in skin lined up against the walls.

– I think I'm going to be sick, Wind choked.

She turned towards Gimmick with something beyond gratitude in her feverish eyes.

– Thank you. Thank you for taking me away from this.

She had stuck to her almost childish outlook of the world, latching onto the perceived strongest in her life and pouring all her gratitude into that. Gimmick forced herself to smile and give assurances confirming the girl's hopes.

The first hall was filled with people and so was the second. It quickly felt like they had been walking under the tall ceiling forever. The cries rose from tortured and dull minds and assaulted Lucinda.

She will save us.

Gimmick frowned.

She will save us.

Gimmick caught the thought rising from the sea of thoughts striking her shore. It didn't come from just one mind, but from several close by, a persistent, feverish repetition.

– BLACK DRAGON WILL SAVE US

The powerful voice and its startling words, shouted with pride shook everyone present and especially the five new arrivals.

The shouting man wasn't hard to find. He sat in a chair and they spotted him immediately, easily separating him from the rest by the force of his health, vigor and the strength and awareness evident in his eyes.

– What do you mean by that? Crimson Mask asked distraught. – What's your purpose here?

– She told me to wait for you at this very spot, he grinned his wicked grin.

– You've met her? Lucinda asked startled, unable to conceal the interest from her voice and features.

His grin turned into a dreamy smile.

– No, I haven't had that honor, he replied willingly, eagerly. – She appeared to me in a vision and told me to do her bidding, told me to go to this place and wait for you until this exact minute.

He looked at his watch.

– SIX FIFTY PM, a loud choir of voices from near and far away shouted.

Lucinda shuddered at her core.

– CHANGE IS COMING!

The cry echoed across the halls and beyond.

Sensor kicked the man in the head. There was a gasp in the crowd. She kicked him again. He crumbled from sitting opposition to being stretched out on the floor.

– A change is surely coming for you, she spat.

Melinda struck the man in the mask and kept striking him until he stopped moving. She checked if he was still breathing and then she found the collar and put it around his neck. He was still conscious while she did it. She watched while the light of will faded in his eyes.

– Stupid prick, she chuckled.

Her wicked laughter echoed between the walls.

– Let's take them all, she declared, – all the supporters of vile Black Dragon.

Wind and Dancer glanced at Gimmick. She nodded with numb lips.

A frenzy caught the five. They started moving from person to person in the hall. Gimmick easily caught those with thoughts sympathetic to Black Dragon and resentment towards them. They knocked them around and beat them up. Just a few put up any fight to speak of, and they were easily dealt with as well.

– *On your feet!* Dancer commanded harshly and they obeyed with hazy eyes.
– *Walk!*

The prisoners, twelve in all stumbled towards the exit, struck and hounded by their captors.

The five Maverick Crew members marched them through the streets, to the nearest police station. Mundane people stared at them. The big avoided their glances. Gimmick read all kinds of thoughts in their minds.

– These were stirring up trouble, Sensor told the desk sergeant. – They belong behind bars, in the darkest, deepest dungeon there is.

– And that's exactly where they will end up, the man cackled in anticipation.

They saw how he and the other cops took great pleasure in handling the prisoners. Gimmick didn't need her mind-reading ability to discern that, didn't need it at all.

The five of them returned to the streets, breathing as much as possible of the stale air.

– That felt good, Dancer said. – It felt really good to show those pathetic wretches where they can stick their worship.

Her voice was quivering, her eyes did flicker.

– You do know what happened here, right? Crimson Mask said. – I wanted to show you how our kind was suffering and we ended up adding to it.

– You're such a conceited bitch, Adeline, Gimmick snarled, unable to keep the poison from erupting.

Crimson Mask shook in anger and resentment and anxiety.

They returned to the headquarters. The walk through the portal cut Gimmick. She felt like she was bleeding from a thousand small wounds.

The moment they stepped through to the other side she turned towards Crimson Mask, forcing herself to hide her discomfort.

– There will be no more rebellion from you, she said lightly. – We will no longer tolerate more of your bullshit. Understand?

– I understand, Adeline replied, once more standing straight like a schoolgirl or a soldier.

– That's a good girl.

Gimmick touched her jaw in beyond patronizing ways.

Sensor, Dancer and Wind looked at Gimmick with deep admiration and respect in their shiny eyes.

– That would be all, children, she joked or pretended to be joking. – You run along, now.

They pulled back, leaving her, their imprint staying in her mind. She lingered for a while, hesitating before moving on.

The hum from the laboratory drew her. She sensed Lady Grace in there, like Lady Grace sensed her. Mechanic was there as well. He was always there.

– She knew we would come, she said, unable to keep the whiny quality from her voice. – Black Dragon had orchestrated everything, preparing for our arrival. Our actions only served to strengthen the resolve of her followers.

Lady Grace looked at her with a frown, a condemning frown, but right now Lucinda didn't care.

– And the portals become more… agitated each time we use them, don't they? Today it was like someone… shook me in there, as if the entire «place» briefly became... energized. It is as if she can screw up Oracle's design somehow.

– Black Dragon is truly a fearsome foe, Mechanic said, shaking his head, clearly revealing a kind of detached professional curiosity that Lucinda had always detested. – She can evidently fight off our powers with ease and turn them against us. I will speculate that she did that with Lavender and at several other occasions as well.

– We will work even harder with toughening up the recruits and ourselves, Lady Grace stated solemnly.

Lucinda knew what she meant by that, knew exactly what she meant by that.

– It's frustrating, Mechanic conceded. – I've made considerable improvement to the surveillance grid, and can see much more of what's happening, but I'm still unable to get a firm grasp of the Cadre's movements and tactical dispositions.

He showed them footage from Tobruk and many other places all over the world. It was a remarkable display and Gimmick felt the familiar ambiguity. Sudden nausea rode her.

Suspicious behavior was marked in red, proven enemy activity in violet. There was much red, little violet.

– The Cadre is gaining more volunteers, not less, Mechanic stated, shaking his head.

Lady Grace and Gimmick were aware of Raven Bird, of her excited state of being well before she rushed into the room, aware of what was on her mind, but they let it play out, feeling quite startled themselves.

– Crimson Mask sent me a message, she said.

She showed them her cell phone.

> «I will stay with you, do my duty, but I will not return to the headquarters, ever. I will stay in contact through Raven Bird, like before and no one else».
>
> Crimson Mask

– That conceited bitch, Lady Grace said softly and Gimmick found herself nodding, nodding, nodding.

Lucinda couldn't remember much of the remaining day. She experienced reality as if everything was cut into ever smaller pieces. It just faded away somewhere in a deep, deep hole inside of her. She recalled talking to Melinda at some point, but only one sentence, one set of words stood out to her.

– I feel so indecisive, so out of whack with myself that I can hardly feel myself.

For some reason those words kept repeating themselves in her mind. She could not stop them from repeating themselves, almost as if they were sentient, as if they had an independent, conscious mind.

She remembered drinking, the taste of alcohol never leaving her tongue.

The door slammed behind her as it closed. She whimpered as she stumbled towards the bed. Her body rested unmoving on the soft surface, but her thoughts kept rambling, kept shifting and prodding her in an unending loop. It surprised her, stunned her that the alcohol didn't keep her powers from working, didn't keep her mind from operating at all, but rather encouraged it to prod, prod, prod and never stop prodding.

She fell into a deep, deep sleep, suffering feverish, confusing and troubling dreams of yesterday and tomorrow.

Part Two:
Black Dragon

Chapter 19

The flashes kept blinding her, kept creating rainbow stars behind closed eyelids.

Lucinda and Melinda danced before the cameras and the photographers, smiling prettily, projecting strength and all kinds of emotions, moving in flimsy dresses and fitting uniforms.

As always, there was a press-conference afterwards. The two of them posed with others for more pictures, more silly questions. Everything went smoothly. Everyone present stayed true to the script. No reporter or interviewer asked anything but the right questions and no one of the model big people gave wrong answers.

The mood was high, even exalted in the wardrobe afterwards.

– They love us, Melinda sighed pleased, with bright eyes. – They just love us.

Lucinda found herself nodding in agreement and smiling with the others, a smile staying in place during the subsequent festivities.

It was more of the same, really, drinking mostly soda and smile pretty and converse with the guests. She kept the smiles coming, carefully masking her face.

– I long to be back out there, in the streets, she said excitedly, – doing my job, my fucking duty.

– Me, too, Melinda agreed. – I'm excited beyond words.

More weeks passed by. Gimmick and Sensor and the others, filled with renewed vigor spent their days cleaning up the streets, filling shipping stations with new batches of big people.

– Move! Sensor shouted, beating up on a straggler.

He was pushed into the back of a truck with the rest. The door was closed and yet another transport left the backyard of the main police headquarters.

– Look at those fat bitches, a policeman cackled to a colleague.

– They've become quite tame, haven't they? His colleague snickered. – Perhaps they wouldn't be adverse to a round or ten in the haystack?

She had no trouble hearing them from her given position, didn't need to strain herself at all. Their lewd thoughts and intent got to her. She felt the low-level arousal rise a notch, then another. It got so bad that she was unable to stand still, and when she moved it got worse. Sweaty and uncomfortable she fought to regain control over herself.

The guards inside the truck had already started undressing the prisoners and quickly began having their way with them, brutalizing them, raping them.

The sensations didn't go away when the truck disappeared from her sight, as she had imagined it would.

– C'mon, she told her squad. – Let's go.

She bloodied her palm by burying her nails in her skin again. It worked. The others noticed, both the pain and the desire riding her. They could not help but noticing, and glanced dazed and confused at each other and eventually at her.

Gimmick led them away from there.

– This is so fucked up, Raven Bird said, – so damned fucked up.

No one responded to her, but they glanced bewildered at each other.

The beyond confusing sense of dread and desire and anger and shame mixed together didn't leave them, kept burning within Lucinda.

Fragments of thoughts, impossibly reached her from nowhere.

Fucktoy, such a great fucktoy.

Her hand hurt. She couldn't make a fist anymore.

The man was big, very big. She noticed him before she saw him, his mind a disorganized vortex spinning her hard. Everybody heard him, blocks away.

Gimmick and her squad of big females turned a corner and they had him straight in their sight. He stared at them, at everybody with his huge, mesmerizing eyes. His madness made them all dizzy, nauseous.

– I'm the big bad troll, he shouted. – I'm the lizard king. I can do anything.

His beyond loud cackle hurt her very flesh.

He wore ragged clothes, but his muscles flexed hard and big. If he had a rough life he didn't seem physically marked by it. He fixed his attention on Lucinda. She shrunk in his presence.

– Aren't you a peach? He said perplexed.

His inane and insane laughter rocked the very buildings surrounding them.

– You're just a puny woman, he breathed. – No matter your powers, you will always be easy prey for any true man.

She laughed him in the face. It came off spontaneous and true and made her feel more than good about it.

He looked startled at her. He started swaying and then he fell to his knees. She didn't do anything, but he clearly crumbled before her eyes. He looked at his hands, his big and scarred hands with horror in his eyes.

– No, he cried out in boundless misery. – NO!

He started clawing at his face. It didn't leave any marks to speak of. There were no nails left on his fingers. The tips were hardly more than scarred flesh. He fell on his side while sobbing uncontrollably.

– No, Gimmick replied to the others' unvoiced question. – I don't feel like returning to the police station, to any police station right now. Let's just leave this poor wretch here. Let him enjoy his misery in peace.

In pieces.

She smiled.

– I feel like having dinner.

They walked straight into the nearest restaurant, one just off the Square. A waiter met them at the entrance, a man flipping nervously at the corner of the menu.

– Good afternoon, I'm Parker. Is there anything I can help you with?

– You have adequate facilities at this place? Gimmick inquired. – The toilet bowls are of sufficient size, I trust.

– They are, Parker assured her.

– Then by all means: a table for five, please.

They sat down by one of the best tables at the restaurant. It became a bubble where the rest of the world didn't reach them. They fed, pretty much with the usual vigor, ignoring the angry stares, the people standing up and leaving the restaurant.

– Life is good, Gimmick said with the huge grin very much visible across the face, in spite of the mask.

The shit burned. It always burned. The injured hand made it more difficult for her to dry her ass. The stall walls closed in on her more than ever before.

– You didn't deceive us, she said with a distinct patronizing flair to the waiter afterwards. – The toilet bowls were truly the required standard. The food wasn't half bad either. We will make sure to recommend this place to our colleagues, won't we gals?

The other four nodded and voiced their over-the-top agreement making the poor guy's skin turn a deep shade of red.

They returned to the headquarters. It was quiet, as always, except for the hum of the machine running all the operations in the building. Lady Grace was here. She filled Gimmick's mind in an instant. Gimmick left the others without a word, heading straight for Lady Grace.

– Ah, there you are, ready and eager to report to me.

Lucinda stopped before the other, the woman looking like a giant in her mind's eye. She reached out a hand and Claudia grabbed it, and their contact, already strong turned even more powerful.

– Nice work, little one, she said pleased. – Nice work!

She let go of the hand, leaving Lucinda somewhat alone inside her own head again.

Lucinda blinked and suddenly there she was, in the training hall with all her teammates, except Crimson Mask, running through Lady Grace's iron hard exercise regime. Sweat poured from their soaked skin, kept soaking already long since wet uniforms. Gimmick kicked a sandbag. She struck it with her hand, with both her hands. It felt good. Each hit felt great. The pain didn't faze her.

– These are our enemies, Lady Grace told them, low-keyed, intense. – Strike them with everything you are, with every ounce of strength you possess. Remember it all when you are out there, fighting for real.

Her words energized them further, spurred them on to no end. They kind of... spotted Flight Captain as well, but he seemed ephemeral, almost like no more than a shadow by the big woman's side.

Gimmick hit Brick, hardly even affecting him. He made a swing at her, but missed by a mile. She struck him again, and kicked him, and kicked him. He struck her. His hand only graced her jaw, but it made her stumble backwards and see stars. He rushed forward to take advantage of it. She dodged him and gave him a boost on his forward momentum, pushing him hard into the wall. It was reinforced metal and didn't break. She kicked him again, hitting him in the lower part of his back. He was pushed at the wall. All the kick's energy hit him. He gasped. She struck him with both her fists in the neck. He went down. She kicked him in the head, smearing his face at the already bloody wall. He hit the floor and didn't move.

The applause filled her ears and Lady Grace's approval her mind. She blushed in triumphant joy.

– Well done, Lady Grace cried. – We may make fighters of you yet.

Brick woke up quickly, shaking his head, not really hurt.

– Do you see what she did? Lady Grace asked the others. They looked slightly bewildered at each other. – She took advantage of her strengths and turned his strength into a weakness. Well done!

The water in the shower hit Lucinda, both hurting and soothing her sore skin.

In the shadow of the water she glimpsed a dark, snarling face and heard a chilling silent laughter, and would have gasped in horror if she hadn't been stunned by fright.

– That will teach them, Sensor spoke excited to her later in the hallway, – teach them that the dynamic duo is no pushover.

The ecstasy brought on by the victory stayed with Gimmick and made her nod and smile in response to Sensor's juvenile display.

– That's right, Kid Sister. They've got nothing on us.

The chilling, silent laughter from the shower didn't fade either, creating an ambiguous sense of dread and bravado within her, so visible in the eyes Melinda didn't see.

Lucinda studied Melinda, studied her hard, hardly able to conceal her cold

338

suspicion.

– Do you want to have some fun tonight? Sensor asked with a touch of her old youthful demeanor. – We could gather all the girls, make it a girls' night out to be remembered for *ages*.

– Sure, Gimmick heard herself say. – Why not?

Melinda's eyes took on an added layer of shine. She cried out in excitement and ran off like the innocent teenager she had been.

Lucinda frowned. She knew she did, knew that particular frown was like frozen on her face these days, but she couldn't wrap her mind around it, couldn't see it in the mirror.

There was a mirror somewhere, in the mist in front of her, but blurry, indistinct.

Raven Bird approached her, anxious, fighting to stay calm, collected. Gimmick sensed that, even though she had always had trouble properly reading her friend's mind. Lisa turned the corner. The interference from her magnetic powers turned even worse. She was clearly excited. Something had happened.

– We must make haste, Raven Bird said, skipping the small talk.

She showed Gimmick a message on her cell phone.

Bring Gimmick. Meet me at second choice, urgent 1

– It's from Crimson Mask, Raven Bird added. – It's a high priority call, not just an ordinary meeting up.

– Lady Grace must sanction it, of course, Gimmick said.

– Of course, Raven Bird conceded willingly.

They ran down the hall. Lady Grace met them there, like Gimmick knew she would. Gimmick showed her the message, even though there was no need for that.

Lady Grace nodded to herself.

– Yes, you should go. That traitorous bitch has an extended network of local contacts and may have important information for us. It is also pretty clear that this is a somewhat special meeting, since she wants «enforcements».

Gimmick couldn't help but pick up on Claudia's patronizing and contempt. She shrunk in shame and perplexity and a despair she couldn't shake.

– Don't let her fuck you around, Lady Grace practically commanded them.

– We won't! Raven Bird assured her, unable to hide her resentment towards the leader.

Gimmick and Raven Bird turned towards the hardly visible shimmer in the air and stepped through the portal.

They emerged in the shadowy alley, stepping out into the bright sunlight, into the quiet, quiet late afternoon. The lack of wind made sweat break all over their body in an instant. They broke quickly into a fast walk, ignoring the strain brought on by the heat.

Gimmick felt pride coursing through her. She walked with an excited smile behind the mask, like a bloodhound tracking prey, and hardly registered Raven Bird's concerned look.

Lisa's mind was harder to read than ever. It was buzzing like a swarm of wasps.

Bzzzz

BZZZ

Lucinda shook abruptly, stark fear pulling her in all directions simultaneously.

Or so it felt.

– Are you alright? Raven Bird asked. – What's wrong?

– Nothing, Gimmick replied with confidence, with a confident voice and stance. – Nothing is wrong!

Their chosen route towards their destination took them mostly through the back alleys and less traversed streets. They were only occasionally spotted and pointed at by the natives.

The old, abandoned warehouse district stretched out before them. Raven Bird noticed easily Gimmick's discomfort this time as well.

– It brings back memories, that's all, Lucinda replied to her friend's casual probe. – I and Melinda didn't exactly have a good time here. Have I told you that we had to scrunch garbage cans for food?

– Many times, Lisa said sympathetically, with anguish in her voice. – It was bad, wasn't it, bad beyond words?

– Big bad males had first pick, Lucinda kept speaking, as if she hadn't heard the other speak, – and we didn't know whether or not they would choose us or the food.

They turned a corner. Buildings without walls appeared on both sides of the «street». Gimmick frowned. The frown cut a deep ditch between her brows.

– It's right ahead, Raven Bird said unconcerned.

They turned another corner. Raven Bird walked to an open spot among all the rubble and Gimmick followed her. Gimmick began probing her surroundings, focusing even harder on making her mind power work a little better, covering a larger physical area. She sensed no one, no other people nearby.

Raven Bird levitated a piece of metal. It floated to the top between the two buildings where they were standing. She made it dance there.

– Crimson Mask is the only one except me that can send such a unique signal, she said with pride in her voice.

Gimmick glanced around her with anxious eyes. There was no one to see, hear or sense.

Crimson Mask approached them from the south, levitating through the air with a new level of accomplished ease inadvertently impressing her teammates. An excited, downright relieved smile cracked on Raven Bird's face and she waved frantically. Crimson Mask didn't return the greeting.

She landed with what approached nonchalance in front of the two.

– That was impressive, Raven Bird greeted her. – You've been practicing hard lately, I trust?

– We must hurry, Crimson Mask said cold and indifferent. – Slave traders are about to move their merchandize not far from here.

– Slave traders? Lucinda gasped.

– Yes, it's your old friend who's back in business again.

Her words made Gimmick hot with embarrassment and boiling anger. Lucinda wanted to know more and a pure reflex made her probe the other's mind, but nothing revealed itself, nothing at all. Gimmick frowned. The thin smile on Adeline Goddard's lips froze Gimmick.

– Yes, I've been practicing, Crimson Mask said. – I've also learned how to keep fucking mindwitches out of my head. Do not attempt to read my mind again.

Gimmick felt like she had been slapped in the face. Crimson Mask, clearly more assertive than they had known her to be started walking, rushing down the street and the two others followed her.

– The three of us shouldn't be at odds, Raven Bird said, slightly out of breath, as if she had kept something contained for a long time. – We should present a united front against... against Lady Grace.

Gimmick and Crimson Mask stopped and stared incredulous at her.

– That's partly why I wanted us to meet here. Raven Bird spoke fast and furry, almost losing her drawl. – I want us to leave the Maverick Crew, flee to another country, one of the few not allied with the United States if need be and take as many as we can with us.

Adeline Goddard's loud laughter shook the derelict buildings and those gathered between them.

– What's so funny? Lisa Carlton spat.

– You are, and your timing, Crimson Mask chuckled darkly. – After all this time you finally grow a backbone, but not a very thick one. You will run away, with your tail between your legs.

Lisa's shame and simmering anger wasn't hard to gauge.

– You don't understand. Lady Grace is so powerful and her position with the government...

She caught herself, then relenting, shaking her head in determination.

– You're saying that Claudia Malone is far more powerful than Lady Grace? Adeline grinned.

There was malice there, thinly veiled. Lucinda and Lisa gasped.

– C'mon, you didn't think it would be so difficult to see through her disguise, do you?

They stood there, like girls caught red handed stealing candy.

– It isn't surprising that the other mindwitch knew, though, and not that she shared that secret with her good friend, the Mistress of Magnetism either.

– I can't say I care much for your tone, missy, Raven Bird said, and now her drawl was back.

They stared enraged at each other, but then, by seemingly solemn agreement they turned towards Gimmick.

– So, what do you think, mindwitch?

Lucinda's mind felt like wool, her thoughts totally disorganized. They turned to her, to her for guidance. She could just about keep herself from uttering a dark laughter similar to that of Crimson Mask.

– Let's handle the problem at hand first, she said, striving to put conviction in her voice and stance.

The three of them nodded to each other, feeling a kind of relief, sick relief because the most important discussion had been put on hold, making Gimmick feel even worse.

Raven Bird and Gimmick followed Crimson Mask into the building. There was a sense of urgency that wasn't hard to gauge. Adeline looked so much like herself, but there was something there, something that had been added, something dark and hard that had been… added.

They ran up the stairs to the upper floor, ran in silence. Gimmick was about to «suggest» that it would be prudent if they communicated through telepathy when Crimson Mask put a finger to her lips. She had certainly become far more assertive.

Gimmick rubbed her forehead. It did feel like something was burrowing itself into her head. Apprehension stalked her. These surroundings…

They emerged into a hall. She recognized it. Cold sweat covered her exposed skin. A toy had been discarded in a corner. Melinda's doll.

– This place…

She stopped. The other two did as well.

– You recognize it, don't you? Crimson Mask said with a wicked grin. – You and your sister spent some unpleasant time here, before Claudia «rescued» you.

And that made fear strike Lucinda like a viper.

– This is it, you know, Crimson Mask chuckled, – the moment you've been dreading for years.

– What *is* this? Raven Bird looked bewildered at them both.

– She's with them.

Lucinda could hardly speak. Her constricted throat felt like lead.

– Yes, I *am* with «them». I have discarded the hypocrisy and oppression represented by the Maverick Crew and its backers like yesterday's laundry.

Crimson Mask struck out with an arm. It was like Raven Bird was struck by an invisible fist. She was pushed backwards and hit the wall hard. Gimmick witnessed how she shook her head and strived to clear it. But she fell and collapsed on the floor.

Gimmick felt herself be grabbed by those invisible hands, by Crimson Mask's power of the mind, before she managed to do anything to counteract anything.

– Off you go!

Gimmick was thrown through the air and through the door, into the other room. The door slammed shut behind her. She cried out in pain as she hit the floor and slid across the concrete.

There was someone else there, but she didn't see who through the haze of her vision.

Her vision cleared. She looked straight at the Catcher.

– Hello, Gimmick, he grinned. – Long time, no see.

She shook her head, half incredulous, half amused.

– What are you doing here, Franklin? She wondered, not very worried. – Did you finally decide to come out of hiding? You haven't joined the freak show, have you? They can't possibly have use for someone like you, can they?

Thought and action were one, when she confidently attacked him… and he slapped her on the cheek. She fell on the floor and stared at him.

– Things have changed, Lucinda, he snarled, – and the sooner you realize that the better… for you. I don't mind playing a little… or a lot.

She had noticed it immediately, how he had changed, how different he had become from that small-time hustler she had caught and put behind bars so often. Hearing him say her name, her civilian name was only one more shocking part of that. She was up in a whiff, both angry and scared, doing her best to ignore the unpleasant thoughts roaming her mind. Her right hand curled into a fist and she attempted to strike him. He avoided the hand easily, and struck her again. She tumbled backwards. He pressed his advantage and attacked her ferociously. His hand hit her jaw, hit it hard and she fell and hit the floor. She kicked upwards. He avoided it and kicked at her. She avoided it narrowly and rolled away frantically. Anger flared inside her, and she decided to stop playing around. She used her mighty mind power on him, but the moment she struck out and attempted to touch his mind pain flared between her temples. She yelped.

– Oh, no, he grinned, advancing on her, taking his time, confident and strong. – There will be no more pulling of tricks for you, little girl. Your edge is a thing of the past.

Panic and fear grabbed her, filling her mind with questions, as she stared wide eyed at her adversary. This was the Catcher, a guy she had had for breakfast for years, without breaking a sweat, and now he was rolling over her.

Distraction filled her mind as well, about the other battle in the other room, where the more powerful, vastly improved Crimson Mask made mincemeat of Raven Bird.

Lucinda glimpsed something in Franklin's mind, something dark and scary, something she had hardly experienced outside dreams, and she knew what it was. She knew!

He struck her again. His fist hit her ribcage, making her lose her breath. She hit him back. It hardly seemed to affect him at all. She jumped away from him, in an attempt to catch her bearing. Her hand raced inside her jacket, drawing the crossbow. One of his ropes struck her hand, making her lose the weapon. The ropes, seemingly independent of each other danced in the air as if they were alive. He had clearly become more powerful and gained a far more precise control over his abilities.

– GLORY TO THE EBONY GODDESS! Crimson Mask shouted, as she pushed Raven Bird at the wall and started beating her up in brutal and cruel ways.

Raven Bird was already half unconscious, but Crimson Mask kept hammering at her with a cruel smile on her lips.

The Catcher struck Gimmick on the jaw with his right fist. Blood flowed from her mouth. She staggered backwards, just about avoiding another hit. She kicked him in the ribs, making him gasp. He still shook it off as if it was nothing. A brief, casual, ongoing study of his fighting technique told her more of how he had changed. She imagined she fought a completely different individual only resembling the Troy Franklin she had faced earlier.

One of the thin ropes struck her like a whip on her butt. She screamed in frustration.

– I will capture you and ravage you first, he snarled, – and then I will repeat it all with your sister, sweet and young and ripe and no longer so innocent Melinda.

There was a cruelty to him, one that hadn't really been there before. He had been a more or less sophisticated burglar, not a thug, not the brutal man she glimpsed in front of her.

The rope formed into a wide noose, one that slipped onto her arm. She pulled the arm backwards, avoiding the snare. Distracted, she practically walked directly into his fist. She attempted to return the strike in kind, but he ducked. His motion was fluid, elegant, as if he had trained or had been trained as a fighter for years.

Months…

The thought struck her in a flash. Only months, since the mass escape from the prison.

– The Cadre trained you…

– Oh, they did far more than that, he chuckled hard. – Don't worry, you will get answers to all the questions burning in your confused mind.

The noose slipped onto her right wrist and this time she couldn't keep it from happening. It tightened around it, tightened hard. It hurt. Blinking sweat from her eyes she made an attempt to remove the noose. It seemed glued to her wrist. The rope pulled at her arm. She tried to resist the pull, but failed again. He struck her on the side of the head. She fell. Desperation, pain, anger and fear, his nasty remarks about Melinda combined in her and without considering the ramifications she lashed out with her mind, pushed deep within him with her power.

He just grinned at her and she stared dumbfounded at him, and then the pain, the horrible pain came and she screamed.

The scream, the horror lasted *forever*.

He just stood there, not doing anything, as she crouched on the floor, as he towered above her, as she kept gasping in horror and pain, as all of it kept echoing inside her.

Another rope tightened around her second wrist. As she watched both ropes began tying her wrists together.

– You're out of gimmicks, Gimmick. I told you, you stupid cunt. You went into my mind, and now you will never leave.

She… tried, but it was as she was… locked inside there, unable to break free. She whimpered and tried to get away, to crawl away, but almost nothing was working. He laughed callously and kicked her in the abdomen. She gasped and collapsed there on the floor, and saw him and the world through a sick daze. He kicked her again and again. She laid still.

– You're nothing, he boasted, – and soon you will be less than nothing.

The ropes pulled her tied hands up, over her head and then they pulled her entire body into the air. She hung there. He struck her several times.

– You will not attempt to kick me, he snarled, – if you know what's good for you.

She felt wasted and weak and couldn't even if she wanted to. She hung there and the pain in her wrists turned worse by the second.

The door opened. Crimson Mask entered the room. The bloody and beaten, more or less unconscious Raven Bird levitated in the air behind her, clearly under her power, not her own.

Raven Bird's arms were raised above her head and she was pulled into the air by Gimmick's side. Crimson Mask found a collar and put it around Lisa's neck.

– This will neutralize your powers, she said softly. – But not do more. We want you to be aware for all the upcoming delights.

And for some reason that word, that single word made Lucinda shake even harder.

– I'm Blood Diamond, Adeline Goddard declared, - am Red Dragon, a servant of the Ebony Goddess and her Cadre, and you are our prisoners. I'm happy to say that it won't be pleasant.

It appeared to Gimmick and the slowly coming to Raven Bird as if the entire building was shaking.

The Catcher rubbed the fabric covering Gimmick's cheek, rubbed her shaking lips with his thumb. That tiny «caress» made her guts do a topsy turvy in her stomach.

– We needed to take away Raven Bird's potentially pesky powers. Yours are of no concern to us, as you have experienced several times already.

He began cutting off her jacket, removing all the remaining gadgets.

Lucinda heard steps from somewhere. Three figures solidified slowly in her hazy vision.

– BRAVO! The biggest man applauded. – I confess I was a bit miffed when we were told not to participate in the fun, but watching was thoroughly enjoyable, too.

Gimmick frowned. His appearance had changed, but she did recognize him through the passive use of her mind power, even though that signature had also been altered. It was Ulysses Rogan, one of the Brewery Boys.

The other two were his siblings, Trevor (that she also had known as Ronald) and Cassandra Rogan. Gimmick didn't need more than a glance at them to see that they had all changed the same way Franklin and Goddard had changed.

Cassandra held a whip, a large bullwhip in her hand. Franklin stepped back. Lucinda and Lisa began shaking their hands in incredulity and terror, starting to form words of protest.

They never made it. The first lash hit Gimmick's back. She screamed again.

346

The next hit Raven Bird's back. Another scream filled the room. The two screamed themselves hoarse as the punishment continued. Several lashings cut through their clothes. Lucinda imagined she smelled blood and saw it flow from her skin. Her screams turned to whimpering, insane wails. She began pulling at the ropes, and rocked up and down for what felt like minutes. Raven Bird had stopped screaming. She just whimpered weakly every time another lash hit her clothes and also partly unprotected skin. They quickly lost count over the number of lashes.

It seemed to go on and *on*. There was the occasional small break as Cassandra shifted position, as she began whipping their sides and front and their thighs, as she resumed the punishment again and again and *again*.

– I'm Stern Mistress, Cassandra Rogan snarled, – am Violet Dragon, and you will learn to pay attention to me and my commands.

Wide open eyes saw nothing. Wide open mouths caught no breath.

The two captives hung there, all strength having left their arms.

The Catcher let go of Gimmick and Blood Diamond of Raven Bird. They collapsed as they hit the floor, blood and tears and saliva covering their bodies.

Cassandra kicked Lucinda, not hard, enough to get her attention.

– You're quite a disappointment, cunt, not at all like the semi-goddess my dumb brothers portrayed you as.

If the woman had ever been a meek teacher, that part of her nature was long done, submerged into the new, dominant personality.

Personality, Gimmick thought dully.

The word didn't make sense or hardly even registered in her stricken mind, but it kept echoing in there, like the memory of a sound and never truly going away.

Cruel and hard eyes studied the two on the floor.

– They're softened up and ready, Cassandra stated pleased.

Softened up and ready, Gimmick thought stricken.

– Look at you, The Catcher said softly, – the incredulity and distress in the wounds you use to look at the world.

The three men fell on their knees and began tearing off the prisoners' pants. The two women began shaking their heads. Trevor Rogan - the Whiffer began fondling Lucinda.

– I will make sure you enjoy it, he spat. – I did it once before, remember?

She did, and that incident suddenly became so much clearer to her. He released pheromones making females aroused, but his ability hadn't been very effective before, easy to resist, just like the Catcher's effort at catching her.

But on that evening in the disco he had already been a changed man, both physically and mentally. She had not recognized him. He, like his brother and Franklin counted among those referred to as standing jokes in the community, and she had never paid much attention to him before.

She realized that she who had been Crimson Mask had probably also changed physically, not enough to see it through the mask, but more than enough that she probably wouldn't have been recognized without the mask.

– Pay attention, bitch!

The Whiffer slapped her cheek.

– You will be pleasing, won't you? Ulysses said. – You don't want another round with the whip, do you?

She shook her head, timid and scared, terror beaten deep into her very self.

– Good girl!

Trevor pushed a hand between her thighs and she howled in despair and sudden, irrefutable need.

– Yes, I will make sure you enjoy it, he snarled. – After we're done you will fervently agree with those saying that women enjoy rape.

She whimpered, howling silently like a lost soul.

– Gimmick is well known as a great fucktoy, the Catcher cackled. – We will do everything in our power to prove that to our satisfaction, of course.

Ulysses Rogan - Sledgehammer struck her with his hard and strong fists, pacifying her before she was even tempted to resist.

All three of them fondled the two women with invasive hands and malicious acts. They removed the masks and Lucinda felt totally exposed and vulnerable.

– That's better, I wanted to see their faces, Ulysses giggled like a girl.

Lisa shook hard, her face bloated and bloody and covered in tears and sweat, and Lucinda knew she was a mirror image of her friend.

The three men undressed. They were excited and ready, their cocks erect and wet at the tip.

The Whiffer grabbed Gimmick's hands. He pushed them at the concrete and mounted her, pushed her body at the crude floor. A knee split her thighs and she couldn't keep that from happening, couldn't keep that from happening either. He moved inside of her. She released a load moan of despair and protest, everything useless. The other brother was on Lisa. His fists hammered her body every time she even tried to resist. Ulysses pushed his seed into Lisa with a triumphant grunt. Lucinda cried out in misery, nausea stuck in her throat like a ball. She felt sick, felt needy, felt horror beyond belief, her wounds burning hotter than hell. He wanted her to enjoy it, but didn't try very hard. It was, in truth not about sex to him, but about power, and she felt a sick sense of relief.

348

The Catcher was inside Lucinda, even more than before. She didn't resist, but just laid still and let everything happen. It didn't just seem to go on forever. It was forever. He made an effort and she choked when she realized that. He touched her, fondled her. He took his time, patient and unrelenting. She shook her head in protest.

– No, she mumbled.

– You want it, he stated. – You're mine. You belong to me like any needy bitch. You have just not yet admitted that fact to yourself.

She writhed under him on the concrete. It hurt. She writhed extra hard. She wanted it to hurt. It didn't. She only felt his hand in her cunt. He slapped her again. She turned limp in his grip. He kissed her and she… she kissed him back.

– NO!

– You're a pain whore, Lucinda, he growled. – You want your man to be tough with you, want tough love. Don't worry, you'll get it. You will come to love it, as I make you more and more mine. The Ebony Goddess has promised you to me. I know it will happen.

– G-goddess?

Her voice hardly sounded like hers anymore, but like that of a frightened, whiny girl.

– Precisely, she will change your life, like she did mine, completing you, filling you with all the power you need and want.

He sounded eager, almost religious in his zeal, and scarier than ever.

– B-black D-dragon?

He began laughing then, laughing hard, so hard that his body practically shook. She shook her head in even worse distress.

– I don't understand, she whined. – Please!

He began moving harder on her, the loud laughter still ringing in her ears.

– PLEASE!

He came and she came, in a howl of shame and horror.

– I love the smell of burned pussy after great sex, he marveled and shook his head in contempt and triumph. – You don't disappoint, sex toy. I felt you, *felt* your pleasure in my mind. It's remarkable. You will be *so* popular!

He pulled out and left her alone there on the floor. The vomit rose from her throat like a geyser and flooded her chest and the floor on her left side.

– That's gross, Ulysses said with disgust in his voice.

He was next. She didn't move, made no attempt at getting away or resist him. He kept going unceremoniously. Her power just went haywire. She came for him, too, and shared her pleasure with him, and with everybody present. Lisa released a shout reminiscent of a moan.

– Oh, Goddess! Ulysses shouted. – Oh, boy!

– I felt that, Cassandra marveled. – I felt it good! This is better than Christmas and Fourth of July and everything put together. I feel so in the mood.

– You bitch! Lisa hissed at Lucinda. – You disgusting bitch!

Gimmick broke in another round of tears, unable to stop herself from anything.

The two, no three faces blurred in her eyes and mind. She confused the slap on her cheeks with the crude fondling of breasts and nipples and cunt. Blood Diamond said something. Stern Mistress laughed loud and wicked.

They had moved on to the bed, the bed where Lucinda and Melissa had bunked in their lean years. The abuse continued, continued and continued and Lucinda saw no end to it.

She crouched on the bed. Her entire body hurt, even more as it was racked with helpless and continuous choking. The three men dressed. The sweet stench of semen made Lucinda sick.

– Look at you, Stern Mistress said with obviously fake pity in her voice. – Poor girl.

– Look at that sweet mug, Blood Diamond chuckled. – A famous feature for sure.

Gimmick looked at her with total incomprehension in her eyes.

– How can you do this, Adeline? Your disagreement with Lady Grace, with us wasn't that bad, was it?

The last two words were hardly even a whine.

– I am transformed, Adeline, mighty Adeline boasted, stated, – released from my paltry, insignificant existence through strife and the grace of the Ebony Goddess. You're just a tame bitch. I'm the Goddess' fierce and cruel servant, one of her *dragons*. Believe me when I tell you that both your old lives are over and done, now. The sooner you accept that, the better it will be for you.

Her dragons... Gimmick frowned, but couldn't reason, couldn't think.

The lash of the bullwhip hit the prisoners' unprotected butts.

– On your feet, tame bitches! Stern Mistress snapped.

They obeyed promptly, no matter how much it hurt.

– Walk, tame bitches!

They walked, guided by the occasional lash from the stern whip. Gimmick heard a choke. She couldn't tell whether or not it came from Raven Bird or herself. They clutched what was left of their uniform and clothes.

– Halt!

Blood Diamond's metal voice froze them in place.

– Get rid of their clothes, she spat. – These wretches have no more use for them.

The three men hurried to comply, the brutal grin painted on their faces.

They began tearing the tattered fabric off the captives' bodies. It didn't take long and elicited no visible protest from Gimmick and Raven Bird. The dull expression never strayed from their eyes. The Catcher grabbed Lucinda around the jaw and displayed her face to his cruel gaze.

– I love those generous cheeks.

She sniffed, unable to offer even the slightest resistance to his invasive touch and scrutiny. A small amount of vomit seemed to be squeezed out of her mouth.

– Poor Lucinda; so confused and conflicted. But we will sort you out, don't you worry.

He pulled back. Cassandra instantly continued the unrelenting punishment.

– What are you waiting for, you lazy cows? Get *on* with it!

Gimmick jumped forward, in a stupefied and totally useless attempt at avoiding the lash. She kept putting one foot in front of the other, imagining that Raven Bird moved by her side, unable to confirm it, her eyes seeing nothing but the thick, thick fog ahead.

The ropes still tightened around her wrists. The tight fit hurt and tears kept flowing from her eyes. She was unable to put a stop to it.

They stumbled down the stairs, fearing they would fall every time they took a step, unable to do anything about it. They were driven off like cattle. When they reached the floor it didn't make them feel any better. Gimmick hardly noticed her surroundings. She noticed the strike of the whip and the harsh voices commanding them and hardly anything beyond that.

The bright daylight felt beyond harsh to her sore eyes. The empty, desolate street shook her further. There was only a short stretch over to the other building. They entered it where there presumably once had been a wall. The fog thickened and the sick buzz in Gimmick's ears grew louder and more distorted. They entered a room filled with sweltering heat. A long row of captives hung in ropes down the line, all of them at least as bad off as the two new arrivals.

Blood Diamond and Stern Mistress walked to the males in the line. There was hardly any reaction in the countless dull eyes swimming in Gimmick's vision.

– Look at you all, Blood Diamond snarled with contempt. – No more than slabs of meat after the easy slaughter. You disgust me!

Gimmick realized startled that, even though this woman resembled the teammate she had known, she was even more changed inside than she might be on the outside.

Cassandra walked straight to a man and began petting him, grabbed his soft cock and rubbed it. He didn't seem to get it, get anything that was happening.

She slapped him. She whipped him. She slapped him again.

– Look at you, she told the wet rag of a man. – So useless, hardly more than a boy facing a woman.

Her words, strangely enough brought a slight change of expression to his eyes, a modest adjustment of features.

– Ah, there you are. Good boy! Perhaps you will survive the ordeals ahead and gain the honor of further serving your mistress?

The ropes began untangling around the wrists and ankles of the prisoners. Gimmick also felt them loosen around her wrists. Those that had been strung up like slabs of meat collapsed on the floor. Stern Mistress was there instantly, giving them no pause, walking back and forth with her whip until everybody stood or rather swayed before her and the other four members of the Cadre.

– Walk! She snapped.

They obeyed dully. Gimmick and Raven Bird joined them, joined the line. There was the louder buzz and the sicker feeling again, and they were outside, walking through a rough terrain in the wilderness. Gimmick realized startled, dully that they had passed through a portal, possibly for the second time or more. Her thoughts churned even more in her mind and made even less sense.

Their brutal captors drove them through a brutal trail making all wheeze and heave for breath. The prisoners stumbled and fell, stumbled and fell, and quickly lost count of the steps. There were breaks, each time Stern Mistress made another attempt at rubbing a cock. When they failed to please her she punished them harshly. Gimmick almost felt sorry for the men. Almost.

She strived for something, any emotion, anything, in vain.

Numb, she was numb. Only her burning skin felt like anything at all.

Cassandra finally had some success. A cock hardened under her stern guidance, and she brightened visibly.

– You're made of sterner stuff, ain't you? Hey, guys, we finally have a winner here.

He ejaculated all over himself. The eruption seemed to go on forever in Gimmick's eyes. The sick fascination in those watching went double for her, as usual. Cassandra let go of the cock and rose. The man collapsed in tears. The long laughter surrounded them. Lucinda couldn't tell whether or not she joined in.

The march continued. It seemed unending, was unending. Erratic, beyond confusing thoughts kept ravaging Gimmick's mind. She stumbled and fell. The lash bit into her skin instantly. She was up in a whiff. More than once she believed Stern Mistress to be everywhere. The numb fear she saw in everybody's faces seemed to support that conviction.

Raven Bird fell. Gimmick hurried to her and reached out a hand. Raven Bird snarled at her.

– Get the fuck away from me!

Hurt and bewildered Lucinda felt her insides harden further. She kept putting one foot in front of the other with added resolve.

That was days, years ago. Everything just faded away, slipped away from her, the more she reached for it. The wheeze of her breath, the hammering of the heart made her turn deaf and mute. She heard Cassandra and her snarls, though, and the other four's spiteful remarks.

In flashes and glimpses she spotted Lisa's accusing glare, and a growing resentment filled her few aware thoughts.

They had reached indoors somewhere. There was a wall there. It seemed to go on forever, up and to the sides. She saw no end to it, no matter which direction she looked. When she looked backwards the wall was there as well. She swallowed hard and the dull terror kept paralyzing her.

The Rogan brothers grabbed a man and threw him into one of the many holes in the wall. Gimmick looked into the deep darkness and saw no end to it.

She crumbled further, if that was possible. A thousand thoughts raced through her head and none made sense. She crouched on the floor, staring at nothing.

Hooks like claws grabbed her soft, malleable flesh and limbs. They threw her into the deep hole and forgot about her. She was sucked in and down, and she fell. It turned her inside out and she could do nothing but let gravity take its toll.

The narrow tunnel and its smooth, narrow passage and the stark, revolting fear became her entire world. She turned practically catatonic on her way down, down, down.

She hardly felt like anything more than a face in smoke. There was nothing there, except the face with the ugly, inflamed scar and even that slowly dissolved into nothing.

Nothing, nothing, nothing.

Chapter 20

She landed in heat, in bright lights and loud screams turning into more pitiful pleas.

Lightning struck an endless field of flesh and terror in the hall without walls. Men and women with bullwhips welcomed everybody emerging from the tunnels. There were many more of them compared to what Lucinda remembered from above. The bullwhip lashes rained down on all those given birth by the dark and narrow horror behind them. There was no respite from the pain, except the terror itself. A man roared something, but it sounded like unintelligible rabble. His voice still terrified everyone hearing it. Undiluted chaos surrounded them.

Most of the raindrops already lay frozen on the floor, understanding somewhat the unspoken message of the whip, but quite a few still rushed about like confused hens.

A woman appeared. Gimmick stared at her and caught everything about her in one single moment. Her lashes, her golden lashes flowed from her arms, her hands and fingers and feet, strains of pure energy. One woman was hit by one. She froze, seemingly in midair. There was no audible scream. They all saw her become paralyzed, immobile the moment it hit her. Others were hit as they watched. It was like every captive present shared their experience. Lucinda knew she had been struck, just knew it. Pain charged through every fiber of their being. They had believed, in their folly that they knew what that was, but had been as clueless as children the first time they had been punished.

It left no visible mark, but burned the deepest thought.

A scream filled the entire collective consciousness of the infinite hall.

Silence reigned in the hellish place. The giant woman stood there, towering above them. Her very speech made them all turn stricken beyond belief.

– I am Hard Whip, the Green Dragon in the Ebony Goddess' court. You will feel my lash and my wrath.

Green, her tattoo was green.

She gave no orders or commands. There was no need. She was so fearsome that they wondered themselves sick with worry over whom or what could make her voice shake at the mention of the feared name.

Gimmick walked again, equal to all the rest that didn't dare stumble. She realized startled that she recognized the woman, the woman so tall and big and strong, so dramatically changed and such an awesome and fearsome sight and felt sick to the bone. The mere sight of the powerful creature made her gasp in terror and awe.

– Lois! She cried out. – LOIS!

She felt the lash burning her core again, and found herself paralyzed, frozen in amber.

The big creature rushed forward and grabbed her, holding every single piece of her in what felt like the worst of vices. Green Dragon held her, held up the hand with the ring, spitting venom.

– Behold, she cried triumphant, – we have a VIP with us today.

The other's contempt and hatred hit Lucinda and made her even smaller and more reduced in her own mind.

Cruel laughter rose in the air.

– We have two of them.

She held them both up, effortlessly, as if she carried feathers in her hands.

The dull faces surrounding them recognized the ring, knew it for what it was, what it signified. A murmur spread among them.

– They're nothing, of course, no more, no less than the rest of you sorry lot.

Mere close proximity to the giant woman hurt Gimmick, like that of the Catcher, the Whiffer, Sledgehammer, Blood Diamond and Stern Mistress had also done, but one casual glance from the hateful creature made it worse.

The blame in her eyes and thoughts was all too evident. Whatever was left of the old Lois hated her guts. Gimmick moaned in distress, eliciting more of the cruel, raspy laughter.

Lucinda found herself in a cage filled with even stronger, torturous heat, one of many in another hall so big that she could hardly even glimpse the walls. Lisa was there, too, a couple of cages away. Big men and women stood outside the bars, slamming big whips at the floor.

Terror ruled every second of the captives' existence. The very idea of resistance would have felt ridiculous if it had occurred to them in any tangible shape or form.

Fires reached high into the ether-like air, turning the heat up even more. There was not much smoke, but what little there was of it burned their throat.

– You're not prisoners, the fearsome creature with the green dragon tattoo on her exposed shoulder, upper back and arm said, as if spitting something vile. – You do not have that honor. You're lower than worms on the ground, but if you endure and do well for yourself, you will earn your place in our army. You may become a soldier, dying for the glory that is the Ebony Goddess.

Lucinda Patterson spotted only pale glimpses of her friend Lois from half-remembered dreams.

She crouched in the presence of the Green Dragon.

Nude females and males stood like sardines in a box, clutching the bars in sore hands.

Green Dragon smiled.

– You're all dry leaves blowing in the storm. You will have to do far better than that.

There was something in her tone, one more thing cute, clueless, sniveling Lucinda could not grasp.

Eternal minutes turned to hours. The caged bird with the scar beneath her eye imagined that the first day in her new prison was done, and that the night had come. There were no guards, at least no one visible. Hunger pains had long since appeared and departed. There was little or no talk. No one looked at each other, except with stolen glances, at musk-covered skin covered in swellings and blood.

Pens, she thought, it looks more like pens than a prison.

Her thoughts leaked like giant holes, gashes in her mind to the others present. She was one of those without a collar, and she wore the ring, the cursed ring. They glared at her, if their dull eyes could be said to be glaring at all. She would have thrown the damn thing away, if she had believed it would have helped. She rubbed it like a drowning woman, held on to it, stubbornly, spitting in their faces, her resentment growing in leaps and bounds.

Many of them wondered and had questions, even pertinent questions related to their situation, but their dull minds kept them from asking them, even in their less articulate thoughts.

Animals, a man flared a weak thought, animals in cages.

Several of the others nodded, half-witted, bewildered, but aware somewhat. Lucinda's thoughts kept leaking. She had no strength to keep it from happening.

They fell down, more than sat down eventually. There was just enough room for all of them to do that. They sat there bundled close together, doing their best to pull away from each other, unable to do so, clutching their legs, their heads resting on their knees.

Much time had passed. Heads rested on other shoulders and between bars. There was the occasional moan, but no one had the strength or the nerve to move much.

The howls, silent and not, rose from the cages, echoing beyond the dungeons.

Lucinda couldn't puke anymore. There was nothing left there to puke. She frowned, fairly certain, but not positive that she had felt the hunger pangs in her stomach some time ago. It had turned into a ravenous black hole not long after that, and now only the dull pain remained.

No one came. There were no guards, no one visibly watching them. People shook the bars a little for a while, but eventually stopped. Anxious eyes glanced at each other, fearing no one would ever come and that they would be left there to rot.

Minds had become empty holes. Eyes stared straight ahead at nothing.

Then there was something, as a procession entered the hall and approached the cages.

Green Dragon led them. Lucinda didn't try to address her or get her attention anymore. She saw little or nothing of her former friend in the fearsome creature.

– On your feet, Green Dragon snapped. – Your face pushed between the bars. Open your mouth.

They obeyed. The thought of not obeying hardly even occurred to them. All movements felt slow, painful. The teat of a big feeding bottle was pushed into their mouth. They needed no incentive to close their lips around it and start feeding. The lukewarm fluid flowed down their tubes into the hungry maw their stomach had become.

– That's it. Good children…

The bottles were empty. There was nothing more to feed on. They let go of the teat, content, still hungry.

– Look at you all, Green Dragon said pleased. – With most bothersome thoughts removed, the hungry beast stands revealed.

They swayed and stared at her with dazed eyes. The first pangs of pain in the belly began even before the Green Dragon and her minions had left the hall. Whimpers rose from sore throats. Lucinda didn't know time anymore and couldn't tell how much of it had passed, but she sensed very little resistance when the shit began pushing at their asshole. Those resisting at all gave in quickly. Shit flowed down their thighs and down on the floor. Stench filled their nostrils.

Sleep, when it came, in the midst of the stench from shit and body odors hardly felt like sleep at all, but a nightmarish dormancy they could not escape from.

They were fed many more times. She knew that, or imagined she knew it.

There was a time when the doors to their cages were wrested open and they were commanded outside, and more lashes hit their skin. They were marched down a corridor by harsh words and lashes and brutal beatings. There was no mercy, not anything even approaching kindness in the snarling guards surrounding them. One hit by Green Dragon's lash hurt more than all the other put together. It paralyzed them, even as it spurred them on.

They were brought to a large shower room. Ice-cold water hit their beyond sore skin. The marks from the lashes hurt like burns.

– You better rub your skin and rub it hard, Green Dragon shouted. – If we find one dirty spot on you there will be hell to pay. You will be clean as infants, or I swear you will suffer an eternity of pain.

Clean, Lucinda thought. Infants.

The cold water chilled her to the bone. She rubbed herself as hard and fast as she was possibly able, in a vain attempt at keeping warm. She had been warm, had glowed like iron. Now, she felt like a popsicle, an ice-cream served straight from the freezer.

She rubbed herself with the towel afterwards, rubbed herself so hard that sensitive skin turned warm and pleasant. The others walked. She walked with them. There were clothes, uniforms feeling fairly pleasant on the skin.

– You all look so cute, Green Dragon cackled, – like little children dressed up.

The voice, like the rest of her was recognizable to Lucinda somehow, but skewed, distorted in a mirror twisted beyond belief. Something or someone had changed Lucinda's friend almost beyond recognition, into a nightmarish version Gimmick could hardly look at.

The face… the face wasn't really that much changed, but the subtle changes put together were, a horrible, focused wrath very similar to what she had seen and sensed in Franklin, Goddard and the Rogan siblings' faces and minds.

Lois touched her jaw, a light, kind touch.

– You might think me weak because I show you kindness, even this little.

More tears jumped from Lucinda's eyes. She couldn't keep it from happening.

– Kindness is a weapon, just like everything else that may bring you advantages. You will know the truth of my words eventually, like you will all truths.

I don't understand, Lucinda wanted to scream at her, but she stayed silent.

– I know, Lois said softly, – you don't understand, but rest assured: you will! Green Dragon straightened again, towering in her might above her captives.

– YOU ALL WILL

The drilling, the brutal exercise began. They found themselves in yet another giant hall without walls and ceiling. The Drill Instructor's thunderous voice burrowed itself into their head.

– You may have some experience with what you perceive to be hard or harsh exercise. Rest assured that you have never experienced anything like this. You better be prepared for it, or you will fall behind and by the wayside, and you will have no one to blame but yourself, your own *weak,* pitiful self.

The heavy sandbags moved in front of them like meat, gaining the face of an enemy in flesh and blood, a distorted, angry face. They struck and kicked them until their hands and feet felt like raw meat. The gauntlet appearing before them resembled the one Lucinda had experienced during her harder than usual boot camp, but exceeded even that by a mile or ten. There was hardly any respite at all. There was fighting, exercise and uneasy sleep and nothing more. They fed now and then, fed like beasts, and then ran and fought themselves forward once again.

Two rows formed and faced each other. This time Lucinda felt positive there was an actual breathing human being there.

– Fight!

The Drill Instructor bellowed.

Lucinda and the rest did. She struck the face and body she glimpsed in the red mist ahead. A bloody lump of clay crouched in front of her. Not long after that it lay unmoving on the floor. The whip made her stop the attack and pull back. She stood at attention, waiting for the next opponent to attack.

One by one or in lumps the victorious presented themselves.

Two rows, not quite that long reformed.

– Fight!

The next set of bouts began. There was more contact between fists and flesh, flesh and feet. It wasn't hard for Lucinda to fight, wasn't difficult for her to muster the will to combat the lethargy within, to probe and dissect her opponents in the cold light of her skills and experience. She worked herself up and fought with hands hard as steel.

Then, as yet another opponent had been vanquished and crouched on the floor before her, she realized that she had used her telepathy to probe him even deeper, and to make herself even stronger.

Lisa stood before her. The drill instructor cried out his command. The fight began.

Flashes of thoughts flowed into her feverish mind, and she realized triumphant that it didn't hurt. Some of the sickest fear let go of her and a focused beam of rage took its place. She struck Lisa. The pain in her hand felt good. Lisa stumbled backwards. Lisa was angry, too, filled with resentment and spite. Lucinda kicked her in the belly. Lisa fell and hit the floor, hit it hard. Lucinda kicked her in the head. Lisa didn't move. Dark, accusing eyes stared no more.

Lucinda stared at the blood staining the brown skin. She raised her hands above her head, accepting the silent accolade.

The day of training and strife ended eventually. They showered again. Later at night, when they stretched out on their mats in the giant hall, Lucinda wondered what number of night or day this was since their capture, but focus and answers eluded her. She knew Lisa rested on a mat with another platoon a few rows away. They hadn't spoken and didn't seek each other out.

– I'm in PIECES!

A man screamed his banshee wail from the darkness to her left.

Mostly silence blessed them, but on occasion such outbursts disturbed their rest.

No one moved from the mats. It was as if there were bars around them, cold metal they could touch and rub.

The cruel treatment and exercise continued the next day, and the next, and the next and the one after that, until she lost count, totally lost any ability to measure time. There was no day or night, anyway, only the same uneven twilight.

They could be roused from their pitiful sleep and run through the gauntlet, at «night», at any time.

It made no difference. It didn't truly change their circumstances at all.

Lucinda struck the heavy bag in front of her. She kicked, kicked it repeatedly, alternately with left and right foot. There was hardly any pain anymore. The lash hurt when it hit sore skin, but it still felt like a light tap compared to the horrible lashing they received each time they were selected for punishment or when the Green Dragon showed up during their sessions and turned particularly zealous. There was no pattern to it, no method they could use to determine when it would happen.

– Repeat the oath! The instructor spat.

They did so instantly. The choir filled the hall, the vast plains.

– WE ARE THE SOLDIERS OF THE CADRE, THE SERVANTS OF THE EBONY GODDESS. WE LIVE AND DIE FOR HER.

Drums, deep bass drums hammered their ears day and night. Lucinda heard them in everyone's minds.

And then there was the laughter she didn't know was real, that only she heard.

There were more fights, integrated in their training, a whirl of blood and pain. Her hands hurt, her feet hurt, her face and limbs, the entire her hurt.

She spotted Lisa somewhere to the right, or to the left, or straight ahead, or all of the above. Lisa, covered in blood, beat an opponent senseless until her opponent moved no more. Lucinda's nausea and fear and deep-seated terror grew. The wicked brown eyes kept haunting both her dreams and conscious moments.

The opponent before her went down, but it never stayed down, no matter how hard she hammered it. She remembered herself falling and not moving on the floor, unable to tell if she imagined her downfall, her failure, the instructor's harsh words.

Even though she could draw on the experience of her military service, this was worse by far. There had been some lenience there, after all. Here there was none.

Numbers dwindled around her, as unmoving, slaughtered meat was dragged from the fighting arena. She noticed that, even though she wasn't sure, sure of anything anymore. Her hands and feet kept striking the moving meat placed before her. She welcomed the constant rage. Even the headache made her feel grateful, made her repeat with passion the prayers to the unseen goddess they honored.

She woke up one day, on her mat to the sound of the reveille. The rising and standing at attention happened automatically, without any discernible conscious thought.

Then the Chief Drill Instructor marched them off. They followed his sound and commands. Disobedience wasn't really on their mind at all.

They dressed. No other choice remained open to them. The daily routine, the training, the service was the only path imaginable.

She stood at attention again, frowning, not frowning, no more than random thoughts and ongoing confusion.

One female was picked from the line, then another and then Lucinda. The Chief Drill Instructor hardly had to wave to make them a follow him. Obeying a commanding officer, a superior had become second nature.

He brought them to his bedroom. It didn't evoke any particular emotion in the three. They kept staring attentive at him.

– Look at you ugly bitches, he chuckled. – You were probably quite pretty once, but no one looking at you will use such a word to describe you anymore.

It hurt when he squeezed Lucinda's jaw. He wanted it to hurt.

– What a waste, he mumbled and shook his head.

He let go of her like he would something vile.

– Undress! He commanded them casually, so confident in his power. – Display yourself.

They obeyed. Obeying this order was no different from all the others. The last part of Lucinda's military training, the special ops instructions rose to the surface of her mind. She gave him an inviting smile, one that widened when he picked her first.

He put her on her back on the bed and began exploring her body. It hurt, hurt no matter what part of her body he touched. She saw him grow hard and big from the corner of her eye. It affected her. She let it, encouraged it.

– I know who you are, he grunted. – Luck has placed you in my arms and I intend to take full advantage of it.

He slapped her.

– Do you understand, ugly bitch?

Her eyes turned big.

– Yes, that's it, he grinned. – I want you to serve your superior, serve with all the skills you possess. I grant you permission. I, your superior, desire your eagerness.

She felt his arousal. It worked on her. Obeying this order was no different from all the others. He fondled her, made an effort she imagined was unusual. The kiss was rough, demanding. She responded to it without resistance. He touched her below. She released a loud moan and pushed herself at him, at his roaming hand. He chuckled in expectation. Saliva flooded his mouth. One of her breasts turned wet when he massacred it with his tongue and mouth. It still hurt.

He pushed into her, took her as his, possessed her. She waited for the nausea, the vomit, but it didn't come. Her body began responding in earnest. Her mind was filled with a pleasant, excited hum.

Yes, she thought and imagined she sent. Do it. Do it. Do it!

His expectation turned into a triumphant grin.

Easily overpowered by his will she did as instructed and… let go. She snorted in pleasure and pain, something sounding like wails in her ears.

Pleasure exploded in her, and engulfed him and the others. He shouted aloud. The two women released two very distinct moans.

– Wow! He marveled. – The rumors about you weren't exaggerated, weren't exaggerated *at all*.

He pulled out of her.

– This is it, bitch. You're mine, now.

She looked blank at him. He slapped her.

– You belong to me, he stated. – Do you understand?

– I understand, she replied dully.

– I think I will call you Lucy from now on. While you're in my care, you'll be *my* Lucy.

– Your Lucy, she stated, adding a sweet smile to her words.

He chuckled some more, adding to his pleasure.

The other females, clearly excited, clearly aroused beyond desire, practically ran to him when he signed for them both.

He studied and measured the three of them some more, very possessive. There wasn't any visible objection to his invasive scrutiny.

– You gals don't look too bad. Some honest men, myself included even think a few bruises on a woman improve her looks.

They surrounded him, pushed themselves at him, like kittens rubbing their master's legs. The continuous feedback overwhelmed Lucinda completely. She just knelt there, on the edge of the bed, swaying back and forth with the other eager girls.

He pushed her off the bed. She made no effort to stop that, but she landed on the carpet pretty much like a cat, looking up at the man like a dog would at her master.

– Lucy… Lucy will sleep on the carpet.

Lucy… will… sleep. She crouched on the carpet. He began pleasing himself with his delicious companions. Lucy began rubbing herself between her thighs. As his play got more intense, hers did as well.

– This is grand, the man marveled. – GRAND!

Lucy writhed on the floor with open mouth, breathing hard while she scratched and scratched and scratched herself and nothing seemed to be enough. Once again she exploded in pleasure. She sighed content and her eyes slid close. Sleep came to her quickly, but it hardly felt like sleep at all, but like an endless and confusing experience of sensations and powerful emotions, of anticipation and release.

She never stopped breathing hard. When she awoke from her slumber, she was exactly in that state of terror and need, only many times stronger. She gasped, as one nightmare creature in her inner vision gave way to one in her outer. Cassandra, fully dressed, rode the instructor, rode him hard, made him pay for each and every slice of pleasure she granted him. The other girls knelt in awe of the startling sight and Lucy found herself doing that as well.

The man screamed. Lucy knew why. Cassandra scratched him across the chest, drawing blood, and she made him feel the pain a thousand times over. She was that powerful, dishing out pleasure and pain in equal measure. Lucy found herself gasping in an awe bordering on worship.

Feeling contempt for the man the powerful being trashed.

Cassandra was done. She dismounted the poor beast. He was barely conscious, reduced to hardly more than a mire of neurosis in her presence.

– Address me! She snapped.

And the three women had no doubt she meant them.

– Violet Dragon, they choired. – S-superior One.

Violet Dragon snorted, not displeased. The three found themselves relieved to the point of ecstasy.

– Yes, you know the truth, know I'm superior to you, superior in all ways. You let this wreck of a male dominate you, while I handled him with ease.

The light scolding felt like the worst possible and they shrunk to nothing faced with her might.

– That being said, you have clearly shown progress, shown *promise* since your arrival. Your betters have singled you out for advancement, granted you the means to that effect or rather that potential.

There was only the slightest pause, but to those kneeling with their eyes cast down, it felt like forever.

– You will come with me!

They did. She left and they scurried nude after her, exactly like those dry leaves in her slipstream, forgetting the conquered, discarded male they left behind.

Lucinda was hardly aware of the other two scurrying by her side, having all her attention directed at the mighty one leading them through more murky hallways and torture dungeons.

She heard the many screams easily, though, both through her ears and her mind. They kept torturing every shred of her perception.

Violet Dragon smiled at her. At least she imagined she did. Lucinda couldn't affect her with the pain echoing from her self, but her two companions clearly were.

Lucinda frowned, striving to make sense of her own jumbled thoughts, her fractured mind.

– You're on the right track, worm, Cassandra said softly. – Our powers are similar. We both have the ability to drive men insane.

It hurt again when Lucinda touched the superior's mind. Even when she didn't do so actively it hurt. But right now it didn't matter or didn't feel important.

A thin sketch of a smile touched Lucinda's lips.

– There is no brainwashing, no significant such. There is just the relentless hammering and breaking.

She stated. It dawned on her slowly, like an unwelcome thought.

No one seemed to hear her. Her unimportant words fell dead to the ground.

– That bright mind of yours never ceases to work its wonder, does it?

The voice seemed to come from nowhere and everywhere around her. It brought repeated chills down her spine.

Cassandra stood in front of her. Her cold, metallic laughter hurt sore ears and minds. Lucinda dressed. Kitty and Luanne dressed, too.

– Let me have a look at you.

Cassandra surveyed them, like pets, for a while, until she seemed somewhat pleased.

The fabric covering them was of simple quality, denoting their low station. It felt like a giant leap forward.

– That's my girls. You don't look like much, but there is potential there.

They followed her down another dark hallway, one more without end.

– Be advised that you shouldn't see this as a day off. The testing is ongoing and your performance today will not be unimportant in determining your standing among us.

Unimportant, Lucinda thought. Standing.

They reached a quiet eye in the storm. Lucinda sensed something in Cassandra's mind then, a flash of anticipation. Stern Mistress opened a door and walked inside. Her three charges trailed her without thought and more than a superficial awareness, and then, abruptly Lucinda discovered the reason for the dragon's smug grin.

A not very tall and big woman knelt humbly on the floor. Lucinda recognized her dimly, brightly…

Alysse Montgomery.

Cassandra acknowledged her with an imperceptible nod. The almost unrecognizable woman rose with lowered eyes.

– Good evening, Alysse.

– G-good evening, Stern Mistress.

– You will now explain your position here to these three recruits.

The woman straightened, focusing, organizing her response.

– I'm a tool of the Ebony Goddess, her dragons and the Cadre, Alysse recited without pride or emotion. – I'm the loyal servant of the Ebony Goddess, now. She finds me useful and I am grateful for her kind mercy. I'm merely a speck in her space, not worthy of her attention.

Her lips shivered. The impression she made on Lucinda and the others were that of a broken doll.

– Alysse will conduct an examination on you, a physical each week, Violet Dragon told Lucinda, Kitty and Luanne. – Though she's inferior even to you, she may address you and pretend she has worth while doing so.

There wasn't even a trace of condescension in her voice. Alysse and the others shrunk faced with her powerful presence.

– Will you step over here, please, Lucinda? Alysse asked with a voice filled with respect.

Lucinda moved to the examination table.

– Will you please undress and lay down on the table?

Lucinda did so, feeling very good about facing the dull, sniveling creature.

Alysse attached electrodes in wires to various points of her body. The pain brought on by the clips and clamps hardly registered in her mind. Alysse turned switches and pushed buttons. The machines began humming.

– Read my mind, please.

Lucinda did. She saw pieces of what her old enemy had suffered since becoming a thrall of the Cadre. It made her cringe.

A spike rose on the monitor.

– You may stop.

Lucinda obeyed, obeyed the dog, the whimpering dog, aware that it wasn't really the dog speaking, but the powerful voice holding its leash.

The examination, tiring, exhausting kept going. The physical workout, the strength and endurance tests followed the display of mind power. Lucinda read undeniable interest and curiosity in the mind of the mundane standing close to her. She saw the other woman's frown and sensed its equivalent in her mind.

Both women easily noticed the interest Cassandra Rogan showed them.

– Run faster.

Lucinda did, inevitably spurred on by the command, unable to withstand its authority, the treadmill practically fading below her.

– Faster, Alysse snapped.

Lucinda did. A few minutes, a rage of blur later she was lifting weights again, once again pushing herself beyond endurance.

– Use your mind on Kitty. Use it to the fullest.

Lucinda glanced at Stern Mistress, but the Superior One seemed both bemused and involved, and didn't show any desire to put an end to the dog's extended experiments.

Lucinda pushed deep within Kitty, not holding herself back in any way, and felt so good when Kitty froze up by the might invading her.

– You may stop, now.

Lucinda emerged from a daze, her mind sizzling with activity and exhilaration.

Alysse removed the clamps and the clips, pulling back the wires.

– There is nothing special about you. I thought I spotted… an anomaly, but a further investigation brought no solid evidence.

A smile lit up her face.

– I can't help but be fascinated by you, though, dear Lucinda. You actually managed to evade my clutches twice and also managed to trick me when I had you in my care. Well done!

A shadow darkened her smile.

– Alas, it matters not. You're not Gimmick any longer, only yet another lowlife scrounging for survival and finding pleasure in simple obedience. I, myself thought in my folly I was so cruel and so devious, but I was only yet another speck drifting in the Ebony Goddess' vast kingdom. You will make the same discovery, if you haven't already.

She was subdued, timid, brought low by the forces ravaging her. Lucinda sympathized.

– You may dress, she said, all business again. – You're done here.

The others' examination put together didn't last even half of the time Lucinda had spent under scrutiny, but Lucinda's curiosity had been whet, and she studied carefully both Alysse and her instruments during the examination of the other two.

– That's it, then, Cassandra said abruptly. Her charges straightened and stood at attention. It happened so easy, without effort on her or their part. – Now, when the formalities are done, we may move on to the better stuff.

She… enjoyed herself, enjoyed herself so much. Lucinda sense of awe in her presence didn't dissipate for a moment. Power emanated from her in waves.

Her three charges followed the former Jaynagar teacher eagerly.

They entered the giant reception hall, where Lucinda, Kitty and Luanne had arrived not that long ago. A new welcoming party had long since started. Whips hammered at the skin and bodies of those newly arrived. Lucinda spotted Green Dragon, the Catcher and the two Rogan brothers out there, dishing out punishment. She remembered how it had been in flashes and re-experienced the disorientation and fear with a sick revulsion gripping her. Yet another rollercoaster emotional turmoil charged through every single nerve-ending.

The entire stage filled her. She could not keep it from happening.

– Oh, I'm SO in the mood.

Cassandra marveled in a mock resemblance of ecstasy.

Lucinda hardly heard her. She could not take her attention off the horrible sensations unfolding before her.

The events of the reception hall played themselves out in front of her, behind half closed eyes.

There was one man, one creature in particular catching her attention.

He was sobbing, not only in pain but in despair, in desolation and every delicious bleak emotion. He made no attempt at evading the lashes.

She found herself chuckling in scorn.

A light prodding was sufficient. She caught Cassandra's attention and straightened, fear striking her gut.

– That's a good girl, Stern Mistress said pleased. – You move to please me, don't you?

– Yes… Mistress! Lucinda mumbled, shame and self-contempt filling her to the brim.

– They're dogs, aren't they, hardly worthy of our notice?

– Yes, Mistress, Gimmick replied sullenly. – No, Mistress!

– Yes, I thought you would say that. I know you want to give your Mistress a hand. After all, you're not without a certain talent of persuasion yourself. In fact you're world famous for your ability to make a dog's tongue hang out.

She signed for her to follow her.

Gimmick frowned. She didn't get it at first.

– C'mon, Cassandra smiled encouragingly, seemingly endlessly patient, – help your Mistress out here.

Gimmick trailed behind her, to yet another male in the line catching Cassandra's interest.

– Use your wiles on him.

Gimmick looked blank and with a sick expectation at her.

– Yes, with that I do mean all the talents at your disposal, including your mind power. Yes, you've been discouraged from using it, but not lately, right? Know that that you're only discouraged from using it against those high in the Ebony Goddess' favor, and this wretch is hardly that, right?

No, please, Gimmick begged her silently, looking at the poor wretch at her feet with sympathy.

But her confused features slowly changed into an expectant grin.

She knelt down and crawled onto the man's lap, began rubbing and caressing him. He didn't try to prevent her or anything, but only looked at her through his hazy vision. She saw that he wore a collar, marking his powers as pesky, potentially dangerous.

His powers perhaps, but certainly not the man. She curled her lips.

– You've dreamed about me, haven't you? She stated softly.

Yes, you have!

And using her powers again deliberately and poised felt so good.

He was dull and weak-minded. She overpowered him easily, feeling strong and tall in the bargain. He nodded like a boy, a child would do to an adult. She smiled to him and knew the smile filled his mind, all the way to the edges. His cock hardened in her hand and triumph filled her, charged her brought-low batteries to no end. He ejaculated in sudden violent pulls and pushes.

Tears filled his eyes, as he collapsed in deep shame and horror.

– That was pretty darn impressive, Stern Mistress applauded. – How did it make you feel, my pet?

– I enjoyed it, Mistress, Gimmick said, unable to keep herself from telling the truth, to withstand Cassandra's indomitable will, – but he was an easy snack, hardly worth the effort.

And then more tears filled her eyes as well.

Pausing a bit, as if really considering it first Cassandra walked to a girl in the line. Her eyes had recently been filled with tears, too.

– So, sweet Pauline, how did that make *you* feel?

– I didn't feel angry with Scott, if that's what you think, the girl snapped. – It isn't his fault.

– He is a dick and it isn't his fault? Cassandra giggled incredulous.

– I love him, Pauline whispered.

Cassandra's giggle turned to loud, menacing laughter.

– Stupid girl, love is only found in books, movies and poetry. Not in real life.

Pauline broke into tears and crumbled right there.

Stern Mistress signed for Gimmick and Gimmick was there in a whiff, attentive and eager.

– This silly bitch offended me. You will punish her for me.

– She…

Gimmick just stopped, unable to proceed.

– You will punish her for me, or you will take her place.

The imposing figure handed Gimmick the bullwhip and Gimmick accepted it with a shaking hand, one shaking so badly that it could hardly hold on to the handle.

She turned towards the girl.

– No, please, no, Pauline begged her. – I can't take more of this. Please have mercy!

– Mercy?

The whiny creature beneath her did something to Lucinda, made something snap inside her. She brought down the whip on already inflamed skin. Pauline howled like a banshee. Lucinda struck her again.

– Please, forgive me, she choked, – I'm a cowardly and weak-willed bitch.

And then she proceeded to strike her subject that much harder.

She felt herself harden inside, felt the nails dig deep into her palms.

– I've been cast into hell, she snarled. – Unfortunately for you…

Exactly at that word she lash struck Pauline's left breast.

– You've been cast here with me and at my mercy.

She let out a shriek only resembling laughter.

– This is great, Franklin marveled. – We should have sold tickets. Hell, we should have brought a camera and documented it all for posterity.

Pauline tried crawling away. She made one tiny move to that effect, but stopped the moment her tormentor stepped up the pace and strength of the punishment.

– You're mine. Your ass and everything you are is *mine*.

The girl on the ground was nothing but a shaking leaf long before the demon was done with her.

– Scott is your brother, and you fucking love him?

The smile turned wicked.

– W-what? Pauline stuttered.

– Sorry, poor choice of *words*...

The patronizing laughter rocked the girl on the floor, even more than the ongoing physical punishment did.

The lash kept hitting flesh, kept making blood flow, and there was no end to it.

Lucinda stood there afterwards, shaking harder than ever. She held the bullwhip and its lash up like a trophy. Blood dropped in spades from its tip, both on the floor and on the woman with the mad taint in her eyes.

– Now, you know you don't know nothing, don't you? Cassandra whispered into her ear using the grammatical incorrect lingo of the Brewery where she had grown up. – You know that a good teacher can snap her fingers and turn a wayward student around in fucking moments...

– Yes, Miss, she who had been Gimmick replied, sounding like a girl in the early teens having a serious talk-to-talk with her teacher.

– That's my girl. I'll tell you what. You're so good at this that I will let you have the whip for the rest of the day. I expect you to use it often and well.

The word «expect» burrowed into Lucinda's head like a badger through the ground. The teacher signed for Kitty and Luanne to join them and they eagerly obeyed. The two of them received a bullwhip each, and led by Lucinda they charged other newly arrived recruits.

– I knew you would fit right in here, Cassandra cried, her voice thick with triumph. – I just knew it!

The trio rushed into the thickest melee, right by Green Dragon's side. Lucinda felt the first or second or ninth stirrings of arousal, as she rained down her personal punishment on the poor wretches on the floor.

She felt nothing but contempt for them.

Slowly, slowly a state of bliss transformed Lucinda Patterson's face.

The four had a great time watching her. The Catcher in particular enjoyed himself.

– Look at her. It doesn't look like we did a very good job with sorting her out, does it? She's more confused and screwed up than ever.

She heard their condescending voices, shaking in horror and delight every time her malicious lash hit more sore skin.

The cruel laughter kept echoing in her mind and she and it kept falling into the deep and dark pit without end.

Chapter 21

She woke up on the Drill Instructor's carpet again, last night's excess catching up with her in waves.

He looked at her, she knew he did. The self-conscious smile touched her lips again.

There were only the two of them today. The others had been given other assignments. Startled she realized that hers here wasn't quite done. She didn't care. Waves of exhilaration charged through blood, bones and synapses.

She remembered his hands on her hips, his awkwardness when she offered herself to him.

– You think you're something special, don't you?

He had been shamed by her elevation of status, her becoming a favorite of the Dragons. She was very much aware of that fact and it was visible in all her moves and smiles.

– No, Master, I'm just eager to serve, that's all.

She stretched on the floor before him, displaying herself, not really self-conscious in any way, except for the certainty that he was attracted to her, that he desired her.

– You will join me today, he snapped. – You will follow my orders to the latter.

– Of course, Master. I can learn so much from you.

He was great with his charges. She remembered, his commanding voice echoing in her head.

She dressed similar to him, in clothes that were basically various shades of leather. Her hands braided her hair and it felt easy, like an old habit. She smiled to him, her mirror. The smile felt both easy and hard.

They walked the short, long walk to the training hall, where Green Dragon waited for them with new recruits.

Lois nodded curtly to the Drill Instructor. Lucinda kept her head bowed in respect and awe. He managed and was allowed to keep his composure. Lois left without a word, snorting in her contempt for her inferiors.

– You may have some experience with what you perceive to be hard or harsh exercise. Rest assured that you have never experienced anything like this. You better be prepared for it, or you will fall behind and by the wayside, and you will have no one to blame but yourself, your own *weak*, pitiful self.

His words kept burrowing into Lucinda's head.

He nodded to her, clearly giving her the word, deferring to her. She looked startled at him. Pride coursed through her. Her nosedive, girl-like gratitude got to him, she knew that.

– You worthless scum better give us your all, she shouted, – or you will be sorry.

They looked like drowned rats, no matter how dry they currently were. She slapped the closest. He fell.

– AT ATTENTION! She commanded.

Everybody instantly obeyed her.

– That was supposed to be at attention? She chuckled in contempt. – You sorry wretches have a long way to go.

She knew she got to them, knew it in every little glance and thought she caught.

The drill, the brutal exercise began. They were marched, made to exercise beyond exhaustion and made to fight, to conquer their opponents in the most brutal, callous way. She watched them, studied them. He didn't see the imperceptible shaking passing through her, she knew he didn't.

Two hesitated. She instantly went at them, struck them down.

– You will fight, she snarled. – You will beat your opponent senseless. You will learn to fight or your demise will be a fucking kindness.

They obeyed, obeyed her, so scared of her that it overrode any sense of dignity and pride they might have entertained.

– Fight! She screamed at them, her bloody whip striking the floor.

And they did.

– Fight! She howled at them.

And they obeyed her with anticipation and boundless apprehension.

They carried slowly cooling bodies from the arena.

It didn't move her.

Some of them had been beaten slowly to death by zealous opponents.

It didn't move her.

The first long training day ended. She licked salty sweat from her lips. The recruits were allowed a brief respite while they were sized up by the instructors, while they were inspected with cruel eyes. She eyed them all with cold, impassionate eyes.

A woman sniffed.

– Which one were you? She said startled and weary, waiting for the shoe to drop.

Lucinda looked at her, holding back.

– I know you're the doll at the front page of magazines and shit, Pauline Walsingham said. – I knew there was something familiar about you, but I didn't recognize you at first, not under all the *makeup*. But which Crew member were you?

The ring still on her finger, of course still marked her. Lucinda shrugged.

– Who I was doesn't matter. Who I have become does.

One stern look was enough. Pauline crumbled. She knelt and bowed her head in subservience, shaking in fear.

Lucinda walked to her.

– I think I will make you my task, my special project... Will you like that, sweet one?

– Yes... M-mistress, Pauline choked.

– That's a good girl. You will strive to be worthy of that honor, I trust?

– Yes, Mistress! The girl said, determination slowly darkening her eyes. – I want to... want to live and I want to thrive in the Cadre's s-service.

Lucinda slowly clapped her hands in a mock applause.

– You better not fail me, then. Know that I'm not very forgiving in nature.

She left the recruit behind, left her to rot.

It was night. They returned to the man's quarters. She turned towards him with excitement brightening her face.

– Did I do good, Master? I did do good, didn't I?

She threw herself into his arms. He grabbed her and held on to her with invasive, brutal hands. She chuckled pleased, clearly easily aroused.

And she knew she got to him.

– You're such a delightful creature, my dear Lucy.

He spoke with spite, but she heard compassion in his voice and sensed it in his mind.

It slowly dawned on her...

He was free game.

She kissed him, kissed him hard, drawing blood.

– You wildcat, he said hoarsely, – You crazy wildcat!

– I'm known as a great fucktoy, remember...

She whispered in both his ears.

– You take pride in that, don't you?

– I do, she replied coquettishly. – Believe me when I say there isn't a single male superhero I haven't fucked. I was their fucking doormat.

– I bet you loved every second of it.

– I did. She chuckled. – I love big bad men.

She sensed how he bristled with macho pride and hardly anything beyond that. He began fingering with the buttons and zippers of her uniform. She didn't pull away, but pushed herself at him with a drowsy and sensual grin.

– Can you hear them out there?

– Huh?

– Our charges?

He clearly pondered her words and stopped in his task of undressing her. The occasional scream and howls of despair weren't hard to catch, of course, but he knew she heard more than that.

– I can hear them, she stated with a dreamy expression in her eyes. – I can hear their far louder screams. Do you want to?

He realized what she was offering him and a big, expectant smile grew on his face.

– Yes, he nodded eagerly. – Show it to me, show it to me right now!

She reached out with her mind, catching the thoughts of the unfortunates dozing off on the mats out in the hall, and transferred them to him.

His grin widened to an insane degree.

– Your fucktoy is a bitch with many talents, she said with visible pride.

– I knew, he marveled, – but I had NO idea…

Her dazzling smile and enticing thoughts offered him the most exquisite exotic delights.

– Come, she pulled him, – come…

She pulled him into the hall, where a score of destitute and ravaged people writhed in their sleep.

– I feared that many troubled minds would take a toll on me, she said, – but most of their thoughts are calm, hardly a challenge at all. They are adapting well to their new reality, submitting easily to the authority imposed on them. There will be no trouble training and molding them to our purpose.

– Good, he grunted. – Excellent!

He acted tough, but she saw straight through him. She saw him glance at her with worry in his eyes.

– I can practically identify those that will act up even before they do so themselves, she said with confidence in her voice. – Just say the word, master, and I will take care of them for you, take care of them good.

She threw herself at him again, grabbing his hair, giving him long, sultry kisses.

– Do you know a special place, one that can be ours, only ours? She whispered. – Can we go there, please?

She spotted it easily in his mind. He wanted to take her there, wanted it so much, a private place where he could have her all for himself.

He grabbed her and put her on his shoulder and walked off with her. She laughed throatily, amplifying her willingness with her mind, her excited mind. He opened a door to a staircase, a place she had never seen before and climbed it with fast, determined steps. She probed his mind. The place clear in his buzzing thoughts was a place close to the control room, where there was no surveillance. He had taken others there before her.

His cock had hardened and turned harder while she watched, while she sensed, practically felt it between her thighs. He rubbed her cunt, rough, uncaring with his free hand. It excited her. Her mouth stayed open. She was unable to close it.

They reached the small atrium. He put her down.

– Look, he whispered hoarsely in her ear.

She did. There were five windows, openings without glass. She beheld five very different landscapes, a wilderness without walls and ceilings. A sense of triumph and determination rose within her.

– It's so great to finally see the sky, she said softly, putting her arms around his neck.

– Too bad you can't fly, he chuckled cruelly.

– I don't want to fly away…

She kissed him.

– Even though the entire place is eerie beyond words.

– It gives me the creeps, he admitted.

She saw in his mind how it confused and befuddled him, how he could hardly find his way from one section to another. A trickle down her spine spread all over her body.

Her hands and feet moved by themselves, or so it felt, even as she debated with herself, whether or not she should wait, wait it out, find more information before she acted. She struck him and kicked him with accurate, brutal accuracy. He went down. She kicked him in the head. He didn't move.

She used the whip to tie him up and put pieces of clothing in his mouth. Then she made sure he would stay unconscious for far longer than he usually would. A small nip in his mind was enough to put him deep under. She giggled in triumph.

The surveillance room was not far away. She rushed there with a kind of controlled urgency. There was no one there right now and hadn't been for quite some time. The woman on duty had a serious case of indigestion. She rocked on the toilet bowl down the hall and looked like she would remain there for a long time.

Lucinda studied the screens, studied them to what felt like exhaustion, going through the system countless times in her mind, her overactive mind, almost forgetting the woman rocking in pain and suffering on the toilet bowl.

The images didn't seem to make sense. There was no repeating pattern, as if everything was changing randomly, as if nothing was ever the same from one camera pass to another. Lucinda frowned, feeling the fear, the distress

376

grow, slowly pacifying her. She returned to the room with the five windows, chose one and attempted to walk through it. She was stopped by something that seemed like a solid wall. A buzz resembling electricity sent a shockwave through her body. She chose another window, threw herself at it, and the shockwave increased to a level paralyzing her. She fell to the floor. The pain made it hard for her to move. She stayed there unmoving for a time she couldn't measure, and the haze didn't lift from her mind.

Then the determination and growing fury returned. She rose and left the room. It wasn't that long to the stairs. She rushed down and forward, and returned to the bedroom she had «shared» with the «instructor». A thousand thoughts charged through her. She strived to focus, to think through everything calmly, using her analytical mind. The plan she had formulated half-conscious earlier proceeded apace. She broke off the legs on the bed with quick kicks and pulls. A little fine-tuning and she had four clubs at her disposal. She returned to the hall where the new recruits slumbered on the mats. All of this, the fast walk, felt longer than it actually was, or so she fervently hoped. She felt like she moved through mud and fought against the hopelessness threatening to overwhelm her.

Come with me!

Pauline Walsingham woke up groggy, her consciousness subdued by an imposed haze. Lucinda did that, she knew she did.

You will not speak. You will come with me.

Pauline's response was confused, disorganized, nothing like the trained minds of Melinda and Lisa.

The brief notion of Lisa faded like a bad memory left behind.

You will guard me, guard me with your life.

Yes, mistress, came Pauline's garbled, humbled acknowledgement.

Lucinda gave the girl two of the broken-off legs.

Pauline walked in front, like a shield, her hands clutching the wood.

We're getting out of here.

Yes, mistress, yes.

Lucinda smiled.

The hallway they, she and her bitch charged through shifted and burned in her senses, her increasingly acute senses. She sensed others in the hallways and halls around her. They moved in her mindscape, like they moved in her physical surroundings. There was no sign of them being aware of the two of them, no pattern suggesting that they knew of the escape-attempt. She couldn't read their mind, but keeping tabs on them wasn't too hard, or it wouldn't be if she didn't also need to keep her bitch properly attached on her leash. The iron-hard focus made sweat cover her forehead far more than the run.

They ran through the maze, one Lucinda could practically see in her mind, never clearly, but well enough. She knew when to stop, when to turn. They stood by a corner as a patrol passed them in a hallway close by, focusing on keeping their breathing even. Five seconds passed, ten, thirty, two. They moved on.

The insane choir of the recruits rose from a thousand throats as they marched, filling their already delirious minds. Lucinda saw two pairs of sentries moving towards them from opposite directions. The retreat was closed off.

Ready yourself, she told the bitch.

The bitch's tongue hung out in eager anticipation.

Charge!

They jumped the two sentries from behind, hammering them with the wood in their hands. Two bloody and battered pieces of flesh and bones fell to the floor. Lucinda and her tail ran on.

An empty hall opened up to them, imposing itself on Lucinda. There was one single door at the opposite side. She sensed the people, more than two people coming from behind, chasing them, the image of the other, battered sentries fresh in their minds. No alarm yet, at least no loud alarm. Lucinda and Pauline reached the next empty hall.

Wait here, Lucinda imposed on the girl, nudging her with her mind, awakening her rage. When they come... Charge! Kill and maim. Fight on to your dying breath.

Pauline stopped. Lucinda, with a sense of pride continued. She was about half across the hall when the group of sentries entered and Pauline attacked them with a vicious snarl. Lucinda ran on, turning her eyes forward, even though her mind, at least partly remained with the fight. Pauline, catching them by surprise decked two of the sentries. Lucinda charged into a third empty hall. Pauline decked the third opponent, even as two others used their powers on her simultaneously. It was as if she was pushed into the air. She flew across the room and hit the wall hard and fell to the floor like a wrecked doll.

Lucinda broke the connection then and ran on, fled the fastest she was able.

There was a new room, and then another, and another. Each new space she passed through was different from the previous, different enough to know that it wasn't the same, only similar, an endless row of rooms lined up before her. No matter how many she breached, there was always another to take its place. Confusion and bewilderment added to itself as it kept getting harder to keep track of those chasing her. Breathless and with a hammering heart she kept chasing forward.

Six, there were six chasing her. She sensed them, sensed their eagerness, the saliva flowing in the hounds' mouth. Her mind, in a desperate move cast forward made her feel a cold dread. There was something there, to her left, something very familiar and horrible. She chose the right door. The moment she threw herself through it she glimpsed herself through the eyes of the hounds. She rushed on to the next door, more than wondering, in her despair, her desperation how big this place could possibly be.

They gained on her. Her fear didn't lie. She tried attacking them with her mind. They weren't impervious to it, like others had been, but she still was unable to affect them in any meaningful way.

She was less than half across a hall when they appeared behind her. Her mind worked overtime. She knew she had to do something, do something soon.

A tall woman entered the room, a creature from Gimmick's worst nightmares.

The six froze and fell on their knees, sore afraid.

– What's the *meaning* of this?

Gimmick, seeing her chance kept charging forward, keeping herself on autopilot to keep herself from crumbling, realizing that this was indeed the creature from her most horrible dreams. The woman didn't stand in the doorway, but had stepped well inside the room, leaving a chance for Gimmick to reach behind her and charge further to freedom.

The creature just stood there, smiling, snarling. Lucinda wanted to stop and crouch in fear, but kept charging forward. She feigned one direction, feigned another, and then made her move.

The tall, powerful figure, moving fast as lightning caught her easily, clutching her throat and lifting her up so their faces were on the same level. A numbing, horrible pain shot through Lucinda, something beyond paralysis. She hung in the grip of her nightmare, totally unable to even defend herself.

She choked and began shaking, scared like a small child.

– You really believe you will be able to escape, don't you, from a high-security facility like this one, like in the comics?

Gimmick's reply came slowly, delayed by fear and the horrible physical pain.

– W-why are you d-doing this, Eleanor?

The beyond chilly laughter turned her deaf, blind and mute.

– Eleanor, huh? You believe me to be sweet, vulnerable Eleanor? I always thought you were the smart one, but I guess I was wrong about that, too, like I was about many things.

Something dawned on Gimmick, something she still couldn't grasp.

– Let me put this in very succinct terms, dear child, in ways you can't help but understand: There's no way you could have escaped from this place. No matter how many rooms you had escaped from, there would always have been another to take its place. I could have let the scenario with your hopeless fight with my underlings play out, of course, but I have other plans for you. And no one is allowed to defile my temple. Everyone doing so will pay, and you will pay, my dear Lucinda.

Lucinda's eyes widened. There was something in the way the regal woman said her name, something hauntingly familiar. She wasn't Cougar, wasn't Eleanor, but…

– J-jolene!

The icy laughter once more cut through Gimmick's flesh and bones and numb mind.

– You would have known that instantly if you had used your mind power, but you didn't. You have learned your lesson there, like you will in all things.

She had changed, both mentally and physically, but it was her, beyond the demonic appearance, the beyond cruel and frightening mind. Gimmick, in her incredulity and paralysis shrunk in her mighty presence.

What had been Jolene Masters, had been Oracle, turned towards her underlings. Gimmick sensed their fear, their rapture without trying.

– You may take your leave, now, she told them.

An expression of infinite relief lit up their faces.

– Thank you, My Goddess, the man in front, the leader of the pack cried.

– HAIL THE EBONY GODDESS, the other five cried.

Then the six, in a brutal, shift move slit their own throats. They fell and bled to death there on the floor.

Nauseous and sick to the bone Lucinda Patterson stared through a thick fog of pain and horror at the woman that had been her friend. Instantly another level of pain fired through her. Her scream was like that of a little girl.

– You don't look at the Ebony Goddess, except when given her explicit permission. Do you understand, worm?

– Yes, Gimmick cried, mumbled with her weak voice.

The Ebony Goddess carried her away, like she would a feather. It hurt, every part of her hurt, and the pain was growing. Each new move the Ebony Goddess made hurt more.

They entered a room, one totally disorienting to Gimmick's senses, to all her senses. It was like the very air there started burning her the moment she was carried across the threshold. A succession of ongoing bright and ghostly blinking, stroboscopic lights practically blinded and paralyzed her.

– Welcome to my Domain, Gimmick. You will be spending some time here, in preparation of your glorious future life in your Goddess' service.

– Never, Gimmick mumbled, hardly audible.

There was no laughter this time, but its icy properties still echoed in her broken mind.

Jolene held her up. Ropes, resembling roots grew from the ceiling and the floor and tied themselves around her wrists and ankles. They felt like hot iron penetrating every cell in her body.

– It hurts, Lucinda howled. – It hurts BAD.

– You don't know hurt, Jolene snarled at her. – You don't know anything about the exquisite pleasure of pain yet, but trust me: you will!

The abused little girl stared at the adult towering above her.

– Why are you doing this, Jolene? She whimpered. – What *happened* to you?

– In a glimpse, a tiny glimpse lasting forever I saw the world, as will you, sweet Lucinda. Your eyes will open so hard that it hurts beyond hurting, and then you will know.

There was something there, something about her wording striking a chord within Gimmick.

Then she got it. Another, equally horrible thought struck Gimmick, like a whip, like tendrils of ice.

– My God…

– What's that, my child?

A clawed hand rubbed the prisoner's cheek, tenderly like a kitten's tongue.

Gimmick looked down, sullenly, with an unending expression of shock and horror in her face.

– We… altered you, Lady Grace and I, changed your perspective towards a more… authoritative leaning, to make you change your view on the protests. I didn't w-want to, but I couldn't say no to her.

– I know. More icy laughter flowed from the snarling mouth.

– You… *know?* Lucinda said perplexed.

– Oh, I didn't at first, not until I had truly changed for the first time, hours after I had inadvertently pointed the finger at poor Eleanor. Then I could easily see through such meager deceptions.

A shaking Jolene Masters stood in the hallway of the Old Brewery building, recovering from the abuse visited on her by Chuck Storm and his henchmen. There was what sounded like a crack somewhere, a ripping of flesh. Her face suddenly twisted in rage, in a matter of seconds, or what seemed like that, she grew in body and mind into a new and beyond fearsome creature.

– I'm sorry, Lucinda choked. – S-sorry!

– Don't be sorry, sweet Lucinda. – You shouldn't be mad at yourself. I'm not mad at you.

– You're n-not?

– Of course not! You did me a huge favor, aiding me in my transformation, helping me see my true nature. How could I be mad at you? I'm actually going to return the favor, by aiding you in your change. That's what we do here, you know, showing the potentially worthy who they truly are.

The icy, wicked laughter didn't let up in Lucinda's ears, never ever.

Gimmick wanted to say more, say something, anything, but her throat constricted in her despair and sorrow and she was unable to utter even a single sound.

– You doubt. The Ebony Goddess chuckled. – That is natural and even right at his point, but soon enough you won't and you will sing your Goddess' praise like all my other subjects.

The chuckle turned louder, menacing again.

– Do you know I actually made the Catcher's collar malfunction when I touched it? I didn't realize I was doing it at the time, of course, just like I didn't know I was wrong about Cougar, but it certainly adds even more irony to everything, doesn't it?

Gimmick caught a glimpse of something moving, of something reminding her of a hose growing from the floor. It had teeth and a mouth and tiny eyes. Lucinda yelped in fear. Then, in a swift charge it attached itself to her belly and began gnawing away at her flesh. The scream was so loud that it shook the room.

– You will need no further nourishment in here. I, your Goddess and All will provide you with everything you need to survive and thrive, and when I, in time come and fetch you, you will be ready for your next lesson, your further education on your path to serve in the Ebony Goddess' eternal Court.

The demonic creature left her lowly servant alone.

Lucinda tried, she did, tried to pull free of her bonds, but the moment she did the creature in her belly snarled and began feeding on her flesh.

There were no more screams. The pain had gone far beyond that right now.

The entire room… Jolene's presence was everywhere, slowly invading Lucinda's very being. The girl didn't resist. She had no more strength left. Other individuals made themselves known to her, but they were mere shades, specters of what they had been. She couldn't see them, only sense them, as ghostly remains of Jolene's beyond almighty power.

– No, please, Lucinda whispered. – Please, no. Please, please, please

How many times she repeated the word she couldn't say, couldn't tell time from its absence when it only existed within her and the room.

The fever ravaged her. Non-existence ravaged her.

The next days and nights and unrelenting time flowed into one, unending nightmare, with moments of cruel, lucid awareness.

There were realizations and the Goddess' teaching pervading her being.

So many things dawned on her, becoming clear as they burned through her ashen mind.

Yes, Lucinda, the voice of the non-present Ebony Goddess replied to her. I am a creature of Shadow, transcending all time, all space. My Might is indeed behind the malady befalling you and your former comrades lately. My power, all its aspects has grown to a razor's edge. I am everything you sense, both material and not.

The other prisoners, the other creatures made in the image of the Ebony Goddess made themselves known to Gimmick only in weak flashes. They were hardly more than ghosts to Lucinda, like she probably was to them. This *was* the Ebony Goddess, her mind, her reality, her universe. Only she was tangible here.

A tall and big man hung in the tangled web like she did, crying out his terror, like she did. A woman, broken and neutered joined them. The wailing became a choir of despair and horror.

Jolene stood in front of her or seemed to, but she was truly everywhere, also in Lucinda's increasingly dull and tormented mind.

– This is merely the Maverick Crew's philosophy of Order and regimentation taken to its logical conclusion, you know that, don't you, child.

– Yes, Lucinda choked.

And then, sometimes during a period of painful peace, the snarling, all-present voice would hiss at her.

– I counted on you and you *failed* me, Lucinda. You were well under way to free yourself from being under Claudia's thumb, but she easily reeled you back in, didn't she? She just twisted her finger a little bit and you returned to her fold like the child you are. I gave you a change to fix everything, to crush her like the bug she is, but you blew it.

The girl hardly remembered anything, hardly recalled herself. She had become a part of the room, of the sentience surrounding her like a viper. There were hardly any thoughts, and no one not being a part of the omnipresent presence in her existence.

Seconds passed, years flowed like water, as everything she was, was digested and spat back out time and time again.

Jolene entered the room. Decades of nothing became *something*, a hope hanging by a thin thread.

– Hello, Lucinda.

Gimmick looked at her through hazes, eternities of pain, slowly ascending, to a point from the nightmare her life had become.

– What is this place? She cried in a moment of misunderstood bravery.

Pain shot through her, far worse than before, unimaginably worse than before. She screamed and kept screaming, as the unrelenting pain ravaged her.

When she had screamed her throat raw she still kept going. It *hurt*. She had never before felt anything even resembling such pain. Hours, days, weeks of torment suddenly didn't count.

It finally let up. She looked at the tall, regal woman through flowing tears, with the begging eyes of a child that had been punished forever.

– *Hello,* Lucinda.

– H-hello, Gimmick gasped, unable to resist the command, the powerful will of the other.

– That's so much better, Jolene said pleased. – Isn't that *so* much better?

– Yes, Lucinda replied numbly, her breathing staying labored, her eyes staying wide, like open wounds.

She shook and couldn't keep herself from shaking.

– This is my place of power, Jolene boasted, not boasting. – There is no mote of dust here I don't control.

One of the large hands touched the bloody, tear-stained face. A claw raked the cheek, creating a long, red line.

– You've never encountered anyone like me before, have you, never been exposed to the cold, hard reality beyond your rosy fantasy world.

It was clearly a rhetorical question. Lucinda didn't speak. She struggled to think, to reason through the dark, muddy waters her mind had become.

– So innocent, Jolene spat, – so weak.

– I'm not weak! Lucinda cried out with her nearly gone voice and absent mind.

A clawed hand instantly grabbed her jaw. Lucinda went away again. It wasn't exactly pain this time. It was worse. She felt as if hot glowing iron was pushed slowly through every piece of her body and couldn't even scream. Her vision faded. A loud, low sound drilled a hole through her head. She couldn't breathe. There were no more thoughts, only suffering, agony and torment. Those things had become her entire reality, and she couldn't sense herself anymore.

She slowly came to, regaining a semblance of self, but she had no control, not over her limbs or even her thoughts. Lips shivered. The muscles in her face, too, were never truly settling. Jolene's demonic face was all she could see.

– We will now establish the ground rules between us. Jolene spoke softly, almost kindly, making the captive shake that much harder. – From this moment on you will never speak up against me. In fact you will never, ever contradict me in any way. There won't be any kind of rebellion, not in your mind and certainly not in any outward manner. An attitude, disrespect towards your betters may have been acceptable in your old life, but that is gone. You're nothing but a lowly servant of the Cadre, now, my servant and your only ambition is to serve with duty and dedication. Tell me, child, are you now ready to behave, to accept your new life?

Lucinda nodded. She wanted to speak, to convey her eagerness, to declare her undying loyalty to the woman towering above her, but was unable to do so.

– You're such a sweet child, so eager to learn, and rest assured that you will.

The ropes pulled back, seemingly removing themselves from Lucinda's swollen ankles and wrists. The hose buried in her belly dissolved. She stood before Jolene with a bowed head.

– Give me your ring. You won't need it anymore. It is the final tie to your past.

She obeyed, quickly pulling it off the finger, giving it away to the terror towering in front of her, and she knew once again that the Ebony Goddess had spoken the truth.

– Undress! You're truly nude, anyway, a newborn, eager to learn the world's secrets.

Lucinda removed what scant rags remained of her instructor uniform.

– Now, that was so much better, wasn't it?

The woman previously known as Oracle made a fist around the metal containing pieces of her body.

– Yes, Jolene, the girl sniffed.

– You're lucky I took a special interest in your case. Your future will indeed be that much brighter because of it.

Lucinda panted a bit, frowning, both worry and curiosity written on her swollen face.

– Ah, you're curious, aren't you? You want to ask me a question?

The girl nodded.

– You may do so.

– W-why the s-special interest?

Jolene chuckled, a dark and terrifying laughter.

– Well, it certainly wasn't for old time's sake or even for the great service you rendered me. You kind of pointed to yourself, of course, with your daring, though silly escape attempt. But the truth of the matter is that I would have come and fetched you to my court anyway. You may be the key, or one of them, if you're *worthy* to bring all the important aspects of the superhuman community under the Cadre's control. The superhuman, and thereby the *world*. There aren't that many telepaths around and even though you've clearly squandered your talent, you will become a powerful and terrifying weapon under the Cadre's tutelage and stern guidance.

Worthy, stern guidance… the words kept ringing through Gimmick's befouled mind, and she couldn't stop herself from shivering.

– On your knees, The Ebony Goddess spat. – On your knees, and beg your favors at your Goddess' feet.

Lucinda obeyed instantly. It didn't even occur to her to disobey or even resist. Not for a moment. She bowed her head, her broken soul.

– You will serve me, then? Serve me unquestionably, eagerly and beyond dedication?

It was another rhetorical question, but one clearly expecting a reply.

– YES, MY GODDESS, the broken creature shouted through snot and blood and haze.

– That's a very good girl, but nothing compared to how good you will become when you're fully trained and groomed and have gained your fated position.

The Ebony Goddess smiled her thin smile.

– Come child, come, my daughter, and we shall continue your education, begin it in earnest.

Gimmick didn't raise her head, didn't speak up or react in any visible way, but Jolene still noticed. A sick, revolting fear coursed through the girl.

– Yes, you *are* my daughter. I've just released you from my womb, into the world, and I will raise you and teach you everything, and you will be an astute and devoted child, until you, if you're worthy can take your place by my side as one of my queens and kings of the world, one of the High Ones executing the Goddess' will, one of her mighty dragons.

Her mighty dragons.

– Yes, My Goddess, Lucinda whispered.

Jolene laughed again, a sound of a knife razing metal.

– Look at you, so timid, so broken, but you shouldn't despair, you really shouldn't, or you'll fall behind by the terrible forces ravaging you, and you will be useless to me. Come, my child, and I'll take you further on your path to Glory, where you eventually will, if you're *worthy* grow into a proud and mighty woman in my service.

The tall, imposing creature turned, disregarding what she left behind like yesterday's waste. Lucinda knelt there shaking, slowly, slowly curling her hands into fists, standing up on her feet and trailing the creature into the hall, down a long hallway stained with blood.

Jolene stopped outside a door, turning towards the smaller figure, touching her cheek again, one of the claws raking her other cheek, creating a mirror image to the one on the opposite side.

– Beware, my daughter. The fact that I personally bring you, that I've marked you will bring you some initial respect, but only to a point. Many of my daughters have turned out to be a horrible disappointment to me, and you will have to be at your best and strongest and cruelest to survive the upcoming trials, but know that I have faith in you.

– Thank you, the girl mumbled. – Thank you, Mother.

And saying those words, admitting them to herself, didn't feel strange or bad at all, but like the greatest joy imaginable. The slow smile transformed her face.

The big doors opened. Gimmick stepped through and died. Everything turned pitch black.

Chapter 22

She stepped into a bright room, fairly small, without furniture or anything, with naked walls and floor. A red light was glowing on one of the polished white walls.

Two people sat with their backs to each wall, one very big and stocky man and one average big girl. They wore clothes or at least rags, even though they didn't hide much.

Lucinda sat down with her back to the third wall. A casual peek told her a lot about the thoughts of the other two. She didn't probe, did little or nothing that could make them aware of her insidious information-gathering.

– Nice scars, the woman said and smiled wickedly, not even attempting to appear benevolent.

– Thank you, Lucinda said in exactly the same, composed and wicked voice.

Another man stepped into the room. He looked visibly nervous, even scared. He sat down by the fourth wall.

The white light flickered a bit, as another door opened.

A young girl wearing no collar, but the marks of the Goddess on her cheeks stepped inside. She looked even worse than Lucinda felt and her thoughts were just as much in turmoil.

No one here wore collars. The significance of that was not lost on Lucinda.

The girl stopped right inside, glancing around, looking at how everybody seemed to cover the entire wall where they sat.

– You may sit with me, Lucinda offered.

The grown woman smiled as she glared at them both in contempt. Lucinda ignored her.

She turned towards the girl, brushing off wet hair from her sweaty face and eyes sore from too many tears.

– What is your name?

– Adriane, the girl sniffed.

Lucinda put an arm around her and pulled her close. Adriane rested her head on Lucinda's shoulder.

The light changed from red to green. The girl bit her lip. She was clearly, visibly distressed.

Lucinda chuckled wickedly. She couldn't keep the laughter from rising to the surface, where everybody could hear it.

– Ugly girl has a sense of humor, the big, stocky man spat.

She still hung suspended in the Ebony Goddess' grip, her domain. The voice kept droning on in her mind, doing so in such a way that she wasn't confident that it wasn't in her ears as well.

Five people enter, one leaves.

Five people enter, one leaves.

Five people enter, one leaves.

Five people enter, one leaves.

Five people enter, one leaves.

The others heard those words, too, in one way or another. She knew it brought a big smile to the big brute's face. He might have been a nice man before he had been captured and pulled into Jolene Masters' cruel grip, but he was so no longer.

— It does sound like a bad joke, she mumbled.

She half expected the brute to speak up, but he didn't. He was a sly brute.

His mind was filled with confusion and hatred and brutal fantasies. She saw all three females in chains before him in his mind, similar to dogs with their tongue hanging out, and himself, the superior male standing above them with a whip in his hand.

— Not in the world as it is, honey, the woman said with a snarl of a smile.

Lucinda knew she was shaken to her core, too, like everyone here, but she was very good at portraying a cool exterior.

— It is insane here, the girl blurted out.

— And this is news, how? The woman said.

— They r-raped me, and tortured me, the girl mumbled, in a weak attempt at shouting.

— Of course they did. You are the enemy. One is cruel to one's enemies. Whether or not that situation will change is entirely up to you.

The girl crumbled further in Lucinda's arms.

— I guess you loved spreading your legs, then? Lucinda said casually, fighting to remain calm, to not direct the stab of pure hatred she felt at the woman.

The woman didn't voice any reply, but if stares could have killed Lucinda would have been nothing more than a wet spot on the floor.

The five measured each other, glanced at each other even when there was no direct line of sight. Tension struck Lucinda like a thousand tiny knives, and she made no effort at keeping it contained. She watched how the other four shook like rag dolls. The girl by her side shook particularly bad. She seemed out of place here. Lucinda quelled the stroke of pity.

You have powers, right?

Adriane looked nonplussed at her.

Lucinda smiled at her, comforted her.

I can read minds.

The girl's face brightened in shadow. She giggled inside.

– Oh…

Yes, she replied garbled. Deadly. I can cut p..pl… am a deadly, deadly bitch.

Good, good, we can use that to increase our changes.

– You look so much like my sister, she whispered in the girl's ear. – We will get out of this, the two of us.

Adriane looked at her with gratitude and hope in her eyes and mind.

– Compassion is a weakness, the outspoken woman spat with a grin.

Lucinda and Adriane ignored her.

We must take out the big man, Lucinda told her. He's the only real threat here. Can you do that, sweetie?

… deadly, deadly bitch, Adriane confirmed.

Lucinda petted her on the cheek.

And so very, very useful, Lucinda both sent and whispered to her.

Adriane smiled.

There was a sound, then more sounds from the wall. The five turned even more attentive. Smaller holes opened and something was thrown through them. Pieces of meat landed in front of everybody.

Only one in front of Lucinda and Adriane.

Lucinda's stomach rumbled.

– You eat it, the girl shrugged. – I'm not hungry.

Lucinda hesitated only briefly before grabbing the raw meat and devouring it. The sound of eager chewing filled the room.

Good dogs, Lucinda thought. Very good dogs.

Adriane inevitably caught the shame filling her. The girl rubbed her cheek in a comforting gesture.

Jolene's hell returned to her being, never having left. She whimpered in the unending horror her existence had become. Her lips hardly felt the teeth biting her lip. She savored the taste of blood, not only in her mouth, but all over her body, in her total surroundings.

– Everybody will do what I say in here, Big Strong Man stated with a silent snarl, – and we will all be fine.

– You must be kidding me, the other man responded, very patronizing, clearly meaning it as an insult.

The hostility in the room lingered in the very air between them. Lucinda savored it, tasting its pleasant flavor.

Eyes stayed wide open. It didn't matter. The nightmare stayed with them, like a constant, never leaving them for a second.

Lucinda experienced the first pangs of pain in her belly. The soreness in her butt followed shortly afterwards. Her mouth opened in frustration and distress. She let herself fall to the side. The feces rolled out of her arse.

– That's gross! The woman groaned in disgust.

But there wasn't much confidence or conviction in her voice when she spoke.

Adriane pulled down her pants and released her soft shit.

The two men relented well before the woman surrendered to her immediate and inevitable urges.

The stench filled the room and Lucinda's self again, what was left of it. She frowned, realizing how little it meant to her. It was like a trifle, a slight disturbance on her surface hardly touching the filthy water soup below.

She saw herself half crouching there on the floor, forming her fingers into claws. It was just in her mind, but it felt so real.

Mind floated away, even as mind remained as sharp as the most dangerous blade. Confidence, brittle confidence assured her that the others weren't aware of her intrusion into their thoughts. The unseen smile didn't waver on her lips.

She blinked. It hurt. Skin against skin hurt. Her awareness flowed slowly up and down, very much like she had always envisioned a dry leaf in the wind. She heard insane music from somewhere. It hurt her ears.

The music, coming from one of the other rooms, or from nowhere at all mixed with Jolene's wicked laughter. Lucinda shook her head. Adriane looked at her with compassion in her eyes. Her thoughts and emotions leaked. Lucinda knew that. She couldn't keep that from happening. She focused on keeping them somewhat contained, on isolating what she most of all needed to keep hidden.

There was no new sweat on her brow, she knew that.

A lot of old stains of just about anything, but not that.

She stretched her body, her mind, touching the firmament surrounding her. Jolene, the Ebony Goddess or at least her essence was everywhere. She always had been. Lucinda shook, a shaking she could not quite hide.

It's alright, she told Adriane. I'm alright.

The big man's knowing grin enveloped her. She wanted to make fists, but held herself back.

She almost drowned in Adriane's volatile mind. It was a mess in there, an insane muddle Lucinda could not quite penetrate.

Time rolled slowly, so slowly, no matter the very evident tension.

They dozed off. At least they feared they did. Lucinda shook as she opened her eyes wide again, uncertain if she had ever closed them, unable to recall yet another bout of horrible dreams.

– I guarded us, Adriane stated solemnly. – Guarded you.

– Thank you, Lucinda praised her. – Thank you so much.

She kissed her brow again. The girl pushed herself even closer to the older girl, the more experienced woman. Lucinda managed, with an effort to contain the wicked laughter rising from her throat.

Adriane slept. Lucinda held her in her protective embrace. Time seemed to be sleeping as well. It didn't move, as far as Lucinda could discern, but stood unmoving at the base of a long, steep climb. It grinned at her, shook her to pieces with its laughter.

Her awareness spiked instantly. She masked her reaction to it, fighting to keep her iron-hard focus, to distance herself from the ongoing chaos boiling her brain. It didn't let up for an instant.

Weak!

The voice in her head hissed.

She felt like she was clutching her head, but in truth she wasn't. Her hands rested in her lap or around Adriane's neck. She heard the almost unnoticeable noise from the outside immediately. The others heard it, too, the sound of the feeding doors being unlocked. Everybody tensed.

The pieces of meat began hitting the floor. Lucinda jumped forward and grabbed the meat in front of her. There were only three pieces this time. Lucinda knew that would be the case before she saw it unfold, and she wondered if she stayed in contact with the time lord's mind, if she always had.

The other woman grabbed her piece.

The two men stared at the remaining meat, what seemed like a huge, juicy piece. The big man went for it first, or so it seemed. He was fast, fast, too, totally catching the other man off-guard. It happened with such speed. The other man went for the food. The big man went for the other man's neck, and broke it like a twig.

The surviving man remained there, at the center of the floor, sitting on the other, unmoving body.

– You know, he drawled. – I don't think they'll object too much if I bring three sweet slave sluts with me out of here.

He was big and imposing and big and powerful. They shrunk in his presence.

Air wheezed from the dead body, an event sounding almost like a blowing of a trumpet.

Lucinda took the raw meat and tore it in two and gave one half to Adriane.

– Feed! She insisted.

After a brief hesitation Adriane did, and Lucinda began feeding as well. The other woman had already begun.

– You better be accommodating, the Man stated, filled with expectation and confidence, his ability to prevail.

Lucinda devoured the red meat in what to her resembled a frenzy. Adriane did her best to emulate her, so trusting.

– You, big fat slut, come here. Bring your girl!

It was a command. She rose, stretching her arms above her head, displaying herself further. Adriane mirrored her movements, but with far more evident anxiety. Lucinda began performing, not too fast, not too slow, just enough to make him impatient, but not too impatient. His cock hardened and pushed against the fabric of his uniform. Lucinda closed and opened her eyes.

She relived the man's fast, deadly moves. His power wasn't just the added strength, but indeed an increased speed as well. She made the final two steps into his reach, slipping unresistingly into his grasp.

– Oh, you're a peach, alright, he growled, his voice coarse with expectation.

He signed for Adriane to come to him, too, and she did, choking constantly, as if she had trouble breathing.

Lucinda smiled seductively to him, unable to hide her discomfort, her apprehension.

He chuckled, a wicked laughter cutting into her.

She unbuttoned his uniform. He tensed when she pushed it down from his shoulders, locking his arms, or at least making him momentarily vulnerable. She kissed him softly. He slapped her. Her mouth was filled with blood. She kissed him again, so grateful for his show of affection.

– That's all it takes, he bragged. – Slap a bitch around and you show her who's in charge.

Adriane helped out coaxing the clothes off his bulky body. He grabbed her uniform by the collar and tore it open in front. She made no effort to conceal her revealed breasts.

Lucinda felt the questions burning in her mind. She did her best to calm the anxious girl, to make her sit back and wait. Eyes met eyes in feverish glances. Lucinda rubbed herself between her thighs, willing herself mentally to get excited, feeling the first hot and sticky pangs of pain, filling the room with waves of her emotions.

– Oh, this is grand, he cried. – Grand!

He put Lucinda down on her back and entered her in one uncaring move of brutality. She cried out. A few thrusts and she began moving under him, moving like a rug, wrinkled and old.

Glimpses she caught of Adriane and the other woman found them writhing in their discomfort, in their growing need.

– My hero, she mumbled, – my mucho hombre.

And by those Mexican words everything easily slipped even more into focus.

He held her and hurt her in any way he could. She smiled at him, infinitely grateful. Hands grabbed his torso, rubbing him up and down, nails scratching and breaking skin.

Something happened then, something eluding her. It was as if her hands hurt, as if they touched something, something not flesh. She studied him, his oblivious, pleased expression. There was nothing there, nothing illuminating the frown on her face.

They both exploded in pleasure. Both cried out in pain. Lucinda's hands felt like they were on fire, one filling her entire body in an instant.

He pulled away from her.

– What did you do, bitch? He said angrily. – What did you do to me?

I don't know, she wanted to say, but her voice failed her.

Now, she sent to Adriane. NOW!

Adriane stood close to him. She put her hands close to his neck, his jugular vein. There was a crack or a sound. The area below his jaw seemed to explode and blood decorated the room. The big, no longer dangerous man died instantly. Lucinda moved, moved with a strength and a speed she couldn't believe. It was still almost too late. She grabbed Adriane's head and broke her neck with a beyond hard pull. There was a sharp pain, even as the dead girl fell to the floor. Lucinda bled from a flesh wound on her neck.

She stood there, breathing hard, turning towards the one remaining opponent in the room.

– No, the woman whimpered, pushing herself at the wall. – Please, no!

Lucinda sensed deception in her mind. She was hiding something. Lucinda reached her with two fast steps and kicked out with her right foot, hitting the head firmly pushed at the wall, anchored there. The kick broke the other woman's skull like an eggshell. She died as quietly as the rest. Lucinda felt another sharp pain. She studied her foot. It practically burned, as if it had hit hot plasma or something.

You were warm, Lucinda nodded. You wanted me to touch you longer, such a sly, but useless bitch.

Her foot hurt. The skin was gone, exposing the practically boiling flesh.

She balanced on her left foot, turning towards the door where she had entered.

– I won, didn't I? She said aloud, in sudden, feverish triumph. – I WON!

There was a click. The door slid open. Lucinda limped through the gate with a proud smile on her lips, the numbing pain in her foot hardly more than a trifle.

Four others met her outside. None wore collars. Everybody tensed, measuring each other. Lucinda dimly recognized, somewhat, Lisa from a far away time and place no longer valid or right in any way she could think of.

The Ebony Goddess appeared from nowhere, accompanied by five she had transformed, elevated to a higher level, to her hallowed standard, among them the Catcher. Lucinda felt the pain in her mind again. She and the other four survivors fell on their knees and lowered their eyes.

– You have done well, my children, the Ebony Goddess said pleased. – You have honored your Mother.

Lucinda found herself nodding. The words made sense to her, made very much sense.

The regal figure signed for them to rise and they did so, excitement charging through them like pure energy.

– I bring out the core in people. You've passed an important hurdle on your path, my subjects. Are you now ready to receive the Goddess' touch, the next step on your ascension to glory?

– YES, MY GODDESS! The five choired, standing defiant but subservient before the Ebony Goddess.

– Follow and honor your Mother then.

They did, the catching in their throat so hard that it hurt.

A hall of mirrors appeared to them, one of the Ebony Goddess' many rooms.

– This is your final womb. When you appear from here you will be born into my world and must make your way in it or perish. Your true path begins.

– OUR TRUE PATH

It took no more than a slight prompting to make them cry out in feverish reverence. She controlled them with casual ease.

She walked to Lisa.

Lucinda sensed no rebellion in she who had been Raven Bird, in any of them, no temptation for opposition at all, only the same, sick triumph, overwhelming devotion and dark anticipation for what was about to commence.

Jolene grabbed Lisa around both shoulders, and it… began. Lisa screamed. Waves of her powers washed over them all. Jolene bled from the nostrils, but she held on. Lucinda watched, so utterly fascinated, unable to look away, as Lisa Carlton was transformed, as she seemed to grow bigger, as her features changed, and power charged through her like lightning.

The Ebony Goddess let go of her.

– Behold yourself and your might, Bird of Prey, the creature towering over them said.

Baptizing her new child.

Bird of Prey beheld herself, her darker skin, her changed hair, the power incarnated radiating from every spot of her skin. She turned and fell to her knees before her goddess.

– I'm yours, she declared. – My life for you!

Jolene turned from her, towards Lucinda. Claws dark as night grabbed she who had been Gimmick, and a power beyond imagination filled her. The scream hardly felt like hers at all. Her mind filled the room and everyone in it, and the pain ceased, the pain grew.

There was sweat, cold and burning to the touch. Then there was calm, a deadly calm, pleased smile, a pitch black, transcendent joy.

She stood before the mirror, looking at her new Self. Her hair had turned black and her skin a darker hue, very much a lesser copy of the Ebony Goddess, like Jolene's other favored daughters and sons.

– Behold the Black Dragon, Jolene declared, – or at least her modest beginnings.

No, no, Lucinda thought. Not that. Not that name, please.

That. The Ebony Goddess nodded and spoke in her mind. It's your destiny, your very fate.

Yes, My Goddess.

It sounded so right, so beyond right. Once realization had been imparted on her, she accepted her new reality with passion and enthusiasm making all previous emotion she dimly recalled not even close to a pale reflection.

Something kept ascending from her vast depths along with the darkness, yet another realization, certainty.

– C-claudia…

The stuttering felt alien to her, now, like a distant memory, making the Black Dragon detest herself. She had to catch her breath as an even more powerful black rage struck her.

She who had been Oracle looked at her with something resembling curiosity.

– She did it to me, too. She modified my mind, from the very first moment she laid her eyes on me. That bitch orchestrated many of the horrors befalling us.

– Yes, the Ebony Goddess confirmed. – You were unable to even acknowledge that fact until I made you stronger, until this very moment.

– Thank you, My Goddess, Black Dragon cried out and fell on her knees, casting her eyes down. – You created me, painted my very soul. I'm yours, until Death.

And the Ebony Goddess petted her, like she would an animal.

The Catcher appeared by her side. He was holding a chain and a collar in his hands. She bared her neck to him. He slipped the simple collar around her neck, like another did with Lisa. It didn't drain power, but was merely symbolic. He pulled her on her feet and she stumbled after him down the shadowy hallway.

The Black Dragon was being held in the chain, the leash. The Catcher took great pleasure in pulling her through many a dark hallway. She was his pet, his hound. He stopped once in a while, to make that fact clear, fondling her brutally all over her body, pushing her at the wall, pushing his large cock into her, making her cry out in need and pleasure and dark passion.

He met with no resistance. She had long since relented, given in to him completely and unreservedly. When he pumped his seed into her she cried out in lust and joy. She grinned at him, and though there might be some shame left in there somewhere, it didn't manifest itself in any visible way. Everything she did, every move she made signaled to him that she was his to do with as he pleased. The triumph she sensed in him found an easy echo in her.

Servants bathed her, dried her with large towels, fixed her face as much as it could be fixed, treated and bandaged her foot, did her hair and dressed her up in her new uniform. She didn't care about those around her. They were nothing but somewhat tolerable flies buzzing in her space, girls giggling and staring at her in awe. There was that word again, making her smile. She studied the creature in the mirror again, through their eyes. The long vertical wounds had healed nicely, but the scars remained. They would always be there. She looked sharp, cold and lethal, an appearance worthy of her name, of Black Dragon. Once more the sinister smile lit up the serene mask.

She stood in a dark room, looking into another bright hall through a one way mirror. There was one single cage in there, one single occupant. She glanced at the man holding her leash, humbly and eagerly calling for his attention.

– What is it you would ask me, worm?

– Has he been there… a long time?

– Yes, he nodded, a little preoccupied, – he was captured not that long after you. He's strong and has endured the torture, but more than anything I get the impression that our Queen has gone easy on him and has saved him… for you, my pet.

– Thank the Goddess! She cried. – Thank you, master!

She opened the door and rushed inside, walking slowly, deliberately towards the cage and the man imprisoned there.

He didn't look up, didn't give any indication of having noticed her arrival. She studied him dispassionately, with her predator eyes.

You may begin, *Hound,* the master holding her leash commanded her.

She nodded in anticipation, in eagerness, slipping into the mind of the man inside the cage with ease, so much more powerful compared to Gimmick, poor Gimmick.

– Hello, Richard, she greeted the wreck of a man softly.

He still didn't look up, but it wasn't hard for her, wasn't hard at all to sense his sudden distress. She grabbed it, began playing with it, licking her lips.

The Bowman looked up, casting anxious glances around him, looking for something that wasn't there.

– You didn't really think you could keep your name hidden from us for long, did you?

He looked straight at her, but still had trouble seeing her. He moved his eyes in an effort to focus his hazy vision, in vain. Black Dragon felt a poignant anticipation, a dark, transcendent joy she could hardly contain.

She recognized him, somewhat, in spite of the hard beatings and punishment he had suffered, recognized his mind below the disfigured features and almost skinny body filled with lacerations and bruises. He was denuded, downtrodden, but still defiant. She smiled, dimly recalling the powerful man fucking her, striving to dominate her, failing even in that, at every turn, not even able to take on poor, sweet Gimmick.

– What did you say? Is anyone there?

– I'm here, Richard. I'm inside you. You're my plaything, and I will never let you go.

He frowned, attempting to think, to reason, but it was denied him. He shook his head, in an effort to clear it, but the haze only turned worse.

Dark, patronizing laughter bubbled to the surface, filling the room, Black Dragon's excited thoughts.

The cage seemed to shrink. The very walls outside the cage seemed to close in on him. There had been a slight case of claustrophobia there, originating sometime in his childhood. She took that unpleasant memory and exploited it, augmented it. Black Dragon probed him, and it hardly proved difficult or even challenging. She discovered, almost second by second how her power had grown, how it seemed to keep growing without pause or limitation.

His… mother, yes, his mother had scorned him, ridiculed him.

– You're just a weak, pathetic boy, aren't you, Richard's mother, Black Dragon choired in his memory. – Such a disappointment!

The walls, mother, he wanted to cry out, but the use of his voice was denied him. The walls *hate* me, mother.

Black Dragon found a memory of another woman in his mind. She made him think of her, desire her, re-experience their fucking, their intense relationship. He was pulled towards the memory of her, of a time when he had been in control, had felt powerful and vigilant. His eyes stopped wavering. The walls and cage kept closing in on him, but he held on, held on hard to the memory of his conquest. Black Dragon smiled.

He wanted to go to her, to the woman smiling invitingly to him from outside the cage, but couldn't do so, of course, since the bars stopped him.

– You naughty, naughty boy, the mirage said, shaking a finger in the air.

He looked confused at her, frowning, clearly out of it, not really getting it, not seeing beyond the cobweb cast on his mind. The woman bent down, grabbing his jaw, smiling contemptuously at him. He grew angry, attempting to shake off her touch, but pain shot through him. Black Dragon touched the pain center in his mind. He wanted to scream, but his jaw seemed fused together. She touched his pain again, and this time he was allowed to scream. His powerful vocal cords shook the room. She grabbed his jaw again, squeezing it. He yelped, as more dull pain shot through him.

– Weak little boy, she spat.

She made him look at her, and suddenly he was looking at his mother again. The contemptuous laughter shook him, empowering her further. She had located his weakness, several of his weaknesses and it had hardly taken any effort what so ever.

The woman knelt down outside the cage. She unbuttoned her jacket in front and exposed her breasts.

– You may touch them if you want. Don't you want to?

He stared at her with his dull eyes, nodding with tears flooding his cheeks. Hands reached through the bars and warily grabbed the breasts. He began fondling them. His cock began twitching, began growing. The face floating before him changed, the sight sending shockwaves through him, dull and horrible emotions.

– That's it, the stern woman mewed. – That's Mommy's boy. Show Mommy, show Mommy how much you love her.

He attempted to speak, but no words or even sounds came from him. His cock grew hard and thick and long, sticking out between the bars, as he pushed himself at them in the futile attempt at reaching the regal figure outside. He gasped frantically, as he grabbed the pulsing limb, and began rubbing it, began pumping it back and forth with his ever faster moving hand, all the while looking at the image of his mother fondling her breasts with an incredulous, confused and anguished look in his hazy eyes. The pain grew unbearable below, as his moves grew even more frantic, as the beautiful smile grew even wider. He came with a cry of pleasure and joy, and semen splashed the floor outside his cage.

The muscular body sagged and collapsed. The intense happy feeling persisted and kept overwhelming him. A hand petted his cheek.

– That's it, my son, she said softly, – you may rest now, may sleep and dream pleasant dreams. Say thank you.

– Thank you, Mother, he gasped. – Thank you, thank you, thank you.

Eyes closed quickly, and not before long, he was sound asleep, and so much more vulnerable to the powerful telepath's machinations. Black Dragon glanced shyly but happily at the master when she returned to the hallway.

– Did I do good, Master? She wondered.

– An excellent job, Hound, he nodded, unable to quite keep the amazement and excitement from his voice and surface mind. – I trust the prisoner will be quite pliable quite soon?

– Oh, yes, Master. He will be ready for the imprint in a matter of days. I give him dreams, dreams he will embrace and that will shape him. Each time he awakens from his sleep he will be more open to my suggestions, until he will be nothing but clay. Soon, very soon he will have forgotten who he was and embrace his new life of service and obedience.

Black Dragon stood before the boy's cell as he woke up, as herself. Her image and form had slowly replaced that of his mother in his dreams.

– Good morning, weakling, she greeted him.

– Good m-morning, M-mother, he replied.

– You're such a disappointment to me, she snarled. – You're not my son.

He shrunk further, covering in her shadow.

– You must earn the right to call yourself my son, you sniveling brat.

– I will, Mother, he replied eagerly. – I WILL!

She opened the door to the cell, smacking the whip at her boots, making him rush outside, and kneel before her. She was so tall, so much taller than him. She commanded him to rise by a patronizing snarl. She towered above him, and he felt so very, very small.

– Look at you, thirteen years of age and still only a boy.

She put a collar with a chain around his neck, and dragged him off. He followed her totally docile and unresistingly. She knew he was ready.

The light at the intersection glowed even stronger than reality in her vision. This was one of the many reception areas, where slaves were brought after their capture and trained in the service of the High Ones.

– You take him, she told the underlings there, putting as much calm and relaxation in her voice as she possibly was able to. – He will be an eager boy, so dedicated to learn his place, to earn his keep.

400

She could hardly contain her pride. When the underlings bowed and showed their further subservience to her she almost cracked open in her euphoria.

When she returned to the Catcher he stared hard at her. Regret and anxiety struck her hard. She whimpered and instantly bared her neck to him, waiting for whatever act he deemed appropriate.

– I think I'll call you Lucy...

He said, granting her absolution.

– Lucy, she acknowledged with sick relief, her eyes filled with love. – Thank you, master!

He walked to her, petted her. She purred and pleased him with her love.

– You are my hound of hounds, he stated. – You will lead the hunt.

She glanced at him with inquiring eyes, but didn't really question him in any visible manner.

He brought her to what instantly reminded her of a kennel, introducing her to the rest of his all-female pack. She dimly recognized Eleanor, she who had been Cougar and now was Predator and also some of the others, including some of her former Furies, all changed, all transformed by the Cadre's powerful machinations.

Predator growled at her. Black Dragon struck her down. Predator whimpered at her feet, eagerly baring her neck to the superior creature. The others followed her example. Black Dragon felt pride coursing through her. She knelt with her pack, before their master.

– Now, isn't that a pretty picture, the Catcher mused, his voice thick with the familiar triumph.

He walked in among them. They moved on all fours according to him. He began feeding them candy. They eagerly displayed themselves in order to receive their vaunted prize. Lucy felt like heaven when it melted on her tongue.

– Into your cages, hounds, he bid them.

They rushed to do his bidding. Lucy knew what to do instantly, watching the others. She moved on all fours into the bigger and prettier cage. He slammed close the doors, locking them inside.

He left the room, closing its door behind him.

The lights dimmed, seemingly by themselves. The dark, always present came to dominate everything.

The hounds crouched there on the floor, filled with happy thoughts. Lucy could hardly turn off her power anymore. All thoughts nearby filled her. She filled them. At the top of her cage she saw a skull of a goat she wasn't sure was actually there. Feathers covered its head like hair, whistling in the wind. Its fleeting image faded away. She heard drums, heard them from everywhere, no matter how low. Dark eyes closed. Black Dragon rose in the darkness, flapping its wings, releasing its fire in the night, experiencing countless feverish variations, the very fabric of dreams, about yesterday and tomorrow.

Chapter 23

It was a stark hot, but brisk morning. Black Dragon was held in a leash with the rest of the pack. She surveyed the terrain, the forest and field before them, sensing the prey somewhere ahead. She turned eager, even agitated in the leash, and the others joined in with their loud barks and wet tongues.

The master let go of the leash. His hounds charged into the forest.

The chase was on.

All the hounds were fast, but Lucy was first into the thick forest, was faster than all of them. Lucy couldn't believe how fast she had become and she marveled in it.

Cougar was not far behind. Her eagerness and blood-thirst spurred Black Dragon further on the path the Ebony Goddess had chosen for her.

The hounds raced forward so fast that the trees turned even more indistinct in their vision as they passed them. The prey turned absolutely frantic with panic. The females and males ahead released whimpers loud and loud in their fear, in their terror. Cougar howled in the premature certainty of a satisfying hunt. Lucy and the others joined in.

The labored breath, the stark fear, the weak limbs of the prey, it was all so clear in Lucy's mind. The taste of blood filled her mouth prematurely and almost turned her insane. They were caught already. The hounds barked and picked up speed. Everything surrounding them became a blur.

The stench of the forest, the oxygen and rot combined made Black Dragon's nostrils bleed. Red mist blew from the dragon's nostrils.

Everything happened so fast, was brief flashes, appearing one moment, gone the next. Black Dragon still noticed everything, even as her attention was directed forward. She had been upgraded to a point she hardly found possible.

The first prey was caught. It was slacking, already exhausted and beaten. A few strikes and kicks and it was down, crouching on the ground, below a snarling hound. The others were cornered and pacified not long after that. One tried to get up. Black Dragon kicked it in the head. Another attempted to use its power. Black Dragon kept it from doing so, keeping it confused and dazed.

Eleanor snarled at those crouching, exposing her claws, drawing blood. She was hardly human anymore, so primal that she resembled her former namesake far more than she did the woman Lucinda had known. Lucy found herself howling with her, breathing the blood and the lust with her. The hounds towered above the shivering captives.

It was over, just like that. Snarls faded to growls, without that making the intimidation any less. It was so easy keeping them subdued. Lucy marveled at how their troubled, buzzing minds failed to touch her. Managing them took no effort at all.

The final distraught screams faded to the occasional whimpers with a few added kicks and strikes and scratches.

– Your old lives, whatever they were, are past tense, Black Dragon declared. – You belong to the Cadre, now.

They were mostly low-lives, not much in terms of powers, and those that were she and Eleanor and the others made to stay down, keeping them from showing any initiative. Fear, terror was the key. The smile mixed with the growl.

The Catcher stepped into the clearing. The hounds instantly lowered their eyes in reverence, even though their attention never strayed from the captives.

– The hunt was successful, Master, Lucy responded to his prompting. – These poor wretches are ready for processing. They won't need collars or any restraining what so ever.

She glowed with pride. He nodded pleased.

– Excellent! Let's be on our way, then.

Black Dragon pulled her whip, one with nine tips from her hip. The other hounds joined her. They began whipping the people on the ground.

– UP, YOU WORTHLESS SCABS! MOVE!

She felt their pain and returned it to them tenfold. They gasped and whined in their mindless horror, as they were driven like cattle out of the forest. Even though a few of them attempted to speak, to protest, they scurried on in mute panic. After just a few steps, what felt like a hundred lashes their minds turned dim, and they forgot all thoughts of resistance and even speech. Their every thought focused on putting one foot in front of the other. Each stroke was like dark lighting dulling their mind further.

Every time a slacker revealed itself the hounds were on him or her. Black Dragon projected terror into their feverish minds, making them even more susceptible to the ongoing and prevailing desires of the Cadre.

– It's amazing, Lucy stated startled. – You are so easy to lead that you could just as well be sheep.

The Catcher's cruel laughter warmed her and made even stronger pride fill her being.

She gave a man another round with the whip. He whined like a child. Her contemptuous laughter joined that of her master and her fellow hounds.

They brought the sheep, or the cattle for an extended run before circling in

404

on the nearest portal. The poor wretches were almost completely drained of strength by then. They were driven through the shimmering air very much like the mindless cattle they resembled. Lucinda realized what hadn't dawned on her earlier: that these portals didn't require a special ring or anything for people to go through.

The thought faded quickly into the unimportance it was.

At the first interception area they joined with several other groups of hounds and their sheep. She sensed some differences between the various packs of hounds, but nothing major. All appeared the same in her mind.

More and louder marching and whipping drained the sheep further, invigorating the hounds. Barks and whines mixed, turning interchangeable. She noticed easily how each pack stayed close to their master, how they seemed like an extension of him or her.

The wall with the openings and tubes leading down to the vast field appeared before them. Everything had long since turned quiet in Lucy's head, except the whining of the prey. She was the first of the hounds to grab a goat and throw it into the hole. The others joined her eagerly. She followed the shrieking beasts down the tubes with her mind, into more pain and terror. Another grin lit up her face.

The Catcher walked off and his bitches followed him. They knew what would follow and the burning increased between their thighs.

There was another portal somewhere, and they found themselves inside the vast Cadre headquarters, the heaven where the Ebony Goddess resided. Black Dragon felt her everywhere, wherever she turned and directed her attention.

The hounds joined their master in his quarters. They undressed with feverish movement and displayed themselves to him. Pain and need charged through Lucy and she yelped in anticipation with the rest. They knelt around the bed, their eyes directed at the floor, their complete attention on the Catcher.

Black Dragon swayed on her knees with the hazy look in her slits, her suddenly so wide windows to her depths.

– That was invigorating, wasn't it, Franklin mused, – such a great appetizer.

They hummed their reply, moaning in their mind-numbing need.

– Come here, lowly dragon, he snapped, – show me your fire.

She was there, in front of him almost before he had finished speaking.

Dull flashes of memory burned her as he grabbed her, from the moment he had captured her, conquered her. It held no terror for her anymore, no possible significance. They had become nothing except meaningless images unaccompanied by emotion.

He placed her on the bed. She waited for him there, on her knees. He undressed, not in a hurry.

– The Ebony Goddess gave you to her trusted man, he boasted. – You are her gift to me.

His triumphant lust charged through her, violating her on the deepest level. Her lips parted. She released her moan. It spread to everyone present. The Catcher chuckled in what sounded to Black Dragon like boundless anticipation. He climbed the bed, reaching her, grabbing her shoulders, squeezing them hard. She hardly noticed. Her wet lips met his, again and again and again.

She bit down on his lower lip, pulling her head back hard, ripping the soft flesh from his face. He cried out short and sharp. She burrowed her hard thoughts deep into his. It hurt. She welcomed the pain, relished it. The snarl of a smile felt so good. She glimpsed his startled expression as she buried her hand deep into his abdomen. He folded with a grunt of pain. She struck his neck. He dropped on the bed. She squeezed his balls, squeezed them hard. She grabbed his arm, dislocating it on his shoulder. His scream changed to an already pitiful whimper. She proceeded to handle his other arm and both his feet. It felt so easy. The snarl of a smile filled the room.

– You bitches better remain still if you know what's good for you…

They did, struck by terror, baring their necks to her, to *her*.

He writhed on the bed, his watery eyes unable to focus on the dragon hovering above him and releasing the flame from her mouth.

– You missed the obvious. You are her gift to me.

She dressed, refitting her uniform, doing so slowly and meticulously. He tried to speak, but was unable to do so, unable to release more than prolonged whimpers. She hardly looked at him, hardly paid attention to him at all.

The mirror revealed her, revealed her more than she could ever remember anything do. She turned away from it, even as she kept studying the scars, the impassive face. Troy Franklin had been totally incapacitated. His cheeks shook. She looked pleased at him, even as she grabbed one of his dislocated arms and pulled him down from the bed and across the floor and his ongoing whimpering turned a little louder. The bedroom changed to the hallway. The hallway changed to a hall and to other hallways and other halls. She did encounter guards on her way. They made no attempt at stopping her.

She knew when she approached her destination. Her surroundings changed in major and subtle ways. The two big doors to the throne hall stood wide open. She knelt by the entrance and waited, clutching the limp arm.

The terrifying creature on the throne looked bemused at her and called her forward. Lucinda dragged the Catcher with her and knelt in front of the elevated and oversized chair.

– Hail the Ebony Goddess, she cried. – Black Dragon has conquered her conqueror. She… demands her place at thy table.

The cruel and pleased grin revealed by the female demon on the throne bathed Black Dragon in its consuming heat.

– So, you don't want to run away anymore?

– No, My Goddess, she said with a head bowed even more. – I live to serve thee. And where should I go? The Ebony Goddess' reach is everywhere, in every little corner, low and high of the world.

– Kill him then.

The words were uttered so casual, so evenly, but Lucinda heard them. They burrowed into her as the loudest drill.

There was no hesitation. A hand moved fast as lightning, ripping out Troy Franklin's throat. He shook a little, before lying still. His red, red blood decorated the floor.

She felt the Ebony Goddess' approval assault her in waves. She gasped in awe, terror and joy.

– Rise, Black Dragon and receive thy communion, the final proof of thy holy stature.

Both women rose. The Ebony Goddess stepped down from her throne. Black Dragon rushed forward to meet her. She stopped right before the imposing figure right after it had stopped, her eyes cast down.

The Ebony Goddess put a hand on her right shoulder. The pain when the burning began was exquisite. Black Dragon had an almost instant orgasm.

It was done. The Ebony Goddess looked down on her dragon.

– This is what you are, now, one of the High Ones executing the Goddess' will, one of her mighty dragons, a storm, a lethal creature of the night, a god preying on mortals.

Lucinda kissed the hand she offered.

– Thank you, My Goddess for this great gift, she cried. – I will cherish it always and strive to be worthy of it.

– I know you will!

The Ebony Goddess returned to her throne. Lucinda noticed a draft in her near euphoria. The others belonging to the all-female host of dragons entered the hall. Among them counted the Blood Diamond, the Red Dragon without a mask and black hair, making her hardly recognizable by her former comrades in the Maverick Crew. The Bird of Prey, the Blue Dragon that had been Raven Bird caught Lucinda's eyes briefly without eliciting any particular emotion.

The giant woman sat on the throne. The eight kneeling before her all had a tattoo of a dragon in various color schemes on their left shoulder. Only Black Dragon had hers on the right. She had been marked, marked as special, even more so than the rest.

– I welcome you to my court, the Ebony Goddess said. – Now, and forever.

Her voice, her voice rolled off her tongue like a rusty saw on metal.

– You are my arms, the foremost extension of my will. Together we will transform the world.

It didn't sound like bluster to them, but like a literal truth.

– Politics is a masquerade. We will splinter the illusion everywhere.

Reality shifted. It was later. Lucinda couldn't really tell how much later. The nine sat around a table. They dined with food and wine. The Ebony Goddess sat by its head. Lucinda couldn't look at her without being lost in her being. Her very presence did that.

Lucinda watched her fellow dragons, her equals, as they watched her, watched the new, transformed Cassandra, Lisa, Adeline, Lois and the rest, all equally lethal in the their own right.

The cracked mirror images of the Ebony Goddess all felt and shared her rage and they swam in its sea, a dark, seething ocean without peer. Black Dragon absorbed and redistributed it, making it an even more powerful experience.

The Ebony Goddess smiled, a snarl filling her subjects with joy.

– My table is finally complete, she stated with her metal voice. – We've been playing with our enemies a bit the last couple of years. Now, the true game begins and our true ambitions are within reach.

They knew the meaning behind her words, knew it like the back of their hand. Expectation boiled within them.

Lucinda fed with the others, gorged herself on the heaps of food put before her. Her appetites had increased tenfold or so it felt, turning her stomach into something resembling far more her impression of a black hole. It made her smile, made her snarl in joy.

– Will you share the reason for your good mood with us, Black Dragon? Cassandra asked casually, but with a distinct sinister subtext Lucinda had no trouble catching.

Everybody studied her with predatory eyes. It didn't bother her.

– It's nothing profound, Violet Dragon, she shrugged. – I just imagined that I knew what hunger was in my former life, but I had no idea.

– There is no limit to Hunger, the Ebony Goddess nodded, – no limit at all.

And her eight dragons nodded in awe and acknowledgement. They kept shivering and burning in her presence.

The dinner ended. The Goddess dismissed them. Black Dragon noticed with glee that there was no pressure in her arse, no rumbling in her stomach, no need to run to the toilet bowl. More dark joy rose within her. There didn't seem to be an end to it.

She eventually went and emptied herself, but the stench didn't bother her anymore. She breathed its air with the triumphant snarl on her lips.

Her quarters had not changed when she returned to them and neither had her hounds or their positions. She had told them not to move and they interpreted that command literally. It made the thin smile on her lips broaden slightly.

– Stand!

Stand!

She told them, with both her voice and her mind.

They were up in an instant. A casual glance into their mindscape told her how she appeared to them, how they viewed her. Terror and worship intermingled in their minds, becoming one, singular emotion of devotion. There hadn't really been a need for her to speak, using either method. They would have reacted and would increasingly react to nuances of movement she might even not be consciously aware of.

She studied them, studied Myra, Eleanor, Jordan, Rhonda, Kelly, Jasmine, Allison, Ashanti, Tabitha, Desmonia, Ruby and the rest, forming them with her thoughts, her will without even trying, tying them far stronger to her than they had ever been to Troy. Now, when she no longer held herself back, it was child's play completing the final part of their education, molding them into whatever she desired them to be.

Look at them, your children, Jolene spoke in her mind. You took them and made them what they are today. You have reason to be proud, Black Dragon.

The words prompted joy and very little shame and regret. There were images of when she had first encountered them and other, earlier moments in their common history, but they only served to confirm the Ebony Goddess' statement.

– You are my hounds, she stated, not telling them anything they did not know, – mine to do with as I please. We will hunt for the glory of the Goddess.

– *The glory of the Goddess,* they breathed.

She nudged them a little, moved her little finger a little, and they fell on their knees again, their eyes cast down. They knelt unmoving while she circled them, assessed them, and they bathed in the glory of Black Dragon's pervasive attention. She found the tattoo needle in her uniform.

– I mark you as mine, within and without. You will be nothing but an extension of my being.

– Your being, they echoed.

Jordan was closest when she stopped, looking at her with enthusiasm and rising joy.

She froze the subservient creature in place with her mind and grabbed her arm, pushing the needle at a point just above the elbow. Jordan shouted short and sharp. Seconds later it was done. A smaller black dragon had been burned into the hound's skin.

– Thank you, Master, she cried. – Thank you so much!

The act repeated itself, until everybody had been marked as Black Dragon's creatures.

She left the room and her hounds followed her. A short walk later they reached the nearest gate. This time, when she stepped through the gate there was no nausea or even discomfort. She felt it only through the others. They appeared in central Jaynagar. Lots of people spotted them as they arrived and in the seconds afterwards. Black Dragon and her pack walked like a dance in the midst of the busy afternoon traffic of people and cars. She walked down streets filled with people and as she watched them, studied them, she saw the strange glare, from the adult big people, but also from young teenagers still not Big. The girl had seen it, right after the Great Darkness and occasionally in the ten years since then, but never with such ease as now.

People pointed, clearly anxious, sensing the threat beneath the fairly mundane image of the pack on a fundamental level. Lucinda realized that her ability to spot big people's dark glare and the weaker dark glare of big people to be was on all the time. Her powers had become so elevated that she would have felt like she was bursting with them, if she hadn't been so calm, so relaxed. There weren't that many big people present. Most of those few with the glare were children and young, undeveloped teenagers. Some glowed stronger, others less. She quickly grew to differentiate between them, to pick those most important.

At her bidding Jordan grabbed a boy, tearing him away from the small parents.

– Rejoice, Black Dragon told them. – Your son will, if he's worthy, be significant and serve the Ebony Goddess and her Cadre well and long.

The mother rushed forward, in an effort at recovering the boy. Myra, fast and lethal swatted her like she would a fly.

– You do not approach Black Dragon, she snarled. – You are not worthy of her dust.

They began gathering more children and also adult big people and met with very little resistance. In less than a minute the fairly peaceful scene had turned into bedlam and chaos. The sky and the very air itself seemed to

410

darken, turning the sun into a moon.

Feel the presence of the Goddess, Lucinda shouted at them and everybody heard her, far clearer than speech.

People attempted to flee, doing so the fastest they were able, but very few made it and big people and prospective children were rounded up, surrounded by the hounds.

The eight dragons and their hounds made their presence felt in eight large cities across the world. Lucinda felt them all. It empowered her further.

– KNEEL! Allison snapped. – Pay respect to your betters. Bow your head to *Black Dragon*.

A male stood his ground briefly, but two hounds punished him until he also fell on his knees.

Black Dragon walked to him, bending down, grabbing his jaw.

– You wanted to say something? She said patronizingly.

– You are the C-cadre? The young boy stuttered, seeing the answer in her burning eyes. – I want to j-join you.

– That's an excellent first step. She slapped him, and slapped him again and he fell to the ground. – We'll see if you ever amount to anything.

He crouched before her with lowered eyes, and she studied him with her cruel stare.

– Black Dragon is already a legend, he conveyed through a mouth filled with blood. – I would follow her anywhere, through hell itself.

– You'll have to.

She turned away, dismissing him.

– On your feet, Jordan spat, walking among the captives. – Light run.

Bullwhips hammered already sore skin. There were no slackers. The children sobbed helplessly, but they didn't stray from their position in the line.

The procession ran through the streets, dominating it. The nearest blocks, the entire inner city filled her mind, like a map, a woven pattern moving and shifting. She directed her attention at the gate, the one that had always been available to the Maverick Crew. There was no activity there, none at all, no sign of them anywhere. She curled her lips in contempt.

They spotted the occasional police officer, but the uniformed men and women held back, practically backed off and hid before the horrible host plaguing their city.

Lucinda recognized the area they walked through. It was Cassandra's old turf. The school loomed dark and gloomy not far away. They rushed inside. The children and teachers alike were cooped up in the classrooms. She enjoyed seeing how attentive their fear made them. The hounds swooped into the classrooms and children and adults were theirs for the picking. More cries of terror joined those already filling the eight cities.

Lois lashed out with the energy power she possessed. Lucinda glimpsed her and other dragons in flashes. New recruits were brought back to the indoctrination facilities in droves.

A man, a guard had drawn his gun and pointed it at them. Desmonia took one step towards him, showing him her sweet, angelic face. Her power had appeared and grown, like with all members of the pack. She charmed the man, turning terror into a vacant stare.

– Such a hard, brave boy, she whispered. – Perhaps you will even survive the upcoming ordeals the Ebony Goddess and her mighty dragons have ordained for you?

They grabbed more children, from several of the classrooms and several other big people that had sought out the school as a refuge from the streets of fire outside.

When they emerged from the building a crowd of men and women Lucinda had long since noticed knelt on the ground, their eyes cast down.

– Black Dragon promised she would come and save us, and now she has, the front man cried.

– NOW SHE HAS!

The others echoed him.

Lucinda held up a hand, a visible, unnecessary part of the nudge she used to hold her hounds in their reins. She walked to the man and his congregation with a slight smile on her lips.

– So, you deem yourself worthy, then?

She grabbed hold of their minds and made it hurt.

– Yes, Honored One, he gasped. – And we will prove it to Your Highness beyond doubt.

Black Dragon curled her lips in contempt. She turned away from them and walked on.

Then four of the hounds were there with their whips and beyond brutal lashes.

– ON YOUR FEET WRETCHES.

And the even bigger procession left Jaynagar, even as they remained there, in the minds of everybody who had seen and felt them. The gate waited for them where they had arrived. They faded away like a nightmare that would never go away.

They reappeared in the wilderness somewhere, in the wild and ragged terrain Lucinda recalled from her early introduction to the Cadre's kindness.

– This is the Trail of Cleansing, she informed the recruits, – the first of

412

many trials in your service of the Cadre and Black Dragon and the Ebony Goddess herself.

A bright young boy stared at her and looked like he wanted so comment on something. She stepped in front of him in an instant and froze him in place.

– You didn't think your pickup was any hardship, do you? She asked him.

He shivered and shook his head.

– No, Mistress, he shouted.

– Good boy.

She touched him with both her hand and her mind, and knew he would give her no more trouble, but become a dedicated and useful servant.

Children and adults alike stared at her with equal amounts of terror and worship in their eyes. Then the whips began hitting them again, and easily prompted they began stumbling forward in the right direction. One hour later only the same dull expression showed in their wet and dirty eyes and features.

They were marched off, nothing but more cattle for the pens. If anyone stumbled and fell, they were whipped back on their feet. Only when repeated whipping and torture had been put to use, and the piece of flesh still didn't move, was he or she left behind. There were only two of those. In one of them Black Dragon sensed how brain activity faded and all body functions failed. The other's body was healthy enough, but the mind had taken a permanent leave of absence. There was hardly more than the mental equivalent of empty space in there. Her power, her blazing power told her in no uncertain terms that the wreck on the ground wasn't shamming.

– Your loss, she spat.

The march stumbled on.

The wall grew out of thin air, as always. She still couldn't make sense of the Goddess' realm, her enormous Place of Power, no more than others could. Awe touched Black Dragon once more, long before she sent the recruits down through the tubes to join their peers, before their screams and prolonged horror filled her mind and the smile broke on her face.

Black Dragon and her hounds returned to her quarters and walked through it, to the throne room, where all the dragons and their people knelt before the Goddess. Lucinda and her furies joined them.

– You've done well. Know that the Ebony Goddess is pleased with you.

– PRAISE THE EBONY GODDESS, everybody choired.

She sat on the throne, bathing in the red light flowing from an unspecified point in the hall. It was one of several signs that here, at the center of the Ebony Goddess' power reality bent and cracked more than any other place. Light, movement, sound and the most exotic scents were all present.

The red light burned eyes, burned skin and vertigo constantly threatened to overwhelm those kneeling.

They kept gasping in overwhelming awe, shaken to pieces by the forces charging them. Strength kept surging through them all.

– You've done well, and it's time for the Cadre to finally claim its place in the world.

She raised both arms, waving both hands. Suddenly, just like that they found themselves observing the Maverick Crew in their headquarters. Eight pair of eyes twinkled in triumph and expectation.

They watched Lady Grace pace the floor around the bigger table and Flight Captain trailing her like the lovesick puppy he was. She spoke, and they heard her speak, but the words were immaterial. The eight dragons observed everything they needed in her sweaty brow and flickering eyes.

The Ebony Goddess, Lucinda noted absentmindedly in her fervor was clearly straining. Black Dragon easily noticed the sweat covering her forehead.

A casual scan brought Black Dragon into Lady Grace's surface thoughts. The confusion and anxiety she felt there made anticipation rise to an even stronger level within her.

– We will bring them and all other teams and loners in, the Ebony Goddess proclaimed. – We will teach them about existence, about the world, like we do everybody. They will join us, join our purpose, become one with us.

– They will grovel at your feet, like all our enemies, My Goddess, Blue Dragon cried.

Lisa was still covered in blood, both her own and that of others, among them her former master, the woman that had met the same unkind fate as the former master of Black Dragon had done.

The Ebony Goddess granted her a smile, gave her affection, one more reason for being.

Black Dragon studied all her old comrades with the same intense scrutiny as everybody else around the table. It was such an amazing three-dimensional experience. They hardly looked any different compared to how the other dragons perceived them: like puppets dancing on the Ebony Goddess' strings.

Master.

Lucinda recognized Alysse's voice, her mind's pattern, imprint, one stronger call among the many thoughts constantly present in her expanded mindscape.

It didn't distract her, like it once would have done. She had no trouble keeping her attention on what happened right in front of her, even as she kept registering Alysse's thoughts.

I have news, Master. Lucinda could feel the eagerness in the pet as its tongue hung out. It's potentially exciting news. If Master would deem this slave worthy of her presence, this slave would be able to fully appraise the Master.

Lucinda curled her lips in more contempt. Her weekly physical was coming up later today, and Alysse had subtly reminded her of that fact.

The audience with the Ebony Goddess ended, with the dragons practically bursting with excitement. Plans put in motion long ago were about to come to fruition. Many lines of thoughts, many levels of consciousness surged through Black Dragon, without one or ten distracting the others.

Alysse welcomed her by kneeling and lowering her eyes. Lucinda acknowledged her and gave her the signal, the permission to rise, speak and act and the servant did so.

Pride surged through the woman, but never reached the surface. She had been broken, neutered and would never be anything else than the eager, obedient creature she was right now.

There was a strange spike when I examined you after you emerged victorious from the Cage of Five. It wasn't an ordinary power spike. I've seen those before and yours is different.

Black Dragon looked at her. Her mental speech remained loud and clear, louder and clearer than before. She had obvious been practicing hard. Something touched the dragon's conscious mind, but faded before she could grab it. She shook her head in irritation.

The Ebony Goddess is kind. She granted her servant a tiny piece of her might.

No, no, Alysse contradicted the master cautiously, it clearly happened before that. Look at the spike. It is far taller than the one following.

Lucinda did look at the screen and a strange exhilaration beyond the love to her Goddess charged through her.

The slave fell on her knees in abject fright and knelt before her superior, fearing she had taken liberties with the Master's kindness, her lower lip shivering.

Continue, worm.

We may find out more if this servant made a thorough examination, Master.

You may proceed.

Alysse directed her to the examination table in the deeper part of the room. Lucinda knew what that was. The pet reserved that to her truly important projects.

Lucinda lay down on her back there. Alysse fastened electrodes to her skin and temples. Alysse looked very much in love when Black Dragon's energies lit up the screens.

– My powers are certainly different from Claudia's, way different, and far more potent, Lucinda said, with badly hidden contempt and triumph thick in her voice.

– You dwarf her completely, Master, Alysse breathed with shiny eyes.

Alysse prodded her, brought her through physical and mental trials, and made notes on the keyboard while doing so, as efficient and skilled as ever.

But nothing remained of the snotty elitist that had preceded her capture. Alysse knelt again. Lucinda relaxed in the pleasant chair.

– Everybody our Exalted Goddess has given her gifts has made quantum leaps in terms of power and endurance, also in the ability to resist other powers they previously could not withstand. It's a remarkable thing to study. You have also finally achieved the control you worked in vain to attain, also with your digestion. She raised you to a far higher, consistent level and also stabilized you. You didn't lose control with more power, but gained it...

Lucinda listened, listened hard, still striving to catch the fleeting thought, the notion she could not grasp, whatever it was that had made her frown lately. She had believed that the Ebony Goddess had brought total clarity, but that wasn't quite correct. There was more... more...

– Many of the big people enjoy two gifts, but you, My Lady seem to have gained a third. You have become both faster and stronger. Your reflexes have increased to a level that is far above what an ordinary power boost would have brought.

Lucinda watched herself through the testing. Alysse had «released» her from the examination table and begun throwing things at her, also sharp and dangerous things like darts and knives. Lucinda had caught all of them with a speed and coordination ability that had been so casual that it had totally failed to stun her.

– This is certainly good news, she said brightly, even gently to the servant. – It means I can be even more effective in my service to our Goddess.

– The Ebony Goddess be praised, Alysse responded automatically, stars in her eyes.

She leaned forward, even more eager.

– What is different with Master continues to elude this one, but I'm confident that I can aid Master in finding out what makes her different from her brethren.

– I'm sure, Black Dragon mused.

She rose. The servant crumbled even more in her deep kneeling position.

416

You will not share your findings with anyone. You will erase them from the databanks.

Of course, Master.

Only an invisible frown accompanied that thought.

It was mostly a redundant command. Lucinda had already begun making the necessary alterations to her mind and memory. The moment Black Dragon left the room Alysse would remember nothing but an ordinary examination and forget that there had been more at all, or that there was any reason for it. She would proceed with the wiping of the databases and invent a perfectly valid and believable explanation for doing so in her inventive mind, and that would be it.

I will find out on my own, Lucinda promised herself.

She had trouble shaking off the feeling of dread flooding her.

Cassandra, with her snake smile approached her in the hallway.

– Everything was in order, I trust? She said with obviously fake compassion.

– Everything was in excellent order, Lucinda shrugged her off. – I'm better suited than ever to perform the tasks the Ebony Goddess, praised be her name, requires of me.

– Praise the Ebony Goddess, Cassandra responded automatically.

She pulled her enigmatic smile. Lucinda saw it, as easy as she saw the flickering shadows in her own face.

– Have I told you how pleased I am with your progress? Cassandra spoke softly. – It has been so great to watch you pull yourself from the mud, to join us at the top of the Cadre's table.

Lucinda smiled, too, not saying anything. The other woman frowned.

– It was easy, Lucinda shrugged. – I merely realized you guys were all beneath me.

She sensed how anger flared in the other form, until it could hardly be contained.

– Our powers aren't similar at all, Black Dragon added with impunity. – Contrary to you I have the ability to drive anyone insane.

Cassandra hissed at her, but it felt as threatening as lukewarm water.

Stern Mistress turned abruptly and rushed off, fading down the dark hallway, leaving Black Dragon alone with her shadows.

Chapter 24

The battle at Coleman Square began just before dusk.

The Cadre appeared in a wide circle, their attention turned inward, at the confused members of the Maverick Crew. Lucinda's former teammates had stepped into the portal and the Ebony Goddess had snapped her fingers and made them appear according to her desires.

The late day's sun had become a moon and the Ebony Goddess cast its wide and deep shadow across the square. Pedestrians, ordinary citizens going about their ordinary tasks shrieked in horror.

Red dust and steam flowed from Black Dragon's nostrils. She stood with her hounds and those under her command, dispersed, like all the dragons evenly around the circle.

Black Dragon was with the Ebony Goddess, there, in the Crew's midst, creating increasing confusion and disarray. Lucinda practically felt Claudia thought by thought, the frown on the woman's brow turning deeper and deeper.

Melinda wasn't there. She had left, practically fled from Claudia's pervasive dominance weeks ago.

All Lady Grace's attempts at reading the army surrounding the Crew were returned to her. She felt it like a wall of thought surrounded her. Black Dragon smiled.

Oil screamed and collapsed.

Lavender froze. She saw a dark shadow appear in front of her.

You thought I was your shadow, but you were totally mistaken in your inane belief. The truth of the matter, of course is that you are mine.

Lavender choked and kept choking and could hardly move a finger, totally frozen in place by an all-encompassing, insane fear.

ATTACK!

The command was given, the battle commenced. Four dragons and their hounds and warriors charged forward as a first wave. The second followed moments later.

The attack force was like an immutable object of flesh and fury. Only a few was struck down and kept from participating in the fight.

Ordinary people still in the line of fire were swept aside, killed by a casual swat of the hand or by ignoring the immutable force moving forward.

It wasn't really much of a fight. The prey at the end of the short run was on the defensive from the start. They were overrun and overwhelmed quickly, unable to offer anything beyond feeble resistance.

Brick attempted to counter-attack, but many of those coming at him were just as big and strong or almost there. He managed to strike down only a few before they started hammering him.

Lady Grace screamed in pain as she attempted to mind-blast her closest opponents and fell to the ground.

Feet and hands contacted with flesh. Blood and pieces of flesh began dancing in the air.

And then it was as if the late day sky started bleeding, and it was no longer moonlight, but a red, thick and dry air stealing the breath from her lungs, a pervasive reality filled with fighting people and the cruelest, most brutal violence.

This was a no killing mission, something becoming clear quickly, as beaten prisoners were chained and a few of them, like Oil were collared.

It was practically over already. Black Dragon could walk among the fighters without being bothered much. She kicked and prodded those already prisoners.

Flight Captain fled, horror stuck on his face. He took flight and took off the fastest he was able. Lucinda ignored him. She studied him, his fear-filled mind, as he was torn between terror and wild, irrational hope the more seconds passed of his doomed escape attempt.

A powerful energy blast hit him. He fell paralyzed to the ground.

They were on him the moment he landed, assaulting him from all sides. It took no more than a few seconds until he had been pacified and taken prisoner like the rest.

A group homed in on the big, sweaty and bruised shaking woman.

– So, this is the mighty Lady Grace? She looks like wet paper.

Two men held her. A woman fondled her with brutal touches. Claudia shook hard. Lucinda strengthened her fear, making it grow like wildfire.

A loud whimper of despair rose from an already sore throat.

– No, a hoarse whisper rose from an already sore throat, – please no!

Loud and patronizing and vicious chuckles assaulted the prisoner at their mercy.

– You will be a great puppy, won't you? Red Dragon chastised her. – Such a great, sweet puppy?

– No, Claudia whimpered, – no.

There was no conviction backing her words.

She crumbled further, by the second, as their invasive intrusion in her private space progressed.

– Okay, people, Black Dragon shouted. – Fun is over. Process them. They're ours, now, and soon they will be us.

It had been so simple. To say that it had been like snapping fingers was an understatement.

The captives were brutally made to stand, with strikes and whippings and harsh commands.

– You never had a change, Blue Dragon taunted Lady Grace. – How does that make you feel, huh? Tell me, tell me, *tell me!*

She slapped the once so feared leader of the Maverick Crew, slapped her repeatedly.

Claudia kept staring straight ahead with dull eyes.

Lucinda started grabbing and squeezing both female and male prisoners, their cocks and cunts and all, making sure they felt bad about it. They squirmed and shrunk under her brutal handling, feeling many times the pain and shame and a horror beyond words.

- No, Mechanic shouted well beyond mind-numbing panic. – NO!

Black Dragon squeezed his balls, making sure it hurt, easily evoking his need. She tore open his pants and underwear, exposing his erect cock.

Malignant laughter mocked him and the rest, making it all feel even worse. They were all stripped of clothes and masks and everything.

The march began. Lois whipped Flight Captain, whipped him hard.

– It hurts, he choked, tears flooding his cheeks. – It isn't supposed to hurt.

– Shut the fuck up, *boy,* Lois snapped, and dealt him yet another devastating lashing.

They were processed, going through all the stages of initiation and inclusion from the Trial of Cleansing and onward established by the Cadre. Black, Blue and Red Dragon followed them every step of the way. The Maverick Crew was merely one of several groups of captives dumped into the field of mist and was met by the same people that had sent them down the tunnels. Lois was also there with the remaining dragons, accompanied by her skilled torturers. She was always there.

The cages were filled, filled beyond capacity. Some captives had to be chained to the floor outside. Sweat, fear, terror and malice seethed in the very air.

Black Dragon felt everyone's despair. She used it, used the loop to make it worse. Distress totally overwhelmed the prisoners and some of them began shouting and shaking in terror. Black Dragon cackled aloud, pleased beyond words.

The members of the Cadre had become galvanized against her methods, at least to a point. The pervasive fear in the air strengthened them, made them shout in contempt and triumph.

Days without numbers had passed since the new prisoners had been added to the pens. They had become hardly more than shaking leaves. Time moved painfully slow, each moment experienced like an eternity.

Four dragons patrolled the pens, looking at those inside the cages with cruel and predatory eyes. Fear grew further in the minds and hearts of the prisoners.

The four stopped outside the cage where Claudia resided. Adeline opened the door with a slight nudge of her powerful mind.

– OUTSIDE, LADY WORM! Lisa ordered the crouching human being inside. – At attention!

She slammed her whip at the ground.

The other captives had no doubt which prisoner the dragon commanded, and they felt both spite and relief.

Claudia moved with desperate speed, standing straight almost before her former teammate had finished speaking. She stared straight ahead with hazy eyes, her lips and limbs shaking hard.

Lisa gave her one single lash on the butt. The prisoner jumped in shock and terror. More lashes followed, until the shaking woman stood still, and just endured the beyond brutal punishment.

– You will not move, Blue Dragon snarled. – You will not move an inch, or you will be sorry.

Claudia hardly moved, but she released a loud whimper dominated by an even more overwhelming terror.

She had long since stopped attempting to use her mind as a power. It stayed on, in its passive mode. Lucinda made sure it did, but she no longer had the ability to influence or dominate a fly.

– Good evening, Worm, Lisa greeted her.

– Good evening, My Lady, Claudia replied with a bland voice and expression.

– Who are you? Lucinda snapped.

Claudia looked at her with a prevalent haze in her eyes, hardly seeing anything, a lasting frown painted on her face.

– I'm Worm, My Lady.

Adeline snickered wickedly.

– Isn't that grand? Isn't the worm a good worm?

Base relief flooded the weary features. Tense shoulders sagged.

– I don't think it is, Lucinda said.

Lady Grace looked bewildered at her, desperately attempting to retain her pride and reason.

– I think it's just pretending.

– No, My Lady, please, no!

A childish wail rose from the big woman.

– I think you hit it on the nail, Black Dragon, Blue Dragon said. – She's just a willful and deceitful *dissenter* pretending to be one of us.

Lisa, the Blue Dragon slapped her and slapped her again. Worm fell and hit the floor hard. Something dawned on her. Doubt became certainty. She looked dumbfounded up at three of the dragons hovering above her.

– Will you look at that, Lucinda chuckled pleased. – She's such a bright puppy!

In her shock and sudden added distress the woman on the floor reacted instinctively, reaching out to Black Dragon, pushing into her mind or attempting to do so.

L-luc…

The scream reached well above the countless other screams in the hall.

You will never do that *again,* the beyond cruel and mighty voice filled her mind, her very self.

The lashings hammered her. Lois mostly held back and enjoyed watching the other three punish the once so powerful Lady Grace. The sudden, extended rage almost overtook them completely. They held back and stepped back with an effort, their faces lit by expectation, not regret.

– Crawl back into your cage, worm, cold, hard Blood Diamond told the bloody and shaking figure on the floor.

Pure hatred poured from Red Dragon, making every guard see red.

The piece of raw flesh and exposed bones obeyed with a sudden, panicked eagerness. Adeline slammed the door behind her the moment she reached inside.

They opened the next cage. Lois picked and grabbed Howard Eisenhouse from the overcrowded space and pulled him outside and began whipping him without delay, reducing him even more in stature compared to the shivering bundle of flesh he had already become.

Black Dragon knelt down by his side, rubbing him with kind, comforting strokes.

– Poor boy, she said softly. – Poor boy.

He began shaking harder. It was as if every single piece of his skin shook, as if he had become a walking earthquake. She squeezed his balls, making sure it hurt far more than it was supposed to do. He crouched there, only dimly aware of his surroundings.

Other dragons played with Brick, with Hans Nielsen. Their physical strength was probably not greater than his, but they were so much faster, and Lucinda knew he would have been no match for them even without the unending torture he had suffered.

422

– You're prime stud material, of course, Cassandra said matter of fact. – You will father many of our second generation warriors. They will be reared by the Cadre, and not suffer from your pathetic weakness.

Lucinda felt the constant warm and pleasant surge roll repeatedly through her. This, all this was such a satisfying task.

– The Ebony Goddess be praised, you are actually purring, aren't you, Black Dragon? Adeline mused, the smile playing on her thin lips.

– I am, Red Dragon, Lucinda shrugged. – Serving the Ebony Goddess and her purpose is such a great thrill. We are… blessed.

There was very little thought beyond those words and the emotion they brought her.

– Praise the Ebony Goddess, the others, the very room voiced, and everybody's mind did as well.

Darkness lit the room, from one moment to the next, and the dragons' joy became rapture. Every single being present fell on their knees and collapsed in a shaking bundle of terror and pleasure.

The Dark God entered the hall. She walked from one door to one of the cages. No one dared look at her or even contemplated doing so.

She walked, flowed to the cage that included Star Bartlett, where darkness already danced and flowed. Its door opened.

– Come, my shadow, the Ebony Goddess called. – Become one with your maker.

She who had been Lavender, but now was hardly more than an ethereal bundle of molecules, crawled out of the cage, and flowed through the air. Jolene Masters turned and left. The shadow tailed her, practically joining with the giant form, fading away to nothing way before they had exited the hall.

Light returned to the dark place. Existence put on hold resumed anew.

The cruel training, the terror regime continued.

The prisoners were fed like small children, and they looked at their captors with infinite gratitude, as their lips closed around the teat and sucked the bottle empty.

Claudia tried, through a rock-hard focus to keep the shit inside. Lucinda studied her with a patronizing grin, and let Claudia know she did so.

The shit burst out and flowed down the thighs. Claudia broke down in a wail of tears and collapsed on the floor, the spiteful laughter echoing in her ears.

Many days and night had passed. Lucinda didn't know how many, not this time either. She saw the recruits march, saw them wash and fight and wash again.

Howard Eisenhouse, he who had been Flight Captain fought. His thick skin made it very hard to hurt him, even though some opponents managed to best him, to beat him into unconsciousness and defeat, but he wasn't really hurt.

– Set Brick up against him next, Black Dragon instructed the Instructor.

The man bowed in servility and did as he was told. He understood and a brutal grin showed that he would enjoy what would follow.

Brick hit Howard in the face, making him stagger. He hit him again and again, and he went down and stayed down. The next time Brick took his time beating him, making him suffer in the process. Black Dragon made Howard feel bad, really bad about it.

He writhed on the mat during «rest», plagued by pain and unending nightmares. She knelt down by him and began rubbing him gently, whispering comforting words in his ears. The tears came quickly.

Suddenly the nature of her treatment of him changed. Her face twisted into a brutal grin and she began striking him and punishing him. She couldn't really harm him physically, but she could make each touch hurt. His expression turned shocked and horrified.

– You're still just a cripple at heart, Black Dragon spat at him.

She grabbed his hand and rubbed it, becoming gentle again. He choked in horror, despair and longing. She didn't even have to make him do… much. It was so clear in his mind, how he practically embraced his new reality, how he bonded with her, how she tied him to her with a thousand strands of the spider's web.

Hands, clever, manipulative hands grabbed his cock and began playing with it. He began breathing faster, fearing and anticipating what was coming.

Listen to me, Howard.

He did and looked at her beyond attentive and eager.

You will become *hard*. Your brethren in the Ebony Goddess' army will come to fear you, and follow you eagerly because of that, because they will know that when you shout your commands, they will be an echo of hers.

His cock grew, hardening between his thighs and in her skilled hands. She stopped just before it happened. He panted in her grip. She slapped him on the cheek. It hurt bad! He released a wail of regret, yet again baring his neck to her.

Good boy!

He ejaculated in her hands, and collapsed in her arms, releasing loud, silent cries of gratitude and subservience. He had submitted to her beyond rejection or recall.

She left him there and walked the dark hallways alone, a banshee hardly even there, never truly alone. They were all with her, in her ever expanding mindscape.

She heard two girls having a hushed conversation filled with awe.

– The Ebony Goddess is so mighty, one of them said. – She *is* a goddess, it's a fact, so far above the rest of us that none of us can stand against her, not even collectively.

The other nodded mute and frozen, the mere thought of the creature in all its glory serving to paralyze her.

Black Dragon froze and shook as well, her well established control slipping into nightmares and terror she had no change of holding at bay.

She walked with fast, measured steps, returning to Claudia. The former leader of the Maverick Crew hardly had any self image left to speak of anymore. It was shrunk, transparent and shredded beyond repair. Lucinda made her re-experience the rapes. It was no easier or harder than anything else she had done. Men and women touched Worm and violated her, and she was no more than a helpless bystander to it all, a passenger in her own body.

Pain shook the wet rag on the mat, filled her. She woke up and looked straight up at the mirror image of her nightmare.

The powerful frame crumbled even further during the first few seconds. She kept disintegrating in all the seconds following.

Black Dragon smiled down on her, filled with triumph and contempt.

– Poor Claudia. I always wondered about your motivation and your seemingly supreme confidence, but now I can easily see the truth: There aren't any. There is nothing there behind the bluster and confident shell.

Lucinda knelt down, towering above the crouching figure, rubbing it in comforting gestures.

– Look at me, *look at me…* little one.

Claudia obeyed, startled, instantly realizing the significance of those affectionate two words.

– So, tell me, Lady Grace, how do you find the Cadre, find the Ebony Goddess' palace? Is it to your liking?

Lady Grace blinked with constantly wet eyes.

– W-what?

Lucinda grinned, a grin she knew to be sinister beyond words.

– You are the true instigator, you know, you and Harold, your conviction of regimentation and order. You took me as a young girl and formed me in your image. Then you made me help you with Oracle, aiding in her evolution, practically causing her transformation. Jolene says the Cadre is the philosophy of the Maverick Crew brought to its ultimate, logical conclusion and she is very much correct.

Claudia tried, tried to resist the endless, invasive probes. Lucinda made her pay for it instantly, giving her even more pain than all contact with her mind would normally give the other, way inferior telepath. Claudia screamed again, whimpering like the child she was. Eyes like wounds looked blindly at the creature completely dominating her perception.

– Don't worry, little one, I'm gonna fill you, fill you to the brim. Eventually there will be no more pain, only the joy of service. You will like that, will actually love it, won't you?

There was a light prodding, demanding an answer. Claudia froze and nodded, unable to stop the sniffing and whimpering.

– That's a good girl. You have just earned a reward methinks.

Reward? A hopeful smile touched lips and features in the tear-wet face.

– Precisely! You will love it!

She grabbed the head of the big girl in front of her with big hands, effortlessly focusing on the task ahead.

– Your name is Vivian.

The woman frowned.

– What are you saying?

– I'm saying that I'm baptizing you Vivian, you dumb slut. Shut up and pay attention, dumb slut.

Shut up. The woman nodded. Pay attention. She nodded again.

– There was a big and tall redhair very full of herself that met her match. Her name is Vivian and she became the maid and hound of Black Dragon.

– But my name is C-claudia, the young woman stuttered. – And I don't have red hair.

– Certainly not and of course you have, Black Dragon snorted. – I'm your master and I, the generous master that I am baptize you, give you a name where no name existed.

The confusion and chaos in there made Black Dragon's words rattle her further. The head with the bewildered eyes practically shook by itself.

– No, NO!

She pulled back and crumbled on the floor, practically fading on the spot, distressed beyond anything, slipping further away by the second.

– Your kind master will recreate you in her image, and you will want for nothing more.

Sweat covered every single piece of skin the crouching figure displayed. Her wide open eyes seemed to be filled with water and dirt. She crawled back to Black Dragon, resting her head in her lap. The regal figure petted her kindly, spoke to her softly.

– Yes, you are clearly improving, but you are not quite there yet. You need a few more physical and mental advances, and Black Dragon, like the generous Master she is, will help you achieve them.

She who would be Vivian sat strapped to a chair in Alysse's laboratory. Black Dragon sat leaned back in a high chair to her left and watched the proceedings with anticipation in her eyes.

Alysse stood close by to her right.

– Black Dragon, in her wisdom has ordained I assist her in making a few necessary changes to your appearance, Alysse said eagerly. – Your fangs must show and they must be more pronounced. You will be a hound in a Dragon's service and must look the part. I will, by the grace of the Goddess make all much needed changes in your features. You will be a work of art by the time I am done with you.

She held up a rather big needle, one attached to a thin rope. The woman, the scared young girl in the chair shook her head in denial and terror.

– Hush, Alysse whispered.

Hush, Black Dragon told her. Be brave, little one. Embrace your new reality.

Brave, the little one nodded. Embrace. She nodded again.

Alysse put a gloved hand into her mouth. Then, with a confident move she made the first penetration of the cheek. The little one felt the pain, but could not move. More tears jumped from her sore eyes. Alysse drew the line all the way, until it stopped when the huge knot at its end stopped at the moist inside of the cheek. She made more incisions and penetrations. Then she repeated the procedure with another needle and rope at the other cheek. She pulled the ropes back, pulled them back hard, and tied them together at the back of the head.

Alysse is an artist, little one. She will indeed make you into a work of art. You will embrace the pain and pleasure of serving me, and want for nothing more.

– Yes, she who would be Vivian panted, mumbling, not able to talk properly, – the pain, the PAIN.

She could no longer close her mouth. Her face felt like it was burning.

– There, the first, modest phase of your change is complete, Alysse said content. – When I am done your beautiful visage will terrify the enemies of the Cadre.

A vision assaulted Claudia, one of a face looking more like a skull than a face. Black Dragon seemed to stand above her, pushing a hand at her cunt. Riles of pleasure rode she who had been Lady Grace.

Alysse held up a syringe.

– This is my own formula, she stated proudly, – a distillation made from Cougar's DNA. It will make your fangs sharper and longer, among other things. It will not change you significantly in itself, will not give you Cougar's powers, but will be one of several factors in your overall change. You will be able to bite and shred your prey. I *know* you look forward to taste the warm blood in your mouth. The mix of surgical and biological procedures will ensure that you will become a great, new creature serving your dragon.

She squealed in delight as she set the needle.

Claudia floated away, her few remaining pieces melting into nothing.

The breaking of a telepath continued unabated even beyond that, beyond reason, until her last remaining defenses crumbled, and she was totally exposed to Black Dragon's cruel and potent machinations.

Black Dragon dreamed the empty shell, filled it with her essence. It was an easy, thoroughly enjoyable task. Lucinda felt herself turn wet and hot below. She chuckled wickedly.

The girl with the red hair was born. She grew up in the service of Black Dragon. She learned early the difference between a pat on the head and a lash on the back and to love both, to cherish her master above all, treasuring the day she received her death mask, the physical proof of her newfound stature as the best in her life. She looked beyond excited at herself in the mirror.

Young Vivian joined Black Dragon's hounds. She was presented to them with lots of snarls and patronizing chuckles.

– She's the lowest among you, Black Dragon told them. – Show her the ropes and all.

Expectation added itself to the quality of snarls and laughter.

She knelt deep and in awe before Black Dragon.

– Thank you, Master, she gave her praise. – I am yours, forever!

And Lucinda Patterson knew that to be true.

The Ebony Goddess picked Alan Prescott, among several promising candidates to serve under Alysse in the laboratory. The two of them together, allowed to a point to indulge in every single depravity they had ever entertained became very useful to the Goddess. He didn't really need much convincing, just a tiny push here and there. Lucinda felt his eagerness to start his new life, felt his dark desire awaken fully.

She was able to study that in detail, able to hear the screams in there even when there wasn't any, as she was able to sense almost anything happening within the Goddess' aerie, the hallow ground of reeducation and teaching. It was a satisfying task watching him, as he put collars around many a slender neck. He relished in his duty, both when he infrequently participated in hunts and in the laboratory. He no longer held back when he tortured his subjects, and he was, with a few, necessary restrictions given free reign. His «educational» skills concerning teaching new recruits their place and duties were almost as effective as that of any dragon.

His experiments began in earnest. Lucinda followed them closely and with interest as well.

Scott Walsingham had been stretched out on the bench.

– He's sturdy this one, Alan said excited to the visiting Black Dragon. – I believe firmly he can take a lot of punishment, and that he can, if he survives be one of the most powerful of us all, and will be able to serve the Cadre and the Ebony Goddess with distinction.

He deferred to Alysse.

– I concur, she said, equally excited. – He's very versatile and has such a wide range of gifts, in spite of his hopelessly weak mind. We learned a lot dissecting his sister's carcass. They are or were very similar in their makeup. We took samples and ovaries from her and have semen and samples from him as well, in case he croaks prematurely, and we still desire more progeny from him.

Lucinda took a closer look, on all levels. Yes, there was power there, in the boy's ravaged body and broken mind, beneath the tear-wet face and ever-shaking skin.

– He looks like just another ragged doll.

She shrugged. Ultimately it didn't matter. He was just one more recruit crushed under the Cadre's relentless training and indoctrination regime, one more piece of the Ebony Goddess' body.

Black Dragon took Ashley Hastings under her wings, as she had done Claudia Malone, even though the former Wind submitted far more voluntarily, practically eagerly to her will and guidance. Wind became Hurricane. Claudia became Domina, yet another dedicated and useful servant.

It was another crisp and bright morning. Another hallowed hunt was about to commence.

The girl's heart beat like a jackhammer. Lucinda felt that and a thousand other things about Kid Sister's body and mind.

Melinda had regained her faculties, her relative independence since she had escaped from Claudia's constant influence and dominance. She led the sorry wretches attempting to flee from the hunters.

Lucinda held Domina and Predator in chains. They crouched on all fours by her side. Hurricane levitated just as eager in the air ahead.

I see them, My Lady. They're exactly where we want them.

Black Dragon nodded pleased to herself. They had been goaded and hounded for weeks, until they no longer saw any other outcome than being on the run, and the true hunt had commenced.

She let go of the chains.

Her hounds charged forward like a force of nature. It was a pleasure to behold. They spread out in the terrain, and Lucinda spread out with them. Hurricane hovered, floating forward patiently, giving Lucinda an angle she hadn't had before.

She had no trouble accessing the thoughts of the prey. It was all the usual panicked abandon, rabbits fleeing before the predators. Melinda tried, tried thinking and analyzing, but it was no good. Paralyzing fright took hold of her as well.

Confident hounds quickly closed in on the prey. Lucinda frowned. She noticed Melinda's totally elevated heart-rate, far beyond what the running, even the panic would cause. And she certainly wasn't dying, but appeared healthier than ever. Lucinda realized startled, actually startled that the girl was growing taller and bigger as she ran. Her body broke the fabric of her clothes. Black Dragon studied the spectacle immensely fascinated.

Melinda Patterson turned and raised a hand. There was no thought, no deliberate action there. Mere instinct made her turn and fight.

The hand and the area surrounding it exploded in darkness.

Everything faded in an instant, not to black, but to nothing. To Lucinda, for the briefest of moments there was nothing, no outside input, no sensation whatsoever, the worst kind of hell imaginable. For her hounds that sensation prevailed. She felt their terror and heard their inner and outer screams. It would take minutes for them to recover, if they ever did.

Black Dragon stumbled on, her senses turning themselves on and off, towards the dizzy and both weakened and empowered giant crouching on the ground.

Nice one, Kid Sister, *now* you've grown. But you're still far behind me.

Melinda blinked.

– L-lucinda?

– Hello, little snowflake.

– You have become…?

– I have, Lucinda answered all her questions. – I have become everything I've ever dreamed of becoming.

Melinda crouched there, still in disbelief and shock, but turning strangely calm, and other, more fundamental urges presented themselves.

Hungry, so hungry!

Of course you are. You've grown big and strong and filled with Hunger.

Lucinda found a bottle with a teat and pushed it at the girl's lips. Melinda

430

sucked it empty in a matter of seconds. Lucinda found another. Melinda sucked on that as well, sucked it dry fairly quickly. She looked up at her sister both apprehensive and grateful.

– You have been bad and will be punished.

She struck her, hurt her on a fundamental level. Melinda howled in pain and misery, pleasing Big Sister to no end.

Lucinda let go of her.

– You will melt, dissolve into nothing and then turn into hard ice, a blade cutting anything and anyone.

Melinda attempted to speak. Unable to do so, she burst with thoughts.

What happened toyou? What have youbecome???

That's the wrong question. We've both become what we've always been destined to become. It's time to put childish and silly questions behind us as well. You made me repeat myself, little snowflake and rest assured that you will pay for that.

Melinda looked at her with eyes like wounds, a growing resentment and determination. Lucinda's heart beat faster in pride.

– You once swore to me that you would join me in vengeance against the world. That time has now come. Are you ready?

Swollen eyes stared defiantly up at her. When the girl spoke, it was with a soft, spiteful voice.

– Aye, Black Dragon. I am, I will be thy dark companion, depriving all thy enemies of their faculties.

– Very good. I'm pleased to tell you that your path through the Cadre's training regime will be harder, much harder than that of most others. When you're done you will be tougher, crueler and better than them all.

She put the collar around her neck, turning off the dizzying power in the new, giant body on the ground.

– When this is removed you will be weak and innocent Melinda no longer, but something truly powerful, something beyond vast and mighty. We will prowl the Earth together.

The hounds did recover, slowly regaining their faculties, shaking their heads in confusion and abject terror both, looking at their Master in both shame and relief when they discovered that she had the situation well in hand.

She edited their thoughts, confusing them with sensations of a harder than expected battle, but nothing beyond that. The prey woke up as well, scared and confused and still the easy prey.

– Process them, Black Dragon shouted, emanating calm and confidence.

Domina snapped at their legs with her fangs, circling them on all fours, terrorizing them from displaying whatever bravery they had left. They looked beyond stricken at her visage.

Another Trail of Cleansing began. Melinda steeled herself against the lashes. Black Dragon made sure she was hit that much harder than the others, made sure she cried out in misery and pain, ignoring, rejecting Kid Sister's pathetic pleas for lenience.

Time ran. Events flowed like flashes, like lightning. A giant combined police and military force gathered around a large area of buildings in a major city. Black Dragon gathered her force of both female and male hounds. Howard Eisenhouse, the eager Hardman placed himself at attention before her. So did Domina, Sledgehammer and many others. That also included Bird of Prey, Stern Mistress and a couple of the other dragons. There was no more illusion of equality between them. They were hers to deploy as she wished.

The attack on the combined uniform-clad force began completely without warning. The brutal and superior forces of the Cadre appeared in the defenders' midst and began exterminating them. Predator swatted a man with much of his armor gone with her claws and practically split him in two. Domina slit a woman's throat with her fangs. Poison Oil made blood flow from open wounds. The others were no less brutal. Black Dragon walked calmly up stairs splashed with blood, flesh, bones and guts. She didn't really participate in the «battle» at all, but just swatted a few flies when they dared venturing too close to her sharp and deadly wings and hot breath.

Black Dragon stood at the top of the tallest building and looked at the city, at the world from all angles.

They placed explosive charges in the entire inner city area. Then they disappeared like ghosts and the charges went off, and the central part of a giant urban area was reduced to rubble, and heaps of bones and stinking flesh.

The Cadre and its influence, its power spread across the planet, slowly, inevitably. It took hold in major cities, subtle at first, but then growing, growing, growing, supplanting plastic, glass, concrete and metals in people's consciousness.

The Ebony Goddess appeared in front of Black Dragon, ethereal, untouchable.

– You've done well, Black Dragon. Know that the Ebony Goddess is pleased with you.

Melinda knelt down before Black Dragon one bright day. She no longer wore her collar and her power glowed within her.

Sense Deprivation humbly presents herself to her Queen. She stands ready to serve her with all the power she possesses, with everything she is.

432

Black Dragon accepts her new servant and takes possession of her and everything she is.

She slipped inside and stayed there, attaching all important parts of her sibling to herself. Melinda whimpered a bit at first, but then the dark, dark smile of boundless enthusiasm lit up her face.

Sense Deprivation is no more than an extension of Black Dragon, a tiny part floating at the edge of her consciousness, a weapon longing to be *used*.

– I understand, Melinda gasped, the rapture filling her. – I UNDERSTAND!

The tiny mark of the dragon appeared on her arm. It did so without Lucinda using the physical branding device. She looked stunned at it.

I don't, she told herself.

But understanding was close, now, as if she could almost touch it, touch what had eluded her all this time.

A bell chimed somewhere, penetrating flesh and mind, the dark, dark surface she had previously only glimpsed.

Still meaningless images and sensations flowed through her mind, her being.

It was the day of the Great Darkness, the seconds before everything turned shadow. She was a young teenager walking the streets with her sister and her friend, the long lost friend, which name she could no longer recall.

Lights and eyes and flesh flickered on and off. She re-experienced the day many years later when she and Jolene had made their magick within the pentacle, when they had touched the firmament of forever.

She's not solid, neither here nor there or anywhere anymore, floating through eternity like a specter, except… except…

Lucinda could ride her, had been able to do so right from the start, from when they first met, ride time back and forth, but just ride, no more, being nothing but a helpless passenger on the Ebony Goddess' back.

Thought brought analysis, brought clarity. The puzzle… put itself together. Eyes turned wide.

Lucinda saw herself as that young teenager. The Great Darkness filled her up, supercharged her beyond imagination.

– Get away from me, you dumb bitch!

Feature by feature older Lucinda recognized for the first time younger Claudia Malone. In the commotion, in the terror after the event Lucinda had grabbed her hips, had dug her fingers, her claws deep into Claudia…

And taken, copied her powers.

The big brute in the Cage of Five:

– What did you do, bitch? What did you do to me?

Copied his powers.

Not only temporary, but…

Forever.

Black Dragon smiled.

It took a lot, she surmised, not mere touch, but angry or frightened or lusty touch or something similar.

Clarity surged through her.

She was finally able to identify the emotion deep within Jolene, within the Ebony Goddess: It was fear, numbing, paralyzing fear for the only creature in existence that might challenge her.

Instant by instant, tick by tock Lucinda waited between those for the one moment… that would liberate her from uncertainty, nagging doubt, mud (nothing but mud) and fear and a horrible, unending subservience.

NOW!

Black Dragon triggered the power within Sense Deprivation. Jolene Masters appeared between them. Lucinda was already on her way forward, her hands reaching out like claws.

The world turned black. Black Dragon recovered quickly. The Ebony Goddess did as well, but she staggered, dazed and confused. Black Dragon grabbed her as she snarled in ferocity unheard of. They both screamed, in pain, in pure, feral rage.

– I AM YOU, Lucinda shouted fueled with hatred, her face becoming like that of an angel of death. – YOU ARE NOT ME!

Fear filled the Goddess, but contempt as well.

They slipped out of existence, out of the material world. Lucinda knew that, because suddenly all of Jolene's thoughts were open to her. The Abyss opened up on all sides. She felt it.

She felt herself being torn apart, even as she viciously attacked her mortal enemy and ripped her flesh, her mind and very being.

Reality, as it was, or might be was ripped apart around them.

Words failed them. All expression, except features twisted in hatred faded away.

They fought on what seemed like a thousand different levels.

Doves flapped their wings, wings falling apart, a thousand doves dropping like flies.

Stench filled her, overwhelming her perception.

An unpleasant truth burned Black Dragon's already fried synapses.

The Ebony Goddess had become too powerful, had grown too much into her power, and in doing so had turned practically undefeatable. Panic, fear and hatred beyond any sensible meaning surged through Black Dragon. She redoubled her efforts, tripled them, drawing on every erg of resources of body and mind and whatever more there was. There had to be a way, there had to…

Reality shifted, and shifted again, a thousand times thousand more in the eternity to come. Locked in each other's deadly grip, they rotated, tumbled through the air in an indistinct landscape of mist and shadow.

There has to be a way

Way

WAY

way

She gasped when there was no air to gasp. She blinked with no eyelids to blink. Everything reached her undiluted.

A billion nails stabbed her from every possible angle of existence.

V2
Part Three:
The Goddess

Chapter 25

Eternity blinked and split in two.

Gimmick and Oracle awoke at the center of the pentacle, as if from a deep, deep dream, letting go of each other's hands, moaning in pain and misery.

Lucinda Patterson, in that very moment saw everything crystal clear, saw how the familiar and deadly cunning supplanted the initial confusion and horror in Jolene Masters' eyes. The second heartbeat followed the first, followed by a third, and then Lucinda lounged herself forward with all her strength.

Her hands, formed like claws buried themselves in Jolene's skin, on both sides of her chest. Jolene screamed, a piercing wail shocking the others to the bone. Lucinda sensed it as if it was her own. With a mighty burst of her power she looked into everybody's mind, even Grace's, and no one was the wiser, no one noticed. She held on to the desperately struggling body and equally struggling mind in front of her, with equally sharp claws of body and mind, knowing beyond knowing she was winning, was overpowering her opponent.

Jolene's wail rose yet another pitch, before it stopped, stopped abruptly, as if cut off by a knife. Wide open eyes closed, as if someone had turned a switch. Lucinda let go of her, and she dropped like wet rags, her head hitting the floor with a dump sound.

She lay still. Gimmick, her eyes filled with tears pulled away from her with a frantic, clearly distressed yelp. The others stood there, frozen.

– It was her, Gimmick choked. – She didn't know, not before we emerged from the trance. I saw it, saw how she became the future nightmare version of herself in her mind. She would have pointed at another, one she felt was the biggest threat to her, or at least one we could believe would be capable of it, and we would have believed her, and she would have gathered her strength and her forces in the shadows, until she had been ready, ready to strike, years in the future. I remember *everything*.

The pentacle dissolved around them, the blood and the powder fading as if it had never been there at all. Lady Grace bent down by the still Jolene.

– Her mind is empty. She shook her head, distracted drying the blood from her nose from her lips. – There is nothing left.

– I shut her down, Gimmick said with shivering lips. – I had no choice.

She rose, drying her tears, standing before them with eyes like open wounds.

– Let me show you, Lucinda said with shivering lips, – let me *show* you what she was about.

Flight Captain nodded first, then Raven Bird, The Bowman and the others, and finally after some hesitation did Lady Grace.

Gimmick raised a hand in a dramatic gesture, replaying the events she recalled so clearly in her mind, to those watching. As they watched an image, a series of images formed in the very air in front of them. They stood there, mesmerized while what would never be played itself out before their eyes. They saw both Oracle and Gimmick emerge from the trance, Gimmick dazed and confused, Oracle sharp and focused. She pointed an accusing finger at Cougar. «It's her», she cried. «She will Change and become Black Dragon, the terror from my nightmares». She showed them, with images forming in the air, how Cougar changed, how she grew taller and grew true claws and a demonic visage, and how she used her greater power to destroy and ruin lives. «That can't be», Cougar gasped. «I would never do anything like that, become anything like that. You can't possibly believe I will»? But they did. It was evident in the sick revulsion and shame in their features when they looked at her. «Fine»! Cougar snarled. «I wouldn't want to be one of you assholes, anyway». She rushed out. «We should stop her», The Bowman said, unusually meek. But no one moved. The last vestiges of their innocent childhood's dream ended right there and then, never to be regained.

Lucinda showed them, showed them how Oracle orchestrated her own disappearance, how she changed from the fairly normal sized girl to the fearsome Black Dragon, how she created the worst terror regime ever seen on Earth. They watched themselves being captured and tortured and brainwashed, and becoming part of her vast and powerful army conquering the entire planet.

– STOP IT! Raven Bird shouted.

She stood there, shaking violently, gasping, having difficulties breathing.

– I can't watch anymore, she said meekly.

The images faded. Gimmick lowered her arm.

They glanced at Cougar. She pretended not to notice.

– She is indeed a late bloomer. Lady Grace nodded while looking down at the unmoving Oracle. – Even though one of her powers manifested itself fairly early, the other didn't.

– And it never will. The Bowman curled his hand into a fist. – Not if I have anything to say in the matter.

The others nodded, the revulsion and horror slowly being supplanted by determination and contempt.

Gimmick stood there with a bowed head, crying, sobbing silently and heartbreaking. Lady Grace walked to her, putting a hand on her shoulder.

– It must have been horrible for you. We only witnessed it, but it can be argued that you actually experienced it.

– It was. Gimmick nodded, while she kept drying her tears. – It felt so real, and there were moments when I feared it was actually h-happening.

– Perhaps it was, Flight Captain said, – in a different reality.

They all sighed, a sick sound of relief they couldn't hide.

– What about h-her?

The others were stunned to hear the catching in Cougar's voice. She pointed, without pointing to the unmovable figure on the ground with a shaking finger.

She didn't press her point, but what she was thinking and what was echoed by the others was clear:

We can't let her live.

– Her mind is gone, Lady Grace stated solemnly. – There is nothing there, nothing even remotely sentient or aware. She is no threat to anyone anymore.

She went and picked her up and held her in her strong arms, like she would a small child.

– I'll take her to a hospital. It doesn't really matter if they recognize her, but I'll remove her costume, and obscuring her, at least in minor ways. They will examine her, and then examine her some more, before concluding that there is nothing to be done, and they will skip her off to a nursing home and there they will care for her, for the rest of her life.

They nodded, nodded again, and it felt, in their despair like it was the only thing they could do. Lady Grace left, with her burden.

Those remaining looked at Gimmick, looking for reassurance, for a sign that the world was sane, and she, at least for now was willing to grant them their heart's desire.

– You run along, she sniffed, she grinned reassuringly at them. – I want to stay here a bit. I need to. I will be fine.

They couldn't get out of there fast enough.

You stay, she sent to the Captain's mind.

He didn't notice a thing, didn't sense even a slight buzz in his mind, but he halted in his tracks.

– We shouldn't leave her alone.

The others took time to nod, before vanishing through the door. He returned to her.

She smiled to him, practically glowing in her girl-scout gratitude mode.

They heard the others leave, heard them move about in the outer room, and then there was only silence.

– It must have been horrible for you, he said, – practically experiencing all that.

– It was. She nodded bravely, sitting there with her hands on the couch, looking solemnly at him. – Thank you for caring, for being here for me. I need it, need it badly.

She beckoned him to her, with her eyes and body and mind, and he came. He sat down by her side. She saw his eyes turn moist in the face concealed by the mask. Her deep blue eyes filled the upper holes of her mask, and she knew he was drowning in her ocean.

– The Black Dragon and her Cadre captured me, she said softly. – They broke me and she rebuilt me in her image. I can't get rid of the revulsion, the fear and shame, no matter how hard I try.

– Nothing was left of the Oracle we know… knew? He wondered.

She knew how desperately he wanted reassurances, a declaration from her that there was at least a semblance of sanity left in the world.

– I remember that I did recognize her, vestiges of what she had been, Lucinda whispered, – and that made it *worse*.

He touched her cheek. She felt his skin, through her mask.

– It will fade in time, she assured him. – I will never forget, and I don't think I should, but I will put it behind me, and regain some semblance of peace.

– Good, he choked. – Good.

She put her head in his lap, resting there, slowly sighing. He put his hand on her head, patting it, in a comforting gesture. She had seen him do the same with Grace, and it pleased her.

– It feels so good, she mumbled, pulling her legs up, stretching her body on the couch.

He looked at her breasts. She knew that and would have known it, even without her powers. Her nipples hardened. She felt it and welcomed it, welcomed everything to follow. He looked at her, his eyes hazy with interest. She reached for his lips with her mouth, crawling onto his lap. There was no response at first, but then there was, and she choked and cried out in her need.

– Please, she gasped, – I don't want to be alone tonight. Please, Howard!

He shook imperceptibly, hesitating for one, two, three heartbeats, before grabbing her arms and pulling her close. She cried out in joy and began writhing eagerly in his lap. Her hips pushed at his, at the growing hardness making itself known in his pants. Heat below turned wet and sticky, and she gasped. She smiled sweetly and began removing the paraphernalia on her

442

uniform, the light jacket, with the gimmicks and gadgets, the belt, until she only wore the strip clothes, the dark grey spotted shirt and pants and the mask. Hands grabbed the lower part of the shirt and pulled, pulled it slowly up. She pulled away from him with an enticing smile, stepping out on the floor, pulling the shirt over her head, revealing herself, her dancing, swollen breasts. Hands touched them in an impatient, confident manner. Hands moved the pants and panties down her thighs, until they rested by her feet. She spread her legs, revealing herself to him. Hands moved to the mask, removing it slowly, but inevitably. The blond hair fell down her back and on her shoulders. Her face smiled to him, fully, for the very first time.

She walked towards the bedroom, with the bed he shared with Grace, with Claudia, her head half turned, her face half exposed, showing him her excitement and need, her explicit and undying love.

– Come, she called hoarsely. – Come to me and make me happy. Love me!

He rose and followed in her tracks. She saw him, saw him undress, in a daze, in a need superseding everything else. She saw him remove his mask and reveal the face she already knew.

The heart hammered in her chest. It beat against the inside of her skin so hard that it hurt.

He caught up with her the exact moment she turned, the moment they reached the bed. She welcomed him into her arms, sighing happily in his ear. Hungry lips sought and found his, granting him sultry kisses. She felt it, felt how his hardening cock pushed at her skin.

– Your skin feels so good, she mumbled.

She knew Grace always complained about it, how it scratched her and hurt her.

There was pain, but she welcomed it, along with the rising pleasure and expectation riding her like a mare, a tide of razorblades. She moaned loud and longingly, telling him in all ways and none that she was his, his to do with as he pleased.

She entered the bed, never taking her eyes off his, giving him a smile filled with promise, promising him the world.

He jumped in after her, ramming into her in his boyish eagerness. They tumbled down on the bed, entangled and sweaty and beyond, way beyond impatient. He pushed himself inside her and she cried out in her pleasure and pain. She pushed back at him and he gasped, gasped hard.

– You liked that, didn't you? She giggled softly.

He nodded, nodded, nodded and nodded, pushing and pulling, pushing and pulling, pushing and pulling and pushing, pushing, pushing. Hands touched her all over, fondled her breasts and roamed below. She cried out in lust, in loud, horny screams.

I am a screamer, she thought.

And that made her laugh, laugh hard. She found it hysterically funny.

She rolled him over, on his back. He looked astonished at her. She bent over, giving him sweet, lingering kisses, moving her lower body up and down, up and down. He pushed, moved his hips. She rode him, using her spurs on him, digging in vain at his hard skin. It was… happening, she knew it was. She felt it rise within, the pleasure, the pain, the Power. He turned hard, hard within her, filled her up, and she wanted him to.

And just as her water flooded his lower parts and she felt his hot flow, she grabbed, dug her nails and fingers into his upper body, from both sides. He let out a cry of pain, and she knew he couldn't distinguish it from the wild pleasure riding him, and she screamed, too, in savage joy, in fury, as the backlash hit her.

She fell on him, and rolled over, half on her side, but staying close. They both rested there, with hard breathing slowly returning to normal. She kissed him on the cheek. Whispering soundlessly:

– Thank you.

Thank you!

And she spotted tears in his eyes and chuckled wickedly inside.

Her lip turned wet, and when she touched it with a hand, the hand turned red with blood.

– Did I strike you? He raised his head startled, alarmed. – I struck you, didn't I?

– It was accidental, she mewed, – in your great fervor. Don't worry about it!

She kissed him, and his lips, too turned red with blood.

– It was *wild!*

She grinned, flashing her teeth, her fangs, and she shuddered in expectation, delight, in dread. The…

– The deed already done keeps happening, she said.

– What?

He looked disoriented at her.

– It was what Jolene said tonight. Don't you remember?

He kept looking at her with his dumb, dumb eyes, and she felt a deep, deep contempt for him.

– Tonight's events are obviously weighing hard on you, he said, patting her cheek again.

She shrugged, once again giving him her best of smiles.

– It is, she agreed. – And you're being so kind to me. Thank you. Thank you.

444

She rubbed herself at him, and her contact with his sandpaper-like skin made her feel needy again. His cock began twitching. She turned her back to him, pushing her butt at his groin. He opened and closed his eyes once.

– Put it inside again, she begged him, with her needy voice. – Please!

He did. During a span of a moment or two he had grabbed her hips, and pushed himself inside her warm and wet nest. She wriggled her butt, rotated it with a pleased hum. His hands, his rough skin on hers, on her calves, her breasts and all over her made her completely ravenous with lust.

– That's my boy, she purred. – That's my boy, my boy, my BOYYYY

– Yes, yes, yes, yes, yes, he grunted, holding his breath just as both their bodies froze, and exploded in one, final burst of energy. – YES!

They fell on the bed, gasping, their loud breathing slowly turning low.

– You are so beautiful, he gasped, love lit in his eyes, – so very, very beautiful.

– Thank you, she whispered, giving him tiny, tiny kisses, – you're so sweet, so very, very sweet.

It was quiet, so very quiet, even in her very sensitive, bursting at its seams mind. She let him coddle her, as she coddled him, as she treated him like the child he was.

Their eyes closed not long after that. She felt both him and herself slipping, slipping into sleep. With no or little effort she stopped that process in herself and transferred it into him, a kind of turning polarity. Yeah, it was very much like that. He fell into a deep, coma-like sleep.

– My dog, she snarled contemptuously, – my good dog. You performed quite well, adequately fulfilling your function.

She rose, disentangling herself from him. He lay still, like death. She felt her body changing, changing further for each new passing second.

The skin on her toes touched the hairs on the carpet. She felt it. Her body moved and the air gave way. She sensed it, as she increasingly noticed the dancing shadows surrounding her. The air whispered to her and she understood every word. She felt rested and calm, ready, eager and poised.

She touched herself, touched herself as she showered, as the water drummed softly at her skin. She felt it, the strange, new sensation. She touched herself and cherished the low burning desire it created. The Hunger had always been there, inside her, but now she knew it would never, ever go away or diminish.

It would grow.

The clothes lay where she had left them, had dropped them. She picked them up and dressed with slow, lingering moves, moves she knew would have driven Flight Captain, would have driven Howard, that sickeningly innocent boy mad with lust.

She walked out into the hall, to the entrance, to Jolene's shimmering gates, her gates now. Passing through the shimmering darkness felt completely different, now, so much more controlled. She appeared in the dark alley, with no ill effects or disorientation at all.

Her mind had also grown stronger. It was a cumulative effect. It took just a little effort and she gained access to every mind in fairly close proximity in the lit street beyond the alley. She stood there for a second or two, considering her options, whether or not to be cautious and walk to the hospital, or climb to the roof and move that way. Then she shook her head. She needed to be patient and careful, not timid.

It took a little focus and a thought, and that was all. She rose in the air, just like she had seen Flight Captain do, and then, just like that she flew over the buildings, in the shadow of the night and her own surrounding shadows. Loud and triumphant laughter bubbled in her throat. The tall hospital-building appeared before her. She came in a little too fast, but experienced no real problems when she wanted to slow down and stop.

Jolene rested in a bed on the fifth floor, her skin as white as the sheets. Lucinda hovered in the air outside a bit, enjoying the moment, before slipping through the window, slipping through it like a ghost. She stood before the bed, looking down at the unmoving figure there.

– It's so funny, she said aloud. – They, Claudia and bunch put you here, of all places.

There was no one else in the room. Nurses passed by outside, and could easily look inside, through the open door, but they saw nothing, heard nothing, nothing but what Lucinda wanted them to see and hear.

– They are such losers, you know, so hopelessly naïve. All that power resting in that frail form of yours, and they leave you *unguarded*.

She paced a bit, both calm and excited, the face behind the mask twisted in a brutal grin, so different from the face both friends of Lucinda and Gimmick knew.

– You know, I actually think the Growth Gene is an added bonus and most people just have two powers, or two sets of powers. It's just that one power may have tons of various applications. I thought my powers were strength and mind reading, for instance, but then it struck me, in that moment of clarity: It is memory and analysis/Touch. I am able to seek out people by spotting their shadow, what to me is as visible and clear as day. I touched Claudia in the commotion just after the Great Darkness, did you know that? That was the first time I felt the pain, the first time I Touched anyone. I absorbed her telepathy and added her physical strength to mine. That's what

446

I do: I touch and hurt people, and copy their powers, augmenting them within me, making them more than they were originally. I have always been more powerful than Lady Grace, but I limited myself, held myself back, but no longer.

Ecstasy lit up the face behind the mask.

– Tonight I Touched you and Flight Captain, and your powers grow and accumulate inside me into something new and different and far more powerful, something that will increase with each new power I absorb. I push and I pull, and I Grow. You kept me in check, you, the Ebony Goddess of that other world, kept me from reaching my full potential, but no longer. I will be patient and will be Gimmick for a while longer, gathering my forces, before becoming Black Dragon and then... the Goddess. The others will look for you, of course, but they won't find you anywhere, and they will fear you are out there, plotting against us, and in a way you are. I'm *so* grateful to you for showing me the way, my enlightened path. I will, with a few necessary adjustments take your place, walk your path, until I change that, too, and make it my own. The others are already divided, distrustful of each other, and I will make sure to widen that chasm, and in time I will make them all mine, even more than the Ebony Goddess did. I remember everything from that other world, every little detail I and you experienced. My other power is definitely Memory, something approaching a Total Recall. Now, in hindsight that is increasingly clear, like so many other things.

Lucinda saw it all in her newly remade, powerful mind, saw the future and its countless probabilities like several strands on a pearl chain. She studied it with a deliberate and obsessive zeal that would have puzzled her just a few hours ago.

Lucinda grabbed the frail form and held it in her arms. The two figures faded away, and the room was once again silent and empty.

A group of homeless was gathered around burning oil barrels, warming themselves. Even the warm night couldn't properly heat their cold bones.

BEGONE!

A chilling voice spoke to them from the darkness. They stood there frozen for one tiny moment, before running off the fastest their legs could carry them.

Run rabbits, run, she cried after them, and they heard her, even though they didn't. She laughed contemptuously.

– And Melanie will become a devoted sister and servant, of course. She has no idea how devastating and useful her powers are, no more than I did.

She tore Jolene's head off her body. It was quite an easy and satisfying task. The body shook a bit, spitting gushes of blood, before becoming totally still and dead. Nothing landed on Lucinda, not a single drop. It passed through her, as if she was a spirit. She threw the head into one of the barrels, and then she tore the rest of the body apart and threw the various pieces into the other barrels. The pieces of flesh burned with a hiss, as the fluid within the body turned to vapor.

– Black Dragon will become a ghost, a specter haunting the land, until she reappears with a vengeance, and her rule becomes something very tangible and potent, a force of Order this world has never before seen.

She tilted her head, frowning at the dancing pieces of ash rising in the air.

– Oh, you think I'm taking the law and order thing a bit too far? Not so. I'm simply bringing the Maverick Crew's existence to its ultimate and logical conclusion. You taught me that, too.

She saw the world transformed, saw it become hers, like slowly solidifying mist.

Her phone beeped. She pulled it from her pocket and looked at the message there with a deep grin.

The woman everybody knew as Gimmick stood there for a long time, looking at the smoke and embers and ashes rising into the night.

And then she faded away, as if she had never been there at all.

She appeared in Broken Alley with just a few seconds to spare. Raven Bird flew in from the south, and they met at the center. Lisa smiled, as she landed, as she and Gimmick greeted each other. They were friends these two, and had a connection beyond the camaraderie of the others.

– You got my message, I see, Lisa grinned relieved. – I wasn't certain you would.

– I heard its beep, Gimmick said distracted. – I followed its call.

– Are you okay? Raven Bird asked her softly, as they embraced.

Lucinda sensed no suspicion in her, only concern.

– I am, or at least I will be, Gimmick assured her with a choking voice. – Life must go on.

Lisa nodded solemnly. She was a simple soul, one never going beneath the surface, never asking obvious, pertinent questions.

Black Dragon was pleased.

– Good, Lisa grinned. – Because the way I've heard it your old friend The Catcher will be on the prowl tonight, and you will get the chance to beat the living crap out of him. He has escaped from prison again.

They glanced at each other, inevitably sharing the same thoughts and discomfort.

Lucinda knew he had, knew that the tip Raven Bird had received was on the money, and she looked quite forward to what would happen.

448

– You're awfully chummy with that songbird of yours? She said lightly.

– She has never let me down so far, Raven Bird replied unconcerned.

Two years from now, Adeline Goddard, the Crimson Mask would indeed let her down, gloriously, and the Raven Bird would sing no more, but squeak, like the Bird of Prey she had become.

Raven Bird looked away for a while, and Black Dragon smiled.

– You seem... different.

– I guess I am, Lucinda acknowledged.

– You are certainly entitled, Raven Bird said softly, in a comforting gesture.
– Perhaps we should let others take care of the Catcher tonight?

– No. Gimmick shook her head. – I need action, need to feel my fists *pummel* the Catcher's face.

– You feel... betrayed, Raven Bird said. – I guess we all do, but she was like a sister to you.

– She was, Gimmick choked, – and she threw it away like it was *nothing*.

Raven Bird once more embraced her, comforting her friend Gimmick.

– *We* are sisters, Gimmick choked harder. – We will do great things together.

Great and terrible things.

– Sisters, Lisa whispered.

And then, just like she had done the first time, like the old, limited Gimmick had done she heard the sound of steps, caught the whiff of the Catcher's thoughts.

She stiffened and raised her head.

Action time, she told Raven Bird and grinned her sore smile, so clever.

Minutes, years rotted like flesh.

The Maverick Crew:

Flight Captain – Howard Eisenhouse
Lady Grace – Claudia Malone
Gimmick – Lucinda Patterson
Oracle – Jolene Masters
The Bowman – Richard Pearce
Cougar – Eleanor Sharpe
Raven Bird – Lisa Carlton
Sensor – Melinda Patterson
Mechanic – Alan Prescott
Energetic – Stephen Marks
Martial Athlete – Errol Lantross
Wind – Ashley Hastings

Members of the Junior Mavericks:

Oil – Floyd Tibbitt
Stalco – Elvis Morano
Dancer – Jenna Morgan

Members of the Asphalt Cowboys:

Lavender – Star Bartlett
Brick – Hans Nielsen
Cracker – Monique Quentin

Members of the Cadre:

Ebony Goddess – Jolene Masters
Black Dragon – Lucy Patterson
The Catcher – Troy Franklin
Sledgehammer – Ulysses Rogan
The Whiffer – Trevor Rogan
Domina – Claudia Malone
Hardman – Howard Eisenhouse
Sense Deprivation – Melinda Patterson
Bird of Prey – Lisa Carlton
Predator – Eleanor Sharpe
Stern Mistress – Cassandra Rogan
Thunder – Monique Quentin
Blood Diamond – Adeline Goddard
Hurricane – Ashley Hastings
Poison Oil – Floyd Tibbitt
Hard Whip – Lois Davenport

Members of the Lustful Carnage Gang:

Ashton Kramer
Lauren Harris

Others/unaffiliated:

Crimson Mask – Adeline Goddard

Author's word

It sometimes looks bad for comic book heroes, but they still triumph over impossible odds, even death. They have to, for Marvel and DC to stay in the mainstream publishing business. The status quo, even though it might be rocked now and then must be maintained.

I have no such restraints, of course. I can, like I always do, with any story take it more than a few steps further.

I was never impressed with Watchmen, for instance. Even though it was hailed as such, it wasn't that much of a departure from the norm, except for those getting off on normality and the average and dull and repetitive storytelling, and I see the praise it received as pure mainstream bullshit.

The Dark Knight was merely one more right wing nut job (Frank Miller) describing his oppressive view of mankind.

But in spite of the frustrations, the fact that most comics insult our intelligence (like most novels published by established publishers also do) I have always enjoyed reading comics. They were a comfort and an inspiration to a child hungering for creativity and imagination. I was able to put aside my skepticism, and embrace the important, crucial «suspense of disbelief» tenet. I learned that a somewhat adult story, beyond the fairy tales also should only be measured within its own context, by its own merit, within the rules established in that particular story.

But my objections remained and Black Dragon is a result of the long, growing trickle of frustration, of all the paths not taken by established comic book writers and editors and publishers. I always kind of suspected that I would write a story like this some night, but I waited, waited patiently until I felt ready, and in 2008, when I started on this one, I was.

The thoughts in my head were ripe and ready to fall off the tree.

You will «recognize» the powers and some of the characters, of course. That is practically inevitable. There are only so many variations to go around. But you will find them skewed, distorted here compared to your expectations and teachings and brainwashing many years of comic book reading has visited upon you. My wish to inject hardcore realism into everything I write is certainly very much present here as well. In short, beneath their powers and masks the people described are pretty much… human, with true faults and frailties and weaknesses, existing in a society not that different from the one you experience every day.

452

The mainstream publishers tried that now and then, I guess. They kept failing, because they brought the constraints of the old and stale with them into the professed new.

This is a novel, of course and not a comic book, not a story told in pictures and words, but «only» in words, but I have been focusing on the visuals even more than I usually do, and people keep telling me I am very good with visuals, with the painting of words.

Black Dragon is the last started on so far of what I deem my fourth generation novels. Obviously I wrote it faster than the others, among them Afterglow Dust. On occasion I had the feeling that it wrote itself and doing so effortlessly to boot.

There is one particular distinct characteristic here you will probably notice...

This isn't a novel *about* comics and shouldn't be seen as such, but an independent and self-contained story. Only its appearance is deliberately comics-like.

It certainly moves beyond any perceived constraints of comics and also mainstream novels. Its *shit-load* of transgression begins early and continues throughout the book.

I'm happy to say that I've gone totally overboard with this one...

If this is ever made into a movie, one indisputably faithful to the novel, it will be a great victory for us in the anti-censorship movement.

I'm quite pleased with the result. The story could have been longer, told in more than one book. It could have been shorter, with a tighter plot. I think it is just about the right length.

And this is a Universe, one I can return to and explore further later, if the imagination (not the fancy) strikes me.

And I probably will.

2008-02-02 – 2014-06-17
Printed version ready 2015-08-08

9 788291 693187